D0897981

HER VICTORY

ALAN SILLITOE

HER VICTORY

GRANADA
London Toronto Sydney New York

Granada Publishing Limited
Frogmore, St Albans, Herts AL2 2NF
and
36 Golden Square, London W1R 4AH
866 United Nations Plaza, New York, NY 10017, USA
117 York Street, Sydney, NSW 2000, Australia
100 Skyway Avenue, Rexdale, Ontario M9W 3A6, Canada
61 Beach Road, Auckland, New Zealand

Published by Granada Publishing 1982

Copyright © Alan Sillitoe 1982

British Library Cataloguing in Publication Data

Sillitoe, Alan
  Her victory.
  I. Title
  823'.914 [F]   PR6037.I55

ISBN 0-246-11872-5

Printed in Great Britain by
Richard Clay (The Chaucer Press) Ltd
Bungay, Suffolk

All rights reserved. No part of this publication may be
reproduced, stored in a retrieval system, or transmitted,
in any form or by any means, electronic, mechanical,
photocopying, recording or otherwise, without the prior
permission of the publishers

Granada ®
Granada Publishing ®

Contents

PART ONE
Making the Break

1

'What are you trying to climb into the freezer for?' George wanted to know.

A plastic orange gift-cannon of the Napoleonic type fell out of the cereal box and pointed its muzzle at his forehead. Such an omen, from behind a barricade of cornflakes, indicated the sort of week coming up that he could well do without. When he glanced at rain clouds forming beyond the half-steamed window there was no mistaking the picture of Monday morning. Yet even that was an advantage, because his habit was to leave the house earlier than on other days. He might therefore have thought it the best time of the week if he hadn't, on coming downstairs, seen his wife Pam wearing a bright green blouse, a dull beige cardigan which she had knitted the previous winter, and a crimson skirt from the New Year's sales. Such colours spun against his retina like a mad woman's rainbow.

'Well, what for, then? The bloody *freezer*?'

Every morning for years she had decided to leave him, but this autumn dawn was different because he had never accused her of climbing into the freezer before, when she was only trying to clean it out. There were times when his sense of humour defeated him and, being shocked, he could only sound like the bulldozing swine he had always been. She said: 'It gets too hot in this kitchen.'

He scattered white sugar over the cornflakes with his dessert spoon, then picked up the cannon and hurled it across the room into the sink. Crackshot. It floated in a bowl of water. 'If you open a window, there'll be a draught. I only got rid of my cold last week.'

Can't you see I'm dying?

Aren't we all? he'd said once too often.

They had been married long enough for him to know that he must rehearse every phrase before speaking, but he had never been able to live up to the high expectations he had set for himself. Nor had it been possible for him to exist under those she had no doubt proposed for herself. 'Remember how long we shopped around for such a good quality freezer? I'll never be able to use it again if you do yourself in in it.'

Airtight plastic bags of peas and beans; kilner jars of blackberries collected from the purlieus of Sherwood Forest; breast of mutton; a length of chops like the red and white keys of some fantastic piano which he had brought home in his car from the cutprice wholesaler downtown; yoghourt-containers of soup and squash; portions of carrots; packets of sausages and kidney; all lay scattered around, extracted piecemeal, he assumed, so as to make room for herself. She had only taken everything out in order to defrost and clean. He laughed when she told him. 'Try gas, then. Or pills.'

He got on well with his workmen, his humour sufficiently earthy and loudmouthed to keep them conscientious, even these days. He'd been in their place himself, and knew every dodge in the book. He also paid above the union rate. 'Give 'em money, and they'll work. And if they work, my profits rise. It's as simple as that.'

It was hard for him to talk without boasting, but at such devastation he could hardly speak: 'And what about all that grub? Think of the trouble we took. It'll go rotten if you don't put it back, sharp.' Terror sparkled in his eyes. If he made what he thought she was attempting to do sound funny perhaps she would stop getting her legs into the freezer-chest, and come back to the table.

She was trying to do no such thing, but before he could say more she glared: 'You're supposed to put me off doing it.'

To laugh was better for his pride than crying. 'Am I?'

'You're my husband. Or have you forgotten?'

She was going too far back in time. Pushing by to get milk from the refrigerator, he pressed a firm hand on her shoulder to show that he owned her absolutely, and said sorrowfully: 'What would be the point in trying to stop you, you see, if you're so dead set on it?'

Ice gripped at the heart. Her purpose had been to clean the freezer, and check what was inside. 'It's stupid of you to try and drive me mad. You know very well I'm not that sort of person.'

'How the bloody hell do you expect me to know a thing like that?'

He wasn't as calm as he looked. A man who prided himself on his sense of humour was always quick to lose his poise. She finished cleaning the freezer, and began to put things back, though it made no difference: 'You were trying to stuff yourself in the ice-chest. I'm not blind. But I do wish you'd make up your puny little mind about it.'

She closed the lid quietly and sat on the kitchen stool to face him across the table. She was one skip ahead, but he wouldn't realize it until whatever happened had passed him by. 'I suppose you would like me to kill myself.'

'Think of Teddy.' He was enjoying his favourite breakfast. 'If *you* kick the bucket, there'll only be me to look after the poor little sod.'

'He's eighteen. And he's at college.'

'Thought it was quiet this morning. He's usually got that jungle-band on his hi-fi bursting our eardrums. When'd he go back?'

'Last night. He was glad to get away. Remember?'

Milk splashed on to the table. 'Of course I bloody well do.'

'There's no need to swear.'

'Oh, but there is. There always bloody was. Teddy's old enough to look after himself now.'

She was happy about that. Her tears were falling. 'I've

11

never known anyone as dense and selfish as you.'

'I sometimes think you've never known anybody at all.' He could be even more cutting when he didn't try to be funny. There had been a time when she had known everything about him, but that was when there hadn't been very much to know, or when she wasn't sufficiently acute to see what was there. But now he seemed a stranger with whom she didn't want to become familiar. She wondered whether he didn't think the same about her, and decided it wouldn't much matter. It was best that nothing ever again mattered between them. She finished putting food back into the freezer.

He lifted the spoon to his mouth, always at his most specific when she tried to make amends: 'You bitch.'

She was hardly audible. 'Am I?'

'You're making my life a misery.' What was the use holding back if she was going to do herself in? You might as well tell her everything you'd always thought but not said for fear of hurting her, before she did kill herself, because if she happened to pull it off you might not get another opportunity.

She imagined such words ticker-taping into his brain, which made it more difficult to detach herself. 'I don't particularly want to know anybody.'

His face showed pain, as if he regretted his words. 'In my plain old view you aren't realistic in the way you look at the world.' His smile was kindly, till he shouted: 'But you're right when you say I'm selfish, if that's what it is. God knows, I realize I'm not perfect. Nobody is, are they? To be selfish is the only way I know to save you from yourself. If I slobbered all over you, and kissed your shoes, pleading for you not to kill yourself, you would do it, out of spite, just so's I'd have to take a few days off work. But you'll never do it when you know I don't give a damn whether you do it or not, will you? Will you, then?'

He was asking her. How much proof did he want? But would she really do it? Maybe he was right, because who would kill herself for him? Trust him to think she would do it

12

for him instead of for herself. Not only did he consider himself to be the centre of the world, but he still thought the earth was flat.

He was reasonably tearful. 'But I do care, anyway.'

So much speaking before midday undermined his self-confidence, and made him sweat. If he were late for work he would never forgive himself. He hardly ever said anything at breakfast, and neither did she. He awoke from sleep as if he were recovering from a dose of poison that hadn't been quite fatal. God knows what he dreamt. On once asking, he answered proudly that he didn't, and never had. He slept like a stone that water dripped on, a torment he was only vaguely aware of on waking up, which made his temper so vile that it was best, they had long since agreed, if neither spoke.

Button-lips, he told himself, was the order of the day. Everything he thought, she spoke usually before he had any notion of saying it. Internal and disputatious life was blocked off. He wanted to make her feel deficient about not properly caring for him, so put on the usual mask of a little boy who had been abandoned by all the supports he had grown accustomed to, the real face underneath surfacing only to indicate that he hadn't had many good things to get used to in his hardworking life anyway. He wasn't aware of this, she felt, so the toll it took of him drained the life out of her.

'I think you've got to have a bit of selfishness to get through life,' she said, still wondering whether she would leave him today.

Her clear statement surprised him. 'Selfishness is next to godlessness,' he retorted and, in the same breath: 'Fry my eggs and bacon, duck. I've got to be going soon.'

'Why don't you leave me alone?' Her request came from the misery of a greater plea that she hadn't been able to make, because to do so would give her even more into his mercy. She tried to see him as if for the first time, hoping not to be so strident in her conclusions. For reasons of self-preservation she adopted the obvious rather than the speculative, seeing a

13

man of five feet six inches in height, and solid like a barrel, with muscular arms and big hands. When he walked, the world made way, especially in his own small factory where twenty workmen at lathes and milling machines turned out precision parts which could not yet be mass produced. He went to work in a boiler-suit to prove he was one of the men, but she had to make sure that a clean one was laid over the stair rail every morning for him to get into. When he stood before a machine to do a special piece of engineering that couldn't be trusted to anyone else, his underlip pushed out in intense concentration, he kept his shirtsleeves rolled down so that a pair of gold cufflinks glittered.

He stood, and leaned towards her. Plain, incontrovertible statements upset him most, as well as the simple pleas which he never had the generous pleasure of acceding to because she only made them after he had already ridden rough-shod over her.

She had never seen him so angry, probably because he hadn't been properly frightened before. 'What, for God's sake, is wrong with asking you to fry my breakfast? How can such a natural request be seen as "getting at you"?'

'That's all you've lived for ever since we met,' she heard herself shouting.

He methodically laid strips of bacon on the grill, and cracked two eggs into the smoking lard. 'In the final analysis,' he called over his shoulder.

When, she wondered, had there been a first analysis? She didn't know what sort of wife he'd be happy with, because it was impossible to decide what kind of woman he himself was capable of making in any way content. It wasn't her. No more of that. The serrated breadknife on the table was not to be resisted. Didn't like it here.

The dazzling backplate of the electric cooker showed what he thought of as the last horror. He turned as the knife spun towards his throat.

She remembered everything as having taken place in

14

silence, though it was conceivable that the neighbours heard the combination of shriek and bellow that came from him. The inner noise of bitter rage which forced her to spring was fit to burst all panes of glass in the house.

In spite of her speed and the spin of the weapon, he parried the thrust with an ease that astonished her. A hand made a painful chop at her elbow and sent the knife across the room. Clenched into a fist, his other hand struck her face, pushing her back and half stunning her at the same time.

She discovered, now that it was too late, that to be violent was to be kind to him. Such a life-and-death attempt was far less disturbing than when she had asked him simply to let her alone, action of any sort being the only form of reconciliation that he could understand. The truth was, he didn't want her to kill herself, or to leave home. Though she had never expressed to him her hope of one day doing so, he sensed the possibility so strongly that he liked to taunt her with the idea.

The bout was over before the bacon scorched. He sat down hungrily, though he wasn't altogether happy, in spite of eating the rind as well, because he was the sort of man who knew that whenever things looked like getting better, they got worse. He was no simpleton, and had built up his business by driving himself more intensely during the good times than in the bad. Her resort to violence seemed a hint that he ought now to relax his continual craving for work and take her out for the day, but as he sated his appetite, the conflict took on another aspect, in that he could afford to feel cheerful now that she had tried to kill him and failed. There weren't many men who'd had that to put up with before breakfast.

She couldn't live any more with the kind of person who made her pay for everything before she'd had time to enjoy what he occasionally led her to expect and never gave her. He felt it, too, and being disappointed in himself turned into a bully, which made him babyish. During twenty years she had been so busy learning about him that she had learned nothing of herself, except that much of what she had taken in

15

concerning his character had bitten so painfully that it had become part of her. She resented such gains at the price of her soul, that had pushed her own self out of the way till she often didn't know who she was when in the same room with him, and she was never away from him long enough to begin finding out. She didn't even know who she was when she was alone, which was worse because it frightened her into believing that her memory was failing as well.

His knees were trembling, but he took his plate to the sink by walking side-on. 'Cheer up, love! See you tonight. I'll try not to be late.'

He didn't know what was wrong, so she felt that whatever wasn't right between them could only be her fault. His eyebrows lifted, an unfailing mannerism: 'No talkie-talkie this morning? It's not that bad, Pam, is it?' He winked: 'Just think how lucky you are. You haven't got cancer, have you? If not, then you've nothing to worry about.'

'Goodbye,' she said flatly.

'You've got good clothes on your back. You aren't starving. You aren't being dive-bombed, are you? Well then, you should be grateful for it.'

'Oh, I know,' she said. 'I thank God for every breath I take.'

He smiled because he'd won. 'That's better!'

The only victory is in being alive, she thought, when he went whistling out of the door. She didn't believe any good would come of giving her meagre victory to him by killing herself. Pulling the living-room curtains aside, she watched him drive on to the street. He rolled the car window down and waved. She gestured back to make sure he went away happy enough to work well and make more money, which was all he wanted out of life. He left her as usual to close the garage door when she went shopping. Steely-edged rain clouds filled the sky, drops already spitting at the privet.

2

A bottle of Golden Miracle Skin Lotion, a tin of Super-Quick Hair Eradicator, a flask of Nutritious Fast-Working Pore Food, and a jar of the most efficient Blemish Flattener that science had so far been able to concoct, broke and scattered under the hammer. A fragment of cream-coated glass hit the dressing-table mirror, and she stopped before the next swing because it seemed that her elbow was about to crumble. Blows from everywhere crossed her heart.

In all justice she had to thank George for having such a wide range of hammers. He could never resist a nice-looking red-handled claw hammer set in a row of diminishing sizes in a shop window. He had to go in and get one. If the income tax had really wanted to know how rich he was they'd have to weigh him in hammers like the Aga Khan in gold. There were probably enough in his tool shed and factory for both of them.

She threw the hammer on the bed, and put a few tubes and lipsticks into her case, then sent the rest of the trash over the carpet so that he would know something had altered in his life when he found the garage door open and the house empty.

She pulled sensible blouses, skirts and dresses out of the wardrobe, folding them into her case. Early risers have plenty of time, so she lit a cigarette, and thought of igniting what couldn't be taken. A few drops of paraffin and up it would go. 'I don't hate myself that much,' she decided, 'so I won't do it,' having to speak her decisions before being able to follow them with action. The thought of such a fire scorched her hands and face, and she stood back from the bed a few moments, rubbing her palms together. Then she took tights, pants, vests, bras and stockings, handkerchiefs already folded, and packed them in neatly, but lifted everything out again to lay shoes on the bottom, and fit in two of the heaviest sweaters.

She sat on the bed, cases full but not closed, failing to leave. Hadn't got this far before. What did you do? How did you do it? It was like waiting for someone to come and haul her off to prison. A better idea was to run away from the house and go over the fields, throwing off her clothes bit by bit till she was naked and could crawl into a wood, go to sleep and never wake up. It was as impossible to run away as it was to die, and felt like one and the same thing now that she was trying.

The dialling tone purred. Didn't want to take her gaze from the beige carpet. The whole day could go by, and he would come home and gently put the receiver down before pushing her on to the settee and shouting it was about time she grew up and stopped giving him such a bloody hard time. She took her parents' small black Bible from the dressing-table drawer and slipped it into her case because she had read it as a child, and the dates of births and deaths were inscribed.

'Oh no,' she said, 'it's not going to be like that,' and dialled a taxi, still hoping the number would be engaged or out of order. It wasn't. When the car came she was glad there was no one to say goodbye to.

3

Her two cases were near an empty platform seat, and she walked to get warm rather than go in the tea-bar waiting-room. Someone who knew her might phone George, but if by magic he came down the steps she would throw herself under the mincer of a non-stop train. She preferred to be in the cold wind where people didn't look at each other, for if they did they might see her, and she wanted above all to be invisible.

There was a smell of smoke and diesel fumes. Shining rain-needles slanted on to the rails. Her life was her own – as cold as the weather was – and no one knew better, but she felt she would never wake up from the disabling fear that made her arms tremble as if she would be unable to lift her cases. She would get them on the train herself, or not at all, had them by the edge and hoped a door would be level when the train stopped.

A station announcement, sounding like wind and marbles thrown at the roof, increased her uncertainty and dread, showing a vision of hauling cases up the steps and out of the station, getting into a taxi and setting herself for home, which made the luggage so light when the train did arrive that she threw both heavyweights up into the doorway and carried them easily to a compartment.

Twenty years of concrete crumbled from her, and she laughed while pressing her cases as far into the rack as they would go, thinking it would be a shame if one fell at some sharp jolt and knocked her brains out at this stage of her departure.

She didn't notice the train leaving the city till it had gone by the castle. Coming from the toilet she saw a middle-aged well-dressed man surrounded by expensive leather luggage near the doorway spit through the open window. He swung quickly to one side to avoid any blowback, as if he'd made the same gesture more than once. A handkerchief was also ready, and half covered his face. When he removed it and looked at her she saw a sallow complexion, dark neatly parted hair, a straight well-angled nose, and good teeth when he smiled. The scent was eau-de-cologne, and the mutual stare was short enough to give a feeling of complicity. She climbed happily over his cases as if she had drunk several tots of whisky yet did not feel giddy.

If someone asked why she had left her husband she wouldn't have said anything because the answer she had been born with was embedded like a stone, not to be pulled

19

prematurely into the glare of day without ripping her to pieces. She had lived and breathed too long with a monster she did not know how or when had been conceived. The heart had no way of creating words and giving it birth. But some day a reason would, with time and patience, be found for the riddance of everything that had tormented her since marrying George, and which had agonized her even before that, if she faced the truth which at the moment her thoughts only hinted at.

There was nothing to do except sit. She heard herself laughing at the fathomless drop opening abruptly beneath. The only space was the compartment, luckily empty, otherwise someone might have led her away as she screamed with amusement at distances opening on every side. She gripped the arm of the seat and pressed her cheek to the cold window. To leave home, husband and son for no good reason means I'm going off my head. She wiped tears and stood to look in the mirror, to find out whether or not she was actually laughing.

She had oblique grey eyes, a tinge of blue at happy times. Too much like a bloody cat's, he had said more than once, now and again with a sentimental stare, but she'd hated her eyes for years because they had betrayed the way she felt, patience only built up and sustained by a false contentment. Her hair was long and brown, with no grey seams as yet. Maybe the grind of life had held it in suspension, and it would turn all at once now that she had left.

It was wrong to look at yourself. Before marriage there had been one mirror in the house, over the bathroom sink. The bond had broken under the strain. She saw herself anew. Her mouth was still full, lips shaped because, unlike most people she had known, she'd got her own teeth, and not yet the rabbit-grip George would have felt much easier living with. The fact of her being a few inches taller had often given him a rankling gaze. The raw bruise down her face was a memento from his fist, a reach that more than made up for his short

20

body. If the knife had gone into his throat she would have left him by going to jail, and there would have been no mirrors there either, she imagined. If she had struck blood yet failed to kill, she would never have escaped from his life.

Lines of washing in back gardens flapped towards the place she was rapidly leaving. Clothes of all colours waved goodbye. The train was bully enough to push through any wind and to clear the clouds away, yet such free air could not disperse the ache that George still made her feel. He could crush himself from this point on. Perhaps he would even relish the chore of getting his own washing done now that she had a first-class ticket to St Pancras in her purse.

Despite pain from the mark he had given, she knew herself to be happy. When tears pushed at her eyes she could visualize his face, and reassure herself how lucky she was. The sensation wouldn't last, but would be so much better for that, providing she enjoyed it while she could, for wouldn't she, after wandering around the shops of London, and eating a nice Italian dinner in Soho, come back tonight and be in the same old bed again?

Happiness existed in a world she didn't feel close to, even though she had separated from the one that had buried her for so long. She'd try not to go back, for all this couldn't be for nothing. On her own, a certain amount of happiness would come from being in control both of herself and of the peace this gave – except that he had bruised her to make sure she would come back.

Frosty breath floated like smoke from the mouths of cows. A tractor and its plough crawled on the brown earth of a field that sloped to the close horizon. A cloud of white birds shifted behind. God was in the oil of the tractor and on the wings of every bird, as well as in the separate vapour from each placid animal. She felt the warmth of their breathing. Perhaps God did exist, since she had made her move and could not explain what else had finally given her the courage to act. She pictured Him living below the ocean, under pebbles and soil at the exact middle of the land, a God of this earth only who directed billions of lives and held the fate of everyone in His power.

On her way through town she had taken four hundred pounds out of their joint account, a poor sort of golden handshake when there was so much more (in his name only) in deposit accounts and building societies and insurance schemes and national savings. He told her little about such amounts that were put away in all kinds of places. At the beginning of their marriage she had known how much there was to the penny, but for a long time she had been uninterested, out of pride and laziness. There was also the house and car, and a catalogue of other items which by rights were half hers. But the money she had drawn was merely the retirement fund from an untenable situation, a bit to tide you over when you lit off in a demented escape without saying a proper farewell. There was also sixty pounds in her purse, cash he had kept in an old cigarette tin under a shoe box at the back of the wardrobe, as well as various rings and a watch which might be good for a meal or two.

The bank manager looked from a half-open door. The girl who took her cheque went to see if she had as much in her account. She had it twice over. It was no business of the girl's, who checked because she was new at her job and didn't know her as the others did. Maybe the manager was looking at someone else. He smiled before closing his door.

How many fields were there in England? There must be somebody alive who knew. They jumped hedges, rolled up hills, were sucked into cuttings, darkened into nothing by woods and tunnels. They opened like fans, and were split by full meandering streams, pure fields of green, ploughed, half ploughed, scrubbed meadows and clattering patchwork by the window as if they would come in and cover her.

The door slid open.

'Coffee, madam?'

He held a tray of sandwiches and drinks, and had come to

22

laugh. He was tall, had fair crinkly hair that was somewhat long at the neck but went back in a vee at the front. There was nothing to do but look at him, and he didn't mind, being fresh at the face and grey-eyed like a cat. His smile was friendly, and his appearance scattered the thoughts which she was glad to be rid of. He looked at her as if she were a younger woman, though perhaps it was his way with all customers, men and women alike.

'Have you got any tea?'

'Certainly, madam.' She thought he added: 'For you there's whatever you fancy,' but she could not be sure, because the train became noisier. He was cheeky, but she was safe, and smiled at him.

Too hot to hold, she set the cup on the hand-sized table. He clacked the door shut and went to other compartments, leaving her to wonder if George would come after her on the next train. Perhaps of a sudden at work he had driven home in a sweat to find out whether she had hanged herself or left him. He would speed at a hundred miles an hour down the motorway and wait by the ticket barrier at St Pancras. Like many men who didn't care what you thought, he could be intuitively correct when his mind was put to it. 'Got you, you whore!'

Let him say it. If he was there she would kill him. No mistake this time. He might say such things, but she had never been with another man since they had got married, though he might have carried on with women for all she knew. The fact that she didn't care had harassed him beyond endurance, robbed him of his manhood, one might almost say. But that sort of game had never appealed to her, though she had known some couples play, using it perhaps as a station on the road to divorce, where most of them had ended up – happier no doubt than she was who in her deadbeat way had chosen another and maybe worse method of getting clear.

He wouldn't meet her in London, would not even know she had gone till he got home, when she would be lost to him. She wasn't an animal to be hunted. However much he searched he would never find her, because the world was a big enough jungle for anybody to hide in.

Most of her life she had lived in a small corner of one that had smothered her nevertheless. When he was away on business for a night she could recollect her dreams next day. But when he lay in bed by her side he fed off them all night long, and no matter how much she strove to recall them she hardly ever could.

On a restless night she might ask if he was awake, and get out of bed at sensing that he was, knowing it wouldn't matter if he were disturbed by her movement. If he hadn't been awake she wouldn't have asked. In the morning she might wake him, so that he could then get up by himself and leave her sleeping for half an hour in warmth and peace. But when she got up in the middle of the night it was because something in a dream which she couldn't remember wouldn't let her sleep. So she would go downstairs and make tea. On her way into the toilet she realized that he had been awake for some time and waiting for her to get up, because he called out cheerfully: 'Bring me a cup of tea as well, duck.' At the shock of his voice she felt cheated. Though not lazy, he was a man who expected her to serve him in everything.

When he scratched himself in bed it felt as if he were trying to saw himself in half. If he succeeded there would be two of him to prey on her. He seemed at times to live in her skin, exerting such pressure that she began to know when her period was coming on because he got so moody. Otherwise she might not have known till the blood flowed. She longed for the day when its onset would take her by surprise. Freedom would be hers. She would feel blood on her thighs, and run into the nearest shop in a fever of embarrassment to buy a box of tampons, then hope to find a place to staunch the flow before going on her way.

The countryside went by in broad ribbons as the train cut a way at furious speed the nearer it got to London. Would she

24

die if she opened the door and threw herself out? The thought was a hook that pulled at her stomach. She felt sick with alarm, and her effort to get rid of it was helped by the sight of the attendant who had come to collect her cup, his smile as grand as ever. He saw the reflection of her bruised face as the train went through a cutting, and was aware of her anguish. I bumped into something. Didn't see it coming. Too bloody feeble. My husband clocked me one, she would say. That wouldn't do, either. Maybe it would be best to say, with tears in her eyes: When my boy friend asked me to go away with him and I said no, he hit me. That might be better, though it was no bloody business of his or anybody else's.

'Looks as if we're going to have good weather in London.'

He didn't wait for her response. He would go home to his wife and children, and they would be happy to see him. She was sure he had photographs in his wallet, and after five minutes conversation with any stranger would flip them out like credit cards and give a long explanation about each one.

For the last few years she had played a secret game. Walking along the street, even though George might be with her, she would wonder what it would be like if it was ordained that she had to live the rest of her life with the next man who came by. What if she were washed up on a desert island with him, for example, the two of them strangers to each other? A personable young man approached, and she could imagine it with pleasure. On other occasions he would by no means be promising, so she would cheat: Well, let's see what the next looks like. Or she would settle for the best out of three. She could easily imagine herself attuned to the ordinary youth or man who hove in sight, whether he was alone or with another woman. She passed, never to see him again. Or she would fall in love with a face that went by and vanished forever. That was as near as she had been to unfaithfulness, though according to the Bible it was just as bad. George had never been able to catch her at it. But then, how could he?

The train felt like home, and she dreaded having to get off

25

at the end of the journey. Walking the corridor she saw the man sitting alone in the next compartment who had spat so violently on leaving Nottingham. Maybe the trip south seemed as long as ten thousand miles to him also. Even though they were only passing St Albans he already had his smart hat, gloves and overcoat on. His luggage was down from the rack, as if he couldn't wait to leap out as soon as the wheels had stopped at the London platform. Neither could she.

4

In his mirror George saw the face of the man in the car behind talking as if he had a passenger by his side, which he had not. The driver appeared to be about forty-five years of age, haggard, unshaven, yet fleshy-faced and as vain as a monkey. He didn't like what he was saying, as if unused to uncertainties in a life which had so far been well regulated. He was telling of something over and over again which had not only affected his life in a fundamental manner during the last twenty-four hours, but had changed that of his non-existent passenger as well.

George thought maybe the man had started from Inverness and was driving to London, and that his talk would last all day, but having just got rid of one yammerer he wasn't prepared to take on another, no matter who he was or what he was saying. He could hear every word, because he himself was that man, and wasn't on his way to London from Inverness, either. In any case, what would he be doing coming so far west? I'm not on the road yet, he thought, laughing to see whether the man in the car behind also laughed. He did. I'm on my way to work, and not even she can stop me doing a thing like that.

His boots slipped on the clutch, feathered the brakes, and nearly made him hit a bus that stopped at the traffic lights. The man behind swore. George always wore a pair of boots for work, and made sure they were polished, what's more. They'll keep me fit and, at a pinch, are a bloody good weapon, legal, above board, yet unconcealed. Good to kick somebody to death sooner or later – the bitch. His workmen wore thin shoes or suede, not much better than carpet slippers, so at that place anyway nobody could tread on *his* toes. George swore at the same time as the man behind.

Under the back seat was a box-set of micrometer, depth gauge, pair of callipers and a spirit level, as well as a ruler and a steel tape measure, bought as a present by his grandfather when he started on an apprenticeship thirty years ago. He had hardly used them. In the early days he left the box safe in his locker while he borrowed, bought more cheaply, or used what the firm provided. They hadn't been calibrated since leaving the shop, but today he'd compare their readings with those on his office bench at work, and maybe use them again, though he would have to make sure they didn't get borrowed or stolen. Such antique quality would spark a light in any roving eye. He'd always carried them in his car, fearful of leaving them at home in case the place was rifled when Pam was out shopping. They fitted snugly into green cloth-lined shapes in the box, smelled faintly of oil, steel and camphor, but instead of being comforted by their existence he saw his face in the mirror of the car behind, which happened to be that of the passenger he continually talked to. He'd always thought himself too old to go barmy.

He'd dreamed of walking into his factory and finding the machines covered in inches of dust. Pam came in from the yard outside and stood naked in the doorway, but when he touched her she changed into a steel drill spinning towards

27

him. His only escape was into a bottomless pit, whirling down the smooth-walled shaft, from which descent he woke up sweating.

The only way to wipe the misery from all three faces was to grin. He owned the three of them, and had to decide whether it was misery or merely a forced smile stamped on each face. There was no middle path. There never was. Pam could have told him that. Didn't look much like a smile, being the sort that often made people think he was having a harder time in life than he really was.

He wished he had never looked in the mirror in the first place and caught that expression of unmistakable pain on his face. He had sent the lovely foreign au pair upstairs to tell his wife her morning coffee had been poured. He heard a scream, and the smiling girl with nice bare breasts came in to say his wife wouldn't be wanting her breakfast because she had killed herself. Dial the police then, you slut, he shouted, tucking into his own. Then come down and sit on my knee.

It wasn't like that, and never could be, and don't I know it? He said the tale aloud so that the man in the next car, who had also stopped at the pedestrian crossing, looked at him, then raced off at the all-clear so as to get out of the madman's way.

His wife had been trying to get into the freezer. Maybe it wasn't the first time. But in full plain view she had gone off her head, and when he had tried to stop her, had come for him with a carving knife. Tell yourself the truth. You had to face facts. If you didn't look them square in the phizzog you might never know how to mend matters. He hadn't been trained as a mechanic for nothing. By completing a few calculations he avoided going into the dark. No, she hadn't been trying to tuck herself into the freezer, but she ought to have done.

He had been afraid of her because she was so strong. She had been frightened of him for the same reason. He had found out now that it was too late. They were vulnerable, kids in a playpen, unable to climb over and grow up. He had been scared out of spite, gone yellow from ignorance. He was nervous everywhere except in his workplace. He opened a window and spat, nearly hitting a biker in a black jacket covered in badges, who lifted his gloved fist in warning then shot forward on to a roundabout, causing a Rolls to brake so suddenly it just avoided bumping a Mini.

The men at work respected him. They might snicker behind his back, but they couldn't fault his work. Most were younger, but even the older ones deferred to him for his skill and precision. He was afraid of Pam because he loved her, and hated himself for having a string of thoughts that led to admitting it. He had made her miserable, and disliked her suffering because it reminded him too much of his own. Yet he was also the mirror of her torments. Both of them had been blinded by their continual heliographic flash from too early on. So he couldn't blame her, or feel guilty about it.

Right from the beginning they had made mirrors for each other. They had, as it were, bought them from furniture shops, auctions, jumble sales and junk markets. They had purchased them by mail order, from the tally man, and from the Classical Golden Mirror of the Month Club as advertised on TV and in the newspapers. They set them up all over the house: gilt-edged mirrors, wall mirrors, swivel mirrors, shaving mirrors, and even a two-way mirror. They furnished the bedroom, spare-room, box-room, living-room, kitchen and, worst of all for him, his car, which was the only space he could be alone in because she hated it more than any other place since he smoked continuously while at the wolf-fur-covered steering wheel.

He had never been able to tolerate her yammering when they sat side by side in bed before turning out the light. When it happened downstairs he was at least able to stand up now and again if he felt like killing her. Looking across the table and wondering whether or not she would stop yammering, on sensing this perfectly natural desire in him, he would walk to the fireplace hoping not to offend her even more, at which her yammering would get louder and absolutely to the point. Thinking his head would burst he would get up from his easy chair and shamble into the kitchen to put the kettle on that played 'Annie Laurie' when it boiled, not to throw water over her, or to get the spout steaming so that she could hurl it across at him, but simply to make the age-old gesture of brewing a cup of strong tea in a crisis. At the same time he would be careful to leave the door open so that she wouldn't think he was maliciously trying to get out of earshot, which would justify her in complaining for another half hour at least.

But once they were in bed and the yammering commenced, or resumed, after a short break during which his cup of tea had really worked its effect of hot flushes or spots before the eyes, or throughout the short time of getting ready for bed, there was no escape, and he had to sit there and listen. The more she went on, the hotter it became in bed, her legs and thighs so warm that his own limbs felt scorched, so that as well as craving to get away from the sound of her voice he was also disturbed by the heat coming from her body and wanted to avoid that as well.

As for why she was yammering, there was no answer to it. She had been at the game almost twenty years, and though he heard (it was impossible not to) he no longer listened, knowing from experience after the first few occasions that it was best not to, since if he did his head would burst with the fiery violence of a paperbag overfilled with her cinder breath. Listening was beside the bloody point entirely, because she just yammered for yammering's sake, though it was also true that she was only a yammerer because he could not bear to listen. If he had been a born listener she wouldn't have been a yammerer, and they would have got on so well that everyone might have called it having a cosy conversation.

What he could not understand was how a man like him, whose favourite pastime never had been listening (neither did he like to talk much, except perhaps when he was away from home), had married a woman who did nothing but yammer.

30

This constant machine-gunning yammer tormented him because there was little he could do except keep his ear tuned to it, which forceput he loathed so much he was ready to kill her, had in fact to fasten his hands to his side with mental sticking plaster to stop them getting up and doing so, but when she began to yammer he listened and that was that.

His misery was a simultaneous three-pronged pain in heart, gut and arse, compounded by a loathing of himself which made him feel he was walking in the ebony darkness of an enclosed cave so that he couldn't move in any way whatsoever. If they were downstairs he could get up so as to give himself temporary relief, though only in order to tolerate another half hour before standing again for the same reason. And he had to be careful, in case she thought he wasn't tuned-in, whereby that accusation would be added to the list she seemed to be reading from with such an accusing rhythm.

Anything wrong with her life, and she blamed him. She blamed him for everything because he was incapable of discussing anything. He saw this, yet even her attempts at 'talking things over' in a husband-and-wife way began by her holding him responsible for the fact that it was necessary for her to make the effort in the first place. He began to think she had only married him in order to have someone to blame for all that had gone wrong in her life. It was conceivable that in the track of such verbal convection he really did end by doing her sufficient injustice to blame him for, but only so that she wouldn't destroy herself utterly by being completely unjust to him.

She seemed to blame him for having been born, because this accusation did not make her feel any better she blamed him for having been born herself. He could see no way out except through death's wide gate, but in spite of her yammering he liked being alive, so what could he do?

The truth was, and he told it aloud to prevent his brain continuing its invidious yammering at *him*, that she had in fact hardly ever yammered. It wasn't in her nature to do so, though he recalled having driven her to it once or twice during their long marriage – which seemed short enough now that she had gone. But, his anger struck in again (though he prayed such destructive wrath would soon leave him alone for good), even once had been too often, and he found it hard to forgive her.

He used to think it was pleasant being married because he had found someone who was as good as a mother to him. She was better, in fact, because his own mother had as often as not ignored him, there being so many kids that she had little time for any of them. So he found in Pam a mother who, by and large, because she was a mother herself, he mostly couldn't stand. By the time he met her he no longer needed a mother, but having married he found himself lumbered with one.

Maybe he would try to find her. On the other hand perhaps he wouldn't, since he had no idea where to search. She was bound to come back, because she had no way of getting money. She couldn't look after herself. No mothers can when they suddenly don't have anyone else to work for. And she had to come back to look after him because if she didn't, who would? Now that he had lost her he realized that he loved her as well. He certainly had no mother to go to, so maybe he would look for her. At the same time, perhaps he wouldn't. She didn't deserve such consideration.

I'll tell the doctor I'm depressed, he decided, having driven round the city centre for the last half hour. He'll give me some pills. But you only went to a doctor if your arm was hanging off, or you had gone blind, or if you were carried in having lost your legs in the wickedest kind of car smash. Otherwise you went on with life, and considered that all such minor ailments would sooner or later pack up and vanish. At least he had disentangled himself from the inner-city traffic system that was so irrationally complicated that occasional motorists from other localities abandoned it after several hours trying to get their bearings, and went off quietly to cut their throats in some leafy lane near Sherwood Forest. He would toss up a coin as to whether he would go to the doctor or not.

He drove by the station and towards Castle Boulevard. I ought to kill her for leaving me in the lurch. The car behind stopped following, was lost somewhere in the one-way spirit-traps. All mirrors had disappeared except his own. He touched the end of his nose to see if he was real, and the tip was ice-cold, so he assumed himself to be healthy. The doctor could stuff his pills up his arse where they should have stayed in the first place.

The only thing he wasn't afraid of was his work, and he was happy when he turned into the cul-de-sac street that backed on to the canal and saw his workshop at the bottom. The men were already waiting for him, and one of them waved a friendly greeting.

5

'Don't like it here.' She might even add: 'Coming home today. Expect me soon.'

'Don't come back,' he would write, if she sent him an address. 'You're dead.'

So she wouldn't send any of the leaden words that clamoured at the end of her biro. The post office was warm compared to her room. She screwed up a telegram form before beginning another. People in the queues looked. She needn't have thrown the paper with such force. Every morning after buying food she called at the post office to write a telegram. It might be better to live with George than rot in the fifteen pounds a week hole of a room she had landed in. Pneumatic drills and traffic shook her nerves, and at night the

Shepherd's Bush hooligans roamed noisily on their way home.

When not walking she wanted to be lying down, but was terrified at never getting up again, so she went along muddy lanes of wintry trees in Holland Park, with a plastic bag of shopping, and several crumpled telegram forms in her pocket. She looked in a pool of water, and saw a squirrel run over her face. The pain of its claws and grey bush paralysed her lips more than the wind, but children passing in a gang from the school were happy, and she smiled at them.

The semi-circular screen of the peacock's tail was blue-gold and veined-red against darkening foliage. She fed bread to sparrows. Her pride would never forgive her if she sent a telegram saying she didn't like it here. She was two people. One was imperious and able to cope, plain but presentable, cheerful, imaginative, solid in all her perceptions. The other person was timid, incompetent, everchanging, and half-mad. She knew them well, often walked with one at each hand, like two illegitimate children that she was forced to drag along for their daily outing.

She was neither of them. She was somewhere in between – but now that she lived on her own each fought more violently for her absolute attention. At her best moments she inclined firmly to the former, and at her worst lapsed alarmingly towards the latter. In spite of such inner turmoil, she liked it here, even though it meant spending most of her time being afraid. A long walk was needed before her thoughts became helpful. She passed Lord Holland's statue for the fourth time, and decided to go home.

Hunger was as real as the rain as she crossed the main road. Motor-cars speeding on either side were also real. She stayed on the island, unable to go back or forward, even when there was no traffic. Time passed, and she was unwilling to reach a decision. Her fingers were frozen. Then she found herself on the opposite pavement without having made up her mind.

She bought a pair of heavier shoes because her own got

34

damp in the slightest moisture. Her second pair were also too thin. She bought grey tights and woollen stockings. In Nottingham, George had driven her in the car, or she knew all the buses, or she would occasionally drive the car herself, but here she was often afraid to do other than walk to get anywhere. There were blisters at both heels and along the tops of her toes, but she refused to limp. Pain wasn't considered while finding a way through the parks to Oxford Street. She got used to the nagging sores, glad when they made her feel that what remained of her was still alive. It was better than nothing.

The door key had been in her hand during the walk up Ladbroke Grove and into Clarundel Crescent. A drizzle beating against her face tasted of dustbins and petrol fumes, making her glad to get inside. The drilling-men had gone, and her footsteps creaked. Halfway up the stairs the automatic switch flipped off and left her in the dark, and she pressed the button again on the next landing. It came up immediately. Last night someone had stuck in a matchstick which kept the light on till morning. So she went up and let herself into her room by feeling the key into the lock.

She looked into the small alcove of a kitchen to make sure George wasn't there. It was colder than being outside. Keeping her coat on, she lit the gas fire, then closed the curtains in case George should look in at her. She turned on the cooking stove to get heat from that as well – not forgetting to open the oven door to check that George wasn't sitting curled up inside, ready to leap out.

She wouldn't have been seen within a mile of such an antique grease-caked monstrosity of a stove when living in her immaculate house furnished with labour-saving knick-knacks from the start of her marriage, but which made no difference because what had she done with any of the time that had been saved? The grease had been washed and scoured, so it didn't stink whenever a chop was laid under the grill.

She put on carpet slippers, hardly noticing the pain,

knowing that as the hours went by she would begin to wonder where she was. Sooner or later her feet would harden and the throbbing would decrease. If George found her she prayed they'd be better so that she could tell him to go to hell before running as far away as she could get.

The knife and fork, on the small table set opposite the bed-wall, had cost a few pence from a barrow on the Portobello Road. So had the saucepan and frying pan. She regretted not having brought half the belongings of the house on a lorry. She ought to have deliberated, not fled, talked to George calmly and made arrangements by first finding a flat in London, then organizing a van from a removal firm to carry down what was hers. It was easier said than done. She had acted like a refugee, had fled in peril of her life, and was now hiding from George and his secret police.

But she liked the surprise of how simple life could be. The only expensive item was the shelter of her room, otherwise frugality attracted her. The pleasure of buying a knife and fork for ten pence instead of new ones for a pound or more gave a moral purpose to her existence. If she had never married, this was how she would have lived. Only the cup-and-saucer was new.

She wouldn't go back even if he crawled every inch of the road on his hands and knees and begged her. Emptying her pockets, she spread the half-filled telegram forms on the table. Why hadn't she noticed at their first meeting his deadly hollowness that could only be filled by whoever he latched on to for life? She laughed. He wouldn't want to see her again, in any case. And he was saying worse things about *her*, she could bet.

No need to see anything. But she dreamed about him, and woke up sweating because he was pulling her back into the trap. He was more interested in his motor magazines than talking to her. As he turned a page his fingers were immediately fixed at the bottom, ready for flipping to the next. He would go on the whole evening if she didn't say something, and when she did he answered in such a way as to make her feel guilty, implying that because he had worked hard all day, which he certainly had, he didn't want to be disturbed by her in the evening.

She had seen half a dozen of his magazines full of coloured photographs of naked women, their show-off figures strangely attractive, though most of the faces brazen or apathetic. Her own body could not compete, but was still firm enough, she thought, for him not to hanker after these pushed-out bosoms. When she mentioned them, he laughed. Most men liked to look at such things, if only for the sake of *beauty*. Some had their legs wide open, with hair and flesh exposed. He had found them, he said, piled up in Ted's room, and had taken them away from him. But Edward's only fourteen, she said. I know, he said. You're right: that stuff's for the youngsters, not chaps like me. You've seen one, you've seen them all. There was a threat in his voice, drawing her towards an area of life that she didn't care to take part in. His eyes wanted her to go on talking. He'd left the magazines under some shirts in his bedroom cupboard, where he had known she would see them.

She'd chosen autumn to leave, the pagan-piggery of Christmas yet to pass, but a season to be ignored because that too had been part of her slavery. Best not to think of the winter drizzle still to come, but to smell the springtime in anticipation, no matter how long it took. The freezing room ponged of mothballs, disinfectant and cold whitewash. Even after a week there wasn't the cleanliness she had striven for. It hadn't been possible to sleep more than a night without swabbing every square inch of the green and brown wallpaper with a bleached cloth. Pans of dust had come from windowsills, pelmets and skirting boards. A rag tied to a sweeping brush had brought cobwebs from every corner. Four buckets of water had been used in flushing the lino and floorboards under the so-called carpets.

While she worked she didn't think. The vacuum cleaner from the cupboard on the stairs wouldn't suck the grit easily.

What was left clinging to the floor had to be lifted with fingers and fed to the nozzle as if the zoo had boarded one of its tamer and more delicately nurtured animals on her for a month while the keeper went on holiday. George had shown her how to unblock a vacuum cleaner by reversing the hose and blowing out the obstructions after switching on the power. She tried. A cloud of rainbow-coloured fluff shot over the carpet, but it took only a few minutes for the nozzle to suck it clean again.

She peeled a potato, an onion and a carrot, and dropped them to boil in the same water. She put a mutton chop under the grill, then set a slice of bread and an apple on the table. Being hungry, she was not unhappy. When the onion brought water to her eyes she no longer felt like weeping. At forty years old, and alone for the first time, she smiled because such misery as she felt made her happy in her own way and nobody else's.

She sat in front of the fire, a woollen hat pulled over her ears, and a hand in her pocket squeezing the tenpence coins because they would keep her warm till morning. She kept her coat and gloves on. In the spring she would get a train to the nearest countryside and smell clean air, even if she had to walk through muddy fields to reach it.

When from her previous warm home she had tried to imagine being so beleaguered, she had seen herself as a cypher without purpose. The spice and anodyne of reality had been missing, and she was sufficiently herself not to feel in any way a cypher, because the process of surviving provided enough reality to be going on with. An advantage she had not foreseen was that you could talk to yourself, and that when you spoke your thoughts aloud they became more coherent than when they stayed locked in. On first hearing her voice she made up her mind that it had got to stop: 'If anyone hears you they'll think you've gone off your head.'

But she had no control over the need to hear herself, and thought that if she didn't control it she really would go mad.

38

Her voice filled the room and proved she was sane. When she spoke, her body was warmer. The noise told her she was alive. She felt more herself when she could listen to her voice, and decide whether or not it was talking sense, than when the same useless phrases spun in silence. She had never heard her voice before. It was worth arguing with. She hadn't been able to listen and know how it sounded when in conversation with George. Her words had been distorted, and emotional confrontation had made them more his than hers, which would not be the case anymore.

Occasionally forgetting to say that she did not like it here, she was most tempted to when on the street, and when she knew that she must under no circumstances talk aloud. The urge had been hard to resist, except for saying the odd word in a supermarket, or while waiting at a traffic light. So she allowed herself to talk all she liked in her room, hoping there would be less impulse to let anything out on the street where others might hear.

Happy enough in her freedom, she couldn't believe George was much bothered by her departure. He wasn't to blame that she had gone, and nor was she. It had taken them a long time to realize they weren't made for each other, though she was sure George didn't yet know, and was mystified at what she had done. He had grown fat through never knowing where his next meal was coming from, having been brought up in a family where everything in sight was eaten in case they never got fed again, a scramble for existence which left him with dulled perceptions where other people's feelings were concerned.

Putting on weight was part of George's getting-on in life. Having more energy than a thin man, he wanted feeding. He made good money, drove himself at his work, and needed to eat, and became stout in his self-assurance. Nobody could blame him for that – but don't expect him to care what you were thinking.

He had become his own boss, which in his family was

everyone's dream if not their ambition, though only he had the force and intelligence to show the way. His three brothers hoped it would come by winning the pools, or by pulling off the Great Train Robbery one rainy night when nobody was looking. They never thought of giving themselves a start by working hard, so that the acquiring of money bred an interest and momentum all its own. George had a passion for it, but first he had an obsession for making objects that were useful to others. He'd had little time for her, in that every hour cost money, and she wondered if any man would have, since she did not seem to possess whatever it was that any man needed from her.

She had lived without thought on the matter, though at the time it hadn't seemed so. But too late was too late, and she couldn't go back. She burned the telegraph forms one by one in the hearth before the gas fire.

The steam smelled good. She prodded the vegetables, and drained them into the sink. The meat spluttered in its fat. She was more famished than hungry, but took the heated plate to the table as if to serve someone else. It was for her alone. She stood back for a moment to look, then sat down to eat.

6

The estate agent had been unsure about letting the room in case, being on her own, she might use it for a particular purpose. She'd read the evening paper, telephoned from a box outside her bed-and-breakfast near St Pancras, gone by tube to Holland Park, and located herself on a London Transport map and by asking the way. The agent was waiting between the crumbling pillars of the gate. He said it was on the top floor, which became obvious, unless they were going to a hencoop on the roof.

'The only other person up here,' he said, pointing to a brown-painted door, as distinct from hers which seemed to be a kind of tawny orange, 'is a merchant navy chap who goes away for weeks at a time. It'll be very quiet. If that's what you want.'

'I do,' she said.

His hair was cut short and combed into a parting. Most men had it dangling over their shoulders as if they were teachers or beatniks, but she supposed that the older they got the shorter it would go again, till at sixty it would be as clipped as their grandfathers'. He had trouble with the lock: 'Are you from the north?'

Did he think she was an Eskimo? 'I'm from the Midlands.'

He opened the door. 'Permanently?'

It was rancid and cold. She hoped he had seen from her face, and judged by her talk, that she hadn't come to London just to have a good time. Hard to remember when she had last told a lie: 'I start a new job next week, in a bank.'

He looked at her, and she expected him to ask for references. Maybe he won't, for such a pig-hole as this. 'A student had it till last week. We haven't had time to clean it yet. When do you want to move in?'

He didn't ask what bank she would work at. Obviously didn't believe her. None of his business. He must be used to people like me. 'Tomorrow.'

'I'll get the woman on the ground floor to tidy it up.'

'Don't bother. I'll have a go myself.' Perhaps her accent hid the irony. Was it possible to clean such a place? She paid a month's rent in cash. Maybe he wasn't as surprised as he looked.

'If you leave me, how will you keep yourself?' George wrapped a serviette around his cut finger. 'Beg on the street? Get national assistance?' He leered: 'Go on the batter and

pick up a man now and again? That's all you'll be able to do.'
Rather than mince words, he threw them at her like stones.
She stayed rigid till his Ford Granada crunched over the
gravel and turned on to the avenue. His wounded hand lifted
in case she waved goodbye. I was only joking, he would have
said, if she had welcomed him home that night. You know
me! Bark worse than bite. Don't mean it.

Let him scoff. Didn't like it here, but she would never go
back, wanted to be as far from any man as it was possible to
get. Shows how little he had learned if he thought she wanted
to pick up men. She lacked energy to do anything except
clean the room. Someone had run a sweeping brush over the
floor, but if a man had been moving in it would probably have
been dusted as well.

After the initial swill-down and polish she bought a square
of coloured cloth from an Indian shop and tacked it on the
wall. She cleaned the window inside, and as far as she dared
lean outside, with newspaper and plain water till it was
impossible to tell there was glass in the frames. Light shone in,
even the sun now and again.

At the risk of breaking a leg she stood a chair on the table
and found that with a wet rag she could wipe the ceiling
white. Such hard labour took a whole day, for each square-
foot needed rubbing several times before cleanliness showed
through. Where plaster had crumbled on the walls she pinned
a couple of old scarves, and a flower poster from the Royal
Academy.

Let George see her now. She didn't like it here, which
wasn't strange, all things considered, but at least she could
live with no future. The idea of getting a job before her money
ran out frightened her, and she refused to think about it.
Having finished making the place habitable, she lived in fear.
She hadn't worked at anything for years, because George had
thought that if she went out to find a job people would say he
was going bankrupt and needed his wife to get money for him.

'We've all the spot-cash we need,' he said when she

mentioned doing more with her life than staying at home. He liked to keep her out of harm's way, and busy whenever he was in the house. She thought he spoke from his need to prove he could care for her, but she should have known better. Men were either too fat to be affectionate, or too lean to be lovable, she told herself when the unreality of life worried her into visions and grudges.

She couldn't do much except office work and housekeeping, though when the time came she would find something and be glad of it. Because she'd had no diverting occupation it had been easier for her to walk out on him. She had saved her energy to make the only move that had any meaning since the one that got her married at nineteen, and to view that event as the most important in her life proved how empty her existence had been. Never again. Hadn't liked it there, either. They had no doubt said they loved each other at the beginning, but she had no memory of it. To get married for life was too long a period. The vows were weighted too much against a woman. If you could only get married on a seven-year licence she wondered how many would apply for a second term.

She pulled the mattress off the bed, dipped rag in a tin of paraffin to wipe the springs and headboard. Bugs could be everywhere. The smell was horrible, but necessary. When she went out she would leave the window open.

They had called it love, which was always something other than what it was said to be, but it could only have been the usual mix up of two young kids. She had wanted to change her life by getting into the adventure of controlling a house as she had previously arranged the furniture and kitchen utensils of her doll's cottage.

Marriage was a way out of the overheated office she worked in. With twenty other girls of the City Transport Company she checked receipt rolls of money collected on the buses, and entered the amounts in ledgers before reckoning the totals. They were busy from half-past eight in the morning till half-past four in the afternoon. It was familiar, and she liked it, but after four years she wanted to get away yet not take another job.

Best not to examine the mattress too closely as she pulled it back on to the bed. Looking in a shop window, events on the television screens moved in silence on their different channels. A few children from school sucked lemonade tins, while a chick was shown struggling out of an egg on a bed of straw. The first hairline cracks appeared, then a split, and a gap before she knew what was happening. After a pause came a webbed foot, and more collapse of the shell, followed by a hole, till a side of the shell fell in, and another panel was pushed out, and the damp feathers of a small moving body became obvious. The rest of the shell dropped around, and the silence and distance created by the glass, and the further remoteness of the event within the television screen, and the continuous rush of traffic and movement of people behind, gave a feeling of having watched a birth that had nothing to do with life at all.

A stack of cardboard boxes by the door were waiting to be carted away. Rummaging, she found thin sheets of plastic, which she folded under her arm, and now used to wrap the mattress top and bottom into an envelope so as not to be touched by the stains from whoever had slept there before.

Marrying George in order to go to bed with him was a part of the uprooting that she had hardly thought about. She had set off for Wollaton one Sunday morning on an old sit-up-and-beg machine with a case around the chain that had once been her mother's. Telling the story as if someone was in the room to listen made her feel as young as when it had taken place.

The long brick walls of Wollaton Park stood clean and distinct after a night of rain. Clouds were high and woolly, and a west wind cooled her face as she pedalled. The main road forked near the turn-off for Martins Pond, and she kept to the quieter way curving between high banks towards the village.

The monotony lulled her, and it was marvellous to be in fresh air after the night in her stuffy home, and five days in an overwarm office. Out of breath going up the slope, she pulled the three-speed backward so as not to get off before reaching the church, which meant half-standing from the saddle and pressing hard. The top of the incline was close, but as she drew near, the chain slipped from the ratchet inside its crankcase.

She leaned the bicycle against a wall in the middle of the village, but did not have the knack or strength to lift the machine and press the pedal with one foot so as to snap the chain back into place. Hands black with grease, she already felt the effort of pushing the whole way home. Trying again, the bike capsized.

His face was almost touching. 'You'll never do it like that, duck.'

'Thanks for telling me.'

'I'll show you.' Leaning his own slim racer by the wall, he pressed the chain on in a few seconds. 'It's the *knack* as yer want!'

'I suppose it is.' She didn't care to encourage his vulgarity, though he seemed nice enough. 'Thanks, anyway.'

'Trust a proper cyclist to rescue a lady in distress! I've been to Heanor already this morning.' He stood upright by his bicycle, head bent back as he tapped a map poking from his pocket. 'To see a pal at work. He broke his arm. Where did you get that old dragon-bike?'

'Oh, it belonged to my mother before she died.'

'I'm sorry to hear about that.'

She was amused at his sympathy. 'That was years ago.'

His foot was on the pedal, as if ready for a race. 'I'll ride back to Nottingham with you in case the chain comes off again. It is a bit loose.'

She would leave the office and get a bus for Old Lenton to meet him walking out of the factory at five. He had only to look at a broken contraption to know what to do. He tinkered with his fingers, prodded a screwdriver here and there, and applied a spanner till whatever it was slotted back into place and shifted in tune when the motor was switched on and electricity flowed through. The women pampered him, and he took their praise as gospel truth, whereas they were on piece rates and only wanted him to mend their machines straightaway.

At the office she was considered barmy going out with someone who worked in a factory. Her best friend asked if he smelt of grease, then said it was only a joke when she saw Pam's anger. But Pam knew she was incensed only because she herself had wondered whether she ought to pack him in, though she liked him enough to see how daft and snobbish it would be to do so.

He had loved machinery, even before leaving school. His claims of proficiency were true, though he wasn't backwards at boasting where his skills were concerned. He saw the thought in her eyes. 'You can't blame me, can you? It's all I've got.'

He was more right than he knew, for he treated anyone close to him like a machine, and only those people he had to deal with in business like human beings. When a factory woman told her how smart he was at tackling machines Pam thought it fortunate both for him and the world that he was. She could feel the woman trying to decide what a young man, the spark of everyone's life, saw in her. She wondered herself, and later thought that maybe the girls in the ticket office had been right when they looked amazed at her marrying someone who worked in a factory no matter how good he was at his job.

Behind his sway walk and wide smile, and his opinions which were more overbearing the less he knew about something, he was as insecure as a rat between three traps, and his loud views grew harder to bear the more she realized how disturbed he was at seeing that she believed less and less in his abilities regarding the human side of life. A livelier wife might have made him feel even more uncertain in his ways,

46

but with Pam he was able to further his precarious self-esteem by appearing happier than he really was, in the hope that he would get more out of life, which stance enabled him to abandon the commonplace and devote himself entirely to his ambition.

He gave up his job, rented a workshop, borrowed from the bank and installed machinery. He called it doing his bit for the export trade, saying in one of their arguments that work was his only happiness because he didn't have to think about anything else while doing it. And Pam was content because the more he had to do the less he bothered her.

She kept his accounts, filed insurance cards, typed letters and bills. His trade prospered, and he allowed her to help as if doing her a favour, so that she would have something to pass her otherwise empty time. They discussed all the administration of his business that seemed too tedious for him to manage. Then he hired a secretary, without mentioning it to her, because he thought the work took too much of her time, and that she would feel better without having the job around her neck.

'That might be true,' she answered, 'but you ought to have told me you were going to get somebody else.'

He hardly gave her time to finish. 'I wanted it to be a surprise.'

'We needn't have got married.'

He looked into her eyes, pilloried by her bitterness, and she was sorry that both were in a situation which could not be remedied without vast damage. His fists curled, as if he would strike, but he went back to the mood of his early days, saying jovially: 'Don't get like *that*, duck!'

She knew that one day, when Edward was fourteen and old enough not to need her any more, she would leave.

With this in mind she became more confident, able to argue, and sometimes keep him away at night when he came at her with his battering love-making. She saw how he had used her as ruthlessly as he used everyone who came his way, employing the half-conscious tactics of the self-made man. He was unaware of his methods, and laughed with disbelief when they were pointed out. He was one of those mainstays of society whose activities were interesting to watch, as long as you kept to one side. At the same time, she believed there was nothing malicious about him, otherwise the temptation to live with him again might become too great to resist.

Through knowing him, she had grown to see something of what she was like herself, and apart from not altogether liking what she discovered, she did not relish the idea of getting through to herself in such a way. While accepting that it was impossible to know what you were like except through contact with someone else, she would have preferred self-enlightenment to have come from others rather than only from him.

7

Workmen were throwing furniture from a house about to be demolished. Two mildewed armchairs thudded down. A fire shot flames into the raw drizzle. Pam paused on her morning walk. A bus at full speed sent icy air against her, and a current on the rebound brought smoke from the fire that made her eyes run. Furniture coming from the house was too old and gimcrack for anybody to want, but an elderly woman wearing an army greatcoat and a piece of coloured blanket for a headscarf watched each piece as it fell.

The sharp-eyed face of a man showed at the first floor, and he threw a chamber pot, which the totter shook her head at in disgust when it bounced from the padded back of a chair and rolled on to the wood-rubble. A second workman at the window lifted his right thumb: 'Wait for the next lot!'

He took a cigarette from his overalls and scraped a match down the window frame. He smoked, gazed at the fire, then tugged something across the floor.

Changing her mind as to the value of the chamber pot, the totter asked Pam to guard her barrow and, looking at the ground so as not to trip on a brick or spar, zigzagged to avoid holes and ruts. A man warmed himself at the fire: 'You'd think she was going to a wedding.'

She wore boots. Rolls of socks and stockings padded her lower legs. Pam wondered whether she herself would soon be like those men and women huddled under the motorway bridge at night. Perhaps the totter once had family and friends, and maybe a house her husband was buying on a mortgage when, after twenty years, she turned wild for no reason, put on several dresses and suits of clothes, and got to the nearest railway station. Who was she to think it would be any different for her?

A crane worked noisily. Pam called, but the woman couldn't hear. Having thought all was clear, the two men at the window got themselves behind the wardrobe and pushed it out.

The woman must have sensed it coming, for she looked, and took a few steps back, and smiled as if thinking she couldn't be close enough. The wardrobe turned on its side and hit a chair, and sprang at her with both mirrored doors flying open. Through the world's noise Pam heard the blow that knocked her down. A bus conductor and the man at the fire scrambled forward, while she ran to a telephone box.

A man inside saw her scared rawboned face when she pulled the door open. 'Can't you see I haven't finished?'

'But it's urgent.'

'Shan't be long.' He pulled the door shut: 'Well, as I was saying.' He wore a smart homburg hat, and leather gloves, and an overcoat that must certainly have kept him warm. His speech was loud, though not clear enough to make sense. A whiff of cigars and aftershave lingered, and Pam assumed the smart Volvo by the kerb to be his. She had seen him before, had probably passed him on her walks by Queensway or Notting Hill Gate, but remembered the stricken woman, and pulled the door again: 'Someone's been injured, and I want to get an ambulance.'

'Why didn't you say so?' He pressed the button, dialled three nines, handed her the receiver, and stepped outside. He looked as if wondering where else he had seen her. When she put the receiver back and came on to the pavement he was driving up the road like the busy man he was, no doubt used to running his own life and maybe those of sufficient others to give him whatever confidence he needed.

When the ambulance and police car arrived she didn't want to go back to the building site and get involved as a witness. They would need her name and address, and if she went to court the case might be reported. She wasn't ready to have George find her and say why the hell don't you come back home?

The woman was carried over the rubble on a stretcher, shouting at the two men through her pain and telling them not to drop her. Smoke and flame against the half demolished house made the scene like that of the blitz she had seen on old news films. The woman's hand gripped the chamber pot. 'Let's hope the poor old biddy gets compensation,' a man by the fire said.

'If she don't, she'll get three months in hospital. Just right for the winter. Shouldn't like to be in the next bed, though.'

'They don't have mixed wards, so you needn't worry about that, Fred.'

She was alarmed that they could laugh at such a tragic event, and decided that, having once done jury duty, she would be a witness if necessary.

8

George got used to running his own life. He no longer needed the confidence she had given him during their early struggles. She wasn't necessary to him anymore, and he released her, but when he realized that her unexpected freedom increased her self-assurance he did all he could to undermine her, where he had never felt the need to before. Arguments became bitter. She resented his new independence, and it seemed that nothing could end their quarrels. He accused her of making him incapable of any sort of work. She wanted to ruin him. Life together had become impossible. All he needed was peace, and she was sorry because she didn't know how to give it to him and herself at the same time. And in any case, why shouldn't *he* give it to *her*?

She went down town two evenings a week to a literature course at the Workers' Educational Association. George stayed late at the office so as to meet her and take her home in the car. He didn't like her going anywhere without him. He made it plain that he didn't understand how she could enjoy herself on her own. There are other people there, she told him. What sort? he wanted to know.

She had seen a poster in the library advertising the course, and thought that the 'workers' of the title had something to do with Trades Unions. George despised and feared the unions, and laughed at her when she said the classes were run by the *Workers'* Educational Association. He sat back in the armchair, letting his coffee get cold while he told her how on walking into the factory at the age of fifteen he was told that he had to join a union. 'I don't join anything,' he said, 'especially when you tell me I've got to.'

He hadn't gone to work to be ordered about by his

workmates. If the gaffers issued an instruction, that was different. He argued by the door, until the manager said that if he didn't enrol he would have no job. 'It isn't my decision. That's the way things are.' The sight of so many machines pulled at his new boots and caused his hands to twitch as if he were trying to struggle out of a dream. He told it in so many words, as he often had and was able to do with something which affected him so profoundly. He certainly hadn't brought half as much discussion to bear where his relationship with her was concerned.

Because he had never forgotten his defeat he made certain that no union members got a look in when he came to setting on men at his firm. If he had been left to choose whether or not to join a union at fifteen he might have thought it a more beneficial institution, but he wasn't that sort. He despised organizations, except the one he had created. The only passionate language she heard was when some stoppage, strike, walk-out or go-slow in another firm prevented vital supplies reaching his own. Components gone astray on the roads or in the post, or delayed at the mill where they were produced, turned him into a promenading wagon of invective that kept her speechless and laughing in turn. His reputation for prompt delivery was threatened, not to mention his living and that of his men, as well as his pride which she suspected mattered most.

As was to be expected, he voted Conservative. It was impossible to live long with a person and not fall in with their habits, and have the same opinions regarding the way the world was organized. But such views had been hers for years before meeting him. If she began to question them now, it was simply because he held them, and because they were the linchpins of so much of his character that she disliked. His taunts about the *Workers'* Educational Association made her uneasy concerning the sort of people she would find there, though because of his attitude she was unable to change her mind about going even if she had wanted to.

At the first session she didn't see anyone resembling a workman. They were the same kind as herself, except for one or two she thought might look down upon her as she had thought to look down on others who in fact were not there at all. During the discussion on E. M. Forster one of the women was staring at her, and under the thin face and grey hair she recognized Eunice Dobson who had once worked at the corporation ticket office.

Pam sat at the large table, conspicuous by her inability to say anything. She had read the books, and shaped whole sentences from her ideas, but couldn't speak. She did not feel stupid, having something to say if only she could get it out. George would have laughed if he had known that she couldn't talk.

She was content to listen to the lecturer, and those who, during the round-table talk, which he cleverly encouraged, were not afraid to state their views, even though they might be shown as mistaken or irrelevant in the summing up. But the discussion was easy and even humorous, and though unable to add anything, she felt happy to be in a different world to the one at home.

When D. H. Lawrence's attitudes to the working class were under discussion, after a reading of *Sons and Lovers*, a young ginger-bearded man commented that in his opinion Lawrence was an Edwardian snob who in fact hated the workers, was a writer whose views were not to be trusted because he made the working people out to be far worse than they were, and totally ignored their proletarian virtues, not to mention their revolutionary potential.

She was compelled to speak at last, her face red from embarrassment, her eyes staring with such conviction that she did not see anyone. Her words were distorted by unnecessary hurry, but the class gave absolute attention to what she was saying: 'You can't talk like that about "the workers". They all behave differently. Some are good and work hard, others are skivers and don't. Lawrence's opinion is as good as anybody

53

else's. So is mine, I suppose, and yours as well. I only know my own family, and my husband's, and I never saw any revolutionary potential in them.'

She sat down. It was politically criminal to look on the workers in the way she did, the man retorted. But she had broken her quietude and didn't care what he said, even if she had sounded a fool. Even if, she thought, I am a fool. Her heart banged against her blouse. She seemed bloodless, and wished the words unsaid. Yet she had done it, and would speak again whenever she felt like it.

As soon as she found something to do which excluded him, George realized that she had done so because there was no part of his life he would let her share. As a way of getting back at her he decided there would be even less in the future.

9

The two workmen from the first floor were talking to the police. She expected argument, vociferation, perhaps pushing around, but they only mentioned what had happened. The younger man tapped at a brick with his foot. The other laughed because one of the policemen made a joke. It hadn't been their fault. The old woman had run across the house-wreckage after her bit of treasure and been struck down. Another onlooker told them how. There were neither shouts nor moans of sorrow, and no one was taken struggling away. The demolishers had not thrown the wardrobe on her, but neither had they looked properly beforehand. It was an accident, like all unstoppable occurrences. But some were lawful and others were not. The men in the house had their bit of fun by chucking objects out of the window and laughing at the smash, but this time they had broken the ribs of a person who, a few seconds before, had thought nothing of grabbing at every little thing to earn a shilling or two.

She felt close to her whom the ambulance had taken. The woman would be looked after. For a few seconds Pam didn't know where she was, and envied the injured woman's fate because day and night had been separated from her senses. Icy rain chilled, and she turned, intending to go to her proper home, as if she had been lost for an hour while walking the streets, and had daydreamed of a woman being struck down. She would make coffee and wait for George to come from work and tell what she had seen. She went as close as possible to the fire, pressing fingers against her eyelids till they hurt, then looked to see in what part of the world she now belonged.

George soon thought better of her evening classes, because they made her less liable to snap and grumble when, about once a week, he wanted to make love. His ramming habit, as she thought of it, maligned her body and left her in despair. Her mind veered off it like a finger from an open wound. The emptiness of space was paradise compared to such memories. In her rented room she could moan like a mutilated animal which had nevertheless got out of the trap. Solitude was preferable to a feeling of annihilation with George, when her spirit had been a particle of light getting further and further away, bruised and disregarded because no other human being thought it of any value.

The hold he kept on her was harder to break the tighter it became. The more he oppressed, the more she was his prisoner, till she felt that even to raise a finger would be as impossible as getting under the world and attempting to walk with it on her back.

Sufficient anger came to indicate what she wanted, but finally it wasn't what she wanted that mattered. Desires and necessities, once she knew what they were, were seen to be of no importance, except that they too helped to keep her a prisoner which, reducing her to impotence, thereby made her feel like a victim. But life went on as if nothing were the matter. Action was denied to someone who could endure for so long. The force that eventually moved her to act existed far below the level of intention. Everything she did was under her control. The insupportable life she led seemed as if it would go on forever, but it felt like something had fallen from the sky and crushed her.

She was finally taken by the scruff of the neck, and what she had wanted to do for so long was accomplished by a part of her that she didn't know existed. Whatever it was had more strength – though still part of her – than she had ever been aware of before. She had sensed it, yet for a long time held back in case it betrayed her by not being strong enough when the time came, but its power at last erupted so positively that she had been taken by sufficient force to get to the railway station. From the beginning she had wanted to be dominated by this act, since it was, after all, her own well-concealed self emerging from its hiding place to prove that it was her victory and nobody else's.

Smoke from the fire turned in her direction, so she stepped aside. The wardrobe lay across splintered laths and a mouldy chair, one of its doors detached. Her reflection was distorted by rain spots hitting the full-length mirror, and she knelt to slide a finger from right to left over the glass. Lakes and rivers formed. She rubbed a place dry with her handkerchief, and saw her face in the few seconds before colourless globs of water disguised it again.

The mirror was heavy in its wooden framework, and she was several streets from home. The fire was a hump of smouldering rubbish, and no one else was on the site. She had never taken something from a wasteground before, but felt no sense of stealing when she lifted the mirror-door to the pavement.

The back was covered with black dust, and dirtied her coat. Hinges torn from the main supports had left splinters, but she gripped above and below, and hoped people would move as she walked down the road, for it was impossible to see unless she swung the mirror aside like a windmill sail.

The man in the telephone box seemed to be looking over her shoulder, his face almost as clear as her own. She had seen him in the corridor of the train that was leaving Nottingham when he spat out of the window to say goodbye. There was no doubt. She hoped he was more satisfied with London which, being a bigger place to spit on, might feel the sting less.

She leaned the mirror against a wall, but disliked stopping, even though it was vital, because of picking it up again. The intervals were made fewer by counting an extra dozen steps when at the end of her endurance. She had never carried such weight for any distance. It was painful against her breasts, and pulled her arms till the muscles deadened. At a corner the wind pressed hard as if to prevent her getting the plunder home.

Wall and pavement-edge were visible, and anything in front seemed unimportant. The mirror faced outwards, and people coming towards her, seeing their reflection, stepped aside to let her by. The screen baffled their remarks. The mirror was a memento, and set against a wall of her room would hide a blemish, and fill emptiness. When polished it would reflect both herself and the room within, and create space to look into when the illusion of being a prisoner wore her down. It would reflect light for someone who had come out of the dark. Should it crack, seven years' bad luck would be in store, so she would have to be careful.

Crossing Ladbroke Grove, she stepped up the opposite pavement. Acquiring the burden might make a different person out of her, for she felt wedded to the weight, an experienced carrier not to be waylaid by the last obstacle of the kerb on the final few hundred yards.

Her toast-and-tea breakfast of four hours ago left her famished. In her exertions she was all awkwardness, and rested before reaching the gate. The rain drove, but the

57

mirror protected her. Water streamed off her knuckles. She spun when a corner of her load struck a lamp post. She scraped a low wall, and the mirror fell.

An elbow-pain tightened her grip, and took the weight of the board which banged into her face. Someone had pushed viciously from the front. George had caught her, and was ready to gloat or kick. She heard herself shouting.

Her burden was indestructible, but she felt the biting ache of her grazed hand. No one was nearby. At whatever cost, every limb had played its part in guarding the mirror. An attempt to break it had failed at the expense of a fingernail, proving that the speed of disaster wasn't always too quick to handle.

She opened the front door, thankful to be out of the rain, and knew that even if she took all day to get her prize up the stairs no one would notice how happy she felt about the bit of old trash she had saved.

10

She had never known what she appeared like till now, because those mirrors previously looked into had been surrounded by things which weren't entirely hers. The histories of such objects had intimidated her to the extent that her features seemed either false or indistinct when she stared back at herself from the mirror. She could never look for long because George was always moving in another part of the house, and could come in any second to distort her image.

A proper upstanding full-length mirror would not only allow her to talk to herself, but to see the motions of her lips as well. If she cared to she could speak without noise, like a dumb person. It seemed less insane to have her features clearly in view. When she spoke she would see that she resembled only herself. The inside of the mouth was as important as the tip of her nose or the colour of her eyes.

The clarity of her reflected features would have been seen only as a flat picture when sitting by her dressing-table in what used to be her home, an image pained and drab which she couldn't bear to look at for long, so that she rarely had to worry about being caught examining herself. A mirror showed what was in your spirit, and there had been nothing more than a mask of indecision hiding what one day, after self-murder or emotional earthquake, might be revealed.

The woodwork around the mirror had been eaten with worm, so she bought a chisel and a screwdriver and, careful not to send any cracks through the silvering behind, eased each piece away. Tall and narrow, it leaned without borders against the wall so that when she stood back her whole form could be seen, enabling her to talk from a distance if anything special came into her mind.

She sometimes saw her son Edward as if he were behind her, sent by George as an emissary to bring her home. Walking through Bayswater he had been coming towards her, or standing on the platform of a bus that turned a corner. He was eighteen, and at college, but in her dreams Edward was eight years old, and talked as if he were herself, and also looked as if he were George, so that she woke with tears on remembering that part of her life. What she had lived could not be taken away, but anguish did not diminish on seeing the first light of another day straining at the window, which could only be pushed back by switching on the light and glancing in the mirror as she passed to brush her teeth at the sink. Change was a poison that had to run its course before healing could begin. But knowing such a thing did not make life easier to bear. Her inability to profit from self-knowledge created a further layer of torment.

59

She could reflect any person in her mirror, but it was another matter when it came to who was allowed into her dreams. The walls of rooms and corridors glowed with pale intimidating light. Such dreams caused her mind to labour all night long among frightening combinations of people she had known, permutations lacking any logic or reason. The underworld dogs of the past were set on her by George and his family now that they were no longer able to get at her above ground. They came through doorways, or sprang in mayhem from the waves of the sea or the muddy banks of rivers. With changing faces they pursued her towards disaster, so that she woke having bitten hard enough on her finger for blood to show. At breakfast it was impossible to reorganize every move of her night's dreams.

If George had been unfortunate in meeting her, he had been even more unlucky with the family he had been born into. Perhaps such was the common burden of the self-made man, because having something to fight against gave inordinate resource and strength. It was impossible to get away from his family, but he never ceased trying, while making it obvious that his effort was as much for Pam's sake as for his own, though she guessed that the process must have started long before meeting her.

They had broken with his brothers on many occasions, and though George felt safer and more at peace she knew that he also regretted the poorer spiritual surroundings in which he found himself. He had sharpened his ambition, and learned that the value of what you strove for was only equalled by the payment you made. Having taught him, she now had to learn the same hard lessons for herself.

George's family despised his endeavours to become better off, gave their opinion that to say he'd been born would be putting it mildly. Hatched was more like it, for a money-grubbing weasel like him. You couldn't deny their humour, as they clacked with laughter behind his back. When George first set up the workshop his three brothers got sacked from

60

their jobs and expected him to set them on, to pay them more than his best men yet allow them to boss it over the others and walk around in clean overalls all day doing nothing, as if that was their right, on the cynical assumption that blood was thicker than water.

George, knowing them better than she did, was more afraid of them. They were a woebegone lot, he complained, always glued to the telly or a pint of ale, a rough bunch who knew nothing more than how to live from hand to mouth.

After one severance of contact they made telephone calls while George was at work.

'Pam?'

'Who's that?'

'Harry.'

'Oh, yes.'

'I'm ringing to ask if you'll lend us ten quid. We ain't got a cent between us.'

'I haven't got it. We've nothing to spare.'

He waited for her to say something else, but she held back, though it was hard to do so.'

'Mean bleeder!' he said at last.

'What do you want?'

'Can we come up and watch a film on your colour telly?'

'No. We're busy.'

'We shan't bother you.'

Pause.

What next? she wondered.

'You set him against us. Our George was all right till he married you.'

'You're off your head. Stop phoning.'

'Why don't you help us, then?'

'We have done. Lots of times. You know we have.'

He lied. 'You haven't.'

'Why don't you pay us back some of the money that you owe us? It's about time you did.'

'I'm out o' wok. How can I?'

'Get another job, then. There's plenty of work these days.'
Silence.

Then he shouted: 'You're a rotten whore!'

They knew what to expect from each other. She put the phone down. She dreaded any of them coming to the house, kept the door locked when alone, and never answered the bell if she saw one of them opening the gate. When she and George came back from the cinema one night a stone had been thrown through the front window. He said it was no use calling the police.

'Why not?' she asked.

'I'm not sure it's them, that's why. But if it is, then I've got something against 'em now. They might be careful before they do anything else, in case I bring this up as well.'

He knew them better than she did.

They had no curiosity beyond that of wanting to pierce the future and find out what teams would score next Saturday, so that they could fill in the pools form for a sure win before sitting in front of the television to watch the match of the day.

There were better families, and no doubt far worse, but to get beyond the immediate cycle of work, food, shelter and sex wasn't part of their lives. Their existence was ordered for them, while they imagined themselves independent. Perhaps they enjoyed life more than if they had striven to get on because, unless Alf's telly popped a valve, or illness clawed Harry down, or the big end went in Bert's car engine (they all had clapped-out motors in which to rattle around the streets), they were happy enough in their way, which blinded them to what the world might be doing to them, and stopped them saving what money they earned in order to better their lives.

These weren't the proletarian revolutionary potential that the young man at the WEA had mentioned – if such existed, and she hoped it didn't – though maybe they would be far worse if someone came along and persuaded them that it was about time they got up and inherited the earth. They had been to prison earlier in their lives, except George, who by a miracle – he admitted – had avoided it.

After the ringing of wedding bells, and the pushing of George's ring on to her finger, there seemed no reason not to be friendly with his brothers. But all they wanted to do at the reception was eat and get drunk. George told her that this was only natural, but in her anxiety she was afraid of them. Coming back from the toilet after the meal she met Harry in the corridor who would not let her by: 'Give us a kiss, duck.'

'No.'

He gripped her arm.

'You're drunk. Get out of my way.'

'Come on, he wain't know.'

She considered letting him have one quick kiss, but knew that if she did he would run straight to George and distress him by showing off about it. Her knees were trembling, and she felt sick. 'He will if you don't stop being so daft.'

'Don't care if he does. If he says ote I'll thump 'im. He's got no guts, our George ain't. You'll have a lot better time if you come to bed with me, duck.'

They had once held George by one arm over the opening of an old mine shaft, threatening to drop him into oblivion, keeping him suspended for as long as their strength lasted. It was good fun. They laughed at his screams for mercy, but George told her that he couldn't forget, no matter how friendly they had been afterwards.

'If you don't let me go, I'll shout for somebody.' She hoped no one would hear, because she was ashamed and angry at not having asked one of the bridesmaids to come out with her.

He swayed. 'Not even a kiss, then?'

There was no difference in their height, and she wondered, as he tensed his shoulders, why she didn't lift her fist to him, but she could only back away as he fumbled for her breasts.

'Come on, let's have a bit!'

The door opened. 'Leave her alone, can't you?' her father said. 'A damned fine bunch she's got us married into!'

Her joy was smashed at his implication that she was to blame. The wedding was his first contact with George's relations, and he liked none of them. Having worked in a shop most of his life, he had kept his family what was still known as 'respectable'. 'I've never had much money, but you learn to keep your head above water,' he said, neither boasting nor complaining, 'as if your neck was made of cork!'

He didn't dislike George less than any other young man who might have wanted to marry his daughter, but had hoped they would separate before it came to a union she would never get out of. He had kept quiet in case his words only brought them closer, and he saw his mistake, though knew it would have made no difference anyway in these enlightened times.

Harry was charming, and sober. 'Don't get like that, Albert.'

'Go back inside,' he told Pam, 'or they'll miss you.' The flower in his button-hole was lopsided, and a strand of well-creamed hair had fallen over his forehead. 'If ever you bother her again' – and the grin of conciliation immediately pulled itself inwards from Harry's face – 'I'll hammer you. You can tell that to anybody else in your lot. And if they don't like it, they'll bloody get summat as well.'

It was difficult to know whether he would have succeeded, but moral force was on his side, which might give speed and weight in any physical dispute. Harry was not cowed, but stepped aside in case there should be any doubt that he wanted the incident to end.

They taunted George, who after the first champagne drank only orange squash. He wasn't man enough to pour real booze inside. Was he frightened he wouldn't be able to 'get it in' later on? Alf was shouted down, but he had said it. Other advice followed which they made sure George heard, such clattering laughter proving their possession of him for as long as he lived.

She sat by her father at the top table, overhearing an

argument. 'It must have been at least five hundred years ago,' Bert said.

Harry sat with legs sprawled. 'It couldn't have been. He was born about two hundred years ago, I'd say. No more than that.'

'I'll bet it was seven or eight hundred.' Bert, the eldest of the four brothers, was tall and thin in those days, as opposed to corpulent now. He had a close-set face, shrewd but not tight, knowing without being predatory, the chairman of the brothers rather than their leader, who thereby got his own way more often than not, and was unassailable in his position. He was more right than he knew in assuming Jesus to have been born above seven or eight hundred years ago, but then, it was in his nature to be so.

'Bet you, then,' said Harry, still truculent after getting no kiss from Pam and being unjustifiably threatened by her father, whom he would forever think of as a miserable bastard unable to take a bit of fun.

Bert called to the next table: 'Hey, Tom, how many years ago was it Jesus was born? This daft bogger said it was only two hundred.'

Tom, his brother-in-law, was more knowledgeable. 'Two bloody thousand, more like. Must a been. The bloody Romans killed 'im, didn't they? Nailed 'im on a cross. I learned it at Sunday School.'

Pam's father leaned: 'Somebody should tell 'em what year it is,' he whispered.

Alf began a joke so that she as well as George would hear, and when George protested that he had heard it all before, one of his friends from work said he hadn't, though Pam knew that even if the whole world could retail it backwards Alf was set on spouting it for her especial benefit. She longed for them to scatter to their various homes, or to the pubs.

He pushed his tongue out as if it needed air, pulled it in as if it had had too much of a good thing, swirled it around his mouth, gave it a drink of ale by way of encouragement, then smiled with contrition as if, because they had waited long enough for his joke, he would now make amends and get on with it. Short and wiry, he was less fit than the others. All his teeth were false, and he'd been operated on for ulcers. But he kept his position of equality among his brothers by sheer pertinacity, and by masking the unshakeable vulnerability of his features with a humour that took account of nobody's feelings, theirs least of all but, most important, not even his own.

'There was this courting couple, see? Ah, pass that ale. I'm dying o' thirst. My tongue's got cramp again: it's blocking my windpipe. Well, they worn't going to get married for a couple o' months, and he was askin' her to let him *have it*. "Go on, duck," he said, "I can't wait. Honest, I'll go barmy if you don't let me *have a bit*." She said no, not till they was married. It worn't right, she said. A proper tight-arse, she was. Well, he kept on trying to get it, and she thought of every way to put him off, but no, no excuse was good enough. She just couldn't stop his gallop.'

Pam knew every phrase, though not what the end of the tale would be. He told it with a glitter in his eyes, raised eyebrows, winks – all the right gestures. She prayed that God in heaven would annihilate him. Her hand held a glass whose tight shape gave comfort.

'Any road up,' he went on, 'she thought of an excuse that he wouldn't be able to get round.' He glanced, to be sure she listened, though knowing she had no option. 'Cheer up, duck! Yer en't lost ote, ev yer? It wain't be long now though!'

He squared himself, held a fist high. They all laughed, telling him to leave her alone and get on with it. 'Well,' he said, 'the daft sod kept on at her to let him have a bit of the old you-know-what, but at last she said: "No, Teddy," or whatever his name was, "I can't let you have it, because it's Lent." Well, our Teddy goes dead white at this, and shouts: "What do you say? *Lent*? *Lent*? You'd better get the bloody thing back then if it's lent, because we're going to be needing it soon!"'

Those who hadn't been listening looked across on hearing laughter as if someone had tapped a rock and let it loose. 'Here, just a minute, I've got another one . . .'

Alf wanted to prove that though he may not have a sense of decency he was at least blessed with a memory. 'It's about this couple who went on their honeymoon. But let me get a quick sup at that Shippoes first. I'm as thirsty as a straw dog in the desert!'

Most of the women talked among themselves at other tables, knowing better than to bother hearing jokes that would make them feel as if every man in the world wanted them only for *that*. Pam counted the minutes as they moved on the clock. She picked up her empty glass with a grip so tight she was afraid it would split.

She felt that those within range ought to tell Alf in no uncertain terms to pack it in; or they might at least give a hint that if he didn't stop they would hustle him outside to cool off. He knew what he was doing, his taunts deliberately set to bring tears. But others were under the spell of his story, even if only to confirm whether or not they'd heard it before. They too relished the spite that all men use when close to women, and want either to shame them or get them on the floor.

Alf sucked three-quarters of a pint from his jar. 'Well, there they was, see, a *young* couple in this room at an hotel. They'd been humping around all night. I don't suppose anybody got a bit of sleep next door, and that's a fact. But when the bloke stood at the blind in the morning, ready to let it up, he went up with it, right to the top and round the roller! One minute he was going up and down like a yo-yo, and the next he was spinning round and round like a catherine wheel shouting get me off, get me off, get me off . . .'

A light of such intensity crossed her eyes at his manic depravity, and the cheering that at last tried decently to drown it, that she would have lost the power of sight for evermore if she hadn't swung back her arm and let the glass fly at his forehead.

There was no thought of throwing it, yet on doing so she wished she had blinded him, instead of which the lame missile struck his pullover and fell to the floor without breaking. She no longer cared, but the so-called joke perished in mid-spate. His pale features widened and, enraged at how close he had been to an affliction of sundry cuts at the face, shouted: 'You fucking bitch!'

She stared, at the shock of his voice, wondering why he had bawled such an insult. Resentment and desolation showed in his face when it should have been in hers, for he suffered because they were in a place where he could not hit her as he clearly wanted to for having humiliated him in front of his brothers and friends.

She was seen by his lot as coming from a family that considered itself a bit above theirs, and before the wedding they had made no mistake about letting her know it. Alf had done his best to make her sling something at him (the fact that she had failed to do damage was only through lack of practice) and by succeeding he had not only dragged her to their level, but made an enemy for life.

'You fucking whore. You pregnant cow,' he shouted against her face while the others tried to pull him clear. 'I saw you trying to nobble our Harry in the corridor a few minutes ago.'

Her cool stare prolonged his fury. She had wounded him in the deepest possible way, for the despair in his eyes indicated that it would have been better for his self-esteem if the glass had hit him square in the face and caused blood to flow. He would have had something to talk about, would have been a figure of significance and interest and, most important, would have borne the marks of her surrender to their way of life.

He was insulted to the core, and diminished himself even further by bringing out such ordinary and expected obscenities that they could in no way be considered harmful. She saw from his expression, as he continued ranting, that he had wanted the glass to injure him. All the bad treatment of

women, by him and his brothers, was because they sometime
hoped to meet one who would pound them into the dust. The
revelation came upon her there and then, but she would not
begin on such a course, and thought how lucky she was that
neither her aim nor her strength had damaged him.

Her father would not let her, and therefore himself, be
treated in such a way. He swung his elbow so violently that Alf
fell like a stone. The anger in her father's face was fierce, and
none of the brothers dared attack him. Only then did George
think it time to take her away.

11

She and George had been as children, half their lives ago. The
determination to have nothing to do with his family was
strengthened by the difficulty of keeping the last few minutes
of the wedding reception clear in her mind. Something had
happened. A quarrel had been broiling, the not uncommon
ending at such functions. She had been glad to forgive
everyone, but only as long as she didn't have to talk about the
fight either with them or George.

Time must pass before she could understand what had
taken place. She had been terrified that Alf would begin
hitting her while everyone either watched or cheered him on.
Only her father would protect her, and he was one among
many. She had never felt such danger, and the man who
should have been by her side, and whom she had just married,
seemed as likely to attack her for throwing the glass as Alf
himself.

The mirror was an aid to her reflections. Memories came

according to her own nature now that she was in her inviolate room, and a woman of forty could not ask for more than that.

In the middle of the day her recollections were so real that in her anguish she wanted to smash the mirror, then find the nearest telephone box and call George. She needed to talk to him, though would hardly know what to say. Now that they did not live together the scenes from twenty years ago seemed as if they had happened yesterday. Their reappearance, however, only confirmed their final end, though she was frightened that after a stumbling conversation with George a conclusion might be suggested that was worse than whatever memories the mirror compelled her to face. She would drop under a tube train rather than let her body agree to such a backwards walk.

Yet the urge to telephone was as imperative as had been her need to leave him, when any considerations there may have been against the move had suddenly gone without trace. She dreaded the act of dialling the number, and on her walks would never go by a call box no matter what zigzag course she was forced to steer through the streets.

For a while the face that came most often out of the mirror was that of Alf, and she was surprised at feeling no intense dislike. In his drunken need to 'make her one of them' he had, it must be said, shown himself more human than the others, who would not have put themselves out to make her anything at all. At the same time she had forgotten as quickly as possible the vileness in Alf's face, but she had also refused to allow any good that might have been there to influence her opinion for the better. He had been more human because she was able to see in his behaviour a warning that sooner or later George would act towards her in the same way, causing her in that instant to wonder also whether she hadn't made a mistake in getting married at all.

George blamed himself for what had happened at the wedding, and her refusal to talk about it only prolonged his feelings of guilt. He had hardly been aware of her existence during the party, wanting to enjoy himself with his brothers who now accepted him as their equal because he had, she heard them say, got himself tied up for life in the same way as themselves. After months of waiting, and the tension of the ceremony, George said that he stayed among his brothers so that she could relax with her workmates from the office. It was understandable, but she had wanted him to sit close by so that his brothers as well as the girls from work would see how loving and united they were.

As time went on George considered that there was no need for such useless recrimination, wondering why he should worry about a little harmless fun on his brother's part anyway. The result of this change in George's attitude was that she felt guilty at having been the cause of the fight, making her think that if she hadn't married him or, better still, if she had never been born, he might have led a less troubled life.

In order to prevent him behaving in the way his brothers were seen to treat their own wives, and becoming more like one of them than was absolutely necessary, considering that he was from the same mother at least, she helped him through the complications of starting his business. There was no guarantee that he would resemble his brothers, of course, because some could be very different, but he provided an answer to that one morning when she was halfway through her term with Edward.

After breakfast and before setting out for work he went, as was his habit, to the lavatory. Having finished, he couldn't find any paper, and bellowed for some as if he had woken from a nightmare that had terrified him beyond endurance. She was unable to act for a few moments, his noise frightening her in quite a different way to the fear that had for some reason stricken him.

With a shout he opened the door a few inches so that she could pass a roll of paper. When he came out, the corners of his mouth were flecked with spit, and he was as pale as if he

71

had been blind drunk and then vomited. He tried to say something, his mouth fighting a stone pressed on his vocal chords. His vacuous hazel eyes demanded to know why she had deliberately humiliated him, as if she would now go and tell his brothers about it so that they could all have a good laugh-up together. She sensed no other explanation for his distress.

'You didn't need to shout like that,' she told him. 'I forgot to put some in last night.'

He stared, but did not see her. She turned to walk away because there seemed nothing more to say about such a small matter, though she realized afterwards that it would have been safer to have screamed at him with fists and fingernails flying.

After a year of marriage she thought she knew him well, but now saw – and felt, when he struck her twice across the head – that he was a stranger impacted with unexplained emotions that no life would be of sufficient length to unravel. In any case, she had enough tremors of her own to take care of, whenever it might be possible to consider them.

Knowing his value, he was often unpleasantly vain, lacking the charm even his brothers might occasionally put on. Some time after the wedding Alf apologized for causing her to throw the glass at him, in such a way that she had to be forgiving. He talked sensibly, and was contrite, and not so light-hearted that he didn't mean what he said. His features, better-looking than when he tried to be humorous, had the usual vulnerability that pleaded with her not to treat him harshly.

She fell against the wall as if the roof had pushed her there, but picked up a heavy wedding-present ashtray as she turned to face him. There was no question of throwing. Her intention was to strike at his head. His eyes came to life, their glitter fixed on the glass object in her hand. Like a cat in his dumb suffering he longed for the blow because he would then have paid for whatever he was supposed to have done. She would have nothing left to forgive him for.

That sort of brawling had gone on all the time in *his* family, physical argument that left its bruises but cleared the air quicker than otherwise. They were used to it, and thrived on it, but she refused to join in and periodically act out the domestic massacre as a way of maintaining unity.

He stepped away quickly when she lowered her arm, surprised not to be crouching by the stairs and staunching blood. Either that, or he was disappointed that she wasn't on her way down town already, to sit in a café with a fag and a cup of tea till the storm had blown by, in which time he would have searched her out and agreed to forgive her.

'Don't ever hit me again,' she cried. 'Do you hear?'

He didn't speak, looked anywhere but at her.

'Never. If there's any more of this, I'm off.'

She dropped the ashtray into a bowl of water to wash away any trace of what she had almost done. When he went to work she wept, unable to understand why he had hit her for something so ridiculous. She once visited her father, and got back too late to set a meal out, but he only joked about that, when he might have been angry after working hard the whole day.

She tried to detach him from his family on the assumption that such a course would separate him from his worst traits. They should see as little of his brothers as possible. He agreed, knowing that she was right.

But to cut him off on all except the superficial level of physical prosperity was impossible, she soon realized. The traits he got from them were, albeit camouflaged, unassailable. He suffered for this as much as she did, at times to an even greater degree, so that she was more sorry for him, at the possibility he had to endure, than she was for herself at being on the end of the powerline. He was like a person plugged into an electrified circuit who doesn't suffer a shock as long as he holds on to someone else.

Yet he felt the current passing through, and wanted to let go – to have as little as possible to do with his family because

73

they had, he once said to her, always regarded him as their chosen victim. He went one day to a travel agent's in town to collect a passport for their first overseas holiday, and on coming out was hailed from the cab of a builder's lorry by his brother Bert. Trying to remember in what half-demolished street he had parked his car, George was swamped by the various worries of his business, till the imperative tug of his brother's greeting cleared them from his mind.

'I ain't seen yer for three weeks.' Bert indicated that he had suffered as if it had been three years. On checking backwards, George found that he was exactly right, and felt unable to refuse the offer of a quick pint in the Peach Tree.

Bert parked on a double yellow line: 'The firm will pay if I get fined,' though to give his employers a sporting chance he stuck a card in his cab window saying BUILDING IN PROGRESS, then followed George inside as cold rain swept along the road. 'That's the trouble with the building trade: when the sky pisses down you've got no wok. Not like you, getting set up as your own boss with a cushy inside job.'

George bought the drinks. 'It's not as easy as it sounds. I'm at it sixteen hours a day, and often don't get a minute to myself. Seven days a week, as well, which is why I ain't seen you or any of the others lately.'

Bert put his cap on the bar. There was a line along his brow, and beads of sweat above, his thinning grey hair dampened by it. Tall and thin, he spoke mournfully. 'I thought Pam had been putting in a bad word about us.'

'She's as busy as I am, bless her. But she needs a rest. I'm taking her to Majorca for a fortnight.' He held up the new and shining book: 'I've just been to get our passport.' For himself, he wouldn't have bothered with a holiday for another few years but: 'She talked to a woman at the supermarket who went to Majorca last July, and said it didn't cost all that much.'

Bert wanted to have another drink.

74

'Can't.'

He laughed. 'I'll pay.'

'Must be going.' He put the passport in his pocket, another symbol of the difference between them. 'I've got to see an estate agent this afternoon, and there's a few things to do before then.'

'You'll work yourself to death.' Bert bumped against him as they stood. 'You only live once, you know.' He was the easy-going sort who would never do anything interesting. George thought it wasn't only due to his wife, either, who was as slack and idle as he was. Though ten years younger, George was a much smarter man of the local world, and felt older, even protective to his feckless brothers as long as it didn't cost time or money.

His car was only two hundred yards away, but Bert drove him there. 'Save you getting wet through. I expect you'll be warm and dry in Majorca. I wish I could get clear o' this effing place for a couple of weeks.'

If he stopped drinking for six months and banked the money he would be able to go to the Bahamas. 'You want to try it sometime.'

Such uncalled-for advice made Bert tighten his lips as he stopped his lorry so close to the back of George's smart Cortina that George expected to hear a crunch of tin and glass. Bert laughed: 'I ain't been driving twenty years for nowt. Your cronky old car's safe wi' me.' He leaned towards him: 'Listen, George, you're my brother, and I'm a bit short this week. Can you lend us fifteen quid? I'll pay you back as soon as I can.'

George opened the cab door. 'Money's tight till I get going in my new premises. I shan't be in the clear till the autumn. Maybe not even then.'

'I didn't think you would, you mingy bleeder.'

George slammed the door as he leapt down, and was searching for his car keys when Bert's voice came sharply

75

through the loud revving of the engine. He waved something, and George saw his dark blue passport held above a pool of water. 'You lost this, I think.'

The precious book corkscrewed towards him, hard to catch as Bert's laugh followed its descent. Any attempt to stop it floundering in the muddy grit would be hopeless.

George had never done him harm or wished him ill, and was grieved that his own brother, on bumping against him in the pub, had slipped the passport out of his pocket. He'd done it as a joke, of course, and then given it back, knowing that George wouldn't doubt where it had gone if he didn't, but was still sufficiently ill-natured to make him scrabble for it in the wet.

It was impossible to explain Bert's dislike. George had done nothing to bring it on. Yet Pam, when he told her about the incident, and now looking back on it, assumed that nothing happened without reason except among those who had been born and would die never having any notion as to what reason might be. Reason was alien to George's brothers, except in so far as they could vaguely sniff out its existence in others, whom they then proceeded to despise and despoil.

It might be extremely unreasonable on her part to believe that such people could ever be taught to be reasonable. You were either born with reason or you were not, and she saw this picture of their joint passport thrown into the squalor as the act of a person for whom reason would never have any meaning no matter how determined an attempt was made to convert him to its use.

The only way they could be induced to accept reason was out of fear, which would be worse than leaving them alone, for such a policy would require unremitting effort on the part of those chosen to impose it, who in the process could hardly fail to instil fear into people already accustomed to using reason in their lives.

George's brothers chose not to be reasonable, and Bert resented the status of a passport – which anybody could acquire who wanted to go out of the country. Apart from despising those who considered themselves to be in that category, he feared the submission you had to endure while going through the necessary form-filling. He abominated the authority that granted the privilege of having one.

Some of this may well have gone through Bert's head when he sent the passport zig-zagging at George waiting below, the action of a person who did not know the meaning of ambition and its all-absorbing work. But now that she had left George she was beginning to see that 'getting on' might not have been such a desirable end in itself, though it was also true that without the individual urge towards self-improvement the world would be a worse place to live in.

George had put himself beyond the range of their pecking order, by marrying someone who did not agree with their ways. They must often have imagined there was still time for her to acquire them – though losing the most vulnerable member of the family when George married out distorted their relationship in such a way that they appeared never to have recovered. In the meantime their hatred was always raging, as if they had been married to each other for decades and not yet found the nerve to climb into bed together.

Whatever the reason, it seemed as if no technique had yet been developed for getting anything from them except the worst. There was no sign of improvement, nor would there be, she supposed, which was just as well because she didn't need to use them as an explanation for her clearing out from George. Perhaps the real reason for leaving had been even more unreasonable than any of his brothers ever knew how to be, but if so she had never done anything in her life that had felt so right.

12

She came out of the hairdresser's with a scarf over her head. Her hair was held in place. The wind could no longer blow it about, even without the scarf. She collected a blouse and skirt from the cleaners, for the more often she changed her clothes the sooner she would know the kind of person she wanted to become, and thereby recognize who she was. She had little enough to wear, so there was no danger of becoming more than one person, though such a thought did not faze her at a time when she didn't particularly want to become anyone at all provided she could recognize herself when she saw her.

Frozen fish was cheap at the supermarket. She bought an orange as well, then bread and a bottle of milk before going back to her room. She could close the door, and no one would be able to come in unless asked. The room was hers. She had no other, and didn't need more than one. The space within its walls and ceiling was enormous when she needed it to be, and also small when raw cold had to be heated by gas and paraffin.

She took off the scarf and walked to the mirror. She didn't know herself, but realized she would have to get used to the face still unwilling to smile back at her. Short hair made her look thinner and harder. She was glad to be different. Maybe even George would have to stare twice before saying hello if they passed on the street.

If she were tired in the morning from having gone late to bed she needn't get up, and if she felt exhausted in the afternoon she could sleep till the onset of darkness which would be transformed by filling the enclosed space with electric light. Short hair, easier to wash than the scrag-ends that George had found 'womanly', gave her the illusion of making a new start. She was more in charge of herself.

But she was still not so firmly in control that she didn't think of George and his family much of the time, knowing that as long as such memories plagued her so did the danger that she might go with packed cases to St Pancras and take the first train north. The inner conspiracy, worked entirely by herself, could lead only to one end. Nightmare came at her happiest moments, and rendered her null and void by a terror that could spread no further. At its worst she was unable to move. The only way to defeat her impulse was to let all recollections swamp over her, to see them in the mirror, and listen to them day and night till they lost the power to torment her and pull her back.

She was obsessed by George's family because she had separated him from them sufficiently to become his only real support, and now that she had abandoned him he was entirely alone. Another version, not so neat and simple, might say he had never relied on her, nor properly cut himself off from his family, though he had often been more vehement about his intention of doing so than she.

When he told his brothers never to come and see him unless they first telephoned to find out whether or not he was at home, he said it was because Pam wanted it that way. He turned down invitations to go with them to pubs at the weekend because, he said, he didn't think Pam would want to go. He later refused to help them with money because, he said, he agreed with Pam that if you once started lending there would be no end to it.

Often it was not George who detached himself from his family as much as his brothers who, after his offhand treatment, wanted nothing more to do with him. George did not accept this, preferring to believe that Pam had been the prime mover in their separation. But now that she had left him he could say whatever he liked.

There was a time when the three brothers tried to follow George's example and 'better themselves' by pooling resources to create their own painting and decorating business. After telephoning for an appointment they came to the house, and Alf described to George how he had been a lesson to them in the ways of hard work, and in setting up schemes for making money without being under the heel of a boss. After they had paid back debts, profits would be theirs to share. They created a vision which George admitted could become reality. With their hundred pounds, and two hundred from him, which they hoped that for old times' sake he wouldn't refuse, they would buy a second-hand van, as well as a set of ladders and a load of paint from a bloke they knew who was just going out of business and wanted to sell everything before declaring himself bankrupt.

Bert said their first job was already arranged, so it wouldn't be long before they would pay back the two hundred pounds. A garage owner in Lenton wanted his premises painted, and Harry had sent an estimate which no sane man would turn down. Alf also knew somebody in Mapperley who needed their house doing up, a big job that would make a few hundred profit if they played their cards right.

George lent them the money, and they swore everlasting friendship as he handed the cheque to Bert.

'If they succeed,' George said to her later, 'we won't have much to do with them, though I suppose that whenever they want more equipment they'll ask us for some cash, or if the business starts to fail, which it well might, knowing them, they'll ask me to save it from going under. We shouldn't have helped in the first place, but they're my brothers, after all, so there wasn't much else I could do.' If success depended on the amount of faith George and Pam had in their abilities, they were doomed.

The profits, as Bert told them when he called one Sunday morning (without telephoning first) in his new Vauxhall car, were rolling in. 'So well, in fact, that we might soon see our way to paying a bit of the money back that you lent us.'

When they made no further effort to get in touch, George thought it was either because they had so much to spend that they forgot what was owed him, or because, which he felt was more likely, their trading of paint for pound notes had, as it were, come unstuck somewhere along the way. If the latter assumption was correct, he did not consider it immoral to gloat on their difficulties, because since they had not repaid his two hundred pounds while they were flush, there was little hope of them doing so in their decline. Such entertainment was, however, expensive, and he was galled at imagining their talk when the first money came in.

'We've got enough dough to pay our George back,' Harry might have said, throwing bills and invoices into an empty drawer before spreading money and cheques on the table.

Bert picked up a ten pound note to make sure it was real. 'Don't be a dozy bleeder. We need this for some paint and another ladder.'

'A new car for all of us, more like,' Alf laughed. 'We don't have to pay our George back yet. He don't need it like we do.'

Bert scribbled a few sums on a sheet torn from the appointments diary. 'He's well-off. He'll be lucky if he sees a penny o' that two hundred nicker, old tight-fisted will. It took long enough to squeeze it out of him. And as for that stuck-up wife of his, you know what *she* wants, don't you?'

George knew that his recording was exact, because he had been one of them for so many years. But he hoped they were doing profitable business, and had at last curbed their feckless habits in face of the stark realities of the commercial world. He added to Pam that he was glad to see a spirit of ingenuity and co-operation between them as well as, it seemed, a determination to work.

He saw proof of this while driving through town one day when he stopped at a traffic light and, looking in the direction of a hooter, saw their van pull up by his side. Alf greeted him, and pointed to the others who were asleep in the open back, dead to the universe and caked with paint.

'We've just done seventeen hours nonstop, slogging all the way!' Alf shouted in triumph, before shooting at the amber and getting half along Parliament Street, a stream of red cloth waving from the ladders tilting up out of the van, before George's careful driving had taken him across the intersection.

13

Still in their working clothes, they came to see George one night. Pam brought them tea and biscuits in the living-room, hoping they would go soon, and not leave too much mess. She disliked herself for such a mean thought about her brothers-in-law who had worked hard all day and were now sitting wearily (and smelling of beer) in her best armchairs.

'We've come to ask,' Alf said, looking as pale, she thought, as if he were on the point of dying, 'whether you'll let us paint your house.'

She doubled the sugar in his tea, and told him to take more biscuits.

'I knew you'd see me right, love!' he said.

George stood in front of the television, legs apart, and hands behind his back. There was nothing to say, though he knew he must not sit down, otherwise he would feel intimidated. Nor must he become too friendly in case he agreed to whatever it was they wanted.

'The thing is,' Harry put in, 'that all we've got on for the whole of next week is somebody's living-room, and we can't charge more than forty quid for that.'

Bert surfaced sufficiently from his executive bout of deep thought to say everybody ought to sit down, but George replied that he had been on his arse all day at the office and preferred to exercise his legs a bit in the evening.

'Not only that,' Harry said, ignoring such a poor excuse, 'but the rob-dogs are trying to get some income tax out of us. I fucking ask you! Income tax! Us!'

Bert shivered, his close features raw with fury: 'I got a demand yesterday for three hundred quid.'

So had they all, or something close, but George said he found this hard to credit because he assumed they got paid for their jobs in cash with no questions asked.

'No,' Bert told him. 'You allus get the bleeder who holds you to the penalty clause and wants you to work to a pulp, and the swine who's frightened to part with real notes and gives you a cheque and wants a receipt so's he can set it against his own tax. Too many o' them meat-grinding bastards in the world' – his tone hinting that George was more than likely one of them. 'Some people won't let you live. If they think you're trying to make an honest bob or two they choke with envy.'

'Wouldn't give you the clippings of their toe-nails.' Harry reached for another biscuit, and knocked the ashtray over so that Pam was obliged to go to the kitchen for a brush and dustpan. They laughed when she'd gone, and George suspected they had planned her removal so that they could talk to him on his own.

Bert spoke hurriedly. 'We're desperate for a bit of work, George. Any old job. It'll only be for a while, because the week after next there's a couple of things that'll keep us busy. Ain't that right, Harry?'

Alf nudged him viciously. 'Wake up, dozy bastard!'

Harry leapt from his stupor and looked murderously at George, as if holding him responsible for the pain in his ribs. 'We're fucking desperate.'

Despite his fearlessness and relatively prosperous, self-employed status, George knew there would be trouble if he didn't promise something. When faced with all three of them he couldn't believe he was a grown man, for in their own way they knew how to reduce him in seconds to feeling like a kid. He recalled when, at the age of ten, a neighbour had given him a box of chocolates for doing a week's errands while his wife had been ill, and his brothers had waylaid him at the man's door to snatch the lot.

Knowing why Harry had knocked over the ashtray, Pam came back quickly, and hoped George at least was happy to see her. She scooped up the mess and laid the pan in the hearth till later. 'There's nothing we can do for you. The house won't need painting for another three years.'

George's left hand twitched. 'She's right. Not as far as I can see, either.'

She imagined the three brothers setting up ladders and scaffolding, part of an army of occupation that would mark the house by leaving its quiet dun-coloured intimacy a complete ruin. They would move from room to room mixing paints, stubbing out their cigarettes, and leaving a litter of beer tins and pie wrappings. In sheltering from the rain they would tread their plaster-covered boots on her carpets, and use her kitchen to fry their dinners and make tea.

George's picture showed them taking clothes from his wardrobe and searching pockets for anything they could slip into theirs, knowing he wouldn't say anything in case a fight started that he was unable to finish. The word must have been passed around town that they didn't take care in their work, which was why they had few jobs. He saw them dabbing their thin and doctored paint over the woodwork, and swinging planks and ladders so that door panels got split and panes of glass shattered. They would lark about and fall out of windows, holding him responsible because they knew he was insured, and would get sufficient compensation to stay six months in bed at a private clinic while their families lived in luxury on the strength of what extra compo they would receive after taking skinflint George to court. It was a watertight plan. They wouldn't fail to prise more money out of him and get their own back for wrongs he couldn't imagine having done to them.

He was businesslike. 'Ring me tomorrow, and I'll let you know if I have any ideas.'

'I don't think you know how bad things really are,' Alf said, seeming remarkably fit and lively, she thought, compared to a few minutes ago. 'I can't put it into words. My voice croaks when I try to tell people, and it ain't only because I want some tea – though I wouldn't mind another bucketful. It's good tea, duck!' he said to her with a smile and a wink.

'I'm dying o' thirst, as well,' Bert said.

She didn't respond, not yet willing to be their slave.

George cleared his throat. 'I'd be quite happy to put you in the way of earning a few hundred if I could, so that you'd be able to pay back what you owe me from before. If you'd like to decorate the house inside and out for that tidy little sum, then that's all right by me.' He turned to Pam. 'I'd like some more tea myself, love, if you wouldn't mind.'

'That ain't what we mean.' The veins stood out on Bert's temples.

Harry tore a patch from his overalls at the knee and put it into his jacket pocket. 'You're too fucking clever,' he said to George. 'That's your trouble.'

'All of us could do with some tea, and that's a fact.' Alf didn't want to be seen hanging back in the common effort. He looked pale again, deprived, as if he'd had no sustenance for a week. They ate plenty of food, she knew, but it was cheap and rotten, though neither she nor George had any doubt of their strength and tenacity. 'But we also want the right to work,' Alf added, after a knowing look from Bert.

Pam washed cups and waited for the kettle to boil. Alf's description of George as having been hatched rather than born revealed that he was disliked far more by his brothers than he ever could be by her. They lacked the sense to realize that whatever they said behind George's back was bound to reach him before a few days were out. Or perhaps they knew it, but didn't care. Their opinions, being totally unconsidered, had to be put into hurtful words at the soonest possible moment, which proved to her that words weren't important to them, since they had no sense of control.

Because they didn't think before they spoke, and distrusted anyone who did, their views on themselves and others, and on anything at all, could never alter. They had always treated George as if he had left them in the lurch by becoming a toffee-nosed bleeder who wouldn't give them two ha'pennies for a penny. On the other hand they could be pleasant enough when it suited their purpose.

Alf, between jobs, once came on a friendly call, hoping they would send him away with a few pounds in his pocket. While drinking his tea he informed her and George what his brothers thought of them (after he had taken the money) though she knew (and so did George) that he would tell the others later what mean bleeders they were for not giving him even a cup of tea at a time when he was on his uppers.

The silent room was thick with cigarette smoke, and she didn't suppose she had missed much more than her imagination supplied. She opened the window. 'I thought you'd have sorted yourselves out by now.'

'It ain't so easy,' Bert said.

Her headache was so intense she thought her period was about to start, though there wasn't much chance while *they* were in the house. Not even George said thanks when he took his tea. 'Some people have to go to work tomorrow,' she said.

'The lucky ones do,' Harry said glumly.

Bert pretended to scrape something from the end of his nose, then made a vicious flicking motion across the room towards George, who half closed his eyes as if expecting a fist to follow. 'So you'll see us go down the chute,' he said scathingly, 'before lifting a finger?'

Pam noted that it was nearly ten, and that if George didn't get to bed by half-past he would be tired and upset in the morning. 'There's nothing I can do,' he told them. 'If there was I'd do it, but there isn't. And that's the cold truth.'

Harry held out his cup, and sighed.

'Why do you always come to us when you're stuck?' She was so angry she even poured him more tea.

'There's no one else,' Alf said.

Which was true, and she was filled with guilt and pity, but how they used the fact to hold her and George over a slow fire! Even so, it was impossible to send them away without help, which they very well knew, and she was hoping for an idea that would be acceptable to all when Bert turned to George with one that must have been in their minds from the beginning. 'I passed your factory the other day.'

This did not sound plausible, since it was in a cul-de-sac, and little more than a glorified brick shed backing on to a canal.

'And it seemed to me – didn't it, Alf? Our Alf was with me, because we'd just took a load o' rammel on Dunkirk tips – that your factory wanted painting. That wall looks terrible. It's the worst bit o' wall on the street.'

'It'll do for a while,' George said mildly.

'We'll paint the lot: doors, roofs, *and* walls for three hundred quid. You won't get a better price anywhere.'

The slight creasing of skin around George's eyes told her that he was considering the offer. So was she. Apart from the fact that they had to do something, it was far better that his brothers should dab over the outside of the workshop than devastate their home. George would be there to watch them, and maybe they'd be able to see how hard his own workmen got stuck in. But what amazed her, when it shouldn't have, was how they had cunningly driven her and George to discussing exactly what they had wanted to talk about since first coming into the house an hour ago. Perhaps their business wasn't slack at all, and this was their normal method of drumming up trade.

Bert sensed her thoughts. 'We did a job like that a month ago for five hundred. We should have got six, but beggars can't be choosers. We'll do yourn for three hundred, George, not for profit, but as a favour, just to keep our hands in between jobs, because it'll only cover the cost of the paint. It don't look good that your factory's like a slum. People might wonder why it's in need of a lick of paint when you've got brothers in the decorating trade. They'll think we've fallen out, and say we're not much of a family if we can't stick by each other.'

The confidence tricks they had worked on George had only been successful due to the amount of blackmail and general mayhem which had been threatened, though after each stunt she had told herself that she should love them and make allowances, because hadn't her father said it was their duty to help less fortunate people, since the Bible said so?

But George's brothers did not seem to fit this condition, especially after they had openly robbed you. To help those who couldn't help themselves was laudable and necessary, because they might then co-operate so that some good would come; but to subsidize those who continually complained, telling you to shut your trap and mind your own business and that when they wanted your sanctimonious advice they'd bloody well ask for it but in the meantime what the bleeding hell were you doing not suffering under the same irritations that they were forced to complain about – was not feasible. Why, they'd want to know with all moral conviction, should *you* get away with it when they had to put up with it? It's all very well you standing there – they'd say – and telling us to get out of difficulties by our own efforts, but in the meantime you're a lot better off than us, so what the bloody hell are you going to do about it, eh?

To complain was not only their life-blood but as often as not a tactical manoeuvre for getting something they wanted but had no right to. All they could do about an irksome situation was complain, as if that were the only way of tolerating it. They grumbled in the face of adversity, whereas real hardship would never have left them time for complaining. After a general election, when there had been a change of government, she recalled that Alf had said to her: 'Now let's see what this bunch of robbing cut-throats do for us. The last lot did bogger-all.'

She asked what he would like them to do.

'Well,' he said, 'they could drop the council house rents for a start, couldn't they? Then they could tek summat off beer and fags.'

'What about road tax?'

He had forgotten that. 'They ought to halve it. It's a bleeding shame how they never do ote for yer, in't it?'

She asked what he and his brothers intended doing for them.

'Well, I suppose yo' would ask that, wouldn't yer? It's all right for yo' and George.'

'Why is it? You've got a house and a car, just like us.'

'Ar,' he said, 'but you *own* your house.'

'We might in twenty years. We're paying off a mortgage at the moment.'

'And your car's new.'

She laughed. 'It goes wrong just as often as yours.'

Those who didn't grumble generated sufficient energy to get clear of their difficulties. The best thing was to keep your sense of humour, though she and George had been unable to laugh on being trapped in their sitting-room by his three brothers and realizing there was no way out of giving them some work to do.

Yet George was sensibly horrified at the idea of them being set on to paint his workshop, a situation to be avoided even if they sat in his front room half the night before agreeing to leave. 'I'll think about it in the next few days. But I'm sure I'll come up with something for you to do,' he said, as if this generous promise would satisfy them.

But it was seen as a weakness, and instead of getting up to go home Bert signalled the others to stay where they were, and then found himself with a further suggestion to make: 'While we was passing' – he put the empty cup to his lips for the third

89

time, and paused to spit tea leaves into the ashtray, some of which went on to the rug – 'I saw that your factory yard was full of ruts. That paving's in a shocking condition. Must be a proper swamp in winter. If one of your employees broke his ankle on a pot-hole you might have a nice whack of compo to pay. I know you're insured, but you'd lose your no-claims bonus, and that'd come to a packet with a factory like yourn. Don't look glum, George. It need never happen. The three of us could repave your yard. Dead easy. We ain't done that sort of work before, I know, but we was only looking at some blokes the other week laying a car park at some offices in Mansfield. We'd do it a treat. I know a chap who's got some hardcore. We'd hire a roller. And in no time at all your yard would be smoother than a school playground. That'd be extra from the painting, though, but it would only cost you about two hundred on top. It's got to be done sooner or later. Next year it'll cost more. Have it done now, and it's a bargain.'

Alf and Harry indicated they would like more tea, otherwise they wouldn't get home, with their throats in the state they were. Pam said she had run out of water, not to mention tea leaves. If they were so dry they had better get to the pub, where they might be in time for a pint before it closed. Beer was the only liquid that would slake such a thirst, she said, providing they tipped enough into themselves for it to slop out of their ears.

Oh she had a way of getting at them, they laughed, but they knew she wasn't as stiff-necked as they'd heard. She was really a good sort who didn't mean half of what she said, otherwise their brother George would never have married her.

George also laughed. He then decided that his factory yard was paved well enough to last another five years, except for one or two worn patches.

'It's your decision,' Bert said.

He hoped his fatigue didn't show. 'It is.'

'I'll tell you what,' Bert resumed. 'Let's have the paths around your house paved, and the inside of the garage. We'd

90

like to try our hand at a little job like that. It'd only cost seventy-five quid. We'll do the crazy-paving while we're at it.'

Pam opened the door wide to let smoke disperse. 'Why don't you go home?'

Alf's fragile and injured good nature impressed her so deeply that she wondered what opportunity or congenital condition had been lacking for him not to have become an actor. He lit a cigarette in such a way as to make her feel ashamed of not having offered it herself, and also of not having put it between his lips, and struck the match for him, and patiently held it while he puffed the fag leisurely into life, even though she burned her fingers before dropping the charred remains on to her carpet.

'There are some people in this world you can't help,' he said. 'You can sit and talk your guts out for nobody's benefit but their own, and in your own time, which costs as much money as their time does, and they're the last people to appreciate what you're trying to do for them. It's not that we're begging for money. It's not that we're asking you to *make* work for us, but we want to do summat for you that wants doing. I can't put it fairer than that.'

George waved a hand for his brother to stop, but Bert interrupted harshly: 'Trying to tell us summat, then?'

'I am.' He sat down at last.

'I should think so.'

'If you'll give me a chance.'

'Go on.'

Alf poked Harry. 'Wake up, and listen to this.'

'I was going to say that you could paint the workshop after all,' George said.

No one spoke.

'I was only saying to myself the other day how run down the place is looking. Wasn't I, Pam?'

They kept silent.

He looked at them in turn. There were no takers. 'Pam, my

91

love, why don't we have another pot of tea between us. I could do with a little refreshment.'

'Depends on how much you're offering,' Bert said.

She felt her stomach turning solid. She was sorry for George, but there was nothing to do except bring in a packet of chocolate biscuits and make the biggest pot of tea they'd ever seen. The situation was not sinister, but simply the way such families worked out their problems.

'We mentioned three hundred pounds.' George had come back to life by surrendering to them, but he was also talking business, so didn't need her pity. None of them did. She was a foreign body that could only jeopardize their decision-making machinery. Blood might be thicker than water, but its jewelled movement ran on the oil of centuries, and she was only a bit of grit temporarily involved. If one of them blew his nose she'd fly out of the window.

'I wouldn't call three hundred a fair price,' Alf said.

'You wouldn't?' George didn't seem upset that they began arguing about an amount that anyone else might have considered settled.

'Would *you*?' Bert said. They were like an orchestra, she thought, and had to be admired for their perfect harmony and timing, inspired as they seemed to be by a conductor invisible to her.

George grinned more openly than at any time that evening. 'Happen I wouldn't. But it's all you're going to get.'

They accepted, as if in their rehearsals they had decided that at this point they must. Pam knew they were laughing. So did George, and the three of them knew that he and Pam were well aware of what they were thinking. Yet everyone was happy, especially George, who put a good measure of whisky into each cup. 'When can you start?'

'Start? Start what?' Bert whacked him on the shoulder, and they guffawed until tea splashed into every saucer.

'I'll have to tell the lads when to let you in,' George explained.

'We've got a couple of jobs to finish first,' Alf told him.

'Make it as soon as you can, then,' said George. 'I just want to know the date, more or less.'

'And we want the three hundred now,' Bert said, 'in cash, so's we can get the paint. I'll come up tomorrow to estimate how much it'll take.'

George looked at her. 'Get my cheque book. It's half now, and the rest when the work's done.'

'I suppose it'll have to do,' they grumbled.

'And I want you to do a good job. I mean that. No bloody messing on *my* premises.'

She thought Alf would weep. 'We can bring you forty references from satisfied customers. When we get stuck in, we're thorough. Thorough and careful, George. Nobody can beat us at our trade.'

He asked them to sign the receipt that Pam brought with the cheque. 'You'd think he didn't trust us,' Harry winked. 'Our own rotten brother!'

Their world was run on brotherhood, not fatherhood or motherhood or sisterhood. Everyone was their brother, to work with, to deceive, to bully or to drink with in the pub. Their God must be the biggest brother of all who knew their wiles and weaknesses, and whom they acknowledged as king only because they would never get the better of him. If anybody ever says anything to me about the Brotherhood of Man, Pam thought, I'll run as far away as I can get.

They signed the receipt, and went far happier than when they arrived. George acted as if he'd brought off one of his best business deals, and Pam didn't give an opinion. Having always believed that charity began at home, she was unable to dispute it now that she had seen it in operation.

14

She put more coins in the gas meter. Don't like it here. She hadn't liked it there, either, and at the moment she didn't know where she disliked it most, except that she was here, and not there, and that her body had after all decided where it most wanted to be. Having made the second biggest jump of her life there was nothing to do except sit still in the knowledge that nowhere was perfect.

Being in a place which often struck her as worse than what she had left – clamped into a freezing bug-hole of a London bed-sitter and not knowing what she would do when her money had gone – she thought how Bert, Alf and Harry would roll on the pub floor with laughter if they could see her. The intensity of her complaints during twenty years of marriage had been known only to herself, but she had been a complainer nevertheless, and though they had turned in on herself, she was not morally superior to those who made them out loud. She had no doubt been tainted by contact with such a family, and years would need to elapse before its spirit was washed out of her, but at the same time she felt that allowances ought to be made for them, especially now that it seemed she would have to make so many for herself.

Frost enfolded the room, and in spite of a turned-up gas fire she couldn't get used to the cold. Her bladder ached, but the only decent toilet was at the tube station, which was too far away, and in any case closed. The one downstairs was broken and filthy, and there was no telling who she might meet in the dark.

The enamelled sink in her room was fitted to the wall and stained like a map of places she hoped never to go to, a whitish bowl with a cold tap that brought forth water as if from the Rock itself. Vibrations shook the wall till it was turned off again.

She talked to herself, and to the pipe that shuddered as if about to burst and drown her. She would talk it into silence. There was often nothing to do but talk. At home with no one in the house she had talked to the knives and forks as she polished them in case they became savage and cut her throat, hacked off her limbs and hid her in such secret places that no one would find her, not even herself. So she talked. Her thoughts came out loud, so she imagined she was going mad. Because her arms might become dreadful and violent, she spoke to them as well. On her own, in her own room, it went on hour after hour, and she knew she wasn't insane otherwise she would stop. She would strike herself dumb. Perhaps she was able to go on talking because she was so happy.

She pushed a rickety chair to the sink and stood on it, turned slowly so as not to overtopple, then crouched and at the same time pulled down her slacks and pants, freeing her bladder of all pressure. Loud-mouthed Jane White who had lived next door told her how, on last year's motor trip to remote towns of Spain with her husband, she had broken at least half a dozen sinks staying at places that hadn't got the facilities. She didn't fancy going along corridors in the dark and looking for the proper place in case she never found her way back, and what would her Ted say then?

Pam hoped the present stance wouldn't bring the sink down while her behind was on it and she was laughing at Jane White's tales, causing those ominously sounding pipes behind the wall to flood her into the street. The guffaws of George's family should they witness her on such a perch would last for the rest of their lives, so thank God they couldn't see her.

Privacy was a luxury she'd never possessed, a wonderful word that could be said to herself over and over, marvelling that such a simple condition could feel so precious. You didn't need more than a normal amount of money for the basis of a good life: food, clothes, shelter, and solitude. When you were on your own no one saw you. They didn't even hear you, unless you talked too loud, and she needn't bother whether anyone heard or saw her, because it didn't matter what she said or did.

Being alone, she was out of the land of secrets for ever. You only feared secrets when you lived among people who took either a generous or vicious interest in you. On your own you could make them but didn't need them. Until now her only secret had been the ever-burning desire that led her to this room, indicating as surely as nothing else what an innocent existence she had led.

She stopped talking, and in the silence heard a door bang, and a car change gear as it went along the street. By keeping the gas fire on for long enough the room became warm. Persistence paid off. A carton of broken Christmas crackers lay in a box outside a stationer's and, acting the born scavenger, she brought them back, trapped one in the cupboard door, and pulled. The thin crack was like breaking the strand with home.

She took off her coat, and cleared rubbish from the floor. Thrift and cleanliness would get her back to reality. She would eat little, live on minimum heating, fit herself into one small room, and make her clothes last for as long as was decent and reasonable. Lacking nothing, she was optimistic, but to be occasionally careworn and frightened only intensified her hours of solitude. She did not need ice-box, television, car, house, wardrobe, garden, tea and dinner services, and a hundred other things that had previously walled her in.

Why had it taken so long to find out? The lowest-paid job would allow her to go on living in this way, sitting in front of the heat when she came home from work, with curtains drawn to keep out cold and the world's noises. On the Underground an advertisement for traffic wardens offered fifty pounds a week, work she could easily take on. If George's family came to London in their cars to look for her, or go to the Soho strip-clubs, she would plaster their windscreens with parking fines.

Safe in her room, she recalled a secret of George's brothers which she didn't doubt would never worry them. When their mother lay dying they crowded into the front parlour to make their last goodbyes. Alf took a hand out of his mackintosh pocket to wipe away tears, staring at the wall as if his grief would break it down. Bert's look of bitterness, the closest he could get to panic, suggested he was about to be robbed of the only prize that had ever meant anything. 'Don't go, mam,' he kept saying. 'Don't go.'

'She ain't going anywhere,' Harry said, hoping nevertheless that she would not.

Alf's terror was buried so deep that he became scathing towards whoever threatened to prise it loose: 'You'll frighten her to death, you silly bleeder!' he called across to Bert.

Up to this point they had felt themselves to be young and indestructible, but now saw that at least part of their world must sooner or later come to an end, and that so must their own. Betty and Maureen, afraid to stay in the parlour, were making tea and cutting bread in the kitchen to feed their kids.

Maud's eyes opened. Pam wiped the sweat with a paper towel, and wondered how much she saw while babbling the names of her sons as if they might do something for her. They had taken her teeth in case she choked on them. Pam's mother had died, and her father the year before. She held Maud's cold hand, and felt her own tears start when the old woman stared. Within the bush of grey hair her face seemed to be receding.

The others hung back. Should they come near, Maud might take them with her. Their hearts would go black and they would die. Superstitious horror pushed them away. But she wanted them to approach, though only Pam could hear her say so. George grasped his mother's hand, but his brothers were terrified that such grief would tear their stomachs to shreds should they let it catch hold. They could no more get close to her than they could to a house on fire.

She tried to raise herself, still muttering their names, as if the appearance of her sons and daughters would prevent her

97

slipping into that endless tunnel of darkness which she felt was opening behind. They could do nothing. She knew them as too much like her long-vanished husband who had always been the worst of men to her. They took after him in even the smallest part, she had told Pam. The last gesture to remind them of what she had once been was a brief smile.

It was a movement of the lips that quickly passed, and which no one else saw. But the smile, if such it was, almost crushed Pam's heart with the intensity of its bitter irony, and the emptiness of expectation which was felt almost as a relief compared to the disappointments she had suffered. The two flows of expression merged to become the last grimace of a dying woman who had let the male predators so often drag her down that she had lost all spiritual contact with normal morality. With that smile she had regained it, but at what a price. She lay back on the bank of pillows, her hand in Pam's becoming colder as she closed her eyes.

Yet Pam willed her not to let life slip away. She had tried the same with her father, but to no effect, though just in case dying could be prevented she was again impelled to fix a similar concentrated strength of body and soul to keep Maud from death if only by a few minutes. She spoke, but in silence, pleading with Maud not to leave them in desolation. Maybe her father had had an extra hour of peace and was eternally happy with it, unless he had been too clouded in mind to know, which must be the state of all the dead, if they were in any state at all. And now she kept Maud alive, or seemed to, for her eyes opened, though it was hard to say how much she saw. Perhaps she wouldn't die as long as Pam begged her with an intense love, tears being part of her prayers.

Someone kicked at an ankle, and she turned at the eruption of a private quarrel or resurrected grudge, to see Bert put a brass candlestick from the sideboard into his overcoat pocket.

Alf jabbed his foot out. 'That's mine. I wanted that.' Not getting it, he reached to the shelf for a trivial seaside souvenir and a heavy metal ashtray.

'You grab-alling bastards.' Harry opened a drawer, clutched a box of cutlery under his coat. She now knew why they wore overcoats and mackintoshes on a warm spring day. They couldn't trust each other to share Maud's bits and pieces in a civilized manner. She wanted to scream at them to stop their looting, but she would alarm Maud whose hand stirred at the noise.

The brothers' wives and sisters, hearing the signals, came from the kitchen with plastic bags. They tried to be quiet (she had to say that for them) but they couldn't refrain from the occasional shove and cry over a choice piece. On the other side of his mother's bed George was undecided as to whether or not he should take something to remember her by. As if, she thought, one needed objects to recall a person. But George was, to his credit, as transfixed by their movements as she was, and knew that he would be pushed aside as being the youngest who deserved the least if he made any such move. Because their mother was dying they were in a mood to manhandle him in a manner which would be speedy and vicious, due to the risk of one of their number snatching something on the sly should the process be too prolonged. And they would have said: 'What do *yo'* want ote for, greedy bleeder? Yer've made a bigger pile than we'll ever make, no matter how hard we wok. So fuck off, and let us tek everything.'

She kept hold of Maud's hand, telling her to rest and be in peace. She wanted a miracle, that she would wake up healed and asking for a bite to eat. The eyes were open, looking at familiar objects being taken out of the room.

'She's still living, can't you see?' Nobody heard, and Maud cried through her, but Pam would say no more, willed into silence because words lost their value as Maud closed her eyes for the last time, perhaps glad to be rid of them. Pam kissed her, and put her hands under the blanket, feeling even colder and smaller than the corpse, as if there was no fire left to draw breath that struggled at her diaphragm. 'Let's go home,' she said to George.

'Soon,' he answered, choking with loss.

One daughter said she was going to tell a woman up the street to come and lay her mother out, but she returned in triumph with a death certificate from the doctor so that she could claim the burial allowance. The three elder brothers leaned against each other roaring with grief, and shed tears that scalded so much they evaporated almost as soon as they appeared. Bert, embracing Harry to soothe the anguish they both undoubtedly suffered, felt into his brother's capacious pockets so as to pick out a coveted object, but Harry noticed the sly hand and told him to eff-off, pushing him away so that a real fight began which Alf and George finally stopped.

It was like the Royal Family in a Shakespeare play, Pam thought, but this was a contest that any self-respecting people would keep secret, though she knew they would joke and laugh about how they had gone for each other over a few bits and bobs, and how at least they had stopped George and his woman from getting their avaricious hands on what didn't belong to them. They were in it together, and ended the day with the stuff more or less shared between them, though George got nothing, because they had fought for what was theirs, just as they preferred to struggle for whatever else they may well have deserved. Any shame they felt would only keep them closer together, and what hate they had manifested towards each other had been merely an emotional device to stop the family breaking up at a time of crisis.

15

By closing her eyes she could look inwards to as much space as she would ever need. She was a window in a wall built by herself, and sat for hours with closed eyes yet stayed awake, knowing that somewhere beyond limitless areas God existed, a universe He had provided for her to look into so that she could have peace.

The longer she kept her eyes closed the less she was disturbed by sounds. She heard but did not flinch. The world was benign because she had found a place that was entirely her own. She could not be attacked by memories that she did not want.

The peace remained when she opened her eyes. She looked into the mirror whose own spaces showed memories that would not destroy her. She had once walked into a chapel and heard a man preaching. A piece of paper given at the door said his text would be from the Book of Isaiah.

His words created space, and his voice filled it. She had gone in not out of the rain but from under a clear blue sky. His words chased away anguish and gave her peace. She had first read such words at school, but hadn't been able to properly comprehend. The most intense sensation lasted only as long as the preacher's words, but they gave proportion and order to what had existed in chaos. His speaking fitted the austerity of walls and windows. His voice held back the cold, and protected each person in their different space. By his words she knew what her soul craved:

> 'For ye shall go out with joy,
> And be led forth with peace;
> The mountains and the hills
> Shall break forth before you into singing,
> And all the trees of the field
> Shall clap their hands.
> Instead of the thorn shall come up the cypress,
> And instead of the briar shall come up the myrtle;
> And it shall be to the LORD for a memorial,
> For an everlasting sign that shall not be cut off.'

Without such words space had no meaning. The words brought a beauty without which life was pointless. And after

101

the beauty came silence (even for the score of people present) and without the possibility of silence God had no meaning.

The man who read, younger than she, stood by the simple table, tall and pale, his dark suit not well-fitting. What little hair he had was lank. His blue eyes glistened as he went through chosen verses for the day. He spoke them from memory, and extemporized his commentaries, looking slowly from one side of the hall to the other as if searching his words out from among the people present, but pausing on his sweep at deliberately irregular intervals so that most might at some time believe he looked especially at them.

She supposed that he worked in an office during the week, and wondered whether he had a wife. If he had children did he love them and make them happy? Did he tell jokes and make them laugh? Did he make them feel good to be alive? There was no way of knowing. He was a speaker of words, a man of fervent beliefs which he wanted to pass on to all who would listen, so that the beauty of the universe grew as he spoke:

'We all sooner or later find the road that has been chosen. No twilight stars shall darken when we come to that forked road. Sorrow is not hidden from the eyes, nor is joy. Infants see the light, and so shall the small and the great when life is bitter in the soul, for God does not condemn those for ever on whom he has placed his mark. He gives our eyes the vision to see into our own hearts and the hearts of others. We are unique in God's sight, and no woman or man shall perish from the earth and have no name in the street. Though terrors on every side make us afraid, and we fear to be driven from light into dark, belief in God will show us the way, for it says that fear of the Lord is wisdom, and that to depart from evil is understanding.'

The space, she felt, was within, no matter where you were. She listened without turmoil, stood with other people yet was alone, feeling a balm that she had craved all her life. She may have known some peace as a child, but if so had not regained it

102

till now, when tranquillity had come simply by walking in from the street. She had heard of women wanting to be together, away from men, but she didn't care to be with women any more than with men at the moment. In her void of silence she needed to be a long time in her own space before knowing whether she wanted to be with anyone else. She was drawn back into his voice, and among his words:

'God,' he said with fervour, 'loves Israel, and all who go through the day and the night with her. They that observe lying vanities forsake their own mercy and condemn Israel, and the chief singer with his stringed instrument in turn forsakes them. Among the tribes of Israel God has made known that which shall surely be. Job, Daniel and Noah shall in their goodness and wisdom reign, while those who rise against Israel shall be overthrown, but if the world come to peace and to God it shall prosper mightily. And I will multiply men upon all the House of Israel: and the cities shall be inhabited, and the wastes shall be builded. It will endure for ever. They shall build houses therein, and plant vineyards; yea, they shall dwell with confidence, when I have executed judgements on those that despise them; and they shall know that I am the Lord their God. Israel rejoices, and mankind is glad that the Lord liveth and brought up the children of Israel from the land of the north, and from all the lands whither he had driven them. And I will bring them again into their land that I gave unto their father. Behold I will lift up mine hand to the Gentiles, and set my standard to the people. And they shall bring their sons in their arms, and their daughters shall be carried upon their shoulders. The abundance of the sea shall be converted unto thee, the forces of the Gentiles shall come unto thee. And he shall set up an ensign for the nations, and shall assemble the outcasts of Israel, and gather together the dispersed of Judah from the four corners of the earth. For the Lord will have mercy and yet choose Israel, and set them in their own land: and the strangers shall be joined with them, and they shall cleave to *Elpis Israel*, the vow God gave to the

Gentiles as a gift and an example, and to the Sons of Jacob as a Promised Land. But before what we seek is delivered unto us we shall be tested with tribulations without number, as the Jewish people were sorely tried before they came into their Inheritance.'

Her limbs were numb, but she willed him to go on for ever so that she would not have to cast herself out into the street. The sky might blacken and the day pour water, but the words were balm on her soul, the voice ointment. At the door she bought a tract of his sermons for a few pence, and had the limp book now in London. She remembered walking into the sunshine, and seeing no name on the white and blue poster at the door. He was the man with no evils whom she was afraid to wait for and talk to, the man with God in his eyes, peace in his presence and the Bible on his lips, whose appearance and voice had given her a feeling of space and poignant freedom that she had not experienced before, but which she must one day come back to.

She could not listen for ever, because he did not speak for-ever. She went out. She could only walk. She walked the three miles home, elated from the words poured like wine into her, and repeated with every step. Her legs ached and her feet were sore, but being worn out enabled her to look at the reality of the streets and people again, so that by the time she reached home the preacher's words had faded to a place in her mind where they would not dominate her spirit beyond endurance, but which helped her to remember them.

George asked where she got to every week. She said she went walking. She called on Eunice Dobson who lived in the Park. They had coffee and talked for an hour about old times at the ticket office. Then she walked back. He thought it a good idea, said it was healthy to use her feet now and again. He was sorry he couldn't go, but was too busy with paperwork.

She stepped into fresh air on her way into town. Better to walk than go in the car, as George had suggested. She only

104

drove often enough not to forget how to do it, otherwise he took the wheel, nervous that she might scratch the precious paintwork or scrape the bumper. The protection which the enclosing car-frame gave against the outside world had the disadvantage that it cut her off so decisively from other people.

The fact that she had thoughtlessly told a lie gnawed at her. She felt defiled and threatened on realizing that no one had as much power over you as those who made you lie. Though there was only herself to blame, she knew that George had meant to attack her by asking so pointedly where she went. It was impossible to walk out freely in a world where every experience had to be shared as one might have to divide a bone with another dog.

The Sunday morning street was empty, breakfast-smelling houses standing back from the pavement. Their bricks were dark and comfortable from having been lived behind for more than one generation, compared to the ten-year pebble-dash boxes on her street. They were permanent and untouchable, and inside she imagined a richer atmosphere than that which nurtured her, who felt she was dying under the weight of a single lie. When she ran screaming across the street a paper-boy came around the corner on his bike, and cursed as he swerved, calling out: 'Fucking old bitch!' while pedalling away.

Her father's Bible was in her bag. She had read it in her schooldays and now, frightened, took it out to hold. Her father's and her mother's names were written inside the cover. She had inscribed hers on the opposite page when she was seven. She stood by a lamp-post and looked at the signatures of joint ownership, until she was calm. Then she walked over a railway bridge and to the main road.

The cemetery was to her right as she went up the hill, a sky of grey cloud with no space between, a mild wind blowing into her face. A bus went along the wide road, a car overtaking, and she felt sweat under her arms from the heat of walking. She stopped by the railings because a blister was beginning at her heel, though the lie she had told burned even more.

A man at the wheel of a shining station-wagon turned down his window. 'Are you lost, duck?'

He stopped by the kerb. 'Do you want a lift somewhere?'

He looked at her through wire-framed glasses, seeming about fifty, with fair hair swept back over his broad head, wearing a sports jacket, cardigan and tie tucked brashly in. She liked his easy smile, and the hand that rested on the window. The click of indicators sounded, and he had left the engine running. 'I'll take you wherever you want. My wife's away for a week, and I'm footloose and fancy free!'

'I'm going to chapel,' she said.

'I'll give you a lift, then.'

'No thanks. It's only just over the hill.'

'What do you want to go to chapel for, anyway? You'll do a lot better coming with me.'

She fastened her coat, ready to walk. 'I can't.'

'Can't? Can't? Do you hear that? She can't!' He appealed as if he had someone else in the car, which he hadn't. 'What reason is that?'

She took two steps forward, tempted by a madness that felt wonderfully sane, to get in and put herself beyond the deadly woodenness of life that weighed her down. There would be no crawling back to the self she would leave behind. He opened the door: 'Come on, then, why don't you? We'll be in Matlock in forty minutes, or Skeggy in a couple of hours. It's still early, so the roads'll be clear.'

For such people everything worked. The devil's arrangements were always to be relied on. There was a glint of something worse than victory in his eyes, which she could hardly blame him for, considering her hesitation. The car radio caterwauled brainless music to help in his enticement. 'You aren't coming then?'

106

If ever she was to leave she would choose her own time. 'No.'

His tone was half between a wheedle and a demand: 'Go *on. Come* on. *Why not?*' – she'd heard it all before. 'My wife won't mind. We do a bit o' swapping now and again. I swap her, she swaps me. It don't mean much, as long as we're happy. In fact it keeps us together, doing a bit of swapping now and again. We're in the Aspley Swap Club.'

She wouldn't be surprised. 'There isn't an Aspley Swap Club.'

'I know,' he admitted, 'but there ought to be.'

She laughed, then was horrified at talking to him at all. If he came out of the car she would swing her handbag with the Bible inside. 'I've said no, so get going.'

He was disappointed, but his smile was fixed. 'You don't know what you're missing.'

She waved as he drove away. He waved back. No harm in trying, he must have thought. When the moment came it would not be with another man. That sort of escapade would mean even less freedom. She couldn't understand the disturbance of a trivial lie to George, and forgot her sore heel as she went over the hill towards the city centre, reflecting that some day she might indeed go away to live on her own in a place too far off for him to come and find her.

The preacher she had hoped to hear was gone. The circuit might not bring him back for another year, in which time who knew where she would be? Perhaps it was for the best. Every month a different speaker came with text and message. 'Grief,' she heard, 'is heavier than the sands of the sea, therefore my words are swallowed up. The things that my soul refused to touch are as my sorrowful meat.'

Her thoughts became settled, in that she seemed for a time to have fewer of them, but she was comforted, and grateful to live secure in her own mind. The weekly hour of peace strengthened her, verse and exhortation soothing the turbulence of her false life.

She walked through the pedestrian area on her way to the bus stop.

'I didn't think it could be you, coming out of *that* place,' Bert said, 'but by God it was! How are you getting on then, duck?'

He used to be good-looking, but his close and interesting features had developed into the face of a ferocious but all-knowing bird about to peck anyone into the ground who got in its way. 'You like going to chapel, eh?'

She could sense his silent laughter in the space behind his face. 'Why not?'

'Didn't think you was like that.'

'I am, when I want to be.'

He glanced at the upper windows of surrounding shops, as if someone might be observing him, or perhaps as if reconnoitring for a way inside, like the old days when he hadn't been averse to doing a discreet job or two. 'Looks like it's going to rain.'

'It might.' She glanced at the clouds. More reason to hurry for the bus.

'I'm just off to the "Salutation" for a couple o' jars o' Shippoes. Do you want to come? I'll buy you a short.'

'I have to get home. Thank you, though.'

He nudged her. 'Lots of 'em do, after coming out of chapel. Meks 'em thirsty! It would me, I know that much. I en't bin in a place like that since I got married, and then it wor a forceput!'

The lie to George had been wasted. She had become a 'religious maniac'. They had seen it happening years ago. Her sort probably gives pots of money to the chapel. Alf phoned George and asked to borrow ten quid, and laughed out the information on hearing him refuse.

She didn't go any more, but it wasn't important, since the only thing she thought was that she would walk out on George, even if it meant leaving Edward as well. It was certainly true that she couldn't take either of them with her.

16

A woman by the outside steps of the house, wielding a sweeping-brush to clear leaves from a flooded grating, scooped several clutches of mould from the end of the drainpipe and flopped them towards the pavement. 'That should fix it for a while.'

'Should,' Pam said.

She looked up. 'Are you the person from the top floor?'

Pam stepped aside to see water rushing into the grille. Even her plastic hood and galoshes hadn't stopped her getting soaked.

'Yes.'

They walked up the steps, and the woman opened the door for her. 'You look drowned.' She hung the brush on a hook by the outside door. 'Come in and have a cup of tea.'

She was tall and dark, and Pam was going to add 'handsome', but wasn't sure it was the right word. A tail of hair swung down her back, and she wore a woolly black sweater, and rather baggy purple slacks so that you couldn't tell whether she was broad behind or not. Her heels clattered on worn lino. The large ground-floor room had two single beds along one wall and a wide divan against the other. Pam thought the place must have been furnished off the junk-end of the Portobello Road, or from a War on Want depot. A series of orange-boxes in a recess made a book case of well-kept hardbacks. One or two lamps were fashioned from bottles and weighed down at the base with coloured marbles. The heavy square table was surrounded by odd chairs and a couple of boxes.

She looked at Pam's face. 'It may not be up to much as a London residence, but it's home to me.'

'It's fine.' She didn't want to become too matey, but on the other hand would not like to seem either stuck-up or daft. She wondered which of the cups she would have to drink from. An electric fire glared reddish-pink from the wall, and a paraffin heater made the room damp rather than warm, producing a steamy atmosphere of uncertain temperature. She opened her coat. 'Have you been here long?'

'Six years. I'm Judy Ellerker.' She poured tea in a cup sufficiently ornate to have come out of Buckingham Palace. Pam had seen her name on the outside door.

'My name's Pam – Hargreaves.'

'Left your husband, then?' Judy laughed. 'Sugar?'

None of her business. 'Please.'

'I can tell a mile off. You look shell-shocked. Happens to us all. It's the only hope for the future.'

'I'm fine,' she felt bound to say.

'Why don't you sit down, then?' Judy faced her across the table on which was a newspaper, a doll with no head, and a machine-gun. She pushed them aside to make room for cups and elbows. 'You *will* feel better, but it's like when somebody dies: it needs a year to recover. Took me longer, if I remember. You're lost. Nothing means anything. No references bouncing back at you from somebody you hate more than you love them. Oh, I remember it very well.'

There was less bitterness in her voice than the words suggested, though one or two lines around her mouth showed where plenty had been. 'I suppose you're right,' Pam said.

'I am for myself, and that's for sure. Fag?'

'Not just now, thanks.'

'You got kids?'

She felt too weary to resent being questioned. 'I've left a son of eighteen behind.'

Her neatly trimmed eyebrows lifted. 'He's off your hands, then. You're lucky.'

'Yes.'

'Wish mine were. Don't let your tea get cold.'

110

She drank.

'Are you looking after yourself?'

'Oh yes, very well.'

'I have no option, with two young kids. That's what a man would like when you leave him though, that you would just fold up and die. That'd make him feel really good, the bastard.'

'I shan't do that.'

'But they'd like you to. Anyway, men are the most boring objects in the world as far as I'm concerned, so I'm glad I hit the lid when I did. What did the man in your life do?'

Don't hold back, she told herself. There's no point any more.

'Ran a small factory.'

'Mine was political – very. Active, as they say. Radio-active was more like it. He was in one of those extreme left-wing parties. He was always jabbering on about workers' rights and the rights of the underprivileged, but when he brought his mates home I was the tea-maker and envelope-licker and general tweeny. I once asked why his party was so small, and he said it was because it was only a splinter group, so I said well you had better get the idle lot from under my fingernails because the next time you bring them here they can make their own tea and sandwiches. He said I was a stupid reactionary woman who lacked political sense, because they first had to free the workers, and then it would be the women's turn. So I said how about letting it be women first for a change? He said we had to work today so as to build the world of tomorrow, so I said I'd be dead by tomorrow, and that if he wanted a little slavey-helpmate he'd better shove off and get one from the Third World with a veil around her face, because I'd had enough. Then he lectured me in the usual baby-language on the realities of the class struggle, and when I thought he would go on for ever I dashed him away with the smoothing-iron and threw his pink shirts out of the window. No more jig-jig, and sleeping with the wet around your arse all night. I didn't know I was born.'

Pam laughed, and listened. Oh lucky woman, who knew her own mind.

'But let's talk about you,' Judy said. 'I've seen you coming in now and again, and wondered who you were.'

The front door slamming sent a tremor under the floorboards and an eleven-year-old boy ran into the room and threw his schoolbag on a heap of old clothes. He went to the stove and poured a mug of tea, then came to the table. 'Mum?'

Judy leaned across and lay a hand on Pam's shoulder. 'Women often don't know how hard it was till they've been free for a while. How long *were* you in the M.G.?'

'M.G.?'

'Matrimonial Gulag.'

'Oh, twenty years.' Pam saw that her face was lined, and yet she was undeniably handsome, with her fine bones, lustrous eyes, and a well-shaped mouth marred only by the sight of two bad teeth when she spoke.

'Mum?' the boy demanded.

'Shut up,' Judy turned to him, 'or I'll cut it off!'

Pam thought it unsociable not to give some confidences in return. 'I suppose I left because I thought I'd go mad if I didn't.'

'There's nothing else to do when it gets to that stage.'

Then she didn't want to talk, thinking the subject best left alone when she was with other people. Judy guessed, and decided not to ask, but fetched a loaf from the bread tin and cut two thick slices. 'Sam, spread this for your tea.'

'I want you to buy me a cassette,' he said, defiantly so that she wouldn't be able to accuse him of whining.

'The jam's over there.' She said to Pam: 'I suppose you'll be wanting to get a job now?'

She felt more friendly. 'What do you do?'

The boy sat down to eat, and said between one mouthful and the next: 'I want a cassette.'

112

'You can't have one, so stop nagging. I've worked as bus conductor, traffic warden, checker-out at the supermarket. You name it, I've done it. I wanted to be a street-sweeper but the council wouldn't let me. I suppose they thought I'd go on the game with my tin barrow!'

'You was a waitress once, don't forget,' her son said.

'I've done a bit of everything.'

'Mum, I want a cassette.'

She leaned over and struck another blow for freedom against his head that would have made someone twice the size stagger.

'I get National Assistance,' she said to Pam, 'and all the other handouts I feel I'm entitled to. Then I do odd jobs like painting and decorating, as well as wallpapering, baby minding, car washing, helping at a stall up the market on Friday, and on Saturday I do the windows of four different flats at five quid each. It's bloody hot in here. The thing is, love, don't ever get a full-time job. Find part-time work, because you can change around, and it's more interesting that way, as long as you don't let those you sweat for know that you do for anyone else. Get National Assistance, don't declare your jobs, and never pay tax. You've got to beat the system, because if you don't it'll beat you, specially when you're a woman.'

She stood up to take off her sweater, her loose and shapely bosom moving under her shirt. There was a warm and not unpleasant smell of sweat. 'I don't get a penny from the father. I don't mind, because if I did he'd only come sniffing around now and again to put his head between my legs and cry. He's in the computing business now, and doing quite well after getting over his political tantrums – which I suppose all his sort do sooner or later – going from one grubby-knickered little dolly to another. I said the service of the dead over him years ago.'

The boy finished his tea, rubbed his injured face a couple of times, then sat on the settee and opened a schoolbook. 'I only said I wanted a cassette.'

'Get a paper round then, to pay for one,' she said.

'I'm too young.'

'Say you're twelve.'

The door banged again, and a ten-year-old girl came in, her schoolbag spewing pens and books when aimed at her brother.

'That's Hilary,' Judy said, 'the other bundle. But at least she's a girl.'

'Am I?' Hilary examined the machine-gun knowingly, unclipped the magazine and set the bullets in ranks on the table, then removed the stock and wondered whether to take the rest of the gun to bits before having her tea. 'I sometimes wonder.'

Judy stroked her hair, then drew away as if the feeling burned her. 'You were when you had your bath last night,' she laughed.

Pam pointed to the gun. 'Is it real?'

'It's a replica,' Judy said. 'My husband would spend hours assembling and taking it down, like saying his beads. We lived in a house then, and he used to practise jumping from the back window fully armed. But one day he broke his ankle. He left the gun when I threw him out, and Hilary took it over. She used to watch him playing with it from her cot. I think she thinks it's him now. I swear to God I heard her call it Daddy the other night. Leave it alone, and get your tea.' She cut and buttered some bread. 'I'm going to take that gun into the garden tomorrow and give it a decent burial.'

Dark-haired Hilary smouldered under the deadly insults, but set it down as she was told. 'No, mummy, please don't. I like to play with it.'

She turned to Pam. 'When you think you're fit for a job, come and tell me. If I hear of anything I'll let you know. Or whatever else you need, just come and see me, even if you only want to rest your head on my bosom and tell me your troubles. I know how it is. It's bloody hard for a woman of any age who pulls out of the slave-state. You work like hell for a

114

Lord of Creation because that's what your mother told you to expect out of life, and you don't even get any good sex for it. I don't think I ever had a thrill from a man, unless he did it deliberately before starting in on me, but I can give myself a thrill any time, and get an even better one from my girl-friend. Maybe you can't always trust a woman, either, but at least you know what to expect.'

Pam stood up. 'I really think I must be going.' Her clothes were damp, and she felt herself sweating in the steam.

Judy laughed. 'Do I shock you?'

She made an effort to smile, and sat down again. Everyone did what they liked, as long as they didn't bother anyone else. 'Of course not. Why should you?'

'I don't know. But I shan't try to seduce you. It only comes on me now and again. I don't do it for scalps, like men. You should see all the notches my husband cut into the butt of that gun. I never knew what they meant till Sam told me, though he was only six. "Daddy cuts that gun with his penknife when he goes with that girl," he said. I'd been so innocent and trusting. Good job I was, I suppose. One day I threw the hot iron at him, and he left in fear of his handsome features, not to mention his life. I was a Judy he'd never seen. Six months later I was shopping on the Portobello Road and met this prissy little fair-haired woman with glasses who worked in Whitehall. She was a ready-made MoD type, and I carried her shopping home. From that moment I never looked back.'

In spite of her confidences Pam noted the occasional fragility of her expression. Whatever she was, her marks of servitude were undeniable, and no one broke free without wounds. Pam liked her for being so friendly and sympathetic. She certainly knew a great deal about herself. 'Do you like living in this place?'

'Why? Want to make an honest woman out of me? I'm always waiting for someone to do it, man or woman, I don't really mind, as long as it's under my conditions and not theirs. After all, they'd be getting more from it than I would.'

'I really must go.' But it was hard to get up. There was much that was likeable about the place, and the people.

'Don't forget, then, any time you want to talk, or watch the telly, just walk in. I let these two look at it for three hours a week. Don't stew too much by yourself up there. If you get depressed, remember that your big troubles are over. You've only got little ones from now on, such as feeding yourself and keeping warm. Come down for a chat with Judy. She's harmless, really!'

'Thank you for the tea. I enjoyed it.'

'Come any time you like. Don't forget.'

'I don't want to intrude.'

'Fucking lesbians!' said the boy.

Judy's large hand clenched and reached out, but she drew back as if thinking he had been knocked silly enough for one day. He didn't flinch. With such an upbringing, he'll probably go out and conquer the world, Pam thought.

'I won't mind if you do,' Judy said to her.

If she didn't move she would be here all night. The miasma of cooking – there was a huge long-handled iron pot on the stove from which a meaty smell emerged – was sending her into a doze. She stood up, but stayed near the door.

'Phyllida never comes here,' Judy was saying. 'She's got a thing about children, which is understandable, considering these two. So I go there. Makes a change.'

'She don't like us,' said Hilary, stripping the gun for a second time, and setting parts over the table, 'but she gives us presents.'

'Now and again,' said Sam.

'That's because you pester her, you scroungers.' Judy lifted a pair of trousers for patching. 'She may hate you, but she's a generous little Phyllida, all the same.'

Pam walked up the stairs, glad now to get away from a series of well-worked-out relationships in which she had no part. Judy had her life finely organized, having the

116

straitjacket of kids to look after. Maybe my mistake, she thought, was not to leave when Edward was three or four, and take him with me.

17

Though her watch said twelve-thirty she didn't have to go to bed till she felt like it. Bone idle, they would have said. Spoiled rotten. Don't know she's born. When she's got to go to work things'll be different. She could sit still when her limbs had no wish to move, keep her legs stretched when she felt no desire to alter her position. She was being born again, without father or mother, blessed with a second life minus the aches and pains. She and the cane-bottomed chair had grown together, a weird animal never to be divided. There had been no such feelings when George was in the room, nor even when he had been out of the house, not in all the years of her marriage. She cringed before those simple wonders which were apparent for the first time.

She didn't want to go to bed, but no longer had to witness George's crippled note of concern as if there were no words left that he could speak affectionately and direct from the heart. 'I'm off upstairs, then,' he'd say. 'You can come when you like, love.'

Every minute by herself carried its own stone-weight of guilt which would have to be paid for by his surly expression at breakfast. If she stayed half an hour she would know from his breathing and decisive tug at the clothes after she got into bed that he was still awake. Wanting to be alone when everybody else was in bed was nothing less than plain selfishness, he said. It wasn't natural for him to go to bed while she stayed downstairs on her own. He liked to know that all doors were locked, that the lights were off, and that she was already by his side going to sleep. If he was already asleep, she was bound to wake him when she came up, and he had to get to work on time hadn't he? It wasn't fair. Separate rooms? He stamped on that one. What did we get married for?

It was time for bed, but she wanted to eat, so stood up without even considering the act of separation from the cane-bottomed chair, and went to the cupboard for cheese, bread and a tin of beer. She spread them on the small round table. George had looked at her, his tone stiff. 'Sickening for summat, love?'

'Just hungry.'

'Fry an egg, then.'

'These biscuits are enough.'

'An egg'll do you more good. Two, in fact, with some bacon.'

'I don't like bacon.'

'Shall I do it? Won't tek a minute.'

'I don't want to get fat.'

'Can't see that happening.'

She hated her apology. 'I just want a biscuit.'

'Wouldn't do you any harm to put on a stone or two.'

Her voice was at the edge of a precipice of sound, and he detected it sooner than even she did. 'It would if I say it would.'

'Don't get like that,' he retorted.

She wondered why she couldn't have a snack without any comment. 'Like what?' – hoping she didn't resemble whatever he accused her of getting like, because it was bound to be unpleasant.

'If you don't know, I don't.'

She didn't, and tried to be calm, but the attempt made her

sound agitated, and she could do nothing because, behind his face of hurt concern, he was expecting her to be upset. 'All I want is a biscuit and a cup of tea.'

'Get it, then.' He had tried to be helpful, and been rebuffed, as usual. He knew what she was thinking, so looked even more offended in order to confirm it for her. 'I only made a suggestion.'

'Does it need all this discussion?'

'You mean we talk too much? Don't make me bloody-well laugh.' Now he was getting at her for having got at him in the past for not being able to express his feelings. As if this sort of sniping was a civilized conversation! He wanted to talk, having first made it impossible for her to open her mouth without a tone of defensive rancour, but would he talk so much, and what would his reply be, if I threw the kettle of boiling water at him? Instead she said, exhausted by the continual fight between them, and unable to do anything about it: 'I'm tired.'

'Then what are you eating for? Why don't you get to bed?'

I'm not a rat, she thought, so stop cornering me. There were scores of accusations that she wanted to express, but searching for words that would hurt neither her nor George crushed them back. As people get older they get more selfish. It's plain a mile off, isn't it, George? No one can deny it, so how was it possible for increasingly selfish people such as you and me, George, to go on living together? It wasn't, isn't, can't be, can it, George?

'I'm dying,' she said, 'that's why I'm eating.'

He wondered why she tormented him so wilfully. 'If you're feeling that bad, why don't you wait till morning and call on Dr Graham? He'll give you some tranquillizers. They'll make you feel better.'

She laughed. 'I've never had that sort of pill in my life, and never will. There's nothing wrong with me that pills can cure.'

119

'All I know,' he said, 'is that you're always making arguments about nothing. Pills will keep you a bit steadier than you have been lately. Don't you see that, duck?'

'And what about some pills to help *you*, then?'

'Don't be so bleddy silly!'

Tears were running down her face. She was bitter with herself at having no control. She envied how he went out in the morning, lucky as he was, and forgot about her till he walked in at night. She didn't know whether she craved more to obliterate herself or him from her mind. When he was absent his voice remained with her. Marriage was a pitiless treaty.

'I feel as if I'm dying in this place.' For the sake of peace she was ready to add: 'Though I think I'll be all right in the morning' – but she didn't, and that sentence she was unable to speak was, in retrospect, the one that separated them.

'Die, then,' he threw at her, and his accusing tread up the stairs thickened the blood at her heart. She didn't feel aggrieved at his response. She had deserved it. The food soddened in her mouth. She stood like a stone and recalled a radio talk in which some man suggested that those who came to life late at night were mentally unbalanced. The question was discussed, and she brooded in her stillness on how strange it was that after being exhausted all day, and wanting nothing but sleep, only the night promised liveliness.

But George could not live in such a way. He had his work. Even if he hadn't, he was a day man, a dawn-to-dusk man, a six-in-the-morning and a half-past-ten-at-night man, a person of habit and probity who had been unlucky enough to marry her.

Yet neither was it her wish only to wake up when everyone was stamping off to bed. The pattern had been forced on her as a final refuge. She did not consider herself in any sense mentally disturbed, and to prove it she had left him next morning and come to London.

18

No more of that. She liked it here because she could stay up for as long as she liked and not think of herself as a mental case. She could eat what she fancied when she wanted to, and think whatever jumped into her mind without wondering what the person in the same room would say if she let him hear her thoughts. She did not have to take into account either her own ill-will, or his resentment if what she said perturbed him in any way. If she didn't like what she thought then she, being the only person that mattered, could rid her mind of it whenever she wanted because there was nobody to keep pushing it back at her after altering it to suit their own image, as if what she had said was only so much spiteful and damaging rubbish. She could even talk aloud to herself, and if that wasn't freedom she didn't know what was.

She was under the authority of her selfishness, that great motivator of the meek after they have gained their independence. In order not to be dead she had to become selfish, and stay that way for as long as it took her to hear what her voice sounded like. The argument went this way, and then that. If you aren't selfish you're dead, but if you're dead you can't be anything, not even selfish. To be too busy among the considerations of yourself taught nothing except that you were coming slowly back to a normal relationship with the world.

It was necessary to know that you were selfish in order not to let anyone steamroll over you with their petty desires and ignorant opinions, often only given so as to hear the sound of their own voice. The new bud on the tree selfishly gets sap and sustenance out of the twig-branch-trunk-and-soil, but later the tree selfishly discards all its leaves. The will to live and survive is paramount in everything. Unless you are selfish you do not survive, and by surviving you may at least one day get to know a little of what you are.

The only contact she had with the outside world was to walk its streets like a person just out of prison, or go shopping for her daily food as thriftily as someone loath to over-consume in case she was thought too greedy by those who might be her judges as to whether or not she deserved such freedom.

She also wondered whether a continual striving after freedom wasn't a mere indulgence that could lead only to the greatest state of selfishness of all, which was self-destruction, and worse than the drudgery of non-freedom. Life – and she had never thought otherwise – was the discipline of having to abide by the choices you made, but if after years of trying to make a particular one work, both for yourself and whoever else it involved, you found that the decision you had made was no longer feasible, then you surely had the right to make another choice.

But having done so, and being where she was, she hated the uncertainty and isolation that often seemed more of a burden than the narrow life she had abandoned. There was no gainsaying that everything was hard to bear, no matter how many choices you made. She had settled for only two in her life, one being to get married, and the other to desert her son and husband, and both decisions had affected her so profoundly that all she had ever learned had come out of them.

She pulled the opener, beer squirted over hand, wrist and up the sleeve of her jumper. She wiped the mess with a cloth, and when she washed her hands at the sink the icy water made her veins ache. She pulled off her sweater, and blouse. It was not so easy to see her ribs any more, for she had put on a few pounds, and didn't mind because she liked to see herself in the mirror, and would have stared longer at the shape of her covered breasts if it hadn't been so chilly. She took clean things from her suitcase under the bed.

She would have felt a fool, and made some self-hurting comment to hide her embarrassment, if George had seen her spill the beer. He would have agreed, always keen to back her up at such times. Or he would have smiled and said: 'Them tins are often faulty, you should know that. They seal 'em with air still inside just to make you believe the beer's fresh. Happens to the lads at work. Goes all over the lathes, but *they* don't care. The suds wash it off.' And so on. Which made her feel even clumsier, and worse than if he had called her something he really felt like saying.

The poor bloke couldn't win. But then, neither could she. Wasn't his fault. Nor hers. Why did you have to be either selfish or not selfish when there was so much interesting space in between? You didn't. By yourself you had the freedom to be neither one nor the other, which was the best of all reasons for liking it here.

She put tea in front of him. After he'd drunk it he pushed the cup to the middle of the table. He did the same with his dinner plate after eating. He always needed space before him, and she had often wondered whether he didn't want to clear her out of the way as well, remove her to beyond arm's length but only so that she could be called back whenever he wanted to make sure she wasn't doing anything of which he disapproved, or when he needed her to supply him with another full plate or cup.

To be selfish was to be happy, but as soon as you knew it with any sort of conviction things were changing, or ought to be. George's three brothers were selfish, a moderate word to label a condition so extreme. Yet who could blame them? They were generally happy. They survived because selfishness was their way of life. They were so absorbed by their business manipulations under the umbrella of selfishness that it would have been pure mischief on her part to try and disillusion them, an attempt which in any case would certainly have failed.

Bert's close-handed resolution was backed by the assurance

that if he didn't get money from you at a particular time then he would find some other way of robbing you sooner or later, as had happened when he and his brothers had bullied George into letting them paint his workshop.

He had given a cheque for a hundred and fifty pounds, but even a week later they hadn't begun their work. George went to Bert's house to find out why. Mavis said she didn't know where Bert was, but thought he might be in a pub somewhere, 'unless,' she went on, 'they're out on a job, which I doubt, because as far as I know they ain't had any orders for a week. I wonder how we're going to live if things go on like this, although they have been drawing the dole, so at least we ain't starving, yet. It's a tussle to get money out of Bert for grub, because he prefers boozing to providing for the kids, who'll be soon needing some new shoes. What with this wet weather, they'll have to have them, though you wouldn't think so to hear Bert talking about how he went barefoot when he was a kid, saying what's been good enough for me's good enough for them. So you see the way things are, George? We're on our uppers, though it's nice at times like these to know there's somebody who'll stand by us when things get so bad you think there's nowt else to do but stick your 'ead in the gas oven. It makes us feel safer, George, to think you're lucky enough to have your own factory. I know you would spare us a bit to tide us through hard times.'

Mavis didn't ask him into the house, he told Pam, but kept him on the doorstep in the screeching wind, causing him to wonder if Bert and his brothers weren't inside, frozen in their silence till he went, when they would resume their game of pontoon or brag. Mavis was capable of playing the part, though on the other hand maybe the brothers weren't at home, because their van wasn't parked along the council-house street. He'd even looked around the corners.

Mavis stopped her pleading, and George said: 'Last week, I gave them a hundred and fifty quid to start painting my workshop, and they haven't done anything yet. So I expect them to make a start tomorrow. As soon as they finish, they'll have another hundred and fifty pounds, and that should buy the kids plenty of shoes.'

When Mavis's mouth closed, her lips went back to their former position no matter what alteration had taken place in her state of mind. Even if George gave her a hundred pounds her expression would have stayed the same. She put on a grim face whenever she saw him, as a matter of policy, but he had heard her laughing loudly enough, from a distance, with a brassy kind of gaiety. There was nothing more intimidating than to be talked at by Mavis, and then to see the uncompromising hard-weather shape of her closed and colourless lips when she had finished.

'Tell 'em,' he said, 'will you?'

He remembered before Bert married her, a highly made-up, round-faced nineteen-year-old wearing a tight skirt and high heels. She laughed loud at any dirty joke, and even in those days was never seen to smile. George was sorry for her. 'She's been with Bert long enough,' he told Pam, 'to have too much of him in her to be trusted, though I don't suppose she would have been a very agreeable customer no matter who she married.'

The men were more easygoing. Pam had seen them so full of fun that even she had to laugh. It was their women who bore the cost of their juvenile ways, no matter what George thought. She hated what they did to their wives and, though with lesser intensity, what the women allowed to be done to themselves.

George stood on the doorstep. 'Just tell 'em I called. I'd like to know when they can start the painting they promised.'

Mavis glared. 'I've got to go out shopping. I shall have to see what I can get on tick.'

'Tell 'em what I said.' He walked down the pot-holed garden path, back to his car by the kerb.

They came to the workshop a week later, at half-past three in the afternoon. George was walking across the yard towards the office with a blueprint under his arm, and saw Bert smiling from the gate, Alf and Harry trying to get in behind.

George wanted to sound amiable. 'You aren't going to start today, are you? Be bloody dark soon.'

'We had a few jobs to finish,' Bert told him. 'That's why we had to put it off for a fortnight.'

They unloaded ladders from the van and carried them into the yard. 'We'll get half a wall done before we knock off,' Alf shouted, as if an audience was present to cheer this announcement.

They reeked of ale. 'You know your business.' George continued his way to the office. They did: he had passed a newly painted house which they told him was their work, and though it wasn't top class it proved that they could do a job well enough when they tried.

He was pleasantly surprised when they arrived at eight next morning. Even a grey sky and drizzle didn't discourage them. On the other hand he disliked the fact that whenever he walked outside to the toilet one of them would call, urged by guffaws from the others: 'What's this, then? Got the shits?' Or, if he were going across the yard to the cubby-hole of an office: 'Hey up, George! Going to cook the books?'

It was as if three malevolently mouthed parrots were half-concealed at different points of his premises to taunt him for his two basic weaknesses. He didn't even look up. They had always needed their bit of fun, though he didn't like them using his first name so blatantly. The dozen workmen addressed him as Mister Hargreaves, but if he asked his brothers to do so, the ensuing ructions would diminish his status even further in the esteem of his employees. It was plain that his brothers knew it, and he should have realized the folly of allowing them to carry out any part of their trade on his property. They were well aware that he regretted his mistake in this respect, and so were determined to make him pay in case he had entertained any hope of them not taking advantage of it.

Their way of working seemed illogical, but they had laboured as a team for nearly a year, so obviously knew what they were doing. George had learned from experience that within reason you must let your workmen do things according to the method suggested by their own temperament, otherwise you were asking for trouble.

But what puzzled him was the way his brothers started work from three of the most widely separated points. While Bert began at the gate, Harry was on a high ladder painting the guttering just under the roof that overlooked the canal, and Alf laboured on window frames at the far end of the yard. No doubt they would eventually come together somewhere in the middle, providing, George thought, that sufficient standing room was left for them to apply the finishing flourishes.

On the second day George was shaping a complicated tool at his lathe when he felt a tap at the shoulder. He was irritated at the interruption, for none of the men would disturb him in his work, unless Edward had been injured when the school bus had crashed, or he had been kidnapped, or Pam had been taken ill, or his house had burned to a cinder. He switched off the motor and sud-tap, then turned to see what was the matter.

'Would you come outside for a minute?' Bert said. 'We'd like a couple of words with you.'

He wiped his hands on a rag, and followed him into the yard where the others were waiting. Three newly painted patches shimmered at different corners of his eyes.

'It's like this,' Bert said.

'Like what?' George snapped. 'I'm busy this morning.'

'We've run out of paint.'

'And you stopped me at my work to tell me that? Get some more, then, can't you?'

'We've got no money.'

If he struck one, all three would surely hit him back. Even to shout would lead to his destruction. 'No money?'

Bert looked grave, as if concerned for the reputation of their old-established firm. 'Not a cent. Not even enough for a pint of ale, let alone paint. Even the petrol tank in the van's nearly empty.'

'And what are you planning to do about it?'

'Not much we can do,' Alf said.

Bert was more reasonable. 'There's a job we can start, up Mapperley. The bloke'll give us fifty on account, and when we finish we can buy more paint and come back here. That's the only way I can see out of it. It's just a little difficulty, George. There's no need to look so upset.'

He had been aware for a long time how much Pam disliked them and their stunts, but she could never know the depth of his loathing. 'How much time will you need then to finish that other job?'

'A couple of weeks,' Bert said, 'if we get a move on, and we *can* hurry, when we set our minds to it. This sort of upset happens all the time, George. Other small firms like ours have troubles as well. I know for a fact that one bloke's been waiting eighteen months for some chaps to finish his house. He had terrible arthritis, and had to sleep in a garden shed all winter. It's shameful what some of 'em are allowed to get away with. But we're not like that, George, so don't look so down in the mouth.'

He should have sent them away, then called in the biggest firm, no matter how high the cost, to finish what they had barely started. In other areas of business he acted with shrewdness and decision, but in anything involving his brothers he was totally unable to follow his intuition.

Bert was unnerved by the silence, and said: 'There is one more way.'

George knew.

'You advance us,' Alf put in, 'another fifty quid.'

George's clipped tone impressed no one. 'Never.'

'And we'll go in our own dinner hour to buy paint so that we can carry on this afternoon, with no time lost.'

'Never. I told you.'

Bert knew when to conciliate. 'That's the best solution I can think of to our difficulties. It's the only reasonable one, in fact. And it's *our* money you'll be giving us, after all.'

'Can't be done.'

'Well, George,' Alf said, as if heart-and-soul were on his side, 'it's up to you.'

It was. He felt as if his face had been blown off by the wind, his feet about to go the same way. He was helpless. They were right. 'The robbing boggers had me over a barrel,' he told Pam, 'so I paid up. But families!' he cried, in the only real anguish she'd ever heard from him, going on to describe her own feelings in a more vulgar manner: 'I've shit 'em, before bloody breakfast!'

Bert solemnly pocketed the ten five-pound notes, and went away with promises to come back soon, spoken as airily as to suggest that they were in no way necessary. The three of them returned some days later, bearing sufficient paint to keep going for a few hours,.after which Harry came into the office and said they needed more money.

George felt as if he'd eaten an apple and got maggots in the head. 'I don't believe it.'

Even Harry seemed to know he was trying it on once too often, and became sullen. 'Well I'm telling you.'

'Go outside,' George said, after some thought, 'and tell Alf and Bert I want to see them as well.'

His sleepy-lidded eyes became alert. 'What for?'

'Because,' George said, 'I don't believe you've run out of paint – again.'

129

'I didn't say that, did I?'

Harry was the next one up in age to George, and they had occasionally played together as children, which made Harry more violently grudging towards him than to the others, and always likely to lose his temper with him in an argument. Knowing that clever George who had got on must realize this, and be afraid of certain consequences (because being 'better off' meant you were scared of getting your skin damaged in a fight), Bert had chosen Harry as his emissary in the task of squeezing more of the money out of him that they had not yet earned but had a more than perfect right to because they *would* earn it if only he would act like a real brother and let them.

Harry had been a fussed-over and spoiled child until the appearance of George, a shock which rendered him henceforth inarticulate except in anything to do with getting what he thought the world owed him. In such a family there was always one kid treated as a pet no matter how hard the life, by way of persuading the others that there must be some kindness in them. Such pampering, however, could only weaken an already vulnerable child, for when he grew older and they got tired of the spoiling they either kicked him around even more than if they had so far treated him normally, or ignored him altogether, so that the victim – which by now he had become – saw that the world wasn't kind after all, and could in fact be bloody barbarous. Hankering in the fibres of Harry's system therefore was an ache for revenge on George whom he saw as responsible for his troubles.

'You didn't say you'd run out of paint,' George said, 'I know, but you're going to, aren't you? You'd better tell the others to come in, then we can get things straight, once and for all.'

Harry dropped his half-smoked cigarette and stamped on it. He even made me waste a whole fag, he would say. 'You think you own the fucking world, don't you?'

130

'Not really' – it was hard at times not to boast – 'only a little bit of it.' His desk was laden with bills, letterheads, die-samples, nuts, callipers, an ashtray, a carborundum wheel, rolls of blueprint, two teacups without handles, a depth gauge, a stamp box, a faded starch tin filled with cutting blades and broken drills, and an old table lamp kept lit all day. This *was* his world, which he did in fact more or less own – and he was proud of it.

He stood up. 'Just the same, Harry, I would like a word with the others. You can understand that, can't you?'

While the upper guttering of the wall above the canal was being painted George had opened a window outwards to get some air into the workshop, and had seen Harry's face mirrored in the water, seeming to look up at him in crosswise fashion, showing a wide waggish grin, pot-eyes and a bristled head, the face shimmering when a breeze caught the water or perhaps a minnow thrust its nose up for air. His face had seemed almost friendly.

Harry looked at the wall-safe behind George's head. 'We've got no paint, so we want some money.'

George hoped for friendship with his three brothers even though they were older, an amity equal and respectful on all sides, but he was only ever presented with their united hugger-mugger front, which left him no alternative except to crave their annihilation. He saw the direction in which Harry's eyes were darting, but Harry didn't see Bill Clawson the tool-setter standing behind him in the doorway, until he stepped between Harry and the lintel to get inside.

'What is it, Bill?'

'I'm wondering what to do with that spindle, Mr Hargreaves. I've got it down as fine as I can, and if I use your centre-lathe I might be able to do it better, but I wanted to ask you about it first.'

George looked at his brother, whose only purpose on earth was to bleed him to death. Then he observed the other man who, as skilful as himself in the shaping and use of tools, deferred to him as one human being to another. 'I'll be over in a moment to look at it, Bill. But in the meantime would you ask half a dozen of the biggest chaps to do me a favour and throw any ladders or paint-pots they can see out into the street?'

'Yes, Mr Hargreaves.'

'And Bill, send a couple of 'em over here first to get rid of this chap, before they deal with the others. They'll know who I mean.'

'Will do, Mr Hargreaves.'

Harry showed him his fist. 'You fucking wain't. We'll come back and *smash* you! We 'ate your guts.' But he sagged from the shoulders: 'You'd do this to your *brothers*!'

'It's nothing to what you lot would do to me if I let you. You'd better leave while you're still in one piece. I'm fed up to the tits with the lot of you.'

He felt upright in spirit, but wasn't quick enough. Though he had been prepared to dodge, a savage lam of Harry's fist flew at his face.

Their materials were laid along the walls and must have been collected during the afternoon, because when George went to his car after the men had gone home, there was nothing to be seen, unless a totter had taken it all away.

He held a steel bar by his trouser-leg in case they waited in the dark, meaning to do at least one of them an injury before they put their six boots into him.

They hadn't smashed his headlamps or let the four of his tyres down, but in case they still had such ideas he would keep them quiet by getting a letter sent on the firm's paper saying that unless they returned the two hundred pounds owed to him, through default on work arranged for, he would put the matter into the hands of his solicitors.

He told Pam about it when he got home with a bruise down the side of his face. He should have let the matter drop and forgotten the money, she said. 'It's cost you far more in worry and lost time. They take advantage of you.'

132

'I know,' he admitted. 'I'm as soft as shit.'

'Forget it,' she told him. 'Don't bother with them any more.'

'I shan't,' he agreed. 'If I see them again at the factory I'll call the police. There's nothing else I can do.'

Then he added that there were a lot of other things in his life that needed sorting out. She asked what that funny remark was supposed to mean, and he said it signified that he got fed up coming home night after night, with a hard day's grind to his backbone, to find her looking as glum as if he had just sneaked in from a three-day booze-up at Skegness with another woman. So she said what did he expect her to be, a mother and dancing girl all in one? He imagined it was possible, she was sure. He laughed and said he wouldn't mind, so she put his boiler-suit in the washing machine while he went upstairs for a bath. Then she got Edward to bed, and cooked supper, waiting for George to come down and tell her the rest of the story.

A bottle of beer from the fridge made him more cheerful. In fact he was in such unusual fettle after the blow at his face that she dreaded going to bed that night, though being his wife she knew there was no way out.

20

Edward was eighteen, and didn't need her any more, but if he came to London and found her, and wanted her to go back home, she wouldn't know what to do.

George had always called him Ted and, for as long as Edward could tolerate hearing the sound, his father would sing-song his little Ted-Ted-Teddy-Bear-baby-name as if he really was such an animal to George's sentimental heart, being thrown so high that his curly head went to within an inch of the ceiling. He once touched the plaster too hard but didn't cry and then, thank God, George caught him as he came down. Sometimes, to make the thrill greater, George would catch him almost at ground level, which needed terrific strength if Edward weren't to break his ankles. From an early age Edward had become used to his father taking such risks with him, so that for years he was unable to take any of his own.

George, strong and always able to catch his son on the descent, was a father any child could trust and love for as long as he acquiesced in being hurled to the sky or ceiling. And sensing how much it pleased the father – and what child doesn't enjoy making daddy happy, especially when he spends little time with him? – he took to it stoically until he became as addicted to the experience as George.

She was pleased to hear them enjoying their evening hour together, when neither noticed her presence in the house while she cooked, made Edward's supper, filled his bath, and heard the laughter of delight and terror as he played the jumping-jack aviator in the custody of George who hardly stopped his Ted-Ted-Ted-Teddy-Bear larking about. With infinite energy and love, after his long day at work, he had only to feel Edward's warm hand in his to be born again.

The word 'Ted' would not shape itself on her lips, and she called him Edward. The difference between the words was so great that Edward had two names. He felt himself to be two people. A totally other sound out of their vital mouths led him to assume that he was one person to his mother, and somebody else to his father, causing him to adopt a certain stance to the first and, of necessity, another attitude to the second.

So Edward was two children, until he grew up, when he

134

became both at the same time, which meant neither, and then he could no longer live with his parents because he was unable to tolerate not knowing who he was.

After the high-chair age, when he sat with them at table, he was Ted whenever George had anything to say to him, and Edward to his mother when something crossed her mind worth mentioning.

She once overheard him on the kitchen floor while engrossed with his teddy bears: 'You're Ted, bad boy,' he said to one, and: 'You're Edward, *good* boy.'

After he'd been put to bed that night she said to George: 'Why do you call Edward "Ted"?'

'Because that's his name, isn't it?' he said from behind the newspaper.

'"Edward" is what's written on his birth certificate. Or was, when I last looked.'

'What's wrong with "Ted", then?' The newspaper was still between his face and hers.

'It isn't his name, that's all.'

He looked at her, and pondered on her meaning. 'It is to me, because that's what I call him. To me he's "Ted", and always will be.'

'And to me he's "Edward",' she said patiently, 'because that's his name.'

He lifted the newspaper. 'Have it your way.'

'It's bad for him to have two names,' she said.

He laughed. 'When I was a kid I was called everything under the sun!'

'That was in your family. I like to think that Edward's upbringing is going to be different.'

The paper shimmered, and he turned the page. 'And we should thank God for that,' he said. 'Let's have some coffee. But I still don't see anything wrong with calling him Ted. And if he does have two names it won't do him any harm. He's lucky. Two is always better than one!'

She plugged in the kettle, and put two spoons of powdered

coffee in the mugs. 'I don't suppose he'll find it funny when he grows up.'

'It won't worry him, unless you make a big issue out of the matter.'

Everything was a 'big issue', and impossible to talk about calmly. But George was right in that it didn't matter whether Edward had one name or twenty as long as they stayed together and he never forgot what any of them were; and she had no intention of leaving George until Edward was old enough to fend for himself, and able to do without either name if he didn't like them, though it often seemed that by such time she would be too dead in the head to care, and Edward wouldn't think it mattered how many names he had.

But she hadn't been too dead to care, and here she was in her own room, and Edward had stayed as two people, though it was still hard to say whether any damage might come of his having been Ted to his father, or if it would manifest itself because he had been Edward to her. Either way didn't signify, since it was too late, and everyone sometime or other had either to sink or swim, and nine times out of ten they had enough resilience to do the latter.

George occasionally thought of him as the Edward seen by Pam, and so looked on an altogether alien person. Not liking his conclusion in the least, he would quickly change the picture back to the Ted he wanted him to be for ever.

When Pam now and again saw him as Ted, perhaps irritated by something George had said about him, thus disturbing the love she felt for her son, she would begin a conversation with Edward to draw him into seeing the kind of youth she knew him to be, and during the process would pointedly call him Edward.

Edward was perceptive enough to see that such an encounter was forced and trivial, and thought she was trying to nag or annoy him on purpose, which she was, and so was George, but feeling that Edward had caught her out only led her to realize that she had made her point, and so was

136

satisfied, even though she felt ashamed at having indulged in such an exercise which, but for George, would not have been necessary.

The only advantage to her was that she became more acute at divining when George was about to embark on the same course. He was always more successful because, being able to act in a bluff and easy manner, he caused Edward throughout most of his childhood to feel far more his father's son than his mother's.

Realizing how he was placed between them, Edward soon learned that they were dependent on him for getting at each other. He might indeed have been two people, each one living up to his separate name, one of them open and the other shut, one happy and the other sly, one vicious and the other loving, sometimes mixed up together, which made it impossible for either of them to talk to him, in which case George said he was her son absolutely, while she averred he was his son completely.

The difference of names only established the fact that, she and George being so unlike, it stood to reason their child would reflect for each of them the unfavourable view of the other when he was intractable, and the flattering version of themselves when he was everything a contented child should be.

By the time he was seventeen Edward didn't care about either of them, and only wanted to leave home and be where they wouldn't bother him. Pam sensed this desire in him long before George, who was too busy to be aware of much, though even he realized the state of the family when, on telling Edward to turn the volume of his hi-fi down, he came in from the living-room and said: 'I've had enough of this place. I'm fed up with both of you.'

He was taller than either. Physically he had the best of them both, but he trembled at what he had said. He was pale. 'I want to leave home.'

'I don't know,' George said, who was even more afraid of

what he now knew was in the offing. 'Just because I asked you to turn that record player down.'

George would have liked him to be wearing overalls, and manipulating the knobs and levers of a lathe in his workshop. He wanted to be showing him, teaching him, watching him respond with utter fascination to his dexterity and knowledge. George would then have seen his own earlier self, and pictured exactly how he had been at that age, which he could not otherwise recall, in such detail as would have been possible by putting his son through a first-class apprenticeship devised by himself. It would be sensible, he said, when they talked about it, though Pam did not want Edward to go into a factory.

Edward refused the possibility of such training because he knew it would have to be done in his father's workshop. George's vision of the ideal father for the perfect son was scorned by Ted, as Pam had known it would be. George reproached her for not agreeing to his plans for Edward: 'He's got to make a living for himself, just like we had to when we was fifteen.'

She wanted him to go to university, though George said that, judging by the way he was struggling for his 'O' Levels, there wasn't much chance of that. He was probably right, but she disliked his pessimism. He gets his cleverness from you, he said, mildly ironic, but it might not be worth all that much when it comes to finding a job. She argued that it was still too early to tell.

When George said they should put him into a technical college to do engineering she backed him up, and George was grateful for that at least, and consoled her for any disappointment by saying that 'you can't have everything' – which was a typical response from someone who expected everything to happen in the way he wanted. She had given him a little consideration, but in return he sought to rob her blind. At such times she caught herself using these apt expressions of her in-laws, phrases she loathed while

138

acknowledging the thrill that ran through her when she spoke them thoughtlessly in occasional talks with George.

She had done her best to save Edward the noise of their arguments, and the density of their matrimonial silences, and right from the time when he had been put into her arms at the hospital, the day when he wouldn't be under her direct protection regarding all other perils was unimaginable. But at sixteen he saved enough of his pocket money to buy hobnailed boots, and clattered in wearing them one Saturday afternoon. He let his hair grow long, joined a gang, and looked like Alf. While making his bed one day she found an ear-ring under his pillow.

At seventeen he said he'd had enough and wanted to leave, and though she had been expecting it, she was too alarmed to reply. After a shouting match in which Pam thought he and his father would end by knocking each other down, they decided that after getting sufficient 'O' and 'A' Levels he would go to a college in Manchester, and be given enough of an allowance for lodgings and spending money.

From imagining she wouldn't be able to breathe if he were out of her sight for more than a few hours, she found the separation easy to accept, reflecting that it hadn't seemed so long a time from the patter of little feet to the clatter of hobnailed boots. Now that she had left, she might never see him again. He was in Manchester. She had departed without thought, and still couldn't fully know what she had done. She was more incomplete than before having Edward – for who had children over forty? – though by the time he became adolescent the golden age of mother and son had finished. He had stopped relying on her, or confiding in her. As long as there was food, money and clothes she hardly mattered, and even George's influence was at an end.

Edward and his father had demanded total devotion so that they could pursue the perfect relationship that George at least must have thought possible. It had certainly looked like that for a while. Now she was out of it, and glad, yet felt an ache and an undeniable panic at having parted from Edward for ever. But losing Edward made it easier to leave George. Sending him to college prised loose the vital brick of a wall that hemmed her in.

It would be possible to see him again. She went by circuitous reasoning to decide that she was not an outlaw or murderess. She could write and tell him where she was. He'd be sure to understand. He would come to London. They'd find a nice place to eat, and laugh at their past life that would never return, and talk about the state of the world like old friends more than mother and son.

They wouldn't. The picture wasn't real. She hadn't left George in order to indulge in dreams. She would stay on her own. She was settled into her proper sphere at last. Yet it was easy to think that her vision wasn't fatally distorted, because Edward was also away from home, an amiable young man now managing in his Manchester digs with a couple of friends. He was a person with firm views, and rules for living his own life. Away from her and George he was doing well in his course. At the end of the first year he had got top marks in technical drawing, proving that it had been the best thing for him to leave home.

The lock that held all three together had burst. Edward had known exactly what to do. His spirit had been fought over till he could stand the strain no longer, and his decisive departure proved that he was neither like her nor George – much better for him in the long run if this were true. She was therefore not unhappy at having fragmented the base which Edward had always looked on as home.

The three-way split had completed itself. She had gone into marriage without thought, and had not been a success. The different places where they now lived marked the triangle in which all such threesomes sooner or later found themselves, and to try and get back to the false life of the past would be like attempting to repair the dam while drowning in the floodwater.

21

Such well-being was too good to waste in sleep, but if she savoured her enjoyment overlong sleep wouldn't come at all when she got into bed. She would stay vividly alert until feverish dreams at dawn eliminated her memory of the calm evening.

Her hope during the day was to end the evening in peace, for if by dawn she could no longer endure the nightmare responsibility of having left George and Edward she would get her clothes on and run to the nearest telephone box in Ladbroke Grove, and while wind beat icily through glassless frames dial the home digits and wait for the bleeps before pressing down on what coins she had. George would ask who is it, and she would say it's me, and feel her spirit die in a silence too long to bear. George was a real man who would make her wait a second for every day she had been away, refusing to say hello how are you? because he wanted her to break and say I'm sorry, and sob and say I've had enough, and can I come back and I haven't slept properly for a week because you and Edward are haunting my life.

Before going downstairs she would take every coin from the shelf above the gas fire. He would be home from work. The coins grew big, and fell on her like circular tokens of hot steel.

'What do you want?' he'd ask.

'Send the rest of my clothes.'

'I don't need those rags around here any more,' he'd say. 'Teddy and me was going to burn 'em tomorrow in the garden, soak 'em in paraffin and have a sing-song around the blaze. They only clutter the wardrobe. Where shall I send 'em?' She would put the phone on top of the box, or let it swing by the cable before walking down the road towards home.

The long evening was to be enjoyed. After closing the door at dusk there were hours to go before the desire for sleep became so strong that she was snared into making the attempt. The fact that she would be punished by insomniac half-dreams after hours free of all problems did not spoil the ease she felt, and she wouldn't give up her enjoyment in the hope that sleep would come as a reward. That would be as craven as packing up and going back to George. Perhaps there was no such connection between the two states, but it was a risk she would have to take. Life was full of such risks. Every choice made created another, more so when you lived alone than when you were cooped up in a family that demanded to be looked after.

Guarding a husband and son had its rules. Cosset them, and they assumed you were spoiling yourself due to the pleasure you ought to be getting. Sometimes they were right, but mostly not, for you drudged along and took no chances, because nothing must jar or be out of place either for them or yourself. You were afraid to miss putting sugar in your husband's tea in case he had a nervous breakdown at the thought that your next move might be a knife in his back. If you forgot to put your son's school bus fare in his pocket, and he found no money when the conductor asked, he'd think you had deliberately committed treachery against him, and would probably hate you as well as all women for the rest of his life. Every act was a form of premeditated lunacy, because you were never allowed to take risks even with yourself as long as you were glued like a cut-out on to the cardboard scenery of a family.

Now it was different. Her eyes in the mirror were not flat and vacuous in their expression any more. They were coming back to life. She had changed continents, and was more at risk because she had thrown in her lot with the rest of the world. She was waking out of a long sleep, which explained why proper sleep was impossible. The excitement of getting to know herself drove away sleep, and she had long been used to the idea that she could not have everything, or even much of anything, and certainly not two states of blessedness at the same time – wherein all choices were impossible to make.

On such evenings that seemed endless she sat by the fire. No one would knock at the door. Those who had known her would never find her. If George were to shuffle on the landing she wouldn't let him in. If he paced obstinately day after day, she had enough tinned food not to go out and be talked into following him home. Should he get angry and smash the door, and knock her about in order to drag her away, she had a carving knife on the table.

Impossible to go to bed. All important moves were made, and her desires could make no impression on the course of action. She felt in the grip of some force too strong to resist, but she would fight it because she didn't like being led into situations where she was not under her own control.

She wondered what had brought her to this room, for she wasn't clear in her own mind as to how she came to be there – or here, she thought. She was living on the outside of herself, and trying to discover what was happening within. The person she saw in the mirror knew far more about her and how she had come to be here than she knew herself. She hoped that, no matter how great the effort, she might soon acquire the knowledge possessed by that sardonic reflection in the mirror. She also hoped that when the two of them were united they would be able to learn about others, not wanting to end the rest of her life with the revelation that she had not actually lived.

She listened to noises that came either from water pipes close by, or from the street. Wind rattled a door. The only way to learn as well as survive was to let things happen as if nothing could affect her. To endure meant walking the streets without flinching at every passer-by. Her life had been lived in a hundred pieces, but at any one moment she had been only a single fragment giving an intense light which she alone could sense.

She had been born inside a fragment of bottle-green glass, and couldn't remember how it had happened. Didn't much matter, as long as she one day got all her senses back. However far she was inside, she both liked it here and liked it there as well. Existence had become too good to wonder whether she liked it or not. Yet to speculate was a condition of not going back into the dark; and being here wasn't painful because, however she had gone into this room, and no matter what her reflection in the mirror said, her own will always told her to stay where she was, especially when she felt urged to go back to the bitter warmth of normality.

Sitting at the fire she was alone yet not lonely, wary but unafraid, hunted though not threatened, and willing to dwell for as long as the mood lasted on why she had been born as a small piece of bottle-green glass over which people could walk barefoot without cutting themselves. Such humiliating pressure had driven her to a place where neither George nor anyone she had known would be able to set the mark of judgement on her more convincingly than she could put it on herself.

Now that she was free it was easier to forgive George, and at the same time admit that she too needed forgiveness. Being the one who had left the happy home she was guilty in the eyes of the condemning world; but knowing that somehow or other she would have to pay made her wonder whether the whole cakewalk was worth the bare reward of being able to go on breathing.

The face in the mirror looked wryly into her sparsely furnished room. She was free. She had left everything behind. Even a few bits of furniture would have made some difference to the desolation. Her father had been apprenticed as a cabinet maker, but left the trade at twenty-five to become a shop assistant. No one knew why. He made things out of wood in his spare time, saying it was a consolation for not being able to do much else. He put together an ornamental mantelshelf for her wedding, with borders of elaborate beading, and six diamond-shaped mirrors along the front, a well-varnished box-like structure to fit over the plain shelf in the living-room. It was out of place among the furniture George and she had chosen, but would stay with him for ever.

She sat through the long evening, the mirror-image telling her that idleness was a sin unless you took advantage of it by wasting time, as her father used to say with a seriousness that deceived her for years. There's nothing wrong with idleness, as long as you don't get into mischief, he would say. Idleness is its own reward, and the greatest pleasure in life, because you can do so much with it.

His only idleness was in those few minutes during which he came out with such homilies, usually between ending one job and starting another. She had never seen him idle. With his peculiar humour he taught by first saying the opposite of what ought to be done, and then setting such an example at doing the right thing that the emphasis was even more sure than if he had plainly told her what to do in the first place.

The occasional idleness did not make her feel guilty, yet she was aware of being so. When idleness turned into freedom she contemplated the wallpaper in order not to feel imprisoned. Each wall was a different colour, its pattern a scruffy map she had damp-ragged to get clean. At first she couldn't tell one direction from another when glancing out of the window at so many buildings. Their bedroom in George's house looked west, the builder told them when they first went to see it, from which she gathered that the front door pointed east, and that the other sides of the box faced north and south, confirmed when winter came on the estate of private houses where crescents curved in all directions.

In London, figuring it by the A to Z, her window appeared to face south-east.

Perhaps four young men had once shared this room, each choosing the paper for his wall. Women would have used pleasanter designs – though the room was certainly too small for four to live in. But suppose she herself had four different

145

people careering around inside her? She would settle a wall on each, and to do so would start on the one with the door.

The rectangle of entrance and exit made the least interesting wall of her abode, since she hadn't come in by it for hours and had no intention of going out till morning, if then. The dullest and the least conspicuous. She turned her back because the brown shade was tonally dead. It had been a plush russet judging by the section curling down under the top of the skirting board, that she had picked out with her longest fingernail when sitting on the floor one afternoon while entranced with a shabby old copy of *Wuthering Heights* got from a stall at the market. The embossed pattern of Grecian urns would have been almost funereal but for the fern and sprig of alfalfa springing from each as if they had just been born and were full of life.

The door was a paler brown, and may have been more recently dabbed on, though this seemed unlikely because down the inner edges of each panel the paint had bubbled and cracked. When she pressed with her fingertips, bits flaked off and darkish green showed underneath. Out of curiosity, she forced the blade of her carving knife against it, and, like going through the archaeological layers of an ancient city, found three more levels of colour before reaching wood.

Those who had watched each seam laid on, or who had spread each one themselves and witnessed the fresh colour glow, and been fascinated at every layer ageing to acquire its own peculiar shade, made her relish the same experience for herself, proving that her eyes and spirit were in harmony. There was no need to explore more surfaces with thumbnail or knife, for she could analyse their complexity as one saw into the depths of a lake without going under the water. On these evenings alone in her room the vision was intense, occasionally painful – but it was always part of herself and never unnecessary. The sensation made her smile, content without turning to the mirror as she scratched an itch out of

146

her clean hair, and pushed the chair back from the fire because her legs were too hot.

As a child she had put a poker between the bars of the kitchen fire till it glowed red, then pressed its point into the brown paint of the cupboard door. The hissing contact sent up a coil of smoke, showing a rainbow of colours before the poker-end reached wood. The effect delighted her, but her father rushed in from the parlour. 'Good God! What's that smell?'

He snatched the poker away, and slapped her because she might have caused a fire. From the earliest age layers were forming under the surface of the spirit, each one covering the one below but none forgotten when the hot iron of piercing experience bit deeply through.

She felt her way anticlockwise to the next wall – such a blank space that any colour could be put there. Its surface did not exist on coming in from shopping or wandering the streets, until she allowed it to show what she wanted portraying. On the Underground between Gloucester Road and Victoria she looked at reflections in the opposite windows. The train rattled up speed. She would stare at the river from Hungerford Bridge, then walk to Trafalgar Square to feed the greedy pigeons before going into the National Gallery for half an hour's peace among the pictures.

A woman four seats along on the same side was observing two young women across from her. Pam counted several times to make sure the position was correct. She wasn't interested in the two girls but in the woman looking at them with quiet avidity and whom she could see tantalizingly reflected. The girls were talking, and didn't register the woman's scrutiny. Nor could the woman be aware of Pam watching *her*, since she for whatever reason was busy herself.

The woman was about her own age, but dressed with an elegance Pam could never achieve. Perhaps she was a tourist from Italy or Spain. Her smooth dark hair showed under a felt hat. Shoes and handbag weren't English. Her pale features vibrated when the speed lessened. The indistinct face at such reflected distance was full of a promise which she could not define. There was a risk involved, and she wondered why, though her curiosity would not let her dwell on it.

She was straining to see her as if in a dream, for the person's head was now and again hidden by the movement of the two girls during their lively discussion. All Pam had to do, however, was stand and walk along the carriage to bring the woman's face to greater clarity. No pretext was needed to look directly on it as she passed. But it seemed as impossible to do this as it would have been to put her hand into a fire. There was in any case a greater attraction in keeping the image remote and mysterious, for in this way her speculations gained in depth, and held off a future she was not yet ready to face.

The train stopped at Westminster, and Pam was disappointed at not seeing the woman before she got off. It was too late, like so much had been, because people between them stood at the same time and blocked her view. She let her go, being left with no other option.

Going to sleep that night she grieved at a loss that could never be made up. She was amazed, as the effect wore away, at having been caught by the force of a shadowy reflection in the window of an Underground train while plain flesh-and-blood people rarely had such influence.

For days she regretted having told herself that she would only follow her out if she left at Charing Cross like herself, and hoped afterwards to recognize the half-seen face during her walks, though how could she say to someone she hadn't met, and who didn't even know she wanted to meet her: 'I saw you on the Tube the other day.'? The woman would look at this short-haired, pale, hard-faced, mad-seeming person speaking to her on the street and say: 'Excuse me,' in whatever language, and push her aside.

The room was too comfortable, weakeningly warm. Rainbow colours swirled on the blank wall, a lit wheel

148

moving against the grain of her senses. The surface spun in its own good time, frightening her adult mind one moment and then intriguing her as if she were a child. To let herself float into the vortex of so much dazzle would take whatever nights and days were left. She could neither go back nor stay where she was. She didn't want to find out what the world was made of, nor be crushed into lunacy by it.

But she had to make up her mind what to do with her life, and the only consolation was in knowing that it was up to her alone whether or not she made an attempt to go on. Her own will was the arbiter, the power she had nursed all her life, and that had preserved her, till the time came when she needed to move in a direction she had always wanted to take, using mechanisms impossible to analyse but whose purpose had always been central to her being, proving that the more hidden the will, and the more shocking the move to her reason, then the more it was no other than her own urge for independence coming into action. The notion that she had lived all her life only to develop the necessary will to leave her husband filled her with a rage that made her want to destroy the wall. If she spread paraffin and put a light to the room, gaudier colours would arise than the tinselly façade she saw by squinting her eyes.

The air was stifling. She took off her jersey and blouse, and put them folded on to the table. Her will had finally done good by landing her in a place whose colours no longer made her shake with dread. Their deadly swirl didn't fascinate, and the wall became ordinary, fit only to stop the outside world from persecuting her.

The window dominated the next wall. She pulled the heavy table and box of books clear, to open the flimsy plum-coloured curtains. A crack in the lower pane cut the door of an opposite house in two. A taxi bringing someone from the theatre or airport stopped near by. If George had tracked her she would bite him like a wolf. The feel of freedom made her wolfish at the idea that it might end. A cat ran from under a

149

parked car to the middle of the street, then walked to another car on the far side. She hated the thought of herself as an animal waiting to be dragged to a slow death in captivity. The lighted needle-end of a plane glided slowly enough across the sky for her to wish she was inside.

The taxi driver must have misunderstood the number he had been given, for he rounded the curve of the street and set his passenger down too far along for her to see who it was. The sodium lights of Shepherd's Bush made the pale moon superfluous. Its yellow orb owned the roofs and chimneypots while she stood at the window and felt as if she owned the moon. Her room was inside it, and she stood at its window looking at herself calmly observing it and not knowing where she was.

The window was the most important wall because it gave her the power to see other people without having to look into her mirror. She drew the dusty curtains, and threw her brassière on the bed. The colours of the fireplace wall were locked inside her with the moon. The room was a home where she could be herself and think what she liked. She could buy tins of paint and decorate the walls with zigzags and circles, stars and ampersands. She could lock herself in whenever she cared to, or abandon the den at an hour's notice and look for another if she felt the refuge growing so familiar that it turned into a prison.

The rectangular block of orange gas-fire warmed the whole room. There were no set meal times, so she had put on weight, and it wasn't easy to undo the catch on her slacks. She folded them, and hooked the hanger on the back of the door. The heat rushed to her legs and thighs. She was tired, and ready to sleep, but relished her detachment in the surrounding space. 'I went into marriage myself, and came out by myself,' she said to the tall mirror carried home from the ruins. 'It is only possible to do things for yourself.'

She took off her woollen drawers but kept her dressing-gown open. It was pleasant to stroke her skin. Her figure was

150

firm, but there was no tension left. Nothing could go on for ever, and the break had been made. She felt her arms, and pressed the flesh, thinking of how she had never been idle in George's house, though he had once said how lucky she was being a woman because she didn't have to go to work, as if domestic service on tap twenty-four hours a day came about by the press of a button. In any spare time there'd been the exercise of cycling to the shops, or going for a walk, or pulling up weeds from the patch of garden. The rule of life was never to be idle, though in the last weeks she had done nothing more than work at her room till it became a home. Now it was perfect, and the time had come to leave, one way or another.

She sat with legs outstretched at the fire, smoothing the life-giving heat along her firm thighs as if the half-seen woman on the Tube train were now observing *her*. But, belonging to herself alone, she let that image drift away, and tried to stay fond of herself in spite of the woman's absence.

Her breasts responded when she placed her palms over them. They had never been big, though she loved them because stroking the warm circle of corrugated flesh around the nipples calmed her. During a bath she could lift and soothe each in turn, and love the body that belonged to her alone. No longer sleeping with someone she didn't love, she felt herself more attractive in the sight of other people when walking the streets. Going to the shops, a grey-haired elderly gas-fitter with a well-lined face whistled softly from a tent erected over a hole in the pavement. He was being ironic, aiming his call at her, even cruel, for a man of his age would wolf-signal anyone, though on the way back he was standing on the pavement, and had looked with more serious interest as she had passed.

Imagining things! But who would want her? It didn't even matter. When she put on the table-lamp her body that she had never much considered lengthened in shadow. The body had cared for her, and rarely made her ill. Aches didn't matter. Pains would go away before a day was out, and if they didn't, and you fainted or screamed, then something was

151

wrong, though it might only be 'a bit of a turn'. She had ignored her body because it hadn't belonged entirely to her, so perhaps she was still lucky to be alive on suddenly acknowledging that at long last it did.

Her white stomach had softened. She crossed arms and caressed each shoulder, she and her body in the same world at last. She would walk more, and decide what work to get. You couldn't live for ever in London, so there must be something for her to do, and if not, there was a bigger world beyond, providing she mustered the energy to push into it.

Such speculations were not material to go to bed on. Her fingers parted the inner lips, and smoothed in a rhythm till an indescribable feeling convulsed her. But she resisted the impulse to rub until the end, suspending her fingers till normal breathing came back, when she drew both legs into the chair before closing her eyes.

The only wall beyond the shape of her own body was the enclosing border of her mind, within which she was beginning to perceive secrets till now concealed, yet still not to be clearly divined in case they sowed chaos and nothing else. Frightened, she would be satisfied with no more than a glimpse of those secrets, hoping that by the time full clarity came she would be willing and strong enough to accept them. From dying alone at the brick-end of a tunnel, like a coward evading all problems, she was recovering within her own warm tent of self-love. The final act was, for better or worse, impossible to resist. Intense and prolonged pleasure drove out shame, and was overwhelming.

Startled by someone treading up the stairs, she quickly put on her dressing-gown. Whoever it was was either vast in weight or carried heavy luggage – and must therefore be a man. The landing floor creaked. Suitcases thudded on to the boards, and keys jingled. He muttered in anger while sorting out the one that mattered. She put a hand over her breasts, as if to stop her heart bursting. He was a few feet away, and she couldn't be sure that the key wouldn't be pushed into her lock, and the door swing open. She stepped across and put on the latch, though any firm tap would smash the lot. What would she do if he did? Fight, scream, cry for George, and raise the street with sounds of murder and mayhem? She felt apprehensive, inexplicably guilty, but no real fear.

He cursed at so many keys packed into one bunch, and perhaps, she thought, at not having used the vital one for so long. In the darkness he couldn't sort them out. She heard a match strike, and hadn't known that such prolonged swearing was possible. He had burned his hand.

The key went into the lock. His door hit the wall, and he dragged the suitcases in. The almost biblical rhythm to his cursing both fascinated and appalled, yet made her less fearful, since the *tone* of his voice held no threat. The slamming of his door vibrated the house.

She was afraid to get into bed. He was moving about. She felt as if he had no right to do so, wanted to knock on the wall and tell him to turn his radio down but, as if he had picked up her thoughts, the noise decreased to become hardly audible. Unlike other nights, sleep seemed neither important nor necessary, even though it was past midnight and she had to be out early in the morning. The day had been good, and she didn't want it to finish. But she got into bed and, on waking up, couldn't remember a time when she had gone so quickly into oblivion.

22

She put a spoonful of coffee and two of sugar in the dry mug, and boiling water sent a tideline to the top, and was too hot for her lips. She took orange juice from the cupboard, some bread, a pot of jam and a saucer of butter. She went downstairs to the toilet in her dressing-gown, leaving her door open. If anyone was so poor as to want whatever was inside they were welcome. The radio was still on in the next room, but only at the same low pitch as last night. He had either gone to sleep and forgotten it, or he liked such moaning through his dreams.

The orange juice was sour, and went down the sink. She threw the crushed carton into the cardboard wastepaper box. Her small wireless sent out the five-minute news in a Donald Duck squawk: industrial stoppages, terrorist assassins killing innocent people, an air disaster, a financial scandal, a by-election with the Tories back, and a pub-yard slanging match between Russia and China, loud-mouthed notifications that had no reality, unless it was you being bombed, shot, kidnapped or burnt to death. If it happened to you it would only be news to other people, and therefore the sort of story you could well do without.

She switched off, and wrote a shopping list on a piece of cardboard: food to be bought, a newspaper to scour for jobs, tampons, a roll of wide sellotape (no, she had got that already), and more coins for the gas, though there was a demon jar full of them on the shelf with angled blue eyes, crooked lips, and fair hair.

The sky was clear, a cold day good to walk in. She would get ten pounds from her post office account, leaving a hundred and thirty. When it whittled to nothing she would not apply for National Assistance. It was worse than death to go begging at government offices where you filled in forms and had all sorts of questions asked. She'd heard Bert, Alf and Harry laughing over it many a time. That's what it must be like to be a beggar, because people in such places always turned you into one. They might not want to, but it was their job, and that's what happened. If you could no longer stand on your own two feet there was only one way to take care of yourself.

Impossible to find ease in the world, but she enjoyed her coffee, and bread and butter. She couldn't go out, even though she also needed a new tub of cold cream to put on her drying skin, but would look at the changing sky while staying in her own safe body. Or she would appear her most responsible at the interview for an office job. Not much chance. They would want a young girl whose legs and bosom they could stare at while she typed. Get work in a chemist's, stationer's, newsagent's, or maybe in Selfridges. She had noticed women the same age, shape, height and aspect as herself – a bit more style perhaps, but that wasn't hard to acquire. Yes, madam, can I help you? Would you kindly put that pair of knickers back on the counter (and that nice Indian headscarf – or is it Italian?) or go to the cash desk and pay for them?

The room spun. She stopped dancing. She put on her best underwear, her smartest skirt and blouse, and zipped up her leather boots. On turning to her favourite mirror nothing looked back. She combed her hair, losing a strand of grey among the brown. If George's mob came on a thieving expedition she would call for the floorwalker and have them chased off. That tall one there: he's got ten tubes of lipstick in the inside pocket of his overcoat. Yes, that's him. Looks like a ferret – or will soon enough. The poacher's pocket, I think they call it. Full of stuff he's stolen. If I don't, and they get caught, they'll swear I said it was all right for them to loot. Then I would get hauled to court. Oh yes, I saw them. I saw them once in fact at a fancy-dress night at the Railway Club, when Alf went – no, it was Bert, of course – decked as a tall woman with a battered face and short grey hair wearing a fur coat. He walked across to George and showed his white satin blouse, and stockings held up by suspenders. The men chaffed him, and the women said how handsome *she* was, and later when everybody got drunk he did a striptease down to his jockstrap, and then changed into ordinary clothes which Alf had brought in a plastic bag. They kicked the women's clothes around the hall, a frolic which ended by Harry getting into a fight with the man who ran the place.

She put ten coins in the gas. Cold in here. She took the extra-wide tape and stood on a chair to close the window. Don't like it. She ate a hearty breakfast when the game was up. The day couldn't be finer for a trip to Ancient China. The transparent paper stuck to her wrist, but she pulled the band free and pressed it firm between wood and wood to keep out the air. In a few weeks it wouldn't be possible. Better now than never. Don't like it here, but where could she like it except nowhere?

She stepped down, satisfied at the job, and threw the empty reel on the floor. The curtains were drawn flick-flick and the light put on. Don't cry, don't cry, or you'll wash out the sky. To write a letter would take what life was left, and she couldn't wait. There was too much to say, and what she couldn't explain to herself was no use telling George or Edward, who wouldn't want to listen. There were too many tales in the world, and too many people who didn't want to hear them, so what was the world for except to get out of?

She was happy. Never been happier. She sang, picked up the brush and dustpan to make sure the mat in front of the fire was so clean you could eat your dinner off it. It was a hap-hap-happy day. That's what she had come down to, whether it was wrong or not. It would be squalid to do it at home. She would do it in peace. That's why she had left. Save all the bother.

She put on the multi-coloured woolly hat and faced the mirror. She couldn't smile. The hat wouldn't do for such a day, so she hid it under the pillow of the made bed, and hoped it wouldn't come out and insist on being where it was supposed to be. She didn't want to, and not look nice. Only her best was good enough. She had been brought up always to

156

be clean and look smart when she was going wherever it was and for whoever she was setting out to see.

None of the hats suited her today. Not a single one. Wouldn't have to matter. Perhaps it wasn't the occasion for a hat, and in any case there were some things you couldn't be bothered with at such a time, though she admitted it was a pity, and wasn't it about time she got going, otherwise it would be too late and she might not do it, and then where would she be?

There was no trouble. The floor was an easy comfort to her back as her bones dissolved and lay restful and flat after a hundred years of breathing. The bars of the gas fire were cold from their all-night holiday when she had warmed herself in bed with dreams that hadn't left her alone. Her hand reached and turned the tap full on. If it seemed the only thing to do, why not do it? Didn't like it enough to stay anywhere. The hiss was comforting.

PART TWO
Home from the Sea

Tom resisted god-damning it when the strap of his suitcase snapped, for such words did no good. Laying everything on his bunk he found a spare belt which, though thin, would hold. During the last few minutes of peace on board he sat with knees apart and quietly smoked, listening to the *Fidelio* Overture and thinking that such music heralded a fine bout of freedom.

Signed-off and paid-up, and through the Customs, who took nothing off him, he went ashore and had supper at the Bull Hotel. Three of the crew were already eating. Tom nodded, and got a smile from one who then turned to go on talking with the others.

The roast beef was like damp cardboard, and all the vegetables (including the potatoes) tasted the same and were too soft. He drank a pint of beer for better nourishment, though neither did that satisfy. The cloth napkin was well ironed, but not perfectly clean. A lifetime spent on the lift and fall of knotted planks was over at last, a fact that might have been something to write home about if he had ever had one except the kind that was called an orphanage.

The waitress brought a double whisky, which he had not asked for. She pointed to the other table, and the men looked at him. 'A goodbye drink for you, sir!'

A white rain blistered the pavement, and thrummed on the station roof. Water made him thirsty, and water made him piss, except when underfoot and full of grit on pavement, wharf or station platform. Luggage at his feet, and mackintosh open, he reached for his wallet. The sea is a place where angels fear to tread, and he supposed even Jesus just about made the shore.

'A first-class ticket to London – single.'

No, I'm not going for a dirty weekend, he might have added, nor have I been here for one. I keep a monk's berth in town for my excess clobber while I'm at sea, but that's none of your monkey business, shipmate.

There was no 'First-class to London? Yes sir!' but a pudding-faced stare and cash slapped down to emphasize that the ensuing silence could go on for ever for all he cared. A Force-Niner pushing from behind had made a hard ride up Channel, and meant no easy job sliding into that concrete embrace of mother earth. You can push around the shoulder in the wind's teeth, but it's another matter when you get kicked at speed like a football to make that turn to port through the eye of a needle. But the Old Man had done it as he always did. They were in, and he was out, had chosen to make his last trip at fifty. From now on land and idleness would be his lot, and he anticipated filling the emptiness with only the good things of his choice.

You could laugh at dirty weather on land, watch its worst from behind the glass of a train window. He set his cap on the next seat, folded his mackintosh and put up his cases. The padded shoulder-bag containing sextant, deckwatch and short-wave radio, needed no more but never to be parted from, stayed by his feet.

He couldn't read with his mind on the spin and half-way round the ratchets, even *Our Mutual Friend* and only a third through the tale. His bald dome with border of reddish hair shone with raindrops on the window glass. He saw his face and didn't much care that he considered it ugly, especially the wide, somewhat flattened nose, broken while boxing and again in a shindig with one of the crew as second mate.

The train ran through darkness and he cupped his hands on the glass to look at stars in the clearing sky. The stars are dead

162

but give light, yet never quite dead because they guide us at sea. Not everything is death. Not all is without purpose, not even me, though I'm damned if I know at the moment what it is.

In spite of a few trips around the islands of Central America his face was pale. Beer-smelling breath bounced, so he pressed the black flake into brown straw between his fingers and filled his pipe.

There was no one to think about except his aunt, who had lived in a large flat in Madeira Square. He had first climbed the stairs at fourteen, to stay a few days after she had written to the orphanage that she was his aunt and had better see him. He felt he had climbed more steps in that building than he ever had at sea, and wondered how she had managed as a woman of eighty. Age must find strength, ashes of heart and muscle proving that all isn't over by a long shot. On his last visit he adjusted his cap, and pressed the bell which he remembered had been sticky as if someone had previously called with jam on their fingers. Most were elderly people, and the stairs smelled of dog and cat piss rather than of cooking food.

But she could see the sea from her lounge windows. 'I got your Marconigram, so knew you were on your way. Probably saw your ship as I was having breakfast!'

At the end of every voyage there was no one else to visit. As a young man he had dreaded seeing her though called just the same, but got berths that kept him longer and longer away. Then he wondered and worried as she aged, and tried not to be more than three months absent, expecting every sight of her to be his last. Each time she kept him a full minute at the door as if to remind him that if it weren't for him she would still have a sister, and he should never forget it.

At the first visit from the orphanage, she had been in her forties, a big old woman trying to frighten him. She had always kept him waiting, yet he never missed seeing her when ashore, which puzzled him often enough, except there was no one else to call on. If she hadn't existed, any other country in the world would have had as equal a claim to be called Home as England.

In the Western Approaches he would get the Sparks to send a telegram via Land's End Radio, as if such personal signals were vital for the ship's navigation, or part of his own safety precautions. He didn't know why, but the closer he came to shore the more he knew there was no option but to visit her. When on watch he allowed himself to think of nothing but the ship, so he was happy not knowing. Otherwise he slept, or listened to music in his cabin on the hi-fi system Clara had given him, one of the birthday gifts since he first went to sea, each preceded by a greetings telegram telling him what to expect. Wherever he was, the message and the package always found him, and during the war they waited at the company's office.

2

At fourteen, stiff in his orphanage clothes and smelling of his own strong soap, he had stood in her large sitting-room among plush furniture, pictures and knick-knacks, and a cage of bright yellow birds that never stopped calling and whistling. He had wavy gingerish hair and soft brown eyes, a few freckles on skin that was otherwise pale. He couldn't look directly at her, his cowardice remembered yet at the present time understood.

She sat in an armchair, and left him standing for half an hour. The tall pendulum clock which told him so was the only object he felt humanly close to. The birds talked to the room and to each other, and the woman who was supposed to be his aunt would never speak at all, so it seemed, though she looked at him.

Beyond the bay of the big second-floor window where she made him stand (and he wondered afterwards, remembering the way she was looking at him when he had the courage to glance at her, whether it hadn't been some sort of plan) he could see a sheet of grey flat water down the square and across the promenade which seemed to lift like a hillside as if some barrier on the beach was stopping it rushing into the streets and destroying the town. The sight was scary, but there was nothing else worth looking at. A wide high sea expanded across the world with no land beyond. He stared as long as he thought his eyes were not getting crossed, hoping that when he turned back to the clock at least another minute would have gone by.

The water was the English Channel. He knew it from geography, and that France lay on the other side, but he imagined the sea went right to the South Pole across thousands of miles of ocean that got dark at night and had shining stars over it. There were lit-up ships there, liners, merchantmen, tankers and tramp steamers, and when you got to the ice you would find men fighting with giant whales as in *Moby Dick*, and when God wasn't *for* them He was *against* them, and from within the hidden nine-tenths of an iceberg lurking underwater, He rose up to destroy men in order to show them His power while Jonah sat in the whale's mouth and looked on in awe yet wondered whether to come out and take a chance on life.

The favoured victims struggled in a fearful sea of grey waves. There was daylight but no sky. The only colour was blood when harpoons struck and the sea monster struggled and died, or the great ice-saw of an iceberg's side ripped the life out of ships and men, as in the grey engravings of a 'Penny Dreadful' yarn. He watched it from the window, then opened his eyes wider to see whether or not it had happened, and saw

165

only the calm sea and, some miles out, several steamers. The superstructure on one ship was so high he thought it a white building on the coast of France. He made up his mind during that half hour what course his life would take, and he knew he would never alter it.

He would go to sea. With neither father nor mother, he would become a sailor and live on a ship.

'Did you hear what I said?'

'No, Aunt Clara.'

'I said don't they ever let you sit down at that orphanage? You can sit down, if you care to.'

He chose one of the hardest chairs, as if a sailor wouldn't want anything softer. 'They do at meals, and in class.'

'*Not* on that one. It isn't strong enough for a big boy like you.' She pointed to a sofa whose curved legs, he said to himself, looked as if they wouldn't support his big toe. But he did as he was told, sitting stiffly in his walking-out suit, and enclosed within his own carbolic whiff, at which she wrinkled her nose. 'We shall have to do something with you.'

He glanced at the window, thinking she meant with his life, and that this was the reason for his excursion from the orphanage. 'I'd like to go to sea, and be a sailor.'

'Yes, you *would*. Just *wouldn't* you?' Her voice was so angry that he felt crippled by his mistake. She saw it, and smiled for the first time. 'I meant that we shall have to do something with you after tea. There's a concert on the pier. Would you like to go?'

He didn't care, but knew he must say yes, which was what she wanted him to say. Therefore, he wanted to say it. The maid brought in tea, with biscuits and chocolate cake, and fish-paste and cucumber sandwiches.

'Don't gobble,' Aunt Clara said. Her most stinging words came quietly and in a nice voice. 'You're not a turkey. Gobble like that, and I'll call you Graham Gobble!'

When he smiled, sternness replaced her amusement. He had eaten porridge and bacon at breakfast, but wouldn't say

166

he'd had nothing since, first because he daren't, and then because he couldn't, and lastly because he wouldn't. But he stopped gobbling. He had been hungry, and you had to do something when there was nothing to talk about. He glanced again at the window, as if the only safety lay beyond, thinking he'd like to smash his way out. It was better at the orphanage, which he liked because he was used to things there.

'So you want to go to sea?' Her anger was not yet gone.

He felt like a wall that would never be pushed down. 'Yes, Aunt Clara.'

The boys would say: What's she like? Does she have big tits? She's an old woman, he would tell them, but the scoff was good.

'I suppose it makes sense.' She called for the maid: 'Eunice!'

He tried not to laugh at her name when she came in, but knew even so that he'd reddened.

'You'd better take that cake away or he'll eat it all, and make himself disgustingly sick.'

Sarcasm ran off him like water. He didn't care what she said. They had already eaten it but for a few crumbs, which she picked up between her fingers, rolled into a ball, and pressed into the birdcage. He decided she must be having a joke in telling the maid to take the cake away or he'd be sick. 'What makes sense, Aunt Clara?'

The maid, nearer his own age, had bobbed fair hair, and he could tell the boys about how, as she came to the table, she winked at him, and that when she was close he could smell her scent.

'Your father was a cook on a transatlantic liner, as far as we could make out. But there was nothing we could do about it. Not that we would have wanted to. Father tried to find out, but it was a big liner.'

She must hate him, but he would take no notice. Instead of puzzling out why she forever said such things he wondered whether the maid's room was close to his. He'd have to tell the boys *something* when he got back. She came into my bed. She

167

did, I tell you. He thought his parents had died when he was born. That's what he'd told himself. He hadn't known anything except that he had no parents. Now he knew that his father had been a cook on a liner. He must have been a chef wearing a white hat and an apron. His mother was the sister of this woman who was his aunt.

She pointed to a large photograph on the flat-topped piano. 'I thought I'd better get it out for when you came.'

He walked over to see. She was certainly better-looking than the maid, or his aunt.

'You feature her,' she said, 'that's one good thing, except for the hair, and the *nose*. Ugh!'

Good or not, he didn't care. The woman was thinner than his aunt, as she looked across at some horses in a field. The maid had eyes that were almost closed, and a narrow mouth that couldn't open. Even when she smiled its size didn't alter, though he thought she liked him.

'In any case, by the time you were born half the cooks had gone to other ships. She died in a hotel.'

He thought she was going to cry because her voice went low and her lips shook, so he hoped the maid would come back because he wouldn't know what to do. 'How did she die?'

'Of natural causes.'

She lied. 'Why did I get sent to the orphanage?'

She would never tell the truth, but one day he'd find out. 'Ask your grandfather,' she snapped.

'Isn't he dead?'

'Yes. There was no one to bring you up. Your uncle was killed in the Great War, and we couldn't be doing with you. Father died soon after. The whole business broke his heart.'

The idea was laughable, but he kept his lips firm. He didn't care what happened, or who he was. He was himself, and that was all that mattered. An oil painting hung above the mantelshelf, of an officer in smart khaki, the grey barrel of a howitzer behind. The face looked unreal, as dead as the man was dead, with dark hair and full lips and slightly protruding eyes. The oftener Tom glanced the more artificial it looked, as if he wasn't absolutely dead but only waiting for one good reason to come back to life. He would jump out of a Christmas stocking, and kill everybody with a revolver.

The teachers had been in the Great War. Cranky Dick had a wooden leg. Old Pepper-pot had half an arm gone, though he was good at throwing the stick with the other if he thought you weren't listening. The matron had her husband blown to bits and no known grave, but it was more than twenty forever-years ago. Passion Dale, they called it. Or Mons, Arrers, Wipers. Poppy Day came round and they had to stand still for two minutes. A poppy in every hat, and he always had a sixpenny big one to wear, for his uncle, he now supposed, the money every year being specially sent. And nobody had told him, but now he knew.

'Your grandfather said he would never recover from losing John, but he did. He said the same about your mother, and he didn't.'

You've got to die some time. Everybody had. He must have died because he was old enough to die. The maid smiled from the doorway. Then she winked. He liked her for that. She put her tongue out at his aunt. That was even better.

'And I stayed single to look after him. There's no other way in life.' Her voice was suddenly shrill: 'If you do that again, Eunice, I'll send you away.'

Tom felt his cheeks redden, as if he had connived in the maid's prank. Clara had seen her reflection in the bulge of a shiny vase. 'And stop your winking. There's nothing wrong with your eyes. Unless you have conjunctivitis as well as St Vitus' Dance! Go and wash the tea things.' She turned to him: 'Can you swim?'

Those over thirteen had gone to Dovercourt for a week last summer. He had learned, with a lifebelt. 'Yes.'

'That's a blessing.' She stood. 'Now wash your hands and face, then we'll get our coats and go to the pier. We shall be late if we don't hurry.'

She made him wash with scented soap. She couldn't put up with carbolic, she said. But it was all he'd ever used.

The water was pink, and seemed still to have the same ships on it as before. As if unmoving, their spring-coils of smoke were fixed for ever. There was a calmness out there, but he couldn't go yet. While laughing at the jokes, with the tide rushing in under the pier supports, and huge banks of white water flooding across the darkening shingle, one part of him pictured ships over the water of a wide ocean, with no land to be seen. His Aunt Clara would write to the orphanage and say that he should go to sea. The promise wasn't yet made, but he knew she would see it done. If not, he'd run away.

He thought she hated him, but half-way through the concert she held his hand hard while laughing at the jokes. Perhaps she didn't hate him after all, not at the moment anyway. Nothing was certain except at sea. The water might drown you, but it didn't hate you, though if it drowned you whether you could swim or not maybe it did.

The next day was Sunday. Church was boring, but he had a way of making time go quickly, imagined he was looking from the window of a train, which made his eyes twice as sharp and brought everything so close that soon he was walking in the scenery and not riding through it, and then he was no longer part of the place he was being bored in, for he could sit down and stand up or sing and pray without disturbing the walks he was having in the landscapes he had gone into. For as long as he could remember he had never been bored unless he'd wanted to be, which sometimes was when he couldn't make up his mind what scenery he should choose.

After lunch she sat in an armchair doing the *News of the World* crossword puzzle. She wouldn't let him read the finished pages, but gave him a *Wide World* magazine to look at. She cut the crossword out and put it into an envelope with a postal order. 'We'll find a pillar box for it,' she said, 'on your way to the railway station.'

'I hope you win five hundred pounds.'

'You never *win* anything in this world,' she snapped, 'and don't *you* forget it.'

'Some people do.'

She looked at him, so that he could only stare again towards the sea. '*You* never will.'

There was no sense in caring. If he were going to sea he wouldn't need to win. Every time you came back from a sea voyage you had lots of adventures to tell worth more than five hundred pounds. If they didn't let him go, he would run away and find a ship on his own. He liked being alive now that he had something to think about.

'All you have to do, Thomas, is study hard in the next year or so, and then we'll get you on to a training ship. You'll be happy in the Royal Navy, and I shall be glad to get you settled. '

She went out of the room. The Royal Navy seemed too grand, too severe, too much like the orphanage. You went in battleships to war. He had seen pictures of HMS *Hood* and HMS *Rodney* on Players cigarette cards. In a battle the ship burned around you, and turned over, and you sank with it. He had counted the guns, and knew the names of fifty warships.

'Before I forget,' she said, 'take this back with you.'

He put the ten shilling note into his blazer pocket. 'Thank you, Aunt.'

'And here's a bar of soap. Use it for when you come again in the summer. Write a letter and tell me what you buy with the ten shillings. I hope you don't spend it on bars of chocolate, because if you do you're sure to be sick.'

He'd never been sick in his life. 'I don't want to go in a battleship, Aunt.'

She poured something from a bottle which said 'Dry Sack' on the label, but it looked very wet to him. 'I suppose it'll be all the same when the war starts.'

Older boys listened to the news on the wireless twice a

171

week, but the voice said one thing, and then it said the other, telling of battles in overseas places. 'Is there going to be a war?'

Her coat was on, and a hat. 'There will be if the Germans go on listening to that silly twerp Hitler. But I suppose you'll be as well off in the Merchant Marine as anywhere. Now, don't dawdle, or you'll be late for the train.'

His mind had been empty. Now it was full of pictures and prophecies. He couldn't wait, but everything would happen when it happened, so he knew he would have to. Unlike any other time, he had something to expect. Eunice gave him a packet of sandwiches tied with string, and Clara held his hand as they went down the steps. Both actions embarrassed him. When the train was half-way to London he went into the toilet and left the soap on the shelf.

3

He had watched her get old, and she had seen him reach the bleaker side of middle age. Her face was a calendar for the passing of his own life, otherwise he would have felt no older than twenty-five, that heady ridge on which the awkwardness of youth is left behind but the plateau of fulfilled manhood is not yet realized. He had left one stage and had not yet been too severely mauled by the other, which may have been what Clara liked about him, if she had ever found anything attractive in him at all. Perhaps she recognized a trait from her own family that he would pass on, though he would not get married while she was alive in case he made a mess of it.

He had never quite thought of her as needing to be looked

at as one adult to another. Frail as she was, he could never be in any but a subordinate place when close to her. The assumption after his last time ashore that she hadn't much longer to live made him feel that her demise might accelerate his own trot downhill. But as she stood at the door, and made him remain for a while outside, she glared as she always had, eyes fierce as if to say he had never known what the trouble of life was about, and that now he was fifty she hoped he never would.

She leaned on a silver-topped stick, and looked at the knuckles of the shaking hand that wouldn't hold still. He recognized stony courage in such an exhibition of unbending formality which she would keep up to the end for his especial benefit. It was as if he expected to be kept waiting, as in his younger days he often was by the Old Man of many a ship. He knew her to be a person without malice, but in her attitude there was an unshakeable dislike that he would be glad to see go.

But in the meantime she would teach him the necessity, and the value, of knowing his place, expecting him to pass the same futile rigidity to others. While she stayed alive it was the only hard time she could give him, for hadn't his appearance put the final touch of devastation on the family? He didn't want to know. She blamed him, but could never make up her mind whether or not to utterly damn him. Until she knew one way or the other he must always be made aware of her dislike in the minute or so she kept him outside her door like a man selling bootlaces.

'Hello, Aunt Clara. It's me, Thomas.'

Her hands were so pale they were almost blue. They were streaked with purple. In the dim hall he wondered where the tall stout woman had gone, saddened by her lack of stature compared even to three months ago when he had thought she could not possibly get any thinner.

'I can see who it is. I'm not blind.'

Instead of finding her sharp voice offensive he wanted to say thank God you can still speak. 'I came straight from my ship.'

She drew her head back, aware that she hunched too much over her stick. 'You smell better than you once did.'

He smiled. 'I was in Jamaica, you know.'

'What a place for a naval officer!'

It was a shame to waste his few bits of conversation in the hallway, yet he didn't know how else to fill in the obligatory time. 'I've been to worse.'

'I dare say you have.' She would get a cold standing in the draught, and looked so tired that he thought she would be wise to sit down. If she fell he would catch her, for it seemed she was almost certain to. On a ship you had to anticipate any emergency in a Force Nine gale, yet needed to be more careful on a calm sea, though you would be a fool to hope for much even at the best of times.

He had stood to attention for enough. 'You might as well come in for a while,' she said. 'No use jawing where everyone can hear.'

The doors of the other flats were solid and heavy. No one could. The large front room was the same as when he had first walked into it as a carbolic-smelling orphanage boy over thirty years ago. Nothing was altered, but everything was faded, and a faint dust had grown on all surfaces. A woman came in by the day to clean, cook a meal, make the bed, and bring drugs from the chemist's. You couldn't find maids any more. They weren't *willing* when you could, she said. They wanted you to pay them the earth. And even so, they didn't *care*.

He sat on the same sofa, away from the plainer but more fragile chair. 'Did you get my postcards?'

He'd sent one from every port of call. 'Came in yesterday. Go tomorrow. I hope you are keeping in good health. I'm fine, as always.' Or some such variation. The picture spoke more than anything he could say: palm trees, volcano, hills covered by forest with a narrow-gauge rack-and-pinion railway slicing to the crestline; waterfront, fort or government house.

174

Hard to know what she thought of such sceneries. The only places she had been to were France, where she had visited her brother's grave near Arras; to Belgium where she stayed in Ostend; and to St Moritz and the Rigi in Switzerland. 'But I have *never* been to Germany,' she told him more than once.

'Yes,' she said tonelessly, 'I got all your cards.'

'We had a rough old time coming back.'

She was not the sort to stand his postcards on the mantleshelf, or leave letters lying around, as he knew happened in some homes. He'd never received any letters from her, nor been thanked for his communications. He mentioned them because he wanted to know whether or not they had reached her. Most did, but a few didn't. He could think of nothing else to say.

'Sailors must expect it,' she said. 'It can get very rough around England. I look out at the water every day.'

When she did, he had to believe that she thought of sailors in general and of him in particular. In any case it was the nearest she'd get to expressing concern for him in his presence. She stood up to make tea, ignoring his offer of help. He looked around the room that had sent him to all parts of the world. He walked from end to end as if on the bridge. Only table lights were on, but the eyes of dead Uncle John in khaki watched him pace about. There was more in the portrait-figure's gaze than dread of the unknown, and he wondered whether he'd ever know what it was.

She would order him to do something, but not countenance the least offer. 'Come and get the tray.'

He brought it from the kitchen. The daily woman must have got the meal ready: chicken, salad, bread, pastry and a half bottle of chilled wine.

No matter how hard the days of heavy weather across the Atlantic might be, he always felt a surfeit of energy as he stepped ashore. But it didn't last. A sudden exhaustion raddled him. A sensation of inner wastage brought on a shameful urge to weep both for himself and his aunt. His

175

vision of a painful world without hope or purpose lasted a few moments. It went away, but left its track.

He shook himself, and she did not notice. In the orphanage and nowhere else had such a mixture of despair and tenderness swept through him. A trace had come abruptly, born from the same despondency of days gone by, but more of a threat than those fragments of former times.

He drank a glass of wine before eating. Several bottles might drown his whiff of anguish. There was nothing to say, but he knew better than to be silent. She looked straight at him. The skin hung on both sides of her face, and she could not help the shaking of her hands on the stick. Even that did not distress her sufficiently for her to acknowledge it. He felt insignificant when with her, but out of her presence no one awed him, a quality that came directly from her, and which had made him an efficient naval officer.

He talked of departures and landfalls during the last few months and, unable to know whether or not she was listening, remembered those moments in the orphanage before falling asleep that were marked by such intense despair that he wondered for the first time in his life why she and her father had got rid of him like a piece of rotten fruit, when they had accommodation where he could have been so much better cared for. The question had come too late. He couldn't blame them, not having thought about it until he was old enough to know he might have acted with the same lack of charity.

'Can I pour you a glass of wine, Aunt?'

Heavy and wrinkled, her lids shifted. Her eyes were wide open. 'I can't drink any more.'

'Wouldn't hurt you, I'm sure.'

'I used to drink a bottle of sherry every day, and felt very well on it.'

He ate his meal quickly, then replaced the napkin into its ring, as if he would be there to use it tomorrow night also. 'I never drink anything alcoholic while on board. Too many ships have been in trouble because of a soddened officer on watch, or a drunken captain in his cabin. I don't touch anything from leaving land to walking off the ship.'

Her stick shifted. Her lips moved. 'More fool you!'

He lit his cigar. The truth she spoke scorched him to the roots. He'd got his master's ticket, but had never been given a command. No complaint had been made about his work, but he left ships at the shortest possible notice, or became ill, or didn't get on with the captain – and didn't trust himself to drink. That's what she had meant. What are you frightened of? Can't you hold yourself in properly? It was a look he got often when refusing a touch of liquor. For some reason he had made it a rule. On shore, it was different. Sometimes he came back to the ship hardly able to get on board. He would collapse into a sleep so deep that he didn't waken till the ship was on the open sea. But no liquor was drunk between ports. The captain pushed the decanter towards him:

'Hair of the dog?'

'No, sir.'

'You stank like a lousy old tomcat when they trundled you on deck last night.'

'That was last night. I believe I was drunk.'

The captain laughed. 'Is that what you call it? I call it rotten and senseless.'

He signed off as soon as he could.

'I drank a bottle of sherry for my health – one a day at the best of times,' his aunt was saying. 'Now I don't, because my body can't take it.'

'Here's to you, then.' He finished the glass, and the bottle. It was no feat to drink someone under the table. He'd often done it, so that no companion would chide him on board for a teetotaller. When they saw him as two people they knew when to leave one of them more or less alone. He walked to the heavy curtains drawn across the window. 'I enjoy coming to see you.'

Her voice quavered out of the silence. 'Don't you visit other people?'

177

That had nothing to do with it. He spoke what was in his mind. There was no other person. He had met women from Galveston to Manila, from Durban to Seattle, even saw some of them more than once, but he had no one else except his aunt because that was the way he liked it. Happiness was in moving across the waters of the world, shooting the sun and the evening star when you could see them, and plotting your position on the chart. When the ship moved and he enjoyed a smoke and thought of everything that had happened to him, or about nothing in particular, he was happy, if that's what it was called, though it had sometimes seemed that all his lifetime's journeying through the cloven wave was an effort to find the dark place he had come from.

When the ship was in harbour or calm waters he could sit between watches on a deckchair outside his cabin and, savouring the homilies while remembering the perils and rough passages, browse through the copy of the Bible given as a parting gift – or shot – by the orphanage. There were also log books and almanacks, pilot books and books of tables in the chart room, but in his cabin were a dozen paperback novels to be read on a voyage and left behind. She was right, however. He had no one else.

'Loyalty has always been thought much of in our family,' she said, 'but you should find a young woman and get married. I should think you've had enough of the sea by now.'

She had prised him into his career, and wanted to manoeuvre him out of it. 'Don't you think it's respectable any more for me to be at sea?'

'I never did,' she returned quickly. 'You chose it.'

She hadn't married, because she had looked after her father till he died. It was too late to marry then, even if she had wanted to. The strong-minded don't need excuses. They are one big excuse for doing exactly as they like. 'If I left the sea,' he said, 'there'd be nothing else I could do by way of occupation.'

178

'A married man is always busy.' She make-believed, to pass the empty hours and keep herself lively.

'I shall need to earn my living for that kind of expensive life. In any case, I'm fifty. What woman wants an old salt like me?'

She snorted, and held herself from speaking, waiting for him to say more. But he wouldn't go on, believing that if he didn't pursue the topic she would not. Perhaps whatever was on her mind was already settled. That was often the way she made decisions, and why he accepted them. Her combination of loyalty and pride was a knife-edged weapon that she could walk on even in bare feet, and pull him along after her. Her hidden and unqualified assumptions had strengthened his emptiness to such an extent that those he worked with considered him hard and ungiving. He remembered how a third mate had once said so to his face.

His overnight room was always ready. She told him to go to sleep before his face fell in the ashtray. The only thing about him that she didn't seem to regard with contempt was his silence.

4

He would call at a pub by the docks, and stay an hour before walking the last few hundred yards through the gates and along the quay, a procedure which would keep him teetotal and morose throughout the voyage. The last evening ashore would blot out the effects of his leave. He'd empty his mind of any sentiment at being on land and seeing people among whom he might one day hope to live.

The more poignant the regrets the better. Walking along

tree-lined London crescents of shabby houses, he noted each passing face. Even the flattest and ugliest seemed to have more life than his own, a fact which didn't strike him as remarkable, merely a point to observe. Perhaps no one felt life's heavy imprint on their own face, though he imagined that his sea experiences during five years of war had marked his features in some way or other. Yet when he passed a man of about fifty, who might also have served on a Murmansk convoy, his face seemed only to show the ordinary marks of those who hadn't been in the war at all. Faces were divided into those that showed the spirit within, and those that concealed it, he thought, unwilling to decide which case he fitted into.

The fact that he would not stay at sea had taken long enough to enter his heart, though in the making of such decisions time – and wisdom – had no meaning. Twenty or thirty years seemed little more than a few days. A day on an Arctic convoy could pass, if that was the word, like a decade without leaving any wisdom in its wake. What remained in the soul after a fortnight of such days was a further emphasis of those characteristics which had allowed him to survive without going off his head.

It was no time for the imbibing of sagacity when ships were sinking into the icy sea and their crews had no chance of being saved before the pitiless cold drew them under, and knowing that without warning your ship could be next from either subs or bombers. You battened down the hatches of your spirit and zig-zagged through turmoil. Any notion of becoming wise through such experience would have added to the dangers by spoiling your set purpose of wanting to be alive at the end of the voyage while in every way performing your duty. Whether you got hit by machine-guns or shrapnel, or somersaulted under into the cold-dark without warning, was decided by something too far off for you ever to comprehend or take advantage of. Otherwise, you were kept going by the

180

practical considerations of your trade, and that was that.

When solacing himself in Murmansk with a bottle of vodka he recalled telling his Aunt Clara as a boy that he didn't want to go into the Royal Navy because such a fleet fought battles. There was no other word for what he had just come through except a massacre, because only a few broken and damaged ships came into port of the dozens that set out.

As he walked by the stalls of an East End market such recollections did not make him glad to be alive. They'd happened too long ago, and connected him to a shadowy self he had once been and wanted to forget.

The lack of such punctuating experiences in life would have made his progress seem like walking through a mist without landmarks. There had been too few, in any case, to prove that he wasn't. Nothing much had occurred since then. Every event that promised to be memorable had turned out to be no more than routine. If he hadn't been fifty years of age he would have hoped that something vital though in no way perilous might still happen for him to believe himself as fully alive as most people passing on the street.

When on shore he walked through whatever town he happened to be in. A rickshaw man who followed him in Penang, hoping for a fare, had refused to take no for an answer. Tom made his way to the Botanical Gardens in his own peculiar half-swaying naval stride, the rickshaw man continually pestering him to get in and be towed there. Tom hardly noticed him, nor even his own sweat from the steam-kettle heat, but finally, still unwilling to ride, he gave the man a few dollars and sent him away.

The monkeys looped their tails over a branch and swung towards him. He bought pink bananas and fed them. One claw came too close to his shirt and he was quick enough to land a blow at the head without being bitten. He laughed at his luck, as the monkey ran to the top of the tree. Then he made his way to the City Lights dance hall in town for a few

181

drinks and a hugger-mugger embrace with a taxi-dancer, before walking as upright as was possible back to his rust-sided ship.

There was no such thing as rest. There was only sleep and work, otherwise you walked, and refreshed yourself by food and booze before going back on board. He was not shy with women but could never see himself on shore with job, wife and children. A few affairs had lasted a voyage or two, but after the third call lack of interest had been mutual, and there were no more letters. He was thankful that the one or two women he had imagined himself in love with at the time of getting his third mate's ticket had not taken him seriously.

Work, duty and the ability to endure were no self-sacrifice, since he gained as much by them as he gave. There was no fairer bargain. Work meant a mind emptied of all possible problems, scooped clean except for those connected with the job in hand. Even on a calm day, crossing the Arabian Sea in good visibility and heading for Colombo, there was enough to observe from the bridge to prevent any of life's considerations getting a firm hold.

Towards dawn, on the surface of a lacquered sea, he could look from the stars down to the horizon for a first sight of the sun. Peace spanned his life, and surrounded him with a tranquillity that held off the forces of battle not yet unleashed. When they threatened on shore he endeavoured to walk them into the ground, to exhaust his body and stave off the night about to overwhelm him – going eventually into the nearest bar to drink his mind into such chaos that sense had no chance of alarming him.

The blue, dark sea turned choppy in the Malacca Passage. The mountains of island and mainland were covered with forest and barely ten miles apart. The ship had steamed into a zone of jellyfish whose grey shield-tops lay close together and covered the whole area from shore to shore. He had seen miles of them down the Malacca Straits, but never as many as in this narrow place. He looked through binoculars at the steep dense woods, then slowly back towards the ship across the living masses of jellyfish.

Fresh from sleep and a shower, in his laundered white uniform, he had the sensation of falling and hitting the sea in their midst, his body dissolving by the force of their electricity and poison.

He was drowning, the thrust of salt water up the nostrils and into the mouth as he corkscrewed slowly with closed eyes into the darkness. Tentacles of jellyfish wrapped around him so thickly they became a shroud he could not get out of, and he saw himself as an infant taken to the orphanage accompanied by the photographed face of his mother.

Memories struggled to get into his consciousness before vanishing with him for ever. He smelled the walls and tiles, sinks and toilets and blankets, the soap and the food, as well as the perfume and perspiration of whoever had carried him. He relived her clean clothes and salt tears so elaborately that he was threatened by a greater extinction than that of dropping overboard: a fear of the unstoppable reversal of life back to what was too painful to know about.

He perceived as many long-buried revelations from his past as he dared, part of him willing to go deeper providing the mysteries of his life would be explained; but a tighter grip on his binoculars brought him back to thoughts of duty and work, and the impossibility of making a choice which might cost so much that he would not survive to enjoy the results.

The wooden rail was sticky with his sweat and the salt sea air. He brought the binoculars to his side, and turned his gaze towards the mainland of Sumatra. A Dutch passenger ship passed close from the opposite direction. People on deck waved greetings. A white point of signal light flashed its name from the bridge telling where it had come from and its destination: 'ORANJE – BATAVIA – AMSTERDAM'. He read the message aloud so as to keep control of himself, each dot and dash a thumb-tack stabbing the brain to reality. The sight of the morsed light and the voice of the man on his own ship reading the words like an echo brought him back to the fringes of his ordered life. He began to sway. He fought, but his legs were weak. He was watched by Sedgemoor at the wheel.

'All right, sir?'

He walked a few paces without falling.

'Touch of the sun,' he called, loud and clear.

Sedgemoor knew what he was talking about. 'Singapore will cure it, sir!'

'Think so?'

He laughed, a belly-laugh from somewhere in Kent. 'Cures everything, sir, me and the lads say, if you know where to go.'

He once asked Sedgemoor where he did roam on his shore leave there, and with a ferocious wink that could have boded no one any benefit, he replied that he was 'off with the others to get fixed up with a nice orgy'.

He laughed. 'But what about curing the cure, Sedgemoor?'

'Don't know about that, sir. But it ain't been necessary yet, touch wood.'

5

He went up on the lift. Trolleys were pushed along the corridor by shouting orderlies who seemed to be clattering the lids of dinner-wagons or linen-tins with deliberate relish. He wondered how anyone could die peacefully in such a bedlam. Though it was day outside, the lights within were not bright enough, and the noise offended him.

A nurse saw him standing, cap in hand and holding a bunch of neatly petalled roses. 'Can I help you?'

'You mean to sort this lot out?'

'More than anybody dare do.'

A sheen of dark hair showed under her cap. She had bright eyes and well-rounded cheeks. 'I'm to see my aunt,' he told her. 'Name of Miss Phillips.'

A little circular watch was pinned at her breast. 'Have you come far?'

He wanted to hold her arm, or take her by the waist. The impulse was so strong that he had to step back. 'West Indies this time. I got in this morning.'

'Lucky you!'

He glimpsed into a ward and saw patients in dressing-gowns sitting by beds or strolling about. 'It was work.'

'You see all those exotic places, though.'

'From the bridge. Or through a porthole.' He had nothing to lose, and perhaps something to gain from a state of mind which said it was immaterial whether or not he was old enough to be her father, a mood which came more frequently as he got older. A pace or two behind, he eyed her waist and shoulders, thinking how delectable she was. He caught her up. 'The islands make wonderful scenery, especially from a distance, at dawn or sunset, say.'

'You make me envious.'

'That's the idea!'

A ticket on the door of a private room displayed his aunt's typed name. Clara was never a woman to be denied a place of her own. 'How is she?'

'Comfortable.'

They never told you anything. The hierarchy was as rigid as on a ship, beneath all the clatter. 'Is that all?'

'See the doctor afterwards. He'll be in the ward by then.'

They faced each other, and he wondered whether Clara, in spite of her illness, could hear them talking. 'Would you like to have dinner with me this evening?'

'That's rather quick!'

'Quick enough, for a girl from a good family?'

185

'And that's rather sharp. But I *could* have said yes.'

'Only what?'

'I have to see my boy-friend.'

He laughed. 'I'm consoled. Matter of having to be.'

'You're sweet,' she said. 'It might have been nice.'

'Thank you. I'll go back to sea a sadder and wiser man.'

'I don't believe you.'

'It's the truth. I always do.'

'You're making me feel disappointed.'

The purpose of his errand told him it was time to cut the banter. He looked through the little square window. Clara was sleeping, and seemed at peace. He went in and placed his cap on the table, the door closing soundlessly behind. No ship's officer could fault the white counterpane, polished floor, clean windows, and flowers by the bed.

Stimulated by his recent closeness to the nurse, he could only stand and look, in spite of the vacant chair, conscious of altitude and not wanting to lose it. Air grated through thin vibrating lips. He could neither sit nor get too close to the breath of this ancient person who did not seem to be the same imposing Aunt Clara he had met at fourteen. He remembered her smelling of scent and sherry, and holding his hand at the pierhead concert, and laughing at coarse jokes while he was aware of her trying not to. If he laughed, she'd stay quiet, but when she laughed out loud and shook her head he was crushed into a silence which he now realized was fear.

The accuracy of a recollection is always distorted by the powerful anchor of the present. Compared to the strength of the present the past was surely dead. Every statement is a damned lie. Sentences ran through his mind, and left him hoping that the young nurse would come in and set his roses by the spinney of carnations.

Her feet twitched. He wanted to smooth them free of irritation and pain. It would be a small service to do for her. She had been the only person to help him, but why was he the most hated member of that family? She had loathed him out of loyalty to the others, but had made him aware that he belonged to them nevertheless. He had been a call on her sense of duty, so she'd had no option but to do what she could. He understood. It had been sufficient.

Even those who in other circumstances might have deserved more, often ended by getting far less. Complaints should never be made. Injustice was not a disadvantage providing you could work, eat, breathe freely and say what you pleased – enough to make any man or woman happy if they had it in them.

One eye open stopped his thoughts. She shook her head, as if to deny whatever was going through his mind. 'You were flirting with that nurse.'

He nodded. The chair scraped as he drew it close. Her fingers were so cold he thought they were wet, and he folded his hands over them, leaning to hear what she said.

'I don't blame you. I would, if I could.'

The light was dim. She was the last remnant of his mother, apart from himself. Standing in the open with his sextant, and taking a sight on a star before there was no more horizon, he felt afterwards while he worked out his calculations that the star was now lost among millions and of no further use. The heavens swallowed everything, and though they might sooner or later give something back to redress the balance, they would take his aunt like those stars he had sighted on in order to get his position before darkness intervened.

The stars denied any purpose in life except when you were close to the flesh and blood of someone you loved, or near to the person who hated you most. It was all the same, whichever way you defined the contact. He believed, and he didn't. The truth, which he could never get hold of with sufficient firmness to find his exact emotional position on the earth, caused a pain at his midriff, which he supposed came from the grief of seeing someone die who had wept at his mother's death, and as someone might see him one day slip out of sight like an elusive star. It was a matter of time. That inexorable eater of human bodies was already hovering. The chronometer in its plush box set to Greenwich, and the deckwatch fixed on local time to record each precise micrometer sighting of morning or evening star, ticked away so many unseen deaths a second, but here in a smallish hospital room he watched the demise of someone whom it had never entered his mind that, because he had lived an existence far from proper human contact, he would one day have to see die. For the sea was only a part of reality. On a ship you belonged to a machine for moving people and goods from one place to another. He had always thought that at sea you were also closer to God than when ashore, but in this room it came to him as a revelation that you were only near to God when you were in the proximity of other people.

The nurse placed the roses on the table. She walked out and made no signals. Clara's fragile lids fluttered as if intense life still went on under them. Her hand moved in his, but the flame of life would not return to her arctic limbs. His own burning fingers made no difference.

His watch ticked until its sound was blotted out by her breathing. She withdrew her hand and put it under the clothes as if to find some weight there and hurl it away. He walked from the window to the door, and then back again. Her eyes opened and made him afraid, but he looked at her calmly: 'You'll be all right.'

She neither saw nor heard. The noise she made sounded like an anchor chain rattling over the side of a ship at the end of a long voyage.

6

In the nurse's office he was given tea and biscuits. She leaned against the table and looked at him. 'I think you're tired.'

He made an effort not to stare at her shapely legs in dark stockings. He had two weeks ashore, but if he were due back on board tomorrow she wouldn't have noticed any exhaustion. 'Tell me your name,' he said, 'if it's not a state registered secret.'

'Beryl.'

'I like that.'

'That's awfully nice of you.' She smiled at her sarcasm, and brushed both hands against her hips. 'My boy-friend phoned. He won't be able to meet me tonight, after all.'

He wasn't interested. A decade had passed since his suggestion. In every grain in his body he felt emptiness at the prospect of an evening out with this vibrant young woman.

'Don't worry about your mother.'

'Aunt,' he told her.

'Aunt, then. She'll be comfortable. Come and see her tomorrow.'

It was settled. 'Let's go, then.'

She came close. Girls today thought nothing of making the first move. She put an arm on his shoulder. 'Will you spin me sailor's yarns?'

He kissed her. Or maybe she kissed him. It was hard to say how it happened. 'And more,' he said.

Her body-heat was intense, and before they moved apart he knew she couldn't have missed the stiffness at his trousers. 'I go off duty in half an hour,' she said, 'but there'll be no strings attached. All right?'

Across the restaurant table he told her what tales came into his mind. She expected it of an older man, listened with a hand at her face as he poured wine and yarned in such a way that she stopped saying how tired he looked. Wine and food charged the veins. She distorted her lips when he smoked between courses. He put the cigarette down. She moved the ashtray to the next table. Clara in the hospital seemed as far away as if he were in Port-au-Prince or Santa Cruz.

They went arm in arm to pick up his bag from the

189

station, then came downhill and walked along the front. Breakers tore against the shingle, an occasional overcharged heave sending spray over their heads. She squeezed his arm as they leaned against the rail. 'Looks murky. Do you want to be out there?'

'I'm happier seeing it from here.' He was at ease on a ship. It was home. Even on watch in a gale he was familiar with all procedures and, unless some malevolent flick of the heavens or waves brought a catastrophe, knew what to do.

'As long as you don't go back tonight.'

'No chance of that.' Having done most of the talking, he wondered who she was, and what she was really like. If he went mad and proposed marriage and she said yes and they settled down in a little suburban house what would he find out? She was such a mixture of deliberate gaiety and nervous anonymity that when neither spoke he felt as if he were vividly day-dreaming during a monotonous watch in the middle of an ocean. Marriage, he thought, might well be like that.

A touch on the arm brought him back. 'You've had enough of the sea for a while,' she said, as if trying to tell him something he might not believe.

His half-formed thoughts could only be of use to him after stewing around for a while. 'I think I'd had enough of the sea when I first clapped eyes on it, but I was fed up even more with something else. Every move you make is an escape from something or other, but I believe I went to sea as a boy because when I first saw such a vast amount of water I was afraid of it.'

They walked across the promenade, back to the shelter of buildings. 'That's how people often get into things,' she said.

It wasn't, he supposed, that young people these days were especially wise, as that someone of fifty like himself had forgotten the wise or clever things he most likely said at that age. The self-assurance of the young often sounded like wisdom.

She took off her clothes in the hotel room. He was tardy, she said, helping him out of his, not even giving him, he told her, time to read the fire-escape instructions on the back of the door. She laughed, and they kissed before moving to the bed. A sidelight was left on, and she pushed him gently to straddle from above, resting on both palms to draw herself back and forth. It was difficult to lean up and kiss her, but he could touch her breasts which bowed warmly down. She kept her eyes closed, making it impossible to say how far away she was in her mind – or even where he was himself. No star sight could decide their positions in the world, and one could hardly expect both body and horizon to be perfectly joined after so little time together.

Her face was a mask. The run of her velvet movements increased, hair and skin opening, hair swaying across her mouth. She stifled herself on him, breathed noises of separation till the distance between both was immeasurable. He felt her contractions, and his own roots loosened. His existence was divested of meaning, and without regret he let himself go to her vigorous sounds of pleasure.

She was too far away to hear the noise from the mouth of his Aunt Clara which had sounded to him like the chain of an anchor going pell-mell down into the water.

No longer able to support herself, she lay on him and opened her eyes. 'That was good. I must have needed it.'

He kissed her. 'You did it by yourself.'

'The other system doesn't work for me.'

'I thought you were taking pity on me.'

'Funny bloke!'

'That makes two of us.'

She lessened her reliance on him, and transferred some weight to her elbow. 'Sorry I've got a boy-friend, in some ways.'

'A beautiful girl like you can't be unattached.'

'I'm not glued to him, though,' she said firmly. 'He has his piece of action now and again, and so do I. As long as neither of us knows.'

191

When she lay under him, he went into her.

'You must have been a long time at sea,' she said.

There was no way of keeping the talk going. She held him, and moved her hips, and even though her eyes stayed open it was as if neither had any connection with her body. She wanted it to be finished. He went on till he knew she wasn't able to respond in the same way as before, then felt an ejaculation of pure fire that seemed to have no liquid in it.

She washed herself at the sink.

'Do you mind if I smoke?'

She came back to kiss him. 'Gives you cancer. Or heart disease. You should stop.'

He embraced her. 'I'm scared to, in case I *get* cancer.'

He watched her dress, then he washed and put his own clothes on. 'Don't come out with me,' she said.

'You're leaving?'

'I have to be on duty at six, to look after your poor old aunt. And a few others. Stay here and sleep, then you can eat your cornflakes – or whatever they give you in a place like this – read your newspaper, and have a pleasant stroll to the hospital. All right?'

It would have to be. He loved her and let her go, thanking God for such lovely kids. Sleep was a beneficial oblivion.

Almost too late for breakfast, he was grudgingly served. He lifted the lid to see one pale teabag floating in hot water. A cook once served the captain with such vile things, and the pot was thrown off the table. He drank the tasteless tea because he was choking with thirst. The sausages were as soft as putty, and even the trimmings were on the blink, he thought, cracking a piece of cold toast that was sharp enough to cut his throat, and smearing butter that looked suspiciously like margarine. The only genuine article was the bill of twenty pounds.

But he left his tip, and sat out his time while he smoked at the table, unaware that they were waiting for him to move. It was impossible to do so. There was no eagerness to go out and

192

find that his life had changed. He already knew it, felt a relaxation so complete that for the moment it paralysed him. He suddenly did not know how to move, waited to do so, unwilling to give himself an order which he sensed would not be obeyed.

7

As a deck officer it was often necessary to pull back into the protection of his own shiftless and brooding mind, solitary contemplation teaching him how to stay sane when he felt as meaningless as the heaving sea outside the cabin. The ability to discipline his threatened mind into quiescence had come slowly, in tune with the growing power of the years to crush him into an uncontrollable blackness. The conscious effort to build a defensive system left no emotional energy for friends, or for the kind of prolonged relationship which might turn him into a tolerable human being. He considered people in the mass to be as threatening in their ever-changing unknowingness as the sea, which often turned wild by some force over which no agency in the universe seemed to have influence, and flew up against him like an enormous and mindless grey wolf intending to take his life away.

The sea at that moment regarded him as nothing, as no one, as a spark to be extinguished on an impulse of fiendishness. Because he knew that the body was fragile, life brief, and existence finally meaningless, he was always wary, continually on the alert to repel danger from any quarter, cultivating a readiness of mind which created a loneliness that over the years made him appear like a man fighting to keep his grip on a deadly secret which was eating his soul away.

Someone might try to get friendly, but he was incapable of taking any steps in that direction. A man of the sea, he was blocked off at all points from the land, and now looked with misgiving on so many years spent in the condition of a prisoner who had clung to the shreds of his soul only by withdrawing into an uncertain peace at the centre of himself. Unless he had done this he would have gone down into unfeeling oblivion. The dread of losing what little he knew about himself gnawed at the tenuous connection he had with the rest of the world, or with that small part which might be concerned as to whether or not he knew of its existence. His mathematical sharpness was continually in tune with the fair conduct of the moving ship between taking departure and landfall, and at times he felt that such faculties would be overwhelmed unless he murdered either another or himself in an attempt to retain the clarity that was necessary for his work. Unwilling to take alcohol, he would long for the trip to be over, but now craved an end of all voyages that tested him to such limits.

Others who were threatened by the same malaise defeated solitude on long trips by an obsessive ingenuity, which for self-respect they called a hobby. A man's need to be absorbed often came to him like the rediscovery of the power of love, and might involve an attachment to some musical instrument, or to a collection of objects which, when laid out, created a design or picture that the heart viewed as a unique accomplishment. Outlandish schemes kept a man sane in what might otherwise have been his darkest moments. A project, no matter how futile, was necessary to keep within bounds that person who felt chaos press too close, and who knew that something effective to fix his mind on was the only solution.

Once on a tedious great circular haul across the northern Pacific, the third mate drew an outline of the world on Mercator's Projection in faint pencil on a large sheet of plywood, but then emphasized the coastlines by sticking live match heads, almost touching, to bring out the shapes of the various land masses. The map included both Polar regions, and took weeks to draw, and longer still to cut off thousands of match heads with a razor and glue them firmly so as to demarcate every gulf, peninsula and large island. The operation went on through several voyages, and Tom wondered where the man found so many matches on a single ship, till he saw him walking up the gangplank at one port of call with two huge parcels.

A closer inspection of the near-finished masterpiece showed that the colour of the match heads varied from dark brown through crimson and scarlet almost to grey, but it was pointed out that when seen from a distance they appeared to *match* well enough. It was impossible to guess what he intended to do with this impressive portrayal of the world, though he did hint that, because he considered it the finest artefact ever devised – and he claimed to have made some really unusual objects in his time – he might give it as a wedding present to his best friend who, in one of his absences, had latched himself to *his* girl-friend.

In blue match heads the third mate had yet to chart those trips he had made while this treacherous love affair progressed to its final stage. The happy couple, he said, with a dangerous flash of the eyes, would accept it as an unusual gift from a loser who had no hard feelings. They would put it proudly on their living-room wall, together with the cheaply framed pictures and flying plaster birds, and one day, as they didn't know what the map was made of, it would ignite in their overheated love nest while they were in bed upstairs doing what he himself should have been at if there had been any justice in the world, which there clearly was not – or at least wouldn't be until his unique map took fire.

He was one of the looniest, though Tom had known some not too far removed, but whose pastimes, no less absorbing, ended almost as spectacularly. On the other hand, not everyone, either on the upper or lower deck, needed a hobby. Those who did were more interesting because they became garrulous with their new interest in life. But those others who scorned the idea of taking up some hobby often did their everyday jobs without complaint. Space did not frighten them, nor time intimidate. They were the salt of the sea, as it were, and also of the earth who were born with a gyroscope of placidity inside, and a self-correcting rudder that kept them on an even keel, so to speak. They did not fight against the monotony, nor were they unaware of it. For days the sky did not unroll its grey pall of cotton wool. The ship pitched with the same unvarying motion, till their faces took on the pallor of disappointment, though what they were hoping for no one could say. Their curses went little beyond their everyday ingenuity. The ship laboured, and work was done. Every man was different. Those who had no hobby considered that there was enough to do, and barely sufficient time in which to do it.

Nevertheless, the days went at a different rate for those who had a pastime. Tom had noticed that time had no meaning to a man fighting boredom and madness, but that as soon as he took up an occupation apart from his duty, having followed a sudden life-saving instinct, time slowed, and every spare minute spent with his absorbing hobby became an hour, a day, a week, a month of salvation. While it lasted he was a new man, and those who before kept as much out of his way as possible on the narrow spaces of a ship, would nod, smile, or pass an occasional remark. He had become safe. His obsession had rendered him harmless, hemmed him in by bars stronger than steel.

He was a believer who had no thought of making others take up the same occupation. He had no wish to convert anyone to his all-devouring view of a tiny part of the world. In fact total mayhem might have ensued, making an *amok* appear as a friendly gavotte, if someone had shown competing interest. But there had never been such a case, for which Tom as first officer could only be thankful, and the *nouveau*-hobbyist

196

was a peaceful man, a menace to no one while he carved, played, scooped, sorted, painted, fluked or fiddled. All was well because it was only the beginning.

From stalking the decks unable to sit still, Sedgemoor filled in a few more numbers of different colours on a canvas which, when finished, would become a passable reproduction of the 'Mona Lisa' fit to hang in anyone's furnished room. Or he arranged his collection of exotic Taiwan bottle-tops on a tray with a sufficiently high rim to prevent them slewing over the floor from the motion of the boat.

The Sparks on one ship rigged up his own amateur radio kit and, when not duty-bound and listening out on 500 kilocycles, tap-chatted to other hams as far off as Chile and Australia, Israel and Japan, thus adding to his wall of colourful QSL cards. Another seaman collected matchboxes and called himself a phillumenist. Someone gathered complete sets of coins from even the smallest of countries, and fixed them into the natty pockets of a large album, while others did the same with cigar bands or stamps, or paper money when their pay ran to it.

An electrician packed his leisure time by adding together all the numbers of the complete London telephone directory, so that he could work out the average digits for the millions of subscribers. He did this even before the days of electronic calculators. After finishing his eight-year task he gave a slip of paper to everyone on board with the mystical telephone number inscribed as if it contained the directions for finding the buried loot of Treasure Island.

Every merchant seaman has come across such people. To an outsider there might seem to be no spare time available, but to a sailor even half an hour can be onerous when the black dog is, as they say, sitting pretty on your left shoulder. Tom had only thought of these varied occupations, a spectrum running through his mind in idle hours, but he had seen others, to their pleasure and their cost, take them up.

A carpenter on one leaky tramp analysed all names on his

home sheet of the one-inch ordnance survey map, counting the numbers of farms, villages, towns and rivers that began with any particular letter of the alphabet. He worked out how many names there were to a square mile, added up trigonometrical points and arrived at the average height, calculated the total length of roads, streets, lanes and watercourses. During the whole voyage he hadn't a minute to spare. In his dedicated fashion he knew that sheet of map better than anyone else in the world – an accomplishment which made him a proud man while his passion lasted.

There was a deckhand who learned navigation, and when the time coincided with his off-duty period he shot the sun at midday or took star sights at dawn and dusk so as to work out his own position of the ship – as if, while he believed God Almighty, he was not so sure about the captain. He had his deckwatch and secondhand sextant, and all paraphernalia necessary for his conclusions. When the captain asked why he didn't sit for his third mate's ticket, the man remarked that navigation was his *hobby*, implying that to be deprived of it would leave him with no further interest in life.

The search for skill and perfection was satisfyingly endless, but a hiatus was sooner or later reached. The attraction of the hobby vanished from one watch to the next. Disillusionment was sudden, final, impossible to explain. Emptiness returned and was more devastating than before. Work and duty were not enough, and with vacuity of purpose came danger. Matchboxes were crushed underfoot, bottle-tops slung into the litter bin, and stamps torn. Paper money stuffed into pockets for spending in bar or brothel would hardly deaden the pain of the hobby's absence. The coins thrown overboard looked like the tail-end of the Milky Way disappearing into a Black Hole.

The captain of one ship devised an intricate game of naval tactics. His rule book took a hundred pages of typescript, and there was an accompanying packet of charts twice as thick. The captain considered his game suitable for commercial reproduction, saying that at the time of retirement, when he had collated every amendment, he would take it to a firm that was certain to be interested. The only thing, he said, with not a glint of humour in his grey eyes, was to finish before someone stole it from his cabin.

Tom, then second mate, did not want to remind him that similar toys were already on the market, but supposed he already knew. The captain mentioned his game on the bridge one night, and Tom asked how many points one would score for landing a shell on the flight deck of an aircraft-carrier as opposed, for example, to sinking it. Or if half a squadron of Seafires were put out of action, would more points be gained than if the aircraft were old Swordfish biplanes that had plopped into the drink?

The captain, pleased at this seemingly serious response, invited him to play a game. Tom found the book of rules complicated and contradictory, but bluffed his way through a few rounds. The captain, however, paused in the course of slaughterous engagements to alter rules which did not seem to work, and in this way Tom lost the Battle of the Coral Sea twice, and the Battle of Midway once, though he came close to preventing the disaster of Pearl Harbor. The captain cast dice, enthusiastically spun funny little tops, and moved his pieces, while Tom played with caution and perhaps, he thought later, too intently.

The game was laid on a table in the chart room, illuminated by a special light, beyond which radius all seemed dark as the ship laboured through the night. Leaning over the table, the captain placed one of his tokens off the Falkland Islands. He stood straight, and stared at the wall. The unlit pipe fell from his teeth, and scattered ash across the Arabian Peninsula. He trembled wildly, then swayed into the darker area. When he screamed and fell, Tom ran to him. The captain's limbs were stiff, but he fought to move them. Pained to see him helpless, Tom attempted to lift him into a chair.

The captain raved when Sedgemoor touched his legs and tried to straighten them. His jaws clamped. Sweat dripped from his face.

The engineer calmed him for a time, but through the rest of the night the captain's demon continued its ravings. Sparkie called the medical service, which radioed back regrets that they had an epileptic on their hands, and sent instructions on how to treat him. Two days later they steamed into Seattle, and the captain was taken ashore, his game neatly parcelled and labelled by Tom, never to be seen by any of them again.

For years he could not pass a toy shop without wondering whether old Captain Robinson had recovered sufficiently to market his weird hobby. He would look among rows of coloured boxed in the hope of seeing that he had. Perhaps the concentration of devising such a complicated and never-ending game had in fact held back the seizure for many years, yet only till such time as would make certain that the first fit would be his last as far as duty at sea was concerned.

Sedgemoor spent weeks blocking in the colours of his 'Mona Lisa'. He one day looked at his masterpiece ('A bit too lovingly,' said the cook), finished but for a few last numbers around the enigmatic yet for him utterly discouraging smile, and deciding he could do no more towards bringing it to life beyond the state of a mere painting, masterpiece though it might be, walked on deck with it, stood on the rail, and fell overboard.

A Filipino deck-swabber saw him go, so that he was soon hauled back. The artist-by-numbers explained to the captain, who had nothing less than murder in his eyes, that he had been taking his painting into the air to dry when a gust of wind caught the large canvas and, acting like a sail, carried him away.

8

The map of the world made from match heads by the third mate was, when complete, the marvel of the ship. Even the captain asked to see it. No one thought to remark on so inflammable a work being kept in one of the cabins. Some must have known that the match heads were lethal, but did not realize the possibility of fire should it rest too long against hot pipes.

Nothing of the sort happened, however. After finishing his object the third mate often placed it on a table, closed his eyes, and ran his fingers along coastlines till he knew it so well that he could tell exactly where he was, as if he were a blind person reading a Braille map of the world. The only man who had not seen it was the cook, and for him the third mate brought out his huge board and set it on the ping-pong table in the crew's rest room. Those who thought they might not get another opportunity of seeing the map also came in.

Puffing a half-smoked cheroot, the cook leaned over to look. Such utter fascination must have its consequences. Hot ash from his foul-smelling smokeroo landed at the top of Norway and, being neglected while he looked at Australia, one match head ignited with a sprout of blue and yellow flame, generating sufficient heat to make contact with those on either side. A handkerchief, or perhaps an upturned ashtray, could easily have doused this initial conflagration, but no one seemed able to do anything except stare.

A line of blue flame went east along the Siberian coast, and another zig-zagged in a southerly direction down Norway and leapt across to Denmark. The cook was mesmerized, so much so that the cheroot also fell, bounced, and hit the top of Scotland, thus encircling Great Britain by fire, and also Ireland when heat seeped to Ulster via the Mull of Kintyre.

Those who looked were either helpless, or they enjoyed the sight of a disaster for which they had no responsibility. Eurasia went up in smoke, and flame traversed the Bering Straits to surround the Americas. From Asia it travelled via the Malay Peninsula to Indonesia, not even sparing Australia. The board was thick enough not to let the universal flare-up damage the table, and no one troubled to save the world. Not even Madagascar was unscorched, because after the white heat had ignited Africa through the Sinai Peninsula, and fizzed its all-destroying track down the Red Sea (joined by fire coming from a flame that had already entered the Dark Continent, soon to be dark no more, by the Straits of Gibraltar), it jumped sufficiently eastwards to reach that island also. Only a few spots in the Pacific and parts of the south Polar regions were seen to be untouched when the smoke became diagonal rather than vertical, and to these the third mate, after much hand-wringing, gibbering laughter, and a kind of tap-dancing rage, took out his lighter and also put a *match*.

The smouldering board was thrown over the side, trailing a few rags of smoke, a sound of conflict as it fought and then made peace with the water. Tom lent the third mate a pair of field-glasses so that he could view his devastated creation floating like a mouldy biscuit in the green sea.

No man's pastime could have ended more satisfactorily. The man had come to the end of hobbying even before the accident, which was why he did not try to stop the powder-train of destruction. He could have saved Africa at least, perhaps half of Asia, conceivably Japan, but the fire combusted from the smouldering in his soul, and he played the malevolent god by letting continent after continent burn. The hobbyman has his own pressurized space within which the obsession plies itself, but sooner or later baleful normality breaks in from the world of so-called sanity, reminding him that even on a ship no man lives alone, and that all were subject to laws which, while not easily comprehended, bound them in ways from which it was impossible to escape.

Tom had noted the dogged preoccupations of the hobbyists which prevented self-knowledge from overwhelming them, or which denied the fact that their prior desolation had been an act of God. They were happy, and good luck to them, but he, apart from the distraction of a few books and records, preferred to let the ocean of twilight and nightly solitude break over him and do its worst. Between watches when he couldn't sleep, read, listen to music or even talk to himself, he would sit in his darkened cabin with eyes wide open, lulled by the sound of bashing sea and consuming engines, to recall details of his life with as much clarity as imagination could muster, warding off despair with a determination that turned aside any notions of self-pity. Not knowing where he came from, he had no ghosts to push aside. Having no places to go to, there were few hopes on which he could with any realism dwell. Hopes that might be close were under the water through which the ship was pushing its way, and no moment passed when he was not aware that he would only find solutions if he sank endlessly down to look for them.

The energy to do much was present, but to seek any other posture except that of sitting upright on the only chair, would be to pull himself towards the water by a force impossible to hold back from. At the worst, the only way to survive was to stiffen against inner temptations which were stronger and more dangerous than those outside. His spirit, composed of the will to fight against emptiness, was opposed by the cultivation of an even greater emptiness, so that he could look on the original with less fear. From such a vantage point, he was safe – yet one shade nearer to the deadness which is called annihilation.

He descended, yet stayed alert, and hours had vanished into minutes when the steward knocked at his door and came in with tea, which he would drink quickly no matter how hot, then walk on to the bridge, thankful that duty intervened as a form of salvation from attacks against which his life seemed the only defence.

His colleagues sensed by the set of his features that he possessed only the moral strength to do his work, which confirmed him as a type with whom they could do no more than pass the time of the day. Nothing further in the way of friendship was possible. He was not at peace with himself, and was to be avoided. His silent and ungiving expression marked him as 'one of the old sort', and they left it at that. He knew what they thought, because the dumb insolence of his own miseries at least had the advantage of making him sensitive to the assumptions of other people concerning himself.

To take up some pastime as a guard against his isolation would be dangerous, for if he later tired of whatever hobby his temperament suggested, the peril of a greater emptiness than had assailed him before would be such that he might find himself beyond all reason for continuing his life. So he became known as the sort of person about whom it was said that his hobby was his work, and work his hobby.

The intensity of the struggle had varied over the years, but it was always present, till he saw that by being a firm part of his existence, such a fight might have saved the only quality his spirit possessed. Safety came to depend on the fight. The effort of contesting his despair pulled him through innumerable voyages. In the valley of the shadow he stayed sane. He remained part of life, fixed into himself, and committed to a battle which became responsible for his survival.

His spirit had chosen the way, because though the price was devastation, there was a reward of a sort, for beyond the turmoil, which there was no evading, was a love of and an enjoyment of life, of belonging to the land and sunsets, and certainly to those storms which, on a smallish ship, and for days at a time, often threatened to make the next minute his last. He was able to observe such manifestations coolly, and do his work, sometimes going from the bridge to the wireless cabin to hear the singing of the morse, and see a weather message written down telling of the storm's increasing force.

The wireless operator on one ship was Paul Smith, a tall and youthful Ulsterman of forty, with long jaw, short sandy hair, and grey eyes that needled rather than looked. Deck officers rarely mixed with the Sparks on a ship, but Tom, friendly towards few, was undiscriminating when he chose to speak.

Paul tapped at the morse key, and shifted around in his armchair as if afflicted with some incurable disease of the posterior nerves, but which was only a habit of certain wireless officers who took pride in the speed and rhythm of their sending. Tom's message from the captain was destined for the owners regarding cargo handling at the next port.

Like all wireless operators, Paul knew how to make himself comfortable. There was a cat asleep on the receiver, a large well-fed unfriendly ginger beast. A tea-making machine lay within arm's radius, and two pots of flowers by the porthole, as well as framed photographs of Paul's family, and scenic views of Ulster set in Union Jack frames and pinned by the transmitter.

'It's where I'm going when my time's up,' he called out. 'There's a message coming, so wait for it, if you like.'

'I will.' He looked along a shelf of books when Paul, with earphones clamped, began to write; glanced through a thin volume whose theme was that the British people were one of the Lost Tribes of Israel. He had never heard of such a notion, though Paul had, because the pages were scratched with annotations. The argument was, Tom gathered, that the British were Sons (and presumably Daughters) of Abraham, who would one day resume their rightful place in Palestine – the book having been printed before the modern Israel was formed. An army of British–Israelite regiments would conquer the country from the Heathen (Gentile) Turk and run the country as part of the Empire before handing it over to the Jews as the heritage which had been promised by God to Abraham and his progeny for ever. The Jews of the earth would return, it being assumed that they would all wish to, under the protection of the British Government, and eventually the Kingdom of God would come about on earth because the Jews would finally become Christians.

Tom thought that the Jews might have a thing or two to say about this last point, but he read a few more pages to discover that the British, being Israelites (tell that to my Aunt Clara, he thought), would keep the world policed from the strategical centre of Palestine under a friendly government of Christian Israelites. For the British were the same people as the Hebrews, while other nations were referred to as 'Gentiles'. The author quoted from the Holy Scriptures, and Tom thought his prophecies remarkable considering the present reality of Israel. He slid the book back on the shelf, and sat down.

Paul had got rid of the wireless message. 'Convinced?'

'I'm not much of a Bible scholar.'

He shook his head. 'But he's got something?'

It cost nothing to agree. 'I suppose he has.'

Electrical chatter squeaked in through the atmospherics, and Paul gave the key a few punches as if to keep them quiet. 'He knew that politics and religion have always been bound together, and always will be. The West is cartwheeling towards destruction because it has ceased to believe it. The Russians know it, and their communism is going full blast to convert the world. The first thing the Russians want are the Holy Places of Jerusalem so that they can control the world. It's been their aim for centuries, and they'll never let go. They want to wipe out our religion, but can't because the other tribes of Israel are already back there to guard Jerusalem. Our great British–Israelite statesman David Balfour made arrangements for this in 1917. He knew that Western civilization and our Israelite religion depended on the

206

existence of Israel, and God was in his right mind when the Promised Land was again made available to His scattered people – to whom you and I belong, by the way. The Jews in Israel have not yet taken to accepting the divinity of Jesus, but no scheme is perfect, and there is still time.'

Anything was possible, Tom thought, from the mouths of babes and radio operators. For ten more minutes Paul proved that at least he was good at scripture, and Tom wondered whether in idle moments he didn't set his transmitter on to an empty wavelength and bash out exhortations in the hope of stunning some lonely radio man into instant conversion.

'You're not listening,' Paul rapped out.

He was, and said so.

Paul's fingertips keyed an outlandish rhythm into the transmitter. 'What were my last words?'

To think and hear at the same time was no feat for a deck officer. 'You said, "For Zion's sake I will not hold my peace, and for Jerusalem's sake I will not rest."'

When Paul leaned, Tom drew both hands back in case he tried to grasp them. 'We British belong to the same Hebrew race by birthright, and you also are one of the annointed of the Lord!' He flipped a switch, which caused water in the kettle to heat. 'Israel is our ally against the Gentiles and Heathens of the world because we too have lived by the Book and worshipped the One Faceless God Who Shall Be Nameless. We have our own nation back again, with eternal Jerusalem as the capital city. He brought us to the dust, but has lifted us to our appointed places!'

Tom was as diffident with his questions as he would want a person to be who thought to ask something of him. A man's views were bound up with his complete mental nuts and bolts, and you had to be careful. 'Have you always known this?'

Without leaving his chair Paul drew milk and cream-biscuits from a small refrigerator by the side of the goniometer.

'Sugar?'

Tom nodded, and passed tea cups from a row of plastic hooks.

'My parents believed, may they rest in peace, that the British were a Lost Tribe with all the characteristics of the Wandering Jews. I might not have talked to you if God hadn't led you to the one book which dealt with this universal question. When I glanced at your face I knew you were one of us.'

He made the best cup of tea on the ship, whatever his opinions and obsessions. 'I'll think about it.'

The effort of talking made Paul sweat more than when he worked at his wireless gear. 'If you believe, the thought comes of itself. Logic falls into place when you have faith. When I took the log to the captain for signing the other day and explained to him that we were all Jews he seemed a wee bit puzzled, but he's a man of learning, and agreed eventually that the State of Israel was vital to our world. Other nations resent it, but that's because the idea of redemption through Israel is anathema to anti-Semites.'

Paul's monologue sung on in the pertinent tones of his native Ulster, and Tom wanted to continue listening, because the voice of this biblical contortionist comforted him like the rhythmical swish of the sea when he was trying to rest. But to stay was a luxury he could not enjoy. 'I have to get back to duty. Then I must write a letter to my aunt – or a postcard at any rate. Save me doing it on shore tomorrow.'

He reached out, and handed the book to him. 'Take it with you. I'd like you to have it.'

Tom put it in his pocket. 'Kind of you. I'll have another crack at it.'

A volume, perhaps on the same subject – he thought all of them were – was dislodged by Paul's haste and fell to the floor, and Tom was amused to see Paul press his lips to the cover before putting it back. He had found a way of filling his days at sea that did not depend on manual dexterity, or the

208

enthusiasm of acquiring different versions of the same object, or the interest of calculations that were an end in themselves, but by a notion that was perpetrated by a belief in God, and reinforced by faith in the destiny of a people to whom he felt linked in a personal and moral way – and who could say how right or wrong he was?

From within his own fortress Tom envied no man, but thought no theory could be insane that kept the radio officer as sane as he generally appeared. Even though he himself needed no religion, and no such bizarre side-issue, he knew that Paul had found more stability than the boozers, gamblers, womanizers, and plain black-dog brooders of the maritime or any other fraternity. He was generous and dependable, good at his profession, and within his simplicity lay imagination and even humour, as well as a keen ability to put forth his argument. He studied Hebrew so as to prepare himself for the day when he would, he said, go to the Promised Land. When it did not interfere with his watch-keeping he listened to short-wave broadcasts from Jerusalem, towards which he beamed an aerial so that he would receive news from the middle of the world: 'On perilous oceans I can, by God's will, hear everything loud and clear.'

The Old Man nobbled him a few days later, and in spite of his sixty years and an air of nothing on earth being set to trouble him, grasped Tom's arm and said: 'Has that mad bloody Sparks been getting on to you about all of us being Jews yet? He has? I can see he has. Don't deny it. I'll have to get rid of him. Can't go on like this. He converted the chief engineer yesterday, and once he gets a bee in his bonnet there's no telling what happens. Not that I've anything against the Jews, mind you – no, not at all, Mr Phillips – but I can't have the blue-and-white flag run up on my ship. You know what the Mozzies are – it's like a red rag to a bull. No, I'll have to get rid of him.' And he went away shaking his head. 'It's a pity, though, a great pity to have such a good Sparks going off his rocker!'

9

He relit his pipe and opened the book while the train was sucked through the lights of Gatwick. Instead of reading, he preferred to sample his own immense space which, if nothing else, made him well off in possessing an area that kept people at a distance, so that he could manoeuvre without harming himself or causing offence to others. Awareness of space had always kept his head clear on meeting the greater and often far from friendly vastness of the sea, for if you weren't afraid of your own space it wasn't difficult to meet that of the ocean which, sometimes denying that space existed, reduced the world to a boxroom of unexpected perils.

Clara had occupied sufficient space in his life for him to send her postcards and telegrams, even the occasional letter, as echo-sounders registering her presence in himself. On their first meeting she had stepped into his space without asking, and stayed there because he realized no person could exist in absolute emptiness. She had gone into a bigger space than he could yet know about, and had left his own space emptier than any in which he had so far existed.

He went to the hospital. His age took on importance now that the one person close to him was dead. He had felt her solid assistance without seriously admitting it, and at the undertaker's kissed her lips for the first and last time. On meeting her he had looked forward to the bigger space seen from her living-room window, and the only other space that lay before him now was the one she had already gone to.

He laid a cool finger on her colder forehead. People moved beyond the curtain. The more subtly you perceived life the more brutal it appeared. He stood straight, hands at his side. She had little space in that narrow box, and would have even less when the lid went down and wet earth was packed around. Who needed more room when the spirit was absent?

He would prefer to be buried into a bigger space than that of soil, for his body to meet water without an encasing box. Either the fishes got you, or the worms. He did not want to die because there was still too much to think about. There would be, right to the end, he didn't doubt. He shrugged, which she would never have allowed, then went out, and walked by the public library and art gallery, to sit in the park by himself for half an hour.

A patient at the hospital told him that Beryl had gone to lunch. Must have seen us holding hands when we left last night. He signed for his aunt's wallet and suitcase in the ward sister's office, then took a taxi to Clara's flat. From the large window he saw the roughening indigo sea on which two boats struggled. The surface changed from hour to hour, but was the same that had press-ganged him thirty-five years before.

He could sit without being told, but looked at the elegant unsafe chair and smiled at the thought of breaking it leg by leg. He took the marble-encased timepiece from the shelf, set the hands and turned the large key at the back, offended to see a clock not fulfilling its purpose. In the kitchen he opened a bottle of whisky and poured half a tumbler before returning to his stance by the window.

The view paralysed him. He sipped at the glass and looked at the sea. Toy boats on a bilious pond. Arms dead except to drink, sea dead except to swallow, landfall every few days, the stink of diesel oil and salt, coffee and disinfectant, stale tobacco and stew. The smell of heat and that peculiar odour of invigorating cold: he did not want to go back. The spell was broken. She had kept him at it long enough. He had searched all lanes and knew it well, yet had found nothing. More years than he had fingers and toes, as an old salt said. His contract had two months to run, then he would take his last sway down the gangplank to ironical cheers, and never a look back from

211

dock gate or customs shed. A mote in the eye for ever as his first love vanished.

Dust flew when he hit a velvet-covered chair. He telephoned the hospital. She hadn't given her second name, but they knew who he meant. 'Are you free for dinner?'

A tone of nothing-doing came from her. 'Boy-friend tonight. Really. All right?'

'Some other time?'

'Try when you can. It was fine last night. Really came off well, didn't it?'

'I liked it, too.'

'Sorry about your mother.'

'Aunt.'

'Aunt, I mean. Must go. Busy-busy! Bye now.'

'Goodbye, old girl.'

He was still a sailor: 'as much at sea on land, as I am on land at sea' – so the ditty went. The vacuum cleaner fell from its cupboard, and he took his jacket off, running the machine along lane after lane of carpet till dusk came and he switched on every table lamp and the overhead chandelier in a flush expenditure of amps that the flat couldn't have seen for years.

A few dozen tins of food stood ready as if for another bout of wartime shortage. He opened asparagus and corned beef. There was a case of wine, and bottles of port and sherry. He found a jar of coffee beans, and tinned pineapple for dessert.

He wandered around the flat while eating. The built-in wardrobe held scores of dresses. A mothball smell when he slid back the door was almost solid. He banged it shut. In a drawer of her desk he found an album with snapshots of his mother which Clara had never shown. She hadn't cared to disturb him, he supposed, by what he had never known. Not wanting to complicate their relationship, she had kept him totally in her power.

He went back to the dining-room to finish his meal, turning off the electric lights and setting out enough candles to see by. Clara had tied him firmly to herself by the simple trick of

212

endeavouring to keep him as far away from her as possible. He regretted not having visited her more often. She had wanted it that way, and could no longer answer his questions. Perhaps her purpose had been to open his mind to speculation the moment she was no longer here.

She had disliked him so much, yet been kind to him. There was no doubt about it. His sextant and deckwatch from Potters had been paid for by her, and she had settled the bill for his third mate's uniform, all by way of accepting responsibility for his fateful glance out of her window.

'Responsibility,' she told him, and he wondered in his young arrogance where she could have read it, 'is the hallmark of maturity. I accept the responsibility for whatever I have caused in this life, and I expect you to act in the same way.'

She had said no more, for he was being taken to tea at the Metropole, where she talked only about the weather, and his career. She checked his appearance and behaviour as if he were still a boy, and he held himself from being cheeky because he knew by then that he was afraid of her.

He fetched a pack of Jamaican cigars from his bag, and smoked by the living-room window so that he could hear the thump of breakers between passing traffic. He notified her death to *The Times*, more to inform himself than to tell anyone who might still remember. On the telephone her solicitor said he would like to see him. 'You're her only beneficiary, and have a fair amount coming to you after probate, taxes, duties and all costs have been settled. Hard to say how much. Something like three hundred thousand, I'd say. She was fond of you. After the funeral will be a good time for us to meet. You will be staying till then, I expect. Keep account of all receipts and expenses regarding death certificate, funeral costs, rates on the flat, and so on. It's your responsibility now.'

A swollen bank book would be an affliction. His savings and pension plan were enough for his needs. Having been free of land-ties all his life he had no worries. See her well buried,

213

get back to the ship, and stay for as long as you can stand by the wheel and lift a sextant, then find a Pacific island where you can live like a king on your bit of income. He'd heard talk of places where you wanted for nothing as long as you didn't want much.

The sea glistened in the morning, ominous blades of light across the surface, that could change all too quickly into a white-capped Force Ten blow-up with four horizons only as far away as the hand could reach. Yet it would alter to a grey and tolerable chop before long. The state of the sea never stayed the same, you could be sure of that, which fortunately applied to everything else as well.

He once heard talk of a sailor who carried a piece of rope in his kit to hang himself if things got too bad. When he showed the rope to his shipmates they had a good laugh and thought what a way to make sure you never did yank yourself up. The tale of the bloke with the portable rope went the rounds for years till he met an acquaintance in Galveston who said: 'Remember Jimmy Hawkins on the old ship *Alinoa* who always had a rope in his kit? Well, he actually topped himself. The Sparks told me, who'd got it from another sparky-bloke who was on the very old tub that Jimmy did for himself. We learned it only a few hours after it had happened. You know how fast news can travel when those mad wireless operators get spirit-tapping away. I expect the story is still bouncing into all sorts of one-eyed french-letter grateholes that haven't heard about it yet. But what misery old Jimmy must have gone through before doing a crazy thing like that.'

No, he wasn't built in any way, shape or form, he told himself, to go the way of Saintly Jimmy. Neither the igloo of his heart nor the fireplace of his brain was set on it, and in any case what would Clara say if ever he did, and they met in the lobby of the 'Nevermore Hotel'?

10

The train squeaked alongside the platform, and stopped to the sound of a few doors banging back against the carriages. He steadied the handle and manoeuvred his luggage. There were no trolleys, and no such people as porters any more. Which was why, Clara said, she hadn't travelled in the last ten years. One needed looking after, but nowadays no one wanted your florins, so you had better stay at home.

He lugged his stuff through the desolate station. There were more down-and-outs on the benches than a few years ago. He found it strange that though there were a million unemployed no one wanted the work of cleaning the station, which was looking more like some God-forsaken place in South America.

At Clara's funeral, sunlight flamed through the windows while the chaplain read his piece. There were more people than expected. She had given money every Christmas to those who worked in the shops, to the milkman and the postman, to rubbish collectors and caretakers, and some came to see her buried.

By the grave Beryl held his hand, her glove curving over his, but he drew away so as to bring his right arm up into a salute which he assumed his aunt would expect. They went to the flat for food and drinks, and when everyone had left he telephoned for a taxi to take Beryl to the hospital. He was glad to be alone.

A few more trips at sea allowed him to ponder on what to do, and to get so fed up with life on board that he had no alternative but to leave. When taxes had been paid from Clara's estate he found it hard to believe that so much money was his. In the orphanage he started with a penny a week, and never had more than the ten-shilling note she had given him till he went into the Merchant Navy. He made certain never to lack a reserve of money. Even with the few pounds a month of those days it was possible to put a little cash into the bank, his self-respect added to by the fact that he had earned it. Instead of spending more than he allowed himself, he found excitement in spare-time reading for his various certificates. He searched secondhand bookshops in Liverpool and Preston for texbooks which, though a few years out of date, served for his studies. After thirty years of varying parsimony he would need no other money than his own to live on when he left the sea, yet the invested capital of Clara's assets would bring in more than thirty thousand a year before tax. Twelve months ago he'd been alone in his simple life, but now he had a lawyer, an accountant, and a broker. The whole of the family money had devolved on to him.

His London room felt more like home than Clara's flat. Five years ago he had seen an advertisement at a tobacconist's, went to look, and rented it. He sat back in the taxi. Cars flashed by on Park Lane. He felt free, lost in space, without a ship and with nothing to do, too disorientated to know whether or not he liked it. The nearest human being seemed as far as the closest star. No one could reach him. Neither could he touch them. He didn't want to. Some hardly visible being ran across the road, and the driver braked: 'Did you see that *meshugge*?'

He slid the window a few inches open. 'I did.'

'Drunk.'

They turned into the Bayswater Road. 'It seemed like it.'

He looked for a star, to reassure himself that he existed, but the sodium orange lights made a ceiling that hid them. Beryl had telephoned some days after the funeral. 'What about tonight, sailor?'

'Tonight?'

'My boy-friend's away.' Her tone clashed with the shield that covered his grief.

'I'm busy,' he said.

The intense feeling of loss surprised him. Except to shop for food he didn't leave the flat till the time to go back to his ship. He looked at the changing sheet of sea during the day, and paced at night with all lights on. He could not say what he thought. Hours of dark and light passed as if the time they spanned did not exist. His life had no meaning. He tried to understand the tenuous connections that held one person to another, and knew that if he didn't find an answer in the place where Clara had lived he would not be able to do so when he went back to sea.

The pull of luggage told him he was alive and fit. The taxi driver carried one case to the kerb and offered to help him upstairs, but Tom said he could manage. A ten-watt bulb on the top landing gave more shadow than light. There was a glow under next door and he wondered who was there, before turning to sort among his wad of keys. He pushed the cases across the threshold with his foot, then hauled in the hold-all. The damp wallpaper smelled as if some occupant had rotted there. He unscrewed the release on the Rippengilles stove and heard the reassuring bubble as paraffin went down into the burner ring.

His only secure space on shore was tidy but needed heat. Before going back to sea the floor was swept and books placed on the shelf. Dishes were washed and put away, and bedclothes folded on to the mattress as neatly as any recruit's. A small wooden box on the table contained rations of coffee, tea, soda biscuits and sardines. There were matches in a plastic case, a two-ounce tin of tobacco, a packet of pipe cleaners, a quarter-bottle of whisky and some cigars. A pile of cheap classics lay on top of his record player. He plugged in the radio, and tuned to the nearest caterwauling transmitter so that the room would have a voice to which he need not listen.

Until the heat took hold he kept warm by unpacking. He put his uniform and spare suit into a shallow cupboard which did for a wardrobe, remembering how an otherwise taciturn

217

old captain once said: 'A good mariner wants for little, and needs little. Necessaries are luxuries, but no luxury is necessary' – a habit of speaking which caused Paul the wireless operator to refer to him as Captain Epigram.

He looked along the spines of his books: a set of Gibbon, all of Dickens except *A Tale of Two Cities* which someone had taken a fancy to, odd compendiums of geography and travel published donkey's years ago, a Bible lifted from some hotel, his old seamanship and navigation manuals, a few maps and novels brought back from various parts of the world. There was no reason to keep them, yet they were the capes and pinpoints of his recollections, each marking an otherwise empty log of a dead-reckoning plot, and never to be replaced by Clara's inherited library of leatherbound editions. If his own motley books had been packed in a watertight container and floated to the beach of a desert island on which he was stranded he would want for little in the way of reading till a banana boat came to his rescue.

The radio broke into his thoughts, and he diminished its noise before turning to make the bed. Tripping against a shoe reminded him that it was time to sleep. He asked what he was doing here, and answered that he needed refuge from Clara's flat where no reflection seemed to be his own. Between these four walls he had never known anyone but himself.

His eyes obstinately fought the dead weight of the body pushing against them. Braying music was halted by the rattle of news and weather: frost was coming, cold and clear, a Force Nothing easterly with chilly sunshine to get the black dog off old Beaufort's back. Water jiggered in next door's tap, though the place was quieter than when a student and his girl-friend used to hammer each other under the sound-umbrella of a pop group that shook the windows.

He screwed down the Rippengilles to bubble itself out, but left the wireless on in case silence should disturb his peace of mind while going to sleep. On a ship, engines rattled the bones for weeks at a time, and there was a vigorous thudding

218

of water to go with it. He needed noise in order to sleep, as if he were still on board and had to wake up in four hours.

The easiest way to attain unbroken repose was to drink alcohol till he was unconscious, but he was no longer willing for such dynamite to blow down the walls that separated him from peace. His patience would get him there in its own good time, and if it baulked at the task then he would lie there till it did.

Clara had never suspected his occasional indulgence in alcoholic blackouts – as far as he knew, though she was a realistic woman who was perhaps more familiar with the world's ways, and those of men who went to sea, than he realized. Even so, she certainly did not imagine the depth of his occasional severance from reality and decency. On wondering whether she had died in order that he could reform, he felt the light of morning behind his eyelids.

PART THREE

Meeting

1

The system of forethought by which he lived made sure that on the next watch, or by the morning after, he would find all necessary items for life and duty laid out in perfect navy order. Such drill, when working with a thoroughness too ordinary for him to admire, made existence easy, for sufficient preparation meant less to think about when the moment of necessity came, though he didn't doubt that if assailed by an unexpected happening his training and intuition would channel him into the right actions. There was no other way of doing things.

Yet despite this eternal striving for perfection there were times when the mind had so much to think about that one essential item was missed in the too rapid litany of the re-stocking procedure. When he got out of bed and looked in the provision box he didn't even curb the foul old clichés of the sailor's trade used whenever something went wrong, that acted like a pinch of snuff to clear the head before remedial thoughts came in.

There was everything necessary in the box except sugar. The blue tin with the fancy lid was empty but for enough discoloured grains stuck to the side to show what the tin was for, but not sufficient to sweeten the coffee that he craved.

He switched off the moaning radio, and scratched his head at this contemptible proof of what ought to be feared as no less than an attack of premature senility. The habit of being prepared had come from a time when every happening could signify the difference between life and death. Such thoroughness didn't matter any more, so perhaps he would stand easy and leave things in future to chance. All he had to do was walk to the nearest shop and buy sugar to put in his coffee, or go next door and ask whoever lived there to let him have a few spoons of the stuff till he replenished his larder.

He had done that sort of thing on a ship only occasionally, careful to indulge as little as possible, but on shore there seemed something lacking in a person who knocked on a stranger's door to borrow sugar when he could easily go out and buy a pack from a shop, the inconvenience a way of paying for a trivial mistake.

In rectifying errors you created others, and therein lay the peril that could arise from insufficient attention to detail. On the other hand a number of errors might more or less cancel each other out, though accuracy was sacrificed if too much reliance was placed on such a system. But he wasn't navigating through half-charted waters any more. His latitude was benign, his longitude comfortable, and he was in a country where quakes were unknown, tremors infrequent, fires rare, and floods didn't reach this far from the river.

What would Aunt Clara have done in the present fix? He had never asked such questions, though thought of a few cases when it might have been wise to do so. He had stubbornly relied on training, tradition, his orphanage upbringing, and fragments of congenital sense coexisting so well with that triple grafting on to himself – which by now could not be spliced into distinctions.

To ask Clara, while she was alive, what he should do in such a situation would have opened him to an influence too powerful to be good. She might have told him to do the wrong thing as punishment for having had the weakness to need advice. He only knew that you managed better on your own, and therefore were never likely to be embarrassed by sharing mistakes with anyone else.

Clara considered that, no matter what purpose other

224

people served, they were there to help her, and if she was in need she would respect their existence by giving them the privilege of doing so. Lacking even so lowly an item as sugar for her tea, she would ask for it with that presence which only those could object to who did not possess what she wanted. The notion that not to ask was mean-spirited would hardly occur to her, for she would do so without the thought going through her mind.

He ran the electric shaver over his chin, washed his face, and reached for a tie. To act as Clara would have done was a form of homage – for which she would no doubt call him a bigger fool than he had ever thought himself.

He unscrewed the fuel tap so that he could light the stove when he came back, then took up his sugar-tin and went out. He'd often wondered whether Clara's gruffness hadn't hidden a subtlety too deep for him to fathom, until he came to feel that much of the deviousness lay in himself. Acquaintances over the years had hinted at such qualities on seeing his obtuse and effective methods in dealing with difficulties among the men, but he had felt straightforward in what he was doing, and thought they were exaggerating his skill out of a wish to become friendly – a gesture which he hardly ever returned, on the assumption that people should mind their own business.

Finally, he decided, as he knocked on the door, you do as you damn-well like. Smells of breakfast came up the stairs. A crying child seemed unwilling to go to school. The place was a bit of a slum, and now that he had money he would get somewhere better. A smell of gas overpowered all others. Must have gone to work and left it on. He leaned close to make sure. People were careless, and he thought so would I be if I lit a cigarette while standing here.

There had been movement earlier, but if someone went out the slamming of the door was followed by a thunderous hoofing down the stairs. So much for his scruples about

225

borrowing sugar. He would light the stove, and fetch his own, and might even get fresh bread instead of chewing damp biscuits.

A sensation of horror and alarm, against which he swore obscenely, caused him to propel himself from the wall in a heavyweight rush at the door, and he had knocked over a table and all that was on it in the darkened room before he stopped.

He ripped at the curtains. Strips of tape snapped at his wrists as he slammed the window up, the cut of icy air as welcome as a dash of cold water in the Red Sea.

She lay by the fire, like someone pulled out of a lifeboat after a shipwreck and left to take a chance on recovery while less serious cases that might survive were seen to first. He turned off the tap, but thought she was dead, and that if she wasn't she ought to be, should be thrown out of the window, and then see what troubles she'd have – provided she landed in one piece.

She weighed enough to be in the next world already. Such a signing-off and homecoming was more than he could be bothered with. Leave her. Seal up the window. Turn the gas back on. Go out and lock the door. She'll never forgive you if you don't.

She was damp under the armpits. He hauled her along the floor. A shoe came off, and he stopped to put it back on. Her foot was warm. The fumes and effort gave him a headache. Your trouble wasn't bad enough, or you wouldn't have tried such a stunt. He worked ill before breakfast and, still holding her, rested to get breath, not wanting to fail with a heart attack and have two suicides found instead of one which, in view of the apparent methods of having brought it about, might at least get them a posthumous commendation for ingenuity.

Laughing at the notion, he closed the door and pulled her to his own room. Too cold to open the window, but she needed oxygen – if she was sufficiently in the world to profit

226

from anything. He took off his jacket and put it on a hangar behind the door. Her face continually changed expression, as if she were having painful and vital conversations with herself.

She lay on the floor. He undid the top buttons of her shirt, then stretched her arms up and began to man the pumps, his head and face sweating after the first half dozen of north-south, north-south and north-south. She's dead, but keep on, he said, keep on, and felt light in the head at having to work again, though it was such hard galley-slavery that if it took five more minutes he would stop whether she came to life or didn't. If breath had been available he might have sung a ditty. The impulse to guffaw was hard to fight, as if it had been laughing gas instead of plain old coal. Pity the new North Sea stuff isn't in yet. Must have known it was coming soon, so couldn't wait.

She'll need a bath after this. For a change we'll have east-west, east-west and east-west, but if anybody asks what I'm up to I'll say I might be performing an act of mercy or doing physical jerks as I do every morning like this on whoever's willing, but thank God you've come to take over the pumps because I'm flagging at north-by-east, north-by-east and north-by-east.

He prayed, and bullied, and laughed at her, and swore at himself, and cursed his bad luck, berating his lack of endurance when the pump wouldn't draw, and rocks were about to rip away the bottom of the ship on which she lay. He had made the effort with men about to peg out from drowning, and to the absolutely drowned – with undisciplined hope but diminishing strength.

In freezing air he steamed from the effort and called on God, and Clara, his father and mother, and anyone else who might listen, but most of all himself and the gassed woman under him till he heard her choke and gag and fart and bite more of the bitter cold welling in through the window. Disinclined to gentleness, he spun her halfway round the compass and hauled her with his last strength to the sill,

227

pushing her over as if he'd had enough and would send her three decks below like a bag of dirty linen at the end of a voyage.

'Breathe!' he shouted.

Shirt sleeves flying, he took in air for himself and held her at the window, looked out from the dead centre on a hundred and fourteen degrees of great circle bearing pointing somewhere or other but right now too much was happening to bother where such a beam might go. A man got out of a car across the street and looked up at their lovers' tiff, then shook his head and walked down the nearest basement steps as if on his way to collect a poor soul's rent.

She gasped, and retched when he forced her to the sink. 'Fetch it up!' Only rough stuff could help in a matter of such life and death. 'Or I'll put my hand down your throat and pull it out myself.'

'Leave me be!' she screamed at the purple world that was killing her.

'Ha! You've found your voice? No more blockages?' He tugged her round as if to aim a deliberate blow at a baby to get it breathing – and sent her spinning into the room. 'Don't try and put one over on me, or I'll hand you over to the plumbers!'

He was so much the old sort that he hardly knew himself. He hadn't left it behind, after all. Should have known better than to think so. Wouldn't it come whenever needed? You couldn't save a life and follow the niceties of polite behaviour.

The whizz-bang circled her head, and the carpet she tasted was not her own. She was in London. A madman had broken into her room. She'd had a nightmare but couldn't remember lock, latch or hinges bursting. Yet the door had come open. He tried to throw her out of the window. Water was pounding into a sink, laughter above everything. He'd made her sick. A pillar of bile had rammed to her stomach and she retched it out, sent it flying. Arms, legs and teeth shook from cold. A star ate into her forehead, while a hammer beat at the bones behind. The star burned. She choked. She had eaten pepper, chewed salt. She looked at grey rods and silver wires. I wanted to sleep. She tried to close her eyes but the burning rods forced them open. Knees came to her chin. What happened? You may bloody well ask, she heard.

He cleaned the sink and filled it. 'Get up.'

'Who are you?' She couldn't see him.

'You'll know, soon enough.'

She smelled sweat when he came close. 'Don't kill me, George.'

His laugh wasn't George's. Never could be, a sound from somebody caught in a trap she'd had nothing to do with. He exulted in his separation from civilized entanglements. The metal grip shook from her eyes.

'Stand up,' he barked, 'or I'll *half*-kill you.'

She tried. He saw that she couldn't. She was lifted, and supported in a walk across the room, her head pushed into a block of ice. She screamed from shock. That's better. Bubbles burst, then floated. He was torturing her, holding her head under water. She kicked him, arms pounding at cloth and bone. She was pulled by the hair.

'No brain damage.' He sounded gleeful, had saved more than he'd hoped for. Her feet kicked against ankle. A hand swung at her wet cheek and pushed her once more into the freezing mist. She might have known that George would catch her. Wrong again. He had paid his brothers' friends to kill her. Never took on his own dirty work. The water leaped at her face till she felt him get tired.

'Thank God.' He sat her in an armchair, and took a clean towel from the cupboard. 'Dry yourself. You might be all right. But no funny business.'

Vision was scarlet, changing to a steel grid, shaking into interchange. The pink face was surrounded by red. He lived in blood. Hands and legs would not stop rattling. Pieces of wood clattered, and a gong was calling the world to dinner, sonorously behind both eyes. She talked, but heard him say:

'Can't make out a word.'

'I want to sleep,' she roared.

His ear was against her lips, and he heard faintly.

'I'll tell you when you can go to sleep.'

He pulled her upright, too exhausted to be gentle. 'Walk. First this foot. And now the other. Left-right, left-right, left-right. Come on!'

'Don't shout.'

He didn't hear.

She stepped obediently, pushing against a cliff of indifference. She dropped.

'I can't go on.'

He caught her. She walked the room and back, then fell off the wall. He sat her down. No use. They spoke together, but neither heard. He put a kettle of water on the stove, not knowing what else to do. Then he walked her again. Shouting and cajoling, he was remorseless. He moved her at the waist, pushed her, walked her again until she clutched at the ceiling and heard a whistle that became a scream of pain. She sat while he turned the gas off and put six tablespoons of coffee into the pot. After water, the lid went on, and he walked her again.

The treadmill was unendurable. 'I hate you.'

'Walk,' he said, 'or you really will go out of the window – without a bloody parachute.'

She walked, though. 'I tried to . . .'

She was inching back to life. He felt wasted to nothing, yet hadn't known such elation since the war, when perils came fast enough to stop youth dead in its tracks – when youth was the ideal state to be in. Brought a whiff of it back, cordite and salt water. 'Yes, I know. I know all about it.'

'Free country,' she said.

Bald, ugly, freckled, she saw him laugh. No devil without cruelty. 'Tell me some more,' he said, 'it's good for you.'

'It's a free country.'

He laughed.

'Stop laughing.'

'So it is,' he said. 'Free as air. You do what you like, and I do what I like. God works in many ways his wonders to perform, even in a free country.'

'I don't like it here. And I don't like you.'

He held her, wouldn't let go. 'Talk, then you'll have to walk less.'

'I don't want to.' Stone on a piece of rope kept banging the back of her head. She asked him to cut it loose. She'd ask anyone if they were here. She told him. He didn't care.

'Maybe you're going to live, after all.'

'I shan't do it.'

At the stove he poured hot stuff into mugs. He put spoons of white powder in. He was going to poison her. She ran at him but didn't move. She told him not to kill her, but instead of her lips moving she felt more tears wetting her cheeks. He put white powder into his own mug as well, but it wouldn't kill him, she was certain.

'I want to go back,' she heard herself saying.

He turned. 'You tried to kill yourself, and that's your business. It's my business to bring you out of it. You're staying here till you're all right, and afterwards, if you still want to chuck yourself off the world, it's up to you.'

He hoped she wouldn't. But she was over twenty-one, and that was a fact. He snapped at the plug chain, and water ran out of the sink. She nodded. He was asking something. He couldn't stand up, and shouted. He was insane. He was in a fit when he said: 'I wonder if you could lend . . .'

She was alarmed. His head swayed left and right. Some new horror was about to be manufactured by his mad but versatile mind.

His laughter subsided, but silence gave him a dignity that didn't fit. 'I was going to ask if by any chance . . . you haven't some sugar in your room?'

It was impossible to know what he meant or would do. She nodded. He was concerned about a matter which frightened

231

her. He would murder her if she didn't escape. The light pushed like a flame against her eyes.

'Where is it?'

She tried to explain, but couldn't tell what he wanted. He seemed to understand. She saw him as dead – and deaf as well as ugly. She wouldn't return to George no matter how much he tormented her.

'Don't fall while I'm away.'

He returned with half a loaf of bread, some butter and cheese, and a packet of sugar, reasoning that with such a full cupboard she couldn't have considered knocking herself out for ever – unless she had been too dead-set on it to care.

She was asleep, and he asked himself, putting spoons of sugar into each mug, and whisky into hers, whether he should call a doctor. He helped her to her feet. 'Come on, more walking along the deck. You're all right' – wishing to God she was – 'so twice to the window for a ten-fathom breather, then back to the coffee pot for a sniff at the bean.'

'Don't like it here.'

'Oh yes, you will, or I'll knock you for six.'

He held her waist, fearful that she might fall, that she'd faint and never recover.

She hated him.

'Why?'

And she hated him even more when he laughed, and said: 'I owe you some sugar. I'll repay every grain.'

Impossible to comprehend. He led her to the seat. She clutched the mug for warmth, and drank blackjack coffee, watching him. At the mirror he fastened cufflinks, adjusted his tie, and put on a jacket. A comb from his wallet went through hair around his head, though she didn't see any.

'A sailor likes to look spick and span.'

'Sailor?'

'First officer – but harmless. I only came on earth to stop you doing yourself a fatal injury. Thank God for what's left of my sweet tooth.' He spread a cloth, and opened sardines over

232

the sink. Knives and forks were in order. Two plates of different shapes and colours drifted from a shelf. He cut bread, split cellophane from biscuits, and set the kettle wailing again. She forgot where she was, and what she'd done or had done to her. Why was she here, in another room? A man was putting a meal on the table in as quick and neat a way as she had ever been able to manage.

Rather mannish and thin-faced, there was something good-looking about her, except that her eyes were bloodshot and her face whitewashed. 'Sorry there aren't any flowers. No funeral today. Let's go once more to the fresh-air box.'

She stood. 'I don't want to.'

But he led her. 'After six good breaths, we'll risk shutting it.'

He closed the door, slammed down the window. 'Do you think you can sit at the table?'

She tried to speak while he lit the paraffin stove, but her chin rested on her chest, mouth open. 'You're not very good-looking like that, though.'

He gripped her arms and shook, held her up. She sat like a sack of onions, he said. 'If you don't feel well, let me know. Be a pity if you fell and broke an arm after all this – or chucked up over my best bed.'

She longed to sleep in her own room until death came, or the headache stopped. A fire rampaged behind her eyes. She sat upright, facing him. He fed her pieces of bread and butter. 'Welcome aboard! The ship's all yours – while we're floating along.'

Coffee tasted like boiled straw. One minute she knew how she had got here, and the next she didn't. She wanted to go to sleep and find out, and then to forget why she had. He'd prevent her because he liked tormenting people, as if she had done him harm (though if she had, she'd forgotten about any incident she'd been through with him in times gone past) and he wanted to make her pay. Like any man, he was unrelenting and unforgiving, and she resented him eating as if the effort of

233

stopping her going to sleep when she wasn't strong enough to fight back gave him an appetite. Then she remembered having lain down by the gas. Couldn't say why. She bit into some bread. Wanted to go to sleep and find the answer, but would she get it?

He talked, seeing that she could not, and believing that silence would be the death of her. He told her who he was, and what he knew of his life. She wouldn't remember. But he talked his snotty drivel, as if she were fully alert, to make her grey unseeing eyes stay open, to stop her head dropping into the borrowed sugar, and to help more food and coffee – however little – into her mouth.

When he handed her a corner of biscuit with cheese, she took it like someone with neither sense nor feeling, and ate as if she were made of glass and he could see the crumbs and flakes going down through her body, the ultimate state of shame and embarrassment like one of those dreams in which you were caught walking naked in the street. She wanted to hide from him who thought he could stare at her: just because she wasn't able to respond for the moment. Didn't like him. She floated as if she were drunk. She felt like a baby which, though hungry, wanted most of all to sleep.

Her nose ran. She couldn't feel it. Her lips threatened to stop moving. He trembled for himself. How could a strong enough woman like this try to get off the world before it shot her loose in its own good time? There was no saying. Maybe only the strong ones did it. He wanted her to fasten her shirt but was too shy to do so or ask. There was gooseflesh on her white chest, and an odour of skin from the faintest swell which was visible. The only procedure he knew was to keep her going till she dropped. He felt he'd need more sleep himself after this, though supposed an hour's dose of air in Holland Park would get him lively. The coffee and food fuelled his talk.

When her eyes flickered in acknowledgement of some half-lost phrase he wondered what was in her mind. 'Are you feeling better now?'

234

'Help me.'

He caught her before she fell. 'You'll be all right after a day or two.'

'I shan't.'

He wiped her face. 'What's your name?'

She leaned against him.

He was afraid. If she slept she would die. He'd been a fool in keeping her from a hospital. His instinct had guided him and had never let him down. But he wondered, and worried.

'I want to sleep.'

'I know you do.'

Her eyes flickered. For a moment she was awake. 'What's your name, though?' he asked.

Her smile turned bitter by the downcurving of her lips. 'Why do you want to know?'

'Better and better.' Perhaps knowledge goeth before a fall, but he wanted to hear her say it. That and everything else. 'My name's Tom, if it'll make it easier for you. Everybody uses first names these days, no matter what the circumstances. I suppose we can do the same.'

He spoke now so as not to frighten her. She pushed him away. He threw coffee dregs in the sink. She watched him wash and dry the mugs. He'd forgotten her. He poured fresh coffee. If an unexpected wave hit the ship out of an apparently calm sea, the fact would register yet give no shock, but his hand twitched at the surprising clarity of her voice: 'What's in that box?'

He went to the table. 'Drink some more. You must be bone-dry inside. I certainly am, and I only got a few whiffs.'

'Beautiful box.'

He opened it and tilted it to show her. 'A sextant.'

'And the other?'

'Drink something, and I'll tell you.'

'I'm not a baby.'

'It's a chronometer.'

She drank.

235

'On a better sort of ship there's what you call a Decca navigator. If you want to know where you are in the middle of the ocean you push a few pearly buttons, and get three lemons. Spot on, every time, though there's no way to prove it. You take it on trust, like so much else. It's like having God on tap. But I was lumbered with these magic boxes to work out my daily destiny. Six months more, and I'll forget how I did it. You get your position by sun-stars-and-stripes across the firmament, up to your knees in books of tables and bits of paper. Sometimes there's neither stars nor sun to be seen, and you can't even get a position-line on Old Nick himself. You ask the radio operator what he can do, though every bearing costs the company a pound or two, so you can't ask for too many. But he has a try, and you end up in a worse fix – unless like one of our blokes you believe in the God of Israel! We go by dead-reckoning, when we're not dead drunk. O yes, it was a sailor's life for me all right, but not any more. I'm fifty, fit, and out of it for good, with nowhere to go and nothing to do but enjoy every minute, if and when I can.'

She drank the mug dry. He passed a clean handkerchief. She could wipe her own mouth this time. His intention had been to walk the four parks to Trafalgar Square, then stroll along Piccadilly to look in the shops. But he couldn't leave. He might tuck her cosily in bed, and no sooner was he out of the door than she would try the same stunt again. And he was in no mood to leave. He filled his pipe and lit it. 'Feeling better?'

She wondered whether the door was locked. 'You don't understand.'

'I don't see how I can. We only met a couple of hours ago.'

The room was warm, and he opened the window an inch. He sat away from her. Life had been divided between a stifling cabin and the grinding wind. Oven or gale was the order of life. One without the other was impossible. Tears pumped from her eyes, another method of getting the poison out. 'You should have left me,' she said.

'I had no say in the matter. I heard a distress signal, or sniffed it, rather, so answered it with my own feet and shoulder, instead of all nine articles of Rule 31!'

The world had no limits. If she stretched her arms she wouldn't reach the outside of herself. She wanted to run. 'Did George send you?'

His face was honest. If anything, he was amused at her fear and torment. He looked like a monk in a film. 'It's the first time I've heard him called that, though I must admit I've referred to him myself in some pretty wicked terms in my time. Who the hell is George?'

'My husband. I walked out on him a couple of months ago.'

She was improving. 'I'm sure you had to. But don't cry. You'll be all right. Every move is for the best. Always keep moving. Any sailor will tell you – that while you're on the move, you're alive!'

She knew. But she had no will, no strength. There was nothing left. She wanted to get out of his sight, but was terrified of dropping into sleep, then of waking up and never knowing again who she was. She clutched at the speeding circular wall when the pinpoint of the sky got smaller.

'It's hard till you get used to it,' he said kindly, as if he knew all about whatever it was.

'Don't belong anywhere.'

He held her hand. She tried to draw it back. 'I'm a doctor of the soul,' he said. 'I shan't hurt you. None of us belong anywhere till we die. Most people don't know it, but I always have. Moving across the oceans all my life and never being in one place for more than a few days was what I chose from early on. It was my work. Now that I've left the service I belong on this island, but where I'll be tomorrow God alone knows.'

She thought he talked to himself. Her eyes were half closed. When she swayed he steadied her, keeping her from sleep as she became more of a weight.

'There'll be enough of that belonging when you're dead,'

he told her. 'That's what I feel, so why peg yourself down and anticipate that zone of oblivion? Not to belong anywhere special while you're alive is a blessed state. Well, maybe not for everyone, but I was set for it as soon as I was born, conceived on the sea by a sea-cook, no less, so it's in my blood and maybe my ancestry on more sides than one for all I know, though that's a tale I may never get to the bottom of.'

The morning light was fading, its promise gone. She fell. Cloud hovered low. He switched the light on. Bed was the best place for her, a horizontal state that even a spirit-level couldn't quibble with. 'You'll be all right as long as somebody's close to make sure you start eating when you wake up.'

What did she care?

He walked her next door, and pulled open her neatly made bed. He gently lowered her, and took off her shoes. Her feet were cold now.

She surrendered to a kind of peace. A hand lay against the side of her face. He wondered what the hell he had done. She certainly wouldn't thank him. He covered her, and went back to his room for a roll of bedclothes, which he laid over her own.

A faint snore sounded as he shut the door. It had been as close a run thing as any storm he had been in. He had risked having a dead woman on his hands, and the police asking questions, and charging him with some arcane mis-demeanour. The world of law and regularity would rush on to him and he would be no longer someone set apart from the rest of the people because he'd inhabited a closed order for so long. A juicy scandal for the papers! He'd left the sea, and Aunt Clara was dead, but there was still a polished procedure to follow in such emergencies. He was forgetting his training and habits. Or they were already abandoning him. Even now it wasn't too late to get her tucked up in a nice clean cot with trained nurses to hover around.

Another few minutes, and who is to say whether she'd have

238

come through undamaged? Or even pulled out of the black pit she'd dug pretty well for herself? He put a coffee-flask and some biscuits by her bed, with the thought that she would be normal in a day or two and that what happened then would be up to her. If she really had a mind to kill herself – no use denying the proper words – no one would be able to stop her. He respected her free will, providing it didn't threaten the liberty of others – his especially.

A frown rippled over her forehead. He had an impulse to kiss her on the cheek before leaving, by way of wishing her a quick recovery, not to mention the luck she would need. He resisted, and fought off the sudden wrack of pure sadness, as if they had met at some forlorn beach after their separate shipwrecks, and might never see each other again. He went out quickly, imagining that on waking she wouldn't even remember him.

2

At the bottom of the stairs he knocked twice on Judy Ellerker's door. 'I heard the first time,' she said, 'but like to make sure I'm wanted!'

He went into the room.

She told him to sit down. 'I thought I heard you huffing and puffing up the stairs last night.'

The place was tidy, except for a thousand-piece jigsaw puzzle on the floor. 'I do a bit every day, and break it up before the kids come home. But every day I get more of it done. I threw the box away, in case the picture made things too easy. Not that I have much time, but I manage the odd half hour.'

'What do you know about my new neighbour?' he asked.

'Can I get you anything to drink, captain?'

'No, thank you.'

'She left her husband, or whatever it was called, a month or so back. Leads a quiet life, poor kid. Still got her brain-damage from an overdose of matrimony, which makes it hard to tell what she's like. I suppose you fancy her, but if I were you I'd leave her alone. Give her a chance to pull round.'

He'd heard her distastes concerning men before, but felt they could have nothing to do with him. 'She's not well this morning.'

'It doesn't surprise me. We all recover in the end, though.'

'She had an accident.'

'What do you mean?'

'Well, let's say she left the gas on by mistake, unlit.'

'And you didn't get an ambulance?' She reached some coins from the shelf.

'There was no need.'

Her face reddened. There was an expression in her eyes for which he knew no other name but panic. She pushed by, and took her coat from a cupboard, then swung to face him. 'No need? Have you been playing mummy and daddy up there? What have you got against her? Why do you want to kill her? Never heard of the social services, you blind prick?'

He was going around Cape Horn with a vengeance, and would have felt more comfortable if mere cliff-like waves were crumbling against him instead of this swell of blind loathing, before which he found it hard to stay calm. Yet in the face of her determination to do something ridiculous he felt he had better explain. 'She'll be all right. Call an ambulance, and they'll think it's a hoax. And if you do get one I might be entitled to ask what *you* have against her. Go up and see for yourself.'

She hesitated. 'You think you handled it, do you?'

'I did what I could. My first thought was for her, not the authorities or whoever you want to run for.'

240

She took off her coat, sipped her tea, decided it was too cold, and slopped it down the sink. 'Even so.'

'Take a look at her in half an hour, to make sure she's still sleeping. I'm going out for a while.'

'You're used to giving orders, aren't you?'

'Not to people like you, thank God.' He had few charts for this kind of ocean, and what he did have were recklessly out of date.

'I'll see to her,' she said.

That's what he called for, he told her. 'The door's unlocked. I won't be gone long.'

'If I think she's not well, I'll call a doctor.'

'I'd expect you to.'

He was past caring, and glad to get into the outside air, as if he too had caught more than a good dose of poison gas.

3

It was chilly on the landing but icy when she closed the door. Pam's head was below the line of blankets, and there was no sign of breathing.

Judy lit the fire. She put her hand into the warm damp bed. She might wake up with pneumonia. On the other hand she would be all right, though so ashamed at what she had failed to do that she'd try again. They all did. But she would talk the message into the darkness of her pathetic brain that no man is worth extinguishing yourself for.

She sat by the bed, knowing that in herself there was a light that couldn't be got at any more. It had almost gone out once or twice, but she'd never tried any such suicidal move as this poor thing, having always said she would rather cut a man up than do herself in, or that if she did think to end her misery it would be a better policy to *take one with you*, so that one of them at least wouldn't get away with it any more. It was as good a reason as any for killing a male of the species, Phyllida had pointed out, for once unable to resist saying what was on her mind.

She lit a cigarette, and poured coffee from the flask. He had been playing house as well as nurse, and seemed quite good at it. He had never confided in her, nor tried to impress her as a man. Didn't need to, she supposed. In answer to the question as to whether or not he was married he told her in a tone that didn't want the matter to turn into a conversation that he was not, and as far as he knew, never would be.

They had remained friendly because he only came to the house every month or two, and regarded her more as a neighbour than a woman which, while proving that he could keep his distance, disappointed her because he was in no way influenced by her as a person. He prized neighbourliness more than he liked women, since he had spent most of his life out of their company. Because he was naturally reticent, it was not difficult for him to treat everyone as his inferiors, though she couldn't fault his politeness, which was always well developed in those who really knew how to treat inferiors. She could read his bloody mind all right.

His speech and manners, and an ability to say little and still have a will of his own, reminded her of Phyllida. She knew nothing of his background, but assumed he had been to some minor public school and, not being bright enough for university, had been put into the navy by his parents so that at least he would be able to earn a living.

She was sorry for shouting at him, because he had, after all, tried to save someone's life, in no matter how risky and left-handed a manner. She hated her own big mouth when it gave her no choice in what she really wanted to say. On the other hand such words as came out often had the right effect, and

242

were what she'd hoped to say anyway, though to think so could only be decided by hindsight when she'd seen the effect on whoever was listening.

Being a sensitive person who could not resist allowing her thoughts to speak for her, she also craved the glamour of appearing enigmatic, and had not yet found a way of combining the two desires. Though you could be more than one person at the same time to yourself, it rarely worked with others. She regretted her outspokenness, and the harsh reactions of those who occasionally revealed her to be someone whom she had thought she was not.

Phyllida was quite the opposite, which was why they were able to tolerate each other. Or perhaps the similarities were sufficiently concealed for them to be able to deceive each other that they did not exist. Mutual but loving deception made existence livable, and men were unable to deceive, she had found, and wanted everything their own way. They hadn't the time, the inclination or the intelligence for it, and they were, in general, too fearful of their own sex and identity. There was a positive side to deception when it was done to enhance a relationship, to build understanding. It became a creative endeavour born of love, and not to be used in a negative way as a weapon or with a view to damage – something you couldn't trust a man not to use even if he was sensible enough to know about it.

Phyllida, who had taught her to be aware of such nuances, at the same time only spoke when she had something to say. Her talk was seldom interesting, though it might have been more so if she had let it out loudly and with a little of the peripheral junk that cluttered most minds. But she couldn't. Or wouldn't. It was too deep to tell. Her speech was prim, measured and, inevitably, to the point. Being well brought up, well controlled, and well trained in her job, she never let go of herself, except at those moments when both choice and intention were taken from her.

Even at nearly forty years of age Judy had not learned how

to be other than she was. Wanting to dissimulate and be more controlled, and knowing that she might never achieve it, caused her to appear more irresponsible and passionate than if she didn't care how she felt. She was occasionally upset by it, though only for a moment or two, because such misery was at least something about herself which she never showed to others.

Either Tom had made the room tidy in his sailor-like way before going out, or Pam had done it as part of wanting those who found her body to realize that even in death she was still a housewife, and who by killing herself had known what she was doing. It wasn't so. She hadn't planned anything, must have realized there was someone next door who would find her before it was too late, otherwise she would have done it the night before.

Judy turned from the mirror and walked across the room to pick up a sapphire ring which glinted under the bed. Strips of sticky paper hanging at the window like streamers from a lost election indicated that Pam's attempt had been more serious than she allowed for. The ring clattered to the middle of the table and lay still. Pam must have chucked it away in a rage before flicking the gas on. It still smelled of the soap she had used to pull it off. Or had she decided to kill herself after thoughtlessly getting rid of it, feeling so vulnerable that nothing else was possible?

Pam turned with a cry to the wall, saying words too garbled to decipher. In her dreams was a dark and frightening barrier. She jerked her legs, and the bedclothes slid towards the floor. Judy pulled them back and covered her, then held her cold pale hand to calm the nightmares, hoping Tom would never come back because it would be nice to sit like this for ever.

She had no work today, and would shop soon with the last couple of pounds till she got the children's allowance, returning by the market stalls to pick up enough vegetables for a soup, an old stand-by when cash was short. She liked the peace of a room that was not hers, a solitude in which she

244

could reflect intensely because another person was sleeping near by who had far worse problems than her own. She could always get money from her mother in Colchester, but disliked the idea of her father answering the telephone, or moralizing over her letter when he came home from the office. They sent clothes for the children, but she would take nothing else.

She couldn't believe in what had made her marry the man she did, was astonished and appalled whenever she looked back on it. Every act had been swamped by a thoughtlessness which drew her to the lowest common denominator of what she then imagined her spirit required. The primal aim had been to brush aside all that her family and friends wanted of her, so as to find out exactly what it was she wanted of herself. She wouldn't let them use her fate for the gratification of their inferior wisdom, and wanted to be free, so without any consideration for them (or for herself, as it turned out) she left university after a year and took a room and job in London. She was too stupid to realize that striving for independence was self-indulgence, and too young to know – which now seemed obvious – that self-indulgence leads only to self-destruction.

At a party she met a little androgynous middle-aged woman who owned a secondhand bookshop in a small country town. Both men and women seemed to fall in love with Judy in those days: but I should have known, she mused, that something was wrong, because I didn't feel love for any of *them*.

Helen lived in peace, with two neutered cats, and whatever girl she happened to pick up for a few months. 'Whether I'm a biological dead-end,' she said on a winter's evening after the shop was closed, and they sat by the upstairs fire toasting bread against the bars, 'is neither here nor there.' She relished her isolation and the power she felt from it, which made her interesting to any young girl.

Judy was fascinated by the way she kept busy compiling catalogues or writing letters, and she never saw her either bored or unhappy with the two rooms of books which made up the shop. Helen knew what to buy, and collectors would drive from London. The bell rattled, and a face showed itself. Sometimes a customer wouldn't appear for two hours after the door was unbolted. At other times a browser would already be waiting on the pavement.

A man stayed for an hour, as if afraid to go back into the rain, looking at every book intently. She observed his medium height, pinkish face, well-lit grey eyes, and straight reddish hair cut fairly short. His open duffel-coat had special pockets, for the thieves' mirror installed on the ceiling showed at least six books go in as he moved around the shelves, and it still didn't look laden.

Helen had gone to a sale. Judy was supposed to call the police, and her hand moved to the telephone. Two shoplifters had been prosecuted before her time. He approached the desk. 'I'll have this.'

You might as well: you've had so much else. A copy of *Middlemarch*. He had taste – but had made a feast. 'Four shillings.'

'Lots of nice books here,' he said, smiling.

His look intensified, for he guessed by her eyes that she had seen him loading his pockets, and he wanted to solve the mystery as to how she knew, when no one had ever rumbled him before. Yet he was prepared to sacrifice the pleasure of an explanation provided she did not try to stop him leaving the shop. She read the condition in his gaze, and when he became convinced that she had, he diminished its intensity but did not smile as pleasantly as before.

Civilization must have taken a big leap forward when the language of the eyes had finally been enriched by words. 'There'll be less now that you've been in here.'

'Only one, I'm afraid.' He handed his coins as if there weren't too many more where they came from. 'I'll try to do better next time.'

'We do *sell* quite a lot of books.' He seemed to have doubted that many people actually bothered to pay in such an out-of-the-way place. 'But not all that many to students, I admit.'

He fastened his coat-toggles. 'Our grants aren't much to write home about these days, unless to ask the old folks to top 'em up a bit.'

She nodded at his girth, which didn't match his thinnish face. 'You seem to feed quite well on it.'

'We do our best.' His head was close. He decided to turn prosaic, and get out as soon as possible. 'We eat communally, fifteen to a pot, a yoghourt pot!'

The bell tinkled as he left. She had been bullied. She hadn't been living with another woman long enough to know how to put men properly in their place. She was angry, and she should know, anyway. After dialling one digit, she replaced the receiver, a failure to act which, she was to recollect, fucked up her life.

She had allowed him to charm her into not reporting his theft, and in being disloyal to Helen. She was supposed to write the title and amount of every volume sold, even if out of the sixpenny box. Helen knew, or seemed to know, every book in the place, and when she missed them Judy wouldn't be able to tell her how they had gone. Maybe Helen would think she had pocketed the money. She wouldn't be trusted any more.

She put a card in the window: 'Back in Five Minutes', and went to the High Street to buy meat for their supper. Looking through the window of Silver's Grill she saw the book thief reading his morning paper.

'Remember me?'

His eyes were deadened by print.

'I work in a shop.' She stood by his side.

He put six spoonsful of sugar in his coffee, stirred, drank, and shuddered. 'Woolworths?'

'No. Nor Marks and Sparks, either.'

'Did I get you pregnant?'

She took off her coat. 'You might at least buy me a cup of something, after I allowed you to steal those six books.'

'Seven.'

'My reactions were slow, otherwise you'd have been in the copshop by now.' His duffel-coat hung over the next seat, and the loot was, she supposed, in the cloth bag by his feet. 'Was that the closest you've been to getting caught?'

His hand went up for the waitress. 'I've had closer shaves. Two coffees, please. I'm eating into my profits, you realize.'

'I could still call the police.'

He looked at her. 'You could, but why?'

'Aren't you ashamed of stealing?' She had never come face to face with a thief before.

'You've got your definitions wrong. But then, uneducated people like you always do.'

He must have done his National Service already, and she also supposed he came from a very middlebrow home – if that – to accuse her of being uneducated. And if he really was educated – if that was the word (though she had every reason to doubt that he was) – such a slur would not have been thrown at her. If he really thought so, he would have kept the opinion to himself.

'You've got your definitions wrong,' he repeated. 'I've never stolen. All goods are produced at the expense of the working class, and wealth is property, and property is theft, so theft is the only way of getting property back into the hands of the working classes where it belongs. A mere redistribution of wealth. So don't accuse me of stealing, you right little tight little – actually rather big – middle-class *tart*. You've blackmailed me into buying you a coffee, and if you insist on calling the capitalist property-guarding class-conscious gestapo-coppers I'll have a long and very circumstantial tale to tell about how you connived in my removing those books from the shop – when they drag me into one of their illegal show-trial courts.'

He was sweating. She had frightened him, and was satisfied – for the moment. 'But what *is* stealing,' she asked, 'if that isn't? If you did it in a socialist-workers' state you'd be in the

248

equivalent of Siberia for twenty-five years.'

'Stealing is only from the working classes, and I'd never steal from them because if I did and they caught me they'd kick me to death – ugh!'

He sounded so simple that she became more interested in him, and said: 'But I work. And the woman I work for works, so we're working class, aren't we?'

At his laughter, people sitting around hoped they had ended their lovers' quarrel. 'Nobody works who puts goods on display. They sell, and make profits. They tempt people. They ask for trouble.'

She was convinced that his parents were shopkeepers, and learned later that she was right. 'Somebody's got to sell things,' she said, 'otherwise people wouldn't be able to buy, would they?'

'In my opinion,' he said earnestly, as if his very soul were weeping for it to come about, 'we should live in a utopian society where people wouldn't buy, but *earn*.'

She shuddered. 'But they'd earn money, and then they'd have to buy.'

He took the bowl of sugar from the next table, and began to scoop it up. 'Only those who toiled would earn. It'll take me a long time to explain it properly to you, and I only teach women who go to bed with me.'

'Do you teach men in the same way?'

He looked more disturbed than when she had mentioned calling the police. 'In any case,' she said, 'when did you last toil in a factory, or a coal mine?'

'I'm beginning to like you. I'm hitching back to Southampton. Want to come?'

It was easier getting lifts with a girl. 'I bloody don't.'

'Suit yourself. I'll be back this way in a month.'

'Don't call at the shop.'

'I'm bound to. I love books so much I have to steal 'em. And I've taken a fancy to you.'

She lost her job. But he was loyal. When she got pregnant

249

he married her, after her parents promised to spend five hundred pounds on the wedding and give them, which turned out to mean him, another thousand to get started.

It was a hell she would never delve into again. The planet hadn't been big enough for both of them. She'd tried to poison him, but had made a mistake in the dosage. I dined out somewhere yesterday, he said to the doctor, and must have eaten something bad. I was too drunk to know where the place was. He had tried to murder her. She had a six-inch scar on the shoulder to show where he had missed. I fell down the steps outside the house and cut myself on the foot-scraper. He was a savage bed-sitter terrorist who gave her no peace because she was the nearest victim, but who modified his depredations after she had broken an earthenware pot over his head. The out-patients' department at the hospital had known her well. During every separate minute she had felt she was living for ever. Now that such torment had long been over she still didn't know who or what she was, but that uncertain condition was by now established as her true self, and accepted with enough equanimity for her existence to be tolerable, sufficiently enjoyable for her to know she would never gas herself as the peacefully sleeping Pam had done.

The struggle to stay alive generated the energy to keep going. Fighting against all hostilities created a pressure that did not allow her to contemplate such a way out. She reasoned, and became less despondent. With her free hand she wiped an eye that had become momentarily wet, and happiness at being alive caused her to squeeze the hand she was holding.

Pam woke.

'Feeling better?'

She closed her eyes and lay back. Nothing to get up for.

'You had a good sleep.' Judy's hand was held firm when she tried to draw it away. Her fingers opened in her anguish on seeing the mark of the wedding ring.

The room was as if shielded by grey blankets. 'I can't see anything. Put the light on.'

Judy smiled. 'I will if you let go of my hand.' There was an aroma of sweat and fear. He had bundled her into bed with her clothes on, but couldn't have done otherwise, being the gentleman he was. 'You should get undressed if you're going to stay in bed. Be more comfortable.'

The light made the room dull orange rather than grey. 'If I do I'll never get up. I've got to phone my husband.'

She'd sent a letter saying what she intended to do, so he'd hot-foot it down and drag her back to the bijou den for a kitchen leucotomy. She looked for an unposted envelope, or screw of paper. 'Why do that?'

'I don't know.' Nothing to hold. 'What else is there?'

'Did you tell anybody beforehand?'

She sat up, and turned her head slowly. 'I must stand.'

Judy held her. 'All right?'

The world was empty. 'I did it without thinking. I can't trust myself.'

Judy laughed. 'Who of us can?' She came from the window. 'If you get some work, and mix with people, you won't do it again. There's no point running back to hubby now that the worst is over.'

'Perhaps she does want to go back to him.' The door had opened too quietly to be heard through her talk. She was meddling dangerously, Tom thought, though considered it best not to say anything further on the matter. He expected a raging come-back, but Judy was like the weather, in that what you anticipated didn't always manifest.

'It's up to her,' was all she said.

He was wet from the rain. 'How are you?' he asked Pam.

'All right.' She was morose – or she couldn't recognize him. He had seen people close to death, and she didn't look far off. But he felt an interest in her, though could ask no questions while she was still in the storm. He was repelled by what she had tried to do, and kept his thoughts clear in order not to condemn. Yet he had entered into her offence by doing what he could to save her. She had been caught by a death-dealing wave, and he had interfered with her fate by stopping it in mid-twist. On your own head be it, he told himself, but he didn't want to let her out of his sight in case another stray wave took her under.

'I bought food,' he said. 'After I get rid of these wet clothes why don't you both come next door and have some lunch?'

Pam felt she never wanted to eat again; and Judy said: 'I must go out and do my own shopping.'

He stood, tense and uncertain. 'I have a screwdriver next door, and some bigger screws. I'll fix the latch back on, that I snapped in my hurry to get in.' There was no answer. He stayed a little longer so as not to leave too abruptly. 'Anyway, the food will be next door, if you care for it.' He expected no response, but heard Pam say, as he turned to go, that she would wash and change first.

She remembered a struggle, but couldn't recall what had happened beyond his cruelty at pulling her out of a warm sleep that ought to have lasted for ever. She had seen his face at a time too far off to remember who he was. She had been drawn from that dream by a long scalding ache. This same man had stopped her going even further back into her childhood dream. In bringing her cold skin into more contact with daylight he had crushed the dream for ever, yet wakened her at the same time.

Some force to touch was missing at the end of her fingers, and her mind raced through thoughts like a millwheel in space. Memories created even thinner air. Nothing inside or out had substance. She looked around the room in the hope of seeing some solid attachment that would tell her where she was.

She shook her head angrily, crushing back fraudulent tears till they seemed to burn her brain. The day was unlike any other, an island unto itself.

She took off her blouse and threw cold water on her face,

over and over again, like an unstoppable machine. Judy was frightened that she would never stop unless her arms were pinned back, and pushed a towel roughly towards her: 'Use this.'

Pam rubbed her face too hard for her skin to stay pale. She would erase all features. Nobody would recognize her, not even herself, no matter how clear the mirror. Having woken out of life's worst dream she did not know what part of her existence to get back to.

Judy held her till she became still, and hardly breathing, as if she had gone to sleep while on her feet. There was a tinderish heat about her, not humid and animal, but a temperature the body provided to keep her inner warmth unsullied by cold from outside.

Judy touched the back of her icy hands. The palms were hot. She stirred, but did not move, her face pressed into a compatible darkness at Judy's shoulder. She would willingly stay, but it was an impossible hiding place. To rest in it for more than a few minutes might tempt her to lie in similar places of refuge. Nothing mattered. Her arms relaxed, but hung around the large comforting shoulders and felt the strong beating of another heart, suggesting a world that would have no interest in wrecking her peace. All she hoped for was to arrange a demarcation within which she could live, surrounding a place where she could flourish and work without pain. If it wasn't possible she would be nothing more than a grain of purposeless dust in the universe.

Different feelings were taking hold of Judy at this long embrace, making her afraid of doing something which would involve them too closely with each other. Impatience and embarrassment urged her to ease Pam away, to say it was time she pulled herself together and got back to normal life. She didn't want to play mummy to a person who would become dependent and give nothing in return. She had often helped, and would do so again, but not by starting a relationship which couldn't but end in a very ragged way indeed.

Pam put on a clean blouse. 'I must go downstairs, before I burst!'

'You poor kid!' said Judy.

She didn't like her tone. 'Thanks very much. I'll be all right now.'

4

He could imagine Judy saying that like every man he was only waiting for a woman to come and look after him. She was right. He was. Yet she was also wrong, because he wasn't. All his life without a woman's company for more than a few days at a time, someone to wash his shirts wasn't essential for him. And for sex, the odd affair would see him right.

He'd been to Salik's Polish delicatessen and bought cheeses, smoked fish, loaves and pastries, and picked up two bottles of Mount Carmel wine at an off-licence. There weren't enough plates, so some of the food would stay on paper. It was easy to live in London, with so many shops, pubs, launderettes and eating places, a cosy and civilized north European refuge in which you wanted for nothing provided you had paper money for it.

He tasted the wine. The fish looked good. He sat in the armchair and read his newspaper. She may not come. It was impossible to read. He stood at the window. He needed a housekeeper for Clara's flat if he was to stay there, someone to caretake the six rooms and other nooks branching therefrom. He would use it as a base to go back to, no matter where he wandered. Advertise for a competent middle-aged woman who wanted a haven and a job.

He wondered whether his soul would always be that of a sailor. With no family life during more than thirty years on board, and none before that, the sea had been his mother and the sky his father, two elements not known for their especial concern for anyone sandwiched between. To consider a room or flat as his settled home made him want to run back to the roughest elements, which would soothe him in a way nothing could on land where whoever he might live among could give that sensation of danger which he needed in order to feel alive. He watched. He walked in limbo, thinking while on the street that everyone he saw was dead. The occasional exception was a shock to the heart, and so rare that it was hard for him to believe that he would live for long in this country no matter how comfortable it might seem.

He thought of George Town harbour, and the cable railway going up the green-backed hillside of Penang Island, that dazzling and incomparable paradise on earth. From the hotel terrace at the top he saw the mainland of Malaya with its grand escarpments and jungle-covered mountains falling back layer by layer into the distance of dusk, or growing more distinct at the onset of a storm, enormous sweeps of monsoon rain darkening the livid foliage. There was a place for any man to languish in!

But there were still wilder and more remote localities, far from everywhere even in this day and age: dense forest on a mountain close by, or the bare slopes of a distant volcano, and the roar of heavy breakers beyond his window, places where typhoons, eruptions and storms were so loud and violent that he couldn't believe they weren't intending to engulf the world. There was meaning in life. But he had to taste it by the mouth and feel in every part of the skin that first plate-glass metallic fall of conjoined waterdrops when the monsoon burst over palm trees and fell in such a way that it seemed as if God had singled him out for a spectacular drowning. The weight of the sky wouldn't let him breathe. Everything smelled of water. He was cold yet not cold. He should have hated it but

255

didn't because it was something to *feel*, an intense wash coming down with a noise that wouldn't allow a normal voice to be heard, and he felt in some perverse way that it was a protective umbrella put over him to stop worse befalling. He was awed, and that too was beneficial. Such flashes of lightning came that, though enjoying it, he didn't feel safe. He could die any moment, though the chances were remote. But he knew only too well that he was alive.

When the ship far from land tipped and tilted its way through a monsoon he also lived. But here he was, and such a life was finished. The floor didn't drop away, or even rock gently, and he stood with dry skin looking out of a window at a street under a plastic-seeming sheet of benign drizzle, wondering why the fierce bite of life had gone out of him.

Clara had died, and done no favour by leaving her money into his keeping, though he had no intention of grumbling at that. At least she had hung on till he was fifty, at which she may well have smiled to herself and known that such an inheritance could hardly ruin him.

His chronometer on the sideboard, attended to at twelve each day by Greenwich Mean Time whether at sea or ashore, had been neglected. He had let go of time by one hour. The ticking, lost in another compartment of his mind, stayed quiet, till something in his consciousness pulled it back again. Not to notice its measured marking of his and everybody else's life suggested that something vital was worrying him. It was, and through his acute irritation he wondered why he had been foolish enough to believe that she would ever care to face him again.

The universal clock could not be forced. Alterations brought by the passing of time stopped or furthered all maturing hopes. A chronometer with accurate pacing was part of a scheme devised by God, but needed the hand of a person to build and keep it going. Even in the stormiest seas, when every next moment could tip you to disaster, he had been on hand to wind the chronometer at its set hour. The

256

regularity had been too long part of his life for him not to be annoyed at his lapse.

On his penultimate run from Central America he reflected, while winding the chronometer one day, that whenever he was back on land this was something he would always do, to remind himself of what he thought he could never bear to leave but was forced to because he'd had no say in the matter. All changes had happened whether or not he wanted them. An alteration in the weather had nothing to do with him, but he often felt himself geared to the elements in too helpless a way to bear contemplation.

He did not like what had caused this condition, though knew that no master even of the biggest ship was ever captain of his fate. A lifetime at the mercy of uncertain sea and malign sky had emphasized his addiction to order and precision, and reinforced his scepticism that his own intrinsic self had ever been responsible for changes in his life.

For the sake of well-being he should put his chronometer and sextant out of sight, throw away log books and mementoes now irrelevant. To be tidy in the past had protected himself and others but, in having forgotten to carry out his daily winding of the chronometer, even if only for an hour, he needed such qualities no more.

He had wound it, nevertheless. Face down in its gimbal ring, he turned the tipsy key gently four and three-quarter turns, and the sound of the ratchet calmed him. The odour and movement of the sea was not to be thrown off so easily. Habits die hard – if ever – in a man of fifty, but in the process of change he felt more adrift than ever, and it was with relief that he heard a faint knock at the door.

She sat by the table, and he poured wine. 'I don't suppose a drop of this will hurt.'

She wore lipstick, eye shadow, face cream. That stuff on women does more harm than good, Judy had said before going out to the shops. I know, she answered, maybe it does. I feel better, though. I haven't used it for a month. She wore no bra – don't need one – a white blouse with an open beige cardigan, and a skirt. A change of clothes might give a new start in life. Anything was worth trying.

She looked at his pale face, freckles, tonsure of red hair, uneven teeth when he smiled, broad nose, well-shaped but pronounced lower lip, firm chin slightly squared: an attractive ugliness, a determined intelligence. Why him, and not somebody else?

He put smoked fish on to their plates, and observed her by glances, unwilling to embarrass by staring. With so much to look at, there was something to hope for, and a long time was necessary to take in what lay behind those angled, intriguing blue eyes. She laughed. 'Do you think I should be starving because I tried to do something daft?'

'I didn't really think, except that you can't have eaten since last night.'

She drank the wine. 'You're right, though.' I don't want to get drunk in front of a stranger. 'I'll give up my room and go back to Nottingham.' She had nothing to say, but the silence, even for a few seconds, alarmed her. 'I've got to do *something*.'

He refilled both glasses. 'If you're uncertain, don't. Whatever's going to happen will, without you interfering in the process. My experience suggests that it's just as likely to be good as bad. The time to do things is when they start doing them to you, and until then the only worthwhile course is to take your mind off what problems you have, by eating something, for example.'

He spoke unhurriedly, a slight pause now and again as if to let her know that at least he thought before opening his mouth, a mannerism which made him sound very right indeed, and also wise, since each phrase touched similar words in her mind. He lifted his glass. 'Let's drink to a long life.'

She sipped.

Neither did he give her time to agree nor disagree with whatever he said. 'In my job I learned that you could anticipate problems, but never create them. They came right enough – how they came, at times! – but it never did to brood about them.'

The room had a timelessness that only an unmarried man could create. The stove gurgled, and they were warm. The ticking of his special clock made it even more timeless. She was sincere, almost fearful. 'I left my husband, and don't manage well on my own.'

To have shelter in a fair haven, provisions and clothes, was certainly a start. 'Do you have any money?'

'Enough to be going on with. But is that everything?'

He put food on her plate. 'Perhaps not. I've always lived by myself, but I suppose it's difficult if you never have.'

'It might not even be that,' she said.

What the hell is it, then? 'You have to ride a storm day after day, sometimes for a week or more. In life it can last months, but eventually it goes.'

'Oh yes,' she said, 'everything goes.' He didn't understand, though his words were true enough, and comforting. It was all right for a man. The depths below her seemed immense, as if she still had a long way to fall. Beyond the room there was an emptiness which she couldn't bear to think about, and whatever lurked out there wanted to annihilate her hopes and expectations.

259

He touched her hand. 'Nobody understands anybody, but if you can look and listen and talk, and even laugh, then a glimmer of a solution might come through the mist. The only person I ever understood was my aunt, and I had little enough information to go on. In everybody's life there can't be more than one or two people they'll ever understand, or be understood by. More than that is too much to wish for.'

She felt numb. 'I suppose so.' She hoped he was wrong. She had come from a land of big families, and couldn't live like that.

'The only reason for staying alive is so that sooner or later you'll understand *one* person. Those who try to kill themselves do so only because they have given up hope of trying to understand one person in their lives. Or they don't know anyone who wants to try and understand them. They may have tried, and think they've failed, and don't have the heart to make another attempt. There are lots of duties in life that you've got to look sharp about. The only thing I was brought up on was duty, and I don't regret it now. It often saved me from despair, and stopped me doing much harm to others. Or so I like to think.'

She nodded, content to listen, and wondered why he was trying to send her back to George.

'But the main duty, bigger than all the others, is to go on living even when you can't bear the thought of facing the world a minute longer. When you feel that way, just grit your teeth and live it out till the threat goes. It's the one duty that matters. If you survive that, whatever else you want will come.'

He only ever spoke in such a way to himself, and feared he was being pompous, but words were taken from his control, and though he didn't like it, neither did he regret it when he saw how she seemed absorbed by what he was saying. When the heart gave out its own words in the form of advice for someone else, that advice could also be meant, he knew, for oneself.

260

'Put your decisions off for a while.' He was glad Judy wasn't at their lunch to accuse him of self-interest. 'And get out of London for a day or two.'

'You don't need to be anxious about me.' She hadn't left George's prison to walk blindfold into another. 'I'll be happy enough living on my own when I know what I'm going to do, and what I'm not going to do.'

He once met a second mate who, he told her, being dead drunk, related that when at home with his wife he always peeled her fruit. He called for a plate of Jaffas to demonstrate, and Tom observed that stripping an orange of its skin was like taking a globe of the world to pieces: cutting off the two poles, scoring with great precision along the meridians of longitude about sixty degrees apart, then pulling each segment off intact, much like an instructor at a navigation class demonstrating a theory of map projections. At the third orange the second mate fell on to the floor and had to be carried back to his ship, smelling as much of citrus fruit as whisky. Even though dead drunk one could be precise, though it was wise not to push the *spirit* too far.

She smiled, and watched his fingers dextrously working as he peeled her an orange in the same neat way. 'You spoil me.'

'You're my guest.' Responsibility for any other person but himself had been shunned, unless within the hierarchy of a crew. His relationship with Clara had been possible because she had been equally responsible for him. Half a packet of coffee went into the pot, and he stood while the grounds settled. It was a day for staying awake. One must never ask questions, but he'd got her back from the dark, and his curiosity was intense.

'I'll wash up, at least.' She smiled, and thought he probably had a pinafore hidden in the cupboard.

'We once had a steward,' he said, 'who threw the dishes overboard after meals. By the time we discovered it, we were eating off bare boards and old newspapers. He was flown home in a strait-jacket, poor chap.'

261

He put a tick against the question as to whether she would laugh. Its sound came as the first real sign of life. 'An aunt of mine died,' he said, 'who left me a flat in Brighton, and I'll be going there in a day or two. I haven't yet sifted through the stuff she left.' He came back to the table. From previously thinking he had nothing to lose by certain proposals, he felt that care was needed because something more was at stake. 'I was brought up as an orphan, so I might find out a few things about my past.'

The food and wine made her drowsy. 'Don't you know enough already?'

'Sufficient to breathe on, I suppose. But who knows everything? There's a lot more somewhere. Wouldn't you think there is?'

'There might be – I daresay.'

'I never asked my aunt direct questions, thinking that any information would come to me in its own good time. I suppose I could have, but now it's too late. For some reason I didn't have the burning curiosity about myself until now, nor to get through to anything even deeper than information, if you see what I mean.'

'I think I do.'

He felt as if he had never spoken what was truly in his mind. 'Young kids these days take drugs to blast a hole in the wall that they think keeps them from knowing themselves. Either it doesn't work, or there's nothing to know, and so they find they've turned into zombies when the smoke of the explosion's drifted away. You can't get through to something that you are not, or even into something that you might wish you were. I prefer to know myself in my own good time, at the rate my mind was born to move at. Maybe there's nothing there, but if not then at least I won't get brain damage trying to find out.'

She sipped her bitter coffee, thinking how lucky he was to be able to talk so easily.

'There are other ways than by drugs.'

262

Perhaps he spoke like that because he'd spent years talking to himself. 'I'm sure.'

He lit his pipe. 'I know so. I've tried a few. But often the sea drained every possibility of personal speculation, except that concerning the existence of God. I don't feel embarrassed saying that, because it's a question which on still waters has no answer, and seems all too obvious during storms. One watch follows another, and such speculations soon lose any relevance they had on taking departure. Days drift by. A storm is one day, however long it goes on, and a calm sea likewise. Every minute is occupied by a routine of vigilance, even if it only means staring at a plate-glass ocean. Life is a drill, slow-motion sometimes, often too hectic for good health, but at least you don't forget anything, or let yourself in for too many systematic, constant, random or probable errors, or fall into a dreadful blunder on getting too near land that sends you to the bottom like concrete. But on shore everything's different, a matter of learning to live so that you don't seem like a ghost to everybody as you walk the streets, and so that you don't feel one to yourself. I don't need shock or drugs to get me to a new state of being, as I read in the colour-supplement magazines that people often do. I have to get accustomed to normal land-locked life, and it's like being born again, which I suppose is enough of a shock.'

Her face was encased in her long slim hands. She had not replaced her wedding ring. He was talking for a purpose. She wanted him to continue.

'I was going to ask,' he said, 'if you've got time to spare, whether you'd like to travel down to Brighton with me. I like to look at the sea now and again, that cemetery of old friends, not to mention myself.'

He was surprised not to feel embarrassment at such disembowelling of the spirit. Sailors' tales with mates or girl-friends had been different, and reflections like these had been kept secret in either fair or foul weather. 'You can go your own way in Brighton, or come to the flat and I'll show you

263

around the old place. It'll be a change for you, and a pleasure for me to have company.'

She wanted to say yes. His offer was too important to refuse, being the only one she'd had. Can I let you know later? I'm not sure how I feel. She didn't speak, but vaguely nodded. To judge by his smile she had accepted. She was too exhausted not to. She needed freedom and ease, to sleep, but not to die any more because she wanted to know who he was. Coloured sparks were spinning in the space where her thoughts were losing themselves. No one had graced her with this kind of talk before.

6

In the dark, at five in the afternoon, she put on the light and got out of bed. Endless time was before her, but why didn't her thoughts stop racing? She drew the curtains, and dressed. The room was cold, so she lit the gas. She listened for movement from next door. He had gone out. She pressed three teabags in boiling water to make a strong drink.

Every move is deeper into a prison when you are on your own. There is no place more secure than that of yourself, which those who are alone go further into at every step. She knew it, but was unable to make amends.

The rain had stopped, but it was cold and raw. She passed a lit-up police station and turned towards the Underground. The rush hour was coming out, pushing up the steps. Traffic was stalled at the lights. An old man clutching a plastic bag searched a dustbin.

She got rid of some tenpenny pieces in the ticket machine.

Few people went down, but the up-escalator was packed. She wanted to walk in lighted places. She craved to be in the dark, on her own. She needed both conditions, and was glad to be alive.

She liked being wherever she was. A train came quickly. Stops flashed by. She missed Oxford Circus, got out at Tottenham Court Road, followed crowds into the fume-laden air, looked at faces behind the glass of Wimpys, Hamburgers, Golden Eggs and Grills.

The window of a sex shop was veiled. She saw books, tapes, films, vibrators, condoms, flimsy underwear that probably melted when you washed it, rubber suits and rubber dollies that perished after whatever was done to them, and contraptions whose uses she didn't try to fathom. The men and few women had perhaps come in out of curiosity like her. There were young people, and the smart middle-aged with brief-cases. Film shows took place behind a curtain. Relaxed and unconcerned, people inspected goods on offer, read labels and sets of instructions, and bored young women at the cash desk checked items out like food at a supermarket.

A man gripped her elbow. 'Will you come with me?'

She snapped her arm clear. There was no fuss. Would she have gone with him if it had been Tom? The answer was no, but he wouldn't have done such a thing. But if he did? Don't think. Don't think.

She looked along more shelves and tables of the sexual-fun market that promised the unattainable. A tourist or passer-by was born every minute to fall for such unkept promises, moneyed customers who bought some mechanical spirit-killer to use in making love, goods to be put in Christmas stockings or to litter desert tents. Love is the last thing it can be called.

The district was a garish beast glutted on all that was false. People come to London and go home clutching some sexual gewgaw as they had once taken a stick of rock and a funny hat from the seaside. Whether they walked out with something in

265

their mac pockets, or stuffed into pigskin briefcases, they had more money than was needed for life's necessities. Goods had to be provided in exchange for floating cash, for they couldn't be expected to *throw* their money into the gutter or keep it in the bank, though she supposed that most of the stuff ended in dustbins that tramps rummaged through looking for something to keep them alive.

Old Compton Street smelled of coffee, oranges and exhaust fumes. People were going to theatres and cinemas. Dirty-book shops flourished. Strip shows did good trade. She had to walk along the roadway because some cars blocked the pavement. Cafés and restaurants were full. Those who lived on their own must feel better at seeing how many others also lived alone. Life went on, which was no doubt an improvement on no life at all.

George, wearing a hat, and his heavy olive-drab rainproof overcoat belted at the waist, looked at a showcase of illuminated photographs. A hand at the side of his face indicated that he was about to go into the cabaret place. The man at the door was cajoling, and George said something inaudible, changing his mind, jerking his head aggressively to make the words plainer. He walked along the street, away from her. The man in the doorway swore after him. When George looked back he still didn't see her. Misery had made him fatter, and made her thin. In bed together, their combined weight would no doubt be the same as before.

He turned the corner into an alley. The right angle of the wall seemed as if to fold over her, but she waited, and hoped it wouldn't, her fingers opening on the brick surface. A woman looked as if she would kill her, then moved on, swaying a handbag like a piece of plate-glass.

She changed her track for Piccadilly Circus. She could have said: 'Take me home. Let's go, for God's sake, and get it over with.' But she hadn't. The sight of him confirmed the pointless existence she had given up for good. Fear that he might have seen her made life in her room seem like a blissful prison in which she could hide when necessary.

Shaftesbury Avenue concealed her. She pushed, and made headway. Four jet engines whined in from a place Tom had no doubt been to. A man in overcoat and cap had the same predatory jaw and fixed grey eyes as Bert. She stepped aside without reducing her pace. She expected him to reach out but, his mouth set in cunning, he pretended not to see her. The banging of machines and the dull jingle of coinage came from an amusement arcade as big as a garage. Perhaps Alf and Harry were among the flash of coloured lights, having sponged George's small change.

She walked in the road to avoid a cinema crowd. When a taxi horn blared she jumped back. Popcorn sellers and hot-dog vendors shivered in the drizzle. Wastepaper clung to the feet as if it were magnetized. She knew the streets better than George and his brothers. The four of them must be out on a spree, or as a last effort to help George find her before giving her up for ever. Women with figures contorted beyond all credulity showed up in vivid lighting. Men came out, and men went in. She walked quickly from juke-box noise and traffic, and people ceaselessly on the alert for something they would surely never find. She wasn't one of them, because what she wanted did not exist where people could never meet or understand each other no matter how many times they gyrated. The area to her was an artificial flower, blazing with light, and rotten to the middle of the earth. The only certain road from it was to cut a straight line for as far as she could go.

Her mind had never been so clear nor her eyes so sharply focused. She had seen George and his brothers, and it was necessary to flee. A young man with flowing auburn hair and a rucksack held high in one hand, ran through traffic to the Eros statue. A girl followed, her laughter screaming above the noise of motor cars. Pam pushed against the tide of people coming from deep under earth, holding the rail as she descended the steps with such determination that a way was made for her.

267

Her last tenpenny coins went into the machine. Yes, I'll go to Brighton with you, she would say, and if he'd changed his mind she would take a trip on her own. As unobtrusive stalkers there were none better than George and his brothers, therefore she got on the Piccadilly Line so as to change to the Circle Line at South Kensington and do a devious if not zigzag walk from Bayswater. In spite of such crowds in Soho George's brothers may have kept her in sight, she being one against four. Yet knowing the system, where she assumed they did not, decreased their advantage. She was a free person, but if they found her lair she would get no peace.

Instead of South Kensington she went to Earls Court and then changed north as far as Edgware Road, when she crossed platforms and came back to Notting Hill Gate, switching on to the Central Line for Holland Park.

She had lost them, if indeed they had lasted beyond the first interchange. But she couldn't be sure – feeling that she had been followed up Ladbroke Grove. In any case it was time to abandon London, look for work in a place with better air, where George and his tracker-dog brothers would never think to hound her down. She would buy a map, but would it be of England or of the world?

7

George sat in his car, looking up at her room. She walked by with Tom. George stared, and rolled the window down as if to speak. He didn't. She was with a person unknown to him. His round face under the usual trilby hat pleaded with her, but she had severed contact, and wondered why he couldn't leave her be. Her life was her own, and he didn't yet know it. When her fear came back she regretted not tackling him, but with every step it was less possible. To delay such a matter would build up a dangerous mood in him, a process she knew well. The day was ruined before it had begun.

Tom waved a taxi in Ladbroke Grove, and put down the small seat to face her. He wore a cap, a brown suit with waistcoat and watch-chain, well-polished shoes, and an overcoat. His leather briefcase was of the kind used for carrying sheet-music. He was freshly shaved and smelled of soap.

She wondered who had taught him to dress, supposing it had been necessary, or who had influenced his choice. Perhaps girl-friends had put him right on harmony and colours, just as she had tried to smarten George by persuading him to get at least one suit made at the best tailors but who, when he had, was too shocked to wear it because of the cost. In the matter of ties, socks, shirts and shoes he had no matching sense at all.

Neither had she, on occasion. If she felt happy, she could achieve a plain sort of smartness with what she had in drawers or wardrobe, but there were also times when a clash of styles showed her unsettled state of mind to the most casual eye on the street. The only way to avoid this was by devising simple permutations at more confident moments – clothes she could put on without thought. But no matter what her mood, she'd always had a sense of judgement regarding George's appearance. While he resented her criticisms, he was careful to act on them, though his training had lapsed, to judge by the odd tie and pullover he had been wearing in the car.

She would forget him, if she could, for today at least, feeling smart and comfortable in her grey skirt, white blouse, heavy cardigan and walking shoes. There was nothing of fashion, but she didn't care for that. Her coat was longer than it should be, but in such weather it seemed an advantage. A headscarf and woolly hat in her bag would help if it got any colder. She wondered that young girls in London didn't perish considering how little some of them wore.

Tom looked out at the overcast sky. The park was dull under its pall of winter. A piece of paper scooted along the pavement when the taxi paused at a crossing. 'Should be clearer on the coast,' he said briskly. 'Still changeable, though. You might need that umbrella.'

He then fell silent, but she didn't feel threatened, didn't have to talk in order to defend herself, or attack him before he sent verbal shot at her. Such thoughts ruffled her ease, but she fought to stay calm. When the taxi came into the station forecourt he slammed up the seat so as to get out first and hold the door open.

He bought single tickets on the assumption that no one could say when they would be coming back. Pam waited by the bookstall, looking over the paperbacks. He had no expectations, no plan except to sort out the family junk, no sense except that of happiness at not going to the flat alone. He looked at the departure boards. 'The fast one leaves in half a minute.'

'Let's run!' She took his hand and pulled him along.

A naval man never runs. Run, and you fall. You can't see what you are doing. You injure yourself, or send others flying. Such accidents might prejudice the safety of the ship. So never run.

But he ran now, cutting through queues and dodging trolleys. The black man at the gate said: 'You'll be lucky, mate.'

The train was moving, and he helped her in.

Clouds flowed, and blue gaps appeared after Croydon. He had forgotten to buy a newspaper, he said. 'Shouldn't have run,' she taunted him with a laugh.

'Often I didn't see one for months. Didn't much hear the wireless, either, though the Sparks kept us informed. With a good wireless operator you never lacked news. Even in sleep they're glued to the set searching the ether! When I came

270

across a newspaper again it seemed as if nothing had happened.'

They wanted breakfast. 'I'm ravenous,' he said to the waiter. 'Bring everything for both of us.'

There was countryside to look at beyond Gatwick. She remembered the waiter in the train from Nottingham, tall and handsome, long since gone.

He held his knife and fork almost at the top of the handles, which gave him a fastidiousness that hardly matched his face. Why had he asked her? Out of kindness, she supposed. It was good to be on a train while you looked at the fields floating by. The world was another place. The worst was outside, and changed with surprising ease. 'Marvellous,' she exclaimed, telegraph wires lifting and falling.

He felt like a youth of twenty because she had agreed to come with him, a competent person who, in spite of her gesture of despair, should have known better than to bother. She was abstracted, as if controlled by a mystery he would never be able to unravel. He was happy. Things rarely worked in conjunction, but today they had. His image in the window-glass was that of a worn and battered man of the world who had experienced too few of its many parts.

There was something untouchable about her spirit. He knew little except that she had been married, and had a son, and had broken the connection, an act which, judging by her sensitive but rawly outlined features, had needed much strength of purpose. She was emerging from the hardship, and he wondered how she had done it, but his need to know could not matter, because such a person never voluntarily explained herself. She seemed to live on an island, surrounded by reefs and sandbanks, that no one else would be allowed to explore. It wasn't important now that she was with him, and he knew himself well enough to realize how inaccurate his impressions might be. He felt as if the weight of his own meaningless life was being taken off his back.

They walked from the station, streets freshened by cold

271

wind. They told each other it was good to walk. Gulls squawked over the roofs, and he wondered how he had lived even for a few days without their sound. He had to get used to not hearing that mocking cry of freedom. In every place he had been the noise had an edge of malice, the over-zealous mimicking of the free calling to the unfree when in fact their sounds were signals to each other and had nothing to do with him. Yet he loved their cries, as if he'd once had the voice-mechanism for making them himself but had at some time been struck dumb.

The noise of the gulls over the seafront was less piercing, their calls were poignant, however, because he was with someone who made him feel unimportant but happy. He saw breakers rolling up the shingle and battering the walls, the tide rushing in like flocks of swans trying to escape destruction. Each wave seemed dead-set for himself, and he wanted a rest from such never-ending force. The sight of their unwearying remorselessness exhausted him.

It was hard to believe he had tolerated the sea-going life for so long – now that he had given it up. But everyone had to earn a living, and he had taken the way of least resistance after looking out of Clara's window and deciding that on the sea he would find both vocation and a living. He was young and, much to Clara's relief, who wouldn't otherwise have known what to do with him, had asked no questions. From an orphanage on to a ship hadn't been much of a big step, and once he had paraded his decision, youthful stubbornness turned it into an obsession.

Few choices had been possible, but when looked back on they formed obvious landmarks whose positions never varied from the place in which the years of life had set them. The big changes of choosing the sea, and leaving the sea, had left him feeling sufficiently elated to want as many more variations as there would be time for in his life, though to consider probabilities would ruin the clarity of the first choice that came along. Perhaps it had already been made, and only lacked recognition, and a gentle altering of course by a few points. At his age such changes could be made with less disturbance than before because they tended to stay more concealed.

'This may be what is called bracing,' she shouted, 'but I'm frozen!'

He gripped her arm. 'Let's go this way. We'll soon be out of it.' The wind blew strong from the sea, and she tasted salt. They went back to the comfort of shops and people. 'It's better to see such water from the inside of my aunt's flat.'

8

He held open the door, and she went in, to a smell of musty cushions. The clock striking twelve seemed that it would never stop. He pulled the curtains open on their rails, then took off his hat and overcoat. 'Make yourself comfortable. There are about fifty bottles of sherry knocking around, if you want a glass. She liked her tipple of sack from sunny Spain.'

'Nothing at the moment.'

They were silent. When she was with another person she felt even more like herself – vulnerable and defensive, isolated and unable to feel she belonged anywhere. She walked around the room. 'What's that picture?'

'An uncle, killed in the Great War.'

She had not seen such a flat before. 'It's a nice place – grand.'

'I'm glad you like it.'

She didn't, particularly, but he followed her as if it was

273

something special. She had meant that it was nice for him, though wasn't sure he liked it either. The atmosphere weighed too much. When in a strange place her first impulse was to leave, but such hasty feelings were a screen behind which true impressions could form, if she had any, or if she gave them time. She opened one of the side windows, and fresh air pushed at the curtains. 'Is it your home now?'

He nodded, and sat down. 'Good job I kept the central heating on. Everything's as my aunt left it. I'm torn between keeping it exactly like this, and altering it so that I can really call the place mine.'

'I suppose you would enjoy that.'

He walked impatiently up and down the room, as if he were embarrassed, she thought, or felt trapped. 'On the other hand,' he said, 'I could sell it, and buy a house in the country.'

'That sounds a nice idea.'

He stopped under the portrait of his dead uncle. 'I like being close to the sea, on the other hand.'

'There must be a cottage,' she said, 'near the coast.'

She followed him into the kitchen. 'Was your aunt married?'

'Not to my knowledge.'

'Did she have any men?'

It was a stark, almost unthinkable question. He had never even wondered. Clara had seemed old and staid when they first met. Yet she had been younger then than he was now. 'I'm not sure.'

'Funny if she didn't.'

He poured sherry for himself. 'I suppose so, but it needn't be.'

'I'll have one, then.' She wondered whether she felt easier only because she was in the kitchen. 'I like her furniture.' She sat at the large table, remembering her own plastic, formica-topped or stainless-steel equipment, all sparkling and clinical, wipeable, washable, dustable and swillable. In this place you had to scrub properly to get things clean. There were rows of wooden-topped spice jars, huge spoons, old-fashioned saucepans and colanders, zinc buckets, beautiful cups and saucers – all solid and homely. The place was tidy, yet hadn't been done thoroughly for months.

He laughed. 'It's antiquated, and needs replacing. Rip it out, put new stuff in.'

She had opinions, backed by a stare from her grey eyes. 'Don't do that. It must be comforting to live with.'

'If I don't make up my mind quickly I'm inclined to do nothing. Let's take our sherry back to the living-room.'

There was something tentative, almost stricken about him. She had never been in the flat before, but was sure she felt less of a stranger than he did. When he stood in the large bay window and looked at the sea there was no unit of distance by which she could measure his separation not only from her but from every person in the world, and especially from himself.

He gazed as if he had never been close to anyone in his life, never wanted to and never would be, whereas George had always been impersonal and distant when talking to her, though much closer in his silences. She was angry at comparing every man to George, and wished she had known more men in her life. She went close, and said quietly: 'You're *here*, you know. You're not out there any more.'

He turned. 'No doubt about that. I'm where you are. Otherwise I couldn't be so certain about my geographical position.'

'It's good to be useful.' She was flippant. 'Can I see the rest of the flat?'

She followed along the corridor, which needed a light even during the day.

'This is where my aunt slept.'

The room was gloomy, but impressive in its bigness, combining the safety and isolation that she would feel if it were hers. She stopped by the door. The wide bed had a bolster across the top of its deep yellow counterpane. Drawers from a chest had been taken out, and stacked at all angles.

'I've had neither the time,' he said, 'nor the inclination to go through her things, except to get at the necessary legal papers.'

There was a dressing-table by one wall, and a bureau against another. 'It needs time.'

He was close, but did not touch, afraid to narrow the gap, or perhaps wise in knowing that the time had not yet come. 'There's so much stuff, but this is nothing: there's also a boxroom full from floor to ceiling.'

'You don't sleep in here?'

'I have the room she always kept for me. No matter how much shore leave I had she never let me stay more than two or three days. Thought it would spoil me to rely on a ready-made bolt-hole. I understood. She didn't like men in the place. Not even me. Or maybe especially not me. That's why I don't think she ever had a boy-friend – as the awful phrase goes.'

'What did she have?'

His smile was almost sour. 'If there's someone you respect you simply block off enquiries about particular areas. She never asked questions beyond a certain limit about me, so I couldn't put any to her. It was easy for me. On a ship you listen to stories, and maybe tell one or two, but you don't ask questions.'

'Women would,' she said. 'Why don't men? I can't understand it. Maybe men aren't so friendly with each other – unless, I suppose, they're as thick as thieves – though even then they probably don't get personal.'

'Well,' he said firmly, 'it wasn't done with Clara, that's all. In some situations people satisfy your curiosity if you have patience and know them long enough. But with my aunt, it was sufficient that she existed, and that she condescended to know me. Hard to put it more accurately than that, but it's true enough that without her I would have been nothing.'

Pam sat on a stool which he must have brought in from the kitchen to reach some high built-in cupboards. 'She liked the fact that you were an officer in the Merchant Navy, though, didn't she?'

He thought about it. 'She would have preferred the *Royal* Navy.'

All the same, she couldn't understand his lack of curiosity, and considered that he and his aunt must have looked a weird pair when they were together. 'Don't you want to know what she really thought?'

He sat on the bed. 'Not particularly.'

'I'd go through everything with a fine-tooth comb,' she said, 'and find out what I could.'

'You sound more interested than I am.'

'Perhaps that's because I've had a more sheltered life.'

'Not more than mine, I'm sure.'

'And you make her sound so mysterious.'

Her curiosity was flattering, and an improvement on her apathy of a few days ago. 'I didn't intend to.'

'I mean to yourself.' His own room was half the size of Clara's, with truckle bed and plain chest of drawers, wash-hand stand and flowered bowl-and-jug set, though there was a small sink in the corner. There was also a table with books, an armchair, a framed map of the world on one wall and an oil painting of a sailing ship in full bloom on the other. 'You were probably the only person she loved,' Pam said, 'though I don't suppose you needed to bring me here to hear that.'

He leaned against the wall as if he had drunk too much the night before, and was only now feeling the alcoholic distortion break into his system. 'Perhaps I did.'

He had meant to reveal something more, but held himself back. There was always the danger of falling and, once started, the death of never stopping. He shook himself. What was there to tell, in any case, except that there was chaos in his mind? All he ever said was superficial, while anything vital was too insubstantial to be put into words. There was no certainty as to final truth, nothing on which to fasten emotions which racked him, because whatever wires there had been were rusted, and would snap at the least touch.

She thought he was going to faint. 'Are you all right?'

Common talk over the years, had he lived in a normal family, would have put all praise and scandal in its place. He had missed the benefit of such revelations which, he thought, was just as well. 'Seems I drank too much last night. There are certain things one ought not to tell oneself, though I suppose there shouldn't be. Clara once said: "Whatever you do, don't have any regrets. Regret nothing – but at the same time never do harm to anyone, and always try to behave yourself, so that at least you don't have regrets of *that* sort." She was strong, plain, generous and, I sometimes think, sentimental to the core.'

He had to get away from a place which was only tolerable because he was here with a person of whom his Aunt Clara would have disapproved. Or would she? He had known better than to bring anyone in those days, and Clara had appreciated his tact. She'd had enough to do in putting up with him.

Pam hoped he was right in the summing-up of his aunt, while wondering whether she was as all-powerful as he made out. 'It doesn't really sound as if she was sentimental.'

Clara had probably deprecated his lack of courage in never bringing anyone to see her. So did he, now that it was too late. 'Let's say she was wise, then.'

Shelves in the spare room held cartons tied with string gone brown with age, and cardboard boxes were piled on the floor. 'It's no use staring,' she said, after they had laid them along the corridor, 'and not doing anything to sort every one.'

He could think of better ways to spend the rest of his life, wanting to throw the lot out for the dustbin men, with a suitable tip for their trouble. He didn't care to know what might be gleaned from so many dusty boxes, each with the year clearly pencilled, and splitting under the weight of albums, diaries, bundles of letters, journals, theatre programmes, receipts, bank statements, tourist brochures, railway timetables, Harrods' catalogues, menus, scrapbooks, newspapers and magazines, drawings and photographs. An investigation of such material would spoil the purity of what Clara had ordained for him. He preferred the rosy miasma of endless speculation to information that would fill the gaps in Clara's life and his own, and even that of his mother's.

'You've lived out of a suitcase all your life,' Pam said, 'or even a kitbag for some of it, so I expect you're a bit scared. Maybe I would be.'

He had never been afraid of anything. If she thought that, he told himself, she didn't understand him. But why should she, when they had known each other such a short time? To inspect Clara's boxes, and relate whatever he found to himself, would be a surrender to the forces of continuity and order, the taking of which path he could hardly be expected to find attractive after a life at sea.

Whoever you were, you sooner or later became part of deaths and departures over which you had no control. It was not fear, he said, but inconvenience, and the distaste at being controlled by the uncontrollable which he had formerly been in a position to put up some fight against. Facing the unpredictable sea, you had training, experience, luck, intuition and native-born sense to match its antics, and so rarely felt total helplessness.

'I once knew a man,' he said, 'who at sixty years of age went to Australia for a two-month holiday. At the end of his stay, while he was still there, he wrote to an estate agent in England, and signed the necessary papers for them to sell the house he owned and auction all the furniture and inherited possessions. Anything not saleable was for the junk man. He never saw the house again, and was not unhappy, with his two-roomed shack near Sydney. He got work, though he wasn't short of money. It would be sensible for me as well, to go somewhere pleasant to live, and forget all this.'

The idea chilled her. He had made the story up, she decided. 'It's none of my business what you do.'

He was startled by her brusqueness. They sat in the living-room. 'I've never known anyone who had much more than what they stood in.'

'You'd better grow up, then,' she said. 'You always had this flat to come to, didn't you?'

'I know, but it's hardly the billet for a seafaring man!'

She was irritated. His argument seemed silly. 'What is?'

'If I knew, I wouldn't be here.' He was aware of what he wanted, but couldn't say it. There was nothing to do except continue talking, until she divined what he needed her to say, said plainly to him what he could not say to her, and mean what she said, till all certainty was gone and he was then able to say it for both of them. It was a perilous course, for though she might know what he wanted, she would strongly resent the onus of choice he put on her. In the meantime she might get bored or annoyed, and walk out, never to bother with him again.

She said ironically: 'And where *would* you be, then?'

'I'm a realist. I suppose I would be where I am at this moment.'

If he doesn't search through the stuff now, she thought, he'll never do it. Without knowing why, she felt it imperative that he look at the papers, because something important *must* be among them. He was aware of it also, which was why he felt an almost irresistible urge to discard the boxes. So much clutter was intimidating. They reproached him for a wasted life, or so he might have thought.

Whatever the risk, she must persuade him to get on with the process which could only eradicate the icy emptiness that took him over when he forgot for a few minutes that she was in the room. She didn't like such a mood in him. It was threatening, almost frightening. She sensed it as much for him as for herself. She was aware of the risk if he opened them, however, and swung to thinking that whether he looked at his papers or not was none of her business. Why was she getting into a thing like this? Was she treading carelessly into a continent of

280

misery? But she had learned something in the last few months, summed up by the fact that it was better to say yes than no.

His hands were cold when she turned and held them. 'You won't have much peace of mind till you get going on that so-called rubbish. I'm sure I shan't.'

Her palms and fingers folded over the top of his fists. He may not have wanted such friendliness, but as far as she was concerned there was no substitute. Little as the gesture might mean, she had no control over making it, and if her motion could be described as letting herself go, she had the strength of mind not to be ashamed or draw back, but held on in all innocence for both of them because there was something he had to do, and she was determined that he do it.

'You're right,' he said. 'They've got to be tackled' – knowing that if he hadn't brought her to the flat he would have slung the lot out with no thought of what was in them.

PART FOUR
The Women

1

Clara began with her mother, whose maiden name was Moss, and first name Rachel. She was born in 1860, and her father was a tea merchant who had settled in London from Hamburg thirty years before. By intelligence and toil he became well-to-do. A birth certificate in the first box was leaved between yellowing paper headed by a stark engraving of warehouse and offices. The engraving for the export house was of a clipper in full sail and, small as the letter-head was, a child had put tiny men on the mast tops with coloured pencils.

Rachel was the middle daughter of three, and the mother had died after the birth of the third child. 'I am big, gawky, with scarlet flamy hair and with freckles like sparks, and I do not like myself,' she had written in a school exercise book. There was a small painting taken at some time from its frame which, though as unclear as if seen through a window beaded with moisture, showed her hair to be plentiful and auburn, as firmly tied by a band as her spirit seemed to be held behind her unhappy eyes and shapely sensitive mouth. She had a high clear forehead, and the only freckles visible on the cracked portrait appeared to be on the wrist which rested on her knees.

A clutch of pages had been torn from her leather-bound diary. The spine was worn away, and the ink brown where it had been black: 'The one I am to marry is an honourable man. He is good and pleasant, but I don't love him. The rabbi who spoke to me about it is an honourable man. My father, whom I love, is an honourable man. They are all honourable. But they are all men. What can I do, being alone as I am? I shall ask questions at Passover, but they won't hear what is in my voice. Miss Silver, who talked to me for so long about free will, denies now that she did, and says I ought to marry whomsoever my father wishes, and that I am lucky a husband has been found for me, and that I am to be taken care of, and that she wished she had a husband and children instead of having to teach for her miserable living etc. But I will not marry Benjamin Green, whether or not he is the rabbi's nephew, because I saw *him* while walking from Schule with Miss Silver last Sabbath, and he saw me, and I know that he followed us down Edgware Road as far as the Park, as he knew I wished him to do. I hoped he would follow me for ever, and that I would walk until Miss Silver could keep her pace no longer, when I was on my own and still walking, and then I would turn and he would be there, and with no one else but the two of us we could meet and talk, just as one day we shall be together always.'

The script varied, as if the ink were from another bottle, or because of an indifferent nib and a nervous style of writing: 'I spoke to him. We were shopping and I saw him on Oxford Street. He saw me, and stayed in one place, and I deliberately avoided Miss Silver. I took his hand and we walked up a court. His name is Percy Phillips, and to me it doesn't matter that he is not one of us. God is not blind when He looks on people, and must see that we are all the same.

'"Why me?" he said.

'"Because I have chosen you," I told him.

'He said he had loved me since he first saw me but couldn't understand why I should love him. I said that I did, and that he was mine, and wasn't that enough? Far more than any *elegant sufficiency*, he said with a smile. We were together for half an hour. Poor people were begging while we were talking, but they were shadows, because I was happy. "I will pass here next week," I said, "and we can meet." He nodded, and told me that he worked in his father's office in the City, from which the family property was managed, and that with so much work he might not be able to come. I said he must, and he agreed that he would. "You must also see me on Saturday evening," I said, "whether we speak or not." He said that, providing the family didn't go to their house on the Kent coast, which they did on occasional weekends, he would do so. I maintained that it would be a better plan if, when we next saw each other, we walked away together. I would never go back to my home. My life there had finished, so why not let our shared existence begin? I could not remain where it was abhorrent to me, nor stay away from where it would be heaven to be.'

A different handwriting, on smaller paper, seemed to be part of a letter. '. . . wrong, because my son tells me he wants to marry your daughter. I realize, as I am sure you also do, that because she is a Jewess, and as we are Christians, this is quite out of the question.

'There is nothing further to be said about it. I would not want to be an obstacle to anyone's happiness under normal circumstances, but nothing in this case promises the possibility of any progress towards bringing them together. It would be understandable to me that you do not want your daughter to become a Christian, and therefore you must see that it is quite unthinkable to me that my son should enter your Faith, even if that were possible.

'This situation must be explained to them, and I shall certainly do my part in the matter, so that it shall not be allowed to get out of our control. You must see, my dear sir, that there is a danger of this, though I emphasize however, and I am sure you will agree, that the status of our families is such that were it not for the matter of Religion there would be no obstacle against the young people being joined in Holy Matrimony. How it began is beyond . . .'

'She did not,' Clara commented in her journal, 'fail to notice the gist of James Phillips' letter. All she had to do was become a Christian. There was no other way. Any self-respecting Jew – and all Jews are self-respecting, perhaps because they are more than usually God-fearing, so I understand – would be dismayed at her action. There was a lot of talk at that time of converting the Hebrews to Christianity, and many societies were formed to make the attempt. I've often wondered why, but I suppose there must have been some feeling among the more sincerely religious English that the only real Christians could be Jews, and that if numbers of Jews became Christians then the Christian religion might begin to appear more Christian than it seemed to be at the time. So the Phillipses would have been happy enough to make things easy for Rachel to become one of them. Their son Percy was an only child, and loving him as they did, and fearing for him as I understand one does for an only son, they did all they could to make him happy.

'But father was never happy. No one could have made him so, though mother gave him more happiness than most. The very fact that he must use all his faculties, and fight every inch of the way to get to know her, kept him spiritually awake right up to the time of her death. With someone of his own sort, whoever that might have been, but whom he might more easily have understood both by heredity and upbringing, he would have quickly become dull and slothful. By continually making the effort to understand her – and at the end he was close enough – he stayed alive. Married to anyone else, his first attempt at suicide would have been his last. I'm convinced of it.

'Rachel was only a lukewarm Christian, and so was he, come to that, though they believed in the same God. No form of worship would have been able to cure his melancholia. He would sit for days in his study as if fixed to the huge mahogany desk, moving only to light a cigarette, or to turn the page of a book or newspaper whose print his eyes couldn't fix on sufficiently to read a single word.

'At five or six years of age I remember trying to look

through the keyhole, or pushing the door further and further open, and waiting for him to waken because mother had said that he wasn't like other people because he could sleep while sitting at his desk. I stood there with Emma one day, who was a year younger, but after a few minutes she began to shake at the sight of our unmoving father, and wept in terror. "He's dead, Clara! Look! He's dead! Why doesn't he go to heaven?"'

He moved neither head nor hands, though Clara knew he must have heard, as she pulled Emma away. He was awake, but paralysed. When he wasn't, he went to his office, sometimes every day for weeks. He would walk in the garden and cut roses. There were occasions when nobody knew where he had gone. He would come home dirty and tired, carrying a picture, or flowers, or presents for the children. Then they would see neither their mother nor their father for days, going quietly to bed at night after spending their evenings in the kitchen with the cook. Clara told Emma that she would never marry. Emma said she wouldn't, either. 'Nor shall I,' John said. 'I'm going to be an engineer, and engineers go to foreign places, so they can't be married.'

'But they get eaten by crocodiles,' Emma reminded him.

'Not me,' John said. 'I shall have a gun, never fear!'

Sometimes their father would go to hospital for a few weeks, and Rachel told them that because he went to sleep at his desk they had to take him away in order to wake him up. People went to hospital either to die or get better, and he went there to get better. An account book gave his income for 1895 as eight thousand pounds, and Clara had kept bills and receipts to prove that he had always gone to the best places.

A photograph showed him at Broadstairs after coming out of the convalescent home. On his own at the time, he had arranged for a local photographer to take the picture in the open air. His hands rested on a silver-headed stick, and he was looking towards the water. Forty years old, he was wearing a derby hat and an overcoat, and rimless spectacles. His thin lips curved down with settled apprehension, and his eyes seemed to be looking at the vision of an eternally receding mountain range whose heights he knew he would not be able to scale. Nor would his thoughts catch up with those fragments of his mind that always eluded him. His faculties at times were clear and active, but there was part of himself that he could never find, and the effort to do so occasionally became too much. Clara thought it was this vacancy in his powers of perception that Rachel had sensed at their first chance passing in the street. Something was missing that yet belonged to him, and she thought that by searching, and firmly tying down whatever it was, she could thereby give it back to him whole, an action that would produce a lifelong stability of soul between them.

Perhaps in more lucid moments he had seen that something similar needed to be done for her. However it was, they sought each other's soul all their lives, and didn't give up even at the darkest hours. Because they did not entirely find in each other that which they knew to exist, though at times they were closer to it than anyone incapable of making the effort, they never stopped being in love. 'Your mother,' Percy said to Clara after he had become a widower, 'was from a devoted race,' implying that she had given everything to him, as he at his best moments had tried to give all that was good in himself to her.

A photograph taken in the garden showed Rachel as a grave-looking women with a high forehead and an abundance of hair. Clara was fifteen, her sister Emma fourteen, and their brother John sixteen. Emma had at this time the same tormented eyes as her father, and a distortion of the mouth which was due as much to having moved as because she was horrified at being fixed for ever at this time with people to whom, she said afterwards to Clara, she did not feel she belonged. But her eyes stayed still and were perfectly caught, vainly trying to grasp a vision that would not come to her. In physique she was slight like her father, but grew taller

290

in the next few years. Her look suggested that she had already experienced much suffering, and would spend the rest of her life trying to forget the ordeal. 'She had seen none at all,' Clara commented, 'though what she appeared to feel might have been a preview of what had yet to happen.'

The cardboard boxes devoted to John were marked NOT TO BE OPENED - EVER! But traces of broken sealing wax showed that they had been examined more than once by Clara. There were school reports, textbooks, letters sent home, a picture postcard from Cromer ('seashells good, weather bad') as well as a cloth cycling map marking a tour through Belgium, on which each night-stop was shown in such heavy pencil that the name of the place was almost obliterated.

Letters from the trip were tied up with a Baedeker guidebook that was falling to pieces. After Ostend, on the way out, John stayed the night at Dixmude: 'A level run of nearly thirty kilometres along a poor road of paving stones which can't be much good for my old bone-shaker. We passed many dairy farms – Lord, how many! It rained some of the way, but my cape kept most of it off. Arthur had a puncture near a village called Keyem, and I think all the children of Belgium watched him mend it. They thought it a great lark when we knocked on a door and asked for a bowl of water to find the hole.

'We got a room at the Hotel de Dixmude (unpretending, but good enough for us), had a wash, then went into the church, and inspected the fine rood-loft my tutor told us about, as well as an Adoration of the Magi by Jordaens. Tomorrow, we go on to Ypres, then east to Menin, Courtrai and Audenarde and, Oh dear, I don't know how many places yet, but I don't doubt, and neither do you, dear mother and father (and Clara and Emma, as well as that horrid little dog), that there will be a letter from each benighted spot.

'I'm sore from the saddle, though am told such an affliction will pass with time and wear, but in all other ways it is wonderful being awheel in flat-as-a-pancake Flanders. I understand that the Ardennes area is hilly! I shall have to stop being silly! All we hope is that the weather stays dry.

'Arthur sits on his bed playing the flute, and if he doesn't *pipe-down* soon I shall throw my pillow at him, and they have very big ones in Belgium. So that you don't know of our fight, dear parents, I will close this fond epistle from the almost benighted bicycle-pilgrims!'

Every letter saved, every hotel bill, steamer and railway ticket from John's holidays, as well as engineering notebooks, drawings and profiles, plans and layouts, and estimates for schemes and bridges. All packed away and hoarded, and for what? Paper well-written on, in a small neat hand as if even a margin would be so much square-inchage of waste. A clever, fun-loving, patriotic uncle dead fifty years before his time, and never known.

Another box was set aside for the war that had to come. John was a soldier at university, and later with the Territorial Force. Photographs showed him at summer camp, and it was easy to pick out the young man with dark curly hair and a handsome hawkish face in his middle twenties. A bushy moustache in later photographs made his face somewhat longer and fiercer. Other snapshots showed him laughing when caught trying to pull down a tent rope, or when a friend was preparing to take the jump at leapfrog. Happy days while they were playing, and Clara noted that it was such a pity that reality caught up with them.

During one of his leaves he stood with a sister on either side, premature regret shaping their set mouths, while John was smiling as if, under the circumstances, nothing less would do. In another photograph, next to a horned gramophone, he sat with a small white dog on his knee. There were scores of letters, neatly tied together, as well as badges and buttons in a cloth bag closed by a drawstring. A dozen damp-stained diaries and notebooks were filled with the same fine hand, except that much of the script was in pencil, and had come back from France:

'I am sitting on a stool in a deep dugout with thirty feet of solid chalk and sandy clay above my head. I feel very safe. I am living with three of my fellow-officers in a place eight feet by twelve. It has been fine all day, and our guns have not ceased pounding. The day for our big attack has been a long time coming, but the whole army is as confident as can be, and will go over the parapet keen as mustard to get into contact with the enemy. Our men know they are his master in all but barbarous acts.

'It is now Monday, and has been a great day. I was interrupted all night long with messages, and so got little sleep. I was up at five-fifteen, and at Brigade HQ at 5.27. At Zero Hour – 5.30 – for our operation, every gun we had opened fire and continued hard as could be until we gained our final objective. It began to rain as soon as the battle started, but stopped about 8.30. Later in the day it snowed, but cleared again. While our casualties have not been light they have not been nearly as heavy as at the Somme. Our men behaved wonderfully well, and I am quite proud of my sappers and officers. They carried things along marvellously, and obtained good results.

'Thursday: Shells were passing over our heads when I was out with my orderly. A wind blew towards us from where the shells were landing and exploding. Suddenly we were both half smothered. We hurried forward to get out of the cloud, but soon were complaining of sore throats and chests from the gas. We should have rested, but went on over the battlefield. The padres were first and foremost. I thought one of them was an Artillery Officer, as he was helping to guide a gun over a soft bit of ground. Large parties were out collecting the dead, and when they got a certain number together, service would be read. The padres are responsible for the proper burial, and for the collection of all papers belonging to the dead. Just as it was growing dark I passed the burial party again still at their work, and I wondered how much longer they would stay. The ground we won looks so hopeless. So many wasted lives. Corpses all around. One of the enemy's support trenches was strewn with dead men from end to end. The fire from our artillery was so effective, and with such a preponderance of it, that a man behind our barrage could not easily escape death or such awful wounds as I have ever seen. I picked up the latest pattern rifle and some rounds from one of these dead Germans, and hope I shall be able to bring it home on my next leave. There are so many stories that I want to tell, but none of my *real* thoughts about what happens here can be put into words. I sometimes feel they never will be. Artillery is louder than all speech. When it is close and continuous even the shape of people's lips is distorted, and they stay calm, though the eyes tell another tale. When the barrage is still I have so much work to do, or I am too numb to think . . .

'The thing I abhor more than all else in this war, after the actual loss of life, is that the dead are allowed to lie out in the open, uncovered and uncared for in so many cases. We see in and about our trenches hordes of ponderous rats. I am not sure what species, but they are certainly carnivorous. There is nothing the men out here loathe more than seeing their lumbering bodies dragging along, knowing they have fattened off their dead comrades, and may well fatten off them if ever the time comes. Numerous rat holes are seen over every grave, and our greatest delight is the destruction of these rodents who, by and large, are the only victors of these battles. And children think that Ratty in *The Wind in the Willows* is a lovable character! What a time he would have had out here! But we shall beat the Hun. We shall go on to the end, and certainly defeat him at his own game of soldiering.'

There was a pile of plain buff-coloured Army Books 152, their pages of squared paper, in which were written factual day-to-day diaries telling what time he got up and went to bed, and what the weather was like. Tom had space in his room to set the notebooks on a shelf for further reading.

When everything had been dragged clear from the cluttered boxroom he discovered a shallow cupboard built into the wall. A zinc lock held the latch in place, but he gripped hard and twisted it from the wood. Inside were measuring tapes, photographic enlargement equipment, a tripod, an engineering level, a miner's compass, a clinometer and some longish thing wrapped in a tarpaulin sheet which he carried to the living-room. The knot had been hammered into a compact ball, but he pressed and squeezed till the individual strands worked free.

'I don't know whether I learned in the orphanage that you never *cut* string,' Tom said, 'or in the Navy, but it's another old habit that dies hard.'

Maybe it's part of his nature, Pam thought, to waste nothing, and to let no job daunt him. 'Makes no difference,' she said, 'as long as you get it undone.'

She took a basket from the kitchen and went out, leaving him bemused with his clues and time-schemes, stooping among heaps of ephemera from which he tried to make sense.

Going up a narrow street from the sea, rain drove against her mackintosh. For half the way, till wind blew it clear, a stench of mothballs enveloped her, because the coat came from the hall cupboard and had not been worn for months. Water filled the gutters, and a car splashed her almost to the waist. She stepped across the street to the shops. He needed feeding. Such delving and sifting ate at him from the inside, and made his face thin.

She walked on, a zig-zag course towards the station. The wider road exposed her, icy rain flurrying when she turned towards the seafront. She would never find the flat. She would knock at a door, and someone whom she hadn't seen before would answer. She would wander around town for the rest of her life wearing Clara's mackintosh and with a bag of shopping on her arm.

'Come in,' he said.

'The weather's foul.' She took the mackintosh into the bathroom and hung it to dry.

He had a rifle in his grease-smeared hands. 'I was going to come with an umbrella and meet you, but couldn't be sure of the direction.'

'I was all right. I didn't get wet. Where did that come from?'

His shirt sleeves were rolled up, and she noticed a tattoo on his muscular forearm, a fearsome dragon twisted around the words 'Death or Glory'. Such things decorating men's bodies made them look like woad-painted people from the Stone Age.

'Youthful indiscretion,' he laughed. 'Done in a drunken moment, if I remember. And I only just do!'

'I meant the gun.'

He held it high. 'John must have brought it back – a genuine German rifle from the Arras battlefield. There are a dozen rounds as well. I'll stow it where it came from. No good to us.'

'Didn't do him much good, either.' She set her basket on the floor. A circular bronze plaque several inches in diameter lay on the piano top. Britannia with trident, and wreath held forth, were accompanied by a lion, surrounded by HE DIED FOR FREEDOM AND HONOUR, and the name JOHN CHARLES PHILLIPS in a rectangle above the lion's head. She put it down quickly, as if it were still alive with grief and loss. The first of two telegrams said: 'I regret to inform War Office reports Capt. J. C. Phillips died of wounds April 26th.' The second contained words of solace: 'The King and Queen deeply regret the loss you and the army have sustained by the death of your son in the service of his country. Their majesties truly sympathize with you in your sorrow.'

'That's how it was done.' He put the rifle away. 'Their son, and my uncle, may well have taught me a thing or two.'

'Perhaps if he had lived,' she said, 'you wouldn't have been packed off to the orphanage.'

296

2

Clara said: 'It was too much to bear. No man was ever more destroyed by the death of his son.' It must have been the same for all fathers, and worse perhaps for all mothers. The ranks of a family would be torn into by such a death as if a cannon ball had gone through, and they would not close for years.

Percy went to the recruiting office to enlist. He was nearly sixty. Too old. He offered money if they would take him. He wanted to go to France and die, or to get his revenge for John's death. 'He went day after day, and mother couldn't stop him. She was too grieved to try. Father was utterly broken down. One of the sergeants brought him home, and mother thanked him with half a crown for beer. The same sergeant accompanied him a few days later, but refused another half crown.

'Mother showed me a letter,' Clara said, 'that she would send to the War Graves Commission. John's grave should not be marked with a cross, because he was Jewish. He must be buried under the Hebrew sign, no matter what religion he gave when he enlisted. Though he had not lived as a Jew he was nonetheless one by the Law, as were all children, she insisted, born of a Jewish mother. Father was apathetic, but when he saw the letter he commented that though John had been brought up as a Christian, Rachel was quite right. And what did it matter, since both Jews and Christians believed in the same God? As far as he was concerned they were one people.'

The reply said that in spite of the case being an unusual one it was quite possible and perhaps even proper for his grave to be marked as that of a Member of the Jewish Faith, but that since his records showed him not to be one, it would be necessary to have the authority of a rabbi before her wishes as Captain Phillips' mother could be carried out. Rachel went from one synagogue to another until she obtained what she wanted from a rabbi who had known her father. Emma went with her, and the rabbi who gave his consent said that she was Jewish too, and ought not to forget it when the time came for her to choose a husband and have children.

'We went to see John's grave after the war. Going through the customs at Boulogne was a tedious business. The French officials were very thorough, and there was a long queue, but we patiently put up with it. Father had by this time sufficiently recovered to motor us to Arras, though the roads were still bad and many villages in ruins. Lodgings were scarce, and Emma and I shared a bed at the Hotel de L'Univers.

'The French people were everywhere sympathetic, though Emma said she smelt nothing but death, and wished she had not come. Father enjoyed the travelling, seeming to forget his troubles and constrictions as we drove along the cobbled roads admiring the scenery. But Emma and I wept at seeing him and mother clinging to each other at the cemetery. At the same time father seemed younger than for many years because, as he said, he felt closer to John than when in England. We took a camera, and there is a photograph of the rabbi-padre standing between father and mother, with Emma and me behind. We were at the grave marked by John's name and the Star of David. The Englishman in charge of the cemetery was much taken with Emma, and pressed her hand a little too hard and long, she said, when we left.'

Percy later sent fifty pounds to the rabbi 'to be distributed, as he thought fit, among charities which would in some way benefit his co-religionists'. Percy had always given to good causes, believing that those organizations for assisting the poor and the lower classes should be amply supported by the more fortunate, who ought to give as much as they could so that it would not be necessary for the state to help – which Percy would see as the beginning of universal corruption and degradation.

Each year he took a notebook and a list from his desk and, without a secretary, stayed at home to perform the charitable duty of sending cheques to asylums, hospitals, medical colleges, missionary societies, fishermen's funds, lifeboat institutions, and soldiers' homes. There were receipts for money he had sent to an organization for 'Promoting Christianity Among the Jews' and another for 'Assisting Jews to Return to the Promised Land' and Clara wondered how much their mother was aware of this, knowing it was probable that Percy never told her.

He had a life-subscription of two votes to an infant asylum for orphans close to London, to which he sent extra money when an appeal was made, or when his conscience urged him – as it sometimes did on recovering from one of his nervous attacks. He visited the orphanage twice a year because, he said, it did his heart good to see children being treated well who were, after all, those beings on whom the future of the British Empire depended.

'Father said that Emma was much like mother had been when young. She had the same reddish hair, as well as a fine figure that turned every man's head. Even women stopped to look at her. Her wit could be scorching, and her humour also had a bite to beware of. Her eyes were not good for any distance, and she tried to do without glasses, though on the visit to John's grave near Arras she wore them all the time, frameless half-lenses which, hardly visible until you were quite close, gave an attractive and mysterious glitter to her face.

'At the restaurant in the evening we were a typical English family making a visit to a dear one's grave, as many parties did in those years. We were also, Emma said, enjoying the good food. Father's pepper-grey hair was brushed straight back, and he wore a dark suit, with a high collar and tie, and a watch at his waistcoat. He smiled faintly at Emma and me when we talked about the events of the day in such a way that the people round about thought we were more carefree than we ought to be.

'Father's illness had improved in the last few years, Emma observed, because what attacks he now had were called grief, and that was something in which he was not alone in those days during and after the Great War.'

Rachel wore a high-necked black velvet dress, and a locket around her neck which held her dead son's photograph. Under it, seen only when she leaned, was a six-pointed golden Star of David. Mostly she sat straight, and it was invisible. Her hair, pulled back and tied, was more ashen than red. To the daughters' amusement and occasional embarrassment Percy would reach across and hold Rachel's hand tenderly for a few moments. She told him not to be silly, though Clara knew that without such gestures she would wither and die. She spoke very little since John's death, and none of us, said Clara, not even father, knew what she was thinking. Her pride was her strength, but her belief in God gave her both pride and strength. Which came first was impossible to say. God was her rock, and she turned into the rock on which the family leaned, though at a cost of denying her basic element which was that of speech. She could not take such weight and yet allow her heart to speak. The tragedy had worn her almost to silence. Speech was painful because her heart could no longer support her gaiety of spirit, and so she became sparing of words, an uncharacteristic state, but one which allowed her to go on living as their mainstay. She thought that because she had broken her father's heart by marrying out of the Faith John had been taken away from her, but Emma said in that case what had the millions of others been punished for?

There was nothing to prove that if she had not fallen in love with Percy and run away from home she would have suffered any the less. Life was tribulation, whoever you were, and whichever way you looked at it, but what she had endured from her husband, and again by losing her son, at last forced her to wonder why she had been so mindlessly in thrall as to have broken connection with her family. She regretted nothing, but speculated on what had driven her to pursue

300

something which, set far beyond Percy's love of her and hers of him, seemed to have vanished in the ashes of life.

The folly of a childish and burning will had, on first seeing her future husband, sent her on a course that was endless. She fell in love with the expression on his face, sensing a vision of the future which, while not clear in its details, drew her even more strongly, a vision of his illness, and perhaps beyond that an intimation of the death of their son. She had been blind to this disaster and suffering that waited in the future, as everyone was, but a hint of it was there, and she knew it, and drove herself even more blindly to the actuality which would never let her go. She had been in the grip of a will so profound and valid as to make her commit the terrible sin of abandoning her family, so that when her parents died she could not go their funeral.

Yet even at this age, after all that had happened in her life, she knew she was the same daughter, except that she lived as if afraid to tread down hard on the soil under her feet for fear she would go on falling for ever.

In order to soothe her pain she lit a candle in a small brass holder every Friday night at the dinner table, which glowed by her side until the meal was over. On striking the match she said a phrase in the clearest Hebrew, and Clara remarked in her diary that while this took place the others remained silent. Rachel said to her daughters: 'This is for John, for you two, for all of us, and for all Jews. We always lit the candle at home.'

She sat at the table of the hotel-restaurant in Arras with a husband who never ceased to say that he adored her, and she smiled and returned the pressure of his fingers over her wrist knowing that each morning she could wake up and thank God that she at least had the blessing of two beautiful daughters. On such a thought she lifted her glass of wine to drink.

Percy lit a cigar, and ordered coffee, and looked at his 'Blue Guide to Belgium and the Western Front' to decide where they would go in the morning. The girls smoked cigarettes.

'It's bad for your health,' Rachel told them every time. 'You should be careful with your health' – which caused them to recall the constant phrase to men friends: 'For God's sake, do be careful! If you aren't, it'll be bad for my health!'

But their mother wasn't to know such details about their lives. Not that Clara had been in love with any of the men. Well, not much, at any rate, though it had been the thing to do with one or two who were special, before they went to France or some such place. The only man she'd really loved was John, and still did, and wept silently at night, knowing he would not be in the house when they woke up in the morning. Now that he was dead she loved Emma, who was eerily like her mother and didn't object any more to being told so. Yet it often seemed to Clara that John hadn't been her brother, nor was Emma her sister, otherwise how could she love them so passionately, and at times with such misery in her heart?

3

Tom emptied a whole box which contained items devoted to the motoring tour in northern France: boat tickets, hotel accounts, petrol bills, maps and plans, pamphlets from the Syndicats d'Initiative, photographs and postcards, and bank receipts on money exchanged, as well as the Blue Guide and a diary kept jointly by Clara, and Emma his mother. They travelled towards the Channel along part of the route cycled by John twelve years before, with the intention of staying at Dixmude, but the place was still in ruins so they went on to Ostend, putting up at the Grand Hotel to eat oysters.

In the morning Percy could not get out of bed. Or he would not. He was ill. From what? He said to Rachel that he did not care to leave the Continent, that he could not bear to go back, and wanted to return to Arras and be close to John's grave till he too died.

Rachel said that she also would like to do such a thing, but what was the use? What God gives, He takes away. She held his hand, wiped his tears, kissed him, and steadied a cup so that he could drink tea. She comforted him, but he wept and would not move. He was ill. But there were no symptoms – no headache, palpitations, vomiting, diarrhoea or sweats. Talk of getting a doctor enraged him. Nevertheless, he was ill, because he would not get out of bed.

The girls pleaded. They had to be back in London because there were people to see, dates to keep, shows to go to. When they suggested getting on the boat by themselves, Rachel's face stiffened in an anger they had never seen. They must wait until their father was well, when they would go home together. Emma said she wanted to leave now, and didn't see why they both shouldn't. Or they could all get on the boat, even father, and have the motoring club bring the car back.

Rachel's voice came close to a shout. 'We've come here as a family, and we will go back the same way, as soon as your father's better.'

Moody and subdued, the sisters wanted something to happen but didn't know what. They walked around the town till, in half an hour, they decided that they had 'done it' and there was nothing more to see. They sat in a café, passing and repassing the diary to each other. 'You write about this place,' Clara said. 'I wrote all that rubbish about the last one.'

'And a fat lot you wrote, after all,' Emma said. 'Only two lines.'

'Two and a half,' Clara said. 'I say, don't look now, but look at that fat old man over there.'

'What fat old man?' asked Emma.

'I said don't look now,' Clara snapped. 'But look! He's looking at us. I'm sure you could do a whole page on him.'

'You do it, then,' Emma suggested.

'It's *you* he's looking at,' Clara pouted.

'I'm bored,' Emma said.

'You're lazy.'

Emma scribbled several lines, then rested the pencil across the coffee-cup saucer.

'Dirty old devil!' Clara said loudly. 'Just look at him.'

'Oh do leave him be,' said Emma. 'He's only reading the paper.'

'He's not. He's *fiddling* with himself. He really is. Would you believe it? And it's an English newspaper he's reading. He *must* be from Birmingham – or Bradford! It really is too much.' She laughed. 'I'll call the manager.'

'Oh don't, please.' Emma knew her to be capable of it. 'He's not doing anything at all. Stop joking.'

'Well,' Clara said, 'I'm bored as well. Damn this life. I want some fun.'

They rented a hut on the beach, and swam in the sea, but the breakers were grey and cold, and sent them shivering back up the sand. At a hotel dance they met two officers on leave from the Rhine, and did not get to their own beds till two in the morning.

Rachel said, with a lift of her eyebrows, that they seemed to be taking very good care of themselves.

'If we can't,' Clara said, 'who can?'

Percy stayed in bed for three days. He was ill, and they weren't allowed to doubt it. From the window Rachel could see boats leaving for Dover. Waves erupted against the groynes. She played cards with him, and at such times he was cheerful and competent. But after a game or two he would throw the cards off the bed, and begin weeping again. He was ill, he said. Why did she look at him as if he was not? No one believed him. The world was a black glove, and he was inside it.

Rachel looked away. How could a face change so quickly – and what was the reason? – from being fairly normal to one streaked and shivering with an agony she couldn't bear to look at? She felt like the young girl she had been when his first

304

attack came on soon after they were married. Now he had something to grieve for, and so had she, but her feeling of shock and pity was the same as it had been then. His despair was so intense that her own wracking sorrow had no chance of expressing itself. He was ill, and it was easy to see that his spirit was fixed in such fear and torment that he was beyond help – though she would never admit it.

She calmed him by reading in English from the Hebrew Bible she carried, comforting him by intoning in her beautiful voice verses from Job or the Psalms. He held her hand, and adored her, and became still. He thanked God for sending her, for only through her did the darkness recede, and the black glove relax its grip. When he was finally calm she fought to stop her own tears breaking forth, something which his illness never allowed.

He got out of bed, and they stayed three more days so that he could recover before going home. Rachel sent the girls back as they wished, and she and Percy were alone. They held hands when standing on the beach, and while shopping, and made love in the afternoon and at night. They drove up the coast into Holland for a distant view of Flushing on the opposite shore that was pinned down by sunbeams from the troubled sky.

4

The kitchen was clean enough, Pam thought, but not *really* clean. Wanting a rest from two hours of reading, she went up the ladder with a damp rag soaked in detergent, and rubbed a circle of cleanliness the size of a large coin that might be taken for a dab of fresh plaster whose whiteness had not yet merged. Then she rubbed until the paint under the grease became as large as the memorial plaque sent by the King and his grateful people to John's parents.

An attempt at proper cleanliness would mean enlarging the pristine area to take up the whole room. She looked from the ladder and saw dust everywhere. Closer to the ceiling there were cobwebs and spiders' nests. The floor had been swept but not washed. It was tidy but not clean, calling for days of work.

Everything clean was not quite clean. Lace curtains wanted washing, and the water would darken when they were dipped. Folded tea towels needed a visit to the laundrette, and cutlery could do with a rinse and a polish. Heavier curtains in the living-room should go to the cleaners. The pelmets and woodwork ought to be washed down. Everywhere called for dusting, sweeping and scrubbing.

Was life worth throwing away on such labour every week, month, year? You took one breath only in order to draw another, and laboured from birth till no more breath would come. Everything you did in life was useless, except that it kept death at bay and allowed you to live with as much ease as could be managed. Cleanliness was comfort if you had been brought up that way – though it's no business of mine who cleans the flat, she thought, coming down the ladder and putting buckets and rags away. He'll have to get someone else for the job.

She read again for half an hour, then peeled potatoes and put them into boiling water, laid lamb chops under the grill, and cleaned lettuce. While he carried, searched, sorted, pondered and evaluated the long undisturbed hoard she walked in and out of the dining-room, setting the table and putting down a first course. The immersion in a different life pattern, as well as the long time since breakfast, made her stomach turn with hunger like a swimmer coming up for air. The corkscrew was difficult to pull. 'I took a bottle of Mersault from the fridge.'

He opened it.

'You look as if you've just done the nightshift in a soot factory,' she said.

He washed, then sat diagonally from her. With rolled-up sleeves, and a shirt open at the neck, it seemed as if he had lived in the flat all his bachelor days. Even his subdued and worried state emphasized the fact. 'You must have had an interesting hour or two.'

He paused in his eating. 'I'll tell you about it.'

'Take your time.'

'I still don't know who I am, but I'm getting a rough idea as to who I might have been, and that's a beginning.'

She put more of the fish on his plate. 'Have you found anything startling?'

'Not yet. I'm not even born.'

'Keep trying,' she said. 'Knowledge is sacred.'

His eyes were troubled. 'This sort is.'

She was glad he had changed his mind about it, though he was further away than she liked. She served hot food, then set cakes and cheeses close so as not to get up till after the meal. '*You* can make the coffee.'

He poured more wine. 'I'll wash up, too.'

'No. Get on with your sorting.' If she wasn't useful she wouldn't be here. The day out had turned into something else. London seemed a thousand miles off. Her past had vanished. No alteration of surroundings had ever lifted her so much out of herself. Even to wonder what was missing from her consciousness did not put her back in touch. The man whose flat she was in was a stranger, as she no doubt was a stranger to him, so they were at ease with each other. At least she hoped she was. She felt almost married, but without the tangled obsessions that came from having slept in the same bed. She liked being here because she could leave whenever she wanted to.

He told her what he had found, describing how each piece of information was laid aside until something turned up from a box to confirm or complement it. He assembled truths and

307

situations into sequences, like doing a jigsaw puzzle or putting a pack of cards in order during a game of patience. He did not go rigidly from A to B, and hurriedly to Z as if afraid to lose his way should he not finish the story quickly, or as if he couldn't be bothered to make the tale good for her since it only concerned him, or good for himself since it couldn't concern anyone else; but he went on calmly with his circumlocutionary report, taking a fact here, a lead there, describing a book, or a photograph, and quoting from a letter or journal, or an unlabelled sheet of paper on which someone had scribbled thoughts seemingly unrelated or information presumably unsought, and circling the loose pieces until a more or less whole picture formed, the assembling of a mosaic rather than an ordinary account which would have been finished too quickly and thereby diminished in the telling for him, and been less absorbing in the hearing of it for her.

'I have to be careful not to allow the stuff to explain more about myself than it deserves,' he said, having spoken in his precise way to the end of the meal. 'I'm still me, after all, and my fifty years of unknowing haven't been exactly meaningless.'

He was fighting his definitions to the last. She wanted to pity him because, though he might not know it, his face reflected a painful ordeal. He would never admit it, she felt sure, yet she did not envy him the ability to hold it in check, or his fate that had decided he must.

They went into the kitchen, and when the noise of the coffee grinder stopped, he said: 'The same things happen to everyone. It's only when you find out about such events that they seem more fascinating than they should. I read somewhere that everyone's more like their grandparents than their parents, and now I'm not sure whether to believe it. You just have to live with what you know, I suppose, or let all revelations slip into the bloodstream, and then more or less forget them.'

She was no longer sleepy. 'You're only half-way through the story.'

308

Unopened boxes lay over the living-room floor like the jellyfish surrounding the ship off Sabang on that tropical morning when he had almost fainted and dropped overboard. Would they sting if he stepped on them? There was no option but to descend. The box nearest his chair released a smell of stale lavender, a vanishing sweetness that he recognized but could not fix in his memory.

There was the usual jumble of liner and railway tickets, whist-drive score cards, sweepstake certificates, death notices, address books, pocket diaries and dance programmes. He filled plastic bags for the dustbin men, not being a detective on the lookout for information who needed evidence to condemn or acquit. The past now seemed relevant enough to tie himself firmly to it. He had been an orphan, but it hadn't mattered. Aunt Clara had told sufficient for him to think it unimportant to know more. If he had persisted, he was given to understand he would lose even her. She would tell him not to come back. 'That's all I know,' she had snapped at him, 'so ask me nothing else.'

'Damn it,' he said to himself, 'I'll scratch among the rubbish till my fingernails bleed.'

5

'What memories I shall be left with when all this is over!' Clara wrote in her large script. It was open, and naïve, and the rounded generosity of individual letters stared at him like faces that pleaded to be believed. But he shook off all impressions, imagining that to attempt to read the character of writing in this way would argue even more naïvety in him.

'I knew the cruise would not end well as soon as I saw the name of the ship. But to think I didn't really know what was

309

going on. How could I have been so BLOODY stupid? Yet even so I couldn't have stopped it. Nobody could. We were together every minute. No one came into our cabin. When she was there, I was with her. But of course I couldn't have been. At night she was on her own. Mother blamed me. Father blamed Emma. Emma blamed herself. And we all blamed THE MAN. But Emma was twenty-eight, and in control of her own decisions. Or was she? Whoever is? She saw him for the first time on the third day out, when we'd recovered from our *mal de mer*, and there was nothing anybody could do from that moment on. But why didn't she make him *take care*? Elementary precautions had always been rule number one, the first thought before enjoyment, such as it was or could ever be.'

Emma's carefree ways did not prevent her from understanding the world well enough to try and snap its bonds, but she did more damage to herself than break free of the values which she looked on with contempt. But she was in love with Alec, a sort of scullion or undercook who should not have been within a mile of the first-class part of the ship, but who was the kind of beetle it was impossible to prevent encroaching.

Clara saw them standing on the lifeboat deck one night after dinner, and almost pulled her from the rail. 'We must have coffee, dear.'

He looked at Clara. 'She'll be all right with me.'

'Perhaps so. But she's coming into the saloon now.'

He was even cheeky about it. 'I was showing her the stars. There's a few around tonight.'

'I dare say there are.'

'What a fuss you're making,' Emma said. 'It's nothing to do with you. I'm not a young girl.'

'I know, dear, but it's father's birthday tomorrow, and we have to write that telegram between us so that we can send it off.'

'Goodbye, miss.' The man walked away.

310

Emma said to Clara in the saloon: 'Don't do that again, do you hear? I talk to whoever I like. He's a pleasant person, and we were just *talking*.'

'With his arm around you?'

Emma's fits of temper never lasted long. 'It's your dirty mind. His arm was nowhere near me.'

'I'm not blind.'

'I wish you were. But if you come up to me like that again and make me look such a fool I'll jump overboard.'

'You wouldn't!'

'I bloody well would.'

Clara laughed. 'What fun!'

'You think so?'

'The ship would stop, and we'd throw you lifebelts. A jolly bosun would haul you aboard, and take you to the captain's cabin.'

Everyone wondered why they were laughing.

'I'd be clapped in irons,' Emma screamed, 'for the rest of the voyage.'

'First-class irons, though,' Clara shrieked. 'Or maybe they'd put you in charge of that Chief Dragon Stewardess in the white overall, and the Lord knows what she'd do with you!'

'Oh, shudder-shudder,' Emma moaned. 'I'd much rather have my little cock-o'-the-walk cook.'

'Stop it. You must promise never to see him again, not someone like him. There are lots of men on board who don't seem to be attached, so why do you have to get mixed up with a bad egg like that?'

'Oh shut up. You don't know what you're talking about. Let's forget it. It's absolutely nothing, you know.'

Clara thought that the fuss had indeed got out of hand. 'If it's so unimportant why can't you say you'll never see him again?'

'Well, I can say it, but I may bump into him walking around the deck.'

'He shouldn't be where we can see him,' Clara said. 'I'll complain to the captain.'

Emma turned pale. 'He'll lose his job.'

'*He'll* be clapped in irons. Or be made to walk the plank,' Clara went on, 'from the top of the funnel.'

Emma wanted no more of her humour. 'Don't do any such thing.'

'Promise, then?'

Clara waited. Emma nodded. 'But if I don't see him again, I'll never forgive you. It's rotten of you to make all this fuss, just because you're having your period.'

A tall thin middle-aged man with a row of medal ribbons on his lapel passed their table. He turned his face away quickly, and walked out of the door to get some fresh air.

'You're awful!' Clara said.

Emma became despondent. 'He must have heard such things before, and if he hasn't, what a poor fish!'

When two people want to be together, nothing can be done to stop them meeting. 'We fell in love,' Emma said, on telling Clara that she was pregnant. Emma couldn't be guarded every minute of the day and night. At the cinema one evening Emma complained, before the main film began, that the place was stuffy and made her feel sick because the ship was rocking. She would go to her cabin and rest.

'I'll come with you,' Clara offered.

She pressed her sister's hand and moved along the row. 'No, don't. I'll be all right. I just want to lie down.'

'And you haven't seen him since leaving the ship?'

'No.'

Clara snorted. 'And you call that love?'

'Yes.'

'You're talking like a mill girl who's been reading *Red Letter* magazine.'

'I don't care. It was marvellous.'

Clara had seen him standing on the quayside helping to unload while they were waiting to go ashore at Southampton.

312

He was a pallid ginger-haired man of medium height, though too far away for her to see much else. He probably had a wife and children, the squalid little runt. On every voyage he had fun with someone or other. How dare he wave at us?

'You must have an . . .' Clara daren't say the word.

'It's too late,' Emma told her. 'I never would, anyway. I want it to be like this. Life was getting too empty for me.'

'I can't think what it will do to father and mother. It will kill them.'

'Do you know,' Emma said, 'I don't care. Well, I do, but it's my life, and my baby – not theirs. I have to choose my own way out, and nobody else's. I can't be doing what other people want from me all the time.'

'Father and mother aren't other people.'

'But they will be if they turn against me for a thing like this.' Emma peered closer and saw her sister's tears, wondering why Clara seemed to think that she had committed an act of treachery against her personally. Such sister-love must come to an end sooner or later. Let it go. She couldn't bear Clara's overweening concern, nor her parents', which was really their concern for themselves and not for her. Yet it was the only love they had, and would never diminish.

'We love you more than we love ourselves,' Clara told her.

'Please leave me alone.'

'Of course, it won't kill them. Silly of me to say that. Times have changed. You can always have it adopted, or something.'

Emma spoke firmly. 'Don't tell me. I don't want to know.'

'Is everything I say wrong?' Clara was alarmed at the fact that it might well be.

'I've made up my mind to go to Cambridge.' Emma sat wearily on the bed. 'I can live there with friends till I get a flat or house of my own. Mother and father needn't know what's happened till the baby is born. I refuse to let anybody ruin my life.'

Clara was beginning to wonder whether their lives hadn't

been smashed before they were born, but knew she must stay with her sister in the hope that she could at least prevent her destroying another one – or two. 'Just tell me what I can do to help.'

'Stay with me,' Emma said. 'If I sleep alone tonight I shall never wake up.'

6

The taxi-cab to Liverpool Street was laden with trunks and cases. Emma took three pound notes from her purse to pay the train fares, and got thirteen-and-fourpence change. Their luggage went before them on a porter's barrow. Emma read *Strand Magazine* as the train steamed lustily out of London. She seemed, while rain washed down the windows, as if she had nothing in the whole wide world to worry about.

In the booking hall at Cambridge she confessed that she knew no one there, and couldn't think why she had suggested coming except that they had been at Newnham. For all she cared, they could just as well turn round and go back home. She didn't want to, however, because nobody could go *back*, no matter where that magical locality might be. She didn't wish to run anywhere else, either, so supposed she ought to kill herself, and certainly would if she weren't pregnant, and if she were on her own.

Her face was so dry, eyes so laden with self-reproach that Clara thought even tears would be a blessing. A fit, like a thunderstorm, would clear the air, at least for a while. She felt there was a barrier in Emma's perceptions that held back notions of self-preservation. Such mending thoughts were not sufficiently plain to her. It was torment. Clara found irresponsibility the worst of sins. Emma's apprehensions were merely somewhat distant, though being faintly sensed by her did not mean that she was mistaken as to their presence. The fact that she perceived them at all increased her trouble – and Clara did not know whether Emma would rather that they had not been there. As it was, they only sent enough indication of menace to confuse her decisions.

Their sisterly connection was firm – always had been – almost as if they were twins. Clara was appalled at the situation, but knew she must make an effort. Rain teemed outside. It would be better to do anything rather than nothing, so she telephoned the University Arms, asking for their best double room and bath for herself and her sister.

She swung jauntily out of the telephone box. 'Come on, my love, cheer up. I've got us a big cosy bolt-hole looking over Parkers Piece. We'll have a long soak in the tub, then go down for a ten-bob dinner.' She called: 'Hey, porter, get us a taxi.' Turning again to Emma: 'We'll leave our trunks in the left-luggage, then talk about what we're going to do when we get to our den. Or we won't, if we don't feel like it. We'll do just as we like!'

They had their cases, and then tea, sent to the room. Emma sat on the bed. 'I'm not unhappy. Don't think that. I just don't care. It's wonderful. I've always wanted not to care, and to have something to care about that I won't care about, and now I don't!'

Clara passed the plate of cucumber sandwiches, glad to see her eat. She could hardly do anything else. 'But I care for *you*. I sometimes think I've never cared about anyone else.' It was true that she hadn't, but Emma seemed to be in some strange land of her own, so it was no use pushing the point. She looked older than she need have, with shadows under the eyes, and even powder and rouge couldn't hide the fact that her skin had gone past its first bloom without either of them noticing. Her eyes were large and feverish, as if straining to see more than would ever be possible.

315

Beauty had gone to her body. The slope from full breasts expanded over her belly when she stood by the bathroom mirror, and faced Clara who was unable to resist spreading her fingers over the warm navel. 'Has it moved yet?'

'Last night it did. I thought it was a squirrel. Or a hedgehog. Then I woke up and remembered I was pregnant. I was glad.'

Clara put the plug in and opened both taps, thinking: If only she would miscarry, and things could go on as before. But the notion showed such horror on her face that Emma gripped her arm. 'For God's sake, what's the matter?'

'Damn! It must be indigestion from those candlefat cakes. I had a pain right here, and it was no baby moving, let me tell you. Maybe I'll go for a walk while you have a nap. Shall you be all right?'

Emma got into the bath, and tapped her stomach. 'I can't run very far with this.'

Clara laughed, and agreed. 'Wash your back?'

She sat on the stool and rubbed the sponge up and down, thinking how normal she looked from behind.

'I can tell what you're thinking,' Emma said, 'when you do it like that. It's too regular. Go round and round a bit. Are you thinking how wicked and stupid I am?'

She had been. 'Nothing of the kind. It's just so steamy in here. Perhaps I need a nap as well. Who wants to walk in the pouring rain?'

'You know what I was thinking?'

'How could I?'

Emma turned. 'I was thinking that sex is awful. I wouldn't care if I never saw another man, and I certainly can't imagine ever going to bed with one, even when I feel passionate. Does that mean I'm going to have a boy?'

'You're going to have something.' Clara held the large bath towel for her to step against. 'Let's have you out. It's nap time for you. You look a bit worn out.'

She stood. 'You are funny when you nanny me!'

Clara disliked such flippancy. 'I'm certainly not funny to myself.'

'Who do you think I take after?' Emma asked.

She was wary. 'How do you mean?'

The dressing-gown made her seem less overwhelming. 'Favour. Am I like mother, or father?'

They went into the bedroom. Clara passed a hairbrush. 'You feature mother, I suppose.'

'And you have father's looks, mostly.' Emma lay back on the bed. 'John was a mixture of both.'

Clara moved bottles and tubs of make-up around the dressing-table as if playing a game of chess. 'Why did you ask?'

'Because mother is Jewish.'

'What's that got to do with it?'

'So am I – that's what.'

'She's my mother as well, but I'm not Jewish.'

'Jewish mothers have Jewish children, but if you don't think you are, then I suppose you aren't.'

Clara lit a cigarette. 'John didn't think he was.'

'Maybe he did. But he is now, though, because mother made him be.'

'He didn't have any say in the matter. Why do you have to be anything?'

Emma stroked her stomach. 'This one will have to be, I'm sure.'

'What makes you think so?'

She lay on her side and stared at the wall. 'Whenever I've been at a party and there have been Jewish people who haven't known who I was they all assumed I was Jewish. I didn't mind, of course. I even felt flattered. One or two who thought I was Jewish imagined I didn't care to say so for very mean or frightened reasons. They were wrong, of course. I was too uncertain. I'd never actually been *told* – except by the rabbi, when mother went to see him about John's grave.' She turned to Clara: 'You're Jewish too, but it wouldn't happen to you.'

Clara grunted. 'I'd clout anyone who assumed I was anything. It's none of their damned business, whoever they are.'

'So if people,' said Emma, 'especially if they aren't Jewish, are going to assume the same thing about my son – if it is a son – I shall want him to know what he is.'

'You *have* been thinking,' Clara said lightly.

'I have to, because I'm afraid. The older I get the more frightened I become, I don't know why. It's worse now that I'm pregnant.'

'You're supposed to go all calm, so I hear.'

'It's not happened to me,' Emma said, as if she hoped it never would. 'Maybe it's too early, and I won't turn into a vegetable till later. Don't think it wouldn't have been the same though if I'd had a man fussing all over me, because it would.'

Clara slumped in the easy chair, as if to escape from the rays of her sister's anger. Emma's moods came from a defensiveness which threatened to crush everything else in her. There was no call for it, but then, there was no need of anything that spoiled the trust between people. The last twenty-four hours had worn Clara out, while Emma seemed far from devastated by her trouble, though she went so up and down that it was hard to say what was happening to her. 'I wish you hadn't told that lie about friends in Cambridge. I could have thought of better places to hole up in than this pile of rainwashed scholarship.'

She leaned on one elbow. 'I did know someone, but when I got here I realized they wouldn't do at all.'

'Who is it?' Clara asked.

'Do you remember Jane Gusie and her husband Frank? We used to call them The Geese because they honked and quacked instead of talked.'

Clara sat upright to stop her laughter. 'No! Not the Honks! Of course I remember them. Perhaps we will call. They might know of furnished rooms we could take for a few months.'

318

'A day at a time is all I can accept,' Emma said. 'If I start thinking about the future I get the willies.'

Clara threw her lit cigarette into the lavatory pan, then knelt by the bed and held Emma's hand. 'I'll take care of you. You have nothing to worry about.' Each sobbing lurch of her shoulders brought out more tears.

'Don't cry,' Emma felt as if she would weep too. 'I hate it when you cry. Stop it, please.' But she laughed instead. 'Or you'll sink the room!'

7

The place was cluttered. Such rubbish, Clara said, taking as much as possible to the attics before having their trunks brought from the station. They put the painted gnomes and well-ironed doilies into cardboard boxes, together with seaside knick-knacks, pot dogs, horse brasses and toby jugs from stands, shelves and whatnots. 'I'm bound to knock them flying if they stay where they are,' Clara added. 'A lot of such priceless gewgaw stuff has often gone down under an absent-minded wave of my clumsy arm!'

The furnished house was in a street off Parkers Piece and cost five pounds a week. An elderly couple had gone to New Zealand for six months to stay with their sons – or perhaps for a year, the estate agent told Clara. 'We'll let you know in good time.'

The aspidistras from front and rear windows went into the garden shed, and two oleographs of Admiral Beatty were wrapped in copies of the *Daily Mail* and pushed under a sofa. 'I'd like to strip off that ghastly wallpaper and whitewash the place, but I don't suppose they'd like it one bit. And we'd lose our twenty pounds deposit.'

319

'We must get a maid as soon as we can,' Emma said. 'I hate making fires. And we ought to let mother know where we are. She'll be shocked at what we've done, after thinking we were only here on visits.'

Clara thought not. 'She's used to us. As long as we're sound in wind and limb, she won't mind.'

'She will,' Emma said.

Rachel received their letter with the morning post. At three o'clock in the afternoon she knocked at the door. 'You know, this is the first time you've left home, and you didn't even tell anyone. Your father has to be in the City today, or he would have come with me. He isn't pleased, and neither am I. You did all this in secret. Why didn't you tell us? You can do as you wish, I know, but you might at least have told us, so that we could have talked about it.'

'Your coat's wet,' said Emma. 'Let me hang it up, then you can sit down.'

Clara, not knowing how they would tell Rachel their reason for being here, went into the kitchen to make tea. Their lives had changed utterly. A few months ago the rest of the world hadn't existed except as a place in which to find entertainment, but now it was there only to threaten them. She could not understand why it must seem as if something dreadful had happened. They were young, comfortably off, and healthy. But Emma had struck a blow to change their lives, and Clara wondered why she had acted in such an un-necessarily perverse way. The wickedest thought, which said what a pity Emma couldn't lose the baby so that they could go back to being their old carefree selves, had again to be pushed out of her mind.

Emma rocked in a chair by the fire, and Rachel looked at her. 'You're pregnant.'

'Yes.'

'I knew there was more to it than changing houses. Your father also said: "I wonder what it is? Something is surely wrong."'

'Why is it wrong, mother?'

She sat on a straight-backed chair at the table, instead of comfortably by the fire, and lifted her hand as if to push the devil away. 'Why is it wrong? she says. Why is it wrong?' She turned as if semicircled by an audience, a hand to her heart. 'Is it so hard to know what's wrong and what's right?'

Clara came in with the tray. 'I see she told you.'

'Told me? She's like a barrel – or will be soon. I knew as soon as I came in the door. She disguised it at home, but doesn't care to here – though I had my suspicions. Why wasn't I told weeks ago?'

'We were afraid,' Clara admitted.

'Afraid? I hope you never have anything more to be afraid of than that.' She was troubled, and angry. 'There's no telephone here. I must talk to your father, poor man. He'll be worried till he hears from me, but I can't think how upset he'll be when he listens to what I have to say.'

Clara set out cakes and poured tea. 'The nearest telephone is at the station. But must you tell him?'

'When did it happen? No, I don't care to know. But who's the father? Where is he, at least?'

Emma was silent.

'Well, he certainly isn't here, and that's not a good sign. It's terrible to think about. We had great hopes for you two after dear John died – may he rest in peace. We thought you would find husbands who'd make you happy.'

Clara was forced to say: 'There aren't so many men now, mother.'

'There are for girls like you.' Clara thought the tears on her cheeks came more at the mention of John than because of Emma. 'You wouldn't even have to try.'

'Mother,' Emma said, 'please don't go on like this. It's my life. I don't care what father says when he knows. I'm not dying, and he's not going to be hurt. It isn't the worst thing in the world.'

Clara shovelled coal from the scuttle and slid it on to the

321

fire. The fumes of soot were bad for her skin. At home they had central heating fuelled by coke from the cellar. She hoped Emma would say nothing, and let their mother talk, for there was little to be gained by making her more unhappy than she was, and perhaps reminding her of what she had been as a young woman. But Emma would not stop, and Clara was to see how those who were most alike knew best how to make each other suffer.

'I fell in love. It sounds stupid, but what else can I say?'

'And did he?'

Emma smiled. 'We enjoyed ourselves. It was as if we had only a week to live. If I spend the rest of my life *paying* for it, I won't mind. He stayed every night in my cabin, after Clara and I had said goodnight.'

Clara would have felt that she too had been betrayed, had she not considered Emma's frankness as self-indulgent boasting designed to hurt herself more than anyone else. 'What a swine he was for not taking care!'

The same bright smile lit her eyes. 'I wouldn't let him. I wanted everything, and he did as I told him.' She leaned forward. 'It was beautiful.'

The world could fall to pieces, and she wouldn't care, adding what a pity it was that she had come away with Clara instead of by herself. She had her own money, and when the baby was born she would bring it up without anyone's interference. Later she would get some kind of job, because she couldn't be idle all her life. Alec had said everyone ought to work, whether or not they had money.

Rachel straightened. 'Alec?'

'And do you know what he was? A pastrycook who did the fancy trimmings for our jaded tastebuds! If it's of any interest he was also Jewish. Maybe that's why I fell for him. He was very handsome, and kind, and we parted friends. But we agreed never to see each other again. He wanted to meet me, of course, but I insisted that we mustn't. In any case, he was married and had children. It would have been too ugly and squalid. He took it very well, though not too well, thank goodness. Luckily I didn't know how hard it would be, though I still wouldn't have done it any other way.'

The clatter of Rachel's falling cup stopped her. Clara went to the kitchen for a cloth. 'You make me so clumsy,' Rachel said. Now that Emma had stopped telling her story there was a veil of childish misery on her face. Rachel looked at herself thirty-five years younger, and the reflection of the mirror shook as if Emma was going to cry at last. When she didn't Rachel said: 'We must find him.'

'You want to make him *pay*?'

'Don't be silly,' her mother shouted.

'It's no crime, so leave me alone. I know my mind, and that's what I want. If it's a boy, I shall have him circumcised.'

'It's the fashion nowadays,' Rachel said sharply. 'Ever since the Royal Family had it done, I suppose.'

'I'll get a rabbi to do it.'

'A *schochan*,' she was informed.

'Whoever it is. You never told me.'

'You never asked,' her mother said. 'But what a shame. What a terrible shame it is.'

She above all knew there was nothing to be done. The ticking of the clock told her. That's what came of giving girls an income as soon as they were twenty-one, and letting them do whatever they wanted. The war had been a disaster in every way, because as well as getting killed and maimed, young people had learned to have their own way.

Clara poked the fire, and a bank of hot coal dropped to a lower level, scattering ash into the grate. She believed that any situation, no matter how tragic, could be cleared up without fuss and bother if everyone had a mind to it. Yet she didn't know what to do or say.

Rachel reached for her gloves. 'I must talk to your father.'

'It'll only upset him,' Emma said. 'I'd rather you didn't.'

'It upsets me even to think about it,' Clara put in.

'You're soft,' Rachel told her scornfully. 'You always were.'

Clara winced.

'I discuss everything with your father.'

'Whether he likes it or not, I suppose,' said Clara.

'I'm telling you not to tell him,' Emma said.

'You don't *tell* me anything. When's the baby expected?'

'I don't know! Oh, in four months, I think. I saw a doctor in South Kensington. He was tall, elderly and handsome. Ugh! Horrible! Shan't see him again. I'd like not to see anybody, but I suppose I'll have to. If only I were on an uninhabited island, and could have it all on my own. I'd feed him on coconut milk!'

'You've been reading too many novels.' Rachel stood, and sighed. 'I must go. There's a train in half an hour.'

'It's too wet to go out,' Clara said. 'Why don't you stay tonight, and travel back in the morning?'

'You think *rain* is a misfortune? I wish that was all I had to grieve about.' She wouldn't change her mind, so Clara helped her on with the unfashionable pre-war coat. 'If you really must go, I'll walk with you to the station.'

'Stay and look after your sister. I know my way.'

'No, I'll come with you.'

Rachel turned from the door. 'Do as you are told.'

Clara stepped back as if about to be hit, as if a cliff were behind her and she would fall into oblivion. She clutched the mantelshelf, knowing that her mother's anger was only directed at her because she was afraid to tackle Emma – who hoped they would both go and leave her in peace.

Clara sat down when the door closed. 'Well, we've yet to hear father's wrath on the matter.'

'They can't kill me. Nor *this*.' She stood up to clear the tea things away. 'They do want to kill me, I know, but I only need to get away from them.'

'You're certainly going the right way about it,' Clara told her.

324

8

They bought material for a maternity dress. After lunch Emma spread it on the table, and as they were puzzling over the pattern the letterbox flap rattled.

Clara came back. 'It's from father. I know his hand.'

Emma told her to read it.

'Are you sure?'

She glanced at the envelope. 'It's addressed to both of us: a pretty cheap trick.'

'I know. But it begins: "Dear Emma", so it's only to you.'

'Read it, though, because I shan't.'

'This is what it says, then. Oh dear! "Mother informed me of your disaster as soon as she arrived. It's not for me to judge. There are too many judges in the world trying to take God's place. What has happened is something nobody could have controlled, least of all *you*. Some things are sent to try us, while other events occur expressly to ruin our lives. You have *despoiled your life*, and I can only pity you, though I have more compassion for your mother because after John's death this is the one thing she should have been spared. There is much in you that must have known exactly what you were doing, and I am sure you measured the consequences to such a nicety that any sympathy for your plight from me or anybody else would be totally misplaced. It is not in my heart to bear this, but neither is it in my mind to pronounce you dead. You are a fully grown woman, and must face the consequences, which in any case you are quite capable of doing. You have your own income and are provided for, and therefore I can only say without any feelings of regret or injustice that it would be best if we never met again."'

Clara put the letter down.

'Is that all?' Emma asked.

'Isn't it enough?'

'It's what I expected,' Emma sighed, 'and half hoped for. I like his style, but not his awful cheek.'

'Are you going to answer?'

'Burn it – to ashes.'

'I'd like to keep it.'

'Do what the hell you like. As long as I never see it again, and you never mention it. Come on, let's get this bloody sugar-bag cut out. I might as well look the part of the fallen woman. There's really not much left to do but enjoy it.'

She had fallen, Clara realized, from such a height that she wasn't yet aware of having landed. She hadn't, and would she ever? Try as she might to get through to her, Emma stayed obstinately and resolutely alone. And the more Clara tried the more distance she felt between them. It was best to stay calm, not make the attempt, and help when the time came. Emma had to be guarded, rather than looked after. The thought haunted Clara that, coming back from shopping one day, she would find her gone. She would go into the living-room and not see her sitting at the table sewing or reading or staring at the wall. Only an echo would answer when she called her name. But Emma was always in some part of the house.

'What are you thinking?' Clara asked after breakfast.

'I don't think any more. Nothing so crude as that. Nothing so grand, either. I just sit and feel this tadpole kick and grow inside me. We're like husband and wife, contemplating the absolutely empty future together. I'm filled, among other things, with dread for this poor thing coming into the world. I keep seeing those thousands of graves we passed on our little trip of homage to visit dear John, and I think: "Will this bloke inside me, if it is a bloke, end up *known only unto God*?" Oh, I've got a lot to think about, if you can call it thinking. I think of mother's romantic beginning with father, and of how they must now see my escapade. It would have been bad enough if I'd done the same, but I've actually gone one better, so I can see how they must hate me. I really have spoiled their lives.

But I don't think, exactly. Things only go through my mind in such a way as to reassure me that I still have one.'

Clara tried to be jovial. 'He'll be all right. There'll be two of us to look after him. It'll be great fun.'

'I hope so. But I wish I could get it over with.'

Clara heard a noise at the front door and went into the hall. After their father's letter she hadn't expected to see her mother again. Rachel shook her head at their surprise, and sat down with them at the table. 'He has his opinions, and I have mine. Whenever I feel like coming to visit you, I'll catch the train. That's what they were invented for.'

'We were just off to the picture palace,' Clara said. 'Emma gets so bored.'

'Don't let me prevent you. I'll be happy to sit on my own. I can read or sew. You should buy a gramophone and listen to music. The mood was so sudden to come and see you both that I didn't have time to send a telegram.'

They took off their coats.

'I left two trunks at the station,' Rachel said, 'not knowing whether you would be in. They're full of things which will be needed for the baby, if it's to be dressed in anything good.' She stood up to take off her hat by the mirror. 'It's a pity you can't find a nice young man for a husband.'

'I don't think there are many, even in Cambridge,' Emma said, 'who would want to marry a woman in this all too obvious state, though I suppose I could go out on the street and try. "Excuse me, kind sir" – and I'd do a very nice curtsy – "I hope you don't mind my asking, but if you aren't poxed-up from the war, or have a false leg, or an eye missing, or a toe gone, I wonder if by any chance you can see your way to marrying me some time in the next few days? I have a thousand pounds a year at my disposal, so you shouldn't have too many regrets."'

When they stopped laughing Rachel said: 'You'll take life seriously one day, I promise. I don't know what we did to make you so foul-mouthed and wicked.'

'You're not responsible,' Emma told her, 'nor is father. I suppose I got into this mess because I didn't know anything about myself. At the moment I'm nothing. When I go for a walk I feel I'm like everybody I pass on the street, and can't wait to get back here so that I can be on my own, and feel like nothing and nobody, and then again like myself, whatever that is. Maybe I'll know a bit more when this thing comes out. Did you know yourself any better, mother, after you'd had three children?'

Clara was disturbed, and only doubted that Emma spoke such rigmarole when her mother replied: 'It was *after* you were grown-up that I began to know who I was.'

'The last few months must have taught you something,' Emma said. 'It has me.'

'I know,' Rachel retorted. 'It's taught you how to quarrel. And how to insult your parents.'

By her silence Emma knew that she was pressing against all their wounds. 'I'm sorry, mother.'

'I think you should be.'

Clara felt pain for them both, and stood up, saying brightly to Emma: 'Why don't you start keeping your journal again? It might help you to sort things out in your mind. I write mine, as and when I can. It keeps me in touch with myself – or what's left of me these days.'

'I prefer to be on my own,' Emma said. 'When people are with me, I'm even more alone, so I don't mind either of you being here. If I kept a journal I might get to think I was somebody else, and I should hate that, even though I don't know who I am most of the time. Only this in here knows who I am, but by the time he's old enough to tell me I won't be anywhere where I can hear what he's got to say. And he wouldn't know by then, in any case. One minute I feel I'm going to live a hundred years, and the next it seems I'll be lucky to get beyond this one. I don't care, really. During the war the world was crowded with happy people who only wanted a good time. Now, it's full of ghosts. Something

328

happened, and I don't suppose any of us knows what it was. Perhaps even having a baby won't make much difference to me. If so I don't know what will happen.'

Rachel went home after three days because, she said, she needed a rest. Clara, left behind, was swept with anguish as she looked at her sister, and heard her, in an ordinary enough voice, say things which filled her with either sorrow or horror. Emma's lips were set firm when she stopped talking. The glow in her eyes, suggesting a far-seeing vision, was due only to short-sightedness.

9

Clara came back from the post office, took off her raincoat and galoshes in the hall, and coo-eed to let Emma know she had returned. With a fire burning, the parlour could not be cosier, but Emma was neither there nor in the kitchen. Clara shouted upstairs, and the maid told her she hadn't seen Emma for an hour.

She put her galoshes back on, and took a dry coat from the hall stand, but did not know which way to go. Sleet blew into her face, so she walked with its main force behind, to open ground beyond Park Side. Someone was cycling, but there were no pedestrians. Protected by houses from the worst of the weather, she made her way to Christ's Piece. They had often gone over Butts Green and Midsummer Common to the river, a pleasant stroll with the minimum of buildings hemming them in. But she kept as much towards houses as possible, and peered across spaces in case Emma was there.

It was muddy by the river and the boathouses. Her nose ran water and her neck was cold. Every step made her doubt that she was going in the right direction, but not to make for somewhere seemed too painful to be borne.

Her instinct was to get back into the warm house, but the knowledge that she must fight against it drove her on. You did what you had absolutely no wish to do far more easily than what you would quite enjoy doing – a reflection which made her momentarily stalwart against the elements, and would comfort her as long as the thought of Emma and her general predicament didn't force itself too close to her powers of strength and decision – thought the dreadful situation could only be absent for a few precious seconds at a time during her surge through the rain.

The green river lapped at its banks. An old man on the other side pottered at some job on a boathouse roof, but then came down his ladder to take shelter, squeezing his hands together as if to get the wet out of them. She called, and asked if he had seen a woman walking alone.

He laughed. 'No, I ain't. Not even a dog, come to that.'

She felt an ache in her chest as if someone had punched her. Chimney smoke and mist hung over the houses. The wind had dropped and rain came directly down. Crossing Sun Street, she was nearly struck by a horse-and-cart, the driver too surprised to shout back when she called him a fool for not looking where he was going.

She went up and down every street, then crossed each at right angles, imagining Emma as quite close in front, but always turning a corner before she could be seen. She considered walking across Parkers Piece to the railway station, then stood by the kerb wondering whether she shouldn't get into the comfort of the house and stop allowing Emma to make both their lives miserable. It was impossible to be still. From the edge of the space she saw someone a few hundred yards away, where the walks intersected at the middle.

The never-ending distance passed by putting one foot in front of the other, and keeping on with head down and eyes fixed at the soaking turf, as if afraid that should she look up the figure would vanish. The rain made no difference. If she had to live the rest of her life under water, so be it. To exist in such a way attached her to the earth and could only be good for her. Every step forward put on another year of life, but Emma had to be reached and taken home because each minute out there might take a year *off* her life.

She looked up every dozen paces to make sure there was still some object to aim for. She laughed at herself. There was no one to hear. Raindrops distorted what she saw. The figure was probably a poor old tramp with nowhere to go. She wanted to turn back, for fear he should jump on her. Girls had been raped on Parkers Piece at night. But it was Emma. There was no mistaking the way she hunched her shoulders. Clara called, and hurried breathlessly on. Emma stood with head bowed, unable to hear.

Clara held her arm. 'What*ever* are you doing? You'll get pneumonia – at least!'

She looked. Her skin was like clay, glazed so that the rain poured off. 'I'm trying to find out what it's like to be alone.'

Clara drew her close. She smelled of rain and sweat. 'I've been looking all over. You might at least have told me where you were going, then you could have been alone for as long as you liked. But just to go off like this for your own crack-brained reason is too much. You've no consideration for anybody except yourself. Don't you think it's time you pulled yourself together and behaved a bit more reasonably? Perhaps it doesn't matter what happens to you, but you ought at least to think about the baby you're going to have.' She gripped her arm. 'So let's go back to the house before you really get ill. You're going to need a hot bath and something to drink if you aren't to get a bad cold. Now come on, and stop all this bloody stupid nonsense.'

She was putting it on, but the severe tone was right, under the circumstances, she thought. We are all Death's prisoners, she had heard a preacher say from his pulpit on the edge of the

331

market one morning. Life was a battlefield from which there could be no survivors. Once the fight begins, losses continually occur, even in the most favoured conditions, till you become one of them. She made her observations and, with so many dreadful events all of a sudden to endure, thought it her duty to record the fact that no family was free of tragic times.

Emma allowed herself to be taken by the hand and led back to the midday autumnal gloom of the buildings.

10

Her bedroom looked over the squalid backyards. 'I'm sorry we couldn't have got a better place,' she said, but Emma reminded her that the inside of the house was clean and comfortable, and they were lucky not to be in China or Russia or Germany, for they had coal, food and clothes, and didn't have to live in the rain with no shelter. They had each other. Life was good when you weren't standing alone in the rain. If she could go on living, she would be happy and have no complaints. She wanted her baby to have a long life, without war, want or inner misery. Her life had been fortunate, she said when Clara sat on the bed and held her hand, and yet on the eve of the greatest acquisition she had a fear of losing everything. A senseless anxiety troubled her day and night. There was no sleep, and no peace. Did Clara think that only a woman could have such feelings?

Clara didn't know. If a question was asked with too much intensity she was always lost for an answer, and Emma never wanted to know anything that would be satisfied by a casual response. Emma didn't wait for answers she knew would never come, or for answers that would never convince her if they did. She then asked if she weren't trying to live out all possible anxiety and hopelessness so that there would be so much less for her child to inherit. Heaven only knows, Clara said, hardly able to endure the torment settling on to her from Emma's disturbed state. She suffered with her, and did not know whether or not Emma noticed. But Emma was aware of everything, and what diference could it make that Clara was equally tormented? The suffering was doubled, but not thereby diminished. Clara had no say in the matter, and went through equal anguish with her sister, a process over which she did not wish to have any control in the hope that by taking some of the burden, Emma would sooner or later feel its intolerable weight shifting away from herself.

Clara thought that if she spent another moment with her she would descend into a madness from which recovery would be impossible. She felt herself saturated with resentment at having to bear so much, but her objections were not directed at Emma, who in her misery seemed either unaware or unconcerned that it was passing with ever-increasing intensity to her sister. The mechanism had been there since childhood, for Clara recollected that Emma's infantile despair had in its own way been equally desolate for her. She, on the other hand, had never in either adult or childish misery witnessed any similar effect on Emma when she – Clara – was depressed, for Emma at such times kept her temperament intact against all influences, not out of callousness but because she was set too firmly into her own sphere to know what was happening. Any sympathy Emma might express was mere casual condolence. She certainly wouldn't waste time on sharing half-imagined woes.

When Emma's mood lifted for no apparent reason Clara, with pain still searing her heart, went to the barometer in the hall to see if the pressure had altered, to find out whether the needle was now set fair when it had previously indicated

333

stormy. She was disappointed to see that it denied her idea, having hoped to find some system to Emma's moods that would help her to counter them. She stayed baffled, because while Emma's upsets undoubtedly served to get her through another few days of reasonable life, they left Clara mentally crippled, and even more so when she tried to hide her anguish from Emma in case it caused another of her fits. She contained herself in the hope that the residue of her own misery would go away and leave them both in peace at last.

This volume of Clara's journal ended with: '*Not beyond here. No point going on.*' But a pocket diary contained occasional remarks and pencilled comments on occurrences she later thought worth noting, and entries in a jotting pad dealt with the coming and going of their mother, the doctor's visits, days when the weather was fine and sunny, and walks into town to go shopping or to the pictures. In an unposted letter she described how Rachel came one day and, finding Emma in one of her 'moods', dismissed it with such astonishing ease and panache that the raucous half-hour quarrel which ensued stung Emma finally to speechlessness and weeping. After a while she became girlish, laughed and behaved normally till Rachel left for the railway station. Clara felt gratitude at her mother's courage and ability. Rachel wasn't afraid to shout, and was in no sense willing to stifle helplessly under Emma's injurious silence or frivolous accusations. She marvelled at her mother, but did not regret that she herself was unable to use the same methods.

11

The night was created from a snowstorm of the previous day, making it easy to imagine wolves howling in the spacious Fens and searching for the blood of infants and the warmth of mothers in the city. No one could avoid meeting them in their dreams, or cease to imagine them in the snowy daylight of dark outside their tight-shut windows. The wolf in Emma was trying to get out by gnawing at her backbone, and her screams kept the street awake. Eventually the wolf would streak away, having drunk all her blood, join its lupine brothers still howling to enter whatever house they could find unguarded. Time had reached a stop, while Clara, Rachel and the midwife kept watch, and waited for either the night or the world to end. Each sound was muffled by snow and bleached by pale gas light as the agony that none of them could reach came and went and came again with an intensity towards dawn that they thought could not possibly increase.

Rachel and the midwife made a show of giving practical advice, but nothing mattered to Emma except that she must reach the end of the tunnel or be torn to fragments by the wolf that had her in its teeth. 'What do you say?' Rachel asked when she tried to speak.

Out of the sweat, and the state for which she knew no word, came: 'Get it away from me.'

Clara waited in the parlour, hoping to die if her sister's ordeal did not stop, wondering why they didn't help her, or put her out of her misery like a dog or a horse – for if I were in the same state, she thought, vowing that she never would be, I'd surely ask them to do a kindness and end it by a single shot, as I would if I'd been left to die on a battlefield. Had John gone through similar agony? she wondered, torn half to pieces, yet not dead, and pleading with one of his men to kill him?

Every baby was born the same way, the mother as if mortally wounded yet recovering. A better system's not yet been invented, the midwife said, in effect doing nothing. Clara made tea. She toasted bread and boiled eggs to see them through the night. They ate, as if to sustain Emma by it.

At ten minutes past eight, when Clara was dozing in the rocking chair, the midwife shook her and said it was a boy.

Did she want to come and look at the eight-pound wonder? I bloody do not, she thought, opening the curtains. The snowing had stopped but lay thick along the street. Children were going to school. A postman struggled through drifts with his heavy bag. How could the world go on at such a time? She walked upstairs, knowing that like the wave the world was permanent – as the song said – and she began to laugh but remembered to stop when opening the door.

The wolf had gone, and left a blanket of snow behind. Emma was asleep, equally whitened by the night, the baby by her side. 'She'll call him Thomas,' the midwife said. 'That's nice, isn't it?'

'It's got to be called something,' Clara answered.

Rachel laid a finger on Emma's forehead. 'I thought her time would never end.' Clara waited for her to say more, but she leaned across the bed and put the palm of her hand under Emma's nightdress, holding it on her left breast till she thought to take the golden Star of David from her own neck and lay it on the table as a present for the baby. 'Please God they'll both be well.'

'We shall have to make sure it's the end of her troubles,' Clara said.

'Nothing ever ends,' Rachel told her, before leaving for London a fortnight later. 'Our lives only go on so that Death can get its reckoning.'

Clara laughed, and so did Emma, who put her arms around her mother and said after a kiss: 'Where did you hear such sombre old twaddle?'

Rachel pushed her away, but Clara noted that it was a playful action. There was an air of affection before their parting.

'It certainly isn't twaddle. Eternal truths need stressing again and again. They always have – especially to one's children. And you're still children, don't forget, till I die, whatever you may think.'

'Eternal truths!' Emma exclaimed. 'Really, they only enslave us, mother.'

'They do if you want them to,' Rachel said. 'But they needn't at all. Eternal truths keep people like *us* civilized. We'd be badly off without them. And they're more than necessary for the rest of the world.'

Emma smiled, and helped her on with her coat. 'I hope not.'

'Hope!' Rachel said. 'You won't get very far on that – though I should hope, I suppose, that you'll both find good husbands before very long.'

But Clara had made up her mind never to marry, and never to have children. Any such process would certainly stop with her. A magazine article said that all women should have children, even if only one, for what woman, the wise man asked, wanted to be 'the end of the line'? It was bad for the woman, bad for society, and bad for the country. Clara threw the magazine across the parlour. If she were destined to be lonely at the end of the line, so be it, she snorted. And what damned line did the fool mean? A clothes line? Let the idiot have children himself, if he could. And if *she* didn't, there were millions around her who most certainly would, so as far as the country went there was nothing to fear. Let the people breed. It would give them something to do in their otherwise empty lives. Nature had organized things very well, except that the country had too many inhabitants for comfort, judging by the queues for buses, trains and picture-houses which hadn't been there before the war. But as for her – no children, she told herself, ever.

12

When the train arrived at Liverpool Street station they said that Rachel had been robbed, and then died from a heart attack, but a farmer found her purse by the railway line and gave it to the police. Nothing was missing. Her lost Star of David, Clara explained to her father when he asked, had been given to the new baby.

Percy wrote in his letter that his dear wife must have passed away in an effort to get out of the speeding train, and dropped the purse during the heart-failure which stopped her from doing so. She had not wanted to die while in the moving carriage, and perhaps she would still be here if she hadn't done such a lot of travelling in the last few months. He wondered if Emma knew that self-centred actions invariably had such repercussions? The strain on her mother had been more than either she or Clara had imagined. He had told her not to go so often to Cambridge, and they had quarrelled about it on more than one occasion. But she had been too devoted to listen, and in such a matter he had not persisted. She was one of the good people of the world, without whose kind we might all become barbarians again.

Across the letter Clara had written in broad red pencil: 'SNAKE! HYPOCRITE!' – and called him as much to his face after the funeral. 'Your sort are the barbarians,' she wrote in the small space left after he had signed his name.

13

'I had a letter from father,' she said.

'You are lucky,' Emma replied.

'Aren't you interested?'

'Burn it – for all I care.'

Clara always mentioned Emma and the baby when she wrote to her father, if only to prove to herself that she was not the sort of person who would become a barbarian if people like her mother ceased to exist. She tried to count herself charitable in her thoughts and at least some of her actions, while aware that she rarely succeeded in doing anything good. Her father's favourite saying was that the road to hell was paved with good intentions, and she decided that what for many people might be a very effective footpath she had made into a Ministry of Transport 'A' Road by concocting in her own mind plans for helpful actions which through inanition she neglected to carry out. Her only kindnesses, she supposed, were those which came to her suddenly and were accomplished with no inner discussion. To mull over doing good beforehand was a way of giving herself the credit for it, though she would never allow herself to receive any when she did help someone.

She wrote to her father frequently now that he was alone, and in one letter added a postcript too quickly to be considered, saying wouldn't it be best if the three of them came to live at home? 'The lease will be finished on this hole of a house in a couple of months, and it's difficult to know where we will go when it is.'

The letter was in the post before she wondered whether her suggestion had been wise. She could hardly go to the pillar box and get it back and had, after all, only done it for the best. 'For the best she had done it,' her mother used to say, when Clara dropped her dinner plate in the nursery, or pulled a plant in the garden, and Emma would take up the call so that Rachel told her to stop or she too would be sent to her room.

Clara waited, till she forgot either to wait or hope, and as the days went by Emma fed her baby with care and assiduity. Time had no meaning now that she was so occupied. 'It's only for a while, though,' she said emphatically. 'I'll want to *do* something soon.'

'Such as what?'

'Work. Act. Get out of this.'

Did she think she could find any sort of job with an illegitimate child clinging to her waist?

'I want to travel.' She put her book down. 'There's no place in the world I don't want to go. But I wish I'd been born a man.'

Clara laughed. 'They have their troubles too, or so I understand.'

'Oh yes, but I'd still be *me*, and things would be easier. I'd be able to do much more. I wouldn't feel so weighed down with unnecessary complications.'

'Things will turn out all right.' Clara lit a cigarette. 'Except, of course, that you have Thomas to care for now.'

'Give me one. You know I like to smoke after lunch. I'll get someone to look after him whenever I go away.'

'A person you can trust, I hope.' Clara could not see herself nursing a baby, not even her sister's. The idea seemed ludicrous. 'Mother would have taken him, I expect, but I can't imagine father setting to.'

Emma lifted her book again. 'I shall find someone.'

On fine days the maid pushed the high perambulator down the street, often when Clara thought the weather too damp and bitter for him to be out. He would get a chill, or something worse. But Emma said he had to get used to the elements, otherwise he would be vulnerable to all sorts of things when he grew up.

Their father said in a letter that the emptiness of the house became more appalling every day. He passed the time in a trance, looking forward to the night, but when sleep did come he woke up because the house was on fire, only to find that it was not. The nightmare came back, and he was afraid that he would be burned to death on a night when he did not dream at all. He wanted to hear real voices instead of imaginary ones, no matter what they said about him. The servants had left, and he didn't know why. Perhaps Clara would arrange things. Emma and the baby could have the large sunny room overlooking the garden.

The letter was not a concession, she knew, but a demand that Clara could not ignore. She reflected on how the world

340

must be full of old, selfish and no longer innocent children. Most had never been innocent, though they had all been helpless. Her father still was. He took care to remind her that he did not have much longer to live. He lied out of self-pity. She thought about his life of recurring and debilitating mental agony that was inexplicable until John had been killed in action, and Rachel had died. He and Rachel had been such sweethearts; right till the end, she thought scathingly; and he would never know how lucky he had been that one of the Chosen had chosen him.

The only hope of getting another house, Clara said, was to take a cottage. It was impossible to find anything in Cambridge. But Emma couldn't bear to be cut off somewhere in the countryside. 'I'm dying of loneliness as it is. In any case, can you imagine me in some honeysuckle bijou rural slum without even room to swing a baby? Lighting oil lamps and getting water from a well? I'd become prim, and eccentric, and as coarse as an old witch. I don't feel like growing old just yet.'

'The Jenkinsons will be back from New Zealand in three weeks,' Clara reminded her. 'We have to move.'

'It'll be fun having nowhere to go. Do you think we'll be put out on the street like vagrants? What an adventure if we have to go to the workhouse!'

'Oh do be serious.'

'All right. If it upsets you, I'll do as you say.'

'Father asked us to go back.'

'You mean he wants you to be his housekeeper?'

'He'd like us to go home.'

Emma was silent.

'Don't pout like that. I suppose he does think we'll make his life more tolerable, but it might suit us. After all, Highgate's a good place to live, and you'll be quite close to town. Maybe we'll get to a show, or go to dinner now and again. Even I fancy a bit of distraction.'

The baby cried, and Emma ran up the stairs calling: 'Anything you like. I'll do whatever you say.'

14

Emma watched her pack. 'You're like the Rock of Gibraltar.'

Clara hadn't thought of it like that, saw herself as stupidly undertaking tasks beyond her strength, and never able to change her mind or complain once she had started, but always more or less muddling through. It was not a matter of assuming her mother's place so much as of facing situations Rachel wouldn't have considered. There seemed nothing but herself standing between order and disaster, yet the chaos inside could dissolve her strength at any moment. She knew she must hold on and not let it happen, and felt frightened at each new responsibility.

The carriers came for their trunks, cases and perambulator. In half an hour a motor cab would take them to the station, and Mr and Mrs Jenkinson would not know that the house had been occupied in their absence. Clara would lock all doors and give the keys to the estate agents on their way to the railway. The maid had been sent off with her box and an extra ten shillings, and there was nothing to do but sit and wait. 'We won't notice the bad weather in London,' Clara said.

Emma sat by the last of the embers with the swaddled baby on her knees. 'The first thing we must do is get a nursemaid, so that we can go out together.'

'It'll be spring on Hampstead Heath,' Clara said.

'We'll have supper at Romano's! London's going to be marvellous. I hope our old gramophone still goes. We'll go to the Alhambra and the Empire. We'll actually see people in Hyde Park! I want to come back to life. I feel I've been cut off for years.'

'You poor thing,' Clara mocked. 'I do hope you won't be disappointed in the great metropolis.'

'I won't,' Emma said vehemently. 'Believe me.'

'Well, there'll be more to do than just go around enjoying yourself.'

When Emma reached to press her hand the baby almost fell from her knee. She caught him in time, but cried out: 'Don't bother me with your sanctimonious advice. I've told you before that I don't like it. I can look after myself.'

Clara sat straight. Perhaps there would be an end to it soon. There had to be. She wanted to go away, be by herself at a quiet resort in Switzerland where the scenery would rest her soul. She would stay at a hotel on the Rigi for a couple of months and refresh herself, and perhaps meet some other woman of the right sort to talk to in the lounge, or go on long walks together.

'I keep losing my temper,' Emma said, 'but I don't mean to. I'm sorry.'

Clara smiled. What nonsense to consider taking a holiday while her family needed her. 'I suppose I'd lose mine if I were in your place. Thank God we're going home. We'll be better off there.'

In the train, thin vomit slopped down Thomas's shawl, and Emma's eyes enlarged with panic. 'What shall we do?'

An elderly white-haired man reading his newspaper moved along the seat for fear he would be showered.

'We must get him to a doctor,' Emma cried.

'I wouldn't pull that communication cord if I were you,' the man said. 'It's a very serious offence.'

Emma turned, forgetting about Thomas. 'It's my bloody baby, and he might be dying, and if he is I'll pull whatever I bloody well like. That's what the bloody communication cord is for.' She passed Thomas to Clara, who lifted him high against her shoulder and patted him gently till the vomiting and screaming stopped.

'Well, that's my advice,' the man said. 'It's not necessary now, is it?'

Emma sat down. 'It might have been. I'd stop the world if I

thought it was necessary, and since it's my baby, I'm the one to know, not you.'

Thomas slept, and Clara gave him back. 'I often get the horrors,' Emma said, 'thinking that something dreadful will happen to him. He sucks me dry, yet seems so frail at the same time.'

'He's strong and healthy,' Clara asserted. 'Look at him. He gets bigger every day, the way he feeds from you, and goes out in all weathers.'

'I know, but I can't help the thoughts I have. I dream he's dead, and when I hear him screaming in the morning because he's hungry, instead of being annoyed at not having slept properly, I feel so glad that I cry as I feed him.'

Clara could only think that maybe Emma was lucky at being able to give such full expression to her emotional ups and downs. Yet she suffered for no real reason, and her dread was a contagion that spread many times compounded, though it was different for Clara who had nothing in her own mind and body by which to give it reality. Emma's misery was based on the fulness of herself, but in Clara it only engendered emptiness or dread.

Percy stood inside the iron gate, looking along the road for their taxi. When it stopped, and Clara was half way across the pavement, he was still gazing in the other direction. He had short grey hair smartly brushed, and seemed younger than when Clara had seen him at the funeral. She called. He turned slowly and smiled. His hand shook as it came out to her. 'I had business in town, but I put everything off so as to be here and greet you both.'

She drew her hand away to help Emma. The cab driver steadied her out, and laughed as he got ready to catch Thomas in case he fell. 'My wife dropped the young 'un,' he said, 'so you could say she dropped it twice, in a manner of speaking.'

Percy sent him away with five shillings so as to stop his foul laughter. He tried to smile while looking at the baby. 'Who's he like?'

'Mother,' Emma said.

'Do you think so?'

'No doubt about it.'

'I see what you mean. And yet I'm not so sure.'

'He's from her side,' Emma insisted.

'It's a bit too early to tell, at any rate so vehemently.' He walked before them to the porch, and rang the bell with great irritation. An elderly woman opened the door. 'Help in the ladies, and their child,' he said. 'Get Audrey to take the cases.'

The cab driver had left their things on the pavement.

15

'I'm going to like it here,' said Emma. 'It isn't raining, the house is big, and father will soon get used to us.'

Clara lay on the bed. 'It's good to be back on my old mattress. Where's Thomas?'

'Audrey's got him. She says she knows about babies because there were nine in her family. She can feed him, as well, when I get him on to bottled milk. I don't want to be tethered for ever like some animal.'

At the first dining-room meal Emma said she was going to call in a decorator and have her room painted white. While it was being done she would have to occupy her mother's room. Percy said he thought she should do no such thing. He wouldn't allow it, in fact. Emma looked at him a full minute without speaking, her caramel eyes glowing as if she would strike him should he say anything further. As soon as he finished dessert he got up and went to his study. They heard his door slam.

Emma opened all the windows. The subtle smell of her mother that remained reminded her of her own. Sunlight cut the bed. She took off the counterpane and turned the mattress, tears falling on to the cloth that covered the springs. I didn't kill you, she said. No one kills anyone. You don't even kill yourself.

'Will you bring Thomas's crib in?' Clara said from the doorway.

She turned. 'Did I kill her?'

The fact that Clara knew who she meant proved that she might well have.

'Of course not. Father's a fool for hinting it.'

Emma dried her eyes. While they spread the sheets she said: 'Audrey can take the crib into her room. Thomas will sleep there. I want to be alone at night.'

Emma knew, she said, that Percy did not like her. She had always felt his hostility, and having an illegitimate baby to their name did not improve matters. He had adored his wife, and had disliked Emma (who closely resembled her) for those faults of Rachel which he had never allowed himself to acknowledge in case they spoiled life between them. Like all people who cherished each other as if they were still children in the nursery, the relationship had only been tolerable when they were mindlessly happy. Percy had known this very well, and had done everything to keep it so. Ruses of brain-fever and nervous breakdown had not been too much to manage, Emma said, when they talked about it in Clara's room.

They had tea brought up from the kitchen, and sat in armchairs by the window. 'You imagine too much,' Clara replied.

Emma's hand shook when she poured the milk. 'Anything I imagine is real. I didn't think that for there not to have been some truth in it.'

'I dare say there is, but it's hardly fair to father. Not to mention mother.' Clara was convinced. Emma's sense of reality was reinforced by the tone of her voice, which Clara knew was not true of herself because she rarely pondered on such matters, or thought them important when she did.

Emma's speculations could also be outrageous. 'I wonder what mother and father were like in bed together?'

'I refuse to talk about it.'

'Well, I wonder. There's no harm in that.'

'Much like anybody else, I suppose.'

Emma broke a piece of toast and passed half to Clara. 'I find it disgusting to think about – in a way.'

Clara's mouth was full. 'Don't, then.'

'I try not to.'

Clara could not let the topic go so easily. 'Is it hard to try not to?'

'I think about it whether I try to or not. But I don't mind. Maybe it's good for me. Such thoughts never occurred to me before Thomas was born.'

Clara changed the subject because there seemed nothing more to be got from it. 'Why do you always wear that Jewish star?'

She held it between her fingers. 'Don't you like it?'

'Very attractive, I suppose.'

'I can tell you don't think so. Thomas will have it when he's old enough.'

'You mean *men* wear them?'

'He can put it under his vest.'

'Why do you want him to, especially?'

'Mother gave it to him, that's why. I'm also glad I had him circumcised. She wanted that, too.'

Clara wished they could be together without so much talk. 'I don't see that it matters, these days.'

'It certainly does. Mother wanted him to be part of her line, not father's. She was getting her sense back at the end. When he grows up he can be what he likes, but if he wants to be Jewish he can be. If I die, at least I'll leave him with a choice, and you can't give a child anything better. Anybody can have good health, good looks, and even a good job, but to have a *choice* to make – that's special! Not that I'm sure which way he'll go. It'll be up to him.'

347

Clara, sighing, didn't know what to say. Her hopes sounded so unnecessary. 'You won't die, silly. He'll be what you want him to be. And he may not want anything to do with it.'

'He will. I only wish mother had given me such a choice.'

Clara thought she had. 'I jolly well don't, speaking for myself. There's enough to worry about, without that.'

'You're so plain and shallow. The more one has to worry about, the more chance there is to think other things.'

'I'm not so sure.'

After a while Emma said: 'Have you seen mother's books?'

'What books?'

'You haven't?'

'Is that why you moved into her room? What a dreadful snooper!' – a riposte for being called plain and shallow.

'Her dresses are still there, so I suppose that when you looked you didn't notice the lid that opens from the inside of the wardrobe. I found letters from father written before they were married, and some he'd sent from the asylum, as well as a few she'd written to him. She must have got them back for some reason, or he gave them to her for safe keeping. They were better than I expected. But there were also a few old books in Hebrew and German – which I'll keep, if *you* don't mind.'

'I don't. But will father?'

'He won't have to. Thomas will have them one day.'

'This Jewish thing has gone to your head.'

Clara was sorry. She had spoken without thought, which one should never do with Emma, who looked anguished, not so much, as it turned out, for what had been said, but because: 'I still can't believe mother's gone. It frightens me to think about her life. If only she'd come back for an hour, for me to say all I'd never said when she was alive. I didn't tell her how much I loved her, and now it's not possible.' She shook her head. 'Life under such conditions is hardly worth while.'

Clara was alert with disagreement. 'You're trying to make Thomas become what mother would have wanted him to be, because she felt guilty at having given up her Judaism.'

'She never did. She was always Jewish.'

'Oh, she wasn't all that deliberate about it. One never is. But have it your way. You're trying to get him back on to the "one true path" then. Is that it?'

Emma's face expressed inner enlightenment. 'Yes, you're right. But there are many true paths. I only want him to be like me and mother. Different to you and father.'

Clara shook her head. 'What rubbish.'

'I want him to be *civilized*. He'll find out what I mean when he makes his choice.'

Clara wanted to be alone. She had nothing else to say. There was a limit to the amount of talk she could put up with. 'I'll be glad to start the spring-cleaning tomorrow. We can do the drawing-room first, and that'll take some work. The place hasn't been cleaned for I don't know how long.'

'A few more days' – Emma stood – 'and it's into town for me. I want to spring-clean my life, not this dreadful old house. I wouldn't care if it fell down, as long as we weren't in it,' she laughed.

She had been glad to seek refuge here, Clara thought after Emma had gone to her room. If Emma was tied in all ways to the baby, *she* was harnessed into organizing the household, and for a while neither could go into town. The most they did was to go shopping or to the bank in Highgate village. Otherwise they kept to the house as if they had rented that also. The upstairs back windows looked south, and they could see the Houses of Parliament on a good day. The sun fitfully blessed the grey sprawl, as if they were on the outskirts of a strange city after two seasons in a distant wilderness. Clara reached to the table for her journal and fountain pen, too weary to write yet too stimulated by the conversation with Emma to resist doing so.

The maid accepted Thomas as if he were her brother or son. She fed him, played with him, and daily pushed him in the pram to Waterlow Park or Parliament Hill, walking along the foliaged pathways and under trees turning to a heavier green as the year went on. In the rain she clipped the hood and canvas barrier into place, so that he was snug against the elements.

With much screaming he was weaned from the breast and put on to bottled milk. Audrey fed him, as well as cleaned him, put him to bed, and got him up in the morning. A new girl did odd tasks in her place and hurried about on errands, and Audrey was solely in charge of Thomas.

Clara looked at him. Emma was in town, and Audrey had not yet taken him out. He lay in his pram, eyes open and staring at her, so clean and calm, so innocent. She wondered how much he saw at six months old, how much he knew of what was going on around him. He was unwanted, and would have to take his chance in life. The choice Emma had so thoughtlessly lumbered him with would be no advantage. He would be better off knowing nothing, at least until a time when such problems no longer mattered. Maybe Emma wasn't serious. In her life of going about town she would forget her ideas, one enthusiasm often being swept away by the onslaught of another.

He saw her properly, and smiled. She was sure he smiled. His lips moved, and his eyes sparkled on opening wide. He stared, as if wondering why he smiled. His thin dark hair already had that subtle sheen of red. She lifted a finger, as if telling him to be still because he had nothing to smile fulsomely about. He reached for her thumb. He made a noise of laughter, and she felt sorry for him, as well as pity for Emma. She knew a moment of grief for her mother, her father, and for herself – feelings she disliked intensely. She touched his warm cheek consolingly, then told herself not to be stupid, and walked upstairs to see why the maid was taking so long getting ready.

Her father, on his afternoon walk, made sure he went in the opposite direction to Audrey and Thomas. He did not have the physical strength to force his face towards the baby when he was anywhere near his perambulator. He passed him as if some form of contamination might leap across.

Since Rachel died he had turned his back on life, as if she had taken his spirit with her. His nerves were no good again, he said, not hiding the fact that he blamed Emma for her mother's death. His face was a mask which prevented any sympathy breaking through. No one deserved it, his expression said. The hurt flesh around his grey eyes indicated that he had had enough of trying to understand. Such efforts hadn't worked and never would. Emma told him there might still be something to live for.

'Father,' she said at dinner, on a rare evening when she stayed at home, 'why don't you get married again?'

The cook brought in a platter of lamb chops, and Clara dropped one before getting it to her place.

'Careless,' Percy said. 'Grip it tight.'

They took food on to their plates, and Clara hoped that her sister would forget her unseemly question. Why must she make more trouble than was absolutely necessary? Or any trouble at all? It was too much to expect.

'I asked,' said Emma, whose place at table was to his left, 'whether or not you might ever think of getting married again, father?'

'Oh do stop,' Clara called.

He looked up. 'I loved your mother too much. Besides, I'm an old man.'

Emma laughed. 'You're not much more than sixty. And if you really did love mother you'd certainly want to marry again. It would be nice for you, and good for the rest of us.'

He was about to smile – Clara was sure of it – but changed his mind. She saw it happening, in his predictable, half-conscious yet deliberate way, all emotions mixed to create the effect he absolutely wanted. And who, she thought, is any different? But she longed to get out of such force-fields, which by their spreading torment robbed you of life's enjoyment. Her ideal state was an existence, if she must pass hers with

351

other people, of placid well-bred diplomacy. Otherwise, she would live alone.

'One usually meets someone and falls in love before getting married.' He spoke less severely. 'I haven't yet seen anyone who would be a likely prospect. A marriage of convenience, or one to suit my wayward daughter, isn't the sort of thing I would care to indulge in.'

Emma persevered. 'You might meet a pleasant young woman. There are plenty about.'

She wanted him – and Clara could see that he knew it – to marry only so that she could then accuse him of never having loved their mother. He'd had enough, however. 'When you yourself get married, I could be in a better frame of mind to think about it.'

'Does Clara have to get married, too?'

'I'd rather go on with my dinner,' he said, 'than put up with your tyranny.'

'I'll never get married,' Clara announced, feeling like a boulder before the floodwater.

'I suppose we're lucky mother didn't feel that way,' said Emma. 'Or are we?'

Clara picked up the handbell and rang for cook to come and take their plates. 'Perhaps she did.'

'Though I suppose,' went on Emma, 'that she would quite like you to marry again.'

'She would *not*,' he said. 'She is now in heaven, and she would be eternally distressed.'

He had thought himself safe behind the palisade of his last request. But he doesn't know Emma. He can't possibly know her, Clara thought, since he didn't really know mother very well, either. Or so Emma believed. Perhaps she was right, having a sure knowledge of people's weaknesses. But he torments her, so she's only getting her own back. No, it feels much worse than that.

He stood, and threw his napkin on to the table. The cook moved around to lift his plate. He put a hand to his forehead and closed his eyes. Clara asked cook to bring in the dessert, then said to Emma: 'Why can't you know when to stop?'

He sat down. 'I must ask you never to mention that subject again, not in any way whatsoever. If you do I will find it impossible to be in the same house with you.'

'You're nothing but a male bully,' Emma responded coolly. 'You have no emotional latitude. This is a dead house, and you make it so. We all live under your conditions, right down to what we can think. But you aren't going to tell me what I can and can't say.'

Clara felt riven by fever, cast between freezing and boiling, one part horrified for her father, the other side of her saying to herself: 'Good for you, Emma, tell him off as he deserves.' She had to admit that in some respects their life had been better when they'd had a place of their own, in that their antagonisms didn't spread.

'I wasn't trying to annoy you,' Emma said. 'You could easily have laughed at my suggestion, instead of creating such a tragic atmosphere.'

Their mother had only been dead a few months, and Clara reminded her that people generally needed a year to get over a loved one's death, if they ever did. Emma may not have been malicious, but she was surely insensitive to go on about it when father didn't want her to.

Percy folded his napkin neatly, put it into its ivory ring, and went to smoke a cigar in his study, where he kept a decanter of port and could sit at his desk and stare at the large leather-bordered blotter till he was roused by the need for more port or to relight his cigar; or he would, with the smouldering cigar between his fingers, cover sheets of paper with automatic scribble-writing, using his favourite Waterman fountain pen, till his fingers ached too intensely for him to go on, or until a length of ash scattered itself on the paper as a reminder that he must stop because there were other things in life, such as a further glass of port and another cigar. He didn't notice Clara set a coffee tray on his desk.

'I suppose,' she said to Emma in the living-room, 'that he's happy, after his fashion.'

'I hope so.' Emma added that by talking frankly about his situation she was only helping to bring his thoughts into the open. That was what he found so intolerable. Well, it was understandable. She wouldn't want hers to be forced out in such a way, in which case she wouldn't worry him again. If he wanted to know what he was thinking he could discover for himself – or not, as the case may be. She was sorry, and would apologize in the morning.

Clara said she ought to, and that from now on she should 'act her age' when at table with father, to which Emma replied that she knew very well what her age was, and couldn't do anything but act it. Her age was part of her. It was a wide age that spanned any number of years, and not a narrow segment of time in which every tight-laced emotion was predictable.

There must be some good in him, Emma went on, because that, presumably, had been similar to what he had loved in mother, and maybe what in the end he couldn't stand about her, because after she had died he didn't want any more of it in the house, at least not from one of his daughters.

'You're wrong about father,' Clara said. 'You probably remind him so much of mother that it's doubly painful when you go on as you do.'

'But mother was always quiet as a mouse.'

'In the last twenty years she was,' Clara replied, 'but at the beginning she was very lively – at least by her own account.'

'Till he crushed it out of her by self-indulgent fits of so-called insanity,' Emma said.

'He'd had them before he met her.' It's no use asking where it all began. Here we are, yet because we must put up with all the questions and upsets we ought to forget about them. But Clara knew that to do so would mean cutting away nine-tenths of thought and talk. Emma stood before the fireplace and looked at the oil-painting of John above the mantelpiece.

354

She gazed for some minutes, as if passing on her reflections to the face that could never give off the same life she remembered from him.

'Father used his illness to try and break her spirit.' She turned to Clara. 'But only John being killed did that. Where's the moral in it all?'

'I don't know. Is there one?'

'There must be.'

'Hating father won't help you to find it.'

'Oh, I don't really hate him, but I do wish he wouldn't die on us every day now mother's no longer here. He's spitting on her memory. Don't you see, Clara? I love them both, yet I'm trying to make sure we have a better life than she had. Her beginning with father was a terrible mistake for both of them, but mostly for her. He's trying to reduce us to the same state she was in most of her life. And I don't know how to stop him!'

Tears were falling down Clara's cheeks. 'It isn't his fault.'

'Nor hers. Nor yours. Nor mine. It just happens. That's worst of all. Things happen whether we want them to or not. It's too horrible to bear.'

Clara cried aloud at the searing notion of her sister making the same mistake as her mother, though on a grander scale. She sobbed, unmercifully torn inside. She reached for Emma and held her tight. 'Please don't go on like this. I can't tolerate any more.'

But she didn't, as Emma thought, mean stop talking about their parents. She was pleading for her not to carry on so senselessly. Don't go into town so often. Don't stay out all night with men you pick up. What are you looking for, trying to find, doing to yourself? Why don't you stay in, sit still, or do something else? She couldn't explain, knew it would be useless anyway, that it would only bring words crushing back, might even drive Emma to worse things.

Emma too was weeping, both bodies burning together, but nothing more could be said.

16

When Emma stayed in for a few days, Audrey would not be allowed either to feed or change Thomas, nor take him out. Emma was with him from waking up to putting him to bed.

The decorators had come and gone, and she was back in the large front room, Thomas's crib in the dressing-room opening off. When the weather was fine she sat on the veranda steps. She looked up from her book at Thomas in his pram below staring at a black-and-white cat walking the branch of a plum tree. She read, or she did nothing.

From the living-room window Clara noticed how often she looked straight ahead with a faint smile towards the wall at the end of the garden, a hand occasionally moving to straighten her hair. At the slightest cry she would be down in a moment to comfort Thomas. Or she would pick him up. His priority was total, and Clara did not know whether she preferred Emma's mood of devoted mother (which excluded everyone else from the union of herself and the baby) or that of the distracted young woman who set off for town like an animal loose out of a cage.

Clara wondered why only these two choices were possible, for neither seemed good for any woman. Clara wanted a stable and predictable order, which guaranteed peace everywhere. She craved the ideal family which did not exist.

Emma's calm was the eye of the storm, and out of sisterly love Clara shared the space there. But when the tempest broke Clara would be looking for that calm zone in order to escape the pain and fury, and when she realized that no peace existed anywhere she would be reduced to a tearful passion that seemed to damage her beyond all possibility of feeling normal again.

She wondered how long such a permanently threatening

state could last. The only danger was to feel that she would not be able to tolerate the disturbance much longer, for she sensed a dismaying fragility in herself that might lead to failure in her duty towards Emma. She assumed that similar thoughts had planted themselves in her father's heart as well, for he did not speak to Emma, and never asked where she had gone.

He rarely talked to anybody, stayed in his study, and often ate his meals there. When Emma wondered why, it was only to add that she didn't care, though Clara knew she suffered by being cast as a stranger in the house. To justify his neglect, her father never let the expression of aggrieved deprivation go from his face while either sister was nearby. The turmoil of his earlier life had taught him how to control his family, and Clara saw that only Emma had the courage to prevent such power going unchecked, though at a cost to her that was alarming to witness. It was as if she suspected him of wanting to drive her to some awful fate in return for having, as he supposed, caused their mother's death.

When Emma was out of the house the pall of her misery shifted to Clara, who could not rest in wondering where she was, and from fretting at what might be happening to her, and worrying about what time she would come back, and how they'd be able to find her if Thomas was taken ill.

Clara stared at him until he moved out of sleep, or the mouth puckered because he could not get free of troubling dreams. She was stricken by a sense of his impermanence, as if at any moment he might stop breathing, or be found not living in the morning, in which case the unity in the family, which even his unwelcome presence had somehow cemented, would be broken for ever. Every live being on earth served its purpose, she thought. Every death reordered the position of those left behind.

Fruit trees blossomed, spheres of pink and white reaching one behind the other as far as the wall, while all beneath was cluttered with nettles and brambles because Percy had

357

dismissed the man who looked after the garden for having taken a few sticks of wood without permission. Percy was too mean to give someone else the job, and when Emma suggested he walk to the nearest dole queue and choose a poor man for the honour, he appeared not to hear. Clara had opened a path with shears but the vegetation grew back to its former density.

White lilac, apple and plum blossom set against sunlight and cloud reminded her that there was nothing they lacked to make life pleasant. They had money, a house, all material things, good health, and yet – Clara turned from the blossom that was so pleasing to the soul – why is it one can cut the misery with a knife?

'I'll tell you,' said Emma, when Clara could not resist voicing her reflections aloud. 'It's because we treat each other as if we'll come to pieces if a cross word is said. I teased father about getting married, but actually did think how good it would be to hear and see another person in the house. Whatever my reasons for having Thomas, one of them was because I wanted to bring a new spirit into the family. I went about it the wrong way, of course. Father would like me to get an upright sanctimonious husband who grovelled with respect for him. So would you. But I couldn't attach myself to any man for life, even if I thought I loved him. Nothing can be done for us. I can't stand it here. I was hoping father would throw me out when I went on about him getting married, but he's too old and soft. He'll probably just cross me out of his will. He'll get his own back, somehow, I know he will. There's only one solution for me.'

'You're not going to leave, are you?'

Emma put on her hat at the dressing-table mirror. 'Do you want me to?'

'Of course I don't. But if you're really fed up you could just take off. With your money you could live anywhere.'

'I wish I didn't have it.'

Clara believed her, but such an attitude seemed like an

attack on her own existence, and she scoffed: 'You'd soon wish you had.'

'You're so sensible. That's something else I can't stand. Suffocating sense! It's impossible to break out of.'

'What do you *want*, then?'

She closed the wardrobe, and surprised Clara by sitting down when she had seemed in a hurry to go out. She needed glasses but hardly ever wore them, and peered into her face. 'Only one thing.'

'What?'

'If anything happens to me, what about Thomas?'

'What do you mean?'

'Well, who would look after him?'

Clara wanted to tell her that the maid was doing quite nicely. 'Nothing's going to happen to you.'

'But suppose I went out, stepped off the causeway, and got killed by a motor-car, or a tram? Or imagine I died of double-pneumonia.'

'You're as strong as a horse. You'll live to be ninety.'

She spoke coolly, yet Clara saw the distress behind her darkened eyes. 'I know. I'm asking you to suppose.'

Some other tone must be used, but Clara's voice overrode the feeble effort she made, and produced a note of impatience. 'I don't imagine Thomas would lack the basic necessities. You can depend on that.'

Emma's face seemed small. She was pleading, but Clara's pain prevented her guessing the reason. 'You're not being sarcastic, are you? I can't always tell.'

Clara faced her. 'Do you think we would put the poor little chap on to the street? Really, why talk like this? You'll have me in tears in a bit, and there's absolutely no need to.'

'I know,' Emma laughed, 'I can't bear to see you crying. It's such a sight: the flower of womanhood in a flood of tears! But I must go. I'm off to the Ritz. I met this wonderful chap, an engineer on leave from the Sudan who doesn't give a damn about anything in the world. So refreshing. We have

359

marvellous fun. I'd love to bring him here, but I don't think it would be appreciated. He'd have the place topsy-turvy in no time. Father would have a thousand fits.'

'What's his name?' Clara asked, desperate to know. 'Let me meet him. I won't run you off, though we might get on better than you think.'

Emma opened the door. 'He's going back soon. They all have somewhere to go back to. He asked me to marry him, but I don't see how I could. I love Thomas too much to have to put him in an orphanage. No man is worth that.'

Clara held her hands. 'You sound as if you're in a bit of a mess. Stay with me this evening. Let's talk. Why don't we go to the Riviera for a month or two? There's a pleasant hotel at Beausoleil we can stay at for a while. Or we can go to Menton. It's a bit quiet, but there are lots of nice walks, and it's closer to Italy. Thomas can come with us. We can get two or three rooms. Let's sit down and discuss it. We can go to Cooks tomorrow, and they'll arrange everything.'

Even while talking, Clara knew that they couldn't leave their father – though they might be able to get him looked after if Emma agreed to the plan. Anything to keep her from the obviously horrible man she'd met.

Emma's expression suggested that she might like the idea, but she said: 'It's too late.'

'How is it?'

'It just is.'

'Why?' Clara looked into her face, smelt her rouge and perfume. 'You don't believe what you're saying. Nothing is ever too late.'

Emma said: 'It is, though. Too late. Too late for me to believe in anything any more. Everything's changed. I don't know when it began, or how it happened. There's nothing left in my mind. It's all empty. Unless I'm enjoying myself I'm frightened. Just a dreadful emptiness. At times, too often, I feel there's nothing there at all. Nothing – nothing. You can't imagine. I didn't want to tell you, but now I have.'

She has mother's spirit, but father's sickness, and she knows she's got it, whatever it is or was, Clara thought.

'But I must go, or I'll be late.'

And she went out.

Clara felt the despair of the one who always stays behind, and could only soothe her pain by imagining that Emma blamed her for not having suggested the same plan for a holiday weeks ago, when it might have been possible.

She lay much of the night waiting to hear the front door open and shut, and fell into thick dreams towards dawn knowing that Emma hadn't come home. She was away sometimes for days, so Clara didn't worry. Yet she was troubled, knowing that Emma was always unhappy when they were absent from each other for very long. The same unease afflicted Clara, which nothing but a curtain of common-sense attitudes on her part could disperse. No matter how unjust, or unfeeling, there was no other way if fate were to be given the free hand that was, finally, impossible to stand up against.

17

There was a certain quality about the air at the demise of spring and the onset of summer, a rich green on the burgeoning vegetation that the year could not possibly show again, a week or two of heavy rain shining on slates and wooden huts in gardens, exposing rails and balustrades that needed paint, and gutters that wanted clearing of dead leaves. Paint crumbled, and the body of iron broke through.

The air was warm, yet the wind could turn chilly, and it

was hard to say whether a topcoat or only a mackintosh was necessary on going out. The seemingly quiet streets were in fact full of traffic, the noise subdued because unable to rise in the heavy atmosphere.

In the parks there was a haunting overweight from vivid grass and the branches of laden trees. The sky was in constant alteration, with rarely a pattern of recognizable cloud, and when the sun shone the heat could be fierce if only because of its rarity, but when covered again by banks of cloud the watery air seemed cold.

The fluctuating pressure and temperature put Clara into a state of nervousness that she could hardly control. Such weather made the afternoons long. To fall into a chaos of screaming seemed possible, except that an iron barrier separated her from it. Thomas cried from the nursery, and he stopped when Audrey picked him up. But he cried again. Nothing could soothe him. She had never known him to be such a prolonged nuisance. The day was bad enough without the disturbance of a fractious baby to worsen her headache. She closed the door to her room. He hadn't grizzled so much since Emma had had him circumcised.

She couldn't be bothered to wind the gramophone, tried to read another chapter from *Vanity Fair*, then sat down to begin a letter to her old school friend Lucy Middleton. For the dread she felt, there was little to say. Life was dull, she might write, after her mother's death. The less to be said, the better for all concerned. She had heard no gossip worth putting in, so why waste the postage to New Zealand simply to say that everything was the same as before? It wasn't, but there was no point in telling anybody. She lifted the pen out of the ink and wiped its nib on the corner of the blotting paper. She felt too unsettled. A rattle at the window told her it was raining again.

She didn't know what sort of a bird it was, just a small common feathery thing that settled on a bush and shook itself. The way its wings fluttered and head turned quickly from side to side made her laugh. Such antics! The feathers were quite beautiful. It had crowned itself king (or maybe even queen) of the bush, so what more had it to wish for? Was it a flapper in the sparrow world with a bijou nest under the eaves? It flew away. A policeman and another man were at the gate. They talked, then came towards the door. The window was open an inch or two, and she heard the crumble of their boots on gravel. Unable to move, she watched one of them pull the bell.

The sound made her muscles leap. She cried out, but didn't care to get up. Perhaps Audrey would. Don't let it happen, whatever it is. Unhappen it, she said. How stupid! When the jangling stopped, she went with straight back and springing steps to ask the visitors in.

Someone had come to see her. The smile must be bright. She never forgot the shape of her lips that went into that particular smile, nor the lurch of her steps. The day had no ending in her life, but she'd hardly noticed its beginning. Ensuing days became part of grief – which creates its own lunar space, she wrote, so that when the sky is clear you can hardly see into it. And neither will you till your own life ends. Perhaps such heartbreak even precedes and waits for your soul as it comes out of life. Her writing deteriorated, the script impossible to decipher.

The idiot smile persisted as she hammered the dead wood of the study door to wake her father. He suffered deep irritation at being pulled from the centre of his daily nap, and with a weepish expression waited, in slippers and dressing-gown, for an explanation.

She was alone, the onus of everything only on her. 'They've come with news of Emma. She's been found dead.'

She couldn't shape the words properly, but took him by the cold hand and pulled him along, making sure he didn't fall down the stairs. How lucky to be old. She sniffed angrily, trying to calm herself. By a few words the world had changed. Wood on the banister was rougher. A glimpse of conservatory plants through an open door seemed to threaten her. She let

363

go of her father's arm to shut out the draught, and muttered that she must pull herself together. The tonic of her usual words did no good. Those she had just heard moved into her brain for ever.

The old gentleman didn't seem able to accept the fact that his daughter had been found dead in a Paddington hotel. To tell anything else would have been to suppose just a little too much, and they weren't the sort of people who would do so, no matter what your position in the world. She wondered if they didn't enjoy their reticence. It had been imposed upon them, but they certainly made the best of it. It wasn't their job to do otherwise. Perhaps it was indeed an accident, but they were trying to find out. They stated that much, that they didn't know what it *seemed*, only what they *saw*. Nothing but scientific conclusions were allowable. They weren't competent on those lines, the detective sergeant said, to offer any more information.

There were no tears on Percy's cheeks. She brushed the skin under her eyes and it was also dry. Mustn't break down in front of them.

'Is it quite certain?' Percy's lips mimicked hers.

The chiming clock released the acid in her by each number. She poured whisky, but none for herself. She didn't drink, she said. Percy's glass fell. She picked it up and set it on the mantelshelf where he couldn't reach it. The bureaucratic finalizing of death would give her much to do. There would be an inquest, and the burial. She hoped it was an accident, and one of the men looked at her. No, no, a thousand times no, I'd rather die than say yes. She fought the words of the common song out of her mind. She used to sing them with Emma when they were children – to annoy their mother. Thinking it permissible, she sat down. If her father slumped she could leap across and catch him. Her calm questions finally made them solicitous. All arrangements would be made. Ten minutes had gone by since the clock had chimed.

She was afraid to look in the mirror in case Emma smiled

364

back. To see even her own reflection would break the strength that being entirely alone gave her. It was a risk she would not take. She could issue orders, and do things, but not with the thought that someone was looking on. Being alone was strength, the more alone the better, for it was easier then to be herself, and if you were as totally yourself as it was possible to be, then you were in control. Nothing could break you down.

But sharp physical pains pierced her, and she fought back the temptation to roar out her soul as she powdered her face and put on her coat and then her hat without looking in the mirror. When she walked to the Green to get a motor cab, in order to go and identify the body, anyone passing on the street would have known that she was not her normal self. Her normal self was tall, blue-eyed, with fair but slightly reddish hair, a proud woman easy to remember and describe. She had been brought up to be, and had always assumed that she was, well-composed and unwilling to feel that any catastrophe could hurt her, though she reflected that it must only have meant those blows directed at someone else. If anything harder than the present blow were to strike she would hope to be conscious only long enough to thank God for it and then die.

18

She recorded the fact that in the midst of death she was in desolation, but rejoiced at the inquest's conclusion that her sister's demise was accidental. Emma seemed to have turned on the gas heater and absent-mindedly forgotten to apply a light. There was a willingness to believe such an assumption after the family general practitioner said that, having known her for twenty years, he considered her a normal outgoing person, of whom it was inconceivable to think that the misfortune could have been anything other than an accident. The exoneration helped them to feel that Emma's carelessness was only another manifestation of her feckless nature. If she had died at home, however much more upsetting it would have been, they might not have been tormented by the suggestion that she had betrayed them after cutting herself off so entirely from help. She did not want to be part of them any more, a feeling that, after the first paralysing weeks, diminished Clara's gnawing pain.

From one stance she changed to another, would sit hours by the fire – even in the summer it was cold that year – while her mind went through endless conversations with Emma as to what had gone wrong. Talking aloud, she would walk between the door and the window:

'But she committed suicide, you fool, whatever the coroner decided. Her man friend went back to the Sudan and she couldn't stand the thought of being alone. Perhaps she was pregnant, and this time didn't want to be. She was alone because we didn't mean enough to her. She cared nothing for my support, nor father's, in the final mood she got into. She'd been in that state ever since I can remember, till her condition became so bad she could do little except find a way out, which must have come easily, whether or not it was an accident. Thank God she didn't do it at home and take Thomas with her, though it might have been a blessing in disguise if she had.'

But she wept at the thought of all that had not been done to stop Emma dying, though when she wondered what she might have done it was apparent that nothing would have been possible, because the time and place of a person's death was decided the moment they were born – and with such words she cleared her mind of futile speculation.

Clutching the door handle in order to go out, she could not

turn it, and had only the strength to get back to a chair. It was impossible to know whether she stayed a minute or an hour. The days were long, and darkness came late. Then she sprang from her inanition and went out of the room, believing that if she had stayed a moment longer she would have been paralysed for life.

She walked along the hall, and entered her father's study without knocking. He sat in an armchair, and put the newspaper to his knees on hearing the door knob rattle. She sat on a stool at his feet. 'I've come to talk to you.'

'I used to read quickly,' he complained, 'but I have difficulty fixing my eyes nowadays.' He took off his wire spectacles and rubbed his forehead. 'I can't sleep, either.' His skin was lined and deadly white, nose thin and bones prominent. Nor did he eat much except porridge, orange juice, or mashed potatoes. Nothing but nursery food. 'What do you need to talk about?'

She had forgotten, but wanted to be near him because there was no one else. Since Emma's death she felt a need to be with him, but was afraid of seeming a nuisance. 'It'll soon be time for dinner. I thought you might like to come down with me.'

'I'll eat in my room,' he said sharply.

'I got some Dover sole from the fishmonger this morning, and cook has made one of her marvellous soups.' She wanted to talk, if only to get a response from a voice not her own. She missed Emma's. There was no speech, nothing but vague noises of Audrey and cook laughing together, or of the baby that never seemed to stop grizzling.

'I won't come down.'

'I'm not going to eat alone any more in this house,' she said.

'Oh, aren't you?' He stood up, and took off his dressing-gown. 'Where's my collar and tie?'

They were hanging on a chairback. She gave them to him. 'Shall I help you?'

His hands trembled. He snatched the tie. 'Get my jacket.'

She found it in his bedroom, and when she came back he

367

had already fastened on his collar and tie.

'We still have a lot to talk about,' she said.

'Have we?'

'I can't make every decision myself.'

His small blue eyes, from seeing nothing, glittered acutely. 'You don't have to. I make them, in this house. Where's my tie? I've been looking all over, and can't find it.'

It was not the time to play jokes. 'You've put it on already.'

He sat down, and placed a hand to his throat to make sure she was telling the truth. 'Did you say there was Dover sole?'

'And soup. And batter pudding.' She held out her hand. 'Come on, father, it's nearly time.'

'You go,' he said. 'I can manage.'

She walked downstairs to the dining-room, thinking that even if she heard him fall she would not help. He wasn't even fond of her. He liked no one. All he had was the power of the man in the house, and he enjoyed that, though she was determined he wouldn't have it much longer. But she was afraid to turn and deride the way he had snubbed her. Her fear of him was as intense as her pride that would not allow her to make one more attempt to become friendly. He blocked himself in, and she locked herself out, but she knew that without being able to speak his thoughts his eyes pleaded for her to come close to him. He was too afraid to ask, and his pride would stop him even if he weren't. Emma once told her that pride was a sophisticated form of fear. The family was rotten with it, but because it was Clara's only means of self-respect, and therefore defence. she would guard it jealously. Emma had thrown hers overboard, and look what had happened.

Percy held the spoon high against his chest as if about to beat a tattoo on a drum. The soup steamed. He looked ahead, unable or not willing to move.

'We mustn't let our soup get cold.' It wasn't possible to begin before he did, though she supposed he might not notice it in his abstracted condition.

He broke his bread and started to eat. The cook had decanted a bottle of burgundy, and Clara filled two glasses.

'*I* pour the wine,' he said. 'I always do.'

She smiled at his petulance, her mouth wired to stop a cry breaking out. 'I've already done so.'

He hung the napkin from his waistcoat. She reminded him again to begin. When cook took the plates she heard the far-off wail of Thomas from upstairs. Thank goodness for Audrey, who had replaced his mother, but how long could it last? 'What *are* we going to do with the baby?'

He spoke, the unexpected precision startling her. 'He must go to an orphanage. That's the only place, when there are no proper parents.'

She flushed warmly at such a drastic and outrageous solution, with which she felt in immediate agreement. She couldn't bring up a child, and Audrey's plebeian ministrations were only a stopgap. 'He's a bit young, isn't he?'

'They'll take him. I know a place. I'll write to the director and make special arrangements. We'll pay the bills by the year.'

She had seen him wearing his napkin in such a fashion after coming out of convalescent homes, and then only until Rachel told him to place it on his knees. Let him use it that way. She didn't mind, except that it gave his aspect an air of childish authority that must have been exercised over him while he was under care. In the present situation he knew exactly what to do, though she was surprised that he would make her share the expense. 'But is it the right thing to do?'

'Somebody has to look after him,' he retorted. 'Will you bring him up? No. You couldn't bring up a flower in May. Can I do it?' He laughed dryly. 'Soon be dead. So the place where he'll be cared for, and get a good Christian education, is the Boxwell Orphanage. Never thought I'd need it for this little matter, but they'll be glad to take him till he's fifteen, after all I've done for them. Then *you* can find a way for him to earn a living.'

369

His scornful laugh made her doubt even more that it was right to put Emma's child into such a place. 'Isn't there any other way?'

He was unhealthily excited. 'Certainly. A very good one. Get a husband, and you can both adopt him.' He drank half his wine. 'If your husband's a good man, he'll be agreeable.'

Would he have done it? Not damned likely, she told herself. But such problems cleared his brain. Even at his most absent-minded he could muster a man's decisiveness. When they were children he would come back from visiting the orphanage he patronized (she only now heard its name) and say how lucky the inmates were in having found a refuge which did not require them to suffer for the sins of their parents. But Emma, Clara and John felt how awful it must be for such children, and their nanny of the time said that that was where all bad creatures went, and quite right too, because where would the world be if there weren't such places for them to be hidden away in?

Children knew nothing, made up their own harrowing fears, and trembled at the wicked world of which they had no experience. Thomas would be provided for. Her father reassured her that it was the right thing to do. It was an orphanage, of course, but it was more like a home, certainly a great improvement on the one that he would have if it were possible for him to stay where he was – which it wasn't. It would be like a boarding school, but starting younger. He would enquire about him now and again, and when the time came she would have to make sure that he was not entirely forgotten. Some time in the future he would be found, no doubt, tractable and presentable, and might spend the occasional weekend with her. She would talk to him, or take him out. She supposed he would be polite, and have lots to say. He would be glad of the change, and grateful to her for giving him some relief to life in an institution. In that sense she would do what she could. When he grew up she would see about a career for him. Her father said that from such places

370

boys went into the army or the navy, or had their passage paid to one of the colonies or dominions. It seemed very suitable. There were no problems because they were trained to expect such arrangements. And what boy in his right mind, however he had been brought up, would want to stay in this country, considering the state things were? He didn't know how lucky he was going to be.

'I must get him put in,' Percy said, 'before it's too late.'

'Too late?'

'While I'm able to do it. I shan't live for ever.'

'Don't say that.' To contemplate life alone, and all the shifts of place and spirit that it must entail, was as yet impossible, like looking over a cliff with nothing in the distance, and no sight of the bottom. In spite of his unpleasantness he was all she had, the last tree of familiar safety, and she knew by now that you loved people as much because of their faults as in spite of them.

'You're a big silly fool,' he exclaimed. 'Don't you know that if you talk of one thing, you must think of another? I've left some of my money to a few charities, but most will go to you. I only hope you'll take good care of it.'

'I'll be sure to.' In a final gesture she touched his hand affectionately, but he pulled it away. If any contact was needed, he would be the one to make it. She felt revulsion now at his instinctive drawing back, shivered as if a cold wind had blown across her. How had her mother put up with this? She hadn't, really, because she was not the person to do so. But Emma at least said that to offer affection only made him more cruel. You have to bully him and baby him, though to show that you really care, she said, don't show him that you care in the least.

Perhaps he read her thoughts, for he seemed unable to look at her for a few moments. They were silent while the pudding was served. He tapped the dish with his spoon, each stroke getting louder. She didn't wait for him to begin, but when he saw she had done so he stopped his maniacal banging and ate rapidly.

His absent-mindedness, and fits of childishness, became more frequent. She couldn't bear to think of her father existing in a state where she would have to take over her mother's role and bully him as if *he* were the child. She had read that old people who turned senile lived longer than those who did not.

He strayed too far on his daily walk, and was found in the street staring at the gutter. He picked up a cigarette packet, took out the picture card, and put it in his pocket. She discovered others in his desk. People round about were familiar with the foibles of this smartly dressed old man who walked along the street looking only in the gutter.

On her way to bed she went into the nursery, where a night-light was left burning. To disturb Thomas would be a blessing, because if he cried Audrey would come from the adjoining room and put him to sleep again. He would like such attention. There would be little enough from now on. Four neatly folded fingers went to his eyes. He turned, and the clean fresh smell of a new world came from his cot. The cot would afterwards go to the attic, though God knew what for. She wouldn't stay long in that house. The sooner she was out the better. Too much had happened. She would find a flat at some place on the south coast.

His lips curled, and he tried to turn over. Discovering that he couldn't, he was about to cry. Her large hand held his side, enabling him to complete the manoeuvre. Then he yawned, and seemed to sleep. She was alarmed at how he already looked like Emma. Why had she done all the things she had done? The question was foolish, as questions invariably were that came too late to get an answer. She put out the light and closed the door, feeling better when she had done so, as if her troubles had gone, and left her empty.

19

'A woman came from the orphanage to collect him,' Clara wrote on an undated sheet of paper which was folded into the book, 'and though he didn't cry – in fact he was quite happy, because he obviously didn't know what was happening – Audrey did when she had to give him up. If I was sorry to see him go it was only because he was the last of Emma.'

At the bottom of the box was a pack of carefully written receipts for money sent by his grandfather to the orphanage. Tom perceived that at two hundred pounds a year the contributions had been generous, when in those days it must have cost little more than fifty to provide for an inmate at such a place.

The family had kept their obligations, so he could not complain. His career as a seaman hardly allowed him to grumble about any conditions of existence. Nor was he made that way. The fact of being alive, in work, and comfortable enough as an officer at sea was more than sufficient to be grateful for.

It was difficult to claim much connection with this family whose lives had been revealed. Neither, at the moment, did he feel any attachment to his mother. And the younger Clara seemed to have little in common with the formidable and elderly aunt he had seen perhaps two dozen times in his life. But then, he wondered, how much connection do any of us have at fifty with what we were at twenty-five?

In the last box he found a cigarette-card album, with pictures of different series stuck at all angles inside. Flowers, kings, film stars, birds, ships, cricketers and butterflies had been fixed unevenly. He assumed they were cards his grandfather had collected from the streets, and that they had been put there haphazardly by the old man's hands. But the more he stared the more he knew that he himself had collected them, or begged them, or had been given them at the orphanage. Or he had traded them, because some had worn edges and turned-over corners.

There was a piercing familiarity about the arrangement as he lifted the album from the floor to the table and sat on a chair to look more closely at these colourful and prize possessions of a cloistered infant, a four-year-old's view on to the outside world. He remembered putting them in one by one as he acquired them, tensing the muscles of hands and fingers to get them straight, with the feeling each time that he had succeeded triumphantly in creating another world whose colours he could walk among.

One day the album vanished, and his days of hope were over. Childhood was knocked down by a hammer-blow, and replaced by the plodding dullness of common survival till the time when he saw ships on the sea from the haven of Clara's front window, a vision distant and unreal enough for him to believe once more that there might yet be a way to give meaning to his life.

The cigarette-card album must have been taken away and sent to his grandfather, or to Clara, perhaps as proof that he liked being at the orphanage, that he was at home there and making progress in his separate existence. He is happy, they said. Look how he spends his time. Maybe his senile grandfather had visited the place before he died and, watching from a distance, saw the album and coveted it for reasons best not gone into. The director had removed the tattered object from his bedside one night, and posted it to his grandfather next morning. Why else would they have robbed him of the only thing that made life possible?

In the garden of the orphanage was a wooden one-floored building called the Recreation Room, set among trees and apart from the main house, and on wet weekend afternoons they were sent there to be out of the way. The hours between lunch and tea lasted for ever. He had learned early what eternity meant, so that no long watch kept at sea was ever in the least monotonous.

Inside the room was a large table, and an old upright piano with no lid that one of the boys knew how to play, and a few shelves of mildewed penny-dreadful magazines, and adventure novels by Ballantyne, Conan Doyle, Haggard, Henty and Jules Verne. He had stuck his treasured cigarette cards into the album to the sound of rain dripping on to the roof from trees outside, as they sat the afternoon hours away in an intense smell of pungent soot from a chimney place that had once been lit but now never was, and of damp books and half rotting timber that took a decade of sea-life to get out of his spirit.

Their grey felt hats could be distorted into the sort that Napoleon wore. Porridge at breakfast was sometimes burnt, often cold as well. They were taken blackberrying in the autumn, to get sufficient for jam the whole year. Church was twice on Sunday, and there was Scripture every morning. Each summer they lived in tents for a week by the seaside. Occasionally they walked the streets, and felt like kings.

If his grandfather had hoped to punish him by sending him to an orphanage because his mother had committed the unforgivable sin of giving him birth, then the old man had not succeeded. Rather the opposite, Tom supposed, for to be brought up in such a family would obviously have been many times worse. The one blow he had been dealt, which was so savage that he preferred to put it down to an act of God rather than to any that man could have given, was when he had been deprived of his picture-card album. Even that, considering how quickly he had forgotten it, seemed to have concerned another boy and not him.

In any case, there were other blows to smooth the way to forgetfulness. Never, he recalled it being said at the orphanage, sit with your hands clenched – as by the age of six it had grown to be his habit. When he had done so, once too often for his safety, a cane had smashed across his knuckles. From then on his fingers had remained straight, even when relaxed. But who could now say, he thought, remembering such sharp teaching for the first time in years, that they had ever since been at rest?

On the inside of the album it said in Clara's handwriting: 'When you think of your mother, say a prayer for her soul.' Of all he had seen and read in this morass of tormenting mementoes, these words struck his eyes as if to blind him. Rage spread to the very tips inside his fingers, so that his hands would not stay still from pain. He tore the page from its staples, and crushed it like a poisonous spider.

PART FIVE
Love

1

'You look as though you've been down a coalmine.'

'I wish I had. It would undoubtedly have been cleaner down there.'

'Do you feel bitter?' she asked, after he had related his findings.

He picked up his grandfather's death certificate, tore it casually in half, and let it drop. 'Everybody's gone, so how can I? Getting to know your past for the first time at fifty makes you feel young again, but without the hope you might once have had.'

He pushed a box under the table with his foot. The curtains were closed and all lights on. The shelf clock struck midnight. Traffic noises came from the seafront. She drew the velvet curtains to one side and saw three ships lit up on the sea. When he pulled a book towards him she looked over his shoulder. 'What kind of writing is that?'

The letters were solid and black, as if they would remain long after the paper had disappeared. They lay in packed lines from top to bottom of the large page. 'It's Hebrew,' he said, 'the writing of the Jews.'

'How do you know?'

'There was once a radio officer who had a theory that the British people were one of the Lost Tribes of Israel. He read the Bible, and was learning Hebrew. I saw him practising the script.'

'Can you read any?'

He ran a finger from right to left across the lines. 'It's all

Chinese to me. But I suppose my mother must have known what it was.'

She touched his shoulder. 'You'll have to learn.'

His features were bare and prominent under the light, and he stared at the writing as if the meaning would be made clear, like trying to read hopeful signs in the weather from gathering clouds. She had never seen anyone who seemed so tired, so emptied. There was nothing in him to make life livable except the spirit of his inner self that might or might not revive. Even the sea had gone from him, all the strength he had acquired with so much effort and will. He looked up from the print. 'I must begin again, unless I'm to die. There's no other way. I have no option.'

He had been on a long journey, and had told her about it in order to decide what of value would be preserved from the rubble of the past. She had been of some use, and was glad. One good turn deserved another. What more could he want from her? But she didn't care to get into a situation from which she might lose the desire to escape. If she began such a life again she would die in captivity. 'I think I have to go home.'

He jumped as if stung. 'Home?'

She was frightened at beginning to feel that she lived here. 'Back to London. I must have some clean clothes at least!'

'It's too late to get a train. I'm afraid I lost count of time, which is strange, considering how obsessed I've always been by it. When I first studied navigation I discovered that there were ten different kinds of time. I'd chant the words to get them into my brain: solar, apparent solar, mean solar, sidereal, lunar, standard, summer, Greenwich Mean, watch and chronometer time. Lives depended on them perhaps, and to lose track of time seems either a disaster or a luxury – I don't know which. Searching through oceans of vacant time with landmarks that I'd either forgotten or not known about made me lose all sense of something I thought even my bone-marrow was made of.'

He wanted to sleep, but felt that his body would never rest again, that his brain would fragment and he'd spend the rest of his life raving like a madman at the conspiratorial emptiness of the world. He ached as if his joints were giving way. 'It's shameful to ramble on like this, but I can't feel any good reason not to. I can't help myself. I never met anybody before who I was able to talk to.'

'Talk, then,' she said, thinking anyone would serve. She would listen for as long as he could go on, because he was a person stricken down, and she already knew the symptoms.

'I don't want you to leave, train or no train. If I spend the night here with the ghosts I've just rumbled, and wake up to face the morning alone, I might do something I won't even live to regret. I don't know who I am, though I know I don't belong here. Not even in this country. There's nothing for me to stay for. Until I know where I want to be, I won't know who I am. I've seen most places, but the vital one has eluded me. When I see the name I'll know it. I'll know what it is, and what I am, when it comes. It's been a long wait so far, but no time is too long, because if you die before you get there at least you haven't made a false choice! There's a hand in the way things have turned out that's not my doing, or anybody else's either, and everything indicates that I should leave here, and the fact that I've no idea where to go isn't important. Moving over the world in the last thirty years has been the same as standing still, but now the real move ought to begin. Not only my own, but some other voice tells me it must.'

'It's as good a way of making up your mind as any.' She wanted him to stop talking, because his eyes, from looking firmly at some point beyond, were turned even more intently on her.

'I've used all methods of making up my mind,' he said, 'of deciding when to alter course to avoid danger or reach clear water, but what mattered was always suggested by a force outside myself, which isn't a way I like, but there's little you can do except ride it as you ride the waves – when they let you.'

He opened a smaller volume from the pile of books. The same Hebrew script on one page faced English on the other. 'Perhaps one of my long voyages would have led me to puzzle the language out. I'd have got a key and navigated my way through it line by line. The reason Aunt Clara didn't tell me anything was because she thought I shouldn't be deflected from my simple life. She didn't send one of my mother's Hebrew books because she wanted to keep her sister's things close to herself. Who needs questions? I want answers, but they're safe inside me and won't come out, nicely marbled together like stones on a beach, all numbered and precisely catalogued – or they will be soon enough.'

They stood. She would find a blanket and sleep on the wide sofa. 'You should go to bed.'

He held her gently. 'Without you I wouldn't be able to breathe.'

She smiled at his close face. 'Any other person would have been just as useful.'

He shook his head. 'Two people like us have been through enough to know that we met in the way we did because neither of us is just any other person. Everything is ordered in the universe, as far as the length of a human life is concerned. When you find your latitude and longitude by heavenly bodies at sea they're always in the place in which you expect to find them. They never let you down. Nothing is left to chance. We're individuals, like the billions of stars. But fate is the great leveller, and all is fixed. No other person would have done but you.'

She put her hands on his shoulders. 'I'm even more exhausted than you look, believe it or not, and would like to get some sleep. But I must go to London tomorrow, because I have unfinished business there.'

'I'll go with you.' He surprised her by a light kiss on the lips. She regretted moving away because she did not know the reason for it. He stood like an island. 'I'll give up my room in town, then move down here.'

He took her unwarranted shift from him as one of those blows of life that you must always be braced to expect. He poured two glasses of whisky, his normal tone making her happy to be with him again. 'Maybe these'll do for nightcaps!'

'I feel frightened about going back to London.' What was she saying? How can I confide in him like this? 'It's something I can't explain.'

'It's when you don't feel dread that something dreadful really happens.'

'I wish I could believe that,' she said.

'So why go?' It would be impossible not to. She felt as if pulled by the scruff of the neck. He drank his whisky, then poured another. 'Learn to follow your heart.'

'Have you?' A bit too sharp, she felt. Still, he shouldn't say words he couldn't mean. 'Don't drink any more after that.' She sat down. 'I have things to settle. My husband wants me to go back to him.'

After a few moments he said: 'Well?'

'I shan't. He's been in London with his three brothers. They've found out where I live.'

He laughed. 'Are they such dangerous monsters?'

'Yes. No. I don't know.' She couldn't, until what she dreaded happened. They were known more clearly by her than any other group of people, yet their presence threatened her with the unknown, to which she couldn't trust herself not to respond.

'Get rid of *your* room as well,' he said.

'Oh yes,' she said, wryly.

'Why not?'

She moved towards him, then stopped. 'I like it there because it was my first refuge from a life I couldn't stand, and from the rest of the world that made me think I was a fool for not feeling I was the luckiest person. I can't let my husband or my own fears drive me out, so I must get a job and exist on my own.'

'Being a sailor has taught me,' he said, 'that no one can live without other people. The independence you're thinking about is only possible providing you don't want to stay human. I've been in and out of that state all my life, but never for too long.'

He was accusing her. After trying to stay silent, she said: 'I'm the only one who knows what's good for me.'

'Yes, I realize that. But we did meet under rather peculiar circumstances.'

She didn't like being reminded, and wondered whether she really was lucky to be alive. Where was she? Who was she with? The room was dimly lit. She wanted to see everything with eye-aching clarity. What had been revealed during the day had pushed her life to one side, but now that it was coming back there was nothing promising about it. Only the effort she would have to make appealed to her, because there was no other way of knowing she was alive. 'The light's too low.'

He went to the switches, and the table lamps turned dim in the white dazzle from overhead. 'Is that better?'

She nodded. It was different.

'I've been thinking of putting an advertisement in the newspaper,' he said. 'It'll go something like this . . .' He reached for a pencil and spoke the words as he scribbled: 'Woman aged thirty to fifty wanted as personal secretary and assistant to help ex-Merchant Marine officer with business affairs. Possibility of travel. Must be independent. Ability to drive an advantage. Fair salary offered. Living-in optional. Own television if desired.'

He passed her the paper. 'I don't want to deprive you of your previous freedom, but you have first refusal of this dazzling situation!'

The writing was impossible to read. She would be nobody's servant. To go to an office every morning from her own room and work for a business firm would be acceptable, but to be a runabout for someone with whom she was friendly was not her notion of a proper job.

'There's work to be done,' he said, 'but the hours will be irregular, though you'll get enough time off. You already know what the premises are like. You'll have a room here, and be absolutely private, I promise you. I know you already, and I like you, though I'll say no more about that. Maybe you know what I'm trying to say, in any case. And I might not get anyone who'd fit the job even if I did advertise. I'm not trying to do you a favour, as much as one for myself.'

She wanted to say yes, but such a way out of her dilemma would be too easy. It would be wrong to take advantage of his loneliness and incoherence. She felt close, yet separated from him as by a high wall. 'I'm helping you already, so why do we need a contract?'

He smiled at her simple notion of the truth. You sign on for the voyage and sign off at the end. Old habits led him to expect regularity. The signature was everything. Such articles were the nuts and bolts of a disciplined service, but they obviously had no place in love. Compartments were not divided by watertight doors, below the Plimsoll Line or not. Now that he had found her he couldn't bear the prospect of being alone, but considering the way they had met there was no certainty of her remaining. Such unpredictability disturbed him. But she hadn't said no, and he would have to be satisfied with that.

2

Her watch said half-past nine and for a few moments she wondered where she was. She had forgotten to get a pillow with her two blankets, and by the time she had undressed and lain down she was too sleepy to look for one. What would George say if he knew she had spent the night in another man's flat – and ended up with a stiff neck? Maybe one of his brothers had followed them to Brighton and, posted outside, observed that she had been there all night, and that she had – he could hardly deduce otherwise with his kind of mind – slept with him. Let him think. She wondered why she hadn't. He'd surely expected her to. She liked him enough, and could easily imagine how pleasant it might have been, but she had been too exhausted, either to allow any move or make one.

She pushed a curtain aside. A gleaming estate car with its lights on moved around the square. Neither of the two pedestrians resembled George or his brothers. The bleak sea was ruffled with feather-tops. She came back to the couch. Yesterday had been like ten years, but as time going in reverse, so that she felt a decade younger. It was as if she had already spent a honeymoon which had been perfect and glorious: she had come out of a long tunnel, exhausted but unhurt, and with a strange feeling of happiness. She looked out of the window again. The car had found a space and parked.

She emptied her bag to get clean pants and a blouse. Having expected him to sleep most of the day, she scooped up her clothes and went to the bathroom. The door was locked. He called that he wouldn't be long. Using her coat for a dressing-gown she went to the lavatory, then into the kitchen to put the kettle on. Not being used to alcohol, her head ached, and her mouth was dry from thirst. She thought of what she knew about him. He was a man, as they said, with a past. So was she, and it was called prison, a long slumber of the unknowing until the bars were suddenly behind instead of in front, and never to be stepped back into by returning to someone of George's sort. They had to cut free.

She resisted singing in her freedom. She was with another man. She liked being with him. She was sparing with words, even with herself, yet didn't want to care. She swung open the huge curtains. An enormous patch of sun from the sea

386

warmed her face. There was no movement in the square. They hadn't traced her, after all. She would stay for as long as it wasn't the beginning or the end of anything, but knew she mustn't hope for too much.

The kettle whistled. Before it reached full shriek he had taken it off and was opening the tea caddy. He was dressed, with tie on, face shaved, shoes polished, fresh-looking as if he had slept deeply, looking different to last night when his agonized face in the shadowy light had given age no chance to mark his features. He seemed free of whatever weight the long search through his aunt's leavings had heaped on him, though on a further glance she noticed that more than a trace remained in his eyes. She wondered what he saw in her face. She was uncertain as to what was there herself now that she speculated on him, wishing she had merely said good morning and then gone in to have her bath.

'Did you sleep well?'

'I'm still coming up for air,' she said.

'Sorry it had to be in the living-room, but I did offer you my bed – I mean, on condition that I took the sofa.' They drank in silence, as if a treaty had been signed not to bother each other unnecessarily. She laughed at the thought. He didn't, and looked up from his cup. 'Someone once said that a person who laughed soon after getting out of bed was hungry. Shall I boil some eggs now, or do you want to dress first?'

'I don't know.' And she didn't. She wanted something, but didn't know what, except that it had to be everything. She couldn't be still, left her tea and walked into the living-room. The light of day made it hard to breathe, but she didn't try, kept her lungs shallow, as if a good breath would fill her with something she did not want, and cause her to lose the feeling of desire. She felt restless and ashamed, not entirely under her own control, yet uncaring. On no other morning of her life had she been so fragmented in her sensations.

She went back into the kitchen and said to him: 'I can't answer questions first thing in the morning.'

387

He frowned, so she didn't doubt that he was wide enough awake to answer any question put to him. But she had none to ask. Questions were finished, for the moment. His intense gaze suggested he hardly knew what to say for fear of uttering useless and puzzling words that would push them apart.

There seemed an absolute end of talking. She took off her coat and folded it over a chairback. He looked, but did not move. She had no wish but to be as close as it was possible to get, as a way through what complications might needlessly build up between them. Any less action seemed destructive. She gave reason no chance, but pulled her nightdress over her head and went to him, thinking as the cool air rushed at her body that since she wanted him so much it didn't matter what was in either of their minds.

<h1 style="text-align:center">3</h1>

Her body had decided, so her will was free. Yet the course her body would take had been decided long ago, though she was not aware when the agreement had been reached. It had grown in her, but she had so far ignored it, a half deliberate neglect that had given the fragile plant a possibility of survival.

The inevitability of their becoming closer began during the total preoccupation with his aunt's documentary belongings, a task which had taken him too far into the area of a peculiar past for her to follow. She had been left alone long enough and in sufficient ease to reflect on her feelings, though she was careful to deny any force which they threatened to assume.

Knowing what she wanted to do, she had been afraid on

waking that she would feel some old-fashioned twinge of shame should the event take place at his convenience. If anyone knew that they had been together she wanted to be able to say that she had not allowed anything to be done to *her*, but that she had started whatever they liked to call it herself, out of the need of her own pride and unsurfaced dreams.

Guided by her own will, all sense of the tawdry had been sidestepped. Having nothing to lose by beginning, neither had she any of the shame which she would have dreaded had it been he who had taken the first step. No one could reproach her. Feeling love, a move had been made, and what came afterwards would be his reaction to the thing she had started, and so could never be a matter of regret to her. She would not be in any way demeaned if he couldn't bear the sight of her and they parted never to meet again, though because her initiative had grown out of the ease she had known since their first meeting, such action on his part seemed unlikely.

His instinct, to wait until what he most wanted happened so that neither would appear to think about how to begin what seemed impossible, had indeed been right. He reflected while holding her warm body that they had mindlessly given in to their need for each other. But all in their lives that had led to it had been by no means mindless. The transition was impossible to detect, a fusing spark that was never to be defined and isolated but which had brought them together.

His regard for her had bred the necessary patience, and had been the true guide of his action. The only value received from his orphanage schooling, and throughout a long age at sea, was to know when to wait and how to bide his time, and he considered that the power of this virtue had not disappointed him now that the first real call on it had been made. Thus every move was a combination of calculated choice and inherited need.

His shirt was wet with her tears, and she smiled at the thought that at least they were old enough to know what they were doing. He held her tight but his kisses were tender. He moved away. His cultivated indifference had succeeded, like everything else, at a cost. But his arms relaxed as he kissed the tips of her breasts. 'It's only a few days, but it seems that we've waited years.'

Her eyes opened. 'There's plenty of time now.' She felt like a child, not yet a woman, an unexpected innocence which had nevertheless been hoped for. Was it only an infatuation which people often said such feelings were? She did not admit the word. There was too much cruelty in it, and for herself it was impossible to use. She smiled that she had only ever held her son with the same affection – when he had been a child.

He watched her bend at the bed in Clara's room to pull down the covers. She was thin, flesh firm at her stomach. It was fitting that they should make love here. There was a small mole on her left shoulder. He held her from behind, and kissed the nape of her neck. She fought off the thrill, and turned. 'I must go to the bathroom.'

She closed the door and sat down. She felt relaxed, yet the body was tense. Had she ever been in love, even when George had fixed her bicycle chain by Wollaton Church all those years ago? He had played the gentleman, and ever after called his bike 'The Courtship Special'. Yet who could say what words had passed, or how much the atmosphere had been in control?

Later, when he had asked her to 'be his wife', they called it love. She couldn't remember, but they must have done. The memory was a torment throughout her marriage. All was distortion. Their difficulties had been fixed and pervasive, nonetheless. There was nothing worthwhile to remember, and little to regret. When considering events from another life, memory was fickle and dubious, and hardly the word to use – or blame. The sensation that remained was one of damage. Being held by Tom could easily be called love, for it eradicated whatever might have been thought of as love yet could in no way have been. Love only came once in life, she had told herself while stroking his chest and shoulders under the shirt which tears had dampened. In those far-off days she had been taken up by the slavery of expectation and mistaken it for love.

A pull at the cord set a two-bar heater on the wall glowing at her back. She turned to the mirror, and though she looked pale, a smile held weariness at bay. Her breasts were small but shapely, reflecting the likeness of a skimpy model, she thought, in the long mirror.

He stood at the window looking towards the sea. The coppery midwinter glow drew back as a cloud closed off the sun. He didn't doubt that it would show again. The sea looked after itself, he thought, as softened footsteps sounded on the carpet.

She came to him, her breasts flattening against the coarse hair on his chest. His expression seemed solemn. Did he already regret what had not yet happened? She hoped not. She was no longer that sort herself, and doubted that she ever had been. 'We've landed ourselves in an unexpected honeymoon.'

He kissed her lips, and answered that they were in the perfect place. She wanted no tomorrow and, passionately kissing him, closed her eyes, legs weakening as if about to fall.

His gentle support moved her towards the bed. He kissed the delicate skin that closed over her eyes. The words that said he loved her were torn from him by forces beyond his understanding.

No loving had ever been so slow and harmonious, yet she still did not finally want it to happen. While knowing that she had committed herself, and that any further struggle was useless, and unjust to them both, she could not let go. It was like the objections to being born. Not to contest the change would have denied its value. She pleaded, and then fought, and closed her eyes to the lack of understanding in his expression.

But as if in her thoughts, he held her, giving in to what she didn't dare ask for. Her silence drew him on, conferring a passion without hurry, going against both her will and his as he touched. She seemed to be at the edge of life, about to fall into a trance before death. Is this what fainting was like? She had never lost her consciousness. She was trapped in a private world of love, and didn't care. They seemed as familiar with each other's interchange of pleasures as if they had been together for years. But he was a stranger, no matter what she knew of his past. His fingers played at her and, keeping her lips on his, she held his hand firmly so that she gave in, and went on until she heard herself.

The shock diminished and spread, and he knew sufficient to stroke her for as long as the pleasure lasted. She felt her tears loosen. His free hand flattened her breasts. He sucked and soothed the nipples. She lifted him and looked at his face. He looked at her, but she didn't care whether or not he saw an intensity that had never taken her so completely – whether or not it made her ugly. She opened her legs, and putting out her hands she drew him in.

4

After ripples of sunlight, rain beat from the sea and the air grew dark. Hail flashed and pattered the glass. She turned to press against him but, feeling weightless, hardly knew where she was. He kissed her down the stomach till he brought her back to consciousness. His tongue would not let go. She tried to get free. No one had done this before. She protested, then gave in to her shame, and in a few moments felt no shame at all. He held her to the pleasure that seemed drawn from outside, and as it began he moved into her with an ease that allowed her orgasm to run its course before she felt his own explosion deep inside.

The dreams floated, and she drifted in sleep. He got out of bed, and drew the clothes over her shoulders. A match scraped, and there was a smell of tobacco smoke. She couldn't move, curled in hiding from the rain which fell against the window. She hadn't slept for years. Yet she wasn't sleeping. His weird battering left her sore. She didn't know him, yet wanted to. His intense and purposeful love made him unknowable. He was a stranger home from the sea and she was a woman in from the storm. He touched her shoulder. 'Here's something to eat and drink.'

'I can't move.' She leaned on her elbow. 'What time is it?'

'It's hard to say.'

The light was on. 'I want to know.'

He held a cup for her to drink. 'My watch has stopped. And I didn't look at the kitchen clock.'

'I feel like a baby.' She sat up, and took the cup. He put the tray down and sat by her. 'You must have been dreaming.'

'What did I say?'

'Couldn't make it out.'

She ate a biscuit. 'I haven't slept at this time of day before.'

'Sometimes at sea you catnap at all hours. Never in a bed like this, though.'

'Did you have hammocks?'

He wore trousers and shirt, but had no shoes on. 'Once or twice. I slept in one four weeks on my first trip to Singapore, and then four weeks back. They were comfortable.'

She brushed crumbs from the sheets. He kissed her breasts. In friendship she felt accessible, and liked it. 'I must get dressed.'

'I'm getting used to you with no clothes on.'

She was not embarrassed, and wondered why. Such freedom had been impossible with George. She felt a remote but friendly pity for him. They had existed, but had not been made for each other. Familiarity and time had failed to bring

393

it about. Yet with someone so new she didn't mind how he saw her, or what they did. She kissed his hand, and placed it between her legs.

He stroked her hair.

No words could explain her feeling of ease and helplessness. Did you have to go through the stage of being with no clothes on before getting to know someone, and was making love also part of it? She knew him, yet did not, but felt there was no need to consider it. She wanted to slide back into bed and dream, but drew the eiderdown around her and stood up.

'We'll go out for a meal,' he said. 'I know a place where they serve food upstairs. It's nice and casual.'

In the street a wind blew the umbrella inside out, and he fought in a doorway to right it, while she stood in the rain and laughed. He held part with his foot and worked systematically to get the circle of spokes into place, but by the time he had gone fully around, the ribs shook themselves out again. He tried to do it more quickly, but the spokes still would not jump back into a firm circumference, so she held half the circle with both hands spread wide, using all her force, and they passed it round and round to each other till the umbrella was usable again. People looked at them as if they were mad. Swinging the umbrella high, rain clattered against the cloth, then he held her arm as they walked.

The room was smoky and warm, with a piercing smell of cooking that either made your mouth water, she thought, or drove you back into the street. She noticed him hesitate at the threshold, as if unsure who should go in first. Perhaps the only places where he had ever felt secure were the orphanage, a ship at sea, and his aunt's flat.

The prolonged love-making in strange surroundings had sharpened her perceptions as if she were at the beginning of a cold or the flu. She was glad to sit down. The candle flame shook whenever the door opened. She took a napkin from the wine glass. 'I feel as if I've been rolled down an endless slope in a barrel. My thighs ache, among other things.'

He touched her wrist. 'I'm not surprised. We must have been three of four times around the world!'

The waitress gave them a folded card to look at. Pam didn't know him. He didn't own the flat at all, but had obtained the key while whoever it belonged to was on holiday. And was he really a retired naval man? Judy Ellerker had confirmed it, though perhaps he had deceived her as well, and the story from his day-long sorting out of the lumber room had also been fabricated. The documents matched his tale, though they could have been assimilated from somebody else's. Maybe he was a man out of prison or back from abroad who had perfected his tricks for living off the land. He brought people into life again, and went on his way. His brown eyes looked dully at some far-off scene, until he sensed her attention. Then he came back with such immediacy she felt nothing but tenderness. She knew so little of the world that anything could be true, though in this case it wasn't, and she decided not to retail such thoughts but say what she would like to eat.

He asked the waitress what champagne they had, and Pam let them sort the matter out. 'It gets around the clubs of Nottingham,' she said, noting what he chose.

'I once took a case of it on board, to bring back for my aunt, but the captain sniffed 'em out, so Clara only saw one bottle. She opened it the first night, took a sip, gave me a swallow, then poured the whole lot down the sink. It was counterfeit, Clara said. She was right. It was worse than vinegar. God knows what it was. But the captain quaffed off eleven bottles without even a murmur. Perhaps it just didn't travel.'

The door opened, and he looked towards the sound. He flinched before turning back to his soup, having seen that raven-dark hair, parted at the middle and smoothed tightly back, in some other place. The skin of her cheeks was fresh, like that of a doll still in bloom, and he remembered her from the time of his aunt's death, and the hour they had made love in the bed-and-breakfast place near the station. He hoped she hadn't seen him, but cursed a large mirror along the wall which made the room seem endless and damned all privacy. He lifted his glass to Pam's. 'Here's to us.'

Beryl came close, and he felt a tap at the shoulder.

'Hello, sailor! A different one every night, is it?'

He stood up. Pam noticed his eyes harden. The woman was good-looking, but brazen. Tom indicated whom he supposed to be her boy-friend standing some yards away: 'Would you both like to join us?'

'No fear,' she laughed.

'Boy-friend?'

'Who else?'

He touched Pam's elbow. 'Let me introduce you.'

Pam said: 'Hello!'

'He's good,' Beryl said. 'Aren't you, sailor?'

Maybe she's drunk, he thought. 'Am I?'

'But I must go.' She nodded. Her boy-friend looked left out of things. 'He's not so bad, either, sailor. So long!'

Tom sat down.

He must know scores of girls. 'Someone you met?'

'She was the nurse on duty at the hospital when Clara died. Is the fish all right?'

She felt stupid at having her mood spoiled so easily. He sensed the weather-change, but there was nothing to do except regret the barometric pressure and curse his luck. 'The sky's turned foul for no good reason.'

She nodded, then drank. 'The sun's still out as far as I'm concerned.'

He called himself a fool. He had swaggered off such a close call more than once, but now felt clumsy and vulnerable, unable to speak for a while – till he noticed a newspaper on an empty seat saying there would be a rail strike as from midnight. 'We won't get back to town tomorrow unless we take a bus, and I don't feel like fighting for a seat. It's inconvenient.'

'Strikes usually are,' she said.

'My pay for the first ten years was enough to bring anybody out on strike, yet it wasn't even thought of. I'd have felt ashamed creeping off a ship and saying I'll do no work till I get more money. But times have changed. Your work is your weapon. Everyone can go on strike now. It's bad for the country, of course, but who cares about that? It's like chipping bits of wood from a raft in the middle of the sea. Sooner or later you sink and become food for the fishes. It's a pity there's nothing anyone can do, because it's rather a good raft, and I've grown to like it, having done some of the work to keep it afloat.'

She thought of George's brothers, and surprised herself by saying: 'I've known people who found it hard enough to live on their money. But even if they have enough not to go short of anything, they want more – on the principle that they can never have enough. If others have it, they must have it. They see the easier lives of others on the telly, so you can hardly blame them.'

He dissected his fish. 'It's more than envy. It's restlessness, and a craving for change without any spiritual values. People who could set an example don't care to any more. They've lost their nerve, perhaps.'

'People want to be happy,' she said, 'and they're persuaded it costs money.'

He was as close to bitterness as she had so far seen him. 'But happiness never comes. They're poor, duped fools. When you have it, you don't want it. Often you don't even notice if you do have it. That's probably the best sort. But as soon as you think to want it, it goes out of the window if you already have it, and becomes unattainable if you don't. It's a tricky kind of balance, all in all.'

'I'm happy now,' she said.

He held her hand. 'So am I. But it doesn't come by pursuing it. Nor by going on strike for more money.'

She had to agree, though after a while asked: 'Do you want to go back to the world of your grandfather?'

397

'Not really. It only led to the one we've got now. But I do feel there are values one ought to hold on to. When I wake in the morning I thank God I'm alive. Every birthday I'm grateful for another year of life. I was brought up to believe that if you didn't work you didn't deserve to eat. When the sea was calm and empty there was time to mull on things. You were blessed with two minds, one concerned for the safety and progress of the ship, and the other taken over by thoughts of what was going on in the world, but rarely with what turmoil might lie within yourself. It's very effective to contemplate the state of the world from the bridge of a well-run ship. But things can happen at sea, all the same, and you live with the thought that your life is not your own, being divided between the company you work for and the sea itself. Your life only belongs to you when you set foot ashore. Not even then, for if there's one thing certain it is that our life doesn't belong to us alone. Get to thinking that it does, and someone else then assumes he has a right to take it over. Self-assertion comes before slavery. If every man believes in God, or at least has infinite respect for a humane and unassailable system of ethics, then no other man has the moral power to subjugate him.'

It was more agreeable when he talked than to be caught in the singular deadness that dominated his silence. The evening was pleasant now that the aura of the nurse's disturbance had gone. But she wondered what was the beginning and end of all he was saying, for didn't he belong to himself, rather than to something like God? She certainly did, and especially so in the last couple of months when she had moved from a lifetime of torment after having been attached body and much of her soul to somebody else. Even in the most enduring union you had to be your own property first, before any satisfaction was to be got out of allowing part of you to belong to someone else, she told him during dessert.

'Without wanting to seem unduly religious,' he said, 'we all belong to the unknown, which I call God. By believing in God

398

we are given the authority for our equality with regard to each other. That's all I mean.'

She didn't like the word 'equality'. 'Everyone is different, not equal. If they were equal you wouldn't have been an officer.'

He smiled. 'They may not be equal in everyday life, but they are in the sight of God. It's vital for everyone to think so, for the proper running of society. Under God and under the law we are equal, and that's as it should be, otherwise you get the barbarism of dictatorship, as in Russia, where people can't even leave the damned place until their spirit's broken, and mostly not even then. Law on its own can be tyrannical, but if you have God then His law, which we must assume to be good and beneficial for humanity, helps to keep human laws civilized. It hasn't always worked out, but it's still the only hope we have. And in the best countries it has more or less done so.'

He was embarrassed. 'I'm talking too much. Sailors are known for it, once they get ashore, though Jonah talked on board ship till he got himself thrown into the sea, and then talked in the whale's belly till God got him spouted out again. Not that he was a sailor.' He tapped the empty bottle. 'There's time for another drop.'

She put her hand on his arm. 'I'll get tight if I have any more. Let's go.'

He signalled for the bill.

'I'll pay half,' she said.

'You bought the food yesterday.'

She looked astonished. 'Yesterday?'

He laughed. 'Yes – yesterday.'

He was right.

'We ought not to get too particular about such things.' He picked up the chit. 'I shan't go broke over a few quid.'

At the seafront he looked up the Pointers to Polaris. There was no more rain. The wind was backing north-easterly. 'We're in for a change to dry and cold, so the train drivers will stay snug in their beds with toast and tea, and who can blame them, unless it's those poor chaps waiting on platforms for non-existent transport?'

They walked a mile towards Shoreham, then turned back. Lights twinkled in the Channel. 'Do you wish you were on one?'

He held her hand. Why did everyone assume so? 'I see no point in thinking about the past. Life on shore makes my existence out there seem emptiness itself. After what I learned about my family I suppose I'm still the same person who worked his whole life at sea, but the connection feels slender at the moment, walking along the front with you. I expect the two lives will merge sooner or later, but it's amazing to think I lived so long as someone I wasn't.'

'Maybe you didn't,' she said.

'I agree. It's hard to be final about it. But if I'd been brought up in that kind of family I imagine I'd have gone to a prep. school as a boarder, and then to a public school as a boarder. Being passably bright, and with a bit of luck, I'd have made some sort of university, and become an engineer like Uncle John. By the time I was fifty my mother and Clara would have died, and I'd be where I am now, living in the flat with the money they'd left. On the other hand I might have been an idler, and broken my mother's heart – or some such thing.'

'I don't think you would,' she said. 'And yet – you might have done!'

He stood by the rail. Light reflected from behind, as breakers thumped and grated at the shingle. 'I still think it's all a dream.'

She wanted to hold him and kiss him. 'Is it a bad one, though?'

Where was the calm impassive sailor she had thought him to be? He looked at her in the half light. 'While I was in the kitchen this afternoon I remembered an incident from just after the war that I'd not thought of until today. It was the sort of thing that might happen to any sailor in a foreign port. My ship had docked in the East River in New York, and I had a day to spare so walked into town. I got something to eat in a Chinese place, then went up Fifth Avenue towards Central Park. I'd been there before, so knew my way. Passing a Moorish-looking synagogue near 43rd Street I saw a tall old man with a long beard, wearing a black broad-brimmed hat. He was shouting a greeting to somebody behind, as I thought, but he came up to me, and babbled in a language I didn't know from Adam. He held my hand and called me by a name, and seemed to be asking questions, his eyes glittering with smiles, and I thought what the hell does this silly old bugger want? What's he trying to tell me? I was young and all stuffy-English, and wanted to push by him and carry on walking, but he was so amiable and familiar that I saw he had taken me for someone else, though it never occurred to me to wonder who it would be. I only wanted to make the most of my day in New York. He realized he'd made a mistake, so waved his hands in the air, almost pushed *me* out of the way, and walked on. Bumping into someone in a town of millions of people happens all the time, but what I didn't know then, yet know now, was that that wise old man, even in his understandable error, saw more closely into me than anyone else. And when I suddenly recalled the incident his face was so vivid and close that I could have touched him. I was about to say something, but realized I didn't know his language. I thought it a pity that we couldn't understand each other.'

The recollection calmed him, and they crossed the road to the square. She didn't want to break into his mind. Each had their privacy, and she was content to guard hers, thinking that her past life would be uninteresting to him. The loss was hers and nobody else's, and there was no one to blame for it but herself. As soon as you cut yourself off from the people who were responsible for your loss, any thought of blame becomes ridiculous. The twenty years that had slipped by so emptily filled her with rage, and she stood for a moment unable to move for fear of being sick. After a day of such loving, the wasted years became a devastation of centuries.

'We've both mis-spent our lives,' she said when they were in the flat. She envied his having discovered a whole new landscape of the past, but knew there was no hope of her doing the same – so became glad for him instead.

He poured a whisky. 'I suppose nearly everyone thinks so. But they weren't *useless* lives. Would you like some?'

She would make herself a pot of tea before going to bed.

'My life was futile,' he said, 'only in so far as *you* weren't part of it, but we've met now, and I'm able to feel how wonderful it is. It's bad for my self-esteem to worry about having been unlucky or stupid, or a victim of circumstance. It simply wouldn't be true, in any case. Life has been good to us in that everything has led to our meeting. We can enjoy it better. It's more important to think about the future than to worry about having been diminished in any way by the past.'

The fact that neither seemed to know where they were in their lives united them so effectively that the bond was, she felt, doubly painful. She wondered how much he really knew of himself, in spite of what he had discovered about his family. When he'd had time to absorb the information – for what it was finally worth – would they still have anything in common? She wasn't able to bring these nagging queries into the open, which worried her because he, without difficulty, said whatever was in his mind. Warped by years of marriage, she felt deficient in not trusting someone she loved. The emptiness surrounding their encounter would indicate, if it persisted, that life was hardly worth living. She ought not to think, but to act instead, and do things. Wasn't to *say* better than to *think*? Twenty null years had robbed her of the ability to say and to do out of her own will when with a man. Yet she had acted this morning because no other course was possible, a daring and positive approach which was not easily undone.

A lamp illuminated the open book. 'I've found an alphabet which gives the key to this writing, so it won't be difficult to get the hang of it. I can exercise my brain – like being back at school, but with the lines going from right to left.'

He was as relaxed as a child with a new toy, as if the imbibing of a different script could change him fundamentally. A spark of mystery gave renewal of life, and put light back into his eyes. 'It's like learning a secret language. There'll be nothing to it when I get a proper start.'

He closed the book. She found it easy to kiss him. 'Secret from me? I'll learn it as well. But it's time to go to bed, unless you intend studying all night.'

'You're right.'

She had disturbed him for no reason, when she should have left him peacefully at his task. He had a future, whereas she could see none, having jettisoned hers by leaving George. With George she'd had a perfect future, of calm and predictable days forming a congealed block of years that would go by until disease or old age carried them off hand in hand. Oh yes, there'd been a fine future there right enough. But she had broken free, and now had none at all, which at the moment she felt was the best kind of future to have.

Nor did she want any share of that which Tom might see for himself, preferring to live until a future formed for her – or not, as the case might well be – even if the desolation should become unbearable. And really, who *had* a future? At forty, as Edward once taunted her, 'you're over the hill'. Only the young had a future, and then not for very long. After forty the shutters began to come down. The string that held them could wear through and snap any moment, leaving you in the dark for ever. At such an age you were lucky to have any life at all. Every day was a gift, every month a victory, but she didn't care, as long as she breathed, and had nerves to her fingertips. She had come back to life by crawling through a tunnel, and was more alive than when she had started the process. 'Don't go to bed. Stay at your work.'

He stood. 'I have all the time I need.'

'Really?'

He smiled. 'Life seems as if it'll go on for ever.'

She took his kisses. They were meaningless. 'I don't need to feel that. I hope you do everything you want to do. If so I'll feel good knowing there's at least one person I'm acquainted with whose life is working out according to plan.'

She was alarmed at his optimism. He was scared by her lack of it. There were dangers that could affect them both. She drew her hand away. He wondered why, but she could not explain.

'We need sleep,' he said. 'A bit of the old cure-all of oblivion.'

No doubt he was right. She felt sickened and weighed down. 'I'd like to be in a separate bed, if you don't mind.'

She fought not to mumble words of apology. Her deepest wish was to be alone. He could stay reading into the night. She found his disappointment unbearable because he knew too well how to conceal it.

'You have the big bed, then,' he said, 'and I'll use my old room.'

She ached to sleep with him, but it needed too crucial an act to change her mind. It would also break something she did not yet want broken, and extend their intimacy whether he wanted it or not. Things soonest done are never mended.

She fell asleep after the most wracking agony of tears. She was glad he couldn't hear. He did. He lay awake, trying to read, steeling himself against going in to give comfort. She wanted to be on her own, so to disturb her would be pure self-indulgence on his part. The muffled noise of sobbing made him realize that he was no longer alone in the world, and never would be again, so he wondered whether that was the reason for the sound being so precious, and the reason why he did not go in to comfort her and put an end to it. His last thought was that whatever the reasons, weeping was a bleeding of the spirit. People needed it. He understood perfectly, because he had never been able to do it.

5

She had taken a shower and dressed, and made breakfast. One minute she felt as if the flat was her own home, and the next she seemed like a trespasser waiting for the real owner to come back and say that if she didn't get out the police would be called. Such an idea made the morning interesting. The weather forecast promised dry, but cold.

She spread butter on the remaining pieces of bread, and set it with a mug of black coffee on a tray. There'd have to be shopping done, unless they ate out again, which would be more pleasant than staying among boxes spilling papers and dust all over the place.

He turned from his book as she opened the door. She was convinced he saw a strange woman. He had not even known someone else was in the flat. Distant noises came from underneath. Or she'd been hired to get his breakfast and clean up afterwards. If she had slept in his bed she would have been a slave from an agency with sex thrown in. Better to be mistaken for a servant than a *tart*. Wouldn't that be his word? She didn't care what anybody took her for.

'This is more than I deserve, or expected.'

She kissed him and passed the coffee. 'It's time you got out of bed and faced the day. There's clearing up to do.'

'There aren't any trains to catch.'

When he got up to dress she saw that he wore the golden Star of David found in the box of his mother's belongings. Hanging at his chest it made him look like a swimmer about to put on his clothes and set off on an arduous dry-land trek. He treasured it like a talisman that would stop bullets or make wounds vanish. But she wanted to hear why he wore it.

'As far as I could gather, it was the only wish my

grandmother, and then my mother, had for me. I'm happy to wear it for them – which also means, of course, that I feel a need to wear it for myself.'

'It looks good on you,' she said. 'I like it.' He seemed less starkly conventional, more human. She thought that making love would bring them together before beginning the day, but he got into his pants and vest, then sat on the bed to eat breakfast.

'I intended getting up early, but got lost in what I was doing. It's part of a sailor's pride not to turn into the sort of a man who can't look after himself, though I've never known a sailor who said no to being spoiled occasionally.'

'Well, I'll do my best not to mummy you,' she said.

He looked at her, as if the more he knew her the more mysterious she would become. She decided it must be so, because she often looked at him in that way. She didn't like him 'weighing her up' so obviously. She did it to him every moment they were together, which he no doubt found equally objectionable. He must smile inwardly at such times. Yet what did two people do if they weren't continually judging one another, and trying to find out what the other thought, or forming opinions which they wouldn't say aloud for fear the other might not like it? The mind raced with words unspoken and unspeakable. More often than not they looked at one another and said nothing, only giving an affectionate smile to signify a truce between their warlike curiosities when they caught each other out but knew they needed to stay friends, which she realized was essential, at any rate for her, while hoping he assumed it was beneficial for him.

The process of his dressing eliminated her thoughts. He put on a white shirt and did up each button beginning from the bottom. Her observation amused him. For order and neatness he took his time. He opened the wardrobe and brought out a pair of grey trousers, held them in both hands, and bent slightly to draw them on, covering the white scar on his lower leg which, he said, had been caused by a piece of shrapnel.

406

She hadn't seen a man dress for years. George had done so while she lay half asleep, sitting on the edge of the bed to get his trousers over his knees before standing to pull them to his waist.

Tom fastened his belt. 'You haven't told me whether you're going to give me a hand in sorting out my affairs.' He pulled his socks on while standing up, then took a pair of brown shoes from under the bed. 'The offer still stands.'

He probably polished them the night before. 'I seem to be doing the job already.'

He stood at the mirror, and double-knotted his tie. 'It's stupid of me to want the matter all wrapped up. Old habits are still dying too damned hard.'

'Maybe if they do die there won't be much left,' she laughed. 'You want to be careful!'

She felt herself trembling to kneel and tie his shoelaces. The physical check on going forward needed all her effort, and she coloured at the thought that he might have noticed. He glanced, then sat on the bed to fasten them himself.

'If I'm to act as your secretary, general factotum, or willing runabout, I suggest we get the boxes you want to save back into the small room, and take the others to the dustbins. Don't throw anything away that you'll regret later. You've got plenty of storage space.'

The arrangement, with no definable boundaries, had many uncertainties, but after existing so long under the terms of a too rigid contract, such a state satisfied her. She could be everything to him, or nothing, just as she liked. She would have fled from a firmer liaison. The unknown force of any emotional ties would have to be dealt with sooner or later, but the undeniable fact was that she liked him, whether or not he was also laying down snares for her. As long as everything remained uncertain between them she was not afraid.

6

The weather promised dry. They bought picnic food and got on to a bus which took them beyond all buildings and traffic. She hadn't wanted to be left in the flat while he went to draw cash from his bank, and once in the fresh air he suggested they go on to the Downs and walk.

He held back so that she could come level. The sea was far off when they turned to look, a midday haze over the town. White gulls swooped the woods to their right as if to pounce on food. He liked the sound. They met ships far from land. The noise of gulls from the English coast had a distinctive sound. Their squawk was shriller, more demanding than in other places. They knew their rights, and would see that they got them. English gulls, sure enough – the epitome of the Australians' 'wingeing Pom'. But they flew more gracefully, performed more subtle aerobatics, and if enough food weren't thrown over the side and sent bobbing around in the wake they shot-up the window of the wheelhouse and made the most unholy mess. That was English gulls for you, he said. They picked up their characters from the land they guarded, and from the air they breathed when reconnoitring Romney Marsh or the Sussex cliffs.

He talked all sorts of nonsense, she thought, glad because it saved her saying much. She felt happy at being with him in the winter landscape. From Ditchling Beacon they looked at sheep stippling the steep banks, and the village of Westmeston tucked at the foot of the hill, smoke coming straight up from cottage chimneys. There was a car parked nearby whose occupants had gone walking along the ridge. Inside another car were people eating so that, Pam said, they might just as well have stayed at home to watch the scenery on television.

The tinny noise of a radio came from their metal tomb. She put an arm around him: 'I'm hungry.'

'For food?'

'It's too cold for anything else.'

They ate sandwiches. 'I haven't walked so far for a long time.'

'At sea I used to pace the deck, and in empty moments dream of doing twenty miles a day or more with a rucksack, sleeping in inns or farms, going through Switzerland, or trekking from Land's End to John o' Groats. Probably my feet would pack in after a week, but I liked to think of moving under nobody's steam but my own. We must do it together.'

Who could blame him for making such a casual suggestion on a day like this? But life was too uncertain for plans, or even the haziest of expectations. 'Maybe we shall.'

He kissed her, yet found it difficult to reconcile the stern set of her face with the passion that gave it such life when they were in bed. Passing other people, he carried the knowledge of their lovemaking, however distant she seemed by his side. 'We must eat the cakes,' he said, 'if only to lighten the load. Then we should go, because the weather looks like closing in. It doesn't rain up here. It snows.'

The cold air penetrated to the bone when standing still. The camel-hair coat, as well as scarf, woolly hat, gloves, woollen stockings and lace-up walking shoes seemed flimsy. Occasional beams of sun shone on woods across the narrow road.

After a mile she was warm. He held her gloved hand as they went along. Few cars passed. The gulls' cries were muted against air threatening to turn into a mist. She felt they were the only two people alive. The land was dark and ungiving, and there was nothing to do but reach the shelter of buildings.

She licked icy drizzle from her lips, tasting salt one minute and soot the next. They stood under a tree to finish the cakes. She folded the plastic bag and put it into her pocket. 'The weather forecast got it wrong.'

409

Her heel was sore. When a car passed they stood in the wet grass to avoid getting splashed. By the time the first houses came in sight they were soaked. She inwardly raged because she had succumbed to his suggestion that they come up to this hellish place for a walk. He felt her mood, but couldn't tell whether her cheeks were wet from tears or raindrops. The misery of one became the wretchedness of the other, but he endured it as he knew she had to. The sky always cleared sooner or later.

They stood a few minutes till a bus drew in and drove them back to town. By now she had conquered her anger, and reminded him that they still had to buy food to take home. The shop was about to close but he put his foot inside, and the bald, thin-lipped, dark-complexioned owner demanded to know what they wanted, because didn't they realize that even a shopkeeper had a wife and children to go home to? He didn't think they would forgive him if he were late, but since they looked like a couple who were starving he might relight the showcase under the counter and let them see what was there.

He smiled at last. Did they want ham from Poland, pickles from Hungary, pâté from Belgium, cheese from France, black bread from Bradford, sausage from Italy, not to mention olives from Greece and honey from Israel? They spent ten pounds and filled two bags, and went down the dark street as if such food would cure the needle-bites of rain deadening their faces.

Her skirt and shirt were saturated. She shivered, laid their coats over a chair in front of a radiator, and never wanted to go out of doors again. Tom drew the curtains, and gave her a half tumblerful of whisky. She poured most of it back into the bottle, not wanting to be wasteful. 'Nor do I care to get tipsy.'

He drank. 'Long life!'

She swallowed the remainder as if it were water.

In the bathroom she turned on the hot tap, and took off her underclothes. Chilblains ached her feet, and gooseflesh

410

showed at the midriff. She found his aunt's dressing-gown in a cupboard and put it over her damp skin. From the bottles she took a container of bath salts. Steam coated the mirrors and gave a layer of warmth. She carried his dressing-gown from the bedroom. 'You'll get your death of cold if you don't use this.'

He sat down to resume his reading of yesterday. 'I will, in a moment.'

'You'll be no good with pneumonia.'

The heat was painful, her legs and torso turning pink as she let herself into the water. She soaked, adrift in the heat, then soaped herself, mulling on this strange existence in which every day was as long as a month. Tom seemed weird, not because she had met him so recently, or because he was ten years older, but because he had never been through the defining process of marriage. She didn't know what exactly to expect from him. She hardly knew what to expect from herself. In many ways he was like a youth of eighteen, but with the worldly experience of his proper age, a discrepancy which put her on her guard when she felt herself succumbing too readily to its attractions. She tried not to let such wariness disturb her, because she similarly felt herself to be a young woman again, backed by the protection of her past marriage and middling age.

They were fresh territory for each other, perilous only in that they clung without realizing they did so. What his advantages gave to her she was able to hand back to him, and as long as he knew it, and she sensed that he did, she didn't feel herself lacking in spirit. She felt easy whenever he was physically close, but out of his sight she was assailed by an embarrassment which would not leave her until she properly knew him. In his presence it did not matter, but she wanted to feel free of such thoughts when away from him.

Nothing mattered. Equality had to be continually considered and, if necessary, untiringly fought for. It was like being sixteen again and meeting someone of the same age for

411

the second time. You worried because you were still too young to know any better. She was surprised at herself. But her thoughts were her own, childish as they might be, and she would deny none. She saw him smiling at her through the steam, but was too drowsy to respond. He put a cup of lemon tea on the broad edge. Wash my back, she wanted to say. He took up the soap, and his smooth hands made her feel large as he wielded the sponge around her. 'Why don't you take off your dressing-gown and get in?'

It was a suggestion she had never made before, but she thought there was no point in not occasionally capitulating to whatever came into her mind, and pandering to what the body needed.

In laying the table and setting out food, he still lived alone, inviting her to share whatever he did for himself. At the moment there was no other way. She was glad, and drank the wine he poured. He had swilled the glass, and not dried it properly. A drop of water hung on the outside like a tear, which she pressed away with her fingertip. Perhaps we will stay this way for ever, each mind our own and never to meet, he with his thoughts, me with mine and wondering what his are. But he spoke, whether she could or not, as if he had been brought up to believe that it was impolite not to fill in the silence with conversation.

'The world doesn't want us unless we contribute,' he replied, when she asked if this was so, 'and I suppose that's quite right. In company, people like to hear about your work and what you've done in your life, or what you intend to do. They're interested in what you think, and in the places you've been to, and any amusing stories attached to them. It all comes out of your work. As long as you have a purpose or an aim in life, you can justify yourself.'

Perhaps the director of the orphanage, or some passing notable who had given the children a lecture, had instilled examples of how to get on in the wide world. Otherwise how could he have known? 'My grandfather must have been

412

certain that the place would set certain standards,' he said.

They talked, and finished the bottle of wine. 'I feel deficient at the thought of your adventurous life. I worked in an office before I was married, though I helped my husband with his business affairs afterwards.'

We'll go on travels to other places, he wanted to say, but felt it was not the time. She would rightly suspect him of wanting to ensnare her. There'll be plenty of adventures one day, he would add, though I don't yet know exactly where. She saw it in his candid and affectionate stare, till she laughed for no reason and turned away.

Talking was easy. Everything was easy for him because he knew how to make it so. With all the inhibitions that might have been created by his upbringing he was not afraid to say what was in his mind. He suggested that this might be because those who had lived alone never found it difficult to chatter away. Not that he minded releasing his thoughts, for what they were worth. All his life he had, as you might say, been a man of action, albeit with little enough for long stretches, and such an occupation had certainly made space for reflection to enter.

They were closer together when they talked than when they made love, but after supper it seemed natural that they should go to bed without discussing the matter. When they were so tired that they could no longer stay awake she walked into the bedroom, and heard him switching out the living-room lights behind her. She lay in bed with her arms around him, listening to the sea's roar between traffic noises.

7

She said to herself: yes, I want; and: no, I don't want. So eventually she wanted, and said yes because she hoped to

413

grow through another zone of understanding. You'll get nowhere sitting in your own room while your life rots like a dead bulb in a flowerpot. She said yes, and could only marvel, full of curiosity at his gladness when he heard her decision to stay with him.

He telephoned a garage and hired a car. 'I have a lot of luggage to bring from town, but we should get everything out in one go.'

A fat young man with pale woolly hair parked the hire-car on a yellow line and, when giving him the keys, said he had better not delay driving away or a warden would do him with a fine. The blaring radio stopped Tom hearing what was said. The young man hadn't turned it off because who in this age would want to be deprived of its frantic jingle? When Tom reached in and stopped it the young man looked with half a smile and half a jeer, as if he had expected a tip but now thought he wouldn't get one.

Tom signed a paper, and gave him a pound.

'Cheers, Captain!' Another car waited on the corner to save him walking back to his garage up the road.

Pam came down. 'The flat's locked up.'

He turned northwards from Worthing, intending to cut into London from the south-west. She had watched him map his route by compass directions instead of road numbers and the names of towns. Land and water on the earth were reversed. All around England was land, which he knew like the back of his hand, while England itself was a sea he could steer a boat across, in spite of it being filled with rocks, wrecks, shoals and reefs – in the guise of islands, towns, villages and woods.

'We'll be on the road all day,' he grumbled, six cars nose-to-tail in front. The way was narrow and twisting, part bordered by a brick wall and high hedges, as if they were in the bottom of a drained canal. Then one of the cars forked left, the leader stopped for petrol at the next pump, another turned off, one broke down with smoke coming out of its bonnet by the fistful, a Rover overtook the car in front on a straight bit at last, leaving only a final slowcoach which Tom, slotting down to third, drove immediately beyond into clear road. You were eternally blocked by a convoy, and then all opposition melted away! You were free, and at last could do more than forty, except that it would be incautious due to ice on bends and mist that hung from trees in unexpected places. A BMW came up on the starboard bow and shot by on a bend, splattering his windscreen with muddy water. He hadn't driven for months. 'I'd feel much safer in a rough old sea.'

She felt secure. He was competent. They were going along the road together, which was all that mattered. She had said yes, and there was no way out. A no could always be made a yes, but a yes was more difficult to alter, in this case because she wasn't entirely sure what she had said yes to. A well-defined yes by clause and contract could not possibly have been as final. What made it so binding was that she was content with her choice.

Little time had been necessary to agree, and he had made it easy by not mentioning advantages. If there were any, they were unimportant. It was the disadvantages that influenced her. She would no longer have her own room, losing everything she had come to value. She was surrendering, as if that much-desired state had cost her nothing, had gone against all that she had thought best for herself, as if it was her nature to do so.

People with the best intentions would have said she ought never to have left her husband, and they might have been right. She could have said it was foolish to give up her freedom now, but sometimes you had to go counter to your best interests if you wanted movement in your life. Any explanation for her decision was better than that which said she was doing it because she loved him.

It was impossible to tell whether day glowed or night shone. Dull cloud came almost to ground level, and what scared him stiff, he said, as much as he had ever been scared in his life, were those little dark cars coloured like the sky or road which, with only the dimmest of side-lights, seemed to appear out of the mist when he was half-way through an overtaking manoeuvre. Their murderous drivers are so stupid, stingy, or just consumed by the killer instinct with their lights so low, that you would think they were saving money on the slot meter they'd installed for economy's sake in case they should wear out their bulbs or batteries too quickly. It was as if they had been on a criminal job, and were sneaking home hoping not to be seen, lacking the imagination to realize that they weren't the only people on the road. They were living in that pristine state of unconsciousness which no amount of persuasion could take from them.

She laughed at his fulminations, but he thanked God for his survival when they crossed Hammersmith Bridge and were threading the last mile of traffic before landfall.

The façade of the house was uneven. Cement had fallen from cracked places, and Pam wondered how much longer it would stay aloft. A note on the shelf inside the hall said: 'I have a letter for you – Judy.' When Tom went upstairs, Pam knocked on the door opposite, and heard a shout for her to come in.

The fat-smoke of frying sausages thickened the air. Judy shuffled them in the pan with a spatula and stirred a saucepan of beans with a wooden spoon. Hilary and Sam sat at the table. Judy turned: 'Back from your honeymoon?'

She smiled. 'Is that what you call it?'

'I'll give you some tea if you sit down. Where's lover-boy? Sam, open that drawer and get Mrs Hargreaves' letter, will you?' She scooped stuff onto three plates, and set them on the table.

'Can't find it,' Sam said.

She pulled him away. 'Incompetent bloody male! Get your tea, then, and let *me* look.'

'You bollocks,' Sam said, flinching. 'You're always on at me, especially when somebody else is in the room.'

416

He wants a father, but Pam daren't say it aloud. 'I'll come down later. It can't be that vital.'

Judy began to eat. 'We had your husband here after you flitted with Tom. He came twice, in fact, then left the letter with me before going back up to Nottingham.'

'He gave me a pound note for sweets,' Sam shouted. 'I like him.'

'I'm not surprised you packed him in.' Judy carved bread. 'I hope your sailor-bloke's a bit better. I didn't like George's mood when he left.'

She wants to start an argument, Pam thought, but felt sorry for her. A half-way sympathetic man would certainly make her happier than she is now. He would have to be strong to deal with the children, and willing to allow her a girl-friend now and again. She supposed that if by any chance he existed, the possibility of them meeting was a long way this side of nil. She put an arm over her shoulder. 'It was nice in Brighton. Perhaps you'll come down some time.' She and Tom would pay their fares, and entertain them for the day. They'd lay on food, or go to the beach for a picnic.

'I can't imagine anybody bothering with a gang like us,' Judy said wearily. 'If these two go anywhere nice they take the place apart.'

'Tom will see they don't.'

'We'll go out with George,' Sam said. 'He promised to take us somewhere.'

'To the Waxworks,' said Hilary.

Judy brought the saucepan to the table for second helpings. 'Don't bank on it.'

'He gave me a pound note as well.' Hilary held out her plate. 'Will he come back soon, mum?'

Judy banged the pan in the middle of the table, and raged: 'Be quiet, both of you, or I'll throw you into the street.'

Pam recalled how good George could be with children. Edward had adored him, up to the age when he realized that his father was merely living his own childhood again through

417

him. George made it as perfect a childhood as love and money could, but Edward wanted only to be left alone, presumably, Pam thought, because with George anticipating all his desires he found it impossible to know what kind of person he was likely to grow into.

'Well,' Sam said, 'he *was* nice. He gave you twenty pounds, mum. I saw it on the shelf after he left.'

Judy smacked him across the face, though the blow lacked her usual gusto. 'I told you to keep your mouth shut about that, didn't I?'

'I'll leave home,' he said, 'if you do that again.'

'I can't wait.'

Pam felt as if she herself had been struck. 'You mean he slept with you?'

'Doesn't matter to you, does it?'

'Oh no. Certainly not.'

'He looked as if he was dying with misery,' Judy said after a while, 'so I asked him to share our supper. One thing led to another. He was too upset for me to be of much use, but I managed to soothe him in the end, which is probably why he was so generous. He needn't have been, for all I cared.'

'Twenty's a lot of money,' Sam said.

Pam had nothing to say except: 'When did he leave?'

'Three days ago. But I wouldn't be surprised if he came back. Men usually do, before they go away for good. They hate you, but can't leave you alone.'

'Aren't all men different?' Pam asked.

'Yes, they are. But they're all the same, as well.'

Pam stood. 'Burn the letter if you find it. That's what I'll do with it, after all.'

Judy took it out of the drawer. 'You'd better have the bloody thing.'

She put the envelope into her handbag. 'Thank you for holding it.'

'No hard feelings?' Judy seemed miserable, and it wasn't necessary in the least, Pam thought, saying: 'No, none, really,' though finding it difficult to say anything comforting. 'We'll be off tomorrow, or the next day at the latest.'

'Are you sure about going away with Tom?'

'Absolutely.'

She cleared the table. 'That doesn't sound very sure. It's too definite. See me before you go, though. I'll want a goodbye kiss and a hug.'

Pam went upstairs thinking how gloomy the place was, but on going into her room felt a tremor of affection for her refuge. She put her bag down and lit the fire, no time between the first hiss and pushing in the match-flame. There was a smell of ice and decaying whitewash. A noise next door caused dread till she remembered who made it. When he put on the radio there was music. The house seemed inhabited and safe. She set a kettle on the stove. Under her happiness was an apprehension that she could not explain. There was no reason, which made it worse. She breathed deeply and became calm, yet the anxiety persisted.

She took George's letter from her handbag, and began to read. 'You are a prostitute, and I'll get my own back for all you've done to me. I hung around waiting to see you, but you had gone off with that bastard, whoever he is. I spotted you, and you wouldn't look at me, but I'll get you for it, doing it on me after all I've done for you, and looked after you all these years. You don't know right from wrong, or you went off your head, I don't know which. Or you just wanted to lead a life that you'd hankered for all your life. Or maybe you'd been doing it before you left, while I was at work. I didn't know. I wouldn't, would I? How could I? But I do ask myself why we had to be married twenty years before you show your true colours. I can't think why, and I wonder if you can. I do know though that if you want to come back you can, and I'll forget all about what you have done to me. I love you, you know that, and always shall. I always did, didn't I? I only want to live with you because life's not worth living without you. I don't know why, but it isn't. I haven't told Ted (Edward) yet that you've left me, but I said you had gone to stay for a time in London. So when you come back he'll never know you've been away. I wouldn't like him to, even though he is nineteen now. He won't think much of me if he gets to know. So if you come back it'll be the same as it was, except I'll take you out more. There's a new nightclub just opened down town, and we can go there. Business is good at the moment, I don't know why because it doesn't seem good everywhere else. I've got a new secretary and she's a real worker and looks after things fine. So how about it? If you give me a ring I'll be down to fetch you, or you can come up on the train if you like. I don't mind. You always did as you liked. I can't wait to see you again. It seems years, but it's not much more than a couple of months. You'd do well to come back though, I'm telling you, because if you don't you'll be leading the sort of life that'll *do you in*, because I know you, and when it does don't come crawling back to me. That's why I say you'd better come now, because that'd be best, and try to make up for all you've done, because if you don't I'll give you no peace. I want you back, I know that, and you know it, and if you don't you ought to, so you have got to come, and if you don't, me and my brothers will come and give you a good talking to, and you know what that means. And if we see that bloke of yours he won't be much to look at after we have finished with him. He can't do what he's doing to *our* family and get away with it. He's playing with fire doing what he's doing to us, so if you've got any sense and don't want anything to happen to you or him you'll pack up and get the next train north, and if you'll phone me beforehand I'll be at the station in the car to meet you. Believe me, it'll be the greatest day of my life because I love you and have never loved anybody else, and never shall. So pack up and come back to me, there's a good girl. I'll be waiting for you. I'll never love anybody else. Love. Love. Love. George.'

The paper shook. Better to have followed her instinct and burned it. She understood why Tom had wanted to do the same with his trash. George would not accept that there was no going back, nor know that she did not live in his world anymore.

She shivered from cold. His letter paralysed her spirit. Anguish set her trembling because he was part of a trap from which escape was impossible. She had gone from him, but his refusal to realize just how far terrified her. The single-mindedness that had set him up in business was now beamed on her, threatening to pull her back into his tyranny and madness. His hungering drive would last for ever. She didn't know where to go. She was her own free self, but he would drive her from any safe place.

She took a carving knife out of the drawer, and ran her finger along the blade too lightly to cut the skin. It would thrust itself into her. She was afraid, and put it back, intending to throw the vile thing away, or give it to Judy with other belongings that she wouldn't take with her. She would deal with George without a knife. The shriek of the kettle startled her back to the life she had forgotten. Music on the other side of the wall reminded her. They would start getting their few things together, and be away by tomorrow. She dreaded any unexpected delays.

She made two cups of tea and took them to his room. He leaned over a sheet of paper, still wearing his overcoat and hat. She wasn't sure he had heard her. His pen shaped a black curve to join a half-line of dots and angles, symbols fixed as if they had been cut out with scissors and stuck there.

'Keeps me warm,' he said, 'coming into a freezing room. It seemed natural to light the stove, draw the curtains, and copy a sentence as if I wanted to send a letter to my mother or my grandmother. Maybe I'm writing to myself. It's like learning for the first time, straight from the heart.'

She stood and watched. 'What does it mean?'

He read the translation. 'Blessed art thou, O Lord our God, King of the Universe, who has kept us in life, and has preserved us, and has enabled us to reach this season.'

'Beautiful.' Her hand was on his shoulder for comfort. 'We want a new life, and a new way of seeing things – or a new way of looking at the old things that gives them fresh warmth and love.' She had felt it for as long as she could remember, but had never told herself until now.

He pushed the papers aside, and returned the pen to his pocket. 'You're part of these letters because you persuaded me to search that roomful of stuff, when I really was about to throw it out. You began the process that can't be reversed, so I never want to be away from you.'

She kissed his hands. 'They write such beautiful letters!'

'I saw a page of manuscript on parchment that shines and dazzles,' he told her, 'which must have taken weeks to copy. When I was in the orphanage we had to read the Bible every day. For years I didn't like the sections dealing with a man who was said to have died on a cross for my sins. I couldn't believe that such an event could have anything to do with me. Somebody had got it all wrong, I thought. My sins are my own, such as they might be, and God will either forgive them or he won't. But it's up to God, not the man who was killed by the Romans on a cross – a piece of barbarism of which the twentieth century has more examples than any other. I could believe in God, and those parts of the Bible which weren't about Jesus. It seemed that God had already had a lot to do with my life, if things had any explanation at all. The so-called Old Testament stories made sense. I had a good memory and learned whole chapters, though I later forgot them. In the navy I hardly opened the Bible, except in some hotel when I might – if I was sober – read a few verses before going to sleep. Later I carried one with me from ship to ship, until somebody walked off with it. It's strange to realize that much of it was written in the script I'm learning to write, and that one of the books which came from my mother is the first five books of the Bible in Hebrew.'

'They're part of *you*,' she said.

She sat opposite, did not care to say anything without

422

thinking first. It was no use blurting the words so as to save the anguish of a decision. Those days must surely be over. She must trust herself to say whatever came to her, otherwise there was no way of knowing whether the thought was false or not. She had surfaced after a life under water, and felt the miasma of self-deception clearing. If what she said meant nothing to him, then her words were at least justified by what was in her heart.

They had seemed more united in his aunt's flat, together but without that seriousness which, in the cold rooms of this half-way house, pushed them apart. She no longer pertained to herself. Nor did he belong to himself. Neither were they primarily attached to each other. Yet even to think so implied a more than possible unity. They belonged to this world but were detached from it, though only by such feelings of separation could the real connection ultimately be made. It had to start somewhere. 'I'm in love with you,' she said simply.

He couldn't tell her that he had never heard a woman say so before, but was silent with a silence that was also part of her, just as she thought that her silence must by now belong to him. He shook himself, as if he had been asleep. His eyes showed an exhausted spirit, that seemed to have received an unendurable shock. She had said that she loved him, and he tried to smile, wondering when she would say it again.

8

She was in a wood but sunlight flowed between black-and-yellow trunks, smooth and tall with no leaves or branches visible. Her head wouldn't turn upwards to look. There were bushes and flowers, and gnarled roots half covered with soil that hindered her walk. Sleep showed as if through a window. Her dream, packed on to the head of a pin before it pricked and woke her, kept out the cold. The sunlight was still hot between the trees, and something was about to happen. She stroked one of the trunks, and caressed the mark of its Hebrew letter. Her tongue went forward, and a root at her foot became a cat which nudged her ankle and leapt up the tree before she could touch. She walked a straight line between trees till sunlight drew off, and darkness came. A muffled bang sounded far away as she was climbing, an easy ascent to follow the light, going towards the inside of an umbrella that had a hole where the centre should have been, floating weightlessly up the inner funnel of a parachute without any thought for the earth, arms and fingers straight above her head so that she could steer through and into a light that would last for ever.

A noise deepened into thunder and tore her eyes open. A mass from the outside world threw itself at her. She sat up. Light came through curtain slits.

'Open the fucking door.'

She hurriedly put on shirt and slacks, buttoning and zipping. Her fingers wouldn't work. She felt sick, and choked back her dread. 'Go away.'

A piece of paper had been pushed in as if it might save her life. She snatched at it. 'Gone out for a while.' George must have watched him leave.

'Let me in, you whore.'

'I'll see you downstairs, at Judy's.' I won't see you. Keep out of my life. I'm finished with you. She shouted, but he banged at the panels, then ran at the door with his broad shoulders, shot latch, lock and bolt apart, and was in the room.

She would not let him see her terror. 'I told you: I'd meet you downstairs.'

424

He had grown stouter, as if in the habit of boozing heavily. He trembled as he leaned against the doorway. 'Pack your things. I've got the car outside.'

Say something, but don't argue. And say it quietly. He was strong and agile, but his skin was blotched. He was grieved, and full of violence. 'I've only just got out of bed. You woke me up. If you'd let me know you were coming we could have met somewhere and talked things over properly.'

The clock said nine. He had set out in darkness, full of energy and purpose, see-sawed with love and loathing, till loathing got the upper hand, as it always did. His eyes had hardened during the long stare of a hundred and forty miles of road, impacted by tar and dazzling light thrown back.

'Pack your stuff. We'll talk in the car.' He looked around the room. 'It wain't take long.'

She stood with hands together to stop them shaking. The only way to evade him was to die, or pray for his instant obliteration. She remembered that for the first time in her life there was something to live for.

He moved closer. 'I ain't got much time. The lads came down with me. We're to be back at work today. There's no time to waste.' His fist banged down and tipped her clock, as if angry that she looked at it and not him. His previously contained insanity was erupting. There was no one else in the world but himself, and the person that he wanted to control – which is me, she thought. No will or object could stand in his way, certainly not an instrument for the marking of time.

In such a way he had been insane since she first met him, and she must have known it, and been ensnared because his maniacal sense of possession had left her with no possibility of refusing whatever he wanted. Her presence during their marriage had kept him on the proper side of normal life. And if much of the time she had seemed out of her mind herself, it was only because she was taking the madness from him so that he could function properly. She would have no more of that.

425

He pulled at her. 'You *will* get in the car, if I have to kick you in.'

She looked around.

'*He* won't help you.'

He had been drinking, kept a bottle in the glove-box. 'What do you mean?'

'Alf, Harry and Bert are waiting downstairs for that git. Our family stands together, you should know that. Twenty quid each, and extra for petrol. A good day's pay, but they stick by me, all the same.'

To pack was easy, and then to unpack. 'Let go of my arm.' He had worked out his plan, so there was no one to help. 'I don't want to come with you.'

'You will, though, let me tell you.'

She opened the drawer. One thrust, and she was up for murder. No one would believe her. He attacked me. Where are your marks? 'And what are you going to do when we get to Nottingham? Do you have a room with bars at the window?'

'Ah, no, duck.' His mood altered. 'Once you're back home, and you see how nice it is, you'll be your old self again. It's warm and clean up there, not like this freezing pigsty. You'll be as right as rain.'

'I don't suppose you've had breakfast yet,' she said.

He sat down, resting on his knees, looking more alone than he could have thought it possible to be. 'We was up at four. I've given *them* two days pay – double time – and a bonus after we've got *you* back home. This little lot's costing me nearly two hundred. So just get packing, or I'll block your throat with your teeth.'

'It's a lot of money,' she said, 'just to get me home.'

His brothers had fed him the filth. 'It ain't right for her to do it on you like this, George, after all you've done for her. I'll bet she's having a real old carry-on down in London. God knows what she's up to, but she's finding plenty to keep her busy. A woman can allus find a man down there when she wants to.

426

Thinks she can get a lot more from him than she can get from her husband. I expect she can, as well. You was never one for giving her a lot of *that*, was you, George? Too busy at your factory, though we can't blame you for that. I suppose she even cracks jokes about you to her new bloke. Wouldn't be surprised, I wouldn't. If I was you I'd go down and give her a bloody good pasting. Bring her to her senses. Get her back home for a dose of you-know-what. That's all they want. If Mavis played the same stunt on me I'd give her such a smack in the chops she wouldn't wake up for a week. She'd be as right as rain, then. That's what you ought to do with your Pam. Do you both a lot of good. We'll help you to find her and get her back, wain't we, lads? Mind you, we've got a few jobs on at the moment and time's money, ain't it, George? You're allus saying so, but we know you'll make it right with us if we give you a hand. After all, brothers have to stand by one another.'

He threaded the fingers of both hands together, so that a whole series of cracks ran along the knuckles. 'I can't wait much longer.'

She dodged as he tried to grab. 'I'll come in my own time.'

Terrorist force was on his side, his unreal calculations taking account only of himself. He lived in the vacuum of his own needs, which admitted nobody else's because he thought his desires were also the world's. His clenched fist flashed at her face. 'You'll come *now*.'

He was quick, and the room was small, but she avoided all but the close-winded rush. She had nowhere to go. The refuge that had taken weeks to construct had turned into the perfect trap. 'I'm not going by force.'

She spoke whatever words would stall him from one moment to the next, but despised herself for uttering such phrases of surrender before the threat of his fists. His eyes, and the brain behind them, assumed she belonged to him because he was stronger, and that she had no life of her own.

He stood back, as if he had won round one, and could afford to wait. 'Take your time. Have a few minutes if you like. I don't want to rush you.'

She was wary. He closed the door. She wouldn't get it open in time if she ran. Tom had no doubt been waylaid by his brothers. Three to one was their style.

He lit a cigarette. 'Want one?'

She shook her head.

He acted like a friend, but was not very good at it. He smiled. 'Go on,' and held the packet towards her.

'No thank you.'

She put a suitcase on the table. She should have accepted the cigarette. Lull him. She took a dress from the wardrobe, and walked to fold it in the light of the window which gave a view up and down the street. Tom wasn't in sight, but neither were the others. George's car was in a meter-bay a hundred yards away. Maybe he had only put enough money in for an hour, and wanted her out quickly because he didn't care to overstay his time. Like most ambitious men who lived in their own small area he was law-abiding, for while he had the born energy and skill to do his job well he did not have the ingenuity to break the law and feel confident that he would never get caught, especially in London. Nor did he have the necessary panache to bend the regulations and not care whether he was found out. Therefore he had put in enough money for the maximum of two hours in case something went wrong.

'I must get some fresh air into the room after sleeping in it all night.' She opened the window. Impossible to jump before he grabbed her. His hands twitched, as if afraid she might try. Perhaps he wouldn't care. If she flashed out of his sight it would make a respectable end to his troubles. Or he would hire someone to push her around in a wheelchair for the rest of her life.

'Yes,' he said, 'the room does pong. You must have been drinking. You never did booze, though. The odd shandy now

428

and again. But I expect you're on the hard stuff every night, with the sort of company you keep.'

He looked wretched again, and threatening. A real woman would have sympathized with his suffering – and been destroyed. But she wouldn't. He could plead as much as he liked. Every word he spoke ate into his self-esteem. Then he became quiet. She too had better say nothing. Yet silence could only mean surrender. He called the tune. The leader led, but where did he take you? You didn't follow. So he was no longer a leader. But the rules he made her live by were so deep in him that he wasn't even aware that they existed. Lucky man. All men were lucky – though they might not know it – by much more than a head start. Yet it was best not to think so, because that too was only part of their unspoken rules and the effect they had on you. How could you be yourself, or know yourself, if you were under that kind of domination? You didn't follow. You did anything but follow. A man with no one to follow him was finished. He was beaten. You just did not follow.

He smiled at her silence. Won again. He didn't even need to say it. The damp air that came coldly in might stir her sufficiently to think properly and find a way out of her peril. Still holding the dress, she went to the chest of drawers. 'I don't drink half as much as you imagine. I can't take it. Do you remember when we went to that club? I had two small gins, and was ill when I got home. All I drink is a glass of wine, and then only with a meal.'

Using her dress as a cover she opened the drawer and gripped the knife in her right hand. There was no other way. The more she spoke the more silent and depressed he became. He pulled back into the bleak spaces inside, his familiar manoeuvre being to retreat with set mouth and glazed eyes, and surround himself with a broken-glass zone of resentment that could only be entered by those who admitted to being the cause of his distress, even if they weren't. It was a trick he had often used, of blaming her for the dark moods that would

429

occasionally envelop him for no reason. She was long used to his expressions. To comfort him was to accept the blame for the way he felt, and not to comfort him was to be blamed because her very presence made him feel worse. It was as if she were back home already. Futile emotional competition once more enmeshed them. Her months of freedom vanished in a moment.

Air from the open window pushed at the small of her back. Her face burned but her body stayed cold. The dress fell to the floor and she held the knife in front. She knew him too well not to love him, but it was the love of pity, not the love between equal human beings. Despair pierced her so sharply that she lunged.

He leapt from his chair and staggered away. The point tore his coat. What she needed to tell him fused into a mass and would not be said. There was nothing to say any more. If he wanted so crucially to lead anyone, let him lead that remnant of himself which might yet redeem him as the good person he could well be in some unreachable part of himself. He saw clearly what she demanded from him, but he would not do it. She lifted the knife again.

He stared at the razorsharp blade in the hope perhaps that she would stare back long enough to be hypnotized into losing her determination. His lips were about to say something. He would try to argue, but if she replied with words it would weaken her stance. Words were finished. When in his presence they seared her too painfully.

He darted, speedy as a cat, to grab her arm. She stood aside and brought the knife against his hand. He squealed. It was real. He went back to the door, afraid to turn and open it in case the knife burned into his back. He held his wrist high, and blood came from an opening cut. The insanity was in her own eyes, and she prayed he would leave. But she would neither ask nor order. He had to go without words. Words were finished.

She flexed her body. He saw the movement. His cry

suffused him with shame at having to plead, but it was a shame which gave him courage to stay where he was. He would fight for his life. He shifted as if to come forward, but it was hopeless because he could no longer take her by surprise. He noted her knuckles whiten at the grip, and her left hand come out as if to give a firm balance.

His smile was a sign of wanting to placate her, almost of surrender, and stopped her hand lifting for its final drive. His features, bunched like a baby's about to weep at some primal disappointment, caused her to brace herself for a sly attack. His life was saved. She lowered the knife, but lifted it not quite so high. She hadn't lived with him twenty years for nothing. No sudden attack was possible, because the gleam of the blade was sharper than any eye.

There was a rattle at the door. Inside or out, she didn't know. His unwounded hand clutched the knob. He didn't want to go, needed to speak, to plead, to get the knife clear and batter her to death. She watched the flicker of his eyelids when he tried to look directly at her. He wasn't able to, as if he would go blind should he succeed. His hand motioned for peace, while his head was fixed at an angle that only allowed him to see the floor.

Her terror was in abeyance while she waited. However abject, he could leap like a tiger, but the cold air kept her alert, and if he ran she would kill. He wouldn't force her. She would force him. The rattling of the door knob was to distract her. His eyes looked up, and she swung the knife.

The sleeve of his suit was soaked. The twitch of his face and the sway of her knife came out of the same impulse. An ache pained him. His eyes pleaded for her to speak. Any words from her would have been balm, but she couldn't trust him. Trust also was finished. It was an all-or-nothing game, and she hoped to die rather than have it go on by his rules.

She knew what he wanted. Her whole being told her to soothe him with a few words so that he would go away as a human being and not some animal set on revenge for his humiliation. That too was another of his tricks, and she wouldn't let it take her over. He would lead her no more. Everything that would be to his advantage contained disaster for her. She must stand where she was and stay alert, eyes never ceasing to look in his direction no matter what the effort.

He made croaking sounds, held up his arm and patted the patch where it was wet. She stepped towards the window-sill till the wall was close. She found it hard to prevent her hands laying down the knife, or letting it fall out of the window, or rushing at him in an unstoppable fury and thrusting the blade again and again into his body till she crumbled under a final desertion of strength. Either course seemed overwhelmingly desirable. It was harder to stay silent and ready. The uncertainty of each second was impossible to bear.

The unexpected touch of the sill at her back was a signal. All air seemed ripped out, either as if she would faint, or as if she had infinitely more strength than she knew what to do with. She advanced towards him with unmistakable intention.

He opened the door and ran.

She shouted at the top of the stairs for him never to come back. The front door slammed, shaking the balustrade.

She gripped with both hands. The knife, hurled after him, had clattered on to the landing below. She went down to pick it up, thinking to run on to the street and shriek so that he would know he had reduced her to the lowest common factor of his imagination as far as women were concerned. This couldn't be the end. Wanting to kill, she was still part of him, and so needed more than ever to destroy him.

After picking up the knife, she stopped. If she maimed or murdered she would be part of him for ever. She felt only humiliation and sickness. If she killed him she would *not* be part of him. It was a lie.

9

With trembling hands she laid the knife in the drawer. Looking in the mirror, there was nothing new in her face except fear. She leaned against the glass and cooled her forehead. She forced a smile, but tears were falling. The grimace mocked her. Setting the clock upright, she saw that only twenty minutes had gone by since her dream had been riven by his banging at the door. She wiped the tears angrily, and felt jubilant.

But she curbed her exultation. It was unworthy, a madness too similar to his. There was much still to be considered. The fight was only half done. It would never be done. She didn't know where they were.

His car was still in the parking bay. She closed the window. Why hadn't he gone? A middle-aged woman walked with a dog along the street. Low clouds were about to spill rain from a darkening sky. A man in the distance already wore his umbrella, and a car went by with small lights on and wipers going. They'll have a rough trip home. She cursed the motorway that put them only two hours from London. It used to take at least double, coming through all towns en route. Maybe he wouldn't be so ready another time. He would bandage his cut by using the first-aid kit in the car, nursing the ache every mile north. One of the others would no doubt drive, if he was conscientious about earning his fee. What year did they imagine they were living in, to think they would get her back with them? Their Neanderthal bellies still thrived on the Wars of the Roses. In this day and age you had to fight with a knife to beat them off. She could hardly believe what had happened.

The door would not lock, but she closed it to begin packing.

The sooner she fled the better. She should get properly dressed, go out, and walk back and forth by the police station. But even that might not do any good. She had to live without safety. At least in Clara's flat there was the obstacle of London to deter them from a quick foray. She washed her tears at the sink, unwilling to let them turn her into the animal they wanted her to be. There was no need to despair, she said, looking into her long mirror.

The window tempted her again, but she was afraid of being seen. She looked, and saw their car had gone. Conscious of victory, she felt proud of having got rid of them by herself. Tom would be back, but there'd be no need to mention her struggle, since both she and he would soon be in a place where such struggles would not occur.

She packed shoes and dresses, folded skirts, blouses and underwear into her case. How many more times would she do it? The oftener the better. It didn't take long. Say goodbye to Judy, wedge their things into the car, then go to the estate agent's to settle the rent. The picture was clean and beautiful. They would drive away. Let the rain come. There would be occasional sunshine from now on. Didn't expect it. Didn't care. A thunderous noise sounded on the stairs.

The door banged against the wall. All four were in the room. She cried: cunning bastards. But she spoke quietly. 'Get out, or I'll call the police.'

Alf took her case and was off with it downstairs. George threw her coat into her face. 'Wrap this round you.' He smiled: the leader had won. 'Come on, you'll need it.'

When she refused he crammed it under his arm, and sent two driving blows, one into her ribs and the other at the side of her head that flung her against the wall. No messing this time. She freed herself from one of the scarves that decorated it.

Harry and Bert pinned her arms. It was no dream. They pulled her out of the room. She kicked till Bert fell at the wall to nurse his bruise. Her shoe had flown with him. From the top of the stairs she screamed for Judy, her voice like a noise

434

that rushed out at her from another door. George snarled. 'She isn't in. Gone to get her National Assistance, I expect.'

They had waited downstairs, impatiently smoking their fags to the stub while George made his first attempt. You didn't bring her? Why, you dozy bastard! You're as soft as shit, George. She had a knife? They laughed all over the pavement. And you let that stop you? Bleddy 'ell! Do you want to get her back, or don't you? Don't cry about it. She ain't worth it. You do? Come on, then, there'll be no pissin' about this time. After all, George, this trip's costing you a bomb. You might as well get summat out of it, even if it's only a bit of you-know-what!

Harry alone was left to help him pull at her, and she struck his face with her clenched fist. She'd never hit anyone in her life before. He must have got out of bed too early to shave that morning. 'For God's sake give us a hand,' he called, as his own hand slipped from her. He stumbled half down the first flight and continued on his way. She kicked again, but a blow landed at her face that sent her back through the doorway into her room.

She leapt at the chest of drawers. When George clutched her from behind she kept her grip on the knobs. His wrench was tigerish, an effort which pulled the drawer open for her, so that she took the knife and swung towards him. He let go. All three were back, and then at various points of the landing.

'You don't need to use that,' Bert wheedled. 'Does she, our George?'

She tore Alf's suit at the lapel. Thinking she had stabbed him, he struck at her face. The wall spun and she was on the floor, still gripping the knife. She kept her eyes closed against the stained carpet, and waited for her chance. A shoe stamped on her wrist, the pain grinding all breath away. She held to the dark as if it were a big foul blanket to crawl under. It comforted but did not strengthen her. She felt herself going, but did not know where. Someone kicked her. Two yellow sparks came together from opposite ends of darkness, then

435

shot apart, and slowly moved towards each other, over and over, forcing her into a tunnel without even a pinpoint of light at the end.

A voice was toned with rough animal-like anger at the fact that they were too long at their simple job. She dimly noted the manner of subdued rage at their stupidity in not being fit to do something which the power behind such a voice obviously would be able to accomplish with no bother at all. She had given in. There was only silence and stillness left in her. She forced back her sobs, all future existence dependent on what pride she could muster. It was the only force she could draw on. Years of dust scraped her face, the detritus of centuries. When the foot ceased to crush her wrist she waited for the last blow to descend, hoping there would be nothing more in life to come.

'What's going on?' The words were distinct, not violent or loud, though they had a promise of becoming so. The voice kept her alive, free of final darkness, not from hope of salvation but out of curiosity, for it seemed hardly human, rang up and down the stairs in a sort of commanding bark that she had only ever heard from someone talking to a pack of dogs. She trembled with dread, but would not move, even if he killed her.

'She took a knife to us,' Alf said.

A dizziness faded into and then away from her. Why should he apologize? she wondered, as she battled against the sensation of fainting.

'Shut your mouth, or I'll take my boot to *you*.' The same voice, an island unto itself, seemed to come out of the roof, with a stridency that had little to lose and nothing on earth at least to be afraid of. The dominating ugliness struck even her in the face, a voice accustomed to making itself heard, understood and obeyed against the noise of engines or the elements, or both – not, perhaps, the voice to command from the throne of absolute authority, but that of someone expounding the law of good behaviour which had been passed on to him. He was finding it no easy task, but in a crisis there was nothing else to rely on, and because the odds were so much against him the transference had to succeed. 'What are you doing here? There's eighteen months inside waiting for the lot of you.'

'It's none of your business,' Alf shouted. 'She's our brother's wife, and she's coming back to Nottingham with us, where she belongs.'

George threw her coat on the floor. 'It's no bleddy use. Let's clear off.'

She looked, and listened, and waited for the ability to get on her feet. He was holding her suitcase as if it were weighted with iron, and he would swing it against them. His reddening face seemed about to burst with a rage she could never have mustered in herself no matter what they did, and that she thought was containable in no human being. She had not known him before. His head was held back, as if to see above any level they would reach.

'Let them go away,' she said.

'Not likely.' He put her suitcase by the wall, seeing Bert making signs to push against him. 'Keep back, sailor!' he shouted in the voice she hoped never to hear again.

'Fuck off!'

His knees lifted, and the sharp smack of bone against Bert's face was followed by a colder thump. Bert was taller, and Tom fell grunting with two dull blows at the cheek, but he recovered, and boxed, and edged himself around, and suddenly Bert was heeling down the stairs. George sidled by, and was out of sight. She couldn't tell how it happened, pressed herself in a corner to stay clear.

He maintained his attitude of defence, knowing that Alf would try to avenge his brother. Because there was something funny and pathetic about his two fists, which seemed childishly deployed, she wanted to laugh – despite her tears and the sharp aches. His fists would shield him, and her, from the world threatening to burst through their puny guard. She

437

couldn't laugh. But there was something comical in being defended.

Alf made one last savage attack, but it ended in a circular kind of scuffling around the landing, occasional jabs going out from both. The skirmish seemed to go on for ever. When she looked it was to see Alf go sideways across Tom and follow a pathway down the stairs.

Tom pursued them below the first landing. 'If you come here again, I'll break you in pieces!'

He breathed as if an engine were locked inside, a weird and distressing effect when he tried to smile. He seemed far away from himself, and separated from her by the agony of breathlessness and pain. The front door slammed, and he walked cautiously down to make sure they were on the right side of it, pressing himself close to the wall on one flight, and against the banister on the next. She supposed he had done such manoeuvres often to be so adept in them.

They had swung at his shopping bag on the way by, all of it spilled and scattered. He thought it cheap at the price. Half a dozen cardboard boxes telescoped into one, which he had brought from the supermarket to serve as containers for their belongings, stood by the door, hardly damaged by their boots in the hurry to get out.

10

She stood in her room, unable to move. Her will had gone. If she sat or lay down she would never get up. She would die, because this was no kind of life. Neither her imagination nor her pessimism had envisaged direct assault. A person could

438

not be secure with such people loose, who felt she belonged to them like a slave to be taken back into bondage.

She didn't, and never had. Never would. She was not connected to them in any way, but they would have killed her rather than let her stay free. He spoke, in his familiar and soothing voice. 'Come into my room, and let's have a look at you.'

'Leave me alone. I feel wrecked.'

He put his arm around her. 'You'll be all right.'

What did he know about it? Her stomach was made of iron when she pressed her fist there. But she went with him. He brought a bowl of water, and washed her face while she sat in the armchair. The rancorous note of his authority was still apparent. 'If I telephone the police they'll catch them going up the motorway.'

'Leave them.' She was unable to stop her hands shaking. 'I'm not really hurt.'

His face was also bruised, the lower lip cut. 'They're a rough lot. But you're a bit of a fighter yourself, to hold them off so well. You just left me with the mopping-up!'

'I didn't think I could do anything.'

He took two pieces of cotton wool soaked in cool liquid, and held them to her bruises. 'You never know what you're like till you get pushed against a wall. But I'm sorry I took so long over my business. When I came back and saw this type coming out of the house with your suitcase I thought he'd rifled our belongings. He gave me some talk, so I put in two quick ones and got him to tell me what was going on. For all I knew, your life was at stake. It certainly sounded like it as I came up the stairs. You get rough lots at sea, even these days, so it wasn't a new situation for me. There's often no hard feelings afterwards, though I didn't like the look of that gang.'

'It had to happen, but that part of my life is finished. If I was in any doubt about it I couldn't go on living.'

The pain of her weeping doubled itself in him. Such an incident could brush anyone. He had known rather more of the

439

world in that respect than she had, but decided that, since it was now up to him, she really had seen the last of them. 'We'll be away by this evening. I went to the estate agent's and settled everything. We're to leave the keys with Judy.'

'I could have paid my own account.'

'I did it to save time. All that's left is to hump our belongings on to the pavement and load the car. It'll be like quitting a wharf we've been tied up to for too long.'

She couldn't stay, yet didn't want to go. Every move was a bad dream. She had agreed, and the idea thrilled her, but her one-time family had spoiled her with dread where before she had been optimistic. She felt unable to eliminate such gall from her soul. It was impossible to imagine the kind of freedom from them that she craved. But the gorge rose as if to vomit them out even against her will. It was a matter of time. She would not let them blight her spirit.

She padded the corners of the case with underwear and socks, and folded his uniform while he emptied the cupboards. 'We must leave things ship-shape, though Judy said she would give a final sweep in exchange for whatever goods we won't be taking.'

He put half a dozen out-of-date Pilot Books in a box, and protected his deckwatch and sextant with newspapers. His short-wave radio was placed by the door. There was a record-player, suitcase, roll of charts, and a kitbag of oddments – the tools and toys that had gone all over the world, moved by ship, rickshaw, taxi and human back, belongings as much part of him as his own fingertips.

There was no hurry, he said. It was best that way. She still wasn't fit. He topped whisky with water and gave it her to drink. He sipped from the flask. They smoked and talked. He took off his jacket and unloaded the shopping, cutting away damp bread where the eggs had broken. He set things on the table and they sat down to eat. She felt better. The stove kept them warm. 'I'll leave it for Judy,' he said, 'and five gallons of paraffin in the cupboard.'

She was in pain on trying to smile. 'With so many things she'll open a junk stall on the Portobello Road. It'll make her a pound or two.'

They cleared away the meal and finished at the sink. All his life he had moved. He still hadn't stopped. But *she* was about to begin. After such a send-off by George and his brothers it was impossible to imagine the future. She was exultant from the whisky, but fought to stay calm and not show tears. Men hated to see women in tears, she thought, though not more than she hated them in herself. She had struggled for her life, and won. Even without Tom they wouldn't have taken her. Because it was her victory she could go with him and feel safe, as much out of her own will as because she was in love. Funny sort of love. But it was all she was left with.

Neither knew where it would end, and that also made the prospect acceptable when all through her life there had either been nowhere to think of going, or a straight road on which it would be intolerable to travel. She did not feel that he would be hard to know, or that to fathom him would lead her to a lake of pitch from which there would be no escape. It did not matter whether or not she got to know him. He was not difficult to be with, so it didn't seem important. The fever of wanting to know a man in order to find out whether he loved you or not, or whether you loved him, was a sure way of destroying any love that existed, or cauterizing any regard out of which love could grow. She had learned her lesson, reflecting that it had taken her long enough – if it actually turned out that she had.

In some ways he was foreign to her, though she couldn't say exactly how or why. Didn't want to. She was also a foreigner to him, she didn't wonder, and a foreigner even to herself much of the time, which was maybe why she had been able to stay alive through much of her past existence. She hoped she would continue to, no matter what happened between them. She flattered herself, she said, in imagining that she could be a foreigner to anybody apart from herself, but no doubt she might be, at her time of life and with the foibles that had surfaced after abandoning her funny marriage. That she felt like a foreigner to all and sundry seemed the first good fact about herself and their relationship. It thinned the emotions, gave them less importance when in operation. Not being 'made for each other' meant there were sufficient novelties of behaviour for affection to fasten on without generating painful antagonisms. Because they were not familiar by temperament and background everything had to be said before the meaning was clear, and so only those meanings were made plain that clarity considered absolutely necessary. So they could be almost uncaring, a mood in which all revelations would come, if they must, in their allotted time.

Because they felt foreign to each other she sensed that it still might be possible to love and yet keep their separate identities. Many couples who lived together for a long time took on the worst traits of the other (and in her case she blamed herself as much as George) and so could not help but enter a battlefield from which neither could get free, an inbred fight in which, the longer it went on, the more impossible it was to call a truce or separate. Two people with common frontiers should cross them with circumspection, or by invitation only.

They talked well into the afternoon, as if unwilling to leave such a haven before emptying their minds of what thoughts it had bred in them. A conversation with long silences went on till she could no longer sit up, and the walls swayed towards her.

She lay on his bed, and was immediately asleep. He pulled up a chair and sat as if to guard her, knowing that they would need the whole world's space before their spirits could be contained. He looked at her relaxed face, which seemed younger than before her experience of the morning. He would provide space, but the word, as he observed while putting her hands under the blanket so that they would not get cold, had no precise meaning except in the picture of a blue ocean and a

442

white sky that were empty for as far as the eye could see, but about to be filled by the first star of the morning.

11

A warm spring wind from the sea ruffled the curtains. He had drawn a six-pointed star on a sheet of cartridge paper, using a red biro and a long ruler, one triangle superimposed on the other so that all six points became small triangles of equal area.

From each point he ran a green line to the centre, and pondered on the diagram. Counting the indentations between the points, twelve directions could be marked off. Aristotle was said to have suggested a circle of twelve winds. The six-pointed star was the Star of David, the *Magen David* of the Hebrews, the Jewish Star, the sign on the flag of Israel. He wore one around his neck, under his shirt, two triangles of gold within a circle. It had belonged to his mother.

A box of instruments was open on the table. The drawing fascinated him, as a Euclidean object, a geometrical conundrum, and as a religious symbol with secular properties. He wondered if it had been used in ancient times as a surveying device, a mathematical instrument and angle-measurer for designing temples or building pyramids. The six points coming out of the centre and reckoned as parts of a circle could be used in finding latitude at sea, the sixty-degree divisions conforming to the sixty-degree angle of a sextant.

Each point could be part of a timing system to mark off the segments of the day. If a cord was suspended from the middle, as a gunners' device with a protractor, and a weight attached, it could have calculated calendars. In a land survey, a complete triangulation could have been based upon it. Science as well as art was cultivated before the Flood. He had read that Josephus ascribed surveying to the Hebrews, who were said to have derived it from the Patriarch Abraham, who brought it to Egypt from Ur of the Chaldees. The Star of David was mystical, yet scientific and rational.

She only half understood what he told her. He didn't seem altogether sure himself, except for the mathematical intricacies. On a desert island, armed with the double triangle of six points, he could within a week, he said, produce an accurate map of his territory. A *Magen David* was a star, a symbol for the spirit to dwell on, a design to exercise the brain in all kinds of technical beginnings. A spaced-out baseline would begin his survey, angles subtended by a fabricated tape to get the perfect equilateral. He rolled the words over and over, wrote them and crossed them out as if he had been born recalling them, from the moment the umbilical string snapped, or on first seeing the golden *Magen David* between his mother's breasts.

With such an inheritance, who needs anything else that the world has to give? A Star of David as the basis for a navigation kit could steer you a course through the heavens or over the surface of the world, keeping clear of hell and high water. You could periodically sell your expertise to the highest and most tolerant bidder for laying out irrigation ditches or building trireme canals on which boats with burnished thrones that queens sat on floated at dawn or dusk. Or you could check the sun's zenith, calculate heights and distances, make contour maps never found four thousand years later when the first marauding Europeans opened the pyramids. Or you made Portolan charts of the oceans for mariners to steer by in their ships towards empires only now crumbling away.

Jafuda Cresques of the school of Majorcan map-makers had his observatory in Portugal for Henry the Navigator, and made the first charts of the oceans, as is common knowledge among seafarers ancient and modern. Joseph of Spain brought the Arabic numerals from India. On his Great Voyage of discovery Columbus took with him Luìs de Torres and four more bearing the Star of David in their hearts. They had prepared astronomical works and made scientific instruments for navigation, and were otherwise intimately concerned with and connected to the guiding star seen also by Columbus, who knew that without such people the Great Voyage would never have started.

Covilhão went to the land of Prester John; Abraham de Beja to India; Wolf to Bokhara; Isaacs to Zululand; Palgrave to Arabia; Vambéry to Turkestan. The race of travellers and star-followers spread far and scattered wide, others ever in their wake. Tom knew that he too had been one of them all his working life, though too ordinary to be noticed, because every ship in the middle of the ocean needing to ascertain its position to within a few hundred yards was in effect (and as far as the navigating officer was concerned) there for the first time, since in the nature of things there could not be the marks on the water of who might have been there before.

With no country of their own, the Sons of Aleph (and of every other letter of their Divine Alphabet) looked at the stars for guidance, and the stars answered with their trust. Astronomical tables of practical utility were drawn up by those without country but to whom Jerusalem was the centre of the world. Prophiat Tibbon produced the quadrant to replace the astrolabe, and Bonet de Lattes invented an astronomical ring. Herschel surveyed the heavens. Beer drew his map of the moon, and Loewy invented his elbow telescope.

The world was a pitfall but the heavens were benign and gave their knowledge to whoever observed their mystery with penetrating reason. In the beginning were the stars, and among that unaccountable number were six which, when the points were drawn together in the mind's eye, became two triangles of guided light superimposed, making the Star of David. But those six stars were never mentioned by name nor delineated as such, though they were known and indicated by some sequential cabbalistic sign in the Book of Tables. They are known yet unnamed, and no one will claim to know them, but they exist and are eternally in their places.

She caught one word in ten as he laboured among his heaps of books and charts: reading, drawing, writing, staring out of the window and pondering on some problem which, he said, seemed useless but which delighted the mind and could not therefore be futile. He constructed a frame of two triangles and covered it with letters and figures to test his ideas, fixing sights and strings, and aiming it at the moon, the sun or the first star of the evening, covering sheets of paper with calculations, or pecking at the keys of an electronic calculator till he obtained answers that either satisfied or sent him back into more hours of frenzied reckoning.

She looked up from her reading, and realized that as far as he was concerned she did not exist. Yet he was happy because no obligatory companionship was necessary, no sense of either of them feeling deprived because the other wasn't ready to vibrate with good or bad emotions at a mere glance. They were cut off from each other, and she was glad, able to sit undisturbed and be herself.

She had prayed many times for such separation. When with George, he couldn't leave her alone. Her silence robbed him of his right to exist. Silence alarmed him, but it wasn't so much the actual silence – only that from within that silence she failed to provide the emotional contact he needed in order to feel alive. As he saw it, by cutting herself off she left him to float in a torment of disconnected space, as if to punish him for something which he knew he must have done but could not remember. He implied as much when union had to be resumed over some mundane detail of running the household.

From her side, she had craved solitude, a moment's peace

in which to inhabit a world where she would find no one but herself. It wasn't selfishness, much of the time not even dislike of him, simply a part of the desired tranquillity that true love should have been able to encompass, but which in their case it could not, since love of any kind hardly existed.

She realized that by occasionally severing herself from George's zone of influence she had acted like a man. He became fretful and at times nasty because her detachment had robbed him of that soothing mother-like consolation which he had grown to regard as necessary and obligatory from her. When she was out of his mental area there was no feminine succour for his masculine needs. By his insistence on permanent comfort and care he had driven her into separating from him in order to avoid what she saw as tyranny.

For a man to withdraw his spirit into pastime or business was normal enough. She didn't object, but considered that such retreats were necessary for her also, and didn't see why she should not have them, though while she had been with George it wasn't feasible unless the house were to be consumed by a deadly aura of resentment that threatened to wither both his soul and hers. No wonder he had tried so wickedly to get her back. It must be difficult nowadays to find someone to fill the place on his terms – though she imagined there might still be plenty to suit him.

Her son also, as was only to be expected from a child who screamed whenever she did not give him full attention, had been a replica of George in his soul, and the image of all children when it came to dominating the mother. They had left her no way out except to find a corner into which she could retreat, a golden space where the light was her own for the peculiar but deep need of the moment.

12

A line of intensely white clouds low on the horizon formed a wall of crenellations as they walked arm in arm along the seafront. When she told Tom about it, he asked why she needed this area of quiet and peace for herself. He didn't disagree that she should have it, but wanted to know out of curiosity, and in order to learn something about her from the answer.

She couldn't say, really. Didn't know. She just needed it so as to stay alive. That's all. There were reasons, obviously, but she couldn't be absolutely clear about them at the moment. When she could, she would, he could rely on that. She preferred to talk rather than answer questions.

He laughed. 'Take your time. There's plenty of it.'

'I will.'

'Enough for both of us. It's something we can keep for ourselves, or we can share.'

'I like the idea,' she said. 'It has promise.'

He did the talking. He told her about the wireless officer on one of his ships who had been a British Israelite, and described the hobbies he had seen men indulge in to save their sanity and occasionally their lives.

She liked his stories. For a man who had spoken little to those he worked with he must have done more listening than most. He had observed without seeming to. In the presence of the garrulous he had only to scratch his nose, or adjust his cap, or light a cigarette for that person to set out on long and perhaps intimate confessions. It was human nature, hardly worth remarking on, except that everything was worth comment. Thanks for the education, she said.

He laughed at her. 'One learned more by keeping quiet,

but now, for obvious reasons, I no longer believe it. My talk is unlocked, you might say, though in those days I would occasionally nail someone, and let go a few distilled drops of myself when on shore. I was never an island: more like a peninsula!'

The horizon, a narrow black band from end to end, changed towards the shore to an equally narrow seam of blue. A light green stretched left and right at the beach, where creaming tongues of snowy foam licked at the shingle. Above the horizon a wide cone of rain came from the low sky, while to the west a dim button of sun prophesied more bad weather.

They walked on. She liked people who told stories, she said, even if they were liars. George always said he had none to tell. Everyone had something to tell. He simply hadn't had the gumption or energy to say much. He was too locked into himself. Some people had to be shaken to the roots before they would open up. Not that she blamed George, though she had, she supposed, merely by thinking about it, and felt ashamed at doing so. He had simply not been born for easy speech, and it was no reflection on his intelligence.

The last shekels of sunlight rippled on the sea. Two ships seemed to have been there since she had first looked out of the window at Clara's flat. He held her arm. 'They're not the same ones, though!'

Smoke from Shoreham power-station made a scene of beauty. She had no reason to blame George for not telling stories, because neither he nor she had ever spun them off in the bright tone that any normal person might have expected. When the spirit was willing all problems vanished. To learn slowly was always to learn too late. The only advantage of such learning, it seemed to her, was that it enriched your reflections when you later mulled on the experience that your learning had been too late to profit by.

There was never any reason not to scintillate, not to say something, at least. Her head ached? What if it did? She was deathly tired? Poor thing! She hated him? No excuse, either, unless you hated yourself as well. If you lived together fifty years and hated one another like hemlock-and-pumice-stone there was no reason not to amuse – unless you hated yourself more than you couldn't stand him. Interesting to see that what had gone wrong was lack of energy, congenital self-hatred, a dose of self-pity, a proneness to self-ruination. What was the point? You learned slowly, or not at all. But she wished she had learned more quickly than she had.

She had fallen into the man-trap again, because didn't you, after all, have to protect your own silence, safeguard your own personal and particular retreat so as not to go totally insane when you couldn't stand even yourself a moment longer? Hadn't a man that feeling as well? What one craved, the other must also, in which case if she and Tom lived together, and loved each other, then the treaty to be alone whenever they felt like it should be ratified from the start.

He needed his silences for reading and study. He sat for hours with books and papers, and when she spoke she felt she was taking him out of some weird dreamscape that he cared to inhabit alone. She loved the fact that, being in it, he did not mind that she at the moment was not, though she would sometimes have preferred to be there with him, and occasionally picked up a book from his pile to read, after the battle to admit it to herself had been won. She was beginning to believe that what was good for a man was good for a woman, but that what was good for a woman was good for them both.

He never stayed in bed later than seven, even if they didn't sleep till after midnight. He liked the day, and woke up so as to get the best out of it. He did a few jumps and press-ups, then spent half an hour bathing and dressing. She got the table set. For breakfast he liked boiled eggs, yoghourt, black bread, cucumber and salted fish. She had grown to like the same meal, which she took in her dressing-gown, and he fully dressed. They talked about the day that had gone, and the day still to come. When nothing had occurred, or looked like

450

happening, it was amazing the talk that could be got from such pleasant vacuity.

She asked, while he filled their cups: 'Could we invite Judy and her kids down for a day?'

'Why not? Next Sunday, if you like.'

'They'd love it. I used to feel sorry for them cooped up in that crumbling room, though she wouldn't like to hear me saying so.'

He pushed the egg-shell aside, and reached for the fish. 'The children wouldn't mind, I'll bet. We'll lay on some food, and take them out. Be nice if the weather is good.'

'They're always broke,' she said.

'I'll send twenty pounds for their fares.'

She touched his arm. 'Let me do it. Judy might prefer it to come from me. I'll write to her this morning.'

'We'll devote a day to looking after them,' he said.

She was surprised at how quickly their existence had become easy – and said so. The only words she could not speak were those which jumped into her mind too quickly to be crushed back. 'Make the most of the situation before you go home to George. One day soon, when I tell you, you'll walk out of the flat in what clothes you have on your back, and set off for Nottingham. You'll have no option but to do it, to obey, because I'll know that's best for you, just as George did when he came down – and still does. You're not cut out for this life. It's false. It isn't you, and never can be. Admit it. Give it up. Get out of it. Who are you to think you can be happy? What right do you think you've got to escape your fate? Or even to embrace it? Grow up, and get back to where you belong.'

Uncontrollable orders held themselves in a secret lair and, when least expected, shot venomous barbs to destroy her happiness. Impossible to guard against, not part of anybody else, they came from within, signalled to appear without her knowledge, so that she was helpless with panic at what might be done with no connivance from her.

He didn't notice. Her mind could be in a state of devastation, but a smile would hide it all.

They stayed in, and cleaned the flat together, and put what he called his 'archives' back into their place. At dusk he switched on the lights and drew the living-room curtains. 'With you I'm happy. My life is changing all the time. It's enriched by you. But we have to change our lives together. Will you go along with me in that?'

She sorted out what to say from too much that suggested itself. She certainly preferred his questions to her own. His were positive, direct, constructive, and concerned, she knew, only for her good. 'There's no proper answer. Is that good enough for you?'

It would have been easy to say 'yes', but caution, although she despised it, held her back. To go with someone through their transformation wouldn't be difficult while you too were changing.

'It's all right.'

He didn't look as if it was, though knew he could expect nothing better. He could no longer cover his nuances of expression, which encouraged her to be frank. 'I have this terrible voice in me which says I shall go back to George one of these days.'

'How can I fight that one?' He winced, knowing that he had to. 'I will, though. I'll fight it every possible way. Would you willingly return to the House of Servitude? I came from the same place, and know I couldn't. We have a common journey to make, to get away from what we have left – in spirit as well as in space and time, and without each other it's a break we can't make. Neither of us are out of bondage yet. We've left the old places, but haven't arrived anywhere. We shall, though.'

He was right. She couldn't go back. Nothing would drive her to self-destruction. But why did she still think it possible? The only safe way was to go forward. 'I've become even more of myself since I met you. I'm an individual again. I can't say more than that.'

He stood up. There was no need to make promises. They would share the adventure. There was no other way but to live with uncertainty. One day passed, and another took its place. That was enough for him.

As long as she woke up with him she did not care. She received answers even before thinking of questions. She had formerly carried a string of questions like chains that became too heavy to let her move, until she was driven half mad, fixed into a nightmare that nearly killed her.

He went to the refrigerator. It was time for supper. She had never seen a man enjoy his food so much. 'For most of my life meals came at all hours. You ate when you could. On board you were too stunned to worry, and no plate of food had a name. When on shore you were often too drunk to care. I thought of regular meals as only possible in a reign of freedom and order.'

He held up a bottle of white wine. 'There's nothing better than this to help our food down – on April 3rd 5737, or however it can be put.' He fetched three glasses and a corkscrew. 'Today we celebrate our release from the state of slavery.' He held her hands, and they were cold, the knuckles more prominent than his own. His hands were also whiter.

The cork was tough, but he wedged the bottle between his legs and pulled. 'We only have each other at the moment, but let's praise God for that. So many people don't even know they have as much.'

He was trying, and his blatant attempt to capture her so that she could free herself made her happy rather than guilty at her own pusillanimous fears. He was from a different world. You persisted in the face of all opposition, persevered in spite of any discouragement. You didn't take either yes or no for an answer in case whatever you accepted served only to divert you from the one real path.

The wood was packed stonily hard against the spout of green glass. When he pulled, with hands clenched, the reddish hairs along the back trembled with effort. 'I'm a bit of a Jonah,' he said, 'but fresh from the whale's belly and full of life. I slept like a stone last night, after we made love. I knew when I woke up that this evening was going to be special, even without looking at the calendar.'

She stroked his wrist for a moment, as if to console him at not being able to get the cork out of the bottle – or perhaps to give a reward in advance for when he succeeded. She didn't know. It was a gamble as to whether or not he would get the cork out. She looked at his struggle, unable to speak.

His elbow shot back against a chair, and the pain must have stung his bone. Bits of cork went spitting on to the carpet. She expected him to curse at the difficulty, if not the impossibility. 'We'll toast and talk,' he said, 'and feast our release from useless bondage – if you'll join me in the celebration.'

He went back to work. It was an engineering problem, as if it were a matter of solving a prime conundrum of Archimedes, an equation of force pitted against the seemingly immovable reinforced by the almost certainly indestructible. Neither was it an uncommon situation, he supposed, given the plastic composition of ersatz corks.

'Why don't you take it to the sink and push the cork in?' she suggested. 'You won't lose much of the precious wine.'

'Oh no,' he said. 'No half measures. That wouldn't do at all.'

He put the corkscrew in down the side of the cork instead of through the centre, leaned the bottle at an angle and, using the spout itself as leverage, pulled perpendicularly until, she saw, he was first red and then almost blue in the face.

She laughed, but watched the cork slowly drawn out of its green constriction. When it came free he filled three glasses. He took one to the door of the flat, and she saw that he returned without it. 'What did you do?'

'I left it outside for the unexpected guest.'

454

She smiled at such formal generosity. 'That's a funny idea, though a nice one. But who are we hoping will call?'

'If Elijah passes, he sees the wine, and if he feels inclined, he comes inside.'

'Is that the custom?'

'It's the custom.'

She still wore the coloured headscarf that had protected her hair from dusting and cleaning. The novelty of a party for such reasons as he gave was hard to resist enjoying. 'I should change into my best clothes, then.'

'You're in them already. To our life!'

She drank to life. The wine was icy. Being sweet, it should have been warmer, but its slender cold shaft went down. He tapped off the shells of two boiled eggs and sprinkled them with salt. 'We must eat, as well.'

She took some dry flaky biscuit, and a spring onion. It was good with the wine. His brown eyes glowed. She didn't know why he was so happy, but smiled and felt glad to be alive with him. 'I will,' she said, 'and then I'm going to change my clothes. I hope this celebration includes that activity.'

He sat down in the armchair, legs crossed as he looked at her. 'Anything you say. We're out of servitude.'

With food spread, they came to the table, a solitary candle lit. He was right. Some line had to be crossed, so much left behind. His celebration defined it, a festival to make and mark a new beginning. 'It's a feast for family, group, tribe, nation, or for the whole world if ever it became so enlightened. My grandmother would have approved. It's quite possible that yours would, though it lacks the finer points. But it's all we can do at the moment. It affirms our getting out of slavery, and living properly with each other. Most people live in self-imposed servitude, or in the slavery they allow those nearest to impose on them. They feel comfortable in the House of Bondage, and don't want to come out and face the terrors of the unknown, which to them is the strongest barrier there is. But it's really the Great Knowing, because when you step into it the fetters fall away. We can find love, respect, work, adventure, and we can thank God for giving us the Jerusalem of the spirit, and the Israel of our strength and consciousness. I say this out of love for you, and love for myself. You look back on servitude and think it was a safe and orderly life, and imagine that the way you're living now has no future, but in servitude the future was blank and the certainty dead, otherwise your suffering spirit wouldn't have brought you to me, who wants you by me for as long as we live.'

She was afraid of his weird outpouring on an evening that was not like any other. The only time she was unafraid was when he lay between her legs and buried deeply in, his hands under her buttocks and her recalcitrant orgasm building up almost against her will and she thought she wouldn't come though was dying to, and sometimes she didn't but at other times she decided not to care and then it rose within her and she clutched him, out of control and as far in love as she thought it possible to be.

Thank God he had stopped talking. She couldn't stand it. She liked him. She loved him. She looked at him. If only he would fuck her, and not talk. She was ashamed at such a thought, and felt herself flushing in a torment of self-reproach. Every day he was different. She didn't know him. Then she looked, and for a few moments knew him better than she knew herself, which made her despise herself, then feel sorry for herself, then love herself more than she ever had, then wonder who she was and where she was, till she finally grew calm in the exhaustion which followed, then held his hands and pressed them, and looked at him for minutes that seemed like years, while she fought back tears whose significance she did not want to know.

'When I came up the stairs a few weeks ago and saw the danger you were in from your husband and his brothers,' he said, 'I felt that the Angel of Death was close. I reverted immediately to the raging bull, and would have killed to get

456

you free. But I felt the Angel of Death pass over us, and was able to do what I could which, thank God, turned out to be sufficient. Both of us were blessed at that moment, by being released. When we came down here, I knew that we had left our troubles and started our wanderings together.'

'We haven't come far, my darling.'

He poured more wine. 'We'll leave the country soon.'

'I'll be seasick!'

'Haven't you ever been on a ship?'

'When I went to Spain, I flew.'

'With me you'll go by boat.'

She sat stiffly. 'And if I want to go by air?'

'Don't you want a new experience?' he laughed.

'Depends where we go.'

'Where do you want to go?'

'I can't think of tomorrow, let alone next week, or next month. Do you mind?'

'We'll stay a bit longer, then.' He lifted his glass: 'To those beautiful blue and oblique eyes of a queen! – and to all else about you.'

She sipped, then had an impulse to embrace him, but didn't. She held back, not knowing why. For no reason – not wanting to make things too easy for him, but most of all not easy for herself. Everything was wonderful, but it didn't seem right. She was happy, yet felt oppressed. The weight was impossible to bear. She felt as if she belonged to the world, and was no longer afraid, but the very idea of fearlessness frightened her. She wanted to go to bed, yet wanted to walk in the streets with him. She wanted to go to Nottingham and sort things out with George before coming back here for good. She wanted to do nothing but what she was doing, which was rushing to his arms and kissing him with a passion that burned them both.

He pushed the headscarf back, and moved from her lips to kiss the damp skin and hair that had been covered by the headscarf since before dusk.

13

The sea rose like a hillside when she looked back. Bitter cold
had teeth, wind trying to eat the empty streets, so the parking
space at the station was empty. They had bought a car.
Choose a colour, he said. She nodded at white, a serviceable
estate model for five thousand pounds. We'll go a long way, as
long as there's petrol. She was almost afraid to step into it,
wanted to put newspaper down for when there was rain.

A door banged open against the carriage before the train
had properly stopped. Sam jumped on to the platform. Hilary
was not so daring. A satchel roped to her back, she had the
replica machine-gun which nearly pulled her arms to the
concrete, as if she had to pick up a golden coin before running
to the barrier. A dark young man flinched, and walked
quickly away from her. The ticket collector patted her head
and advised her to wait for her ma, but she told him to leave
her alone or she would phone the police, then pushed through
and went skipping towards the newspaper stall. He shouted:
'Hey, where's your ticket?' He asked Judy as she went
through: 'Are them kids yours?'

She shivered after the heat of the train, and showed him a
ticket. 'They're bloody not. They've been terrorizing
everybody all the way down. They should be done away with,
the little bastards.' She pointed to an elderly woman in furs
coming along the platform, a chauffeur carrying her luggage.
'I expect they belong to her.'

'I'm glad you were able to come,' Tom said.

'I'd have taken any chance of a trip to Brighton.' She
looked full of cares, but her eyes smouldered with haughtiness
and resentment. A mischievousness about the shape of her
mouth set her apart, and might warn anyone to keep out of

her way. She wore slacks, and a three-quarter coat. Pam thought she looked more mannish than when they had last met. 'I don't see why I should pay anything for those two little drag-bags. They're going to enjoy it too much to have their fares paid as well. They ran in at Victoria, and ran out here. If a collector gets on the train going back, they can jump off and thumb a ride home. Got to learn what life's all about. When it happened before, they came home in a police car. They'd been given tea and cakes, a mouth-organ and a doll. I clouted them as they came in the door, and told them not to get lost again – even though it had taken some initiative. I nearly died of worry, I said. I'm not sure whether the copper was convinced, but for the next few days they were threatening to leave me and go and live at the police station.' She turned, shouting in a voice which, Pam thought, must have carried for miles: 'Come back here, or I'll tear your goldens off!'

There was a car to get into, so they rounded themselves up without trouble. 'Listen to the seagulls.' Sam snatched at his sister's machine-gun which was pointed at their noise. 'Don't shoot 'em!'

'We'll go to the flat first,' Tom said. 'Not much opens till midday.'

The children settled in the back with Judy. 'I want to see the sea,' Hilary called.

'It won't run away,' Tom said, 'not very far, that is.'

Sam leaned forward, and said into his ear: 'You mean that the tide'll be out. How far does it go?'

'We'll look at a book of tables that tells you all about it.'

'I want to be a sailor,' Hilary said. 'Will you take me on a ship, Tom? I want to go to Australia on a ship with sails.'

He laughed. 'They have engines now.'

'With an engine, then.'

'Women don't go on ships,' Judy said. 'Unless you whore yourself out to the captain, or work on a liner as a skivvy.'

'You'll get sea-sick,' Sam jeered.

She screamed into his face: 'Yah, yah, yah – and I'll spew

all over you!' She unclipped the magazine, and ammunition thudded on to the floor. Her legs in the air were reflected in Tom's rear mirror, shaking around while she found the bullets. Then she came up, fitted them in, and levelled the gun at a car behind. 'I don't want to whore. I'll dress up as a man. I'll borrow your trousers, mum.'

'Maybe by the time you grow up it'll be different.' Tom was encouraging. 'A woman could do any job on a ship if she was trained.'

It amused him to imagine a crew of women and men, and said so.

'I expect there'd only be as much fucking around as there is with an all-man crew,' Judy laughed.

'Less,' Sam said, looking at the seafront.

Hilary lowered her gun. 'More, I'd say.'

'What do you little mistakes know about it?' Judy asked.

'You haven't lived,' Sam told her solemnly. 'I go to school, don't forget.'

'You'll go to a fucking orphanage if you don't shut your fat little trap. I didn't come down here to bicker with kids on the facts of life. Just look at the wind and listen to the sand, then you might learn something.'

The boy groaned. Hilary laughed, but they sat quietly. Tom winced with disapproval at her swearing. She would make a rough sort of captain, he thought, and no doubt keep any crew in order.

Hilary ran up the stairs with the gun, inspired by the liberty of being able to enter an unfamiliar building. Sam followed, and it seemed to the adults coming behind as if they were a storming party to get terrorists out. 'They eat too well, and too often,' Judy said when milky coffee and a plate of cakes were set before them. 'The town won't be safe today.'

The dining-room table had five places laid. Yesterday had been for shopping, and today getting the meal ready. A soup was to begin, and a trifle to end. Tom peeled potatoes before breakfast, scrubbed carrots, cut cauliflower, and washed for

460

three different salads. A piece of beef was on a low light. He bought cakes, bread, chocolates and half a dozen cheeses, enough to feed twice as many. The larder and refrigerator were stocked as if they were on a ship about to steam across the world, or as if a catastrophe would force a long siege on them.

He wondered how long it had been since the noise of such mayhem had bounced from wall to wall. They leapfrogged up the corridor and down again, and chased each other in and out of the kitchen. Probably never. There had been no children here except himself as a boy on parole from the orphanage, and his voice had never been audible from more than a few feet. He had a vision of himself as a trapped insect, afraid even to jump. Shameless. He rubbed it away.

Judy sipped black coffee. 'I hate the sight of 'em, though I wouldn't be without 'em. You might not believe it, but they're doing well at school, after I gave 'em a good talking to. "If you want to beat the system," I told them, "pass your tests and exams better than anybody else. Do it for me. Learn all you can. If you don't work for me, I won't work for you. You'll have to live on bread and water then".'

She expected to be complimented on her determination and sagacity. 'You're a good mother,' Pam said.

'Not really, love. I'm only their guardian till they're big enough to fend for themselves. Then, it's out into the snow – the deeper the better.'

Tom thought they were lucky. Judy knew that life was a battle, and was teaching them to fight in a world which, contrary to what everyone thought, got harder and rougher. But everything had its price, and the contest seemed to be wearing her out. He only hoped that her philosophy of living off the land didn't encourage such bright children to go too far, and get into trouble with the police.

He led her and Pam into the main bedroom, and showed them the wardrobe of Clara's clothes. Judy stood back at the heavy taint of mothballs, then went forward and ran her hand along the dresses. 'They look gorgeous.'

461

'She was about your size, in her heyday,' Tom said, 'so help yourself.'

'You mean it?'

He nodded.

Hilary pushed through: could she have a skirt and a blouse? Judy held her. 'Maybe I'll get a stall, and sell them on the market.'

He had intended throwing them out, he said. 'But if you can make some money on them – fine.'

Judy looked at Pam with an expression hard to fathom, a smile that was an invitation. To what, Pam didn't know – unless it was simply to be without the kids for half an hour, a desire she could well understand. 'Why don't you take the children to the beach?' she said to Tom. 'Then Judy can try one or two dresses on. I'll stay with her.'

He got his overcoat, scarf and hat. Why not? Get the kids off their hands. And took up his binoculars. 'I'll do my best not to get them drowned, or run over, hauled off to the clink, or otherwise missing presumed glutted on ice-cream.'

'Not as easy as you might hope,' their mother called.

A wind blew, cold and sharp, and Hilary played at being thrown back inside the door, till Tom and Sam were half-way down the square, and then she followed. Sam went in front, sliding himself by parked cars, using the handle of each door to draw himself along, but putting on a pressure to find out whether or not the doors were locked. He would not, Tom felt, go inside and take anything at the moment. It seemed more like a practice run for when he was on his own. He called: 'Come here!'

Sam turned, pale and scared. 'You mean me?'

'And quickly. Run!'

He walked towards him, upright but as if expecting to dodge a punch.

'Listen to me,' Tom said. 'And stand still! While you're out with me, I don't want to see you trying to open car doors. Do you understand? If I catch you at it again I'll knock your head

462

off, and then hand you over to the police station. And what's more, I don't want you to do it even when you're not with me, because sure as hell somebody else will haul you off. Do you hear?'

'Yes.'

'Never, at any time. Not only will you be for it, but your mother will get it in the neck as well. And you don't really want to hurt her, do you?' Damn, the poor kid was about to cry. But he had to put the fear of God into him. It's not his fault, because he sees his irresponsible mother getting up to stunts that can only land them in trouble. When they go back tonight I'll put them on the train with tickets, to show it must be done. He held his arm, and spoke quietly. 'We're going to look at a ship, and if it's ten miles away these binoculars will bring it down to a mile. Do you want to try?'

He nodded.

'We'll have a good time. But don't forget what I told you.'

'All right,' he said.

'I take that as a promise. Do you understand?'

'Yes. OK.'

He tapped his binocular case. 'Carry them for me.'

Hilary held his hand.

'You can take turns looking at ships or birds,' Tom said, 'and I'll tell you about 'em.'

'I want first go,' Hilary said.

'We'll cross the road before getting them out, then spin heads-and-tails for it.'

'She can have them,' Sam said.

'The coin decides,' said Tom.

They waited for cars to pass, then he let them go, over the grass to the railing. There was a blue hole in the clouds, with towering cumulus close out on the Channel. Ships were outlined: tankers, ocean freighters with enormous white superstructures so that Sam wanted to know what those buildings were, and a few coasters which seemed almost to disappear in the swell. Tom looped the binocular strap

463

around Hilary's neck, and told her to look. Visibility was good, but rain would soon hit the seafront.

14

Pam sat on the edge of the bed. Clothes were spread over the floor, draped on chairbacks and stacked on the dressing-table. Judy laid aside the last twenties-style suit: 'I'll start a new fashion in West Eleven if I get this lot on the barrows. Wouldn't mind wearing a few myself.'

Pam hoped she would try some of them on. She'd be sure to look marvellous in such clothes. There were shoes and handbags to complete the picture of a new woman.

Judy took out silk blouses with pearl buttons, elaborate garments with lace cuffs and collars attached. 'I wish the rich hadn't loved mothballs so much, though.'

She pulled off her sweater, and unbuttoned her shirt. 'They'll fit you, as well. You're nearly as tall as I am.' Her breasts were oval-shaped, well-fleshed and only slightly hanging, nipples facing upwards rather than out. She smiled at Pam looking at her without knowing she was staring so intently. 'I had a bath last night so it's all right, as long as you can stand the carbolic smell of a woman who doesn't bother with men!'

Dark hair showed at the crotch of her flimsy red knickers. She took them off, and rummaged in a drawer for underwear, holding up camisoles and stockings. 'What delights! Come on, you change as well.'

Pam wished she had taken her clothes off earlier, because Judy had already put drawers on and a slip, a blouse and a

464

long skirt. 'Don't worry, love, it's just that I like seeing another woman. You do too, don't you? But how do you keep that slim figure? The trouble with me is I eat whatever I can. I feel like the character in that N. F. Simpson play who calls at houses to finish off leftovers because it's her job. Whenever I'm offered anything on my charring round I never say no. I eat when the kids come home from school. Then again when they're in bed, and at breakfast with them in the morning. I never stop.' She opened a cupboard and inspected more drawers. 'Here you are, get this lovely underwear. It makes me feel sexy. See what it does for you. I feel like a schoolgirl just wondering how to . . . I suppose not having kids around helps.'

Pam saw her mistake, if such it was, which had led her into becoming trapped at a game she didn't want to play; but it had been her own idea and there was no getting out of it, so she took off the rest of her clothes and searched among the underwear. Embarrassment was stupid. There was nothing to lose with someone as friendly and easygoing as Judy.

'There are even hairpins in the bowl.' Judy untied her ponytail and sat at the dressing-table to put up her hair. 'It's a treasure-house. I feel as if I'm stealing things.' She stood to finish buttoning the cuffs of her blouse. She was tall and straight-backed, and would become stout if she didn't take care. Pam couldn't stop herself saying: 'You look beautiful.'

Her figure was verging on full. She had been going to say: elegant, handsome, even dashing in an old-fashioned way. Strange what clothes could do, though she suspected they did little enough for her. She looked in the mirror, and found it amazing how they both resembled women of the period.

'I'm not bad for nearly forty, am I? You look quite fine yourself, though.' She lit a cigarette, and passed it to Pam, who hesitated, then told herself not to be so rigid, smiled her thanks, and tasted the damp end when she put it between her lips.

'Come here,' Judy said, 'and I'll finish fastening your buttons for you.'

She smoked, then gave it back. 'It's nice to play at dressing-up.'

'We'll give the others a surprise.'

Pam held out her arms. 'I wish I had hair as long as yours, that's the only thing.'

Judy laughed. 'You can have it, if you give me your figure.'

'Your figure's . . .' She was going to say 'lovely'.

'Don't go on.' She grimaced, and Pam didn't know what she had expected. 'Do you love him?'

'Who?'

'Your ex-sailor man,' Judy said.

'Can't you call him Tom?'

'Tom, then.'

She was going to say: it's nobody's business. But: 'I think I do. Yes.' There was no one else she loved, and if this wasn't love she thought she would never know what was – but wouldn't speak of it, hardly aware as to why, except that she felt such a declaration would sadden Judy, or – and the words flashed at her without warning – as if they would imply some kind of disloyalty towards her, a form of gloating, perhaps. She was hot with an embarrassment she couldn't explain, hoping it would go away before Judy noticed. She was sure she already had. Judy noticed everything.

'Don't blame you. He is pretty good – for a man. I hope you're sure, though, because he's the sort you'll have to follow. He's got lots of firm ideas behind that brow of his.'

Pam was surprised at this opinion. She wouldn't follow anybody. Or would she? She would if she cared to. If she did it would be out of her free will, and nobody's business but her own. 'How do you know?'

'He's the type, isn't he? Does things, rather than thinks them out. Forceful and secretive, I suppose you'd call it. My husband was the opposite. Nothing but talk. Never did anything till I pushed him into the street. His parents wouldn't have him back, but he soon found someone to iron his shirts and make his bed. Men always do, even these days.

466

But Tom's different, I can see that. I once went upstairs for something or other, and through the open door I saw him ironing a shirt. I'd never seen such a thing. A man ironing a shirt! I'd always thought it was impossible. I just stood and looked, till he stopped what he was doing and shut the door in my face. Well, I suppose you've got to admire a man who looks after himself in that way. Though I don't know why. I don't think it strange when a woman irons her things. You're certain to be better off with a man like that than with most others.'

Pam was amazed at how coolly she had analysed him, and how much she admired him. It was unmistakable. A tremor of surprise went through her. 'Did you ever have an affair with him, then?'

She could tell lies to a man, though she'd never found it easy, but not to a woman, which she considered to be one of her weaknesses – while having the strength to know that it was one worth cherishing. 'I wouldn't call it that. I once kept him company for a night or two between voyages, a couple of years ago. Nothing since, absolutely. I didn't want to. Nor did he. We stayed good neighbours.'

Pam knew she could never be a free woman in that way, but was pleased to feel no sense of jealousy. Its effect was rather to make her more affectionate, though a faint diffidence kept her from saying anything at the moment.

'Maybe I shouldn't have told you,' Judy said. 'But there was really nothing in it.'

'Don't make it worse! I'm glad it happened to you both. Why shouldn't we be fond of each other?' Pam stopped herself going too far, though it would never have occurred to her to say much, being so close to Tom, for it would seem like betraying him. She expressed this to Judy, who said: 'You'll have to stop thinking like that. I suppose he wonders the same about you. It's only natural. No man is a cabbage. Nor any woman, either.'

They finished the cigarette. 'How's your life?' Pam asked.

'Personal, you mean?'

She nodded.

'Smashed. My prissy little civil servant girl-friend took umbrage when she saw me with a woman I used to know, and imagined the worst. Or the best, except that there wasn't any best about it, and the worst didn't happen, not with her, anyway. But I'm too busy looking after Sam and Hilary to go in for much philandering. We'd better change back into our everyday rags.'

'Oh no, keep yours on. You really do look marvellous.'

'It's nice to be praised.' She went to the mirror. 'I'll play the drag queen today – but what a let-down when I get home. Do you fall in love easily?'

Pam sat on the edge of the bed, and felt obliged to say: 'I sometimes see a man in the street I think I could go for. But I'm attached to Tom, and that's love, as far as I'm concerned. I didn't have affairs when I was married, so I feel a bit lost regarding experience, though I don't really feel a lack of it.'

Judy sat at her feet. 'I've had quite a bit, but I'm not sure it's done me much good. I suppose it's better than not having had any. It's impossible to have just enough to equip you emotionally for getting the best out of life, but not sufficient to ruin your feelings.'

In her new dress Pam saw Judy as if she were younger, calm, without children, and able to talk properly instead of swear like a villain, almost as if they had met in some hotel far from their normal lives. It was restful to talk to someone in this inconsequential way, and she wondered if it could happen with any person other than Judy. The distance between them narrowed. She felt far closer to her than when she had been with 'normally married' women in the past. With them she would turn stand-offish, especially if the acquaintance threatened to go in the direction of a heart-to-heart talk, as if there was something shameful in their similarly closed lives, much like two prisoners talking in jail and forgetting that a free life existed.

468

The narrowing gap generated more intimacy than she seemed to want. A resonance in Judy's voice was pleasant yet disturbing, at times irresistibly caressing. She looked down on elegantly piled hair, at the flushed face pressed against her thighs. 'My feelings weren't finally spoiled,' Pam said. 'As soon as I left my old life they began coming back, though it was so painful that I thought once or twice I wouldn't be able to make it.'

Judy looked at her. 'I know. It's like a diver coming up for air from a long way down, after the air-pipe's not been working properly. You get the bends. But gradually the agony goes, so I understand.'

Who but another woman would acknowledge that she had been right to abandon a man? To her, such understanding could only be termed affection, and she laid a hand against the side of Judy's warm face.

Judy looked up in pleased surprise. Her larger hand took Pam's, and she kissed the opening palm, her tongue warming across. They stayed silent for some minutes, then Judy's long fingers went slowly under her skirt, and though Pam's face burned like fire she could not turn them back.

15

After Tom had put five .22 bullets into the black circle, Hilary wanted a go. The man in charge of the rifle range said that children had to be fourteen, though he would stretch a point if she could get on tiptoes and stand high enough to lean on the counter at least. Tom opened the breech and drew back the bolt so that she could slide the round in. He pulled the butt tightly into her shoulder. 'Now, squeeze the trigger, here – but gently.'

The sharp noise of firing startled her. Then she blinked, and pushed her hair back. 'Did I get the bull's-eye?'

He pulled the bolt open, and the empty case came out. 'Fire the other four, and we'll see how you did.'

Sam waited. Each bullet cost five pence, and he trembled at the amount being spent. Hilary fired more quickly. Between the noise Sam heard waves coming through the pier supports and shouldering against the beach. He collected the empty shellcases for trading at school. Money flowed like water into the hands of the attendant, for he and Hilary had thirty shots each before Tom reckoned their smarting shoulders might tell them it was time to leave. But Hilary's headache came first, and she had to get out. Sam was so pale it seemed he would be sick either from excitement or the peculiar powder-like smell of the airless place. They took their cardboard targets, to compare scores at the end of the pier.

He watched their zigzag antics on the Dodgem Cars. There was no straightforward life for them or anybody, even though they were looked after to the top of Judy's ability. He supposed there was intelligence on the father's side as well, yet they were being brought up as if they would one day have to function like bandits in the hills. They weren't getting what they deserved. It wasn't easy to say exactly what they lacked. A father, most likely, though he found it difficult to believe there was no better solution than that. But it was also true, as he had occasionally found in life, that the most obvious solution was often the only one possible, and in many cases the best.

He bought them ice-cream with a stick of flaky chocolate. Flickering cold rain made them fasten their duffel coats as they trekked against it to the road, each holding one of Tom's hands as if they would belong to him for ever.

16

Pam closed the door, no click to the latch, unwilling to feel guilty or ashamed. She had forestalled Judy's pleading. Did I? Was that how it happened? Impossible for her to have initiated it, or to deny such a thing with her, so out of an exquisite regard which was now a vital matter to them, and of no concern to anyone else, she had let her.

They had their secret, and she was not unhappy. No one could know how much pleasure they had given each other, and as for having a secret from Tom, what love had value which was without a secret to give it depth and solidity? It could not wreck their love, though if he knew, would he consider it a danger? If it had been with a man he no doubt would, and if he didn't she would be hurt and amazed. She could only hold back those thoughts which threatened to bring shame, guilt, and self-condemnation on every count. She'd had enough of that.

Surrounded by dresses, skirts, blouses and underwear, Judy slept as if she hadn't rested for months. Among scattered clothes she seemed dismembered, though her spirit, reflected in her face, was as calm as if set in stone. She needed peace, love, money, or a job she liked, Pam thought, unable to break the gaze at her whose transposition to calmness was more complete than that given by a change of fifty-year-old clothes.

There was a noise as if a sack of apples had been thrown against the front door. She opened it at the bell, and the children fell in, pink-faced and breathless. 'We shot bullets,' Hilary cried. 'Real bullets from a rifle, Pam. Look at my card: you can see the holes!'

Tom took off his overcoat. 'There's a shooting gallery on the pier. The only thing that would keep them quiet.'

'I'm frozen,' Hilary said. 'That rain had needles in it.'

Pam pulled her close, a smell of wet clothes and soapy scalp. 'Go in the kitchen then, where it's warm.'

But she wouldn't. 'I'm starving-hungry, as well.'

'Me too,' said Sam, to be in competition.

'They're packed tight with ice-cream,' Tom told her, 'so they can wait for dinner.' He looked: 'Where's Judy?'

'She fell asleep. I left her among all the clothes. She certainly looks a picture!'

'She's always falling asleep,' Hilary said. 'She's got sleepy sickness.'

Sam held out his arm. 'Can I look through your binoculars again, Tom?'

Raindrops flecked the window panes. 'You won't see much at the moment.' He hung them round his neck. 'Sit on that chair, and tell me if you see a ship coming towards us. Then we'll take evasive action!'

'I'll wake Judy.' She left him opening the wine. Impossible to disturb her. She closed the door and knelt by the bed. There was hardly a breath, only a faint tremor at the breast, and at the closed eyes. She moved to kiss her lips, but held back. She could only go so far, must be met at least half-way before she would dare such sweetness. A kiss would wake her, and Judy would know why. Kisses that didn't waken were impossible. There might be a reason, if she were seeing her for the last time. And she didn't want that. Friends in her new life affected her profoundly. Her brain had turned about. She smiled at the difference in consciousness. If Judy were awake a kiss would be easy. Or would it? She had never kissed a woman on the lips before today, at least not when it meant so much. She stroked her forehead, unable to believe such gentleness could be felt through the curtain of Judy's sleep, the pad of her finger ends going backwards and forwards along the faint lines.

It was hard to regain control of her feelings so that the experience could be put behind her. She wanted to look back on it, instead of being ever-worried by its implications, which

472

was the only possibility of keeping it as marvellous as she had found it, and the one way she wanted to think about Judy when they faced each other again – without guilt, as the only moments of freedom in her life, if freedom was the time when what you did had not only no connection whatever to the thought within but advanced your consciousness in a direction you never suspected was possible, in such a way as to allow you the choice as to whether or not you wanted to go there at all.

The idea expanded, and warmed her. She felt a more malleable affection than before, as if she had been inside the moon and was still glowing from its heat, though she assumed that Judy would think nothing of their encounter, and that they would probably not meet in such a way again.

Her eyes opened. Neither spoke. Judy looked, as if wanting to know where she was before trusting herself to say anything. 'I haven't enjoyed it so much for a long time,' she said.

Pam nodded.

'I didn't expect it.' She held her hand. 'And so quick!'

'Secret?'

There was mischief in her glint. 'Yes, sure.' She sat up. 'I slept ten hours in one. You've changed back to your own clothes.'

'I know. But keep yours on. You look grand in them.'

Judy stood. 'I need a wash. Now I know why you asked me to come down!'

'That wasn't the reason.'

She laughed. 'Have the children been good?'

'Tom says so.' She watched her fasten her skirt and blouse, then tidy her hair at the mirror. 'I can't believe how different you look.' When Judy kissed her on the lips she stiffened.

'Relax,' she whispered in her ear. 'I won't hurt you. Or eat you!'

'It isn't that. But we'd better go.'

She was held firmly by the waist. 'If you come to London I'll ask you to stay with me.'

473

She would never be there again, she supposed. At least not alone. 'All right.'

Sam and Hilary played on the floor with the colour supplements and a packet of felt pens, elaborately vandalizing the advertisements, while Tom read an article in the Sunday paper by a Member of Parliament who began by calling himself a friend of Israel and then went on to consider it right and proper that Israel should surrender its provinces of Judaea and Samaria (and therefore its secure borders) as well as Jerusalem the capital city, as a mark of goodwill to the Arabs, for the sake of international peace, not to mention oil supplies to a Europe which, Tom reflected with disgust, had never been reconciled to the existence of a Jewish State.

A feature on how to decorate houses seemed genuine because it made fewer demands on credulity and credibility, but he was diverted by someone coming into the room whom for a moment he did not know.

The sky turned dark outside, and with only wall-lights on, the shadows lengthened Judy's pale face. Her features were stilled at his gaze. The long skirt and high collar turned her statuesque, made her severe and formidable, an apparition until she spoke. She had stepped from one of his memories, as if an acquaintance of his mother's or aunt's had reappeared with a disturbing suddenness that would silence any speech.

She sensed the unwanted effect, deciding she had been foolish to dress up and that Tom regarded her transformation as either an act of thievery, deception, or cheek. Hilary got up from the floor and ran to fasten her arms around her mother. 'What's the matter with you, mummy? What happened?'

'Stop crying, and don't be so bloody silly.'

She smiled at Tom, and was again recognizable. Hilary's octopus grip was hard to break. 'I hope you don't mind me having looted your family's rag-trade heirlooms?'

'I said you could.'

'You look as if I'm back from the dead, though.'

474

Such clothes enhanced her beauty. 'I did wonder, for a moment.'

The oil-painted face above the mantelshelf seemed to be observing her deliberate pose. 'Almost feel it myself,' she said.

'You look splendid.'

She rested a hand on the piano, a distorted reflection filling the polished top, broken when she turned savagely on Sam for his continued stare. 'Never seen a woman before?'

'Take them off,' Hilary whimpered.

Judy walked over and stroked her daughter's hair. 'At least you're normal. But don't worry. I'll be back in my old drag-clouts soon. Then you can feel safe again.' She turned to Pam. 'That's the trouble with kids – you never know what to do for the best!'

'Perhaps if you take to wearing such clothes,' Tom suggested, 'you might civilize them.' Yourself as well – but he wanted peace while they were here, and said nothing.

'I told her how marvellous she looked.'

Pam wished she had kept silent when Judy scoffed in reply, piqued perhaps because everyone seemed determined to undermine her: 'You should be the last person to want to straighten me out.'

Her attack, veiled as it was in her own sort of humour, was noted by Tom, and also by Sam who had turned pale at this apparition in unfamiliar dress. The seriousness of the insinuation was marked by a twitch of alarm on Pam's lips. Judy relied on her reputation for outlandish remarks in order to evade the responsibility for what she said, whether it had been true or not, but this time she knew she had gone too far, and tried to make amends, a move which to any acute person, which Pam thought meant everyone in the room, could only confirm the truth of what she had implied.

'After all,' Judy added with a laugh, 'you said I ought to try *something* on.'

'I'm glad you took her advice.' Any words from Tom were

475

better than none, relevant or not, and he spoke only to break the lull following Judy's assertion which, open to more interpretations than could be fitted in now, was most likely a jocular comment that meant nothing to anyone except herself. Certainly, Pam's frown vanished as soon as he turned to pour drinks for the three of them.

PART SIX
Adrift

1

He packed the car as if it were a small boat in which they
would be going around the world, with few ports of call from
which to get provisions. He had filled an alphabetical
notebook with lists of what was to be taken, and had
assembled separate collections of cases, kitbags and
cardboard boxes on the living-room floor. All feasible
preparations had been made. At five in the morning he
carried stores and luggage to the hall. He made many trips
down the stairs, and needed no help.

The last item put into the car was his sextant.

'What do you want that for?'

'The Lord only knows,' he said. 'But I'll take it.'

He was a star-gazer, but with his feet firmly on the earth.
She did not ask when they would be coming back. He said
they would be away some time. She replied that as far as she
was concerned it could be for ever. Already boxed, the sextant
was wedged with newspapers into a separate carton.

I'll go with you, she had said, adding that by so doing she
would be accompanying herself like a jailer, because there
was no other way to stay in the world and prevent a return to
George. Once a change begins, alterations never stop. If you
stop, you begin to retreat. You are lost. So no half measures.
She liked that. She might find what she had always wanted,
but which up to now she hadn't known that she *had* wanted: a
destination without salt or tears, wherever it might be. She
was his ally in the adversity of having been born and, at her
most tender, felt sensations that made all areas of love seem
unexplored.

She slept and dreamed till six o'clock. No sense in both of them getting up, he said. Stay awhile. She sank under water and earth, but could only clamber on to a gaudy fairground roundabout that spun too quickly and made her feel sick. The booth of the headless woman was flashed now and again into her sight. She rushed to the bathroom just in time. Childish to be so excited over a bit of travelling. You look like the miller's daughter, her face said from the mirror, while she wondered what food of the last few days had made her vomit. A hand scraped around the inside of her stomach as she got on to her knees at the toilet bowl. She went back to bed till he called, and in her sleep knew she was dreaming, till she forgot there would ever be a time to wake.

It looks as if we'll need two cars, not one, to shift this lot, she had said. He kissed her. 'It'll fit in. Means a bit of judicious packing, that's all. Balance the weight, to keep the car stable on turns and bends.' He had already washed the car, and cleaned it inside. She got food, to last a few days. 'There are restaurants,' he said on seeing so much. 'And cafés.'

She had premonitions of being unable to find a hotel, of dusk creeping down on a road that ran through a gorge where they would stop the car and hear silence but for icy water speeding over rocks. The road was crumbling in places, dangerous to continue in such bleak twilight. Near a wide part of the road, too close to rushing water to feel easy, they would open the back of the car to get at the primus. While he erected the tent under a tree she would open a few tins and slice bread for an evening meal. Or she would put up the tent, and he would do the cooking. Wolfish noises would sound over local music plinking from the radio. But they'd fill mugs with red wine to swill down what they ate. They were on the road and the road led wherever they wanted it to, whether hairpin or straight. Day after day they would pay less attention to the tattered maps, and on parking by the roadside would notice a tin thrown away on last stopping at that spot. They were going round in circles, and would soon

480

get weary. The moon would disappear, never to come back. They would not have the will to continue, nor the energy to return. There would be nowhere to go, and nothing to look for any more. They had been everywhere, yet had arrived at no recognizable destination. When wolves threatened, and it seemed death to take another step, the Wandering Jew would call to God and become strong again. Or would he?

No hotels would accept them. They would park in a field and bed down in the car, no water to wash with and no food to speak of. The land, ordinary enough except when not pretty in its pastoral way, was inhospitable, and without accommodation. It would rain. The earth, smelling of soil and water, would soften into mud. The car would sink to its axles. They would get out. They had feet: they could walk. They had legs: they could abandon everything and move. With travellers' cheques, even at walking speed, they would eat and pay their way. But they might lose the cheques, or be robbed in their sleep. Deprived of protection and sustenance, they'd be collected into a group of similarly bereft travellers and left to perish, or deliberately killed for what possessions they still had. They would die without anyone either knowing or caring. Or if they did know, the other people of the world would be glad they had been put out of the way, because they wouldn't then be a bother with their problems any more. Yet if they were murdered they would cease to torment themselves, which would annoy the world even more, no matter how aggravated the world had been by their existence, because as long as they were present the world could torment them. You couldn't win. They travelled, and had no country. What business had they to travel, and have no country into the bargain? If they had no country they shouldn't travel. If they travelled they shouldn't be without a country. If they stayed where they were they should move. If they moved they ought to have stayed where they were. The only answer was to have a country, and they would have one to hold for ever, but at this moment, before the matter was rectified, they were

481

chased through a forest in which it was muddy underfoot. The menacing breath of deadly hunters close behind was like the noise of an animal as high as the sky and about to pounce.

He kissed her forehead. 'My love, everything's in. It's a quarter past six.'

She hadn't slept well. On her various holidays it had been impossible to get much rest the night before departure, either going or coming. 'Are we really leaving?'

'We have tickets, passports, money and a loaded car. I seem to feel we are.'

She sipped her coffee. 'How's the weather?'

'The sea will be calm.'

'I've never been on a ship.'

'You'll enjoy it. Can you eat scrambled eggs for breakfast?'

'I'd rather have bread and jam. I feel queasy.'

'Excited at leaving?'

'I suppose so.'

'So am I.' But he wasn't. All travelling was going home, and she was coming with him. It was as simple as that – on one level. Where they were going seemed hardly to concern either of them. The move couldn't be said to matter to him, being part of his mechanism that no longer needed attention.

They would get to the mainland and wander. She felt at peace with herself and in no way worried at what was to happen. She relinquished the knowledge that she loved him. The word had no meaning anymore. They were together, and she was free, hoping he felt the same.

He drove carefully so as to accustom himself to the load. By eight o'clock they were half-way to Lewes. A letter on the table explained to Judy where the rubbish was to be put, how to work the central heating, and what ought to be eaten first from the provisioned refrigerator. He was systematic. The lists were prominent and legible. 'It's not much trouble,' he said, 'and makes life easier for everyone. Judy will be glad of them, I'm sure she will.'

Could one live without advice, information and

482

instructions – iron orders couched in the velvet glove of a request? She supposed not. She could figure no alternative to giving such help. Perhaps he knew Judy better than she ever could.

A cheque for five hundred pounds lay on the piano top, and a note that his solicitor would pay her every month now that she was caretaking the flat. A van hired by him had been sent up to London to move her goods, and three railway tickets had been posted in a registered letter.

When they had seen Judy in London and told her, she had not believed them. The argument was fierce, almost final, and she only agreed half an hour after they had stopped pleading for her to accept. It had been done because her need seemed great, as was that of the children. They would get something of what he and Pam had. With the monthly cash Judy would live without going out to work, or skiving (Tom had thought it diplomatic not to soften his words), and the children might enjoy the sea to the south and open country to the north. He would do what he could for them.

Waiting at a traffic light in Folkestone, she noticed that his hand shook when he lit a cigarette, and touched his wrist. 'It feels right to be on the move.'

'I think so.'

'We should have met twenty years ago.'

He frowned. 'Why do you say that?'

Youth was too sure of itself to think of the future, and middle age too despondent, but Tom reflected further that at fifty the possibility of endless time could be sensed, where it had formerly seemed hardly worth waiting for and living through. There was now a change, and if there was to be any time at all, and he felt there must be, it was to be reached by crossing a wilderness which his life of wandering had taught him how to sow and his spirit to make fertile.

He found it impossible to define what had guarded him in years gone by, except to assume that there had been an unconscious and unassailable strength accompanying him on

483

those journeys which had seemed no more than an end in themselves – everyday work encased by the discipline of a mariner's certificate. There had been a purpose in all he had done by way of duty, and in what had happened by way of destiny.

Life's neat pattern had never allowed any escape, having shown that while no one was the master of his fate, some were the victims of their destiny in such a way that they were shown a fair distance towards what their fate had in any case ordained. He could, at the moment, think of it in no other way, merely claiming as a flourish to his reflections that since he had been a Jew without knowing it, the Wandering Jew must now take over in order to give purpose to his peregrinations, which he would pursue to that point where great circles and loxodromes converged at the centre of all graticules.

'If we had met twenty years ago, I would have been younger for you,' she said.

Due to ambiguous signposting on the one-way system he made two attempts before getting into the harbour area, but then drove past the terminal buildings and joined a queue of cars. 'It makes no difference,' he replied. 'If we had met then we wouldn't have met when we needed each other most. It's better this way. In two years we'll be able to marry.'

She had registered her separation from George with a solicitor, but wanted no more of matrimony. Having been poisoned once, she had found the drug to have terrible withdrawal symptoms. Tom did not see things the same way because he had never been married, and one of her reasons against it was because she did not want the responsibility of inflicting such a state on him.

Sun bleached the car roofs. A man came limping up the line taking tickets, and sticking a number on each windscreen. He was stout and elderly, had a leathery face and pale blue eyes. Tom took out his RAC wallet of reservations, insurance vouchers and travellers' cheques. 'Hello, Brian!'

The man, wearing a nautical jersey and cap, bent his head close to the window, and sounded as if he would have thrown in a few curses if a woman hadn't been in the car when he growled: 'How do you know my name?'

She thought it wrong and uncharitable of Tom to play a joke on the man who was, after all, only trying to do his job on a hot day. 'The first mate never forgets a face. Or a name. At least I didn't. Sedgemoor, isn't it?'

'What's it to you?'

He mentioned a ship, then his own name. 'In 1956. Don't you remember?'

Now he did. She had never seen a smile emerge from such unpromising features. Tom got out, and they shook hands. 'Are you still painting by numbers? That "Mona Lisa" was very good, in my view.'

Sedgemoor glanced at Pam. 'I've got four kids to think about, Mr Phillips. It's a different life nowadays, but I don't regret the old one.'

'You always did want a cushy billet! But I think I noticed a limp as you came up, didn't I?'

Sedgemoor winked, so that only Tom could see the huge lid close over his eye, and the gargoyle twist of his mouth – and the fist that indicated the apex of both legs. 'It ain't *wood* yet, though it ought to be. Gets harder to straighten, and no sawbones has got a remedy for it. One says this, and the other yaks on about that, but they all try something while it goes on getting worse. It does its main work, mind you, and between you and me, my missis don't complain – though I'm getting to think as maybe she ought to!'

'Then that's all that matters,' Tom said, having measured his drift.

'Yes, but women are funny creatures, and don't we know it, eh? When mine gets on to me I say: "Why did you marry me, then?" And she says: "Well, it was because I thought seafaring natures be very good for shorn lambs!" And she laughed, and I don't deny she's got something there!'

485

Tom agreed that no one could. Meeting an old sailor was a pleasant way to see the time off while waiting for a boat to France.

'Let me get your car out of this lot,' Sedgemoor said after a while. 'I don't like to see you in a queue, Mr Phillips, especially when you're going on holiday with your wife.' He gave another wink, bent down to look inside the car. 'You'll be all right with Mr Phillips, missis. He was a good officer.'

She smiled, and thanked him as he began motioning the car behind to get back and out of the line, but Tom declined. 'We'll find space, don't you worry. I'll look for you on the way in, and maybe we'll have some time for a drink.' He gave ten pounds to buy something for his children, and Sedgemoor, saying that duty called, went on to the next car whistling a lively tune, in spite of the obvious pain of his limp.

Tom drove down the rattling gangway and into the ship. 'I thought you were going to get into an argument,' she said.

He parked between lines of buses and lorries. 'He was a good man to have on board. However much things change, you'll always have his sort in the Service. A dirty old devil, but as good as gold. The Old Man once said that Sedgemoor looked as happy as the day was short. He certainly seems more contented now than he was then; but he was never as rough as he looked. Only hard. He's the sort that if he hadn't been a sailor would have been a rougher, perhaps brutal man. It was a case where the hard life had an opposite effect to what you'd imagine.'

She felt he knew what he was talking about. He'd got on well with people like Sedgemoor. The open deck was crowded with people on day trips to Boulogne. A gull flew crying alongside, turning its head with button-eye to observe them. 'You must feel good,' Pam said.

There were no vacant seats, and they stood by the rail to look at the town and cliffs. 'It's certainly a change being a passenger, with no work to do or decisions to make. I feel a bit like a log of wood, but it's not unpleasant!'

486

She carried some food, as well as her handbag, and he had the briefcase with money and papers. They walked the length of the ship, then queued for tobacco and drink from the duty-free shop. At the radio officer's counter he wrote a telegram to book a one-night room at the Hôtel de L'Univers in Arras.

'Do you remember the name?'

'Does the place still exist?'

'I checked it in the Michelin.'

They were well out from land, but mist reduced visibility to a few hundred yards. Engines vibrated underfoot as if to remind her that she had cut herself loose. How long would it be before Tom seemed familiar? It had not yet happened. Her eyes looked from the middle of a stone that would never dissolve. To break out was to know him absolutely, but being on a ship emphasized how hard a move it would be. There was too much of him that she did not know, because there was so much of herself she had never known. Leaving the flat had robbed them of what familiarity they had gained.

Did he feel the same, or was he more sure of himself, or less caring? Greater confidence diminished the importance of the problem. He assumed her attachment to him, and was content with the quality of his to her. He had often set out from coastlines in his life, and on every occasion alone, so how did he view the present departure now that he had company? The newness of everything eased her speculations. She was new to herself, yet trusted to whatever might happen. She had accepted, and couldn't swim back. As Sedgemoor had said, 'He was a good man,' though perhaps she had gambled at setting out with him. She repeated the word whenever another ship passed by. Every move you made in life was a gamble, big or small. Hard to know whether she had done right or wrong. The main thing was that she had done it. Yet she felt that leaving England with Tom was of absolutely no importance. It was impossible to explain. She could not regard it as in any way significant, being tired of considering every uttered word as vital, of looking on all her moves in a way that seemed crucial.

There was less mist near the French coast. Buoys and breakwaters could be seen, and Tom was interested in observing the ship go in. Her resistance was breaking down. But resistance to what? The boat rocked faintly as it made a turn. Before the change that mattered, any resistance formed by the past must finally crumble away. When an announcement said they should return to their cars she followed him down the companionway.

2

Every car started at once, and their exhaust fumes made her feel sick, but when on the ramp and in the open air she felt better. They passed the police and customs posts, and drove by railway lines towards the town. He went with care, not heeding that cars behind wanted him to get a move on. 'I'll speed up when I'm used to this side of the road.'

A red sports car, flat as a bug, shot out and overtook, and narrowly missed a French van coming the other way. 'Probably going to Barcelona,' Tom said, when they found the car waiting at the first set of traffic lights, 'so you'd think the odd minute wouldn't matter.'

She could tell he was glad to get out of the built-up area. He felt his freedom. So did she, with the wide rising fields on either side. French cars came towards them like bullets along the tree-lined roads. Threading Montreuil, as he said, for the hell of it, he thought aloud that he had read of Sterne's passing through on his somewhat sentimental journey, and hiring a servant there.

'I haven't read it,' she told him.

He laughed. It was a long time ago. 'One reads all sorts of books,' he said, 'in the Merchant Navy, from the misadventures of Elephant Bill to Charles Dickens and the Bible. You scan whatever you come across. My mind's a tuppenny bin, and I remember them all.'

Beyond Montreuil it rained a few showers. Then the crooked road became straight, and the sky cleared. High white clouds let them through. At Arras he drove along the Rue St Aubert and turned into the hotel courtyard.

Fifty years before, his grandparents, mother and Aunt Clara had made their visit in a family motor with the spare tyre on the outside. A cap and cloche hats had been in fashion, as magazines and photos showed. Now he was here himself. A few months ago, he had not known. How had he lived so emptily? He hadn't even known other things. Now he was someone else. You were composed of what information was revealed, the sort that took a grip because it was the deepest truth. Someone died: it hit you like a road accident in which, among the injuries, your soul was so smashed that you needed to be completely refurbished by the plastic surgery of memory. It was still going on, but he had already learned to live with the final effect.

The paving and surrounding windows seemed familiar, and he heard Clara shouting his mother's name for the echo. 'Ah yes, Monsieur,' he expected an old woman in black at the reception desk to say, 'I remember them well. Such a tragic family, come to visit the grave of their dead son!'

A pretty girl asked for his passport: name, address, nationality, and date of arrival to write on a bilingual form in exchange for a door key. Would they eat here? Yes, he told her. He'd never been inside France, he said as they walked up the stairs, though some harbours he knew. Their room overlooked the yard. She liked the flowered wallpaper. On trips to Spain she had stayed in new hotels with white walls, balcony and shower, and built-in noises from people in a similar box next door to embarrass you as much as your own sounds were doing the same to them.

She sat on the bed. 'I'll put a dress on.'

'Then we'll go to the Grand Place,' he said, 'for coffee and a sandwich.'

'Do you know where it is?'

'There's a town plan in the guide book.'

'Useful things.' She opened the case. 'Or maybe a cake to eat.'

He put his arms around her. 'Why not? France is a good place to be hungry in.'

She stood in her slip. 'Then again, maybe we won't go out. It's sexy, being in our first hotel room. So intimate and strange, don't you think?'

'I chose the right place,' he said, 'especially for you. There's a guide book to sexy hotels, comes out every year, and this one has four stars!'

'Really?' She half believed him. Anything was possible these days, with so many sex shops, strip shows and dirty films everywhere. And who am I to talk? Here I am, a married woman, come away with a man I hardly know. Yes I do. I already know him more than I ever did George. It's easier to know someone who is more complicated than someone who is not. He kissed her, and pushed the straps of her slip over her shoulders. She touched his face. Why not? Most hotels are still like this, he said. Shall we? He had to ask, and she wondered why. Shall we? she asked in her turn, smiling, kissing his face and throat. Yes, he said, unclipping her brassière to run his hands beneath, then lowering his face to the nipples. The air was humid, and she stood in her pants. While he undressed she pulled back the bedclothes, freeing the top sheet to cover them against the draught. She didn't want anybody to see them, and drew the curtains.

I'm tired, really, she said. I hardly slept last night. The pleasure had not been all hers, she knew. But she couldn't sleep now, either. This was the only thing left if you did not know what you wanted out of life, or didn't have any idea as to where you were travelling. How many more times are you going to say it? She wanted him with her all the time, his finger playing at her so that she never failed to come, then feeling him inside her as far as he was able to get. He filled her, nothing sacred any more. Her own smell excited her. He had explored in all ways, every other part, discovering responses that she herself had never known. Such orgasms left her feeling as if there was no spare flesh on her body. Immediately afterwards she knew how much they had separated her not only from him, but also from herself.

In the street her sight was sharper, all senses keen. In utter exhaustion, she was set totally within her own spirit. She laughed that she knew why it was that all the nice girls loved a sailor. He took her hand. It was as if the scale of their exhaustion was manifest only now that they were in another country. People spoke a different language, so they were more enclosed in themselves. She had not expected to make love during the afternoon, had imagined a decorous though perhaps less passionate encounter after a celebratory supper. Its intensity had divided her from him at a time when she wanted to be close, though the detachment seemed more in her than him. His care and attention was twice as necessary to get her back into the orbit of his affection, and therefore into her own. As time elapsed her tenderness and desire would return, and he was always sensitive to her when it did. What had started as an affair had become a prison that she could not bear to escape from, a prison in which she felt herself to be at least his equal because she was also her own jailer as much as he was his, prisoners and jailers both. He didn't like the comparison, he said, but supposed it ought to be thought about, though for himself he never felt so liberated in his life – being on an extended holiday with someone he loved.

'And it doesn't frighten you?'

'No. It's unfamiliar, so fear can't get a look-in. All I can do is thank God I'm alive, and enjoy it.'

They drank champagne at supper. 'We're not far from Reims,' he told her. 'When a German brigade had to pull out of the town in 1914 every man had two bottles in his knapsack. But we'll drink to us, not robbery.'

She had never felt so deeply imprisoned in herself, packed hard into her limits by her own choice. It was a freedom she had often dreamed of, and wondered whether she could live with. If the spirit died, it would live again. Everything mattered. Her finger ends ached when they met against his limits. She liked it in her own prison, she told herself as he undressed her while she lay on the outer covers of the bed, taking the walls of prison within prison away. She wondered why she liked the prison of herself so much, why she preferred it here, and in fact whether she finally did or would for long. To be a prisoner meant that everything was so much clearer beyond the barred window. She could see it, but not yet get out.

Her clothes came off, and she couldn't move, dead yet able to feel what he was doing, unable to look at him, and then spread out naked: I'm a respectable woman, and saying, 'Fuck me!' even while rage against having her unrelenting modesty violated went through her, and he organized her orgasm while any feeling at all was still with her and she felt that, as she came in a way that pierced her with both pain and pleasure, she was not any more or by any means a respectable woman, and hoped she never would be on feeling the implosion of his life discharging into her.

3

He moved her shoulder gently to and fro, and kissed her mouth. He was washed and dressed, spruced up in his jacket and open-necked shirt. She fought to focus, so that details of the room would become clear. Through her sweat she smelled his aftershave.

'Time to get out of bed, my love.'

There was a knock at the door, and she pulled the sheet to her breasts. A maid came in with breakfast, and set the tray down, then gave a single accusing sniff (or so it seemed) and went out.

She wanted to shrink into the bed. 'I've never felt so wrecked. Can I stay in oblivion for a week? Then I might recover.'

He smiled. 'You look younger. Travelling agrees with you.'

She moaned, and wondered why he was so blind. She felt ninety. 'For how long, though?'

He broke a croissant, and put a piece to her lips.

'You're spoiling me!'

'Don't you like it?'

'When you do it, I do.' He was right. The world's weight had fallen away. She sat on the side of the bed and looked for her nightdress. It was on the back of a chair, across the room. He ate hungrily, but paused to give her more coffee, pouring whisky from a leather-covered flask into both cups. 'There's nothing better for starting the day.'

Her underwear was on the floor, but she didn't care. He picked it up and laid it on the bed, as if she ought to. But she liked it here. She was no longer respectable, and wanted to stay for weeks. 'I wonder how Judy and the kids are managing?'

'Well enough for us not to worry. While you're having your bath, I'll be downstairs paying our reckoning. Then I'll nip along the street to visit a flower shop.'

4

The large-scale map, with burial grounds marked in green ink, had been specially produced from a War Office original by the War Graves Commission to illustrate the position of cemeteries in the Arras area. Percy had had it dissected and mounted on cloth, and folded into a leather case, with a flap which closed and buttoned over the front, and his initials embossed in gold lettering under the clasp.

Tom drove out of the valley of the Scarpe, and on to a minor road through Roclincourt towards Vimy and the Ridge. There was open land all round, and burial plots appearing by the roadside like allotments on well-fertilized soil sprouting their rows of headstones. She navigated him beyond the village and down a lane till they saw the green nameplate of the one they were searching for on a wall. He stopped on a gravel forecourt and switched off the ignition. 'I'll go in for a few minutes and find my uncle's headstone. Do you want to come?'

She would, even if only to exercise her legs. He took the bouquet of lilies and carnations from the back seat. Such a notion of respect was an attempt to bring someone he had never known back to reality and place him squarely in a life they had never had together. At the same time, everything he did – she thought – seemed as if it would be the last action of its kind, a finality in each unfolding scheme, which made her feel unbearably sad, and protectively tender towards him. That he could be more vulnerable than she had ever been came as a shock, but that too helped to make their life together possible. She preferred not to ask what his plans were, wanting the childish satisfaction as each intention was revealed in action. She liked to indulge in the pleasure of receiving surprises, yet knew she had constructed these deceptions in order not to worry him with the desires in him which were so deep and personal that to bring them too abruptly into the open would cause him grief. Out of love she had manoeuvred this consideration of equals, assuming he would always do the same for her, since in so many ways he already had.

They walked between hundreds of headstones, some worn or slightly mildewed, but all in perfect alignment, the gravel neat, the grass clipped, not a weed to be seen. Most had crosses embossed, many had names, but scores were also nameless and bore the words KNOWN ONLY UNTO GOD. After sixty years they were cared for, perhaps still remembered in the families from which they had come.

He went a few yards in front with flowers held low. She was weeping with pity and a wracking pain, with terror and helplessness, sorrow and chagrin. She stopped. It was too much, this lake of graves. She hoped he would not see or hear, the wind turning her skin cold from tears that flowed on to her coat.

She rocked uncontrollably to and fro, with more despair than she had ever felt or given vent to, as if the collective spirit of so many dead were tearing out the life that so far had only raged uselessly in her. She couldn't stop, but walked towards him.

He looked at the grave of Captain Phillips, Royal Engineers. Not under a cross, but the Jewish Star of David that his bereaved mother had arranged to be put there. A British soldier of the Star of David, he said. An officer and a gentleman in Jewry's Book of Honour.

She held his arm while he talked. There were Jewish soldiers in the German Army too, he went on, Jews on either side doing their duty, and no doubt it happened that a bullet from one would find the heart of another. In the last war all Jews were on our side, except those who were caught and murdered by the Germans before they could be.

Her tears had stopped, though felt close to breaking out

495

again. 'There's a lesson,' he said. 'We must never fight against ourselves. The two tribes in biblical days did, until the First Exile. Then it stopped, because there were other forces to contend with. After the so-called Emancipation, the European Jews served their countries as good soldiers, and as good everything else. But now we have a greater force against which to unite, and still for the sake of those countries that as often as not despise us.'

He placed his flowers under the Star of David. She kissed his cold face, and when he looked into her eyes he noticed her tears.

5

'Where to now?' They were back on the main road.

'Boulogne. Navigate us via St Pol and Fruges,' he said.

When the route became straight, he turned out behind a car to overtake. A horn screamed from close by, sending him in again. The driver of a yellow Ford pointed angrily to his side mirror to tell him he should be more careful.

'He's right,' Tom said. 'I must get a wing mirror to make it safer.'

'When you want to overtake,' she said, 'let me know. I can look.'

Near Boulogne he followed signs for the port, and she wondered whether he had forgotten something in England that was important enough to go back for. If they made the crossing, she would feel Judy's warm kiss, and tell her how full of uncertainty she was, how far afloat in spaces she did not understand, how lost among forces still incomprehensible.

She would find comfort, even if only in talking for a few hours about things that didn't much matter. It had taken her a long time to learn that one woman could mother another and call it friendship, and at the moment that's all she wanted.

They were not going to England, but joined a queue by a railway line set apart from the *quai*. 'We put our car on the train,' he said, 'and in the morning wake up in Italy!'

The heat burned into the car. They stood outside, and there was no breeze. She strolled to the end of the queue, wondering how to get a ticket and go back on the next ship whether he came or not. She could be with Judy by evening. She could be in London by tomorrow, and in Nottingham the day after that. She opened her bag. There was enough English money. But there was nowhere for her to go, nowhere she wanted to go to, only someone she needed without knowing why. It had become unthinkable not to be with him.

As if knowing what she thought, he left her alone. He would think the same. He stood, smoking a cigar, looking at long wagons on to which he would drive the car before they took their seats in the carriage. Their tickets were checked. The train was half an hour late in leaving, and he cursed the heat. A man in front cooled himself with a folded newspaper. Cars began to move. She watched him drive up the ramp. She had made her choice. On the way down, carrying their overnight suitcase, he didn't get low enough under a girder, and bumped his head. When he swore she laughed.

6

He held her hand. 'Let's get on board.'

They leaned back in their seats and dozed, taken smoothly from the coast. By half-past five the train was east of Paris, stopped under a sunny sky among green fields, woods and orchards, with low hills in the distance. A halted train opposite was full of Spaniards, one of whom called out that they had come from Belgium and were going home on holiday. The heat was uncomfortable. A young Englishman understood Spanish, and translated what was said. There was a lot of unemployment in Belgium, they told him.

Pam was thirsty, and they went to the restaurant car. Tea and cakes cost five pounds, and she called it extravagance. 'Blame the exchange rate,' he said. The train rolled south and south-east. He took out a cloth map to show where they were. His grandfather's signature was on the hardboard cover: 'But the railway lines are the same.'

Window glass reflected their faces when it got dark. Inactivity made her sleepy. The noise and rattle was soporific. With darkness outside it seemed like travelling through an endless tunnel. They would never hit daylight again and see landscape. She would doze for ever, while Tom assiduously studied a multilingual phrase-book.

On her way from the toilet she opened the window of an outside door and heard the rush of wheels. If she unlatched the door and slipped she would be sucked underneath. The difference between life and death was a thrusting forward of the body, a twist of the foot. Even if there was nothing else to do she would never do it. Such impulses made life seem valuable.

'I thought you'd got lost,' he said.

'I was standing by myself. One has to now and again. I might not be able to for much longer.'

He closed his book, wondering what she meant.

'It sounds idiotic,' she said, 'and impossible perhaps, but I think I'm pregnant. I haven't had a period for two months. Either that, or it's something worse. But I don't think so. I've been as sick as a dog the last few mornings.'

He hadn't noticed. He should have done, he said. She'd mentioned it, but neither had made the connection. They

498

hadn't cared to. Neither had she – until now. So what else could the poor bloke do but smile? Pull the communication cord? He asked if she were sure. Who would be till it popped out? But the signs were there. It's incredible, she said. I'm forty-one. She had lived in a dream and taken no pills. Maybe she was mistaken, but it had been impossible not to mention in this timeless train driving through nowhere. He was happy, she supposed, and certainly wouldn't mind. She wondered whether there was any occurrence he would be disturbed at. If not, it was just as well.

He hoped it was true, he said. He could think of nothing better, leaned across to hold her and say he was sorry there was no one else in the compartment to hear the good news. He loved her, he said.

'At least we can kiss in peace.' If I'm pregnant, she thought, you should take me home. Ought that not to be his first consideration? If he could not get himself to take her home, at least he might say that he would like to. Was he daft, dead, or made of iron? He was unaware of the problem. They were light years apart. She had invented a reason for returning to England, but he hadn't fallen for it. All the same, it seemed she was pregnant, and she was glad they couldn't turn round and go back the way they had come.

At dinner they shared a table with the fair-haired young man who had translated the Spaniards' talk. His name was Aubrey, and he was going to Italy on a three months' tour, he said. In the autumn he would work in his father's car insurance firm. Next year he'd marry, get a house in Boreham Wood, and travel to town every day. Yes, he was looking forward to it. Whatever happened, however trivial, was an adventure. He was philosophical: there was no such thing as an ordinary life. Dullness was in the heart of the beholder. England was a wonderful country, but he liked being on the Continent, as well. When he had a family he would buy a caravan and go touring. He ordered his dinner in excellent French, and called for a bottle of wine, saying he couldn't sleep on a train unless he was half sloshed. Tom, agreeing it was the best thing, asked for champagne.

'Celebration?' He looked at Pam.

'Not particularly,' Tom said. 'I have a liking for it.'

Pam was surprised at her appetite. Something to throw up in the morning. For a train meal it was good. Tom insisted that Aubrey share their bottle. They drank to themselves and to each other, to every letter in the alphabet, never to meet again. Tom was, Pam thought, used to such encounters, which is why he'll never let me go. The idea frightened her, but it was a fear that came out of love. There was no firmer treaty. With both parties willing, what hope of parting?

Perhaps they were too unlike ever to part. Similar people repel each other, like brother and sister, and generate negative energy, whereas different people attract, and create a good – or at least positive – flow between them. She couldn't think of a better reason why they were still together, and felt so relaxed that she didn't want to. Maybe it was the drink, the sacred wine affecting the spine and brain.

Tom told Aubrey about his life at sea, and ordered another bottle. 'An average of one each isn't excessive,' he said, but Pam drank little, and felt tipsy enough on that. They stayed till all others had gone, and the staff were impatient. They shook hands and exchanged addresses. Tom said he and Pam were touring around, with no definite itinerary. Maybe we'll collide at the same night-spot in the next week or two. Aubrey staggered, and apologized for being drunk. 'That second brandy,' he admitted, 'did for me.' Pam thought him a nice, English sort of person.

Tom guided her along the swaying train. She confessed that she too felt pissed, but he laughed and said he would let her sleep it off tonight. The attendant had put down their beds, and they undressed in the small space. Naked, he reached out to kiss her. She still had her pants on, and wondered: What if I start in the night? A packet of tampons was under her pillow.

500

The train swayed at a hundred miles an hour, then stopped at a station, voices shouting up and down the line, white lights shining through slits in the blind. The carriages juddered, started to move, stopped, then rolled almost without noise so that her brain felt as if it had a steel ratchet fixed there for the whole train to go through. She slept, and did not sleep. It was impossible to say what was sleep and what wasn't.

The attendant was to waken them at six, but she was dressed by half-past five, unable to get into even the shallowest layer of rest. Tom slept on the top bunk. Her bladder seemed about to burst. There was daylight behind the blinds, but she didn't want to lift them and wake him. Her breath was vinous and foul.

She came back and cleaned her teeth, then went along the corridor to the door-window. Other people were awake. Aubrey whistled to himself, and didn't notice her when he passed in his pyjamas. She flattened against the wall to let him by. The sky was clear. The train stopped, showed station buildings of beige walls and red roofs, and luminous vegetation. There was the overwhelming sound of birds. We'll wake up in Lombardy, Tom had said. A package tour to Rimini had been nothing like this. She smiled with pleasure at travelling with a lover, instead of a husband who had always despised himself for liking her.

The wayside station was nondescript, yet exotic. If they stayed in the nearest village what would their life be like? Couldn't imagine. An elderly man who stood on the platform some way from other people wore a grey suit, a panama hat, a flowered shirt and smart tie, and held a briefcase. He crossed the line to their train, but a station official called roughly that this was not the right one and that the train to Milan would be in soon. Or so she assumed. The man took the brusque words with dignity, and went back to where he had first stood. She wondered where he could be going at six on Sunday morning.

She let up the blinds. Tom's voice was half-way between a growl and a moan. 'Oh my God, where am I?'

'You may well ask,' she said. 'But I'm not surprised you don't know.'

He looked down, and reached for her stomach. 'Is it true?'

'I hope so, though I don't think I'd hope so with anyone else but you.'

He let himself down from the bunk. 'What a stupendous thing to happen!'

He didn't know what he was in for, but she let him say it, because he had never been into that area of life. 'Wait and see,' she said with a smile.

She went out to make room while he dressed. He was there to look after her. She'd be safe with him, he said. But she felt bloody sick. What else could he say? She wanted to be by herself, get on to land and traipse across country she had never seen, walking and thinking, then walking but not thinking, to enjoy the flowers and trees, and watch the slowly changing view hour by hour and day by day, stopping when she liked, wandering like a mad woman between Alps and Lowlands, burned by sun and saturated by rain, but always alone, and when the first pains struck she would either live or die till she could be no more alone.

The train ran south through the shabby outskirts of Milan. He stood at the door with the overnight case between his feet. Red scrawl marks on walls were passed too quickly to be read. Hoardings and advertisements exhorted them to buy cars, sewing-machines, typewriters, essential goods and gewgaws that would save them time from the labours of life which, though they might not know what to do when they had saved such time, must nevertheless be saved. She thought of the labour-saving gadgets in her own long-gone house, and reflected that time thus conserved had in fact been all too often time lost in dreaming of what she would do with time saved if she had been really free. And now that she was, it didn't matter any more.

They were given vouchers to get breakfast at the station restaurant. At half-past six the air was already hot as they

502

walked with other passengers to the main hall. The restaurant was barred from within and picketed without by a line of waiters offering leaflets to explain their complaints. They were good-natured, even regretful at the inconvenience, and none of the travellers seemed particularly thwarted by their strike.

'We'll find a place to eat on the motorway,' Tom said.

Some people walked to a kiosk on the pavement which was doing a trade in coffee and a sort of cake-bread. Tom elbowed his way forward. 'Hit the capitalist system in one place,' he observed, 'and somebody else steps in to take advantage. It's very resilient.'

She stood by the railway buffers while he went along the catwalk and got into the car. He came off and circled the yard, then stopped to rearrange luggage and bring a packet of maps to the glove box.

7

She was amused at his punctilious fastening of the safety belt. Did he expect to escape if the car turned into a ball of flame? He was sensible to take precautions. As a man he no doubt wanted to live for ever, but for herself – the next car coming either had her name on it or it hadn't. If it did, her worries were over; if it didn't, they were yet to come.

A grey flower passed, or a black flower pounced. Air heated her elbow at the open window. 'Keep your arm in that position for half an hour,' he warned, 'and it'll be cooked three layers down.'

She drew it in. Learn step by step and brick by brick. 'Where do we go?'

'Back.'

'I'm never going *back*.'

He smiled. 'But gradually. Home again.'

I have no home. 'Why change our plans?'

He pointed out roads as if he had been on them before. He hadn't. But the map was clear, and coloured, although signposts were more visible from her passenger seat. On the motorway insane drivers at their steering wheels were set to overtake, or die if they couldn't. She had a near view of their faces. They had stumbled on to a Sunday morning hippodrome to rehearse the national sport for the bigger mayhem of midweek. She was beset by roars, revs, hooting, smoke and eye-bludgeoning from different shapes and colours of metal motor-cars that went by like rockets. Yet the faces of the drivers seemed remarkably relaxed.

'I had a lovely scheme cooked up,' he said, 'to roam the Balkans for a couple of months, then go to Greece and visit one or two of the islands. But it's got to be altered now.'

She hated being responsible for any disappointment. The land was flat, with too much haze to see the mountains which, indicated on the map, lay north and south.

'Your earth-shaking news from last night makes that prospect seem about as exciting as a fishing trip to the Sago Sea. You can't expect me to carry on as if it didn't mean anything.'

'So what do we do?'

'Go to a nice quiet town on the coast for a few days,' he said, 'then wend our way north. It'll be holiday enough.'

He didn't have to remind her that they were in Italy, but the word had a loving and homely sound when he did. She wanted to get to a town so that she would really know where they were, instead of being encased in a metal shell and taken somewhere not exactly against her will but in a direction which up to a few hours ago had not seemed possible. She fastened her safety belt, and saw the faint smile. He wanted to please her. His will had changed to hers. He thinks that at forty I'm more fragile than a young woman, which is

504

ridiculous. Being the first time for him made him young again, and apprehensive. She laughed to herself, felt fewer years pressing her down. She wanted to please him. 'We don't need to run back so soon. I feel fine. There's plenty of time before I have to take care.'

He stared at the road, intent on keeping them alive but locked in his purpose of covering distance by nightfall. She saw, side-glancing, that he was not only fearful of the road but was fleeing as if before demons, on his way to a place where he thought safety lay. Demons would be waiting for him there also. They had driven him out and would beckon him in, the same with her. She read it clearly in his features, that they were leaving a point on the earth like refugees, and felt that her own soul was built into the same escape plan. She was as much the power of their progress to wherever it was to be, as he was the mechanism of hers. They were set on a combined course towards what both had wanted since the beginning, yet neither knew what it was. She touched his wrist gently.

'There'll be plenty of time for roaming, afterwards,' he said. 'We can always put the baby in the car and take off, spend a few years on the road before he or she has to go to school.'

She was blocking his escape route, turning him back by her revelation. If they stayed somewhere long enough she would take a specimen of her water and get her pregnancy confirmed. She was sure, but wanted to be certain. She wanted it to be female, yet was glad there was no way of knowing. It was sufficient for the moment that she had caused him to change plans. Perhaps he was happy that her condition had made him want to, because he was now part of her more than he could ever have been before. If he had not said anything, she would have gone wherever he wanted, though the pride that would insist may have been no more than supine behaviour. Something more important than either of them tampered with his decisions. She resented the interference for her own sake, but not for his. For him it was

505

the appearance of a storm in mid-ocean, an inconvenience to be circumvented. He would alter course. He knew a routine for dealing with it. That part of his temperament she could never affect – just as there was much about her that he couldn't change.

She could have told him she was pregnant before leaving England, but such an early switchback of his aims wouldn't have had the significance of the alteration he was making now. She had left telling him, to see whether or not he would do so. It had to mean something, and he had passed the test – her test. Maybe he was scorching with resentment, and she would never know how hard the decision had been for him. But his happiness was obvious. She didn't know whether to be glad that he wasn't angry. Now that she had told him, and he wasn't, had she really wanted him to cosset her as a fragile girl? She could only accept that for the moment she had. The tune would be called by her, or not at all, though perhaps it was just as well that the situation was bigger than either of them.

South of Milan the speedometer read nearly a hundred. The southern hills were showing themselves out of the haze. 'We'll take off in a bit.' But she wasn't afraid.

'Over those mountains we'll get to the Mediterranean.' He slowed down. 'There's a long way to go yet.'

He parked in a picnic place under trees, and topped up the radiator with cool water from a tap. He refilled the supply in his container, and washed dead insects from the windscreen. The air was humid. Birds and butterflies flitted over a meadow. A few families at benches ate an early lunch. Tom took off tie and jacket, and rolled his sleeves. There was food she had bought in Arras: rye bread, pâté, hard-boiled eggs, salt and spring onions from an icebag, and some congealed cake. He took a small stove from the car, boiled water and made tea, putting lemon and sugar-lumps into two mugs.

She laughed. 'You should have brought a table and chairs.'

It was close to midday. 'I could take a sight on the sun with the sextant.'

'Have fun. Where are we?'

'You tell me.'

'Italy.' Her mouth was full. 'Wonderful!'

He nodded. 'No place like it – to hear such news. It didn't really sink in in France.'

Steam from the tea smelled of citrus, and mingled with her sweat. She leaned against the car, void of speculation. The sky was blue. She undid two buttons of her blouse. The intense heat cut her feeling of exhaustion. She wanted to describe everything aloud in case it vanished, but to pull words from her mind would be a negation of life in this idyllic place.

A British car, luggage topped with plastic ripped by the slipstream, was full of kids and coloured buckets. He passed all but the sportiest vehicles. At such a rate it was possible to see the fuel gauge sliding to zero. The straight road crossed the plain of Lombardy, a hundred kilometres flowing while she leaned her head and dozed. She awoke, startled but not alarmed at her dream of rainy streets. They stopped for petrol, black coffee, and to use the toilet.

The wide road curved into the hills. Milky white ribs of cloud looked like the pale x-ray plates of a ghost. There were grey outcrops, and chestnut trees near farmhouses. He drove to make distance, and to get away from the pull of the place he had set out from – before having to get back to it, as if circling the calm exterior of the storm while gathering courage to steer into the middle. She also felt that life wasn't like this, and she was sure that he also knew. He looked haggard about the eyes, with a tenseness at the mouth she had not noticed before, though when driving by cliff-like menacing lorries his features softened.

'I dreamed of your aunt last night,' she said.

'What about?'

'I don't know. I just saw her. She was trying to tell me something. She was screaming, and upset. So was I. A bit frightened, I think. She was in the flat, in the bedroom. Funnily enough, I couldn't tell what she was saying, but it was more than just trying to get me out of the place.'

'I suppose one could figure it out,' he said, 'though I'd rather forget it.'

'So would I. It was only a dream. I'd forgotten it until now.' She searched for a Kleenex to wipe her face. 'After a night on the train, and all day on the road, I'm going to need a bath.'

'We'll find a hotel on the coast.' He pushed in the cigarette lighter at the dashboard. 'I've pencilled places on the map where there'll be accommodation.'

The road descended towards the signposted smoke of Genoa. 'I can smell the sea already.' He was joyful at the prospect.

It was easier to love a happy man. He must have been marking the map last night while I was asleep, using a pentorch in his upper bunk to change routes from those he had intended. In the cardboard box she had seen tourist pamphlets on Greece and Israel.

He tuned in to her thoughts. '"Thalassa" is the only Greek word I know. Hard to forget, if you've read the *Anabasis*. One of the masters made us read Xenophon's piece at school, but I've read it again since. I actually liked it, even though I was forced into it.'

She felt ignorant. 'I don't know it.'

'There are so many books.'

But she would read.

He told the 'March of the Ten Thousand', of the struggle of Xenophon and his Greeks through the snows of Anatolia towards the benign sea that would take them home, a tale that whittled away the kilometres till the pale Mediterranean came into view for them also. Travelling was still his life. Being on the move meant nothing to him. He was taking care of everything as if it signified little to her. But it did. She was out of her element, a child again, wanting to be away from the car and in control of her own movements. It was hard to know

508

what you wanted till you hadn't got it, especially when you didn't know whether or not you already had what you wanted. Equally hard to know what you wanted when you were in love, and even harder to know anything at all when you were pregnant. But what she wanted was what she had, and what she had was more than she'd ever had in her life, and because she had all she wanted at the moment she didn't doubt that there was far more to come – as much as she ever would want, in fact. A disturbing lack of doubt told her it might never be enough, whatever it was, and made her wonder at this stage if everyone had to settle for far less than they perceived it was possible to have.

Behind the city he turned west towards blue sky along the coast. They threaded tunnels and caught vivid sights of the sea. All windows were opened. She felt more carefree now that palm trees and villas were visible, and small villages that looked good to live in.

'There are at least three hotels in town.' They drove off the motorway. 'And it's only four o'clock. Plenty of time for a stroll along the seafront.'

8

She sat in the car, and hoped there would be a room. Single-storeyed cottages were angled between eucalyptus trees and set on different slopes. The larger building had a café and restaurant. People were sitting in shirtsleeves and cotton dresses at outside tables. He tapped on the window, holding a key. 'Plenty of rooms.'

He drove around the complicated lane system to their allotted dwelling. There were two beds and a wardrobe, desk, chairs and a telephone, as well as a bathroom. She liked its

509

space and cleanliness. He washed his shirt at the sink, then put his underwear into the water, while she stood under the cool shower, a pleasure all the greater for the change she was going through. Impossible to think about getting back to the place they had left.

She ran a finger through her pubic hair, and let fingers stroke her belly. She had needed to pull him from death's cul-de-sac before seeing a way out of her own. In that sense she was connected to him for ever, and he with her, whether or not they stayed as man and wife – whatever that might mean. For who knew whether she would want to remain with him or he with her? To expect comfort from the future was no more than a pathetic cry for help. You could only live in the present, and trust that the way would be shown.

She soaped herself, and held her face to the downrushing water. With blinds drawn, they lay on their separate beds. When she awoke, two hours had gone. Her oblivion had been without dreams, or any indication of having been asleep except that she felt weak, and hardly rested.

He sat reading. 'I couldn't lose consciousness. The road was still rolling along under my eyelids.'

She stood by his side. 'I haven't looked at the Bible for a long time.'

'I thought I'd bring something to read, for those empty moments when one needs solace. It's a book that reinforces my moral fibre. There isn't much left either in me or the rest of the world. It's on the wane, but we must get it back. My spirit is solidified by this, for instance:

'"Give counsel, execute justice;
Make thy shadow as the night in the midst of the noonday;
Hide the outcasts; betray not the fugitive."

'At one time I would have needed a sledgehammer to get such precepts into my senses. Every word is like bread:

'"And I will rejoice in Jerusalem,
And joy in my people;
And the voice of weeping shall be no more heard in her,
Nor the voice of the crying."'

What caused her anxiety at hearing him quote such poems? She felt either fear or joy at the change she had seen in him, at the alterations in herself. Nothing in between. There was no anchor, no stillness or fixity for either of them. But they belonged nowhere if not to each other. He was someone come to life whom she had known but had forgotten, yet still did not know who he was. Was that the same with everyone – for the rest of their lives, no matter how long they were together? The mystery that could never be solved was to be the cement of their unity. The insoluble joined them more firmly than the certain or commonplace. He was going away from her, yet would never get so far that they would lose each other, all the same.

He sat by her on the bed. 'You looked beautiful when you were sleeping, but even more so now.'

She put an arm over his shoulder, thinking they would make love. It didn't matter. She was disembodied, feeling affection more than passion. The air from outside smelled of flowers and pine needles. Their window looked up a hillside. He put on a grey light-weight suit, with shirt and tie, and she wore a cardigan over her dress because the air seemed cool.

They drank a bottle of Valpolicella before they began the dish of ravioli. 'I wonder what happened to Aubrey?'

He broke the powdery bread. 'Aubrey?'

She reminded him. 'Your drinking companion of last night.'

'Seems years ago. I expect he's in Rome by now.'

'Would you like to be roaming around on your own?'

Was he, sailor or not, out of his depth and unable to admit that he wanted to end the jaunt? She was elated, then depressed, within a space in which no time passed. Either that, or it went backwards. Her spirit fled. It came back –

511

always. Did he want to turn around, but his mouth wouldn't say so? To plan travel in the isolation of his aunt's flat was a pleasant way to pass a few evenings. All experience said so. But how about the reality of being with her? And her reality of being with him? Feeling lost, she knew that he wondered, too, and held his hand. It was getting dark. A few couples were dancing to the music.

'I've roamed enough on my own,' he said. 'More than thirty years. I love you, and love being with you. There's no one else, and never will be.'

He looked at her as if also asking why he was in this place with a plain strange person who was a million miles separated from his worldly mentality. He looked at her, she thought, as if he knew more about her than he was easy with. She saw too close, and too deep, and he couldn't know it. But was she wondering whether he wanted to go on because she herself couldn't bear to ask the same question? The idea frightened her. She didn't want to ask. It was unnecessary because it was unanswerable.

'Tomorrow . . .' he began.

When the music stopped there was the deafening cro-ack of bullfrogs on the hill-slope. Talk, she knew, cured all doubts – and pulverized all queries.

'We'll go on to San Remo,' he said. 'It's not very far.'

They needed another bottle for the scaloppine con Marsala. The waiter was young and quick, with wonderful eyes. There was a beautiful man at the next table, with an even more beautiful woman. It was a pleasure to look at other people. She could love them both. 'Do you want to?'

'There's nothing else to do,' Tom said.

She knew that he was alarmed. So was she. But he hadn't answered. He might at least reply to her question by asking if she wanted to go on.

'We've hardly begun,' was all he could say.

He was right in thinking she lacked courage. But she would acquire it by experiene, the only way she knew. It was too late

512

for questions. Who needed them? Questions only occurred to those who found the uncertainties of life too painful to bear. Yet she did, because to let go was to die, especially during changes that seemed incomprehensible.

He stood up, and she wondered what for. Was he about to leave because he could take no more – dump her – make the excuse that he was going to the lavatory, then walk quickly to the room for his luggage and drive away? Would he join Aubrey in Rome, or find himself a proper woman who would take care of him with no holds barred – as they say? He looked tired, but smiled, a hand at her shoulder. 'This jungle music's better to dance to than listen to. Let's have a try!'

She looked. He took her astonishment to indicate that she would not be able to act, so held her arm firmly till she got up and followed. They moved around the floor. He was right. The noise wouldn't let them talk. Unlike the other couples flinging about, they stayed close, her face at his shoulder, his arms around her and hers about him. The dance wouldn't let them look at each other. It was better this way, more comforting. Nor did he seem to mind. Both were lost in their separation. She liked being close to him yet alone. He kissed her, then stepped away and swung her back and forth, spun himself, and turned her. She laughed, jolted uncomfortably into freedom. You don't have to care, he said, and it's called enjoying yourself. She laughed again. The walls of the room ran around her. He was one side, then the other. His face was not part of her, but his body was, as he came near and spun off again. She missed a table by inches, and stepped back, close to him. She had never danced in her life, and now she had. He was quick, and even her clumsiness vanished.

He took a torch out of his pocket to light the path back. He liked the way to be plain, his uncertainties resolved. For her to have everything clear in life would be like having no head. She'd left all that behind. She would sit beside him in the car with no head. At the fair as a child there had been a headless woman. She remembered her terror on seeing the lit-up and

513

gaudy poster. She had not dared ascend the wooden steps and see the woman with no head. Lost it in a terrible accident at some factory in Lancashire, a man beside them said. Every fair has a headless woman, her father scoffed. It's the same one, the other man told him, travelling around. She makes better money, I'll bet, than she did when she worked in the mill. Does she, though, her father wondered. She gripped his hand, and questioned why it was always a headless woman and never a headless man.

'In tropical places,' Tom was saying, 'we didn't walk anywhere without a torch shining at the ground, because of reptiles.'

Back at the room she said: 'I care for you more than I've ever cared for anyone. It may not help at the moment to say it, but I want you to know, all the same.'

He stood in silence.

'I'm sorry I'm such a misery,' she said. But her soul was her own – sorry or not. In the uncertainty of degradation and homelessness she was herself. He did not attempt to control her by trying to share her despair. She did not need such assistance. He would not do it. He endured her feelings as far as it was possible to do so, but left her free with them, the only attitude which might help to detach her from an agony that would not release her. The nearest he would go to acknowledging her plight was to say, as he undressed: 'We'd better get some sleep. We'll both feel better tomorrow.'

What else could the poor bloke say? Unable to speak, she held him in a strong grip. He moved with her to the bed. She was a long way from anything she had known. He knew she was tormented, but there was nothing he could do. He was not the sort of man to do anything except allow her to endure while not being totally devastated himself. She had to break the ropes of past attachments, and weave new ones with her own unaided strength and will. She was remaking the life of another man, as she had first made the life of George by marrying him and getting him started in business and in life.

She had brought up one child and would now bring up another. Was that to be all she would do with herself?

It was as if she were simply passing the years before starting something real, but by the time she was able to she would be dead. As far as she was concerned there was no other life but this, and she had to do what she wanted while there was still time. She had not come on earth to shoe-horn men out of their suits of armour and bring up their children, even though they would be called her children as well.

She had to decide – either end it, and do what she wanted, or leave things alone and live like a cabbage. The way was clear, and wide open. Every course was possible, desirable – or out of the question. She was trapped because the breadth of space was boundless. There was no firmer trap than that. She was caught beyond all possibility of movement because all movement was possible and no direction closed to her.

To leave one man and meet another – where was the sense in that? To abandon one child and have another – wherein lay the difference? To depart from one man she had never loved, to one she believed that she did, was that sufficient? The altered landscape clarified her ideas on the matter. The unknown language around them brought out only what was important. There was no time for dross, no space for former confusions. If she weren't to die she must know what she wanted.

Men were more or less taken care of from the womb to the coffin. So were women – if that was what they wanted, but she was herself first and a woman second. She knew that now. He had been a sailor before being a man, but she had never been anything except a woman. The only strength was in being an individual. Even in the world at large – if it mattered to think so – the more individuals there were, instead of married couples, the greater the strength of that society. Double the number of individuals in a society and it would be indestructible. But if so few of them wanted to be individuals she would at any rate be one herself, as far as it was possible to be so. Only in that way could she survive.

515

Without any foreplay she pulled him into her, and in a few moments felt him ejaculate. Thus soothed, she fell asleep, only awake long enough to know that he had moved across to his own bed. The next thing she knew she was having vivid dreams and beginning to wake up.

9

He bought a box of *antico Toscano*, gnarled, dark-brown, foul-smelling cigars that nevertheless tasted ambrosial. No other word would fit, he said. He had looked more and more like a schoolboy since she had got the laboratory report that spread his smile beyond all doubt.

An Italian gentleman at the next coffee table leaned across to say it was customary to cut the *antico Toscano* into two and smoke half at a time. The tobacconist kept a special pair of scissors for the purpose, he added.

The palm-lined promenade was in sunlight. Tom preferred to smoke his roots in one long sixteen-centimetre stick, though he had thanked the Italian for his kind advice. They walked under the palms. 'I mustn't,' she said, 'forget to buy some insect repellent from the chemist, though I suppose if you smoked those all night and sat by my bed they wouldn't stand much of a chance.'

'I love you,' he offered. 'Of course I'll do it.'

She believed him, whether said lightly or not. They loved each other, but didn't know why. How could you know why? Only a fool would want to know. The reasons were obvious if you looked for them. The answers were always there before the questions. But he couldn't convince her when he said this in all the seriousness of his easygoing manner. Oh how mixed that sailor's manner was – far more so, it seemed, than when she had first met him.

He said often that he loved her, like a perfect gentleman who had been used to obeying and getting obedience all his life. But he never said why, and she was ashamed at telling herself that it was not enough. She couldn't let him know what she wanted, yet couldn't bear to wait for him to say what she needed to hear. If he couldn't tell her why he loved her she would rather be told why he hated her than have him say nothing in response to the basic question. She hadn't gone through the misery of leaving one marriage in order to accept something which was not good enough for her, and, since she loved him so much, was not good enough for him either.

Yet every gesture and action proved that he certainly did love her, a new experience that was overwhelming, making her the victim of an intoxicating see-saw of emotion which at times she doubted her ability to live through. The intensity of her new life (was it new, and why?) daunted her to such an extent that she couldn't finally say that she wanted it. There must be something else apart from this – and death.

He seemed made for the sun, walking by the blue sea and smoking his cigar without any cares, happy with her, adoring her. She had never been adored before. There was nothing she lacked. If anyone had asked if she were happy she would say yes. She was. There was no other answer. They had been here a week, so long that it had become timeless. They never talked about leaving. No question of pushing on. No discussion of what new place to see. Neither joy nor anguish on the merits of staying for ever in one place. Every morning he woke at six and went for a swim. He got out of bed with more alacrity and punctuality while travelling, as if he were still at sea perhaps, and had his duty to perform, than he had when at home and needed to rise by the alarm clock.

They walked the same route, drank coffee at the same place. But the afternoons were different. 'Tell me something,' she said.

'I'm an afternoon man,' he told her. 'Having been a morning man all my life, I can now afford to be. My faculties don't prosper till the afternoon, even though I'm an early riser.'

She stopped at a stall and bought a postcard for Judy. 'I miss her.' She counted the ships on the sea. 'Strange as it may seem. There's a part of me that's always wanted to be independent like Judy.'

They walked across the road. Water flickered into grits of white, visibility sharpening on the horizon. 'You mean that you would like to live alone, as Judy does?'

'I wanted to for years. It seemed the nearest thing to heaven. But I didn't make the break when the longing was most intense. I got used to the torment, and so couldn't snap free. I grew resigned.'

'You did it, eventually.'

'In a somnolent kind of way.' They walked along the shore. 'But I didn't make a dramatic exit like Judy.'

'Who knows what her exit was like?' He laughed. 'I'm sure no prize was ever offered for the most lacerating departure, though I imagine it was just as difficult and agonizing for you as for Judy.'

'But it took me nearly twenty years.'

They watched cars driving along the road. 'And you still want to live alone?'

'I was doing so when we met.'

He remembered.

'I actually thought I was enjoying it, and maybe I was. But presumably the state didn't suit me. Do you ever remember the time when you saved my life?'

'I relive it occasionally, hoping you'll never think I did the wrong thing.'

She held his hand as they walked. 'What day is it? I've lost count.'

'Friday, according to *my* almanac.'

518

'I didn't want to live alone.' She added after a pause: 'What surer proof could you want?'

'It's not only me you're living with,' he said, stopping to relight his cigar by cupping the end in his hand against the wind.

She stopped, and looked at him. 'How do you mean?'

'Well, it's not only *you* I'm living with, is it? It's your past, your ideas, and all the different people in thousands of years who have gone to producing you. It's your nationality, religion, dreams, battles, great migrations – if there were any; struggles and miseries, all the human permutations of every kind of change, which there obviously were; the strife and jubilations, which I hope there were. You wanted to escape, but I pulled you back into them. I shan't remind you of that again. I never intended to, but it still seems to be what we're talking about. I belong to you and your millions of bits and pieces for as long as you'll allow me to. I'm part of them, just as you are a part of mine, and you know as much about my past as I do myself, because we went through that heap of intimidating evidence in the flat, and I told you everything bit by bit as it came to light. So neither of us can live apart from each other. Even if we went away this minute and never met again we wouldn't really separate. By living together, we are interdependent, yet still independent, in a peculiar sort of way. I see you as more truly liberated than Judy, more courageous. You've been through a great deal more, and I know you are still going through it – though I'm not diminishing her suffering, either.'

She saw his face, the same she had glimpsed while driving and thought so empty. Did he teem with speculations every minute of the day? It was the same face she had woken up to after killing herself. She was amazed, yet glad to hear him talk, for how else could she know what was in his mind if, as was generally the case, she was too craven to question him directly, or too indifferent to want to know anything.'

519

She walked on in order to maintain her smile of equanimity, for she was exhausted by uncertainty and self-distrust. He saw more in her than there was, she thought, something he wanted to perceive but which did not exist. He was doing his best in every way. Or maybe it did not exist – whatever it was – because she did not wish it to. Who was he to say that it did, or she to say that it did not? – this mysterious quality she could not get hold of. She didn't want to disappoint him by denigrating herself, though it was hard not to. But if all that he mentioned was a reality then it was something she herself could neither see nor feel, and therefore if it was present to him and not to her there was an imbalance in their association which, however she tried to correct it, would be the end of her independence for ever. He spoke in this way because he wanted something from her which she did not know existed, and which she might not want to give even if it turned out to be there and she eventually discovered what it was.

He also wanted to give something to her. That was certain. He already had, but she found it harder to receive than to give, and was terrified at becoming enmeshed by it. But perhaps it had already happened, and if so, there was no cause to be afraid. She had abandoned everything, but was there nothing else to be done but go on with him?

In the old town there was a market selling an abundance of vegetables and fruits, as well as olives, spicy sausage, cheeses and bread. He bought a bag full, did the buying, chaffing at the women as if he spoke their language perfectly and not just a few phrases which, she had to admit, he mimicked pretty well. They loved him, she saw. He flirted and they flirted. It was their way. And they smiled as if they loved her as well. She bought a melon while his back was turned, and the woman who handed it to her knew she was pregnant.

They drove along the coast to where it wasn't too crowded.

'I thought sailors couldn't swim,' she said, taking her clothes off.

'It's not that they can't. It's often that it does them no good when they have to try.'

She had a horror of treading on something she couldn't see. He drew her along, and out. 'Can you swim?'

'After a fashion.' She dived forward, feeling a wave of water as he followed. He swam around her, then she broke out of his circle and went ahead in a rapid side-paddle, turning to see how far off she had left him. She felt safer when she could no longer touch bottom, dipped under and corkscrewed up for air, spouting water at the sun's heat. She laughed at his slow progress, and did a languid breast stroke towards him.

They sat on a slab of rock in their swimming suits, a towel over her shoulders so as not to scorch. 'I'm getting dehydrated,' she said.

He went to the car on the road and came down with the stove, provisions and a canister of water. Ships in the distance stood waiting to go into harbour. She couldn't eat in the early morning, but her appetite came as the day wore on. Sea creamed over the rocks, a ragged string of phosphorescence coming in and going out.

'It's polluted,' she said. 'We'll probably die after our swim.'

'I don't believe it. But if it is we'll have to get used to it.' He made tea, then sat and looked at the ships through his binoculars. She couldn't tell when they moved, but didn't doubt that he could. They were monuments to the patient sailors who worked on them. Graven, and unable to move head, arms or shoulders, he was a statue set above the dreamy sea. She was apart, and let him be alone, not wanting to know what he thought. He was filled with his own back-and-forth contemplation. When he lowered the binoculars his eyes continued to look in a half squint towards the horizon as if he could see beyond the dark blue line.

She wanted less and less to know what kind of vision he saw. His vision was part of him. His, and his alone. He had a right to it. What did she want it for? She had her own, however unclear it yet was and would perhaps remain. But her own.

521

That was what she wanted. If she showed interest in his she might not understand what he would say, might not recognize her own when it became manifest, if one day it magically did. So how could she take a chance on such a vital question, which in any case wasn't specifically hers? Perhaps at the moment he had even less to tell than she had, that he was also empty, and content in spite of all.

The sun warmed her thighs. She lay back, her head on the folded basket, lids closed against the sky's glare, smelling trees and a mild breeze from the sea. She weighed nothing – because of the heat, the touch of grit under the calves of her legs, her closed eyes and the sense of emptiness given by sea and sky. The vacancy of space produced a peace no force could touch. Her senses floated. She could broach all limits. Within her weakness she felt a semblance of not quite forgotten strength returning from many years ago. Or perhaps she was recalling a life she had never known, a reflection sent back from the future telling of what was yet to come, but designed only to lure her into unimaginable turmoil.

Such feelings of renewal were impossible to trust. She preferred to push them away into the fanciful mists, and instead enjoy the timeless moment with a hand over her eyes to keep off the sun's damaging glare, yet be ready for whatever might come.

He looked at the sea, and said that for the first time in his life he did not want to move. He wanted to stay where he was for ever. The great blue had meaning only because she had come with him. She was here. Why go on? Tennyson had a few choice words on the subject, he laughed. What did it matter where he lived? His ancestors could look after themselves.

He turned to her. 'I've lived three whole lives: orphan, seaman, and now I'm a Wandering Jew. The last I didn't know about till recently, which makes it more important than the others, because it really was the first. It means everything

– and yet nothing, as long as I'm with you.'

God had already taken care of them, he went on, just as they would yet be taken care of. He felt weary to a depth he could never have imagined, though knew he had no option but to move, as if he had a fatal illness and was determined to die only in a particular and chosen spot of the earth, so that he could be content in knowing that he had done the right thing even unto death. He refused to believe it, however. It wasn't like that at all. They still had a whole life to live.

They collected the things together and put on their clothes. She should have been afraid but wasn't. When he revealed himself so absolutely her optimism came back, the unalloyed and joyous sort with no catches to it. Yet it didn't last long, though the residue left her with the desire to do something, to move, to act. When they were driving along she said: 'I want to go back to England.'

'All right,' he answered. 'We'll light off in the morning.'

'Not in the morning. Now.'

He would obey. He has obeyed all his life, she thought.

'We'd better let Judy know, then,' he told her.

'Send a telegram.'

'Why not phone?' he suggested. 'Do it from the hotel while I pack.'

10

'Judy?'

'It isn't Judy.'

'Who is it, then?'

'It's Hilary.'

She hadn't recognized the voice. It had sounded like that of a boy she didn't know. 'Why didn't you say so?'

'Why should I?'

'Is your mother there?'

'No, but Judy is.'

Now she knew what she was going back to. 'Get her for me,' she said sharply, 'or my fist will come out of the telephone and clout you one! I want to talk to her.'

There was a bang, as if the phone had dropped on to the floor, or had been thrown there. She waited.

'We'll only get two hours along the road before we have to stop and look for another hotel,' Tom said, folding his trousers into a case. 'We might as well stay here tonight – we'll have to pay for the room, anyway.'

She could tell he thought her more stupid than determined.

'Start early tomorrow,' he went on. 'We'll be half-way up the Rhône before evening, maybe even beyond Lyon.'

She nodded. 'I want to go now.'

'Judy?'

'Yes.'

'This is Pam.'

'Pam?'

'Pam.'

'Pam! Where are you, then?'

'Italy.'

'You sound next door.'

'So do you.'

'I wish I was.'

'Wouldn't it be nice? We will be, soon.'

'I couldn't sleep for days after you left. What do you mean? Are you coming back?'

While with Tom she felt ten years younger. With Judy she felt that even twenty years had been taken off her life. 'I've got news for you. I'm pregnant.'

There was a drop in the tone of her voice. 'Oh.'

'Tom's happy, as you can imagine.'

'I'll bet he is.'

'I am as well. I hoped you would be.'

Judy forced a laugh. 'That'll make three kids we've got.'

'I don't expect there'll be any more, though, do you?'

'Let's hope not. Boy or girl?'

'I can't tell yet.'

'Let me know as soon as you can.'

'I'll try!'

'I'm interested. See you in a few days, then.'

There was a pause.

'Do you want us to move out?' Judy said.

'For God's sake!'

'Well, do you?'

'What an idea!'

'We'll make very picturesque refugees, sitting on the steps of the town hall. We'll be in all the local papers. Or maybe we won't, because I saw an empty house in Hove yesterday. We can become squatters.'

'Don't be daft.'

'Can't you tell when I'm joking?'

Pam couldn't always. 'Isn't our place big enough for you?'

Judy laughed, a more genuine resonance. 'I hope so. We'll all live happily together I expect.'

'There should be space for all of us.'

'We'll talk about it when you get here,' Judy said.

'We don't need to.'

'All right, then. It's settled.' She sounded glad. There was some disturbance from the children, and Pam heard her shout: 'Shut up, you pigs. Tom's coming back. He'll sort you out.'

There were cheers.

'We'll phone from the docks – maybe Newhaven, after Tom's worked it out. He sends his love.'

'Can't wait to see you.'

'Nor me you.'

'You'd better hang up,' Judy said, 'or you'll have no money to get back on. Love and kisses to you – both.'

525

She turned to Tom on putting the receiver down. 'That's that. All fixed.'

He clipped his case shut. 'Will she be glad to see us?'

'She will now. The children certainly will. She had imagined we'd be away for a couple of months, but it'll be only a fortnight.'

'That,' he said, with more satisfaction than she liked to hear, 'is fate. Everyone is at its mercy.'

'It wasn't fate that got me pregnant.' She turned to her own clothes.

He ignored her remark, and said: 'She'll be all right. We'll look after them. There's enough room in the flat for everybody, as I heard you telling her.'

'Or maybe it *was* fate,' Pam smiled.

11

There was nothing in her mind except the force to get out into the open what little was in it, that much being all she had and therefore of the most vital importance to her. An east wind buffeted the car. He didn't even see the low hills lifting to left and right. She said: 'You are destroying me.'

His hands on the steering wheel gripped more than formerly. She had struck at the middle, and found a rock of truth that she had been feeling for since coming out of that miasma of gas when they first met. And he knew it, she thought, at which he could only keep quiet so as to be able to stay driving safely on the motorway. Their lives seemed more vital to him than anything she could say.

'You're trying to destroy me, that's it.' She was not willing to spare him. The pain was so unremitting that she could not even spare herself. Why did two people live together if they could not confess what pain they felt? Now that she had spoken she seemed more in danger than he could ever be. He knew that, as well, and if he didn't respond, or reply, she would leap at his hands and bloody her teeth on them, tear at the dark hairs on those fingers confidently curled around the plastic-covered wheel so that he would run off the motorway or into some other vehicle. Death seemed easier than silence. She would reduce him, because the prospect of reducing herself was too final to be borne. The cost to her was infinite, but to him it would be little enough. All her life she had wanted to meet someone strong enough to sustain her central fire of attack, an attack into which was built the very substance of herself. The end had come, and she would fling herself into death; because anything less was worse than death which, though it meant life, she would not live with. She was his equal, and wanted him to know.

'And I won't be destroyed, not by you or anyone else, but above all not by you.'

He smiled, but was in agony. Unlike at first meeting, his face was no longer capable of concealing secrets. The ability to create mutual agony was at least a measure of their progress towards each other, as was the happiness they had known an indication of their intimacy. The driving of the car held his pain within bounds. Like the man used to obey, and to obedience, he kept a straight course, still conscious to the extent of moving from lane to lane while overtaking other vehicles. 'You can't destroy me,' he said, 'which is clearly what you want.'

He spoke as if out of despair, but she detected a note of triumph. The vivid light and stink of motor fumes made her feel near to death. Any split second, being at the outer limits of a life to which she had brought him, he might swing the car at the bank of a bridge support and end the misery he must feel but which she now told herself she did not. Death was better than no feeling. Without feeling you did nothing but that which brought death about. If she was dead she would wake him up, make his heart ring and vibrate to what was in her. He had come from the sea and usurped her place in the world, before bringing her back to it in his fashion. He was all compact and formed and finished beautifully by training and circumstance and heredity, while George had been a millpond of nothingness and she a mere appendage of that. She loved him and she didn't, but her own terms were made as nothing by his monolithic self-assurance, against which she must prevail so as to save herself from destruction. He was the spirit to her flesh, and she would make them mix on her terms as much as on his. But all she could say was: 'I won't be destroyed, whatever you may want.'

She lacked words for the outside. They were there by the thousand but would not be spoken. She wanted them but couldn't find any that would tell him what she meant. He loved her, so knew what she wanted to say, but it wasn't enough unless and until she had been allowed to say everything.

'I love you.' Each word was as clear and as uncomfortable as grit in his throat. 'Isn't that sufficient?'

It no longer was. She had glimpsed something else. It had taken time, but another light was beginning to expand. She told him that no, it wasn't enough, as a matter of fact.

He drove on. 'It will have to be.'

She was sure he understood, but knew he might not be able to follow. He overtook an enormous lorry, hands relaxed at the wheel, and went on to put another juggernaut behind them. She struck, smashed, crunched her fist at his hands. 'It won't have to be. It won't.'

He instantaneously gripped. His expression was unchanged, she struck again, the lorry wheels seeming higher than the car, a cliff-face sliding along with engine roaring and smothering theirs as if they were gliding in silence. He changed gear, flicked on blinkers to reach an inner lane, his lips making imprecations which might have been at the lorry as much as at her. For no reason he switched on the windscreen wipers, perhaps as if to wash her pestering spirit away. They were around the lorry obstacle, and for good measure he swung out again and left two cars behind. He thought he was safe, that he had survived a crisis as he'd triumphed in the fight when George and his brothers had attacked her.

She recalled the set-to, filled with shame and, forgetting the peril she'd been in, felt that her brothers-in-law had been hard done by. They'd stood little chance against his cock-of-the-walk sailor-bully who tricked them by bluff rather than fair fight.

The motorway curved, banks of rock and yellow soil close to the side. Heavy gunmetal clouds lay up the Rhône valley ahead. She struck again, fearing to vomit if she didn't – blows more unexpected than the first and even more forceful, screaming at him to stop the car. He looked at the front, tightened his grip, and drove on. He thought she had finished, worked out her demons as if she were a mutinous deckhand whom he had to polish off by the old one-two. When she struck at him on a clear patch of the road his fist spun and knocked her head against the window.

'Be quiet,' he said loudly, 'and pull yourself together.'

There was no other way. She was carrying his child. He would make sure no death occurred while he had control. And for the moment he had. But they were finished.

South of Lyon, a coppice of tall pipes speared into the air, blazing flames of gas burning at their tips against a dark underbelly of cloud. The tips of flame rippled like flags of victory against the world of darkness. She noticed him look at it yet watch every foot of the road. The zone the chimneys covered was immense. Her head turned to stay with them as he drove by. The rhythm of their waving flame-tips calmed her.

At the night-stop hotel, placed between the main road and a railway line, their room was only a few steps away from the dining-room, a bungalow sort of settlement which, he said, would have to do because you were forced to put up with what you got while on the road. She hoped he wouldn't refer to her fit of rage that day, but he said: 'I don't particularly mind when you try to kill me, but I object to you wanting to do yourself in, not to mention the child you're going to have.'

She stopped herself, by an effort as violent as when she had lunged at his hand on the steering wheel, from saying she was sorry about everything. Couldn't help myself. Don't know what got me going. Never.

He stood in his underpants to shave, face hidden from her, thinking that what he had said was the end of the matter.

'Life's not real any more,' she said.

He laughed. 'Isn't it, by God? It's real enough for me. You sometimes make it too bloody real for words, I'll say that for you. Not that I want to talk about it, though not to do so would be worse for me than for you, so I suppose I have to.'

She felt exultant at his admission, petty as it was, sly as all get-out, and did not regret anything she had done or said. His eyes, when he turned, were troubled by a fire in the void behind them, which was more intense and painful than he would admit even to himself. Thus he could only smile, fresh-faced and smooth, a cut below the ear from which blood oozed. The smile was a shadow of his acquiescence to whatever demands she'd make, and he clearly expected many. Whether or not he guessed anything specific about them was unimportant, his expression said – which made her run to him and hold him.

Weeping with relief, she drew the flat of her hand over the rough hair of his chest. Every day ended in victory, when it had not seemed possible, when it had seemed that even defeat would be denied. Life might not be real, but the fight was, and so was the happiness she felt that came after it.

12

He cruised north-west along the motorway at between sixty and seventy knots. They had left the south, what little had been seen of sea and luxury-green. She was not saying farewell for long. The hills were bare and gentle, and to get north did not seem so imperative. They were behind a high, broad-wheeled safari sort of wagon laden inside and out with bedrolls, jerrycans and canvas bags. Tom kept at the regulation distance. The vehicle looked dependable for all terrain, an All-Europe construction heavy with purpose, yet capable of speed. It must shine well in advertisements and glossy brochures. She asked if he wouldn't like that sort of thing, assuming that part of his character was similar to its virtues.

He nodded. 'Maybe. I'm not sure. But I've often thought of driving through Turkey, Persia and Afghanistan to India, so it would do, certainly, though I read that there's now a paved road all the way from Calais to Katmandu. An ordinary car like this would be good enough.'

'If you go on that kind of journey,' she said, 'I'll come with you. Sounds just the kind of trip for us.'

He laughed. 'As long as you promised to behave!'

They watched the safari wagon move briskly, almost brusquely out, and increase speed so as to overtake a saloon car that appeared to be dawdling by comparison. Tom looked in his mirror. 'Maybe I'll overtake as well, for a change of view.'

'OK to go,' she said.

He swung to the outer lane.

She felt a twinge of worry. The heavy safari car swerved, skidding as they followed. Had the driver fainted? Had a heart attack? It weaved ponderously across the motorway, smoke pluming from the rear wheels and filling their own car with the smell of hot rubber and scorching bakelite, plastic and tin.

He braked slightly, some of his tension transferring to her. She was too fixed by her stare to speak. Bits were breaking off the wagon, now to their right-front, and a car steaming up close behind seemed about to come through his rear mirror. Her feet treddled as if she also could slow the car.

The height of the safari wagon diminished, its body nearer the tarmac, while pieces from around the back wheels were spat up and away by the force of rims hitting the ground. The wheels appeared to be disintegrating, as on a stricken aircraft that had touched the runway too fast.

The only safety lay in speed. He knew it instinctively. Pam was fascinated, no fear possible. She watched the falling to pieces of the car, the helplessness of the man at the wheel as his vehicle hit the side of the road and was carried back towards the centre, then again to the side and in a more or less straight line as their own car with a few inches of gap shot by and suddenly had the whole motorway to itself.

Tom slowed when it was safe, seeing the damaged car stopped on the hard shoulder behind. 'It was a close call,' he said, 'but I think they're all right.' He set hazard lights going. 'I'd better have a look, though' – and backed a few hundred yards to get close.

The driver was laughing. Tom might have been, he supposed, in a similar plight. Not much else to do. The man's face was pallid, his one concession to fear. He knew he'd been breathed on by death, so was letting his wind out by noise. He bellowed, amused at his own luck.

Two children and a woman were silent inside, as if blaming him for what happened. If he had been gibbering with guilt and hopelessness they wouldn't have been so ready to blame. He treated the collapse as a bit of a lark, unwilling to get down and pray thanks for his deliverance. But he couldn't do that because maybe he'd forgotten how.

Perhaps he had been driving the car too roughly for its own

good, Tom said, when he had been told there was nothing to be done. The man didn't want anyone to share the harvest of his downfall. Since it had happened, he would relish this crack-up. It would be his and his alone, an experience that, dangerous though it may have been, and (perhaps fortunately) rare enough in one's life, was not to be divided with anyone, or diminished by an offer of help, which could not alter the fact that he was stranded on the French motorway miles from anywhere, after his car-marvel of automobile technology had so undeniably packed up on him.

Tom read this and more into his face, and thought he wasn't far wrong. The man thanked him for the offer of help, and motioned him away, not wanting any other being to come between him and the breakdown gang or the one-way alley to the knackers' yard. It was understandable, yet childish; and while Tom thought he really ought to consider his wife and children (though perhaps they weren't his – who was to say? If they were they had every right to be far more angry), the man held up his other hand and waved a sheaf of insurance papers which, to judge from the wide grin, would bring all the necessary assistance, and pay for it, and put them into the best hotel while his wagon was repaired or replaced, or transport of the plushiest category was provided to get them home. He had no problems – but thank you very much.

Which was all very well, but there was a risk of explosion and fire from leaking petrol. It was a hot day. Tom explained, in spite of the man's grinning vociferations turning into anger, and opened the doors gently to get the passengers out. They climbed the barrier off the hard shoulder and walked fifty yards up the slope. The driver, clutching his papers, thanked him very much, and went to find a telephone.

When he saw a breakdown car already on its way to the stricken landboat Tom drove on. 'What I would like,' Pam said, 'is to get off at the next exit, and go up to the Channel in a leisurely way on ordinary roads.'

'All right.'

'Do you mind?' She sensed danger, especially in speed, and on the motorway. The needle rarely showed less than eighty. Her hands shook. The wreck of the safari-wagon had been a little too close.

He grimaced, as if he did mind. I do and I don't, his expression said. 'The motorway ends in a few miles, in any case. One day I expect it'll go right to the Channel. Maybe even under it in three hundred years.'

He liked the thrusting forward along the great wide road that would get him quickly back to the English water. On the other hand she was right: it would be more interesting from the point of view of scenery and navigation to go slowly along minor roads, forgetting any notion of time or a schedule for reaching home. As long as they were pointing generally north nothing else mattered, though the course would be modified from time to time. 'We'll go north-west for a while, and get into the valley of the Loire, then head through the beautiful belly of France and curve around Paris to the west. Schlieffen in reverse. We'll zig-zag through Normandy, and cross from Dieppe.' If the car came to pieces on a Route Nationale, and there was no knowing that it might not let them down, they would find a couple of days extra added to their time. Speed not only killed, it wore the car out, and that was worse, he jested, telling himself that a rear-tyre blow-out at seventy could mean coffins for them both. Off the main roads there seemed less chance. But he was going to miss the excitement of the solo cavalry charge along the broad road, the tension of high speed and the hazard of so many overtakings a minute.

When he drove at such a rate he was hard to talk to. She felt the intensity of his concentration and didn't want to break it. On an ordinary road he would go slowly and they could talk. It would be more human. Also, she said, it'll be much cheaper not having to pay tolls every hundred kilometres. Well, he replied, so it will. But there'll be an extra night or two on the road, though that should be a pleasure for us both.

The green and wooded hills rolled into a central French

fairyland of châteaux and self-contained villages. In one they stopped at an *épicerie* for food, and bought bread from next door. She left him in the car and stammered her bit of French, pointing when that failed.

They parked among chestnut trees. The place was wet and she avoided mud on stepping out. The air was dank, and she reached into the back for a sweater. Tom primed the stove and made tea on the blue flame. She pulled the long bread apart with her fingers and forced Camembert in between. 'This is the best of being on the road. I feel like a tramp. Nothing in life matters, because I've got nowhere to go, and there's nowhere for the moment I want to go. I certainly never thought this feeling was part of me.'

Could he still love such a person? Wouldn't much matter. Couldn't matter. She loved him in so far as it didn't interfere with her being herself and doing whatever she wanted to do. Travelling not only broadened the mind, as it was said, but opened it where all had been closed before. If somebody loved you, and she believed him when he said he did, they loved you in spite of you being yourself. They saw something more mysterious than yourself to be in love with. She felt the same with regard to him. There was an equality in a relationship that cemented them in spite of all surface imperfections, of which she sensed there were many.

He was busy, and didn't care what she thought. Even when her speculations were spoken aloud he did not seem to concede their importance.

She felt less sleepy after food and tea. 'Tell me if anything's coming. I'm going behind that bush.'

He repacked the stove, then himself went to piss.

She said: 'When we set off, I want to do some driving.'

He gave her the keys.

She began slowly, going barely thirty miles an hour. The road was curving, undulating, and in places narrow. He sat with the map on his knees, and she felt that every mile seemed like ten to him. 'You don't need to worry. I've driven ever

535

since George got his first car. Not all that often, because he never liked me using his precious possessions, but I can drive all right.'

At this rate, she saw him thinking, we'll be a week on the road before landing anywhere. 'I can look at the scenery for a change,' he said.

'Well, do it, then.'

But he observed the road as if he were still driving. He'll get used to it, she thought. He worked out every gear-change and brake tread, looked in the (for him) non-existent rear mirror whenever she needed to move out and get by stationary cars in a village. At junctions and crossroads he looked to see if it was clear.

'I'm not nervous at all,' she said, 'and I'm the one who should be. So don't you be.'

He laughed. 'You caught me out.'

'Hard not to.'

It began to rain. 'Which switch works the wipers?'

He reached across. 'That one.'

'Thought so.' A few miles further on she said: 'Where do we stay tonight?'

'Wherever we land. Most places have a hotel of sorts, and I expect they're pretty much the same.'

So they could drift. Just as well, at the rate I'm going. It was more interesting, and in a way more relaxing, to drive instead of twiddling your thumbs as a passenger in the cabbage seat. 'You just tell me when you've had enough,' she said. 'Then we can find a place to eat and sleep.' A car coming from the opposite direction flashed its headlights. 'What was that for?'

'Well,' he said, 'he's either warning you to slow down because there's a police speed trap ahead, though I don't think that can be the reason, or you're just a shade too far to the middle of the road.'

'You're so bloody diplomatic.'

'It's my nature.'

'Just as well.' On a straight piece she increased to fifty and overtook a 2CV van. He tried to count the trees as they went by, but they rippled along his vision like a washboard. The *chaussée* was certainly *déformé*, but she seemed not to have noticed. Or it didn't matter.

At seven o'clock she drove into the square of a large village. The blonde middle-aged landlady of the Hôtel des Charmettes showed them street-floor accommodation across from the hotel. All other rooms were taken. He went back to fill in the passport form. They walked before dinner, sharing an umbrella along streets of grey houses that were mostly shuttered and seemingly minus inhabitants, despite the Michelin's claim that the village had eight hundred. She liked the clean air and occasional touches of rain when a corner was turned. 'It's marvellous to be in such a place,' she said, 'and know we'll be gone in the morning.'

A mildewed statue to a local philosopher of the last century glowed with the sheen of sunlight between showers. 'I've turned you into a sailor,' he said.

'I always was one, perhaps. And maybe you always weren't.'

'I think I'm tired of continually wondering what I was, and trying to find out who I am. I don't think it much signifies. I don't know, and don't want to know. Or I know, and don't care. Whatever happens will happen, and that's all that matters.'

Each word was an ache to his spirit. Confusion was never far below the surface, and he couldn't stop indications of it breaking through. To that extent she had ruined him, or humanized him, though the turmoil would have been there no matter what childhood he had gone through, or what life he had led. Whatever he wanted he hadn't yet found, and she suspected he knew very well but wasn't capable of discussing it. He was lost, more lost than she had ever been. His tightrope of despair underfoot had turned into a razor-blade. He did not want to speak because he felt that changes were coming over which he would have no control, and that whether good

537

or bad came from them they would be better by far than the perilous uncertainties that embroiled him.

But it was nothing to do with her. The fact that she was close would not make things easier for him. He knew it also. Love should be made to support only so much. She knew what she wanted, and it was up to him to know what he wanted. She wanted not to want, and at times felt close to that state. He wanted to want, and was nearer than he imagined. In a way it made some kind of harmony out of the chaos, a space at the centre of the storm in which she could stay calm. If she could thus be at rest she would be able to help him, and to that extent love could go a little way towards their support.

They got into the soft double bed at eleven and kissed goodnight, turning away into separate sleep. Every day generated absolute exhaustion. It wasn't possible for the bones to be more tired, softened and ready to melt. But sleep fought away from such a body. Traffic went by outside, beyond the narrow pavement. The worst was the motorbikes which, though rare, cut the silence like an enormous saw. Someone upstairs finally dropped his second boot and got into bed.

The ceiling was made of paper, and when she heard him pick his boots up there was light at the window and she realized it must be dawn. Dreams, though unremembered, still weighed heavily, so she snuggled against Tom in the soft cave of the bedclothes until nine o'clock, when he moved away and got up.

They crossed the road for breakfast. She felt a sharp pain in the middle of her back, unable to take close to a full breath, or make a complete yawn which it seemed vital to do, giving her a tense expression that Tom remarked on as she poured the coffee.

'The bed was damp,' he said. 'Steamy, in fact. Maybe you'll feel better when we're on the road.'

The old cure-all, she hoped. She was hungry, which was a good sign. When she managed to get a full breath she expressed gratitude at being alive.

13

They packed, paid, and set off, Pam at the steering wheel. The road twisted through lush country, and after a few miles she came up to a gaggle of lorries impossible to overtake. She resigned herself to the trundle, holding back from the one in front while Tom stared at the countryside. A long stretch of road was needed to overtake, but when there seemed sufficient, vehicles were always coming the other way. There was nothing to do, he said, except sweat it out. Only a lunatic would try to shoot by. According to the map there would be some dual carriageway in twenty miles. And the land would get flatter by the river.

The ache in her back was as if a large pin had stuck there which only let her take a full breath if she began slowly and hid her intention of breathing at all. Before she could succeed in her purpose she would often come full-stop against a barrier of pain and anxiety that forced a retreat back into shallow breathing. She would try again, using the same tactics, and when a full breath came the relief felt like victory indeed.

The road was empty from the opposite direction, but other cars out of the queue behind were already racing by. She wanted to stop driving, but it was impossible because the rheumatic pain and heavy dreams of the night goaded her on.

She also felt the tension in him when he was no longer interested in the scenery. He was impatient because she could not overtake the lorry and get on. He lit two cigarettes and passed one, but after a few puffs she left it in the ashtray. Speed was slow, but they progressed some miles, as he must have seen from the map. She only wanted to cover more of the road. Being a driver had its compensations, in that you forgot yourself. Who or what you were was of minor importance. You simply had to get ahead, and stay alive. Life was simple.

'Is it clear?'

There was nothing behind.

'Yes.'

'I'm going!'

'Now?' he urged.

It was a game with basic rules, and they were in it together. It was her throw. She came down to third gear, moved into the clear, and accelerated forward. The enormous arse-swaying lorry seemed by her side for ever, as if maintaining speed however much she increased hers.

'Bit more gas,' he said coolly.

'More gas!'

A bend was close, perhaps half a kilometre, but a hundred-mile-an-hour Citroën coming around could reduce it to nothing in a few seconds. Her indicator was already flashing for when it would be necessary to nip sharply in.

She was at the front of the lorry, then beyond it. A car from around the bend was flashing headlights as it came towards her, a jungle-monster out of the bush and dead-set for her death. The lorry behind signalled with its light, and she got safely in, swaying slightly then straightening as she took the bend.

She felt triumphant, as if she had passed a test, but decided from then on to be careful.

The lorry she had overtaken was only a foot behind her rear bumper, keeping a full battery of headlights beamed into her mirror.

'The sod! He knows it's a woman driving.' She increased speed so that he fell behind.

'At the next place,' Tom said, 'there's a *Relais Routier* eating-house where we can have a proper meal.'

The pain was acute in her chest and back ribs, but a full breath came more often, the tension relaxing as they shared a bottle of wine over lunch. She wondered whether a lorry man who came in hadn't been the driver of the one she had overtaken. 'It's good to have a co-driver to share the labours of the road,' Tom said.

'Hard to believe.' But he meant it, she knew, touching his glass with hers. 'Your turn when we set off.'

A youngish cadaverous-looking man came in clothed in black leather, probably a motorcyclist, she thought. His tall figure, pale face and staring gentian-blue eyes attracted her. He took a table by the curtains, as if he wanted to observe traffic going by, even while eating. He disturbed her, though he didn't care or even realize. The waitress took him a litre of wine, and Pam turned away, to go on with her meal.

They walked the town for an hour, stood at the ramparts by the church and looked down a steep declivity with heavily wooded banks. She saw the black-clad motorcyclist travelling along the road they had come in by.

Tom drove as if to make up for lost time, back on the cavalry charge when the road straightened, overtaking traffic as if hoping to get in front and have an empty highway to himself.

Impossible, he knew. There would always be someone ahead as long as you were in life and not death. But the striving was there which, he supposed, would never leave him.

There was no hurry, she knew. Embroiling dreams pulled her from the ever-rolling road, the motorized dragon-roar of traffic passing from the opposite direction, and high flat clouds over the riverine landscape. She went willingly to sleep, giving herself to a change from the eternal sound and motion of travel. George, pursuing and ranting, followed into her dreams. She was glad to wake when the map fell from her knees, and was happy to see Tom's face. 'Was I dozing long?'

'Half an hour.' She glimpsed his profile as he concentrated on his work. She wanted to kiss him, but to do so might smash them to pieces, and bring their return more quickly to the kind of end they would never hope for. He felt her scrutiny. 'How are you feeling?'

'The aches and pains have nearly gone.'

He smiled. It was easy to make him. His face, difficult to

focus, turned into George's, and she heard an unstoppable scream tear itself from her ribs. I was only wondering whether it was you and not somebody else.

The car slowed. 'What is it?'

'There was something in my eye. An insect. It's gone now.' He was troubled. Who wouldn't be? 'How far's the next place with a hotel?'

'Fifteen kilometres,' she told him.

'We've done enough today.'

They went into the town, trees along the road, people walking the pavements. They lived here, worked here, were born and would die here, most of them. She envied them. Life seemed calm. Young girls strolled with their boy-friends. There was a public square, with a newspaper kiosk and garden seats. The streets were narrow, and shops open. It was like being back in the world when he parked and they stood upright on the gravel to stretch themselves. She belonged nowhere, only to herself. Yet she belonged everywhere she came to, and to nowhere in particular, the only certainty was that she was with Tom, covering the trail of a journey without end.

The hotel was modern, their room on the fourth floor. Out of the window she saw river and country beyond immediate roofs. 'We must look like tramps coming out of the car.'

'People are used to seeing such things.'

They washed and changed.

'We'll soon feel human again,' he said.

He lay on the bed, and no sooner was his head on the pillow than he was asleep. It was still light outside, so she picked up the car keys and drew the curtains so that he wouldn't wake till dinner.

She walked across the road to the parking space and unlocked the door, wanting the basket so as to buy food for tomorrow's stint. To reach Dieppe by evening and get on the Channel ferry wouldn't leave time for a sit-down meal. Broad daylight invited her to turn on the ignition. She backed out. A hundred miles would roll before he awoke. Traffic was leaving town, and she joined it, cars behind and in front, hers anonymous and unremarkable, one of the crowd.

Rolls of cloud lay on low hills ahead. If she met Judy by the kerb of the tree-lined road she would give her a lift, providing they were going to the same destination. It was laughable to be free. The ease of driving with no one else in the car was so much greater. She could go on for ever, until coming bang up against frontier or coastline, when it would be seen that the car wasn't in her name. Even then, she might get through.

She would ride awhile and go back. She loved him too much to let him worry. He must be wakened for supper. She saw him sleeping, his exhaustion at last in repose. It was rare enough, these days. She wanted to be with him, and looked for a place to turn.

At a traffic island she went left instead of right. A car from the opposite direction smashed into her left side. Too late to avoid or beneficially stop. There was a rending of metal, a smash of windscreen and headlight, and a fearful jerk at the neck that spun her eyes into blackness.

14

By nine at night Hilary and Sam were so deadbeat that few squeaks or mumbles were still to come. They'd had their baths, been fed and sent to bed, and nothing could break the tranquillity of the hours that followed. Traffic noises diminished, and even the muted beat of the sea contributed to peace.

The security of living in Tom's flat, minus the tension of

wondering where the next tenpenny piece was coming from, made her feel more bodily worn out than she ever had. Having no worries, she decided, will be the death of me, unless I get used to it. The fight was worth making, considering, as she did, that her struggle had been sufficient to pay any debt towards sin and sloth that she might at some time have incurred.

She put her supper plate on the piano top, and set up the card-table by the fireplace. Her unease was caused by wondering when such good fortune – there was no other word for it – would end. She tried not to care. Her body and spirit wallowed in the succour that had dropped from heaven in the shape of this seaside flat and the money Tom allowed her.

The painting of the dead officer above the mantelpiece was taken down the day they came in, and stood in the hall where no one could see it. Sam had cracked the canvas by a nudge from his elbow, and a stab from the heel of his boot, on a race to the door with Hilary, injuries which distorted the pink-glo cheek and changed the angle of the gun barrel. But she joined the cracks with glue and coloured them with a child's painting set, and hoped the wanderers wouldn't notice on their return. She couldn't remember when Sam had last shed tears, and his distress at the damage to what she considered to be the vilest bit of painting she'd ever seen almost brought tears to her own eyes.

She cooked at midday so as to have an easy time in the evening, when she fixed a cold supper of bread and cheese, and made a pot of black coffee in the fancy alchemical percolator of Tom's old aunt. The kids had a dinner at school, and more or less looked after themselves, but she gave them breakfast and kept the flat in order, and spent any spare hours reading her way through shelves of novels by Trollope and George Eliot. Time passed, but the golden days would end, because Pam had phoned a few days ago to say they were on their way home. She expected them any moment, and then where would she be?

544

She sipped scalding coffee between bites of sandwich, trying to decide who she was in love with. The absence of Tom and Pam emphasized the isolated unreality of her feelings, which she hoped wouldn't be altogether denied when they got back. She had been surprised by the realization that there had to be a man as well as a woman in her life. Perhaps such deficient people as myself, she thought, need both, but if so I don't mind being in that category, especially if it leads me to become less deficient.

She was consoled by the fact that she could admit the truth at last. To indulge in dreams was a cure for exhaustion, a necessary exercise because at the moment there was neither man nor woman to comfort her. Perhaps there never would be again. They'd surely be too involved with each other to give any attention when they got back, especially now a baby was in the offing, but at least she would have passed time in that twilight aura of knowing there was one way which would allow her to live fully. And anything better than nothing was as good as having everything. If her hope to be with both of them turned out to be no more than her favourite fantasy, the knowledge of her possibilities would remain, and perhaps lead to a resolution of some kind.

After the children got into bed she changed to wearing one of the long skirts and high-necked blouses from the cupboard where Tom's aunt had stored them. Slacks and sweater were slopped around in during the day, or put on to go out shopping. If it was chilly she donned Tom's Merchant Navy overcoat, which seemed to be fashionable among the young these days. But for evenings she needed to feel different, hoping to reach part of herself long since forgotten.

She walked the room, and poured a glass of brandy. The telephone sounded, but she let it ring. Poured into coffee, the brandy warmed her. Most likely it was a wrong number, or a heavy-breather wanting his night's sport. There had been such cases lately. She sat in the armchair with legs resting on a stool. If the noise went on for a long time she had enough will

545

to last it into silence.

One had to know the basis of one's relationship to love before connecting properly to life. Most people had the facility, she thought, because they reached the extent of their capacity early on, or imagined they did, which was the same thing. A proper existence must be founded on a correct appreciation of the half-hidden love that inevitably surfaced, and she knew that she had been in the presence of an enduring lustful affection which she called love ever since meeting Tom, and from the moment Pam had walked into her room one day out of the rain. It was an event of the lost meeting the lost, and feeling a sense of fulfilment as soon as they were in each other's presence, or arms.

She remembered that they had needed cornflakes and butter for the larder, so went into the kitchen to scribble on the shopping-list before she forgot. The vital pushed out the banal. To bring food into the flat was at least as important as her thoughts, though she'd never known a time when space hadn't been found for both.

The ringing stopped. She refilled her glass, the last drink before going to bed. Sleep would encircle her, like a ring of flame never to be broken out of. She would not take pills, though scores of boxes were in the bathroom cabinet. Most nights she lay with a book, sipped her drink and read till she fell asleep with the light on, and Sam woke her at half-past seven with a cup of tea. She would then get up and make breakfast, foul-tempered and zombie-like in her movements. Established in their new school, they went happily out at half-past eight, but not before looking downstairs for postcards from Tom and Pam. They had run back up with a few to show. He had written and told them to find the places on the map, like the good father he ought to have been.

She would not leave when they got back. They would surely fit into the scheme of the flat. Not wanting to be idle and live off anyone, she would look for a job, only wanting to stay with them, and know that life was settled for a while.

Such effrontery made her laugh. She called herself a fool, yet saw no reason not to indulge in such expectations. In the morning she would be her old self as she shouted at the kids to make sure they were clean before going to school. The raw day was a good cure-all. We are made up of dreams that can't be real. Anything that becomes real was never a dream, but a hard-headed idea. Dreams were gorgeous, nonetheless. When the telephone sounded again she snapped off the receiver even before the second ring, her fingers ready to press out any obscenity:

'Hello?'

'Judy?'

The horror was that her husband had found the number, and was trying to get back with her. He had lost his job, flat, dolly-bird and car, and was on the streets with nowhere to go, and nothing more than the rags he stood in.

'This is Tom.'

She laughed. They were at Newhaven, and would be here in half an hour. There would be no sleep that night. They would drink and talk till dawn about their adventures.

'Tom! You sound half-dead.' He must have whacked himself by driving day and night.

'Listen, Judy . . .'

'I'm hearing you. Where from, though?'

'In the middle of France.'

'That's a fine place to be!'

'I have to tell you about Pam.'

'What the hell do you mean?'

'Bad news, I'm sorry to say. Where were you all evening? I couldn't get through.'

'I was in the bath, I suppose.' She must have found she's not pregnant after all. 'What news? Tell me, for God's sake!'

She pressed a hand across her breasts, undoing a button of her blouse and fastening it while he tried to speak.

'She had a smash in the car.'

'Oh no!'

'She went for a drive on her own. But I do feel *dead*. You're right.'

She broke in. 'How is she?' – thinking that the bloody fool had got her killed.

'Neither of us are, though.' He tried to laugh. He was putting a good face on it – the bastard.

She couldn't hear what he said. 'Speak louder.'

'She took the car, and had an accident.' The pause lasted years. I'll go grey twice over. But she wasn't dead, or he would have said it as the first item on his official report.

'What happened, then? How is she?'

'She'll be all right – in a while.'

'What do you mean "All bloody right"?'

'We thought she had broken her neck. She's badly bruised. A few cuts. The baby will be all right. We won't be back for a while. There's a lot to say. I have to square the police.'

'Don't say that. They may be listening.'

She thought he laughed. 'It's nothing like that. Just a bit of form-filling.'

'Thank God.'

'I saw her tonight. She's in the clinic here. She sends her love.'

'What place are you at? Tell me, and I'll come down. The kids can stay here. They're very good at looking after themselves.'

'Bless them!' he said.

He sounded drunk. Must have been at that flask again. Tears came to her eyes, but she clamped them back. 'I'll get to where you are by tomorrow evening.'

'It's all right. But thank you. If there's any need I'll phone you. I'll phone tomorrow, in any case.'

She couldn't talk. Neither could he. Then she said: 'Give Pam my love. And my love to you as well.'

'We'll be all right. Keep well.'

'I love you both.'

'I must hang up now,' he said.

She put the phone down. Goodbye, you poor stupid kids without me to put in a harsh word. You don't need Judy, either, do you? But what have you been up to? Wait till I get my hands on you. They don't know how to look after themselves, because they have no idea what real love is all about.

Her drink unfinished, she went to bed without a book, and slept – though not before wondering whether to tell the kids when she woke up in the morning. But they were too grown up not to be told.

15

The smash had come from pink dust and white lights. She would tell Judy when she saw her that the explosion had shaken every molecule of her bones. The explanation ran through her mind while they stood silent on the platform waiting for the quick train to Paris. Tom paced up and down, but always came back in case she needed anything or wanted to speak.

Not even time to jam the brakes on, she would say, by then perhaps able to laugh about it. Why did I turn left on the roundabout, instead of right? The old subconscious was dead-set on my assassination, she supposed. Good to know it wasn't as all-powerful as she had often given it credit for, since the plot or impulse had clearly failed.

The other driver was a woman, and neither had she put her brakes on. All happened too quickly. Good job she had been a woman, and hadn't hurt herself. More helpful than angry she was, a schoolteacher on her way home, young but with a severe face, dark hair pulled back to show the shape of her skull, features I'll never forget, but most likely won't see again, though Tom in his appreciation left our address so that she could stay in England any time. He was always quick with the generous thought when someone did a favour, especially if it was for me. A wonder he didn't have an affair with her while I was in hospital, but he couldn't because he spent nearly every hour at my bedside.

I blubbered at the trouble I'd caused, but he laughed, and said it didn't matter as long as I was all right, and I was, because everything turned out even more superficial than they had thought. 'I got both of us, and the car,' he said, 'insured to the limit before we left, so the motor club can bring the car back when it's fixed, and we'll have a leisurely return by train and boat.'

The schoolteacher came to see me in the clinic, and brought flowers, as well as a get-well card from some of her pupils. I could have fallen for her myself with her English as good as mine, and probably more correct in its grammar. She was very charming – and generous. Tom took her to dinner one night, and I was glad, otherwise he would have drifted around the town like a lost soul, as if he'd just come off one of his old ships, or stayed in the hotel room supping on his bottomless whisky flask.

Why I turned left instead of right I'll never know. I was happy and unthinking, a wrong state of mind because how can you be responsible if you are so stupidly relaxed? You have to pay for the air you breathe by being vigilant all the time, no matter how wearing. In the flash and crunch that followed I was in despair because he would think I had taken the car to do myself in, or get myself an injury so that I'd be in hospital for months and not have to worry about anything. Then he would wash his hands of me because I'd tried a silly stunt once too often. He'll leave me high and dry, I thought when I was collapsed like a piece of regulation jelly outside the car, and then what will I be able to do except make my own way back and cry on your bosom for the rest of my life?

But when I told him it was no more than an accident, he believed me absolutely, a man of trust who takes things as they come, without panic or reproach.

16

The early train to Paris ran smoothly, and it was hard to believe that by midnight they would be home, except that the speed told them so and would not be gainsaid. The weeks had been difficult for him, and he must have fought his way through a few hard facts while she lay in the clinic. He sat opposite, looking at the pictures in *Paris-Match*.

'Did you think of leaving me?'

She used to imagine abandoning George every morning, though only considered it now and again with Tom, a game which, she knew, must sooner or later be given up.

He rested the magazine on his knee. 'I feel we've been married for decades, so why should I?'

She laughed. 'What a load for you to bear, poor thing!'

He had carried bigger ones. 'My shoulders are fairly broad.'

'Well, why don't you leave me?'

'You want problems?' he said. 'Be careful. They only bring others, often worse.'

She felt light-spirited. 'How can you be sure?'

He had read somewhere (though who needed to read it?) that a man without a woman was not a human being. There was equal truth in saying that a woman without a man was not a human being, either. He held her hand, and told her so.

'I'll never leave you. If ever you want us to separate, you'll have to be the one to do it.'

He's a sharer, she thought, all open and above board, who imagines that to pay for one's mistakes is merely showing a sense of responsibility. 'Why put everything on my shoulders?'

He leaned back in his seat. 'I don't believe in that kind of self-sacrifice.'

She kissed him. 'Don't worry. I won't go through that again. I don't want to leave you. Nor do I want you to leave me.'

'Why talk about it?' He rolled his magazine into a baton and tapped the window, as if testing its strength, she thought, before hitting me over the head.

'I talk about anything,' she said. 'I wondered how you felt.'

'Now you know, my love.'

The seat was empty, so she sat by his side and caressed his face. 'I do.'

'Does it make you feel better?'

'Even happier.'

'So while you're happy, I'll tell you, once and for all, not to do anything like that again.'

'The third time will be final,' she said, 'but I hope I'll be ninety years old by then.'

'God might have a thing or two to say about that.'

A provision trolley stopped at the door, and he bought two large oranges. She sat back in her place, bones still aching from the bruises. 'Do you believe in God, then?'

'Certainly. The fact that I'm a Jew might have something to do with it.'

'Is your God like the captain of a ship, steering the big world from the bridge?'

He took out his penknife, cut two circles in the top and bottom of the first orange, then scored the sides. 'He's nameless, faceless, and formless. That's how I think of Him. But He has His people, and His people, though scattered over the world, have their country.' He pulled off the segments of skin, and took the fruit neatly to pieces before passing them to her.

'In many ways,' she said, 'I don't feel I have a country any more.' Her mouth was momentarily full before she squeezed the delicious fruit into juice and felt it pour in and revitalize her. 'I don't know why, but I seem to have lost it. You and I, and Judy and the kids together – maybe we're our own country.'

He dissected an orange for himself. 'I have two countries,' he said, 'if I want them – England and Israel. And my country is your country. That's how I feel. Every Jew has the automatic right of return to Israel – and that means me. I'm lucky to have two such places, which both have great merits. If they joined forces they'd make an unbeatable combination. The two peoples Hitler hated most in the world, so I read in one of my potted history books, were the British and the Jews.'

He took some Kleenex to the toilet and dampened them so that they could wipe their hands. When he came back she said: 'You seem to have been thinking while I lay in my bed of pain!'

'The only time I'm not is when we're making love, which I suppose is a fairly normal state of affairs. One day we'll go to Israel, and you'll see what your other choice of country would be like.'

She gazed out of the window at suburban houses. The future, as always, was impossible to handle. Thinking about it never brought anything but trouble. At least it hadn't so far. But she said: 'Maybe I'd like that.'

'I'd expect you to think about it.' He joined her gaze out of the window. 'We'll soon be in. We'll get a taxi to the Gare St Lazare, and snatch something to eat before setting out for Dieppe.'

'We ought to be home by ten,' she said.

Because the sea would be rough he obtained a cabin for her before the ship sailed. She was glad, for her back was sore and she wanted to lie down, fearful of going home now that they were so near, but excited at the idea of seeing Judy, and staying in one place for a while. Tom sat by her, as if afraid she might get up if he didn't keep guard, and go on deck to throw herself overboard. Simple man who was too good for her. She only wanted to sleep an hour or two. 'I'll be all right. You go up and walk around the deck.'

He stood by the open window of the radio officer's cabin listening to the singing of the morse, but from thinking of Paul and his outlandish theories of British Israelitism he retreated into his own musings. The squall cut visibility, and the old unsteady rolling of the boat put the familiar strain back into his legs. He was a blind man at sea – *l'homme qui rit* – wanting to find a way off the eyeless ocean to a land he could feel was his for eternity – even if only to be buried there. Nothing had been his since being carried in his cradle to the orphanage, not school, ship, furnished room or the flat of his Aunt Clara, not motor-car nor even the deck or ground he stood on. His shoes burned and would not let him be still.

Cold water beckoned, but he spat into the lee of it, walked the length of the deck and back. Figures huddled on seats were covered by capes and raincoats to get away from the stench of frying and cigar smoke where they would assuredly have been sick. He stood at the rail to be alone, the sea in front, no ships visible. Life seemed endless. Only a happy man would see an end, and he hadn't yet found an existence which took happiness into account. After the age of fifty something happens. Time regains its meaning. When one was young, he thought, time also had significance, with the difference that most of one's years were still to come, whereas two-thirds were now behind.

With little time left, it must be treated with a new respect. There was less to waste, and far more to do before none remained. Yet one still can't act – know or not what you want to do. One could create a positive end, but the ensuing blackness and silence is the final rebellion against God, and suicide the last rebellion against yourself, the vilest form of murder and no more to be thought about, a passing reflection as he turned and laughed so loudly into the wind that one of the huddled figures stirred and a pretty young woman with a face made tragic by the motion of the boat looked at him crossly for disturbing her. He resumed his pacing, smiling at the notion that even the long fart he gave sounded like a cry for help, and knowing that the only course to follow was to endure till a landfall came that he and Pam would somehow make together.

Before the boat docked he found a steward to take tea and biscuits to Pam's cabin. She had undressed, and was resting between the sheets. The rough bumping of the sea had made her drowsy, did not let her sleep but scraped continually at the cabin to the rise and fall under her bunk, more soporific than the train, keeping nerves on edge while relaxing her limbs. In her waking dreams she seemed deep under the sea. The capsule she lay in was at the whim of unseen currents. She couldn't imagine being in a normally lighted room, with the floor unmoving and no other noise than laughing and talking, with Judy and the kids. If the sea came in she would be glad, yet use her last strength to stay alive.

She was surprised at being left alone for nearly three hours. He couldn't desert her on board ship. Where would he go, even if he wanted to? They were in it together, and would stay that way. Her belly was taut, increasing in size. Was the baby swimming in its own inland sea? There was no future while it was, but she didn't doubt that it would start one day. Would all hell be again let loose? She had no option but to wait and see, and endure, until the future, with a great cry, turned into the present, which would, she supposed, cry even louder.

The cabin was hot, and after her tea had been put down she got out of bed and stood up. He knocked and came in, wearing his heavy gaberdine raincoat, and cap which he took off. 'We'll be in in a few minutes. Newhaven's ahead.'

'I don't feel the same person going back as I did when we

left.' She pulled on her dress. The only way he could respond was to go up for air and light, and watch the ship sliding into harbour while he laughed into the wind.

17

Judy didn't like living off a man, and told the bastard so in no uncertain terms. Certainty of meaning in such cases was a letting go of the self, and she had, she decided in that floating ecstatic moment before speech, as much right to it as anyone else. But her voice was not too loud, nor her terms so brash as the throbbing in her veins had led even her to expect. 'I shall be leaving as soon as I can get something fixed up that won't let the kids down too badly.'

Tom was no fool. Nobody thought so, himself least of all. Let the sky come down, but he would not raise his voice beyond the normal pitch to meet any onrush. 'All right,' he said, 'but listen to me. I'll talk to you as to a woman. Or a man, if that's what you want. Or any other being you care to imagine yourself if you'll just tell me what it is. Whoever and whatever you like.'

If a woman (or anyone) slammed into him he slammed straight back. No messing. It was the stiff-necked part of him you could always reckon on coming into operation when you least expected it. Judy had had enough, though, Judy had, she told herself, and Judy – thought Judy – would sling her bloody hook no matter how deep in anybody's back it was buried. But there was no stopping him, until such time as she got up and walked. For some reason or other she couldn't, and meanwhile he went on:

556

'I'll tell you, what's more' – he tapped a two-fingered rhythm on the piano top to mark off and emphasize each phrase – 'that the money you're too scared or too proud, or too mean (let's face it) to share with us, isn't mine, and never was. It came from my family – if you can call it one – by no other route except that of accident. That was the only way it got to me – and therefore to us.'

Fed up with such confrontations, Pam would have told her to go if she wanted, though knew she would be out-voted on the matter. But there was more to the clash than mere argument suggested. There always was. Whoever loved each other could do so from a distance, for all she cared. She wondered whether Judy hadn't wanted Tom to respond in exactly the way he was doing. A person like Judy didn't know anyone until she had made them angry, though it had to be admitted that she was sincere in all her principles, and fervent in any sacrifice she would make for them.

Judy needed an emotional base, however, and once it was found she considered it too good to relinquish easily, as Pam gathered from their conversations in the darkness of the bed they had twice shared since coming back. Judy had discovered ease not in material things, which to her were dispensable, but in the security of communal friendship not before experienced. The seeds of trust had slipped into her and taken root, but the rougher part of herself that sometimes demanded change threatened her with havoc.

While it was reassuring to know that everyone was a battleground, the consequence when those battlegrounds came into contact with each other could be anything but pleasant. Yet she saw the justice of Judy's case. Judy wanted formal and open avowals that she and her children could stay, to be cemented by anger as much as with friendship and love, enabling her to agree before both Tom and Pam as witnesses, so that from then on she would not be tempted to thoughtlessly leave. Any arrangements half-defined, or allowances given on sufferance, or terms made plain yet not specifically numbered, were no good to her. It was too English a method – too, in a way, oriental. Only the rich could live by it, but in the present case an unspoken agreement to hang on as long as you liked suited no one, certainly not Judy, and Pam saw immediately that she was right. It must be roughed out (in anger if need be), drawn up, ratified, and thoroughly understood.

Pam loved him for falling for such tactics, or for falling in with them, which was more likely, as he continued: 'And the money's now in my name, but don't let that gall you. We can do something about that – since the notion clearly does.'

Judy played the game her way, while he made the moves his, and Pam marvelled how neatly the methods dovetailed when they met. She coloured at his deviousness, and at Judy's, and at her own when an occasional small contribution came into effect. Either that, or they all had a well-developed talent for self-preservation in the midst of an incipient chaos.

Then another truth came to her, the one that said he would promise anything to Judy because he knew, she thought, that as long as she stayed so would I. This made her feel trapped, and also angry, but it was a trap she herself had engineered, every twig, leaf and piece of bait. She had deliberately made it, walked into it willingly, and feathered it almost without knowing. Now she was to give birth in it. What had she left the old one for? The question was as unnecessary as it was for her to say that she liked it here.

'As far as possible,' Tom said, 'I'm trying to make out that we own the wealth – if that's what it is – in common. I don't really know how far back it goes, and don't much care, because I have no guilt feelings whatsover about using it to our advantage. My grandfather accumulated property. He bought stocks and shares. Maybe he owned half a coal-mine, and inherited a few miles of some branch-line railway. It could be that he even sweated the proletariat in sundry mills and slate quarries, as your former husband might have put it. But now the residue is ours. Ours, not mine, and if you don't want any advantage from the money, that's your decision. But if you take your children back to anything like the life you were living in West Eleven, then you'll be far more immoral than staying here and living off money you think is tainted because it supposedly belongs to a man.'

His face had reddened. It was not in his nature to justify himself, neither to man nor woman, especially at such length. But it was part of him to be just, and he suppressed much of his anger lest it lead to a state where he could not be so.

Judy's shrug was a milder reaction than Pam expected from someone of her views. But there was more to her response than the glimpse of a protected existence for her and the children. The picture of her leaving was desolation indeed to Pam, who knew it had always been possible to wake up one morning and find her packing before final quittance. Now it wouldn't be, mainly because the reality of her departure with the children had also been unthinkable to Tom, who had handled its prevention in such a way that everyone had thought they alone were responsible for winning the skirmish.

Later in the evening while Judy was taking a bath she said to him: 'I'll stay with her tonight. I think she needs me. Is that all right by you?'

He nodded.

18

When the baby was born Tom felt he was present at the birth of himself. Clara had described him, on his own first appearance, as having fine reddish hair matted on a fragile skull. Lips pouted and arms waved, and her small nose was like his mother's on the photograph. They called her Rachel.

He had explored the antique shops in The Lanes for a cradle befitting the status of his daughter and firstborn, but finding nothing to suit, they had gone out together and bought a utilitarian new one from a department store.

While Pam was still in the hospital he had overheard Hilary say 'Mum!'

'What?'

'Who do you love most – Pam, or Tom?'

He never heard the answer. He would have closed the door himself if she hadn't slammed it, not wishing to know, or to pick up any evasions. No one should be called upon to answer such a question, though if children asked, then you had to find one. Children see everything. They had observed him go into Judy's room a few nights ago, and though they had said nothing he knew that the question as to whom she loved most was their way of telling Judy that they weren't as blind as she might in her new life have grown to believe and hope. It had been once only, and he had gone afterwards to his own bed. But one of the children had got up to get a drink of water, he supposed, and eternal curiosity had pulled at them. He had come back from the hospital, and Judy had put supper on the table.

'How is she?'

'A real live daughter. All sound in wind and limb.'

She didn't seem joyful, or even much interested, and perhaps her mood made what followed even easier. 'Another female in the house!'

'Suits me,' he said, 'very much.'

'Eat, then,' she told him.

'And you?'

She lit a cigarette. 'I've had mine.'

But she sat close by, and when he poured wine she reached for his glass and drank. He stood up to get another glass from the cupboard, but she held his wrist firmly. 'I'll drink from yours, if you don't mind.'

He refilled it. 'I don't.'

'I haven't thanked you yet,' she said, 'have I?'

He smiled at her strange mood. What could she mean? He had taken Hilary and Sam to look at ships in Shoreham harbour, and on recognizing an old face had been able to get them on board.

'There's no convincing you, is there?' she said with a tenderness he had only seen her use with Pam.

'I'm sorry,' he said. 'But what do you think you have to thank me for?'

'That's better. You know very well what I mean.' She crushed a piece of cheese on to some bread. 'You've done such good things for me, and for the kids especially. I think you're a nice person.'

He felt pleasure at this, till he realized it couldn't be true. Then he thought he had better consider it as true enough, if only to be fair to her. 'It makes me happy to hear you say so.'

'I have to,' she said, 'for my own self-respect.'

'Oh.' He hoped she would let the matter go.

'I mean it. You're really all right.'

He couldn't resist saying: 'Even if I am a man?'

She laughed. 'We live, and sooner or later learn.'

'Yes, we certainly do that, if we try.'

'From each other,' she said, 'but not all that much from ourselves, do we?'

'You may be right.' He drank half the wine, then passed the glass back to her. She stood up unsteadily in the overlit kitchen. He had made sure there were brilliant lights all over the place, every corner vividly seen. When she or Pam put only a couple of wall-lights on he became silent and sleepy. He thought she was about to fall, so he held her closer than he had intended, softened breasts against his shirt, and wine-tasting lips pressing at him.

Afterwards she said: 'I like having a man *come* into me now and again.'

'You came as well.'

'I know. Who taught you how to do that?'

The bad dream made him sweat. He wondered how to get out of it. 'I'm glad I was able to help.'

'It's all right,' she said. 'You don't need to worry. We shan't make a habit of it, though I wouldn't need to think like this, and neither would you, if we were able to face the truth.'

He touched her full body, and stopped himself saying that he loved her. For the moment he did. But the truth was more complicated. It was like fire. You touched it at your peril. 'I can't be treacherous,' he said. He already had, and knew it, but his mark of affection proclaimed innocence, which ordinary sense told him might be possible.

She guessed his inner debate. 'It's only a way of getting to know each other.'

He smiled, wanting to agree. He did so. He stroked her breast, as if his touch was sufficient to let her know he was near to her, and to explain all she might find puzzling about him.

'Why don't you say something?' she asked.

'I was wondering whether it's possible to love two people at the same time.'

She pulled him close, and almost robbed him of breath. 'No, it isn't,' she said between her sobs, 'and don't I know it?' She was silent, and then: 'Of course it bloody well is!'

19

Pam came home from the hospital, and no longer belonged to him. He had expected her not to, he said, at such a time. It ought not to be difficult to accept, she answered, because she never had. Belonged to him, she meant. She never had belonged to anybody. He laughed. It was only a manner of speaking, of course. Perhaps so, she said, but she was her own woman and he, she didn't mind supposing, was his own man. If life was to go on, and for her part it certainly was, that's how it would be.

Love was not a matter of belonging to anyone, he mused on one of his walks by the sea, but of mutual protection whenever necessary, which must never become onerous. Dependence grew, and obligations developed. They were bound to. There was responsibility, and no freedom except what was earned by unremitting though diffident attention. He could do no more, and sensed that she didn't want him to do less, either.

She fed Rachel by the window that looked out to sea. The primal tug at her nipple was pleasant. The fine hand and warm fingers at the flesh of the breast, and the small face already so alert, made her own smile impossible to hold back. It was a smile such as no other could be.

The light calmed and fascinated Rachel, and after her first slake she would stare at any pattern that danced or dazzled. When they occasionally did not, her head turned back to resume feeding, but her eyes flickered around as if to make sure no bogyman or shadow would appear unbidden. Hilary held her finger, and Rachel took it while she fed, her hand gripping and relaxing as the milk went in.

'I don't know what you find to boggle at,' Judy remarked when Sam looked on. 'You'll never be feeding a kid, and that's for sure.'

'I know I won't.' He had passed his eleven-plus, and went to the local grammar school. Hilary would follow the same path in a year, because Tom had worked it out that way. He took Sam to the barber every month so that his hair was kept short and parted. Sam polished his shoes every morning, and his clothes were neat. Maybe it won't last, Tom thought, but let the future look after itself. Judy was amused at her son's self-absorbed industriousness, only critical of Tom's regime when Sam seemed less connected to her than in his former outspoken days. But she thought such a change would have come anyway.

'Don't sound so sorry about it,' she said to Sam, ushering them into the kitchen for their suppers. 'Then you can go to your rooms and do a bit more homework before sleep time.'

After putting Rachel to bed Pam was exhausted. 'She drains me.'

'They all do,' Judy replied. 'It never stops, one way or another.'

'I remember it from before.' She went from one end of the emotional spectrum to the other – a wicked see-saw impossible to jump from. But that's how she was, feeling no guilt about it, nor any particular wish that it would end.

'We did the same to our mothers, I expect.'

Tom was setting the table in the dining-room for their supper. The large oil painting of his Uncle John was back above the mantelshelf, but the piano had gone so as to make more space. It was the mainstay room in which they could eat, live, or study.

She fed Rachel. If she threw her out of the window would she die? I dropped her. I was looking at the view while getting some fresh air. She moved. She slipped from my hands. Terrified at the nearness of disaster, and full of love for her daughter, she shut the window with a bang, then held her gently to stop her crying. She recalled a similar urge with Edward, wanting to end it all, even then. But at least now she knew what she was doing, or what she was not going to do.

'Is this life everything?' she said to Judy the following day, when the sun shone full into the large room.

'What do you mean?'

'Well, it can't be, can it?'

Judy put her arms around her. 'You're insatiable.'

'I mean, it's just not possible.'

'What more do you want?' There was a tone of exasperation in her voice. 'You could live on your own and be a rag-picker, if you liked. Or you could do the Open University. Or you might try going into industry – whatever that means. There isn't much, unless you want to join the army, or be a stunt-rider on the Wall of Death. Of course, we could get a loan and run a boarding house, or manage a pub in Cornwall, or open a boutique like everybody else. Life's short. Options are limited. It's too early to go around the moon on a camel and write a book about it. Anyway, you've got a lovely kid, and you're in love with Tom. You're not supposed to be on this dissatisfaction kick.'

She was in the mood to say whatever she felt. 'I'm in love with you, as well.'

'I know, and that's marvellous, but don't tell me too often, because Aunt Judy's got her own sales-and-wants column roving around inside her. You'll feel better when Rachel's a year or two old. I love you as well, but it can't mean as much as your love for Tom and Rachel, and sooner or later you might have to choose between me and them.'

'There are too many damned choices.'

'So there ought to be.' Judy took a bottle of red wine from the drinks cupboard, fixed in the corkscrew, and raffishly winked at her as she pulled. 'This will help us to relax.'

'When I was with my husband,' Pam said, sipping the wine, 'and thought I could never get away from him, a story kept coming to me, repeating itself over the years. Funny how I'd forgotten it, and it suddenly springs on me again now. I must have dreamed it more than once, and the scene built itself up when I concentrated hard to pull it together. A heavy plank of wood was floating down a river in flood. At one end the husband stood, and on the other, the wife. Both wanted to get off and save themselves, either from the flood or from each other, or both. If the husband jumped first, the plank would tip and the wife would probably drown, and he didn't hate her so much that he wanted to kill her. If the wife leapt free the husband's end would go and he would drown, and she didn't despise him sufficiently to want his death. They passed the occasional sandbank or overhanging tree, when it might have been possible for one or the other to have made a grab for it. But neither could jump. And they were coming to a five-hundred-foot waterfall. Only a miracle could save them. If not – over they'd go.'

'Sounds familiar,' Judy said. 'But go on.'

'Well, during the time when the plank was floating, they could have moved to the centre and got closer to each other. They could have then discussed matters with regard to jumping together, so that both would have been saved – or at least had a chance. But the torrent made them unwilling and afraid to move. They thought the effort wasn't worthwhile, because they'd be able to jump free at any moment, and it wouldn't have been necessary to get close anyway. It was obvious they should never have shared that floating plank, no matter what they thought they were escaping from. But they had, and that was that. It was called a romantic story, which was bound to have a tragic ending. That's how the woman saw it, but she didn't tell him. How he saw it, she wasn't much interested, because he was no longer there to ask in any case. They had leapt from the plank half-way down the waterfall, neither of them thinking of the other. They had gone their separate and individual ways to death, which were more or less the same except that in every kind of distance they were very far apart. They missed the sound of the river, and the passing moments of tormenting indecision, and the noise of that fatal waterfall getting nearer and nearer. It made their life exciting, but was absolutely intolerable at the same time.'

She was silent for a while, then Judy said: 'Does all this mean you're going back to your husband, after all?'

'No. That's unthinkable. Finished. But in five years I don't want to feel like that with Tom.'

Judy refilled their glasses. 'You won't, though I understand your fears. Tom's the sort who won't let that happen. Plenty of knock-about life is in store for you yet, I'm sure.'

'But will he ever feel like that with me?'

'I don't expect so, but who knows? None of us is God.'

566

20

The choice came to Pam as a blinding revelation one night after Rachel was in her cot and Judy had gone out with the kids to the cinema. She looked over his shoulder at the Hebrew grammar and said: 'You'll never know the language properly until you go to Israel to live, and hear it spoken all around you.'

'I don't suppose I will. Yet I went into the local synagogue last week and heard it there.'

'That's liturgical. I mean as an everyday language.'

On most Friday nights a solitary candle burned on the dining-room table. The children liked it, and even Judy was tolerantly quiet. Tom wore a black cap hardly visible on the back of his head, and hurriedly murmured a prayer. He opened a bottle of wine and, to the children's delight, poured a glass for everyone. That was the extent of his Sabbath.

'Haven't you ever thought about it?' A recollection forced the question into her mind, of seeing the preacher clearly from ten years ago, in the chapel she had wandered into like a sleepwalker. She had found comfort in the strange words, and had gone back love-sick week after week to hear this unprepossessing yet mysterious man tell of the virtues of ancient and modern Israel.

Tom admitted that he had considered a visit to his second country, but so many things had happened to divert him from such an idea.

'I don't mean a visit,' she said. 'Wouldn't you like to live there? After all, your mother was Jewish, her mother was Jewish before her, and so was her mother. It would make sense, absolutely.'

He stood up and smoked a cigarette by the mantelshelf. She

looked at him: fragile, vulnerable, uncertain. From the beginning she had known all too well what he must do, and so had he, but he had chosen to deceive himself so as to let her be the one to tell him. By doing so she was being more herself than she had ever been.

She had seen him looking at maps of Israel. For a year he had read continually books on Zionism and Jewish life, and studied intensely in his spare time, but the exact place of his yearning in modern terms had seemed too remote for her to divine the answer or him to make the connection. It was amazing how distant the obvious could be. But now she knew. If she hadn't sensed his ultimate destination right from the beginning she would not have lived with him and had their child. She would not have set out with him on such a long and perhaps endless journey. As for her independence, didn't she know that a passion for it carried to excess was a sure recipe for getting nowhere?

She would initiate the change, move him. She felt herself drawn towards Israel, because he saw it as a land whose light was as yet too far away. The preacher's sermons told of how the Jews were at last able to go back to the Promised Land, and she felt that circumstances had carried her inexorably this far towards it. Events always moved you to what was most profoundly wanted. She recalled the preacher's face, and his voice, and heard again what he had said, blushing at how she had gone week after week, unbeknown to George, to sit gawping like a young girl before a pop star.

He pressed her hand. 'I don't know. I really don't know.'

But he did, and she knew that he did. He always had known. She had surprised him again. She surprised herself. She loved him because it was possible, and always would be possible, to surprise him. People went to Israel for holidays much as they did to Majorca or Italy, she said. The place isn't so remote any more, nor so strange, she supposed, unless you were like me who happens to be madly in love with someone who has a birthright connection with it.

568

It's part of my life to go there, she thought, to a country like any other, yet a place that nowhere else can resemble. Being Jewish was more significant to a person than being anything else. She hoped so. She knew so. She had seen the effect on him when he first found out about his mother. He still hadn't got over the shock. She would help him, and there was only one way. He was more than half-way there. She had seen him put money into the collection boxes on the counter of the delicatessen. She knew where they belonged.

He sat down. 'It's something to think about.'

'No,' she said scornfully. 'If you have to think about it, it's impossible. One doesn't think about a thing like that. The thinking has already been done, though you haven't noticed, I dare say.'

She distrusted herself. No, she didn't. All motives had a thousand strings attached. Ignore them. No, don't ignore anything. To ignore is to fly in the face of God. Did she merely want to get out of the country because she couldn't bear to bring Rachel up in this same old place? Would going anywhere else be better? She couldn't bear to be seen pushing her about in a pram, a woman of her age with a child on the street, and old enough to be its grandmother! If she stayed she would really drop her out of the window, all love pulled away to create a vacuum wherein she didn't know what she was doing. And that would be the end of them all. In any other country such an action would be unthinkable. The idea surfaced vividly to convince her, but seemed merely another motive that, unable to deny, she had to contend with and finish once and for all.

Nor could she bear to love two people at the same time. It was impossible for peace of mind, and tore her in two. Sleeping with Judy was like being back with her mother, a sensual restoration of all senses, which she ought to have outgrown long ago. Nothing but a sea-change would suffice. And yet again, why should she? She would always love women if she felt like doing so. She was tired of learning lessons when it was perfectly safe for certain parts of her to drift the way she wanted. All the same, you could not give in to such distractions if you wanted to guide your life in any positive way.

They were surface reasons perhaps, excuses and nothing more, yet the words had come spontaneously because whatever reason had put them there would never be defined. If it wasn't already obvious, yet utterly buried at the same time, there wasn't a reason and never would be. She didn't know which it was, and didn't care to. They would go to Israel, or she would return to living in a room of her own. She had said enough. He must do the rest himself.

'Is that an ultimatum?'

It was.

He knew what he wanted, he answered. Nobody knew better, but he didn't know whether what he wanted was what she really wanted, that was the trouble. Even though she had suggested accurately enough that he wanted to break off the present life – and he did, if only to end it – he had to be sure she wanted it as well. The idea that she was merely, if unintentionally, tormenting him could be countered for the moment by saying nothing. Be still, and know that I am yours, he wanted to tell her.

He said it.

She already knew.

It was irrelevant, he felt when he had said it.

So did she.

So much was.

How could it not be?

But to the extent that you had to say it, it wasn't.

Nothing was.

Forget it.

Know that even love was something that had to be endured, a fact which, when realized, did not make him unhappy. Rather, it made him feel less numb than before he had said it.

He said it again to himself while walking through the park by the Pavilion on his way back from the public library on a fine April morning. She wanted him to go on his own, and then they would see, but if he did he thought he might lose not only her but Rachel as well. It was too much to ask.

But the chance had to be taken. He was never anywhere except in the middle of a storm, the never-ending turmoil of life. Momentous decisions had always to be considered and quite often taken, a state of mind not unfamiliar, nor even unwanted. Life at sea was like that, and the whole of life was being at sea, until you went under into the dark. There was no reason not to smile about it, as he did when catching a glimpse of himself in a shop mirror on his way through The Lanes. She wanted him to go to Israel by himself, and then he could tell her when she and Rachel were to follow, and though he couldn't bear to leave his two-month-old daughter for as much as an hour, he would brace himself to do it.

In other words, he would leave his daughter with a feeling that recalled his mother's action when she had taken a last look at him in his cradle before going out of his grandfather's house never to come back. That event, and the one that felt too uncomfortable to contemplate, were close enough to produce a crushing overlap as he turned and walked with more speed along the seafront, a memory still too near for a proper decision to be made.

But having said it, it was as good as done. Speech was the point of no return. Discipline would take over. Otherwise what were words for? Blue sea worried the shingle with a roar before going out again. There was one last journey to travel, and nobody could say he was afraid to make it.

Sunlight was doled on to the water by a wind manipulating gaps in the clouds. Glistening acres came and went as he looked from the end of the pier. Smokestacks were alive, energy and purpose in their acute angles as when he had first been mesmerized by the expanse. They ran on diesel now and were plain blocks battling their way, but all alteration was progress, one way or the other. Sloth, which was sinful in the eyes of the righteous, meant in him a self-induced form of death that was far worse.

He had given no proper and binding answer. To make it firm – so that he could not turn back for fear of damaging his pride to the extent that he would never have the spiritual strength to move more than five miles beyond where he lived for the rest of his life – they would have to talk about his departure before Judy and the children.

21

'Israel!' Judy exclaimed. 'You must be stark raving bonkers!'

They talked on Saturday afternoon when it was raining too hard for any of them to go out. Pam thought Judy might be envious, and also afraid, because she seemed, after all, less adaptable to change than any of them. What she or anybody thought was unimportant. While holding Rachel to her chest so that she could look at the children playing Monopoly on the floor, Pam felt that once changes began out of a centre of consciousness, as they had with her on leaving George, there was no stopping further developments spreading in their wake. She was no longer safe or happy at being settled. She had opted for adventure, and even the final conversion, wanting the new life to go on, no matter how disturbed others would be by her wanderings. If they were in the same state would they consider her? She doubted it, and would not blame them if they did not.

Judy stood by the mantelpiece, a hand at the side of her face as if Tom's information had struck and left a mark there. 'There's a war every five minutes,' she said.

'They have them everywhere these days,' he answered, 'or

are likely to. You're never far from the riot, or the terrorist psychopath with his so-called explosive device. There's no use worrying about that sort of thing any more, or using it as an excuse not to act. If anything happens to me, all I have goes to Pam, but if we both end up dead before our time, which I consider unlikely, by the way, then whatever's left goes to you. You'll be taken care of, in any case. As I've told you before, there's enough for everybody here.'

She knew he was Jewish, but even so, didn't you only go to Israel if, say, some nut like Hitler came up from the sewers? 'They don't even have proper frontiers,' she said.

'They will have. Every country starts that way.'

'You like to make things all neat and tidy,' Judy said. 'But that's not what I mean. Your sort of tidiness makes me want to puke. You can't move us around like pieces on a chess-board. I love you both, so I don't want either of you to go.'

'I'm not going,' Pam began.

Judy put a hand to the other side of her face, as if that cheek was also in pain. 'What?'

'Well, not straight away.'

'I can't get a proper answer on that matter,' Tom said. 'Things aren't as tidy as you think.'

They looked at each other helplessly, as if they would have rushed to be physically close had no children been by. Judy went into the kitchen. 'I'll leave you to sort yourselves out.'

He settled himself in an armchair, and lit a cigar.

'I think you offended her,' Pam said.

He puffed smoke towards the fireplace. 'What? By talking about money? Possessions?'

She looked out of the window, her back to him, raising her voice to make sure it was heard in the kitchen. 'Perhaps. But it's you she doesn't want to lose. She doesn't care about anyone else. You can hardly leave yourself to her in your last will and testament.'

He put his cigar in the ashtray and stood. 'Is that why you want us to go?'

'I wish you'd sort yourself out,' Hilary said to Sam. 'All you've got to do is sell Piccadilly, and one of your railway stations, and then you'll have some money left to go on playing.'

Sam groaned. 'I know. But I don't want to lose any of my complete sets.'

'She told me about it last night,' Pam said, after a silence. 'What happened when I was in the hospital.'

He held her shoulders, feeling the warmth under her blouse, and looking down over inflated breasts at Rachel peacefully sleeping. 'I'm sorry about that.'

She was surprised that it did not matter. And she told him so. 'Somehow, it doesn't, not with Judy.'

Nevertheless, he thought, it was best forgotten. 'I'll be unhappy to leave Rachel,' he said softly, 'and more than sad to leave you. I'll also regret leaving Judy, and those two.' He nodded towards the children on the floor. 'But I have to go, whether or not I want to, or whether or not you now want me to. I'd have come to it of my own volition, otherwise I wouldn't have agreed to your wish, suggestion or command, or whatever you like to call it. But it's easier for me to go knowing that you won't be left here alone, and that you and Rachel will come to me after a while.'

He was rational and cool, and she was afraid as she turned to him, and wondered why he insisted on tormenting her and everybody, till she remembered having pushed him towards the move. 'What if I said don't go? Forget what I said when I was in a stupid and destructive mood? Somebody told me at the hospital that her husband never took any notice of what she said till the kid she'd had was a year old.'

He was bewildered. There was, she knew, no greater suffering for a man of his sort. He was fearless, and probably cared little about pain, but chaos inside was intolerable. She weighed him up as he looked at her, and such total consideration was the only act of love she could muster at the moment. That she loved him was indisputable, but she wanted him to go, if for nothing more than to prove that he recognized her love, and loved her in return. It was the only test she could make. Having grown to a state when she could confidently test a man whatever the risks, she felt that she had achieved some sort of equality at last.

The children were looking at them, and listening with interest. But it was open-house for that sort of thing.

'Yesterday,' he said, 'I collected my plane ticket to Athens, and my boat ticket to Haifa – both one-way. I prefer to go in by sea, to land from a ship. Even the remnant shall return. The sand of the sea shall be washed on the shore. That sort of thing.'

Before she could ask the date of his leaving, Sam called: 'Can we come with you to Israel, Tom?'

'Why,' he turned with a laugh, 'are you going to be Jewish, as well?'

Hilary pushed the heaps of false money aside and stood up. 'I am. I'm Jewish, Tom. Daddy was Jewish, wasn't he, mummy?'

'No, he bloody well wasn't.' Judy came in with the tea.

'And the strangers shall be joined with them,' Tom said. 'To it shall the Gentiles seek.'

Hilary wept with chagrin. 'Oh why wasn't he?'

'He was no bloody good, that's what he was.'

Tom grimaced with disapproval. 'He was no more no-good than most, I suppose.'

'You know nothing.' Judy's words were so fierce that all were fixed by them. 'I loved him. No matter how much of a swine he was, and I knew he was bad, I loved him, even though I knew I ought not to, and felt ashamed and degraded that I couldn't help myself. I went on loving him through more than I dare tell about, and it went on for years, and that's what I can't forgive myself for. And he didn't love me, not a bit, though I was handy as a bit of furniture, and to scrounge money from. I was pregnant when we got married, but had a miscarriage just after the wedding because he got

575

drunk one night and pushed me a bit too hard. That was at the beginning, but he calmed down, for a few years, till I had these two. Then one day he saw me kissing a woman who came to the house. He'd probably already had an affair with her, though I wouldn't have known. But the penny must have dropped, because from then on he was in love with her. It was disgusting the way he crawled and grovelled. Either that, or he would go into such fits of violent hatred, far worse than before, that the danger finally got through to what bits of goodness were buried deep inside him, which even he only caught a glimpse of about once in ten years.'

'I shan't be like him,' Sam said.

'Nor me,' Hilary put in.

She looked at them. 'I knew I had to get rid of him then, or me and the kids would be more deranged than we'd ever be on our own, even with me going on all the time as if I've still got brain-damage from it. But what's the point?' She sat down, as if totally worn out.

'I'm sorry,' said Tom, 'but you ought not to talk like that in front of – us.'

He meant the children, and Pam supposed he was right. Someone had to advise her against it, but Pam thought he was hardly the right person, being a man, and certainly more at sea than he'd ever been. Judy, however, looked across at them with an embarrassed smile. 'I'm sorry too, but I won't mention it again.'

She's upset about us going. Pam sat by her and held her hand, while Tom pulled Hilary to him and stroked her hair. 'Now stop crying. It's more like the beginning of the world than the end. You can come to see us in Israel after we get settled. I promise. You can bring them,' he said to Judy.

Sam took Rachel when she cried, and rocked her gently. It was a happy family, but all happy families sooner or later disintegrate – cruel, Pam thought, as it may seem. She was tired of it all, and watched Tom set out cups and pour tea.

'I'm going to Israel,' he said, 'because it's the only solution.

My past will be put into its proper place.' He turned to her. 'And so will yours be. I want you to come because we were lost in the same ocean together, and came out at the same time. I can't carry you there forcibly, but more than anything I want you and Rachel to follow as soon as possible.'

She wouldn't give an answer, though there was a positive one somewhere in her. The time for thought was over, especially of the kind that degenerated into worry. Having been so long in the beam of chaos, she wanted the futile roundabout to stop. She had changed her life when the odds against doing so had been too heavy to contemplate. She had married blind at twenty, and had come out at forty with her heart so bruised that it seemed as if she couldn't do anything except turn into a cabbage and rot in the earth. There was only space for one victory in her lifetime. Who needed more? Her spiritual and bodily strength hadn't been made for victories, she often thought. It took more strength to achieve them than to sustain defeats. The victory she felt in possession of, though it might seem less than ordinary to anyone else, already felt unique to her.

She did not have to say anything in answer to his question because she felt as safe with him as she hoped he would ultimately feel secure with her. He did not appear threatened or unmanned by her silence. That much had always been obvious. What better love could there be between them? What more did she want? Nothing more. She felt older than the thousands of years he sometimes talked about, but it was part of the victory that her heart blended with his, their beginning already being far in the past. She would go to him when the time was ready, and stay no matter what, because hadn't the preacher's message been that Israel was her country as much as it was his?

Damn the preacher, she thought with the next inner breath. If he had ranted the opposite she would still be where she was, and of the same mind, because it was the only place in which she could find peace. Tom had, after all, brought her from the valley of the shadow of death.

Those who at one time might have said that she had had everything hadn't known that to her it had been as nothing. And now that they could say she had nothing, she felt as if it were everything. Her heart had been unable to live without the almost sensual desire to go into another state of being, proving to her that only by complete change was it possible to learn. The embers of the heart had turned to ash, but they had retained their warmth and were ready to burst into life again. She was rebuilt by endurance, and though she still felt much of the time that she was alone, she also knew that the three of them would find an existence in the place that had been devised for them. With love they would re-create their lives in a new country, and stem the rages that would no doubt continue to torment them. But at the moment she would tell him nothing. He must go without her and Rachel, or not at all.

'Me come as well?' Judy said. 'Can you imagine me picking oranges? Still, I might try it for a year: Judy Ellerker, the blight of the Holy Land! I'd love being in the sun, all the same.'

'You'll adore it,' Pam said, 'I'm sure you will. I can already see you there.'

'Do all Jews go to Israel?' Sam's hand hovered around Rachel as if he was playing with a kitten.

Tom put down his cup. 'Only those who want to. And those who have to.'

'I wish you weren't going, though.'

'I'm one of those who have to.'

'But do you want to?' asked Judy.

'I don't suppose I'll know the answer to that one until I get there. But there's more to it than just wanting to. It's bigger than that, beyond discussion, like so much else.'

'Now you're *talking*!' Judy mocked.

He stood apart, conscious of the fact that in a week he would no longer be with them. They knew it. Hilary held his hands tight. 'Will you play Monopoly with us, Tom?'

'It's no use,' he laughed. 'You always win.'

She pulled at him. The sleeve of his coat covered the back of his hand. Everyone else's need was greater than your own. He smiled when Hilary said: 'Not every time, I don't.'

'We'll let you win,' Sam promised.

'All right, then,' he said. 'My last game of Monopoly!'

'Leave him alone, you little vampires.' But Judy took the baby from Sam, because she knew Tom would play a game or two with them.

22

'While waiting for the ship at Piraeus I walked along the boulevard by the docks looking in shop windows, but nothing interested me. Since leaving you and Rachel I was an empty skin, able to move but not think, capable of facing the future, but not daring to wonder about the past. I felt part of a system, if such it can be called, that was pulling me to the centre, sleep-walking me to a conclusion that can turn out to be nothing except a real beginning. It's a relief to be without options at last.

'Like the normal passenger I was I loitered till it was time for the ship to sail, but felt more lost than I'd ever been during my sailor life when I hit a funny port and wondered how to pass the time before going back to my cabin.

'I was in a state of well-being, but sorry to have left you, knowing from experience that it is always more depressing for those who stay behind, no matter what the circumstances. To that extent I felt twinges of guilt and uncertainty. In fact it might be true to say that what I didn't feel would hardly be worth writing about! I was also obviously sorry at leaving Rachel, though perhaps on her part she'll miss me less at the tender age of three months than she would if I had left my departure till much later. The quicker the move, the healthier for everyone.

'The ship didn't leave until two o'clock, and much loading had to be done, as I saw from a stroll along the quay. I probably walked around the docks to the shipping office to get my ticket checked more times than was necessary. The ship would be full. People had boxes, bundles, plastic bags, rucksacks, suitcases, trunks, and cardboard boxes tied up with string. Bedding (including a whole bedframe) was going up the stern gangplank. A line of cars was waiting to go into the hold. All luggage was being searched, in case a terrorist should plant something there.

'I strolled back to the dock gates. There was still no hurry. I repeated to myself that I was going to Israel, said the word over and over like an incantation, and a port worker who went by must have thought I was going a bit crackers in the midday sun. Perhaps I was. Perhaps I am. I would get to Haifa, so then where would I go? Jerusalem is the capital city of Israel, I said, therefore it is natural to go to that place. But would I lodge there for good, or fix something up near the desert, or work in orange groves on some kibbutz or other, or stay close to the sea? Sooner or later I would have to make myself useful. Where would I pray if the need arose, as it surely will? I'd find a synagogue – no difficulty there! – to give thanks for my arrival. I had my *yarmulka*, so they would let me in. I hadn't left my old life in order to settle for less. Israel was, I told myself, the only country in the world I could go to after England. It will supersede England in my mind – a great change, but it will be done. For once in my life I have to prove myself right in a fundamental choice, not out of fate, egotism or force of circumstance, but due to a religious reason that is at the very middle of me.

'I walked back to the boulevard. A tram was going by, and

580

I almost ran after it. Both sections turned a corner before I could make up my mind to get on. My body and spirit played a game, joining forces to perform a trick I didn't fall for. A car bonnet passed close as I crossed the road, its hooter screeching. The heat was terrific, coming out of an emptiness I thought had been left behind. (They said there was a heat wave in Greece at the moment.) That emptiness was caused by my leaving you and Rachel. I sat on a seat by some stunted bushes, a huge ship rearing on the other side of the railings. It is impossible to leave anything behind. The past stays with you, or that's how it feels at the moment, a part of your irreducible torment that you see reminders of again and again, memories that render down and become one more contribution to the unconscious.

'The whistle of a departing ship reminded me that time went on and there was less possibility of retreat, no matter what going forward might mean. We will survive, the three of us, whatever happens, because in our different ways we have already learned never to be afraid.

'The ship set off through industrial mist and sailed among the isles of Greece. I ate a meal, slept for an hour, then looked from the rail at rocks and ashy mountains poking their summits out of the clear blue mirror of the sea. It was only now, seeing the last markings of my departure from what to me was the old world, that all nerve seemed to go, and the questions began. The effect was terrifying, striking at the most vulnerable part and at the worst moment – as of course it must. I had not expected it, when I ought to have done, though even if I had braced myself, the effect would have been no different. There was little use denying or avoiding it. I was down among the jellyfish, make no mistake about that.

'Everything I thought appeared to me as the truth, and the denials that immediately countered it were also nothing but the truth – as if the experience I had let myself in for was determined to change even the basic chemistry of my mind. The journey so far had been full of interest. I had been on the move, and there had been little time to think, but now, not only was I alone, and a passenger who had nothing to do while crossing the sea, but I was back on a ship, in the place where I had spent most of my life before finding out who I was and what my connection with the past had been.

'I should have known. I had not given sufficient forethought to avoiding the most obvious pitfalls of my transference. Not only was I back in my former life with an intensity neither desired nor anticipated but, having no connection with it in a working capacity (nor any urge to be so), was doubly lost. Every facet of me that I was, or had been, or intended to become, fell away and left me as a monument of nothingness. I felt ice inside me, growing every second as I stood at the rail, a coldness that made my teeth clatter and my body shake, the extent of the ice inside me increasing until its volume went far beyond the size of my body and became an iceberg into whose space and constituents I had entirely disappeared.

'I don't think I would have come out of it – I would have thrown myself overboard and drowned, that's one thing I am certain of – if one word had not come to my rescue. I don't know how much time passed: perhaps not much, but in a few moments the word had dissolved my paralysis. The sound activated itself from the disciplined service I had been part of for thirty-odd years, but it also formed the definition of something that had been with me ever since I had been born. The word, which began to melt the iceberg that encased me, was *fear*. Fear had been with me for as long as I could remember, a fear mostly half-buried, usually totally so, from as far back as even before I was born. It had led me into every situation of my life, perilous or not, thrown me into all changes, even this one. It had earlier ushered me into becoming a merchant seaman, a very good move, thus allowing me to conquer fear, as I thought, once and for all. Perhaps it also pushed me into the present move, and that's why I allowed it to happen.

582

'As I stood by the rail therefore, contemplating my final move out of the iceberg and into the sea, the word *fear* spoke itself plainly through to what remained of my consciousness. I heard it, and the spark that struck warmed me back into the world. "You're afraid," I said to myself, "stricken with unholy and destructive fear." And discipline took up the call, and expanded on it with words that made me sweat, but which stopped my helpless trembling. That single word brought me back to life, but the word attached itself to many others, before I banished it for ever. Early in my seafaring life an old captain said to me: "Fear God, but nothing else!" The natural and no doubt healthy scorn of the young caused me to pull the saying into myself and then forget it. But as the word came to me I realized that all my life I had been driven everywhere by fear, and even had feared life itself. During the final move that was being made away from it, which when completed meant that I would be able to fear God and nothing else, savage fear made one last attack upon me, but as I walked a free man away from the dusk and down the companionway, I knew I had defeated it.

'I slept in the oven of a cabin, and woke the next day refreshed and calm. The boat was crowded and scruffy, and I sat by the stern with my Hebrew grammar. After calling at Cyprus I felt almost home. I was impatient to see the hills and coastline of Israel, at times wishing I had gone there by aeroplane, but consoling myself with the fact that tomorrow I would be in Jerusalem, that next year would have become this year! In the morning I dressed and went on deck. There was a breeze, the ship rolling slightly, but no sight of land. I wondered how I came to be on a ship, waiting to see Israel rise out of the dawn, such a vast change to a year ago. But I couldn't think backwards any more. There would be no more of that. I would like it where I was going because there was nowhere else. Every move in my life had been to the same end, but this time there was a motive for my shift of vision, a connection which I had often sensed, but missed because the

583

evidence of my feelings had not been there.

'The decks were crowded. Somebody claimed to see land, but it was nowhere in sight. Israelis, pilgrims and tourists jostled for a place at the rails. After breakfast we saw the coast clearly. The ship waited for a pilot boat to show us our moorings. A police launch stood by with machine-guns mounted – or maybe it was part of the Israeli Navy. The only Hebrew I spoke was that of having to do with First Seeing the Land.

'The mist cleared. I looked through binoculars at the coast and the old Crusader town of Akko till my eyes ran from the strain. I saw the docks of Haifa, and the long back of Mount Carmel with modern buildings crowding the northern spur. A notice said no photos were allowed. It was a busy harbour, with plenty of traffic. People were waiting by the sheds to greet lucky passengers. There were cars and lorries beyond the dock gates, and pedestrians in summer clothes. Gangways were lowered, but it took an hour to get through tedious landing formalities.

'By sharing a taxi I was in Jerusalem at midday. I sat in a café with my suitcases, watching people go by and sampling that smell of musk and spicy food on Ben Yehuda Street. Using the café telephone I located a hotel with a vacant room. It turned out to be somewhat modest, and I was told I was lucky to get it with so many tourists crowding in, but it was a place to sleep and leave luggage while I wandered around.

'There was less heat than on the coast. The sky was blue when I stood below a windmill and saw the crenellations of the city walls. I wanted to reach out and touch them, but they were too far away. So I looked. I looked at the walls and at Mount Zion for half an hour, impossible to exult or brood after so long, only to stand still and look with steady recognition at a scene I had heard of and read about even from my Bible days at the orphanage. The agony of being without a past was over, however bleak the future might be.

584

'Many tourists were coming and going, bringing a babble of languages from all over the world. I walked at my usual quick speed between some houses and down the hill, as if I had been there before, across the valley and up to the Jaffa Gate. At the open space inside I bought a glass of freshly pressed orange juice, glancing at the people as I stood and drank.

'Pushing my way down David Street, I had to step around places where the road was up. It was as if I had arranged to meet someone and was already late. I stopped a soldier and asked the way to the Western Wall. It used to be called the Wailing Wall, but I learned in the taxi, when one of the passengers corrected me in a very brash way, that it doesn't have that name any more.

'So much space in the middle of a cramped city came as a surprise, but once you're in there's no doubt where the Wall is. A soldier examined my haversack, for bombs, I suppose. Then I put on my *yarmulka* and went into the enclosure. There's a place for men, and a place for women, which I suppose neither you nor Judy would like! I stared mindlessly for a few minutes, before letting my hand touch the stone. When the Hashemites from over the River Jordan occupied this area no Jews were allowed in, I was later told. The Wall cut off the sky, but was a lightning rod in contact with it. A few people on either side were praying, wearing shawls and weaving back and forth. Without intending, my forehead was touching the Wall. How long I was there I don't know. I was with you. Then I was with myself only. I was mulling on all I had discovered about my mother, reliving every event up to her death. Perhaps if she hadn't died we would both have been here.

'I lost a sense of time when my hands touched the Wall, unable to let go because it seemed alive. If ever there was a man in a dream that man was me, but the dream knew what it was doing, even if I didn't. I pressed the Star of David from my mother to the rough surface to prove that one of us had

585

come back to where we belonged. The action comforted me, however outlandish it might seem to you – and in some ways seemed to me when I realized what I was doing.

'After dark I walked to the Jaffa Gate and out of the City. Back in my room, with a dull bulb glowing, I felt calmer. It is my home for the moment. I'm reminded of when you were in your room in London, as I try to stamp my own personality on to it, even though I may be here only a few days more. My half dozen books are on a shelf, my map on the wall, and the sextant on the dressing-table. All I need for the moment is this small room, and I feel richer than Solomon at knowing it is in Jerusalem.

'I still don't know why I left you and Rachel, but there was no other way. I feel pared to the bone by the mindless search which has now come to a stop. The fact that there is no going on will take getting used to. Unless the unified heart is wholly committed to life, no one can truthfully speak of the oneness of existence. There had to be a stop. It is irreligious to strive for the absolute, which is beyond human comprehension. A deeper meaning can only be found by searching within a closed circle, through actions rather than words, but actions that are good rather than evil. One must cultivate justice, love and mercy, in so far as one's life and one's country are spared to let you do so.

'The place I have chosen is the one that by birth was chosen for me. I am under no illusions. That too would be a sin, because we know, or should, that illusions pave the way to greater evils than those which might already be close by. Israel is in the middle of the world, and I can't help feeling that it is a rock on which the stability of the world depends. At the same time it is a country like any other, while also like no other country. You have to be here to feel it. First impressions count for much, even though they might amuse those who have been here so long they have forgotten what their first impressions were – if such a thing is possible.

'I speak to people in the cafés, and my poor knowledge of

Hebrew – though it *is* improving – brings comments as well as a few laughs, but I use it without any self-consciousness. Someone generally speaks English, so it's not difficult to start a conversation. I mostly listen, however, to what goes on among the others, being too diffident about putting in my no doubt naïve opinions. What they are, I have formulated over the past year, and confirmed during the time I have been here. If I had no such opinions how could I have been here in the first place?

'While life is normal, one senses a faint electricity of danger in the air. At least I do, though perhaps that's because I'm still a stranger. Maybe it's only a more-than-usual feeling of existence, an urgency, liveliness and tension coming from three million people back in their own land after having been denied it for so long, and determined to survive in spite of all adversities. But such a feeling as mine only makes life seem more real, because I've long been used to the feeling, as one always was on a ship, and especially during the war. Maybe it's best for me to have come, after all, to a country where danger of some kind is never felt to be absent. Not that there isn't a need for such vigilance everywhere. Explosions occur in London as well as in Israel, and no doubt will continue to do so – though I haven't heard of any here as yet. It is a factor of modern life, and also the kind of evil that has always been with us, which indiscriminately strikes every time at the innocent. Various countries have no option but to live with it, and to contain it till, like a visitation of the plague to which a healthy country cannot finally succumb, it goes away. Whatever there is to live with will, after a while, seem ordinary enough. To be surrounded by enemies is a form of reality, and in this country life goes on as normally as anywhere else. It is a new nation still, not thirty years old, going through flux without end, from inside and out. But it will endure, no matter what, and to be here fills me with a joyous will to live.'

23

She read the letters from Tom after supper. There were no secrets from Judy. They placed their armchairs by the fireplace, each with their separate side-light and pot of coffee, enjoying that silence when children are in bed. Tom had been gone a month, and until each letter came it seemed to Pam as if she had never known him. But the letters brought him vividly back, even more so when she read them to Judy. The only part that remained was Rachel. When Tom was present Rachel looked like him, but when Tom was away it was Tom who resembled Rachel, so that whatever she felt, she was fundamentally linked with him. Life with Judy and the children seemed settled, yet the flat was only a half-way house until the time came to be on the move again.

The end of his letter ('I'll start looking for a place for us to live tomorrow. It could be anywhere between Dan and Ophira, and from the Mediterranean to the River Jordan. I'll hire a car and reconnoitre') had been followed by one in which he said that he had found a flat for the time being in Jerusalem, and wanted her and Rachel to join him as soon as she felt they were able to make the move. He could come and get her if she liked, and they would make the trip by plane. He'd see that Judy and the kids were all right, unless, he added, they would like to come as well! Even that could be done.

'The pair of you certainly seem to have got all that was possible out of each other,' Judy remarked, 'considering how it looks like ending up.'

'Nothing is ended yet, that's the joy of it. I hate to think of endings.'

'Yes,' Judy said, 'I suppose beginnings are more in your line. But you will go, won't you?'

She leaned, and filled her cup. 'What would you do, if you were in my place?'

'I'm not, and never would be, thank you very much. But if I had the chance, you mean?' Her voice quavered, and broke. 'Well, I don't know. I love you too much to want you to go. You shouldn't ask questions like that.'

It was unfair, Pam saw. There was too much pressure between them. She complimented her on her honesty. 'Do you want brandy in your coffee?'

Judy noted how affectionately they cared for one another, and how soon it was to end. 'Sorry, whisky.'

She went to get it.

'But I mean' – Pam poured it into both cups – 'I'm asking what you would do in my place – exactly that.'

'You've made the bloody coffee cold,' Judy said. 'We have as near a perfect life as I can imagine at the moment. Trust a man to ruin it.'

'He made it possible.'

'Damn him!'

They were silent, Pam hardly able to look at Judy who gazed intently at her.

'I'd go,' Judy said. 'That's what I'd do. But don't let me influence you, for God's sake!'

'I won't,' Pam said. 'But I suppose I shall go.'

'"Suppose!"' She saw some hope. Then the light went out of her eyes, because any uncertainty from Pam only brought a certainty closer. Seven negatives made a positive. She poured more whisky. Close to crying, you must laugh. 'Shall you dip Rachel in the Jordan?'

'I doubt it. Whether I'll stay in Israel or not, I can't say. Depends on a lot. I'm too free a person to commit myself, though I suppose that, too, is an illusion. In one way I'm frightened, but on the other hand, to go to Tom in Israel is something I can't not do. Not to try it would be cowardice. Since we met I've really given him a hard time. I can't imagine how anybody but Tom would have put up with it.

There'll be no more of that, though, from now on.'

Judy sat at her feet, and put her arms around her legs. 'If you go, it'll be for ever. I know.'

'That's being melodramatic. Nothing's for ever.'

'Maybe not. But I know you, absolutely. You'll go, and you'll stay, even though you may well come back now and again to say hello to old Judy.' She looked tired, as if she would feel a weight off her when there were no more decisions to be talked about. 'It's front-line stuff out there. You know that, don't you?'

'It's where I want to be, though. There's no other place.'

'No, I see that. Not for you there isn't.'

'I'll begin arrangements to move in the morning. I see no use in holding back once my mind's made up.' She smiled. 'There are certain things you have to do, and you'd never make any beginnings if you couldn't act until you were able to see the end.'

She spoke without much consideration. Life seemed empty, but the weariness was finished, and she could only gird herself for the future. 'After all, it's my victory as well as his. And the fact is, there's no such thing as a victory, unless you have someone else to share it with.'